# PICTORIAL
# PRICE GUIDE
# TO
# AMERICAN ANTIQUES

# 1984 - 1985 EDITION

# PICTORIAL PRICE GUIDE TO AMERICAN ANTIQUES

### and Objects Made for the American Market

## OVER 5000 OBJECTS IN 300 CATEGORIES ILLUSTRATED AND PRICED

*by*

# Dorothy Hammond

*A Dutton*  *Paperback*

## E. P. DUTTON / NEW YORK

Published in the United States by E. P. Dutton, Inc.
2 Park Avenue, New York, N.Y. 10016
Library of Congress Catalogue Number: 82-71301

ISBN: 0-525-48093-5

Published simultaneously in Canada by
Fitzhenry & Whiteside, Limited, Toronto
W

10 9 8 7 6 5 4 3 2 1

First Edition

# CONTENTS

# INTRODUCTION

The Sixth Edition of PICTORIAL PRICE GUIDE TO AMERICAN ANTIQUES provides the antiques dealer and collector with an accurate market value of items sold at auction galleries in the United States between July 1, 1982 and November 1, 1983. Each entry is keyed to the auction house where the item was sold. A state abbreviation has been included for the readers' convenience, since prices vary in different locations across the country. Also, the year and the month the item sold has been indicated.

Now that the economy is on the upswing, the antiques market is enjoying a brisk recovery. During the fall of 1983, collectors began showing more interest in antiques and collectibles, and major auction galleries began realizing many record sales. Once again, top-quality items brought good prices and sold quickly. Overall, the market seems to be on a more solid footing with added buyers. Many of this latter group are showing an increasing interest in memorabilia — ranging from Campbell's soup, to cartoon art and Star Wars items. With all the increased activity, the antiques market is showing more stability with each passing month, and this is most encouraging.

I am greatly indebted to the following auction galleries who so generously provided pictorial material in order to make this undertaking possible. Thanks are especially due to: Richard A. Bourne Co., Hyannis Port, MA; Early Auction Company, Milford, OH; Robert C. Eldred Co., East Dennis, MA; Garth Auctions, Inc., Delaware, OH; Willis Henry Auctions, Inc., Marshfield, MA; Lloyd W. Ralston Toys, Fairfield, CT; Robert W. Skinner, Inc., Bolton, MA; and Adam A. Weschler & Son, Washington, D.C.

In addition, I would like to thank Dolores Payne, Project Coordinator, and Kurt Heimke, for their assistance with the varied details in organizing the many entries. I am also very grateful to my staff — Modena Spurlock, Jeanne Billings, and Wanda Clapp, for generously aiding me in assembling the material for this book.

Every effort has been made to record prices as accurately as possible in this publication; however, the writer cannot be responsible for any clerical or typographical errors that may occur.

*Dorothy Hammond*

## ABBREVIATIONS USED WITHIN THIS BOOK AND THEIR MEANING

| | | |
|---|---|---|
| A. | Auction | |
| A.C.B. | Acid Cut Back | |
| Alter. | Altered | |
| Am. | American | |
| Amt. | Amount | |
| Attrib. | Attributed | |
| Blk. | Black | |
| Br. | Brown | |
| C. | Century | |
| Ca. | Circa | |
| Comb. | Combination | |
| Cond. | Condition | |
| Const. | Construction | |
| D. | Deep | |
| Decor. | Decorated | |
| Dia. | Diameter | |
| Drk. | Dark | |
| D.Q.M.O.P. | Diamond Quilted Mother of Pearl | |
| Eng. | English | |
| Escut. | Escutcheon | |
| Ext. | Exterior | |
| Fr. | French | |
| Gal. | Gallon | |
| Gr. | Green | |
| H. | High | |
| Ht. | Height | |
| Illus. | Illustrated | |

| | |
|---|---|
| Inc. | Incomplete |
| Int. | Interior |
| Irid. | Iridescent |
| L. | Long |
| Litho. | Lithograph |
| Lrg. | Large |
| Lt. | Light |
| Med. | Medium |
| Mfg. | Manufactured |
| Mkd. | Marked |
| M.O.P. | Mother of Pearl |
| M.W. | Mt. Washington |
| N. Eng. | New England |
| N.E.G.W. | New England Glass Works |
| Orig. | Original |
| Pat. | Patent |
| Patt. | Pattern |
| Pcs. | Pieces |
| Pr. | Pair |
| Pt. | Pint |
| Q.A. | Queen Anne |
| Ref. | Refinished |
| Remov. | Removable |
| Repl. | Replaced |
| Replm. | Replacement |
| Repr. | Repair |
| Repro. | Reproduction |
| Restor. | Restoration |

| | |
|---|---|
| Sgn. | Signed |
| Sq. | Square |
| Unmkd. | Unmarked |
| Unsgn. | Unsigned |
| W/ | With |
| Wh. | White |
| Wrt. | Wrought |

**State abbreviations used within this volume are:**

| | |
|---|---|
| CT | Connecticut |
| DE | Delaware |
| LA | Louisiana |
| ME | Maine |
| MD | Maryland |
| MA | Massachusetts |
| NH | New Hampshire |
| NJ | New Jersey |
| NY | New York |
| OH | Ohio |
| PA | Pennsylvania |
| TX | Texas |
| VA | Virginia |
| WV | West Virginia |
| WA D.C. | Washington D.C. |

A-MA July 1982    *Richard A. Bourne Co., Inc.*
*Row I*
**ROYAL BAYREUTH NUT SERVICE,**
7 pcs., wh. roses on yellow ground, mkd.
"Hand Painted Ivory," Bayreuth label
............................. $130.00

*Row II, L to R*
**PORCELAIN SUGAR & CREAMER,**
hand-painted, unidentified ware ... $70.00
**R.S. PRUSSIA PLATES,** set of 6 (1 illus.),
red mark, 6" D. .............. $100.00
**PORCELAIN COMPOTE,** hand-
painted, 5⅞" D., 4" H. .......... $40.00

*Row III, L to R*
**R.S. PRUSSIA BERRY BOWL,** red
mark, ivory ground color, elaborate decor.
of roses w/floral border, 10½" D.
............................. $135.00
**R.S. PRUSSIA RELISH DISH,** red mark,
lilies on wh. ground, 10⅛" L. ..... $70.00

A-MA July 1982    *Richard A. Bourne Co., Inc.*
*Row I, L to R*
**LIDDED SUGAR OR TEA BOWL,**
Chinese-style polychromed decor., 6" O.H.
............................. $120.00
**SUNDERLAND LUSTRE OPEN JAR,**
4⅜" D., 3⅞" H. ................ $45.00
**CHINESE EXPORT PORCELAIN
BOWL,** ship decor., badly cracked, 5½" D.
............................. $150.00

*Row II, L to R*
**STAFFORDSHIRE CHEESE DISH,**
form of swan, professional repairs, some
discoloration, 10½" L., 7" H. .... $425.00
**STAFFORDSHIRE HANDLELESS
CUPS & SAUCERS,** set of 4 (1 illus.),
rose lustre & blue-gr. flower decor., slight
discoloration ................. $70.00

A-MA July 1982    *Richard A. Bourne Co., Inc.*
*Row I, L to R*
**BENNINGTON PARIAN FIGURE,**
kneeling & praying child, 4¾" H.
............................. $230.00
**PARIAN ORNAMENT,** greyhound rest-
ing on cushion, attrib. to Bennington, 5⅝"
L., 2⅜" H. .................... $200.00
*Row II, L to R*
**BENNINGTON PARIAN SYRUP,** Palm
Tree patt., lt. br. w/raised wh. patt., minus
pewter cover, one chip on rim, 7¼" O.H.
............................. $75.00
**BENNINGTON PITCHER,** Paul & Vir-
ginia patt., drk. blue glaze w/raised wh.
patt., 10¾" O.H. .............. $325.00

A-MA Aug. 1982    *Robert W. Skinner Inc.*
**COMBWARE SHALLOW BOWL,**
Eng., 18th C., molded form, notched rim,
yellow glaze w/br. slip decor. of a straw-
berry hanging from tendrils, old repr., 13¾"
D. ......................... $4250.00*

A-MA Aug. 1982    *Robert W. Skinner Inc.*
**WHIELDON CLOUDED WARE,** 2-
pcs., Little Fenton, Eng., mid-18th C.,
footed & lidded cream jug, br. mottling,
5⅜", pepper pot, br. & yellow mottling &
vertical gr. stripes, 3" H. ....... $850.00*

A-MA Aug. 1982    *Robert W. Skinner Inc.*
*L to R*
**WHIELDON CLOUDED WARE
OPEN VEGETABLE DISH,** Little Fenton, Eng., mid-18th C., oval shape w/br.
sponged decor., glaze roughness on rim,
11¾" L., 9" W. .............. $110.00
**WHIELDON-TYPE SHOP PLATE,** possibly Eng., mid-18th C., round shaped-edge
form w/br. sponged decor., glaze roughness on rim, impressed on bottom w/script
monogram "J" & "AS," 12⅜" D.
............................. $325.00*
**WHIELDON CLOUDED WARE MUG,**
Little Fenton, Eng., mid-18th C., cylindrical
shape on a rounded foot w/br. sponged
decor., damaged, 4⅛" H. ....... $80.00*

A-MA Aug. 1982    *Robert W. Skinner Inc.*
**WHIELDON CLOUDED WARE CUP
& SAUCER,** Little Fenton, Eng., mid-18th
C., handled cylindrical cup w/relief orna-
mentation, br. & gr. mottled glaze, dam-
aged, cup 3-1/6" H., saucer 5⅜" D.
............................. $210.00*

A-MA Aug. 1982    *Robert W. Skinner Inc.*
*L to R*
**WHIELDON CLOUDED WARE
BOWL,** Little Fenton, Eng., br. sponged
decor., 4-13/16" D. .......... $210.00*
**WHIELDON CLOUDED WARE,** set of
4, (1 illus.), Fenton, Eng., mid-18th C., br.
sponged decor., deep plate 9⅜" D., two
plates 7½" D., octagonal toddy plate 5-3/16"
D., glaze chips on deep plate, others are
damaged & restor. ........... $160.00*
**WHIELDON CLOUDED WARE IN-
VALID CUP,** Little Fenton, Eng., br.
sponged decor., spout & handle restored,
2⅝" H. ...................... $50.00*

*Price does not include 10% buyer fee.

A-MA July 1982 *Robert W. Skinner Inc.*
L to R
**DEDHAM POTTERY BUTTER PATS,**
set of four (one illus.), star shaped, MA,
dated 1931, outlined in blue, 3⅝″ D.
............................. $600.00*
**DEDHAM POTTERY COVERED
ROSE JAR,** ca. 1930, MA, full blue ground
w/wh. prunus motif, glaze imperfection,
4¼″ D., 4¾″ H. ............ $1400.00*
**DEDHAM POTTERY PAPERWEIGHT,**
ca. 1920, MA, form of rabbit, slight glaze
imperfection, 3″ L. ........... $400.00*

A-MA July 1982 *Richard A. Bourne Co., Inc.*
Row I, L to R
**DEDHAM POTTERY RABBIT FIG-
URE,** unmkd., small imperfections, 3½″
L. ............................ $350.00
**DEDHAM ASH TRAY,** Swan patt., ca.
1929-1943, 4″ D. ............... $230.00
**SMALL DEDHAM BOWL,** flat rim,
Rabbit patt., ca. 1929-1943, 5½″ D.
............................ $120.00
Row II, L to R
**DEDHAM PLATE,** Magnolia patt., ca.
1929-1943, 6⅞″ D. ............. $90.00
**DEDHAM COVERED BOWL,** Magnolia
patt., ca. 1929-1943, one small chip, 7½″
D. ............................ $240.00

A-MA July 1982 *Robert W. Skinner Inc.*
**DEDHAM POTTERY PLATES,** ca.
1930, MA, 1 w/Magnolia patt., other
w/Azalea patt., minor chip in 1, 8½″ D.
............................ $100.00*

A-MA Oct. 1982 *Robert W. Skinner Inc.*
**VASE,** Boston, MA, ca. 1905, Grueby Art
Pottery, sgn. & initialed "M.S.," glaze
imperfection on rim, 11¾″ H., 7½″ D.
............................ $750.00*

A-MA Oct. 1982 *Robert W. Skinner Inc.*
**VASE,** Boston, MA, ca. 1910, Grueby
Pottery, rim chip, hairline, 21½″ H.
............................ $800.00*

A-WA D.C. July 1982 *Adam A. Weschler & Son*
**DERBY REPOUSSE WARE VASE,** late
19th C., relief flowers & foliage in gilt w/gr.
& rouge highlights, 11″ H. ..... $350.00*

A-MA Oct. 1982 *Robert W. Skinner Inc.*
**NEWCOMB POTTERY VASE,** LA, ca.
1897, sgn. "M.W.B., JM, VC, Q, R35,"
decor. by Mary W. Butler, thrown by
Joseph Meyer, 7½″ H., 3¾″ D.
............................ $875.00*

A-OH July 1982 *Early Auction Co.*
**PORCELAIN PLAQUE,** round mkd.
"K.P.M.," w/biblical figures, in gold
florentine frame, 6″ D. ........ $450.00*

A-OH July 1982 *Early Auction Co.*
**PATE-SUR-PATE VASE,** pink w/2 Pate-
sur-Pate plaques, 1 has wh. cherub & floral
design, 1 has wh. garden tools, flowers & a
hat on br. background, gold ring handles &
gold decor. at bottom of vase, red mintons
mark on bottom, sgn. on 1 plaque
"Lawrence Birks (L.B.)," 7½″ H.
............................ $275.00*

**PATE-SUR-PATE VASE,** gr., flat-sided
on 4 gold feet, 2 wh. figures, sgn. Sanders
who is a listed artist in Minton's book of
Pate-sur-Pate, 7½″ H. ........ $325.00*

A-OH July 1982 *Early Auction Co.*
**GREENTOWN BOWL,** chocolate
footed oblong, Geneva patt., 8½″ L.
............................ $80.00*

**GREENTOWN DOLPHIN,** chocolate,
chip on dorsel fin, roughness inside base
top ........................ $100.00*

**GREENTOWN WHEELBARROW,**
chocolate, flake on handle, chipped foot
............................ $475.00*

A-MA Oct. 1982 *Robert W. Skinner Inc.*
*SATURDAY EVENING GIRLS
POTTERY*
**TEA TILE,** Boston, MA, ca. 1913, sgn.
"S.E.G.F.L. 10.13," rim hairline, 5½″ D.
............................ $110.00*

**PLATES,** set of 6, Boston, MA, ca. 1913, 1
broken, sgn. "S.E.G F.L. 10-13," 8½″ D.
............................ $425.00*

**TEA CUPS & SAUCERS,** 6 cups, 3
saucers, Boston, MA, ca. 1913, hairline,
sgn. "S.E.G.F.L. 7-13" ........ $225.00*

*Price does not include 10% buyer fee.

*L to R*

A-MA July 1982        *Robert W. Skinner Inc.*
**PORCELAIN VASE,** ca. 1890, gilt rim, wide simulated metal molded band w/ rosette medallions on blk. ground w/cobalt flowers, repr., 5¼″ D., 17″ H. .... $50.00*

A-WA D.C. July 1982 *Adam A. Weschler & Son*
**SEVRES ORMOLU MOUNTED URN,** late 19th C., sgn. T. Quentin, 29″ H. ............................. $775.00*

A-MA July 1982      *Richard A. Bourne Co., Inc.*
*Row I, L to R*
**PARIAN COVERED DRESSER DISH,** cracked, slight roughage, 5″ L. .... $35.00
**PARIAN RING HOLDER,** 4″ H. ......................................... $40.00
**PARIAN HEAD & SHOULDERS BUST,** 6″ H. ................... $25.00
**SMALL PARIAN JAR,** raised grapevine design, slight roughage on rim, gold highlighting slightly worn, 3⅜″ H. ..... $30.00
**PARIAN FIGURAL VASE,** slight roughage, 7″ H. ..................... $40.00

*Row II, L to R*
**PARIAN EWER FORM VASE,** mottled flowers & grapes around body of pc., some damage, 10″ H. ................. $75.00
**PARIAN VASE,** reversed fluting & raised grapevine design, 7¼″ H. ....... $45.00
**PARIAN FIGURE,** 8½″ H. ...... $70.00
**PARIAN BUST,** of Sir Arthur Sullivan, Eng., 7¾″ H. .................. $25.00

A-MA July 1982     *Richard A. Bourne Co., Inc.*
*Row I, L to R*
**WEDGWOOD JASPERWARE BOX,** blue, 7¼″ L. ................... $80.00
**WEDGWOOD JASPERWARE VASE,** lavender & wh. raised designs on gray ground, 3½″ H. .............. $210.00
*Row II, L to R*
**JASPERWARE CABINET VASE,** blue, 5″ H. ........................ $25.00
**WEDGWOOD VASE,** blue, 5″ H. ......................... $110.00
**GLAZED PARIAN MILK PITCHER,** lavender on wh. ground, made by S. Alcock & Co., Eng., 6″ H. .............. $80.00

A-MA Aug. 1982        *Robert W. Skinner Inc.*
*L to R*
**WHIELDON CLOUDED WARE PLATE,** Little Fenton, Eng., mid-18th C., octagonal rim w/gadroon edge, mottled br., gr. & yellow glaze, glaze chips, 8¼″ across....................... $925.00*
**WHIELDON CLOUDED WARE PLATE,** Little Fenton, Eng., mid-18th C., shaped rim w/relief ornamentation, mottled br., gr. & yellow glaze, glaze flake, 9″ D. ...................... $280.00*
**WHIELDON CLOUDED WARE PLATE,** Little Fenton, Eng., mid-18th C., br. tortoise shell mottling accented w/gr. spots, rim chip, 9-1/16″ D. ..... $220.00*

A-MA Aug. 1982        *Robert W. Skinner Inc.*
*L to R*
**WHIELDON CLOUDED WARE TEA POT,** Little Fenton, Eng., spherical shape w/relief ornamentation, restor., 4¼″ H. ............................. $300.00*
**WHIELDON CREAMWARE PINE-APPLE TEAPOT,** Little Fenton, Eng., mid-18th C., spherical shape, fish shaped handle, restor., 4½″ H. ........ $300.00*
**WHIELDON CLOUDED WARE TEA POT,** Little Fenton, Eng., spherical shape w/br. & gr. tortoise shell coloring, spout chipped, 3″ H. .............. $750.00*

A-MA Aug. 1982        *Robert W. Skinner Inc.*
**WHIELDON CLOUDED WARE TEA CADDY,** Little Fenton, Eng., mid-18th C., cylindrical shape w/relief ornamentation, br. & gr. mottling, pewter cover, rim chip, 4⅜″ H. ...................... $500.00*

A-WA D.C. July 1982 *Adam A. Weschler & Son*
**SEVRES PICTORIAL PLAQUE,** late 19th C., central portrait of Louis XVI, gilt decor., 17¼″ D. .............. $300.00*

A-WA D.C. July 1982 *Adam A. Weschler & Son*
*Row I*
**DRESDEN SERVICE PLATES,** set of 12 (1 illus.), wh. ground w/blue decor., 11″ D. .......................... $300.00*
*Row II, L to R*
**PORCELAIN SERVICE PLATES,** set of 8 (1 illus.), French, retailed by Tiffany & Co., 10¾″ D. ................. $150.00*
**PORCELAIN SERVICE PLATES,** set of 8 (1 illus.), German, Carlsbad, gold etching on wh. ground, 10½″ D. ....... $225.00*

A-WA D.C. July 1982 *Adam A. Weschler & Son*
*Row I*
**LIMOGES GAME PLATES,** set of 6 (1 illus.), T & V, late 19th C., sgn. Senamoud, gilt scrolling, beaded edge borders, 9″ D.
............................ $150.00*
*Row II, L to R*
**LIMOGES BOTANICAL SERVICE PLATES,** set of 12 (1 illus.), sgn. William Shoppe, gilt decor. on wh. grounds, 9½″ D. ........................... $350.00*
**LIMOGES GAME PLATES,** set of 6 (1 illus.), France, late 19th C., sgn. Emile, gilt scalloped & beaded borders, 8½″ D.
............................ $275.00*

A-WA D.C. July 1982 *Adam A. Weschler & Son*
*Top to Bottom*
**MEISSEN PICTORIAL PLATE,** late 19th C., 10″ D. .............. $650.00*
**MEISSEN PICTORIAL PLATES,** set of 2, late 19th C., 9½″ D. ........ $900.00*

A-WA D.C. July 1982 *Adam A. Weschler & Son*
*L to R*
**MEISSEN FIGURE,** Cupid Blacksmith Repairing Broken Heart, late 19th C., 7½″ H. ........................... $450.00*
**MEISSEN FIGURE,** Cupid Binding Winged Heart, late 19th C., 8″ H.
............................ $350.00*

A-WA D.C. July 1982 *Adam A. Weschler & Son*
*Row I*
**MEISSEN ALLEGORICAL FIGURES,** pr., late 19th C., 5¾″ H. ....... $350.00*
*Row II, L to R*
**MEISSEN ALLEGORICAL FIGURES,** pr., late 19th C., taller: 6″ H. ... $725.00*
**MEISSEN FIGURE OF SEATED LADY,** late 19th C., 7½″ H. ... $600.00*

A-WA D.C. July 1982 *Adam A. Weschler & Son*
**MEISSEN FIGURE OF STANDING MAN,** modeled by Joseph Frolich, ca. 1777, 9¼″ H. ................ $1050.00*

A-WA D.C. July 1982 *Adam A. Weschler & Son*
**LIMOGES PRESIDENTIAL OYSTER PLATES,** set of 3, Haviland, for Rutherford B. Hayes Service, ca. 1880, 8¾″ D.
............................ $400.00*

A-WA D.C. Dec. 1982 *Adam A. Weschler & Son*
**MEISSEN FIGURE OF FLOWER LADY,** underglaze blue crossed swords, 18½″ H. ..................... $450.00*

A-WA D.C. July 1982 *Adam A. Weschler & Son*
**MEISSEN DINNER SERVICE,** 145 pcs., wh. ground, gilt scalloped border
............................ $2500.00*

A-WA D.C. July 1982 *Adam A. Weschler & Son*
**MEISSEN ALLEGORICAL FIGURES,** pr., depicting Spring & Fall, late 19th C., 11½″ H. ..................... $950.00*

A-WA D.C. Dec. 1982 *Adam A. Weschler & Son*
**MEISSEN MONKEY BAND,** 4 pcs., blue overglaze crossed swords, 6″ H.
............................ $900.00*

*Price does not include 10% buyer fee.

A-MA July 1982    *Richard A. Bourne Co., Inc.*
*Top to Bottom*
**MAJOLICA STRAWBERRY DISHES,**
pr., by Minton, 1 blue, other pink, 8⅝″ x 8¼″
.......................... $125.00
**AUSTRIAN MAJOLICA ASPARA-GUS SERVER,** lrg. tray w/separate
sauceboat, 16½″ L., 13″ H. ...... $140.00

A-MA July 1982    *Richard A. Bourne Co., Inc.*
*Row I, L to R*
**METTLACH STEIN,** ½-litre, 9″ H.
.......................... $575.00
**METTLACH STEIN,** ½-litre, upper area
of inside shows deterioration of glaze, 8¾″
H. ........................ $200.00
**POTTERY STEIN,** ½-litre, German, 10″
H. ........................ $50.00
**STONEWARE FLAGON,** German, br.
heart design on blue ground, 12″ O.H.
.......................... $75.00

*Row II, L to R*
**METTLACH CASTLE STEIN,** 15¾″ H.
.......................... $5200.00
**METTLACH LRG. FLAGON,** 18½″
O.H. ...................... $2500.00
**METTLACH FLAGON,** 11″ O.H.
.......................... $325.00

A-MA July 1982    *Richard A. Bourne Co., Inc.*
*Row I, L to R*
**HUMMEL FIGURE,** "Feeding Time in
the Chicken Run," flecks of wh. paint in
areas, 5½″ H. ................. $40.00
**HUMMEL FIGURE,** "Sensitive Hunter,"
mkd., flecks of wh. paint, 4¾″ H.
.......................... $35.00
**HUMMEL FIGURE,** "Signs of Spring,"
mkd., 5¼″ H. ................. $45.00

*Row II, L to R*
**HUMMEL FIGURE,** "Stormy Weather,"
mkd., slightly rough area on boy's hair, 6½″
O.H. ...................... $90.00
**HUMMEL FIGURE,** "Mother's Darling,"
mkd., few specks of wh. paint, 5½″ H.
.......................... $65.00
**HUMMEL CANDY BOX,** "Playmates,"
.......................... $90.00

A-MA July 1982    *Richard A. Bourne Co., Inc.*
*Row I, L to R*
**CHINESE CLOISONNE PLANTERS,**
pr., engraved brass feet & teakwood bases,
minor damage, 6⅜″ L., 4¾″ W., 4¾″ O.H.
.......................... $150.00
**CLOISONNE LETTERHOLDER,** slight
dent, 4⅞″ H. ................. $150.00

*Row II, L to R*
**LRG. CLOISONNE COVERED
BOWL,** Chinese, 19th or early 20th C.,
8½″ D. ...................... $175.00
**CLOISONNE VASE,** Japanese, late 19th
C., poorly repaired, sm. chip, 11½″ H.
.......................... $100.00
**COVERED CLOISONNE BOWL,** teak-wood base, Chinese, late 19th or early 20th
C., 5″ D. .................... $130.00

A-WA D.C. July 1982  *Adam A. Weschler & Son*
**CROWN DERBY COFFEE SET,** 3-pcs.,
retailed by Tiffany & Co., NY, Imari
patt. ........................ $250.00*

A-WA D.C. Dec. 1982  *Adam A. Weschler & Son*
**ROYAL CROWN DERBY JAPAN
PATTERN DESSERT SERVICE,** 92
pcs. (place setting illus.) ...... $2100.00*

A-WA D.C. Dec. 1982  *Adam A. Weschler & Son*
**MEISSEN DINNER SERVICE,** 69 pcs.
(some illus.), oval covered tureen, 3 nesting
platters, round platter, 2 oval covered
entree dishes, 2 oval open vegetable dishes,
double-lidded sauce boat w/attached
undertray and ladle, 24 dinner plates, 12
salad plates, 12 bread & butter plates, 10
rimmed soup plates & a fish platter, wh.
ground w/floral bouquet medallions & gilt
festoons & inset borders ...... $2600.00*

A-WA D.C. Dec. 1982  *Adam A. Weschler & Son*
**LIMOGES GAME SERVICE,** oval
platter & 12 plates (2 illus.), each has
different game in landscape medallion, sgn.
"de Solis," platter: 18½″ L., plates: 9½″ D.
.......................... $650.00*

*Price does not include 10% buyer fee.

A-WA D.C. Dec. 1982 *Adam A. Weschler & Son*
L to R
**SEVRES MOUNTED URN & COVER,**
late 19th C., gilt metal, amorous scene
medallion, sgn. "C. Roy," other side has
river landscape, on a pink ground, 26" H.
............................... $600.00*
**SEVRES ORMOLU MOUNTED URN,**
late 19th C., one side has bacchant &
cupids in flower garden, other side has river
landscape, handles in cobalt blue & gilt
enamel, sgn. "C. LaGarre," 28" H.
............................... $1600.00*

A-WA D.C. Dec. 1982 *Adam A. Weschler & Son*
**GEORGE JONES PATE SUR PATE
VASES,** pr., ca. 1885, decor. by Frederick
Schenk, one sgn. "Schenk Sc," deep olive
gr. round w/gilt highlighting, 8" H.
............................... $800.00*

A-WA D.C. Dec. 1982 *Adam A. Weschler & Son*
**RUDOLSTADT CAPO DI MONTE
URNS,** pr., S-scroll handles, egg & dart
flaring rim, 15½" H. ........... $500.00*

A-WA D.C. Dec. 1982 *Adam A. Weschler & Son*
**POTSCHAPPEL LONG-NECK
VASES,** pr., late 19th C., amorous scene
medallions within a floral encrusted &
butterfly field, 12" H. ......... $400.00*

A-WA D.C. Dec. 1982 *Adam A. Weschler & Son*
*MEISSEN FIGURES*
L to R
**TAILOR,** late 19th C., underglaze blue
crossed swords, mkd. "0176," 4¾" H.
......................... $225.00*

**WOOD CUTTER,** late 19th C., underglaze blue crossed swords, mkd. "L154" &
"58," 5¾" H. ................. $300.00*

**SEATED CUPID HOLDING HEART,**
late 19th C., underglaze blue crossed
swords, mkd. "L103" & "93," 6¾" H.
......................... $325.00*

*Row II, L to R*
**TE PRENDS MONESSOR,** late 19th C.,
underglaze blue crossed swords, mkd.
"T11" & "111," 5¼" H. ........ $275.00*

**ALLEGORICAL "WINTER,"** late 19th
C.,underglaze blue crossed swords, mkd.
"K116" & "151" & "37," 5¾" H.
..................... $300.00*

**WARRIOR,** late 19th C., underglaze
crossed swords, mkd. "C39," 5" H.
......................... $275.00*

A-WA D.C. Dec. 1982 *Adam A. Weschler & Son*
*ROYAL WORCESTER TROPICAL FISH*
Row I, L to R
**BLUE ANGELFISH,** limited edition #82,
11" H. ..................... $450.00*
**SPANISH HOGFISH & SERGEANT
MAJOR,** limited edition #160, 10½" H.
..................... $400.00*
**ROCK BEAUTY,** limited edition #20,
issued 1963, 9" H. ........... $350.00*
*Row II, L to R*
**RAINBOW PARROT FISH,** limited
edition #34, issued 1967, 10½" H.
..................... $450.00*
**SQUIRRELFISH,** limited edition #56,
issued 1961, 9½" H. ......... $450.00*
**FOUR-EYED & BANDED BUTTER-
FLY FISH,** limited edition #203, 10¾" H.
..................... $400.00*
**RED HIND,** limited edition #31, 11¾" H.
..................... $475.00*

A-WA D.C. Dec. 1982 *Adam A. Weschler & Son*
L to R
**MEISSEN COVERED URN,** late 19th
C., underglaze blue crossed swords, mkd.
"29" & "39," 10½" H. ......... $600.00*
**MEISSEN ALLEGORICAL FIGURE
OF THE ARTS,** late 19th C., underglaze
blue crossed swords, 13" H. ... $350.00*

A-WA D.C. Dec. 1982 *Adam A. Weschler & Son*
L to R
**MEISSEN MONKEY BAND,** 7 pcs., late
19th C., underglaze blue crossed swords,
mkd., maestro: 6¾" H. ....... $2100.00*

*Price does not include 10% buyer fee.

A-WA D.C. July 1982  *Adam A. Weschler & Son*
**CANTON BLUE & WH. PLATTER,**
mid-19th C., 17¼″ L. ......... $425.00*

A-MA July 1982    *Richard A. Bourne Co., Inc.*
*Row I, L to R*
**EXPORT PORCELAIN SOUP PLATE,**
Chinese, late 18th or early 19th C., 9″ D.
.................................. $100.00
**EXPORT PORCELAIN CANDLE-
STICK,** Chinese, 18th C., armorial decor.,
6⅜″ H. ......................... $300.00
**IMARI PLATE,** Japanese, 19th C., 8½″ D.
.................................. $100.00

*Row II*
**SMALL EXPORT PORCELAIN PLAT-
TERS,** pr., Chinese, late 18th or early 19th
C., 10⅛″ L. .................... $450.00

*L to R*
A-WA D.C. July 1982  *Adam A. Weschler & Son*
**ROYAL WORCESTER JAR,** late 19th
C., floral medallions on ivory ground, 7½″
H. ............................ $100.00*

A-MA July 1982       *Robert W. Skinner Inc.*
**ROYAL WORCESTER PORCELAIN
TEA POT,** Eng., ca. 1894, polychrome
floral decor. w/gold detail on tinted ground,
9″ H. ......................... $400.00*

A-WA D.C. Dec. 1982  *Adam A. Weschler & Son*
**ROYAL CROWN DERBY JAPAN
PATTERN DESSERT PLATES,** set of
22 (3 illus.), 9″ D. ............ $950.00*

A-MA Nov. 1982    *Richard A. Bourne Co., Inc.*
*Row I, L to R*
**BLUE & WH. CANTON SAUCER
BOAT,** 19th C., intertwined handle, slight
roughage to glaze at spout, 7″ L.
.............................. $175.00
**BLUE & WH. CANTON PINT MUG,**
19th C., twined handle, 4 small rim nicks &
glaze roughage to both rim & handle, 4″ H.
.............................. $225.00
**BLUE & WH. CANTON CREAM
PITCHER,** 19th C., 2 small chips in spout,
4″ H. ......................... $100.00
**BLUE & WH. CANTON SM. PITCHER
OR CREAMER,** 19th C., lt. glaze
roughage around upper rim, 1 small glaze
chip on side of handle, 5¾″ H. ... $250.00

*Row II, L to R*
**BLUE & WH. CANTON POT,** 19th C., 1
very minor glaze roughage, minus cover,
5¾″ D., 4¼″ H. ................ $150.00
**BLUE & WH. CANTON TOBACCO
LEAF DISHES,** pr., 19th C., several small
glaze roughages to rims of both, 8⅜″
.............................. $325.00
**BLUE & WH. CANTON TOBACCO
LEAF DISH,** 19th C., several small upper
surface glaze imperfections, 7¼″ L.
.............................. $150.00

A-MA Oct. 1982       *Robert W. Skinner Inc.*
**CANTON RETICULATED BASKET
& TRAY,** China, 19th C., painted in
underglazed blue, blue willow pattern, 9½″
L. & 9¾″ L. ................... $400.00*
**CANTON CIDER JUG,** China, 19th C.,
8½″ H. ....................... $850.00*

A-MA Nov. 1982    *Richard A. Bourne Co., Inc.*
*Row I, L to R*
**BLUE & WH. CANTON PITCHER,**
19th C., elaborate landscape scene, slight
glaze roughage along edges of handle,
shallow chip on inside of foot ring, 9½″ H.
.............................. $500.00
**CANTON BLUE & WH. BOWLS,** pr. (1
illus.), 19th C., 1 small rim chip (unillus.),
one has larger rim chip, 9¾″ H.
.............................. $750.00
**SHELL-FORM BLUE & WH.
CANTON SERVING DISH,** flat handle,
3″ age crack, 10″ x 10½″ ....... $275.00
*Row II, L to R*
**BLUE & WH. CANTON VEGETABLE
DISH,** 19th C., 1 shallow rim nick, 8½″
x 7¼″ ......................... $275.00
**BLUE & WH. CANTON COVERED
TUREEN,** 19th C., boar's head handles,
12″ L. ........................ $1100.00
**BLUE & WH. CANTON UNDER-
TRAY,** 19th C., reticulated "Forget-Me-
Not" patt. rim, 2 small raised flowers
chipped, 1¼″ age crack in upper rim
.............................. $300.00

A-MA July 1982    *Richard A. Bourne Co., Inc.*
*Row I, L to R*
**CANTON PLATE,** Chinese, 19th C.,
minor repr., 9¾″ D. ............ $100.00
**CANTON PLATE,** Chinese, 19th C.,
polychromed int. scene w/6 figures, minor
repr. for chip, 9¾″ D. .......... $90.00
**CANTON DEEP DISH,** 4-panel decor. of
fishing villate, retouching of rim area, 10¼″
D. ............................ $120.00
*Row II*
**CANTON ROSE MEDALLION FISH
PLATTER,** w/drain, wear to gold rim,
18¾″ L. ....................... $900.00

A-MA July 1982 *Richard A. Bourne Co., Inc.*
*Row I, L to R*
**BLUE CANTON MASTER SALT**
.................................. $230.00
**BLUE CANTON COVERED SUGAR
BOWL** ........................ $170.00
**CANTON ROSE MEDALLION
BRUSH POT** ................. $90.00
**CANTON ROSE MEDALLION COV-
ERED JAR,** 1 sm. inner rim nick, 4¼″ D.,
4″ O.H. ..................... $185.00
**CANTON ROSE MEDALLION COV-
ERED DISH,** wear to gold on rim, 5½″ L.
.................................. $190.00

*Row II, L to R*
**CANTON ROSE MEDALLION
VASES,** pr., surface flaking of glaze on
both vases, 7⅛″ H. ........... $225.00
**EXPORT PORCELAIN COVERED
TEA CADDY,** Chinese, 18th C., 2 bird
decor., repr., 5½″ H. ....... $40.00
**EXPORT PORCELAIN TEAPOT,**
Chinese, late 18th C., sm. medallion
decor., minor damages, repr., 5½″ O.H.
.................................. $200.00

*Row III, L to R*
**CANTON ROSE MEDALLION COV-
ERED SAUCE BOAT,** gold on handles &
finial shows wear, 7½″ L. ....... $400.00
**BLUE CANTON FRUIT BASKET &
UNDERTRAY** ............... $575.00
**KUTANI VASE,** Japanese, 19th C., sgn.
in red, 6⅝″ H. ................. $125.00

A-WA D.C. Dec. 1982 *Adam A. Weschler & Son*
**CANTON TABLE ARTICLES,** 4 pcs.,
19th C., pr. rectangular entree dishes,
rectangular covered sauce tureen &
undertray ..................... $700.00*

A-MA July 1982 *Richard A. Bourne Co., Inc.*
*BLUE CANTON*
*Row I, L to R*
**FOOTED EGG CUP,** 2⅜″ H. . . $100.00
**TEA SERVICE,** 3-pcs., slight roughages
.................................. $410.00

*Row II, L to R*
**DEMITASE CUPS & SAUCERS,** set of
6 (1 illus.), slight rim nicks or roughages
on saucers ..................... $160.00
**PLATES,** lot of 15 (1 illus.), 1 w/minute rim
nick, 8½″ - 9″ D. .............. $400.00
**LRG. CUPS & SAUCERS,** lot of 6 (1
illus.), non-matching, rim nicks . . . $200.00

A-WA D.C. Dec. 1982 *Adam A. Weschler & Son*
**CANTON FAMILLE ROSE MEDAL-
LION VASES,** pr., Chinese, late 19th C.,
applied salamander collars w/Foo puppy
handles, 13″ H. .............. $600.00*

A-WA D.C. Dec. 1982 *Adam A. Weschler & Son*
*L to R*
**CANTON FAMILLE ROSE MEDAL-
LION PUNCH BOWL,** Chinese, last half
of 19th C., interior & exterior decor., 16″D.
.................................. $1000.00*
**FAMILLE ROSE OVAL PLATTER &
STRAINER,** Chinese, late 19th C., butter-
flies & insects within foliage on wh. ground,
16½″ L. ..................... $375.00*

A-WA D.C. July 1982 *Adam A. Weschler & Son*
*CANTON CHINA*
*Row I, L to R*
**DINNER PLATES,** set of 8 (1 illus.),
Famille rose medallion, late 19th C., 9½″ D.
.................................. $150.00*
**DEEP PLATES,** set of 6 (1 illus.), Famille
rose medallion, late 19th C., 8¾″ D.
.................................. $100.00*

*Row II, L to R*
**SHALLOW BOWLS,** set of 2, Famille
rose medallion, late 19th C., 1 sq., other
lotus shaped .................. $275.00*
**DOUBLE-LIP SAUCE BOAT,** ca. 1860,
Famille rose medallion, strap handles on
flaring base, 8″ L. ............. $200.00*
**CUPS & SAUCERS,** set of 9 (1 illus.),
early 20th C., rose medallion . . . $100.00*
**DINNER PLATES,** set of 19 (1 illus.),
19th-20th C., Famille rose medallion, 9″ D.
.................................. $200.00*

*Row III, L to R*
**COVERED VEGETABLE DISH,** ca.
1860, Famille rose medallion, 10″ L.
.................................. $275.00*
**COVERED VEGETABLE DISH,** ca.
1860, Famille rose medallion, 8¾″ L.
.................................. $250.00*
**COVERED VEGETABLE DISH,** ca.
1860, Famille rose medallion, 8¼″ L.
.................................. $225.00*

A-MA Mar. 1983 *Robert W. Skinner Inc.*
**CANTON COFFEEPOT,** Chinese, 19th
C., tall tapering cylindrical form w/shaped
spout, entwined handle, 8″ H. . . $450.00*

A-WA D.C. July 1982 *Adam A. Weschler & Son*
**CANTON PUNCH BOWL,** ca. 1860,
Famille rose medallion, gold ground, 15¾″
D., 6½″ H. ................... $450.00*

*Price does not include 10% buyer fee.

A-MA Aug. 1983   *Richard A. Bourne Co., Inc.*
*L to R*
**ROSE MANDARIN GARDEN SEATS,**
pr., minor wear, 18″ H. . . . . . . . $4500.00

A-MA June 1983   *Robert W. Skinner Inc.*
**SATSUMA VASES,** pr., 19th C., polychrome decor., raised gold accents, some
gold wear, 14½″ H. . . . . . . . . . . . $425.00

A-MA July 1983   *Robert W. Skinner Inc.*
**COVERED BOX,** Korea, 19th C., porcelain, applied insects on cover, cover &
base w/minor chips, 5½″ D., 4″ O.H.
. . . . . . . . . . . . . . . . . . . . . . . . . . $220.00*

A-MA Aug. 1983   *Richard A. Bourne Co., Inc.*
*BLUE & WH. CANTON*
*Row I, L to R*
**RETICULATED FRUIT BOWL W/
UNDERTRAY,** handles chipped away,
8¾″ L. . . . . . . . . . . . . . . . . . . . . . $250.00

**DEEP DISHES,** set of 10 (1 illus.), 3 w/age
cracks, 1 w/chip, 10″ D. . . . . . . . . $400.00

*Row II*
**HOT WATER PLATES,** pr., minute rim
roughages, 9½″ L. . . . . . . . . . . . . $450.00

*Row III, L to R*
**OVAL PLATTER,** 11¾″ L. . . . . $200.00
**PLATES,** set of 7 (1 illus.), assorted, 2
w/slight rim nicks . . . . . . . . . . . . . $175.00

A-MA Aug. 1983   *Richard A. Bourne Co., Inc.*
*ROSE MEDALLION CANTON*
*Row I, L to R*
**PUNCH BOWL,** 15⅝″ D. . . . . $1700.00

**PUNCH BOWL,** 11½″ D. . . . . . $750.00

*Row II*
**LIDDED TUREEN W/UNDERTRAY,**
slight wear to gold rim, 14½″ L.
. . . . . . . . . . . . . . . . . . . . . . . . . . $2600.00

A-MA Aug. 1983   *Richard A. Bourne Co., Inc.*
*CANTON*
*Row I, L to R*
**BUTTERFLY TEAPOT,** slight wear to
gold, 1 sm. rim nick, 6″ O.H. . . . . $375.00
**FISH PLATTER,** rose medallion, comp.
w/drain, 18″ L. . . . . . . . . . . . . . . $1000.00

*Row II*
**COVERED DISHES,** pr., hot water
compartments, 10¼″ D. . . . . . . . $1800.00

A-MA Aug. 1983   *Richard A. Bourne Co., Inc.*
*BLUE & WH. CANTON*
*Row I*
**TOBACCO-LEAF DISHES,** set of 3, not
a matched set, 6″ to 8″ L. . . . . . . . $400.00

*Row II, L to R*
**COVERED CONDIMENT JARS,** pr.,
1 w/roughage around foot, 3¾″ H.
. . . . . . . . . . . . . . . . . . . . . . . . . . . $140.00

**SM. CREAMER,** sm. nick, 3½″ H.
. . . . . . . . . . . . . . . . . . . . . . . . . . . $175.00

**COVERED SUGAR BOWL,** berry finial
& strap handles, 4½″ H. . . . . . . . $250.00

**TINY PLATTER,** 7¾″ L. . . . . . $175.00

*Row III, L to R*
**CREAMER,** sm. glaze roughages to rim &
handle, 4¼″ H. . . . . . . . . . . . . . . $200.00

**TEAPOT,** 6¼″ H. . . . . . . . . . . . . $200.00

**COVERED VEGETABLE DISH,** minor
nicks in glaze of rim, 8″ L. . . . . . . $200.00

*Price does not include 10% buyer fee.

A-OH Mar. 1982 *Garth's Auctions, Inc.*

*Row I, L to R*

**SPATTERWARE,** handleless cup & saucer, blue, rose decor. on saucer, repr., damage to cup ................ $25.00

**SPATTERWARE,** handleless cup & saucer, blue & gr. rainbow, close mismatch, flakes on cup ............ $85.00

**SPATTERWARE,** miniature cup & saucer, br. .................... $60.00

**SPATTERWARE,** handleless cup & saucer, blue, mkd. "Davenport," repr. ............................ $30.00

**SPATTERWARE,** handleless cup & saucer, red & blue, simple flower in red & gr., mkd. "Harvey," chips on table ring of saucer ....................... $35.00

*Row II, L to R*

**SPATTERWARE,** handleless cup & saucer, purple ................. $115.00

**SPATTERWARE,** handleless cup & saucer, blue, surface chip & hairline in saucer ....................... $30.00

**SPATTERWARE,** handleless cup & saucer, yellow, blue dots ........ $210.00

**SPATTERWARE,** handleless cup & saucer, blue, paneled, center blue dot ............................ $50.00

**SPATTERWARE,** handleless cup & saucer, purple, inc. mark "--- & Sons, Pearlware, Fenton," flake on top edge of handle ........................ $20.00

*Row III, L to R*

**STICK SPATTER,** handleless cups & saucers, pr. (1st & last items), floral design in red, blue & gr. ............... $50.00

**SPATTERWARE,** sugar bowl, red, blk. stripes & well-formed handles, flakes & hairline, 5¼" H. ................ $105.00

**SPATTERWARE,** oversize cup & saucer, blk. ......................... $85.00

**SPATTERWARE,** saucer, blue transfer of a Chinaman ................... $35.00

A-OH Sept. 1982 *Garth's Auctions, Inc.*

*SPATTERWARE*

*Row I, L to R*

**HANDLELESS CUP & SAUCER,** red & yellow rainbow, thistle in red & gr., flaking ....................... $425.00

**HANDLELESS CUP & SAUCER,** red & gr., rainbow, thistle in red & gr. ............................ $300.00

**HANDLELESS CUP & SAUCER,** blue, floral spray in red, gr. & blk. .... $250.00

**HANDLELESS CUP & SAUCER,** blue & purple rainbow, rose in red, gr. & blk., some damage ................ $230.00

**HANDLELESS CUP & SAUCER,** red & yellow rainbow, thistle in red & gr., flaking & repr. ............... $425.00

*Row II, L to R*

**TEAPOT,** blue, cockscomb in red & gr., some damage, 5¾" H. .......... $175.00

**CREAMER,** blue, peafowl in orange, red, gr. & blk., 3½" H. ............ $225.00

**OBLONG PLATTER,** blue, thistle in red & gr., some damage, 9⅜" L. .... $475.00

**CREAMER,** blue, dahlia in red, blue & gr., 4" H. ...................... $275.00

**TEAPOT,** blue, dahlia in red, blue & gr., some damage, 5" H. ........... $300.00

*Row III, L to R*

**PLATE,** red, peafowl in red, blue, gr. & blk., impressed "J. Heath," repr., 8⅝" D. ............................ $250.00

**PLATE,** blue, peafowl in orange, blue, red & blk., 7⅝" D. ............... $285.00

**TEAPOT,** blue, octagonal, tulip in red, blue, gr. & blk., repr., 8½" H. ... $400.00

**PLATE,** blue, pomegranate in red, blue, gr., yellow & blk., 6⅝" D. ....... $275.00

**PLATE,** blue, tulip in red, blue, gr. & blk., 9¼" D. ...................... $275.00

---

A-MA Nov. 1982 *Richard A. Bourne Co., Inc.*

**LARGE SERVICE OF MULBERRY IRONSTONE CHINA,** (1 illus.), Eng., mid-19th C., "Corean" pattern, bottom of teapot has old repr., few pcs. slightly discolored, covered vegetable dish has faint age crack, 1 of smallest plates has faint age crack, 1 of middle-sized plates has poor rim repr., 1 of large plates is discolored ............................ $550.00

**MULBERRY IRONSTONE WASH BOWL & PITCHER SET,** "Corean" pattern ...................... $275.00

A-OH Mar. 1982 *Garth's Auctions, Inc.*

*Row I, L to R*

**STICKSPATTER CUP & SAUCER,** gaudy floral decor. in blue, gr., ochre & red, mkd. "Maestricht" .............. $20.00

**STICKSPATTER WASTE BOWL,** gr. & blk., mkd. "Staffordshire England," stains, flaking, 5⅝" D., 3" H. ..... $15.00

**STICKSPATTER TRAY,** gaudy floral design in red, blue & gr., mkd. "Adams Titian Ware," 7½" L. ............. $30.00

**GAUDY IRONSTONE WASTE BOWL,** floral decor. in red, blue & gr., mkd. "Staffordshire England," stains, hairline & chips, 6⅜" D., 3" H. ... $12.50

**STICKSPATTER CUP & SAUCER,** floral design in red, blue, gr. & blk., rim flakes on saucer ................ $10.00

*Row II, L to R*

**STICKSPATTER PLATE,** floral design in red, blue, gr. & yellow, mkd. "Wild Flower, Made in Scotland," 9⅛" D. ............................ $45.00

**STICKSPATTER CAKE PLATE,** gaudy floral decor. in red, blue, gr. & blk., mkd. "Maestricht," 12" D. ............ $75.00

**STICKSPATTER PLATE,** gaudy floral decor. in red, blue, gr. & purple, Davenport Anchor mark & "Made in Great Britain," 9¼" D. ....................... $7.50

*Row III, L to R*

**STICKSPATTER PLATES,** 5 (1 illus.), red, gr., br. & blue, mkd. "Staffordshire England," 4 have hairlines, 8⅝" D. ............................ $25.00

**STICKSPATTER PIECES,** 10, (1 illus.), match to above, 7 plates 6" D., 3 saucers, some stains & edge chips ........ $35.00

**GAUDY STICKSPATTER PLATE,** floral design in red, blue, gr., yellow & purple, mkd. "Villeroy & Boch," stains, 10" D. ............................ $25.00

**STICKSPATTER WASTE BOWL,** gaudy floral design in red & blue, 5⅝" D. ............................ $32.50

**GAUDY STICKSPATTER PLATES,** 5 (1 illus.), match to above, one has rim flake, 7½" D. ....................... $40.00

*Price does not include 10% buyer fee.

A-MA July 1982    *Richard A. Bourne Co., Inc.*
*HISTORICAL STAFFORDSHIRE*
*Row I, L to R*
**PLATE,** drk. blue, "Gilpin's Mill On The Brandywine Creek," by Enoch Wood & Sons, 9⅛" D. ................. $325.00
**PLATE,** drk. blue, "Commodore Mac-Donough's Victory," by Enoch Wood & Sons, 9⅛" D. ................. $250.00
**PLATE,** drk. blue, "Fall Of Montmorenci Near Quebeck," by Enoch Wood & Sons, 9-1/16" D. ................... $150.00

*Row II, L to R*
**PLATE,** med. blue, "Dam & Water Works, Phila.," slight discoloration in glaze, 10" D. ................................. $200.00
**PLATE,** drk. blue, "Constitution," by Enoch Wood & Sons, glaze worn around inner rim, 10⅛" D. ............. $150.00
**PLATE,** med. blue, "Bank Of The United States, Phila.," by Stubbs, faint age & glaze cracks, 10" D. ................ $150.00

*Row III, L to R*
**PLATE,** drk. blue, states of Am. & Independence by Clews, chips, 10⅝" D. ............................... $100.00
**PLATTER,** drk. blue, unidentified maker & patt., slight wear on inner rim glaze, 14½" L. ............................... $300.00

A-MA July 1982    *Richard A. Bourne Co., Inc.*
*HISTORICAL STAFFORDSHIRE*
*Row I, L to R*
**PLATE,** drk. blue, "Southampton, Hampshire," by Enoch Wood & Sons, 7¾" D. ............................. $150.00
**PLATE,** drk. blue, "The Kent East Indiaman," by Enoch Wood & Sons ◀
............................... $125.00
*Row II, L to R*
**PLATE,** med. blue, "The Landing Of The Fathers," by Enoch Wood & Sons, 10¼" D. ............................. $100.00
**PLATE,** drk. blue, unidentified maker & title, edge crack in rim, 10⅛" D. . . $80.00

A-OH July 1982    *Garth's Auctions, Inc.*
*HISTORICAL BLUE STAFFORDSHIRE*
*Row I, L to R*
**CREAMER,** medium blue floral transfer, 5½" H. ........................ $65.00
**PLATTER,** med. drk. blue transfer, "Kidbroof, Sussex," impressed "A. Stevenson," minor scratches, 10⅜" L.
............................... $245.00
**CREAMER,** drk. blue transfer "Mount Vernon, The Seat Of The Late Gen Washington," rim & base flakes, 4½" H.
............................... $220.00

*Row II, L to R*
**PLATE,** med. blue transfer, unmkd. sheltered peasants, 10⅛" D. ..... $45.00
**SOUP PLATE,** drk. blue transfer, "Villa In Regents Park," impressed "Adams," 10⅛" D. ........................ $130.00
**PLATE,** med. blue transfer, unmkd. sheltered peasants, 10⅛" D. ..... $45.00

*Row III, L to R*
**SOUP PLATE,** drk. blue transfer "Landing Of Lafayette...," impressed "Clews," cracked & glued rim & rim flakes, 9⅞" D.
............................... $35.00
**SOUP PLATE,** med. drk. blue transfer of "Villa In Regents Park," impressed "Adams," 10⅛" D. ............. $105.00
**PLATE,** drk. blue transfer, "Landing Of Gen Lafayette," impressed "Clews," cracked & rim chips, 10⅛" D. .... $30.00

A-OH Oct. 1982    *Garth's Auctions, Inc.*
*COPPER LUSTRE*
*Row I, L to R*
**PITCHER,** wh. band, brick-red transfer, 5" H. ........................ $65.00
**PITCHER,** wh. band, brick-red transfer, 4⅝" H. ........................ $45.00
**PITCHER,** wh. band, brick-red transfer, minor wear & flaking, 4⅛" H. .... $25.00
**PITCHER,** canary yellow band, br. transfer, 4½" H. .................... $75.00

*Row II, L to R*
**PITCHER,** pale yellow band, br. transfer, 5¾" H. ........................ $65.00
**PITCHER,** br. transfer, polychrome enameling, flaking, 6¼" H. ....... $35.00
**PITCHER,** polychrome enameled flowers, 6" H. ......................... $40.00
**PITCHER,** purple band, polychrome enamel, glued break, 6" H. ....... $35.00

*Row III, L to R*
**PITCHER,** burnt orange band, blk. transfer "Cornwallis" & "LaFayette," wear & scratches, repr., 7½" H. ........ $105.00
**PITCHER,** gr. enameled band, 6¾" H.
............................... $70.00
**PITCHER,** wh. bands, flake, 4⅝" H.
............................... $15.00

A-MA July 1982    *Richard A. Bourne Co., Inc.*
*L to R*
**PLATTER,** drk. blue, from the French series by Enoch Wood & Sons, grapevine border, 18¾" L. ........... $400.00
**HISTORICAL STAFFORDSHIRE PLATTER,** drk. blue, from the Vine Leaf Border series by Ralph Stevenson, slight discoloration, 20¾" L. ........ $1050.00

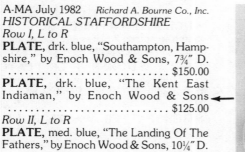

*Price does not include 10% buyer fee.

A-OH July 1982          *Garth's Auctions, Inc.*
*Row I, L to R*
**YELLOWWARE MUG,** w/br. bands, 3¾" H. ........................ $75.00
**ROCKINGHAM SOAP DISH,** small flakes on base, 4½" D. .......... $45.00
**ROCKINGHAM TOBY PITCHER,** 5¾" H. ........................... $45.00
**ROCKINGHAM SOUP DISH,** rectangular, chip on base, 3⅞" x 5½" .... $50.00
**ROCKINGHAM MUG,** 3½" H. ........................... $95.00

*Row II, L to R*
**ROCKINGHAM PIE PLATE,** some int. surface flakes, 11" D., 1½" H. .... $75.00
**ROCKINGHAM BOWL,** some glaze flakes & wear, 7" D., 3¾" H. ..... $25.00
**ROCKINGHAM PIE PLATE,** small surface flakes, 10⅜" D., 1½" H. ... $85.00

*Row III, L to R*
**ROCKINGHAM PIE PLATE,** some wear & old rim flake, 9½" D., 1½" H. ........................... $60.00
**OPEN VEGETABLE DISH,** flint enamel, rim & foot chips, cracked, 8¾" x 12½" ........................... $105.00
**CUSTARD CUP,** putty colored clay w/br. & blue sponging, edge flake, 3⅞" D. ........................... $30.00
**ROCKINGHAM PIE PLATE,** 9¼" D., 1⅛" H. ........................... $85.00

A-MA July 1982          *Richard A. Bourne Co., Inc.*
*L to R*
**BENNINGTON NAME PLATE,** drk. br. w/wh. mottled glaze, applied wh. porcelain letters, 6⅝" L., 3¼" H. .......... $225.00

**BENNINGTON PICTURE FRAME,** flint enamel, blue, br., & yellow mottled coloring, 7⅝" x 6½" ............ $400.00

**ROCKINGHAM COW CREAMER,** tiny nick, 7" L., 5" H. .............. $150.00

A-MA July 1982          *Richard A. Bourne Co., Inc.*
*Row I, L to R*
**ROCKINGHAM PINT FLASK,** colonial tavern scene on one side, 6" H. .. $90.00
**ROCKINGHAM PITCHER,** hound handle, mkd. Nichols & Alford, small chip, 8¾" H. ........................... $225.00
*Row II, L to R*
**BENNINGTON WASH BOWL,** 12-sided, mkd., br. & yellow glaze, 14½" D. ........................... $300.00
**BENNINGTON TYPE FOOTWARMER,** med. br. & tan glaze, small chip & repr., 11⅛" H. ................. $100.00

 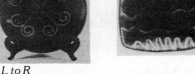

*L to R*
A-MA July 1982          *Robert W. Skinner Inc.*
**SLIPWARE DECORATED PLATE,** Am., early 19th C., hairline crack, 10¼" D. ........................... $425.00*

A-MA Aug. 1982          *Robert W. Skinner Inc.*
**REVERSE SLIP DEEP PLATTER,** Eng., 18th C., oblong molded form, rounded corners, notched rim, drk. br. glaze, wh. slip decor., cracked, 10¼" x 12¼" ........................... $1050.00*

*L to R*
A-MA Aug. 1982          *Robert W. Skinner Inc.*
**YELLOWWARE HANDLED POT,** Eng., 18th C., combed marbled decor., rim chips, small crack, 5" H., body 5½" D. ........................... $1900.00*

A-MA July 1982          *Robert W. Skinner Inc.*
**SLIPWARE DECORATED PLATE,** Am., early 19th C., 9¾" D. ..... $225.00*

A-MA July 1982          *Richard A. Bourne Co., Inc.*
*Row I, L to R*
**SCRODDLED WARE CUSPIDORE,** br. colored glaze, faint age crack, 8" D. ........................... $250.00
**SM. POTTERY JUG,** Eng., gr. glazed leaf patt. around shoulder, yellow-br. glaze on bottom, 4½" D., 4¾" H. ........ $175.00

*Row II, L to R*
**POTTERY JAR,** Am., drk. mottled br. glaze, once had cover, 8" H. .... $110.00
**POTTERY PITCHER,** Am., mottled glaze in lt. gr., lt. reddish-br. & drk. olive gr., 7½" H. ................... $110.00

A-MA July 1982          *Robert W. Skinner Inc.*
**LRG. SLIPWARE DEEP PLATTER,** Am., early 19th C., rim chips, 11½" x 18", 3" H. ........................ $800.00*

*L to R*
A-MA Aug. 1982          *Robert W. Skinner Inc.*
**REVERSE COMBWARE DEEP DISH,** Eng., 18th C., large, molded deep round dish, deep br. glaze, combed wh. slip decor., body loss on back, crack, 14" D. ........................... $800.00*

A-MA Aug. 1982          *Robert W. Skinner Inc.*
**REVERSE COMBWARE DEEP DISH,** Eng., 18th C., medium, molded deep round dish, notched rim, br. glaze w/wh. spiral decor., 11" D. .............. $1500.00*

*Price does not include 10% buyer fee.

A-OH Jan. 1983          *Garth's Auctions, Inc.*
*ROCKINGHAM GLAZED WARE*
*Row I, L to R*
**MUG**, 3¼" H. ............. $60.00
**BOWL**, minor flaking, 6¾" D. .... $45.00
**SOAP DISH**, crack & chip, 4½" D.
............................... $40.00
**BOWL**, 6¼" D. ............. $45.00
**MUG**, bubble in glaze, 3¼" H. ... $60.00

*Row II, L to R*
**PITCHER**, embossed, minor glaze flakes,
7½" H. ..................... $85.00
**ENAMEL CANDLESTICK**, Bennington
flint, flake on base, 7¾" H. ...... $400.00
**BOWL**, embossed rim, minor flakes, 7" D.,
4¼" H. ..................... $85.00
**BOWL**, minor wear, 8¼" D., 1¾" H.
............................... $40.00

*Row III, L to R*
**PLATTER**, minor wear, 10" L.
............................... $115.00
**COVERED JAR**, cracks & flakes, 8¾" D.,
8¼" H. ..................... $90.00
**SERVING DISH**, minor wear & scratches,
10" L. ...................... $115.00

---

A-OH Jan. 1983          *Garth's Auctions, Inc.*
*Row I, L to R*
**SPONGEWARE BOWL**, br., blue, wh.
on cream, 5¼" D. ............. $45.00
**WHITE CLAY PIG BANK**, Rockingham
glaze, 6" L. .................. $45.00
**SPONGEWARE PITCHER**, br., blue,
red & wh. on cream, 5" H. ....... $95.00
**WHITE CLAY PIG BANK**, clear glaze,
red, br. & amber, flakes, 5⅝" L. .. $50.00
**SPONGEWARE GYPSY KETTLE**, blue
& wh., lid, chip, no handle, 4¾" H. ... $55.00

*Row II, L to R*
**SPONGEWARE JAR**, lid & wire handle,
damage, 6" H. ............... $110.00
**SPONGEWARE COVERED POT**, wire
handle, blue & wh., 11" D., 7" H. .. $295.00
**SPONGEWARE COVERED JAR**, gr. &
wh., flaking, 5½" H. ........... $95.00

*Row III, L to R*
**SPONGEWARE MIXING BOWLS**, pr.,
gr. & wh., 10" D., 4½" H.
............................... $170.00
**SPONGEWARE JARDINIERE**, br. glaze,
7½" H. ..................... $55.00

A-OH Jan. 1983          *Garth's Auctions, Inc.*
*Row I, L to R*
**ROCKINGHAM SOAP DISH**, 6" D.,
2⅜" H. ..................... $95.00
**ROCKINGHAM CREAMER**, flaking,
4½" H. ..................... $40.00
**ROCKINGHAM OVAL DISH**, minor
wear, 5⅛" x 7¼" ............. $65.00
**ROCKINGHAM MUG**, sm. flake, 2⅞" H.
............................... $50.00
**ROCKINGHAM CREAMER**, chip, 4⅜"
H. ......................... $15.00
**ROCKINGHAM TURK'S HEAD
MOLD**, 6⅝" D. ............. $85.00

*Row II, L to R*
**ROCKINGHAM PITCHER W/LID**, em-
bossed, flaking, 9¼" H. ........ $300.00
**ROCKINGHAM OCTAGONAL PLAT-
TER**, minor wear, 11¼" L. ..... $125.00
**ROCKINGHAM MUG**, flaking, 2⅞" H.
............................... $30.00
**ROCKINGHAM MUG**, vertical ribs, 3"
H. ......................... $55.00
**HOUND-HANDLED PITCHER**, Ben-
nington flint enamel, embossed, flaking,
8½" H. ..................... $250.00

*Row III, L to R*
**ROCKINGHAM PIE PLATE**, 11" D.,
1¼" H. ..................... $115.00
**ROCKINGHAM PIE PLATE**, 9" D., 1¼"
H. ......................... $85.00
**HOUND-HANDLED PITCHER**, wh.
clay, olive gr. dappling, embossed, flakes,
6¼" H. ..................... $175.00
**ROCKINGHAM PIE PLATE**, some
wear & chips, 10½" D., 1¼" H. ... $55.00

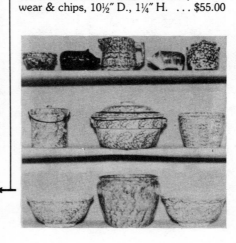

A-OH Mar. 1983          *Garth's Auctions, Inc.*
*Row I, L to R*
**CUP & SAUCER**, br. spatterware, mkd.
"Staffordshire England" ......... $20.00
**CUP & SAUCER**, red w/blue border
spatterware, mkd. "Staffordshire, Eng-
land," flake on table ring of cup ... $15.00
**FOUR CUPS & SAUCERS**, (1 set illus.),
spatterware, Gaudy floral decor. in red, gr.
& blue, mkd. "Wm. Adams, Tunstall,
England" .................... $100.00
**CUP & SAUCER**, spatterware, mkd.
"Staffordshire, England," minor glaze
flakes on back of saucer ......... $25.00
*Row II, L to R*
**PAIR OF CUPS & SAUCERS**, (1 pr.
illus.), red, blue & blk., stains & chips
............................... $15.00
**COPPER LUSTRE FOOTED SALT**,
tan band, blue dots & lustre foliage,
pinpoint flakes, 3" D., 2" H. ...... $40.00
**WASTE BOWL**, spatterware, floral
decor. in blue, br. & gr., overlay of blue
spatter, mkd. "Wm Adams, Tunstall," tiny
rim flakes, 5⅜" D., 2⅞" H. .... $45.00
**DISH**, blue & wh. spatterware, mkd.
"Schenectady Exposition 1924 Weber
Electric Co.," 2⅝" D., 1¼" H. .... $20.00
**CUP & SAUCER**, blue & wh. spatterware, mkd. "Davenport," minor edge wear
............................... $15.00
*Row III, L to R*
**FOURTEEN PIECE TEA SET**, (6 pcs.
illus.), spatterware, br. & wh. w/red stripes,
many pcs. mkd. "Staffordshire, England,"
teapot, sugar, creamer, 5 cups, 3 saucers, 6
plates, 5⅜" D. ................ $125.00

*L to R*

A-MA Aug. 1982          *Robert W. Skinner Inc.*
**REVERSE SLIP DEEP PLATTER**, Eng.,
18th C., oblong form, rounded corners,
drk. br., purple glaze, wh. slip decor., 12⅜"
x 14" ...................... $2100.00*

A-MA Aug. 1982          *Robert W. Skinner Inc.*
**REVERSE SLIP DEEP PLATTER**, Eng.,
18th C., oblong molded form, rounded
corners, drk. br. glaze, wh. slip decor.,
chips & cracks, 13" x 14⅜" .... $2300.00*

*Price does not include 10% buyer fee.

A-OH July 1982          *Garth's Auctions, Inc.*
*Row I, L to R*
**ROCKINGHAM PITCHER,** 4⅜" H.
............................ $135.00
**ROCKINGHAM MUG,** hairlines, 3¼" H.
............................ $15.00
**ROCKINGHAM BOWL,** cracks in base,
6⅝" D., 3½" H. ................. $15.00
**ROCKINGHAM MUG,** glazed over chip
on lip has a tiny flake, 3⅜" H. .... $25.00
**ROCKINGHAM PITCHER,** short rim
hairlines & a rim flake, 3¾" H. .... $70.00

*Row II, L to R*
**ROCKINGHAM PLATE,** small rim flake
& a small int. hairline ........... $65.00
**POTTERY BOTTLE,** figure of girl on
both sides, one side impressed "S. Bedford,
94, Fore Street City," 2 tone putty br.,
flakes on base, 7" H. ........... $45.00
**ROCKINGHAM BOWL,** cracked, 9" D.,
2½" H. ...................... $20.00
**ROCKINGHAM PIE PLATE,** 10" D.,
1⅜" H. ...................... $95.00
**REDWARE FIGURAL BOTTLE,** man
on barrel w/inscription on barrel head
"What Do You Think Of Me 1838," lip has
been ground & has flakes, drk. glaze, 7⅝"
H. ......................... $55.00

*Row III, L to R*
**ROCKINGHAM JAR,** 6¼" H. .. $35.00
**ROCKINGHAM PITCHER,** hound
handled, very minor hairline in handle, 10"
H. ......................... $100.00
**ROCKINGHAM JAR,** gothic arches
w/foliage, chips & lid is missing, 7¼" H.
............................ $12.50

A-MA Mar. 1983          *Robert W. Skinner Inc.*
**BENNINGTON SPICE SET,** 19th C., br.
slip, 8 sm. covered crocks each mkd.
w/spice name, 2 larger crocks mkd. "Tea"
& "Coffee," & a batter pitcher, some sm.
crocks show finger marks from glazing
process, minor glaze chips, spices 4¼" H.,
tea 7¾" H., pitcher 8½" H. ..... $750.00*

A-MA Nov. 1982     *Richard A. Bourne Co., Inc.*
**BENNINGTON FLINT ENAMEL
SAUCER BASE CANDLEHOLDER,**
ring handle, glazed in olive, yellow-br. &
br., impressed on base w/letter "J," 3¼" H.
............................ $875.00
**BENNINGTON ROCKINGHAM
GLAZED COW CREAMER,** long glaze
crack running down cow's spine, 5⅜" H.
............................ $175.00
**ROCKINGHAM GLAZE STAFFORD-
SHIRE-SHAPE MASTER SALT,** yellow
& br. glaze, minute rim nick & faint age
crack, 2⅜" H. ................. $350.00
**BENNINGTON ROCKINGHAM
GLAZE PAPERWEIGHT,** yellow & br.
glaze, "1849" impressed mark underneath,
2¾" H. ...................... $650.00
*Row II, L to R*
**BENNINGTON FLINT ENAMEL
BOOK FLASK,** "Life Of Kossuth," glazed
in blue & br. w/yellow, 6" H. .... $658.00
**BENNINGTON FLINT ENAMEL
BOOK FLASK,** "Departed Spirits,"
glazed in yellow & br., 5½" H. ... $575.00
**BENNINGTON FLINT ENAMEL
"TULIP AND HEART" PATTERN
CREAMER,** glazed in blue-gr. & br., repr.
to handle, 6" H. ............... $300.00
**BENNINGTON FLINT ENAMEL
COLUMNAR CANDLESTICK,** glazed
in blue & yellow-br., 6¾" H. ..... $325.00
*Row III, L to R*
**BENNINGTON GLAZED SEATED
TOBY PITCHER,** "1849" mark, 6½" H.
............................ $450.00
**ROCKINGHAM GLAZED BOOK
FLASK,** probably NY, 4 small chips, some
glaze wear, 7¾" H. ............ $200.00
**BENNINGTON ROCKINGHAM
GLAZED COACHMAN TOBY BOT-
TLE,** repr. to brim of hat, 8½" H.
............................ $625.00

A-MA Aug. 1982          *Robert W. Skinner Inc.*
**REDWARE,** 2-pcs., Am., 19th C., baluster-form pitcher w/rim chips, 9¾" H.,
slant-sided bowl is damaged, 6" H., 13½"
D., lead glaze w/mottled manganese
............................ $450.00*

A-MA Nov. 1982     *Richard A. Bourne Co., Inc.*
*Row I, L to R*
**BENNINGTON FLINT ENAMEL
PITCHER,** faint impressed "1849" mark,
slight glaze flaking on handle, 9¾" H.
............................ $500.00
**BENNINGTON FLINT ENAMEL
SCALLOP PITCHER,** drk. br. glaze,
impressed "1849" mark, small repr. to rim,
9" H. ....................... $450.00
**BENNINGTON FLINT ENAMEL
BOOK FLASK,** br. & yellow glaze,
hairline glaze crack, 10⅝" H. .... $500.00
*Row II*
**BENNINGTON FLINT ENAMEL
SCALLOP CHAMBER PITCHER &
MATCHING BOWL,** olive gr., blue & br.
glaze, bowl impressed w/"1849" mark,
bowl has 2 slight age cracks, pitcher 12¾"
H., bowl 15" D. ............... $700.00

A-OH July 1982          *Garth's Auctions, Inc.*
*BENNINGTON W/ROCKINGHAM
GLAZE*
*Row I, L to R*
**MUG,** chips on base, 3⅞" H. .... $17.50
**MUG,** 3⅝" H. ............... $75.00
**SHAVING MUG,** embossed Toby on
each side, rim flake, 4¼" H. ...... $85.00
**MUG,** hairline in base .......... $20.00
**MUG,** 3¾" H. ............... $100.00
*Row II, L to R*
**PLATE,** 8⅜" D. .............. $110.00
**INKWELL,** w/reclining doe, flint enamel,
both ears are repl. & have some deterior-
ation, 8¼" L., 6½" H. .......... $725.00
**PLATE,** 8½" D. .............. $105.00
*Row III, L to R*
**PIE PLATE,** 11¼" D., 1½" H. ... $125.00
**COVERED JAR,** oval, small flake on one
ear & on rim of lid, 8¼" H. ...... $150.00
**PIE PLATE,** 11¼" D., 1½" H. ... $155.00

*Price does not include 10% buyer fee.

A-MA Jan. 1983    *Robert W. Skinner Inc.*
*L to R*
**STONEWARE CROCK,** 4-gal., cobalt blue, "J. C. Waelde, North Bay," 11¼" H. .................... $1500.00*
**STONEWARE JUG,** 2-gal., cobalt blue, "J. & E. Norton, Bennington, Vt.," glaze damage, 14" H. .............. $950.00*
**STONEWARE CROCK,** 3-gal., cobalt blue, "New York Stoneware Co., Fort Edward, N.Y.," cracks & chips, 11½" H. .................... $700.00*

A-MA Jan. 1983    *Robert W. Skinner Inc.*
*L to R*
**STONEWARE CREAM CROCK,** 4-gal., cobalt blue, "N. Clark & Co., Lyons," cracks, chips, flaking, 12½" H. .................... $525.00*
**STONEWARE CROCK,** 4-gal., cobalt blue, cracks, 10½" H. ......... $400.00*
**STONEWARE CROCK,** 5-gal., cobalt blue, "Ballardvale," cracks, chips, 12" H. .................... $575.00*

A-MA Mar. 1983    *Robert W. Skinner Inc.*
*L to R*
**STONEWARE CROCK,** 6 gal., "M. Woodruff & Co., Cortland," cobalt blue rudimentary flying eagle, crack, 13½" H. .................... $550.00*
**STONEWARE CROCK,** approx. 1 gal., "Whites Binghamton," cobalt blue portrait of a side wheel steamship on water, crack & chips, 7" H. ............... $725.00*
**STONEWARE CROCK,** 4 gal., "Troy N.Y. Pottery," cobalt blue pecking chicken, 11½" H. ............. $375.00*

A-MA Mar. 1983    *Robert W. Skinner Inc.*
*L to R*
**STONEWARE CROCK,** 5 gal., "Riedinger & Caire, Poughkeepsie, N.Y.," minor rim chip, 12" H. ............. $450.00*
**STONEWARE JUG,** 4 gal., "Whites Utica," cobalt blue two-handled basket beneath a garland of flowers, "1865," 17½" H. .................... $900.00*
**STONEWARE CROCK,** 3 gal., "C. Braun, Buffalo, N.Y.," cobalt blue running spotted dog, base chip, 10¼" H. .................... $500.00*

A-MA Jan. 1983    *Robert W. Skinner Inc.*
*L to R*
**STONEWARE CROCK,** 5-gal., cobalt blue, "New York Stoneware Co. Fort Edward, N.Y.," chip, cracks, 12½" H. .................... $750.00*
**STONEWARE CROCK,** 5-gal., cobalt blue, "J. Burger, Rochester, N.Y.," rim chip, 12½" H. ......... $1000.00*
**STONEWARE CROCK,** 6-gal., cobalt blue, "New York Stoneware Co. Fort Edward, N.Y.," rim chips, 13½" H. .................... $575.00*

A-MA Mar. 1983    *Robert W. Skinner Inc.*
*L to R*
**STONEWARE CROCK,** 5 gal., "J. Burger Jr. Rochester, N.Y.," jumping deer w/palm tree, rim chip, pebbly salt glaze surface, 12½" H. ............. $1750.00*
**OVOID STONEWARE CROCK,** 8 gal., "S. Hart, Fulton," cobalt blue walking dog holding a basket in his mouth, chip, glaze imperfections, hairlines, int. staining, 14" H. .................... $1400.00*
**STONEWARE CROCK,** 4 gal., "I. Seymour, Troy," cobalt blue elongated fantail peacock & 3 scrolls, chip, cracks, 11½" H. .................... $400.00*

A-MA Jan. 1983    *Robert W. Skinner Inc.*
*L to R*
**STONEWARE JUG,** 2-gal., cobalt blue, "J. & E. Norton, Bennington, Vt.," 14" H. .................... $800.00*
**STONEWARE JUG,** 3-gal., cobalt blue, "Fort Edward Pottery Co.," repr., restor., 15¼" H. .................... $1050.00*
**STONEWARE PITCHER,** 2-gal., cobalt blue, "J. & E. Norton, Bennington, Vt.," cracks, repr., 13" H. ......... $525.00*

→

A-MA Jan. 1983    *Robert W. Skinner Inc.*
*L to R*
**OVOID STONEWARE CROCK,** 5-gal., cobalt blue, "J. Burger, Rochester, N.Y.," chip, 13½" H. ......... $600.00*
**STONEWARE WATERCOOLER,** 5-gal., double handles, cobalt blue, "Satterlee & Mory, Ft. Edward N.Y.," chip, damage, 19" H. .................... $575.00*
**STONEWARE CROCK,** 6-gal., cobalt blue, "J. & E. Norton, Bennington, Vt.," cracks, salt glaze loss, 13½" H. .................... $1650.00*

A-MA Mar. 1983    *Robert W. Skinner Inc.*
**MINIATURE STONEWARE CANTEEN,** mkd. "White's Pottery, Utica, N.Y.," cobalt blue lettering, 2¾" H. .......... $150.00*

A-MA July 1982    *Richard A. Bourne Co., Inc.*
*Row I, L to R*
**STONEWARE CROCK,** 2 gal., by F. B. Morton & Co., Worcester, MA, cobalt blue bird decor., cover missing, 2 chips, slight discoloration, 11¼" H. ......... $150.00
**STONEWARE CROCK,** 2 gal., by F. B. Morton & Co., Worcester, MA, cobalt blue decor., 2 chips, slight discoloration, 11" H. .................... $175.00
*Row II, L to R*
**STONEWARE JUG,** 4 gal., by E. & L.P. Morton, Bennington, VT, cobalt blue decor., slight discoloration, 16" H. .................... $150.00
**STONEWARE CROCK,** 4 gal., by NY Stoneware Co., cobalt blue decor., cover missing, rim chips & age crack, 14" H. .................... $75.00

*Price does not include 10% buyer fee.

A-MA Mar. 1983     *Robert W. Skinner Inc.*
**OVOID STONEWARE WATER COOLER,** approx. 5 gal., "M. Tyler & Co., Albany," applied Masonic decor. incised w/"Ed. Raynsford," device name, minor chips, repr., crack, 17½" H.
............................. $3300.00*

A-MA Oct. 1982     *Robert W. Skinner Inc.*
**OVOID STONEWARE JUG,** CT, early 19th C., 4 gal., cobalt blue, 17¼" H.
............................. $2100.00*

A-MA Mar. 1983     *Robert W. Skinner Inc.*
*L to R*
**OVOID STONEWARE CROCK,** 4 gal., "I.M. Burney & Son Jordon," cobalt blue bug-eyed bird on leafy branch, cracks, 13½" H. ...................... $475.00*
**STONEWARE PITCHER,** "R.C.R., Phila" in octagonal cartouche, cobalt blue leaf & floral design, chips, 11½" H.
............................. $575.00*

A-MA Mar. 1983     *Robert W. Skinner Inc.*
*L to R*
**STONEWARE CROCK,** 5 gal., "Lewis & Cady, Fairfax, Vt.," cobalt blue drooping bell-shaped bouquet, crack, 13¼" H.
............................. $175.00*
**STONEWARE WATER COOLER,** 5 gal., barrel-shaped, "W. Gardner," cobalt blue spread-wing eagle on cartouche in relief, floral swatches at sides, 15½" H.
............................. $1300.00*
**STONEWARE WATER COOLER,** 6 gal., crock-shaped, "S. Hart, Fulton," cobalt blue double crossed birds on branch, 13" H. ............... $425.00*

A-MA Mar. 1983     *Robert W. Skinner Inc.*
*L to R*
**STONEWARE JUG,** 3 gal., "A. White & Co. Binghamton," erect cobalt blue fantail bird on floral branch, potstone near name, 15½" H. ....................... $400.00*
**OVOID STONEWARE CREAM POT,** 2 gal., "H. M. Whitman, Havana, N.Y.," cobalt blue American flag, chip, 9" H.
............................. $1250.00*
**OVOID STONEWARE CROCK,** 2 gal., "J. Norton & Co. Bennington, Vt.," cobalt blue decor. slightly blurred, 10¾" H.
............................. $650.00*
**STONEWARE JUG,** 2 gal., "W. Roberts, Binghamton, N.Y.," cobalt blue fantail bird, leafy floral bower, lrg. chip, 13½" H.
............................. $625.00*

A-MA Mar. 1983     *Robert W. Skinner Inc.*
*L to R*
**OVOID STONEWARE CROCK,** "J. Mantell, Penn Yan," 2 lrg. cobalt blue brush stroke flowers emanating from lrg. central leafy stem, cracks, 13½" H. .... $225.00*
**OVOID STONEWARE CROCK,** 6 gal., "N. Clark & Co. Lyons," cobalt blue sunflower w/leaves, chips & hairline, 15" H.
............................. $400.00*
**OVOID STONEWARE CROCK,** 4 gal., "W. H. Farrar & Co. Geddes, N.Y.," blue lineal bird w/leafy spray, cracks, 12" H.
............................. $500.00*

A-MA Mar. 1983     *Robert W. Skinner Inc.*
*L to R*
**STONEWARE CHURN,** 6 gal., "J.J. Hart, Ogdensburg," lineal cobalt blue anchor w/swatch, streaked & stained, 18¼" H. ..................... $375.00*
**STONEWARE CHURN,** 6 gal., "John Burger, Rochester," two lrg. cobalt blue flowers, cracks & hairlines, 19¾" H.
............................. $700.00*
**STONEWARE CHURN,** 4 gal., "John Burger, Rochester," lrg. cobalt blue 8-lobed flower, hairlines, repr., 17½" H.
............................. $450.00*

A-MA Mar. 1983     *Robert W. Skinner Inc.*
*L to R*
**STONEWARE CROCK,** 5 gal., "E.A. Montell, Olean, N.Y.," cobalt blue floral spray, chip, cracks, repr., 11½" H.
............................. $150.00*

**STONEWARE JUG,** 2 gal., "Cortland," cobalt blue peacock, 14" H. .... $500.00*

**STONEWARE CROCK,** 6 gal., "C.W. Braun, Buffalo, N.Y.," blue-blk. flower on leafy stem, crack, chip, 12½" H.
............................. $220.00*

A-MA Mar. 1983     *Robert W. Skinner Inc.*
*L to R*
**OVOID STONEWARE CROCK,** approx. 1½ gal., cobalt blue, "Commeraws" on one side, "Stoneware" on other, breaks, chips, 11½" H. .............. $1100.00*

**STONEWARE CROCK,** approx. 3 gal., "C. Crolius, manufacturer, Manhattan-Wells, New York, in cobalt blue decor., minor chips, 13" H. .......... $450.00*

**OVOID STONEWARE JUG,** approx. 2 gal., "C. Crolius, manufacturer, New York," in cobalt blue decor., chips, 13" H.
............................. $400.00*

A-MA Mar. 1983     *Robert W. Skinner Inc.*
*L to R*
**STONEWARE CROCK,** 5 gal., "Evan R. Jones, Pittston, Pa.," tulip emanating from 4 leaves, minor rim chips, 13" H.
............................. $300.00*

**STONEWARE JUG,** 3 gal., "Whites Utica," pr. of cobalt blue birds facing each other, a leafy spray at center & the date 1862 above, crack, blurred edges, 16" H.
............................. $120.00*

**STONEWARE CROCK,** 5 gal., "Somerset Potters Work," cobalt blue basket of leafy flowers, winged insect on each side, rim chips, 12" H. ............. $150.00*

*Price does not include 10% buyer fee.

**ABC PLATES** - Alphabet plates were made especially for children as teaching aids. They date from the late 1700s, and were made of various material including porcelain, pottery, glass, pewter, tin and ironstone.

**AMPHORA ART POTTERY** was made at the Amphora Porcelain Works in the Teplitz-Tum area of Bohemia during the late 19th and early 20th centuries. Numerous potteries were located here.

**BATTERSEA ENAMELS** - The name "Battersea" is a general term for those metal objects decorated with enamels, such as pill, patch, and snuff boxes, door knobs, etc. The process of fusing enamel onto metal—usually copper—began about 1750 in the Battersea District of London. Today, the name has become a generic term for similar objects—mistakenly called "Battersea."

**BELLEEK** porcelain was first made at Fermanagh, Ireland in 1857. Today, this ware is still being made in buildings within walking distance of the original clay pits according to the skills and traditions of the original artisans. Irish Belleek is famous for its thinness and delicacy. Similar type wares were also produced in other European countries as well as the United States.

**BENNINGTON POTTERY** - The first pottery works in Bennington, Vermont was established by Captain John Norton in 1793; and, for 101 years, it was owned and operated by succeeding generations of Nortons. Today, the term "Bennington" is synonymous with the finest in American ceramics because the town was the home of several pottery operations during the last century—each producing under different labels. Today, items produced at Bennington are now conveniently, if inaccurately, dubbed "Bennington." One of the popular types of pottery produced here is known as "Rockingham." The term denotes the rich, solid brown glazed pottery from which many household items were made. The ware was first produced by the Marquis of Rockingham in Swinton, England—hence the name.

**BISQUE** - The term applies to pieces of porcelain or pottery which have been fired, but left in an unglazed state.

**BLOOR DERBY** - "Derby" porcelain dates from about 1755 when William Duesbury began the production of porcelain at Derby. In 1769, he purchased the famous Chelsea Works and operated both factories. During the Chelsea-Derby period, some of the finest examples of English porcelains were made. Because of their fine quality, in 1773 King George III gave Duesbury the patent to mark his porcelain wares "Crown Derby." Duesbury died in 1796. In 1810, the factory was purchased by Robert Bloor, a senior clerk. Bloor revived the Imari styles which had been so popular. After his death in 1845, former workmen continued to produce fine porcelains using the traditional Derby patterns. The firm was reorganized in 1876 and in 1878, a new factory was built. In 1890, Queen Victoria appointed the company "Manufacturers to Her Majesty," with the right to be known as Royal Crown Derby.

**BUFFALO POTTERY** - The Buffalo Pottery of Buffalo, New York, was organized in 1901. The firm was an adjunct of the Larkin Soap Company, which was established to produce china and pottery premiums for that company. Of the many different types produced, the Buffalo Pottery is most famous for their "Deldare" line which was developed in 1905.

**CANARY LUSTRE** earthenware dates to the early 1800s, and was produced by potters in the Staffordshire District of England. The body of this ware is a golden yellow and decorated with transfer printing, usually in black.

**CANTON** porcelain is a blue-and-white decorated ware produced near Canton, China, from the late 1700s through the last century. Its hand-decorated Chinese scenes have historical as well as mythological significance.

**CAPO-di-MONTE**, originally a soft paste porcelain, is Italian in origin, The first ware was made during the 1700s near Naples. Although numerous marks were used, the most familiar to us is the crown over the letter "N." Mythological subjects, executed in either high or low relief and tinted in bright colors on a light ground, were a favorite decoration. The earlier ware has a peculiar grayish color as compared to later examples which have a whiter body.

**CARLSBAD** porcelain was made by several factories in the area from the 1800s and exported to the United States. When Carlsbad became a part of Czechoslovakia after World War I, wares were frequently marked "Karlsbad." Items marked "Victoria" were made for Lazarus & Rosenfeldt, Importers.

**CASTLEFORD** earthenware was produced in England from the late 1700s until around 1820. Its molded decoration is similar to Pratt Wares.

**CHINESE EXPORT PORCELAIN** was made in quantity in China during the 1700s and early 1800s. The term identifies a variety of porcelain wares made for export to Europe and the United States. Since many thought the product to be of joint Chinese and English manufacture, it has also been known as "Oriental or Chinese Lowestoft."

As much as this ware was made to order for the American and European market, it was frequently adorned with seals of states or the coats of arms of individuals, in addition to eagles, sailing scenes, flowers, religious and mythological scenes.

**CLEWS POTTERY** - (see also, Historical Staffordshire) was made by George Clews & Co., of Brownhill Pottery, Tunstall, England from 1806-1861.

**CLIFTON POTTERY** was founded by William Long in Clifton, New Jersey, in 1905.

**COALPORT** porcelain has been made by the Coalport Porcelain Works in England since 1795. The ware is still being produced at Stroke-on-Trent.

**COPELAND-SPODE** - The firm was founded by Josiah Spode in 1770 in Staffordshire, England. From 1847 W. T. Copeland & Sons, Ltd., succeeded Spode, using the designation "Late Spode" to their wares. The firm is still in operation.

**COPPER LUSTRE** - See Lustre Wares.

**CROWN DUCAL** - English porcelain made by the A. G. Richardson & Co., Ltd., since 1916.

**CUP PLATES** were used where cups were handleless and saucers were deep. During the early 1800s, it was very fashionable to drink from a saucer. Thus, a variety of fancy small plates was produced for the cup to rest in. The lacy Sandwich examples are very collectible.

**DAVENPORT** pottery and porcelain were made at the Davenport Factory in Longport, Staffordshire, England, by John Davenport—from 1793 until 1887 when the pottery closed. Most of the wares produced here—porcelains, creamwares, ironstone, earthenwares and other products—were marked.

**DEDHAM (Chelsea Art Works)** - The firm was founded in 1872 at Chelsea, Massachusetts by James Robertson & Sons, and closed in 1889. In 1891, the pottery was reopened under the name of The Chelsea Pottery, U.S. The first and most popular blue underglaze decoration for the desirable "Cracqule Ware" was the rabbit motif—designed by Joseph L. Smith. In 1893, construction was started on the new pottery in Dedham, Massachusetts, and production began in 1895. The name of the pottery was then changed to "Dedham Pottery," to eliminate the confusion with the English Chelsea Ware. The famed crackleware finish became synonymous with the name. Because of its popularity, over fifty patterns of tableware were made.

**DELFT** - Holland is famous for its fine examples of tin-glazed pottery dating from the 16th century. Although blue and white is the most popular color, other colors were also made. The majority of the ware found today is from the late Victorian period and, when the name Holland appears with the Delft factory mark, this indicates that the item was made after 1891.

**DORCHESTER POTTERY** was established by George Henderson in Dorchester, a part of Boston, in 1895. Production included stonewares, industrial wares, and later some decorated tablewares. The pottery is still in production.

**DOULTON** - The Pottery was established in Lambeth in 1815 by John Doulton and

John Watts. When Watts retired in 1845, the firm became known as Doulton & Company. In 1901, King Edward VII conferred a double honor on the company by presentation of the Royal Warrant, authorizing their chairman to use the word "Royal" in describing products. A variety of wares has been made over the years for the American market. The firm is still in production.

**DRESDEN** - See Meissen

**FLOWING BLUE** ironstone is a highly flazed dinnerware made at Staffordshire by a variety of potters. It became popular about 1825. Items were printed with the patterns (oriental), and the color flowed from the design over the white body so that the finished product appeared smeared. Although purple and brown colors were also made, the deep cobalt blue shades were the most popular. Later wares were less blurred, having more white ground.

**GAUDY DUTCH** is the most spectacular of the Gaudy wares. It was made for the Pennsylvania Dutch market from about 1785 until the 1820s. This soft paste tableware is lightweight and frail in appearance. Its rich cobalt blue decoration was applied to the biscuit, glazed and fired—then other colors were applied over the first glaze—and the object was fired again. No lustre is included in its decoration.

**GAUDY IRONSTONE** was made in Staffordshire from the early 1850s until around 1865. This ware is heavier than Gaudy Welsh or Gaudy Dutch, as its texture is a mixture of pottery and porcelain clay.

**GAUDY WELSH**, produced in England from about 1830, resembles Gaudy Dutch in decorations, but the workmanship is not as fine and its texture is more comparable to that of spatterware. Lustre is usually included with the decoration.

**HISTORICAL STAFFORDSHIRE** - The term refers to a particular blue-on-white, transfer-printed earthenware produced in quantity during the early 1800s by many potters in the Staffordshire District. The central decoration was usually an American city scene or landscape, frequently showing some mode of transportation in the foreground. Other designs included portraits and patriotic emblems. Each potter had a characteristic border which is helpful to identify a particular ware, as many pieces are unmarked. Later transfer-printed wares were made in sepia, pink, green and black, but the early cobalt blue examples are the most desirable.

**IRONSTONE** is a heavy, durable, utilitarian ware made from the slag of iron furnaces, ground and mixed with clay. Charles Mason of Lane Delft, Staffordshire, pattented the formula in 1813. Much of the early ware was decorated in imitation of Imari, in addition to transfer-printed blue ware, flowing flues and browns. During the mid 19th century, the plain white enlivened only by embossed designs became fashionable. Literally hundreds of patterns were made for export.

**JACKFIELD POTTERY** is English in origin. It was first produced during the 17th century, however most items available today date from the last century. It is a red-bodied pottery, oftentimes decorated with scrolls and flowers in relief, then covered with a black glaze.

**JUGTOWN POTTERY** - This North Carolina pottery has been made since the 18th century. In 1915, Jacques Busbee organized what was to become the Jugtown Pottery in 1921. Production was discontinued in 1958.

**KING'S ROSE** is a decorated creamware produced in the Staffordshire district of England during the 1820-1840 period. The rose decorations are usually in red, green, yellow and pink. This ware is often referred to as "Queen's Rose."

**LEED'S POTTERY** was established by Charles Green in 1758 at Leed, Yorkshire, England. Early wares are unmarked. From 1775, the impressed mark, "Leeds Pottery" was used. After 1800, the name "Hartly, Green & Co." was added, and the impressed or incised letters "L P" were also used to identify the ware.

**LIMOGES** - The name identifies fine porcelain wares produced by many factories at Limoges, France, since the mid-1800s. A variety of different marks identify wares made here including Haviland china.

**LIVERPOOL POTTERY** - The term applies to wares produced by many potters located in Liverpool, England, from the early 1700s, for American trade. Their print-decorated pitchers—referred to as "jugs" in England—have been especially popular. These featured patriotic emblems, prominent men, ships, etc., and can be easily identified as nearly all are melon-shaped with a very pointed lip, strap handle and graceful curved body.

**LUSTRE WARES** - John Hancock of Hanley, England, invented this type of decoration on earthenwares during the early 1800s. The copper, bronze, ruby, gold, purple, yellow, pink and mottled pink lustre finishes were made from gold-painted on the glazed objects, then fired. The latter type is often referred to as "Sunderland Lustre." Its pinkish tones vary in color and pattern. The silver lustres were made from platinum.

**McCOY POTTERY** - The J. W. McCoy Pottery was established in 1899. Production of art pottery did not begin until after 1926, when the name was changed to Brush McCoy.

**METTLACH**, Germany, located in the Zoar Basin, was the location of the famous Villeroy & Boch factories from 1836 until 1921 when the factory was destroyed by fire. Steins (dating from about 1842) and other stonewares with bas relief decoration were their specialty.

**MOCHA WARE** - This banded creamware was first produced in England during the late 1700s. The early ware was lightweight and thin, having colorful bands of bright colors decorating its cream-colored to very light brown body. After 1840, the ware became heavier in body and the color was oftentimes quite light—almost white. Mocha Ware can easily be identified by its colorful banded decorations—on and between the bands, including feathery ferns, lacy trees, seaweeds, squiggly designs and lowly earthworms.

**NILOAK POTTERY** with its prominent swirled, marbleized designs, is a 20th century pottery first produced at Benton, Arkansas, in 1911 by the Niloak Pottery Company. Production ceased in 1946.

**NIPPON** porcelain has been produced in quantity for the American market since the late 19th century. After 1891, when it became obligatory to include the country of origin on all imports, the Japanese trademark "Nippon" was used. Numerous other marks appear on this ware identifying the manufacturer, artist or importer. The hand-painted Nippon examples are extremely popular today and prices are on the rise.

**OWENS POTTERY** was made from 1891 to 1928 at Zanesville, Ohio. The first art pottery was produced after 1896. Their different lines included Utopian Ware, Navarre, Feroza, Cyrano and Henri Deux. Art pottery was discontinued about 1907.

**PISGAH FOREST POTTERY** - The pottery was founded near Mt. Pisgah in North Carolina in 1914 by Walter B. Stephen. The pottery remains in operation.

**REDWARE** is one of our most popular forms of country pottery. It has a soft, porous body and its color varies from reddish-brown tones to deep wine to light orange. It was produced in mostly utilitarian forms by potters in small factories or by potters working on their farms, to fill their everyday needs. Glazes were used to intensify the color. The most desirable examples are the slip-decorated pieces, or the rare and expensive "sgraffito" examples which have scratched or incised line decoration. This type of decoration was for ornamentation, since examples were rarely used for ordinary utilitarian purposes, but were given as gifts. Hence, these highly prized pieces rarely show wear, indicating that they were treasured as ornaments only. Slip decoration was made by tracing the design on the redware shape with a clay having a creamy consistency in contrasting colors. When dried, the design was slightly raised above the surface. Because these pieces were made for practical usage, the potter then pressed or beat the slip decoration into the surface of the object.

**RED WING POTTERY** of Red Wing,

Minnesota, was founded in 1878. The firm began producing art pottery during the 1920s. The pottery closed in 1967.

**ROCKINGHAM-** See Bennington Pottery.

**ROOKWOOD POTTERY -** The Rookwood Pottery began production at Cincinnati, Ohio, in 1880 under the direction of Maria Longworth Nichols Storer, and operated until 1960. The name was derived from the family estate, "Rookwood," because of the "rook" or "crows" which inhabited the wooded areas. All pieces of this art pottery are marked, usually bearing the famous flame.

**RORSTRAND FAIENCE -** The firm was founded in 1726 near Stockholm, Sweden. Items dating from the early 1900s and having an "art nouveau" influence are very much in demand these days and expensive.

**ROSE MEDALLION** ware dates from the 18th century. It was decorated and exported from Canton, China, in quantity. The name generally applied to those pieces having medallions with figures of people alternating with panels of flowers, birds and butterflies. When all the medallions were filled with flowers, the ware was differentiated as Rose Canton.

**ROSEVILLE POTTERY -** The Roseville Pottery was organized in 1890 in Roseville, Ohio. The firm produced utilitarian stoneware in the plant formerly owned by the Owens Pottery of Roseville, also producers of stoneware, and the Linden Avenue Plant of Zanesville, Ohio, originally built by the Clark Stoneware Company. In 1900, an art line of pottery was created to compete with Owens and Weller lines. The new ware was named "Rozane," and it was produced at the Zanesville location. Following its success, other prestige lines were created. The Azurine line was introduced about 1902.

**ROYAL BAYREUTH** manufactory began in Tettau in 1794 at the first porcelain factory in Bavaria. Wares made here were on the same par with Meissen. Fire destroyed the original factory during the 1800s. Much of the wares available today were made at the new factory which began production in 1897. These include Rose Tapestry, Sunbonnet Baby novelties and the Devil and Card items. The Royal Bayreuth blue mark has the 1794 founding date incorporated with the mark.

**ROYAL BONN -** The trade name identifies a variety of porcelain items made during the 19th century by the Bonn China Manufactory, established in 1755 by Clemers August. Most of the ware found today is from the Victorian period.

**ROYAL DOULTON** wares have been made from 1901, when King Edward VII conferred a double honor on the Doulton Pottery by the presentation of the Royal Warrant, authorizing their chairman to use the word "Royal" in describing products. A variety of wares has been produced for the American market. The firm is still in production.

**ROYAL DUX** was produced in Bohemia during the late 1800s. Large quantities of this decorative porcelain ware were exported to the United States. Royal Dux figurines are especially popular.

**ROYAL WORCESTER -** The Worcester factory was established in 1751 in England. This is a tastefully decorated porcelain noted for its creamy white lustreless surface. Serious collectors prefer items from the Dr. Wall (the activator of the concern) period of production which extended from the time the factory was established to 1785.

**ROYCROFT POTTERY** was made by the Roycrofter community of East Aurora, New York, during the late 19th and early 20th centuries. The firm was founded by Elbert Hubbard. Products produced here included pottery, furniture, metalware, jewelry and leatherwork.

**R. S. PRUSSIA** porcelain was produced during the mid-1800s by Erdman Schlegelmilch in Suhl. His brother Reinhold founded a factory in 1869 in Tillowitz in lower Silesia. Both made fine quality porcelain, using both satin and high gloss finishes with comparable decoration. Additionally, both brothers used the same R.S. mark in the same colors, the initials being in memory of their father, Rudolph Schlegelmilch. It has not been determined when production at the two factories ceased.

**SAMPSON WARE** dates from the early 19th century. The firm was founded in Paris, and reproduced a variety of collectible wares including Chelsea, Meissen and Oriental Lowestoft, with marks which distinguish their wares as reproductions. The firm is still in production.

**SATSUMA** is a Japanese pottery having a distinctive creamy crackled glaze decorated with bright enamels and oftentimes Japanese faces. The majority of the ware available today includes the mass-produced wares dating from the 1850s. Their quality does not compare to the fine early examples.

**SPATTERWARE** is a soft paste tableware, laboriously decorated with hand-drawn flowers, birds, buildings, trees, etc., with "spatter" decoration chiefly as a background. It was produced in considerable quantity from the early 1800s to around 1850.

To achieve this type decoration, small bits of sponge were cut into different shapes—leaves, hearts, rosettes, vines, geometrical patterns, etc.—and mounted on the end of a short stick for convenience in dipping into the pigment.

**SPONGEWARE,** as it is known, is a decorated white earthenware. Color—usually blue, blue/green, brown/tan/blue, or blue/brown—was applied to the white clay base. Because the color was often applied with a color-soaked sponge, the term "spongeware" became common for this ware. A variety of utilitarian items was produced—pitchers, cookie jars, bean pots, water coolers, etc. Marked examples are rare.

**STAFFORDSHIRE** is a district in England where a variety of pottery and porcelain wares has been produced by many factories in the area.

**STICKSPATTER -** The term identifies a type of decoration that combines hand painting and transfer-painted decoration. "Spattering" was done with either a sponge or a brush containing a moderate supply of pigment. Stickspatter was developed from the traditional Staffordshire spatterware, as the earlier ware was time-consuming and expensive to produce. Although the majority of this ware was made in England from the 1850s to the late 1800s, it was also produced in Holland, France and elsewhere.

**TEA LEAF** is a lightweight stone china decorated with copper of gold "tea leaf" sprigs. It was first made by Anthony Shaw of Longport, England, during the 1850s. By the late 1800s, other potters in Staffordshire were producing the popular ware for export to the United States. As a result, there is a noticeable diversity in decoration.

**TECO POTTERY,** is an art pottery line made by the Terra Cotta Tile Works of Terra Cotta, Illinois. The firm was organized in 1881 by William D. Gates. The Teco line was first made in 1902 and was discontinued during the 1920s.

**VAN BRIGGLE POTTERY** was established at Colorado Springs, Colorado, in 1900 by Artus Van Briggle and his wife Anna. Most of the ware was marked. The first mark included two joined "A's," representing their first two initials. The firm is still in operation.

**VILLEROY & BOCH -** See Mettlach

**WEDGWOOD POTTERY** was established by Josiah Wedgwood in 1759 in England. A tremendous variety of fine wares has been produced through the years including basalt, lustre wares, creamware, jasperware, bisque, agate, Queen's Ware and others. The system of marks used by the firm clearly indicates when each piece was made.

Since 1940, the new Wedgwood factory has been located at Barleston.

**WELLER POTTERY -** Samuel A. Weller established the Weller Pottery in 1872 in Fultonham, Ohio. In 1888, the pottery was moved to Piece Street in Putnam, Ohio—now a part of Zanesville, Ohio. The production of art pottery began in 1893 and, by late 1897, several prestige lines were being produced including Samantha, Touranda and Dickens' Ware. Other later types included Weller's Louwelsa, Eosian, Aurora, Turada and the rare Sicardo which is the most sought after and most expensive today. The firm closed in 1948.

A-MA Aug. 1983 *Richard A. Bourne Co., Inc.*
*Row I, L to R*
**LADY'S WALTHAM WATCH,** 14K
yellow gold, not running ....... $150.00
**LADY'S WALTHAM WATCH,** 14K
gold, French-style cross hatch covers
w/shields for initials, minor dent
.......................... $125.00

*Row II, L to R*
**LADY'S PENDANT WATCH,** 14K w/7
jewel movement ............... $70.00
**ELGIN LADY'S WATCH,** gold plated
foliate engraved case, 20-yr. warranty, 15
jewel movement ............... $50.00

A-MA Aug. 1983 *Robert C. Eldred Co., Inc.*
**AM. TRIPLE DECKER SHELF
CLOCK,** ¾ size, w/label of Daniel Pratt,
Jr., strike & time, mahogany veneers, 28½″
H., 19″ W. ................... $400.00

A-MA Aug. 1983 *Robert C. Eldred Co., Inc.*
**AM. TRANSITION CLOCK,** w/label of
Henry C. Smith, Plymouth, CT, strike &
time, eagle finial, painted dial, mahogany
veneers, 34″ H., 16½″ W. ....... $175.00

A-MA Aug. 1983 *Richard A. Bourne Co., Inc.*
*Row I, L to R*
**HUNTING CASE WATCH,** 18K yellow
gold, works by John Beasley, needs bezel
............................ $200.00
**CASED WATCH,** 18K 5-colored gold
w/Fusee movement, by Sebastian Konz,
chip on porcelain dial .......... $400.00

*Row II, L to R*
**HUNTING CASE WATCH,** gold, silver
& niello, mkd. Balvelez & Co., 15 jewel
movement, minor damage, no bezel
............................ $75.00
**HUNTING CASE WATCH,** gold plated
& enameled inlay case, made by Hyde &
Sons, London & Paris, comp. w/key, loss
of enamel .................... $300.00

A-MA Aug. 1983 *Richard A. Bourne Co., Inc.*
**WAGON SPRING CLOCK,** by Birge &
Fuller, CT, orig., center glass cracked, 26″
H. ......................... $3100.00

A-MA Aug. 1983 *Robert C. Eldred Co., Inc.*
**TIFFANY REPEATING BRASS CAR-
RIAGE CLOCK,** w/calendar dial & alarm
dial, 6″ H. ................... $1900.00

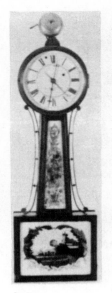

*Left*

A-MA July 1982    *Richard A. Bourne Co., Inc.*
**WILLARD TYPE BANJO CLOCK,**
eagle finial & brass brackets, assembled
clock, bears label of Daniel Pratt, door &
throat glasses flaking, 32¾″ H.  . . $450.00

*Right*

A-MA Nov. 1982    *Richard A. Bourne Co., Inc.*
**BANJO CLOCK,** by E. Howard & Co.,
Boston, 19th C., weight missing, orig. blk.,
wine & gold door & throat glasses, 29¼″ H.
. . . . . . . . . . . . . . . . . . . . . . . . . . . . $1400.00

*Left*

A-MA Oct. 1982    *Robert W. Skinner Inc.*
**FEDERAL ALARM BANJO TIME-
PIECE,** Boston, ca. 1820, mahogany, 8-day
weight-driven movement, painted iron dial
inscribed "Aaron Willard, Boston," restor.,
33″ H. . . . . . . . . . . . . . . . . . . . . . $850.00*

*Right*

A-MA Jan. 1983    *Robert W. Skinner Inc.*
**FEDERAL BANJO TIMEPIECE,**
mahogany & gilt, inscribed "No. 1907
Aaron Willard Jr. Boston," 8-day weight-
driven alarm movement, missing alarm
mechanism, 29½″ H. . . . . . . . . $1700.00*

A-MA Oct. 1982    *Robert W. Skinner Inc.*
**FEDERAL TALL CASE CLOCK,**
Providence, RI, ca. 1800, mahogany,
painted dial inscribed "Caleb Wheaton,
Providence," base restor., 92½″ H., 18″ W.,
9¼″ D. . . . . . . . . . . . . . . . . . . . $10,000.00*

A-MA Aug. 1983    *Richard A. Bourne Co., Inc.*
*L to R*
**ANSONIA MANTEL CLOCK,** blk. iron
case, 8-day movement, 10¾″ H. . . $75.00
**MANTEL CLOCK,** blk. slate & marble
case, by U. S. Clock Co., keyless 8-day
movement, 14″ H. . . . . . . . . . . . . $250.00
**FRENCH MANTEL CLOCK,** blk. slate
& marble case, 8-day movement, porcelain
dial, 15½″ H. . . . . . . . . . . . . . . . . $125.00

A-MA Aug. 1983    *Richard A. Bourne Co., Inc.*
**BANJO CLOCK,** E. Howard Co., limited edition production, 59¼″ O.H.
. . . . . . . . . . . . . . . . . . . . . . . . . . . $1000.00

*Left*

A-WA D.C. Sept. 1982 *Adam A. Weschler & Son*
**FEDERAL SHELF CLOCK,** ca. 1836-40,
stencil decor., Romes' & Darrow, Bristol,
CT, 30″ H. . . . . . . . . . . . . . . . . . . $600.00*

*Right*

A-WA D.C. Dec. 1982 *Adam A. Weschler & Son*
**DRESDEN FLORAL ENCRUSTED
MANTEL CLOCK & STAND,** late 19th
C., 19″ H. . . . . . . . . . . . . . . . . . . . $650.00*

*Price does not include 10% buyer fee.

A-MA Aug. 1983 *Richard A. Bourne Co., Inc.*
*L to R*
**FRENCH SHELF CLOCK,** brass & silvered, 19th C., 8-day movement, slight wear, 14½" H. ............... $300.00

**FRENCH MANTEL CLOCK,** ornate brass, 8-day movement, porcelain Roman numerals, 16" O.H. ........... $275.00

**ART NOUVEAU CLOCK,** gold finished wh. metal case, by Gilber Co., CT, 8-day movement, 12" H. ........... $100.00

A-MA Aug. 1983 *Richard A. Bourne Co., Inc.*
*L to R*
**MINI. STEEPLE CLOCK,** ebonized case, brass 30-hr. movement, alarm, orig. Eagle & Flag trademark on inside, minor restor., 15½" H. ............. $250.00

**SETH THOMAS COTTAGE CLOCK,** Vic. walnut case, orig. glasses, 10¼" H. ............................. $90.00

**ANSONIA-BEEHIVE CLOCK,** rose-wood case, brass 8-day movement, orig. label, orig. glass, 18¾" H. ....... $800.00

A-MA Aug. 1983 *Richard A. Bourne Co., Inc.*
*L to R*
**SHELF CLOCK,** mahogany, pillar and scroll, by Mark Leavenworth, CT, 30-hr. wooden works, orig. label, restor., 29⅞" O.H. ........................ $800.00

**SHELF CLOCK,** mahogany, pillar and scroll, by Norris North, CT, door glass repainted, 30⅜" O.H. ........ $1200.00

A-MA Aug. 1983 *Richard A. Bourne Co., Inc.*
**GIRANDOLE CLOCK,** by Elmer O. Stennes, MA, 47" O.H. ........ $1750.00

A-OH Oct. 1982 *Garth's Auctions, Inc.*
**BANJO CLOCK,** mahogany on pine case, gilded bracket, orig. reverse paintings, "The Constitution Escape from the British Squadron," brass works sgn. "M. D. Dedham, No. 10," wear, flaking, replm., repr., 40¾" H. ............... $1000.00

A-MA Aug. 1983 *Richard A. Bourne Co., Inc.*
**FIGURE 8 CLOCK,** E. Howard & Co. repro., limited edition, 34½" H. .. $750.00

A-MA Aug. 1983   *Richard A. Bourne Co., Inc.*
L to R
**GINGERBREAD CLOCK,** walnut case, by E. Ingraham & Co., CT, branded sgn. in bottom, orig. glass, 22¼" H. . . . . . $125.00

**GINGERBREAD CLOCK,** oak case, by Seth Thomas, CT, applied brass scroll work, orig. glass, 22⅝" H. . . . . . . $200.00

**VIC. COTTAGE CLOCK,** gilded decor., adj. pendulum, 19" H. . . . . . . . . . $200.00

A-MA Aug. 1983   *Richard A. Bourne Co., Inc.*
L to R
**SM. STEEPLE CLOCK,** rosewood veneer case, by Ansonia Clock Co., NY label, orig. glass, decor. worn . . . . $200.00

**STEEPLE CLOCK,** rosewood cased, by Waterbury Clock Co., orig. glass, 19¼" H. . . . . . . . . . . . . . . . . . . . . . . . . . . . $450.00

**STANDARD STEEPLE CLOCK,** by Daniel Pratt & Sons, MA, walnut & mahogany veneered case, 19⅝" H. . . . . . . . . . . . . . . . . . . . . . . . . . . . $450.00

A-MA Aug. 1983   *Richard A. Bourne Co., Inc.*
L to R
**ENG. BRACKET CLOCK,** 8-day Fusee movement, no strike, inlaid mahogany case, minor repairs needed, 14" H. . . . . . . . . . . . . . . . . . . . . . . . . . . . $225.00

**GERMAN MANTEL CLOCK,** maple case w/brass 8-day movement, ref., 14" H. . . . . . . . . . . . . . . . . . . . . . . . . . . . $100.00

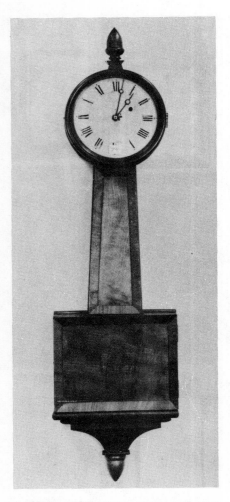

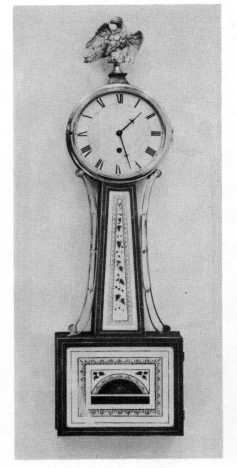

A-MA Aug. 1983   *Richard A. Bourne Co., Inc.*
**BANJO CLOCK,** mahogany case, orig., 39½" O.H. . . . . . . . . . . . . . . . . . . . $750.00

A-MA Aug. 1983   *Richard A. Bourne Co., Inc.*
**LYRE CLOCK,** by Elmer O. Stennes, MA, 45" O.H. . . . . . . . . . . . . . $800.00

A-MA Aug. 1983   *Richard A. Bourne Co., Inc.*
**REPRO. WILLARD BANJO CLOCK,** made for Tiffany & Co., 35" H. . . . . . . . . . . . . . . . . . . . . . . . . . . . $500.00

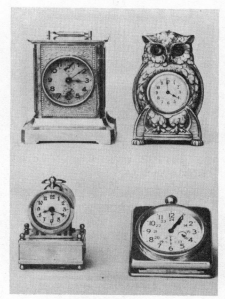

A-MA Aug. 1983   *Richard A. Bourne Co., Inc.*
*L to R*
**CALENDAR CLOCK,** by Ithaca, H. B. Horton's patt., iron case, sm. glass between dials missing, 21" H. . . $1250.00

**WALL CLOCK & BAROMETER,** iron case, mounted side-by-side w/thermometer in between, 16" H. . . . . $150.00

A-MA Aug. 1983   *Richard A. Bourne Co., Inc.*
*L to R*
**DUTCH DELFT-CASED MANTEL CLOCK,** 8-day movement, sgn., 17½" H. . . . . . . . . . . . . . . . . . . . . . . . . . . $800.00
**DUTCH DELFT-CASED MANTEL CLOCK,** 8-day movement, open work pendulum, repr., 18½" H. . . . . . . $700.00

A-MA Aug. 1983   *Richard A. Bourne Co., Inc.*
**MANTEL CLOCK,** E. N. Welch, iron front, 8-day movement, mother of pearl inlay in iron . . . . . . . . . . . . . . . . . . $175.00
**NEW HAVEN MANTEL CLOCK,** iron front, bronze finished decor., 18" H. . . . . . . . . . . . . . . . . . . . . . . . . . $100.00

A-MA Aug. 1983   *Richard A. Bourne Co., Inc.*
*Row I, L to R*
**GERMAN CARRIAGE CLOCK,** nickel plated, music box alarm, 6" H. . . . $75.00
**GERMAN NOVELTY CLOCK,** form of owl w/blinking eyes, 6¼" H. . . . . . $325.00
*Row II, L to R*
**MUSICAL ALARM CLOCK,** nickel plated grass, 5" H. . . . . . . . . . . . . $160.00
**WALTHAM AUTOMOBILE CLOCK,** 8-day movement, 15 jewel, partially working . . . . . . . . . . . . . . . . . . . . . $160.00

A-MA Aug. 1983   *Richard A. Bourne Co., Inc.*
**CALENDAR CLOCK,** by Welch, Spring & Co., rosewood case, 8-day, orig., 33" H. . . . . . . . . . . . . . . . . . . . . . $1000.00

A-MA Aug. 1983   *Richard A. Bourne Co., Inc.*
**ITHACA REGULATOR - CALENDAR CLOCK,** upper dial repl., lower dial orig., 41½" O.H. . . . . . . . . . . . . . . . . . $2100.00

A-MA June 1983   *Robert W. Skinner Inc.*
**SHELF CLOCK,** enameled, France, late 19th C., 8-day time, 14½" H. . . . $150.00*

*Price does not include 10% buyer fee.

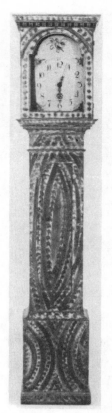

A-MA Oct. 1982 *Robert W. Skinner Inc.*
**TALL CASE CLOCK,** N. Eng., ca. 1800, grain painted, replaced hood & seat board, 86½″ H., 17¼″ W., 10½″ D. ... $1400.00*

A-MA Oct. 1982 *Robert W. Skinner Inc.*
**CHIPPENDALE TALL CASE CLOCK,** New London, CT, late 18th C., walnut attrib. to William Gillespie, 8-day weight-driven striking movement, 91″ H.
........................... $3100.00*

A-MA Oct. 1982 *Robert W. Skinner Inc.*
**FEDERAL TALL CASE CLOCK,** N. Eng., ca. 1790, mahogany inlaid, French feet ref., 91″ H. ............ $3250.00*

A-MA Aug. 1983 *Richard A. Bourne Co., Inc.*
L to R
**SHELF CLOCK,** rosewood case, by E. N Welch, Gerster patt., 8-day movement, paperweight pendulum, 18½″ H.
............................. $1300.00
**VIC. SHELF CLOCK,** walnut case, by Ingraham Clock Co., 8-day movement, 24″ H. ............................. $275.00

A-WA D.C. Sept. 1982 *Adam A. Weschler & Son*
**FEDERAL TALL CASE CLOCK,** ca. 1810, mahogany stained pine, Thomas Dicker, PA, 79″ H. ......... $1100.00*

A-MA Aug. 1983 *Richard A. Bourne Co., Inc.*
**ANSONIA FIGURAL CLOCK,** Crystal Palace, cast wh. metal figures, brass movement, glass dome cracked, clock 15″ H. ........................... $325.00

A-MA Mar. 1983    *Robert W. Skinner Inc.*
**FEDERAL TALL CASE CLOCK,** ca.
1790, inlaid mahogany, 8-day weight driven
movement, label of Aaron Willard on door,
parts missing, minor damage, 87″ H.
..................... $12,500.00*

A-MA Mar. 1983    *Robert W. Skinner Inc.*
**FEDERAL TALL CASE CLOCK,** ca.
1800, N. Eng., cherry, 17″ W., 9″ D., 80″ H.
.......................... $2300.00*

A-MA July 1982    *Robert W. Skinner Inc.*
**CHIPPENDALE STYLE TALL
CLOCK,** Walter H. Durfee, RI, ca. 1870,
mahogany veneer & brass inlay, brass ball
finials, weight driven time & strike movement, 101¼″ H. .............. $3000.00*

A-MA Oct. 1982    *Robert W. Skinner Inc.*
**TALL CLOCK,** ca. 1910, mission oak, 8-
day weight-driven movement made by
Waterbury Clock Co., ref., 73″ H., 20½″
W., 14″ D. .................. $600.00*

A-MA Mar. 1983    *Robert W. Skinner Inc.*
**CHIPPENDALE TALL CASE CLOCK,**
late 18th C., mahogany, Josiah Gooding,
Dighton, MA, 8-day weight driven brass
movement, old finish, weights & pendulum,
90″ H. ................... $13,000.00*

A-OH July 1982    *Garth's Auctions, Inc.*
**TALL CASE CLOCK,** PA, walnut, brass
works w/repainted iron face, door hinges
are old replm., brass escut. is orig., age
crack in base & minor old repr., old
alligatored varnish finish, 91½″ H.
.......................... $2600.00

*Price does not include 10% buyer fee.

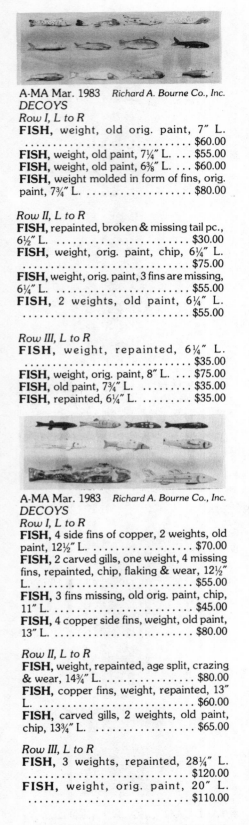

A-MA Mar. 1983   *Richard A. Bourne Co., Inc.*
DECOYS
*Row I, L to R*
**FISH,** weight, old orig. paint, 7" L.
.................................. $60.00
**FISH,** weight, old paint, 7¼" L. ... $55.00
**FISH,** weight, old paint, 6⅜" L. ... $60.00
**FISH,** weight molded in form of fins, orig. paint, 7¾" L. .................... $80.00

*Row II, L to R*
**FISH,** repainted, broken & missing tail pc., 6½" L. ........................ $30.00
**FISH,** weight, orig. paint, chip, 6¼" L.
.................................. $75.00
**FISH,** weight, orig. paint, 3 fins are missing, 6¼" L. ........................ $55.00
**FISH,** 2 weights, old paint, 6¼" L. .......................... $55.00

*Row III, L to R*
**FISH,** weight, repainted, 6¼" L.
.................................. $35.00
**FISH,** weight, orig. paint, 8" L. ... $75.00
**FISH,** old paint, 7¾" L. .......... $35.00
**FISH,** repainted, 6¼" L. ......... $35.00

A-MA Mar. 1983   *Richard A. Bourne Co., Inc.*
DECOYS
*Row I, L to R*
**FISH,** 4 side fins of copper, 2 weights, old paint, 12½" L. .................. $70.00
**FISH,** 2 carved gills, one weight, 4 missing fins, repainted, chip, flaking & wear, 12½" L. ............................ $55.00
**FISH,** 3 fins missing, old orig. paint, chip, 11" L. ........................ $45.00
**FISH,** 4 copper side fins, weight, old paint, 13" L. ........................ $80.00

*Row II, L to R*
**FISH,** weight, repainted, age split, crazing & wear, 14¾" L. ................ $80.00
**FISH,** copper fins, weight, repainted, 13" L. ............................ $60.00
**FISH,** carved gills, 2 weights, old paint, chip, 13¾" L. ................... $65.00

*Row III, L to R*
**FISH,** 3 weights, repainted, 28¼" L.
.................................. $120.00
**FISH,** weight, orig. paint, 20" L.
.................................. $110.00

A-MA Aug. 1983   *Robert C. Eldred Co., Inc.*
**CARVED DECOY,** painted, RI, Canada Goose, 24" L., 13" H. ......... $350.00

A-MA Mar. 1983   *Richard A. Bourne Co., Inc.*
MASON'S FACTORY DECOYS
*Row I, L to R*
**PINTAIL DRAKE,** w/premier stamp on bottom, age split on right upper half
.................................. $700.00
**BLUE-WINGED TEAL DRAKE,** premier grade, wear & age splits .... $315.00
*Row II, L to R*
**MALLARDS,** pr., premier grade, sm. chips ........................ $525.00

*Row III, L to R*
**BLUE-WINGED TEAL DRAKE,** tack eyes, orig. paint, ¼" hole drilled through body .......................... $475.00
**BRANT,** orig. paint, in-use flaking, sm. chip .......................... $1100.00

A-MA Mar. 1983   *Richard A. Bourne Co., Inc.*
WILDFOWLER DECOYS
*Row I, L to R*
**REDHEADS,** pr., balsa bodies, orig. paint showing much in-use wear ...... $100.00
**MALLARD HEN,** hollowed body, repainted, age splits .............. $80.00
*Row II, L to R*
**MALLARDS,** pr., balsa bodies, orig. paint
............................. $200.00

*Row III, L to R*
**CANADA GOOSE,** balsa body, orig. paint, age split, tail area slightly chewed by dog .......................... $175.00
**HOLLOW CARVED SWAN,** orig. paint, heavy mildew ................. $140.00

A-MA Mar. 1983   *Richard A. Bourne Co., Inc.*
MASON'S FACTORY DECOYS
*Row I, L to R*
**BLUEBILLS,** pr., premier grade, repainted ........................ $210.00
**MALLARD HEN,** premier grade, repainted ........................ $80.00
*Row II, L to R*
**BLACK DUCK,** premier grade, repainted
.................................. $90.00
**REDHEADS,** pr., premier grade, repainted, bill of hen has been replaced
.................................. $160.00
*Row III, L to R*
**REDHEAD HEN,** premier grade, repainted ........................ $90.00
**CANVASBACKS,** pr., premier grade, repainted ........................ $140.00

A-MA Aug. 1983   *Robert C. Eldred Co., Inc.*
*L to R*
**MINI. CARVING OF RED HEAD DRAKE,** by A. Elmer Crowell ... $375.00
**MINI. CARVING OF WIDGEON DRAKE,** by A. Elmer Crowell ... $375.00
**MINI. CARVING OF WOOD DUCK DRAKE,** minor damage to bill tip
.................................. $450.00
**MINI. CARVING OF BUFFLEHEAD,** sgn. C. S. Crowell, MA ........ $400.00

A-MA Aug. 1983   *Robert C. Eldred Co., Inc.*
MINI. CARVINGS
BY A. ELMER CROWELL
*L to R*
**BLK. DUCK** ................ $350.00
**GROUSE** .................. $425.00
**BLK. DUCK** ................ $375.00

A-MA Aug. 1983   *Robert C. Eldred Co., Inc.*
MINI. CARVINGS
BY A. ELMER CROWELL
*L to R*
**BLK. DUCK** ................ $350.00
**MALLARD** ................. $400.00
**GOLDEN-EYE DRAKE** ....... $400.00

A-MA Nov. 1982   *Richard A. Bourne Co., Inc.*
*Row I, L to R*
**WING DUCK,** cast iron, painted blk.
.......................................... $120.00
**MASON STANDARD GRADE BLUE-
BILL,** glass eyes ............... $240.00
*Row II, L to R*
**MASON'S STANDARD GRADE
BLUEBILLS,** pr., drake & hen, drake has
glass eyes, hen's eyes have been repl.
w/tack eyes ................... $170.00
*Row III*
**MASON CHALLENGE GRADE
BRANT DECOY,** paint worn off end of
bill, glass eyes, bears brand hard on
bottom, slight age split in bottom
.............................. $225.00

A-MA Nov. 1982   *Richard A. Bourne Co., Inc.*
*Row I, L to R*
**FLAT YELLOWLEGS DECOY,** by A.
Elmer Crowell, tack eyes, orig. paint
............................... $1050.00
**FLAT YELLOWLEGS DECOY,** pr.,
nail bills & tack eyes ........... $140.00
*Row II, L to R*
**MASON YELLOWLEGS DECOY,**
spike bill & tack eyes, right side of head hit
by shot, old repaint ............ $125.00
**FLAT LESSER YELLOWLEGS
DECOY,** nail bill ................ $70.00
**FLAT YELLOWLEGS DECOY,** spike
bill, chipped at base of bill, lightly struck by
3 bird shot .................... $60.00

A-MA Aug. 1983   *Robert C. Eldred Co., Inc.*
**MASON RED HEAD DECOYS,** prem-
ium grade, pr. ............. $2000.00

A-MA Mar. 1983   *Richard A. Bourne Co., Inc.*
*SHORE BIRDS*
*Row I, L to R*
**YELLOWLEGS,** by Ira Hudson, mostly
orig. paint, replm., lightly hit by shot
............................... $400.00
**YELLOWLEGS,** by Dave Watson,
carved wing tips, possibly orig. paint
w/considerable wear, bill partly broken off
............................... $400.00
*Row II, L to R*
**KNOT,** by Leon Pierson, paint worn to
natural wood, replm., age splits .. $100.00
**EASTERN VIRGINIA BLACK-
BELLIED PLOVER,** worn old paint
............................... $350.00
*Row III, L to R*
**KNOT,** carved wing tips, worn mostly to
natural wood, replm., some restor.
............................... $400.00
**KNOT,** orig. paint w/in-use wear, replm.,
chip, dry rot .................. $250.00

A-MA Mar. 1983   *Richard A. Bourne Co., Inc.*
*CHESAPEAKE BAY, VA & N.C.
DECOYS*
*Row I, L to R*
**MALLARD DRAKE,** by Lee Dudley,
sgn., old repaint, age splits ..... $1600.00
**PINTAIL DRAKE,** by Mitchell Fulcher,
extremely rare, sgn., mostly orig. paint, in-
use wear ................... $3000.00
*Row II, L to R*
**MALLARDS,** pr., by James Holly, good
orig. paint, slight age splits ..... $2200.00

A-MA Mar. 1983   *Richard A. Bourne Co., Inc.*
*CANADA GEESE DECOYS*
*Row I, L to R*
**HOLLOW CARVED,** by Harry Shourds,
old in-use repaint, age split & chip
............................... $425.00
**HOLLOW CARVED,** in-use repaint,
crazing, repr., split ............. $175.00
*Row II, L to R*
**HOLLOW CARVED,** in-use repaint, age
split ......................... $180.00
**HOLLOW CARVED,** by John McLough-
lin, very old paint ............. $350.00
*Row III, L to R*
**HOLLOW CARVED,** by John McLough-
lin, carved raised wing tips, old paint
............................... $350.00
**HOLLOW CARVED,** by Harry Shourds,
repainted by Shourds .......... $400.00

A-MA Mar. 1983   *Richard A. Bourne Co., Inc.*
**HOLLOW CARVED BRANT DECOY,**
by Nathan Cobb, exceptionally rare,
slightly carved indentations around the
eyes, carved "N" sgn. in bottom, very old
mostly orig. paint, some overpainting on
the blk. area, in-use wear .... $28,000.00

A-MA Mar. 1983   *Richard A. Bourne Co., Inc.*
**CANADA GOOSE DECOY,** by Walter
Brady, retains worn orig. paint, possibly
some overpaint .............. $5400.00

A-MA Mar. 1983   *Richard A. Bourne Co., Inc.*
**HOLLOW CARVED PINTAIL DRAKE
DECOY,** by Gilbert Maggioni, rare,
carved raised wing tips, inscribed "G.
Maggioni/For Lu & Roy/Bull," orig. paint
.............................. $450.00

A-MA Mar. 1983   *Richard A. Bourne Co., Inc.*
*IRA HUDSON DECOYS*
*Row I, L to R*
**HOLLOW CARVED BLUEBILL DRAKE,** good orig. paint w/some in-use flaking & wear . . . . . . . . . . . . . . . . $2400.00
**HOLLOW CARVED BLUEBILL DRAKE,** ca. 1920, orig. paint, slight age splitting to body . . . . . . . . . . . . . . $900.00
*Row II, L to R*
**BLUEBILL DRAKE,** orig. paint, restor., age splits . . . . . . . . . . . . . . . . . . . . . $350.00
**RED-BREASTED MERGANSER HEN,** balsa, orig. paint, age split . . . . . . $500.00

A-MA Mar. 1983   *Richard A. Bourne Co., Inc.*
*IRA HUDSON DECOYS*
*Row I, L to R*
**CANVASBACK DRAKE,** in-use wear repaint, age splits . . . . . . . . . . . . . $175.00
**WIDGEON DRAKE,** old repaint, slight age splits . . . . . . . . . . . . . . . . . . . . $250.00
*Row II, L to R*
**BLUEBILL DRAKE,** old repaint . . . . . . . . . . . . . . . . . . . . . . . . . . . . $200.00
**BLUEBILL,** paint worn to natural wood, areas of dry rot, many age splits . . . . . . . . . . . . . . . . . . . . . . . . . . $100.00
*Row III, L to R*
**BLUEBILL HEN,** heavy wear, several age splits . . . . . . . . . . . . . . . . . . . . . . . . $110.00
**BLUEBILL HEN,** repainted showing little wear, restor. . . . . . . . . . . . . . . . . . . $90.00

A-MA Mar. 1983   *Richard A. Bourne Co., Inc.*
*ILLINOIS RIVER DECOYS*
*Row I, L to R*
**MALLARD DRAKE,** by Charles H. Perdew, retains orig. weight, age split in neck . . . . . . . . . . . . . . . . . . . . . . . . $850.00
**PINTAIL DRAKE,** by Robert Bradbeer, very old paint, age split in neck . . $250.00
**GREEN WINGED-TEAL DRAKE,** by Hector Whittington, stamped on bottom and dated 1958 . . . . . . . . . . . . . . . . $675.00

*Row II, L to R*
**MALLARDS,** pr., by Thomas Chida, very old paint . . . . . . . . . . . . . . . . . . . . . $225.00
**PINTAIL DRAKE,** by William Kohler, some repaint, some restor., shows wear . . . . . . . . . . . . . . . . . . . . . . . . . . . $160.00

*Row III, L to R*
**MALLARDS,** pr., by Henry Holmes, restor. & repaint . . . . . . . . . . . . . . . $170.00
**MALLARD DRAKE,** by Leonard Doren, regluing, minor flaking . . . . . . . . . $125.00

---

A-MA Mar. 1983   *Richard A. Bourne Co., Inc.*
*HURLEY CONKLIN DECOYS*
*Row I, L to R*
**GREEN-WINGED TEAL,** pr., hen's head turned to left . . . . . . . . . . . . $275.00
**HOODED MERGANSER DRAKE,** . . . . . . . . . . . . . . . . . . . . . . . . . . . . . $200.00

*Row II, L to R*
**SHOVELERS,** pr., head on drake turned to left . . . . . . . . . . . . . . . . . . . . . . $375.00
**REDHEAD DRAKE,** scratch feather painting on back, excellent cond. . . . . . . . . . . . . . . . . . . . . . . . . . . . $175.00

*Row III, L to R*
**RED-BREASTED MERGANSERS,** pr., slight wear to paint . . . . . . . . . . . . $525.00
**REDHEAD HEN,** . . . . . . . . . . . $110.00

A-MA Mar. 1983   *Richard A. Bourne Co., Inc.*
*DECOYS—DECORATIVE CARVINGS*
*Row I, L to R*
**BUFFLEHEADS,** pr., by William H. Cranmer . . . . . . . . . . . . . . . . . . . . . $325.00
**CARVED HALF-SIZED DUCK,** by Stephen Ward, carved raised wing tips, inscribed, unpainted . . . . . . . . . . . $400.00
*Row II, L to R*
**HOODED MERGANSERS,** pr., by William Cranmer, sgn. . . . . . . . . . $350.00
**GREEN-WINGED TEAL DRAKE,** by Bob Kerr, carved raised wing tips, scratch feather painting . . . . . . . . . . . . . . . $575.00
*Row III, L to R*
**BLUE-WINGED TEALS,** pr., by Davison Hawthorne, sgn. & dated, carved wing tips . . . . . . . . . . . . . . . . . . . . . . . . . $375.00
**BLUE-WINGED TEAL DRAKE,** by Bob Kerr, carved raised wing tips . . . . $225.00

A-MA Mar. 1983   *Richard A. Bourne Co., Inc.*
*MASON'S FACTORY DECOYS*
*Row I, L to R*
**COOT,** repainted . . . . . . . . . . . . . . $80.00
**BLACK DUCK,** glass eyes, repainted, age splits . . . . . . . . . . . . . . . . . . . . . . $60.00
**CANVASBACKS,** pr., premier grade, orig. paint, much wear, restoration . . . . . . . . . . . . . . . . . . . . . . . . . . . . $200.00
*Row II, L to R*
**WHITE-WINGED SCOTER,** repainted showing little wear . . . . . . . . . . . . . . $90.00
**BLACK DUCK,** premier grade, old repaint, chip . . . . . . . . . . . . . . . . . . . . $55.00
**WIDGEONS,** pr., premier grade, restor. & repainted . . . . . . . . . . . . . . . . . . . $175.00
*Row III, L to R*
**BRANT,** some overpaint, age splitting . . . . . . . . . . . . . . . . . . . . . . . . . . . $200.00
**BRANT,** overpaint, moderately hit by shot, one eye missing, age split . . $220.00
**CANADA GOOSE,** premier grade, restored & repainted . . . . . . . . . . . . $450.00

A-MA Mar. 1983   *Richard A. Bourne Co., Inc.*
**HOODED MERGANSER HEN,** by Ira Hudson, rare, carved tail & scratch feather paint, orig. paint, age splits . . . . . $7000.00

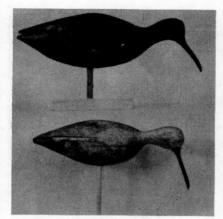

A-MA Mar. 1983 *Richard A. Bourne Co., Inc.*
**SHORE BIRDS**
*Top to Bottom*
**CURLEW,** from Cobb Island, carved wing tips, worn to natural, replm., age splitting, dry rot ...................... $500.00
**YELLOWLEGS,** from Eastern VA, in feeding position, carved wing tips, mostly worn to natural wood, replm., age splits ............................ $400.00

A-MA Mar. 1983 *Richard A. Bourne Co., Inc.*
*NEW JERSEY DECOYS*
*Row I, L to R*
**BRANT,** old in-use repaint, minor flaking & wear, chips ................. $100.00
**BRANT,** old in-use repaint, flaking & wear ................................ $160.00
*Row II, L to R*
**BRANT,** by C. McAnney, old in-use repaint w/little wear ........... $160.00
**BRANT,** by Otto Wrenger, old paint, moderate in-use wear .......... $230.00
*Row III, L to R*
**BRANT,** by Capt. Jesse Birdsall (Barnegat), old in-use repaint, age split in neck ............................ $160.00
**BRANT,** old in-use repaint, 2 age splits in neck ....................... $250.00

A-MA Mar. 1983 *Richard A. Bourne Co., Inc.*
*HURLEY CONKLIN DECOYS*
*Row I, L to R*
**BUFFLEHEADS,** pr. ......... $225.00
**WOOD DUCKS,** pr. ......... $400.00
*Row II, L to R*
**RED-BREASTED MERGANSERS,** pr. ............................. $375.00
**SEAGULL,** carved & raised crossed wing tips ......................... $325.00
*Row III, L to R*
**WIDGEONS,** pr., branded "H. Conklin" on each, carved wing tips ....... $300.00
**BLACK DUCK,** branded "H. Conklin," carved tail & wing tips ......... $180.00

A-MA Mar. 1983 *Richard A. Bourne Co., Inc.*
*CANADA GEESE DECOYS*
*Row I, L to R*
**HOLLOW CARVED,** old repaint heavily worn, restor. ................. $225.00
**HOLLOW CARVED,** by Gene Hendrickson, orig. paint ................ $350.00
*Row II, L to R*
**HOLLOW CARVED,** in-use wear repaint, chip, slightly hit by shot ... $200.00
**HOLLOW CARVED,** by Lloyd Parker, in-use repaint, chip, age split .... $225.00
*Row III, L to R*
**HOLLOW CARVED,** by Hurley Conklin ............................. $375.00
**HOLLOW CARVED,** old paint, possible restor. ....................... $320.00

---

A-MA Mar. 1983 *Richard A. Bourne Co., Inc.*
*DECOYS BY SELECT CARVERS*
*Row I, L to R*
**CARVED BRANT,** by Charles Birch, good orig. paint showing minor in-use wear ............................. $3300.00
**MALLARD DRAKE,** by Ken Greenlea, carved in sleeping position, old paint w/little in-use wear ............. $850.00
*Row II, L to R*
**HOLLOW BRANT,** by Ira Hudson, excellent orig. paint w/little in-use wear ............................. $1400.00
**BALSA BRANT,** by Ira Hudson, in preening position, w/carved wing tips, old repaint showing flaking & wear, slight age split to neck................. $1900.00

A-MA Mar. 1983 *Richard A. Bourne Co., Inc.*
*SHORE BIRDS*
*Row I, L to R*
**BLACK-BREASTED PLOVER,** metal spike bill, orig. paint ............ $150.00
**YELLOWLEGS,** "HD" carved on bottom, old paint, age splits, replm. ............................. $200.00

*Row II, L to R*
**CURLEW,** paint mostly worn to natural wood, replm., heavy coat of varnish ............................. $400.00
**YELLOWLEGS,** old paint, much in-use wear, lightly hit by shot ........ $125.00

A-MA Mar. 1983 *Richard A. Bourne Co., Inc.*
**IRA HUDSON DECOYS**
*Row I, L to R*
**CANADA GOOSE,** carved wing tips, old in-use repaint, age splits ....... $600.00
**CANADA GOOSE,** in-use repaint, age splits ......................... $600.00

*Row II, L to R*
**CANADA GOOSE,** repainted, attached right side, age split ............. $325.00
**CANADA GOOSE,** repainted, restor., age splits ..................... $300.00

A-MA Mar. 1983 *Richard A. Bourne Co., Inc.*
**BLACK DUCK DECOY,** by Nathan Cobb, extremely rare, sgn. "N" on bottom, orig. paint worn mostly to natural wood, old in-use repaint to split in bill ..... $7000.00

A-MA Oct. 1982   *Richard A. Bourne Co., Inc.*
*BISQUE DOLLS*
*Row I, L to R*
**SOCKET-HEAD GIRL,** blue glass sleep eyes, open mouth, jointed composition body, incised "111," 8" H. ....... $300.00
**SOCKET-HEAD GIRL,** blue glass sleep eyes, open mouth, jointed composition body, incised "1907/R/A DEP/1 8/0," 10" H. ........................... $90.00
*Row II, L to R*
**SOCKET-HEAD BABY,** blue glass sleep eyes, open mouth, jointed composition body, incised "151/2," 11½" H. .. $160.00
**BISQUE-HEAD BABY,** blue glass sleep eyes, open mouth, jointed composition body, orig. skin wig, incised "G Made in H/Germany/JBK/211/12," 13" H. .............................. $325.00

A-MA Oct. 1982   *Richard A. Bourne Co., Inc.*
*BISQUE DOLLS*
*L to R*
**SOCKET-HEAD GIRL,** blue stationary glass eyes, open mouth, retains cork & nice br. wig, pierced ears, jointed composition body, incised "1907/12," mkd. w/blue paper label "A. Gesland/Fque De Bebes/& 5 Bis Rue ₇Beranger/En Boutique/Paris," sm. damage, 26" H. .......... $1300.00
**SOCKET-HEAD CHILD,** br. sleep eyes, open mouth, pierced ears, jointed composition body, incised "119 13/Handwerk/Germany/Halbig," 26" H. ....... $300.00

*Left*
A-MA Oct. 1982   *Richard A. Bourne Co., Inc.*
**BISQUE-HEAD GIRL,** swivel head on Bisque shoulder, br. threaded glass stationary eyes, closed mouth, pierced ears, leather body w/Bisque arms, incised "Bru Jne/6," and "Bru Jne," & "No 6," head restor., 17½" H. ............. $1700.00

*Right*
A-MA Dec. 1982   *Robert W. Skinner Inc.*
**BISQUE-HEAD DOLL,** Germany, early 20th C., jointed composition body, mkd. "33 G 165 K 14 Germany," damaged & repainted, 33½" H. .......... $300.00*

A-MA Dec. 1982   *Robert W. Skinner Inc.*
**AUTOMATION ROCK-A-BYE DOLL,** pat. 1902, bisque-head mother doll, jointed composition body, mkd. "192 3/0," bisque jointed baby in wooden cradle, base mkd. "Rock a Bye Doll patented Apr 5 1902," 8⅛" W., 11" L., 12" H. ........... $550.00*

A-MA Oct. 1982   *Richard A. Bourne Co., Inc.*
**BISQUE SOCKET-HEAD GIRL,** br. eyes, brushed eyebrows, closed mouth, pierced ears, orig. cork & blond wig, jointed body, incised "4," stamped w/blue Jumeau stamp, some damage, 12" H. ... $1900.00

*Left*
A-MA Oct. 1982   *Richard A. Bourne Co., Inc.*
**BISQUE SOCKET-HEAD GIRL,** stationary br. glass eyes, brushed eyebrows, closed mouth, blond wig, pierced ears, jointed composition body, dressed, incised "S & H/939," some damage, 15" H. ........................... $1200.00

*Right*
A-MA Oct. 1982   *Richard A. Bourne Co., Inc.*
**BISQUE-HEAD GIRL,** blown blue eyes, brushed br. eyebrows, closed mouth, br. wig, dressed jointed composition body, incised "J. Steiner/Bte S.G.D.G./Paris FIRE A.15," damage & repr., 23" H. ........................... $400.00

*Price does not include 10% buyer fee.

A-MA Dec. 1982    *Robert W. Skinner Inc.*
*L to R*
**SHIRLEY TEMPLE DOLL,** ca. 1938, Ideal Toy Corp., orig. wig & dress, damage, 18″ H. ...... $100.00*
**SHIRLEY TEMPLE DOLL,** ca. 1936, Ideal Toy Corp., jointed composition body, damage, repl. wig, 21″ H. ..... $140.00*
**SHIRLEY TEMPLE DOLL,** ca. 1936, Ideal Toy Corp., dressed in cowboy outfit for "Texas Centennial 1936," sm. volume of "Shirley Temples' Favorite Poems," crazing, 16″ H. ........ $150.00*

A-MA Oct. 1982    *Richard A. Bourne Co., Inc.*
*BISQUE DOLLS*
*Row I, L to R*
**SOCKET-HEAD BABY,** blue glass sleep eyes, open mouth, jointed composition body, incised "Made in Germany/H W-S/9/0," damage, 9½″ H. ........ $50.00
**BISQUE-HEAD BABY,** flange neck, blue sleep eyes, open mouth, celluloid wrists & hands, incised "AM/Germany/3514/0," 9″ H. ........ $90.00

*Row II, L to R*
**BISQUE-HEAD BABY,** flange neck, blue glass sleep eyes, closed mouth, orig. diaper & stockings, incised "C (in circle) 1923 By/Grace S. Putnam/Made in Germany," damage, 10½″ H. ........ $225.00
**SOCKET-HEAD BABY,** blue glass sleep eyes, open mouth, jointed composition body, incised "Made in Germany/2," damage, 11″ H. ........ $80.00

A-MA Oct. 1982    *Richard A. Bourne Co., Inc.*
*BISQUE DOLLS*
*Row I, L to R*
**SOCKET-HEAD GOOGLY,** German, blue glass sleep eyes, closed mouth, blond mohair curly wig, jointed composition body, incised "Armand Marseille/Germany/323/A410M," retains prize-winning ribbon "Third Prize/United Federation of Doll Clubs/10th Annual Exhibition/Kansas City/1959," shows some wear, 10″ H. ........ $500.00
**SOCKET-HEAD GOOGLY,** German, blue glass sleep eyes, closed mouth, drk. br. wig, jointed composition body, dressed in sailor suit, incised "Germany/323/A5/om.," 10½″ H. ........ $650.00
*Row II, L to R*
**SHOULDER-HEAD BOY,** intaglio eyes, closed mouth, red-blond painted hair, leather & cloth body, Bisque hands, incised "217 14/0/E.H.Germany/D.R.G.M.," head is loose, 12½″ H. ........ $150.00
**SWIVEL-HEAD BOY,** blue glass sleep eyes, open mouth, painted br. hair, jointed composition body, incised "KH/1661/0," 10″ H. ........ $300.00

A-MA Oct. 1982    *Richard A. Bourne Co., Inc.*
*DOLLHOUSE ACCESSORIES*

A-MA Dec. 1982    *Robert W. Skinner Inc.*
*L to R*
**BISQUE SWIVEL SHOULDER-HEAD YOUNG LADY DOLL,** France, ca. 1875, kid body, mkd. "6," damage, 15½″ H. ........ $700.00*
**JUMEAU BISQUE-HEAD DOLL,** France, ca. 1880, jointed composition body, mkd. "8 E.J.," damage & repaint, 16½″ H. ........ $2600.00*
**BISQUE-HEAD DOLL,** Germany, early 20th C., jointed composition body, chips, 14¾″ H. ........ $625.00*

A-MA Oct. 1982    *Richard A. Bourne Co., Inc.*
*BISQUE DOLLS*
*L to R*
**BISQUE-HEAD GIRL,** blue stationary eyes, orig. blond wig, orig. cork, pierced ears, closed mouth, mkd. in red "Depose/Tete Jumeau/Bte S.G.D.G./4," body stamped in blue "Jumeau/Medaille D'Or Paris," 13½″ H. ........ $1750.00
**BISQUE-HEAD GIRL,** paperweight eyes, closed mouth, orig. long blond wig, jointed composition body, stamped in red "Depose/Tete Jumeau/Bte S.G.D.G./2," 11″ H. ........ $1700.00
**FRENCH CHILD,** rare Bebe Schmitt doll, swivel-head girl, pale blue threaded eyes, closed mouth, jointed composition body, mkd. "2/0/Bte S.G.D.G.," body mkd. w/Schmitt shield mark, some damage, 13″ H. ........ $4500.00

*L to R*
**PARTIAL TEA SET,** (5 illus.), doll's tea set w/transfer decor., approx. 18 pcs., minor chips ........ $110.00
**PLATE,** Kewpie design by Rose O'Neill, slight surface scratching to front of plate, gold border shows wear, diameter: 9⅞″ ........ $150.00

A-MA Dec. 1982     *Robert W. Skinner Inc.*
*Back Row, L to R*

**TETE JUMEAU BISQUE-HEAD DOLL,** France, ca. 1878, stationary glass eyes, jointed composition body, mkd. "Depose Tete Jumeau Bte S G D G 8," repainted, 19½" H. .......... $1150.00*

**JUMEAU BISQUE-HEAD TALKING DOLL,** Paris, ca. 1880, stationary glass eyes, jointed composition body, mkd. "Depose Tete Jumeau Bte S G D G 9" & "Bebe Jumeau Diplome d'Honneur," repainted, damaged talking mechanism, chips, 22½" H. .............. $1100.00*

**JUMEAU BISQUE-HEAD DOLL,** France, late 19th C., stationary glass eyes, jointed composition body, chip & repr., 15½" H. .................... $2500.00*

**J. STEINER BISQUE-HEAD DOLL,** Paris, ca. 1880, stationary glass eyes, jointed composition body, mkd. "J. Steiner Bte S O D G Paris Fire A 15," repainted, crack, 22" H. ........ $1650.00*

**BRU FISQUE-HEAD DOLL,** Paris, ca. 1885, stationary glass eyes, jointed composition body, mkd. "Bru. Jne. R 9," damage, repr., repainted, 21" H. ........ $400.00*

*Front Row, L to R*

**JUMEAU BISQUE-HEAD DOLL,** France, ca. 1880, stationary glass eyes, jointed composition body, mkd. "Jumeau Medaille D'or Paris," repainted, chips, 14½" H. ........................ $1000.00*

**BISQUE-HEAD DOLL,** Germany, late 19th C., stationary glass eyes, kid body & limbs, swivel head & shoulder plate, damage & chips, 14" H. ....... $350.00*

**JUMEAU BISQUE-HEAD DOLL,** Paris, ca. 1880, stationary glass eyes, jointed composition body, mkd. "5" & "Jumeau Medaille d'or Paris," wear & chips, 13" H. ................ $1550.00*

**BISQUE SHOULDER-HEAD DOLL,** Germany, late 19th C., sleeping glass eyes, kid arms on cloth body, mkd. "G" & "No 7," 18" H. ................... $350.00*

A-MA Dec. 1982     *Robert W. Skinner Inc.*
*L to R*

**BISQUE-HEAD CANDY CONTAINER,** Germany, early 20th C., Dutch boy, paper & wood body, bisque hands, mkd. "70-16," 7½" H. ......... $80.00*

**MUNICH ART DOLL,** Germany, ca. 1912, by Marion Kaulitz, jointed composition body, orig. clothing, roughness & damage, 13" H. ............ $525.00*

**BISQUE-HEAD CHARACTER BOY,** Germany, ca. 1925, jointed composition body, mkd. "Simon & Halbig 126-16 Germany," 6¼" H. ............ $250.00*

**BISQUE-HEAD CHARACTER BOY,** Germany, ca. 1910, cloth body, bisque hands, mkd. "Germany, M? DT5," 12" H. ............................ $140.00*

**BISQUE-HEAD DOLLS,** (third from right & far right), Germany, ca. 1925, both have jointed composition bodies, girl mkd. "Just Me Registered Germany A 310/11/ O.M.," 7½" H.; boy is Ernst Heubach Googly Eye doll, mkd. "Germany EH 262 15/O D.R.G.M.," damage, 6¾" H. ............................ $370.00*

**BISQUE DOLL,** Germany, early 20th C., jointed shoulders & hips, repr., 9" H. ............................ $120.00*

A-MA Oct. 1982     *Richard A. Bourne Co., Inc.*
*FRENCH FASHION DOLLS*
*L to R*

**BISQUE-HEAD LADY,** swivel head on Bisque shoulder plate, gray & amber tinted eyes outlined in darker blue, closed mouth, pierced ears, cloth body, newer leather arms, mkd. "(block) H," on head, "(block) H," on left shoulder, slight damage, 18" H. ............................ $1400.00

**BISQUE-HEAD LADY,** swivel head on Bisque shoulder plate, blue glass stationary eyes, pierced ears, cloth body w/leather arms, 17" H. .................. $1600.00

A-MA Oct. 1982     *Richard A. Bourne Co., Inc.*
*BABY DOLLS*
*L to R*

**BYE LO BABY,** flange head w/blue sleep eyes, closed mouth, painted br. hair, celluloid hands on cloth body, incised "COPR. by Grace S. Putnam/MADE IN GERMANY," body stamped "BYE LO-BABY/Pat. appl'd-for/copy/by/Grace/ Storey/Putnam," 14½" H. ...... $350.00

**ORIENTAL BABY,** sleep eyes, open mouth, blk. wig, jointed composition body w/curved arms & legs, incised "Germany/ 243/JDK/Made in Germany," body stamped "Made in Germany," 13" H. ............................ $1700.00

**BISQUE SWIVEL-HEAD BABY,** blue sleep eyes, open mouth, reddish skin wig, jointed composition body, curved arms & legs, incised "152/LW&Co./11," 18½" H. ............................ $350.00

A-MA Oct. 1982     *Richard A. Bourne Co., Inc.*
*MISCELLANEOUS DOLLS*
*Row I, L to R*

**CHINA-HEAD LADY,** painted blue eyes, closed mouth, milliner-type leather body, wooden arms & legs, 7¼" H. .... $350.00

**CHINA-HEAD GIRL,** painted blue eyes, closed mouth, china arms & legs on cloth body, foot chipped, 6½" H. ..... $175.00

**CHINA-HEAD DOLLS,** lot of 2, (1) nursemaid and baby, china shoulder-head, cloth body, orig. clothing, Frozen Charlotte baby in arms, 3½" H., (2) cloth body, china arms & legs, 5¾" H. ............ $70.00

**PINK-TINGED CHINA SHOULDER-HEAD LADY,** painted blue eyes, cloth body, china arms, china shoes, 4½" H. ............................ $70.00

*Row II, L to R*

**SOFT PINK-TINGED CHINA SHOULDER-HEAD GIRL,** painted br. eyes, cloth body, china limbs, damage, 8" H. ............................ $40.00

**PINCUSHION FROZEN CHARLOTTE,** painted blue eyes, closed mouth, Frozen Charlotte in pocket of pincushion skirt, outfit is lined in clear beads, 7" H. ............................ $60.00

**CHINA SHOULDER-HEAD LADY,** painted gray-br. eyes, closed mouth, creamy pink china, 8" H. ....... $400.00

**CHINA SHOULDER-HEAD LADY,** painted blue eyes, 8" H. ......... $40.00

A-MA Oct. 1982 *Richard A. Bourne Co., Inc.*
BISQUE DOLLS
*Row I, L to R*
**GERMAN LADY,** socket head, blue sleep eyes, closed mouth, jointed composition body, incised "Cod/Germany," 14" H. ............................ $900.00
**SHOULDER-HEAD LADY,** blue stationary eyes, open mouth, orig. br. wig, straw-filled cloth body, composition limbs, mkd. "3," & "22," & group numbers, 13¾" H. ............................ $550.00
**SHOULDER-HEAD BLACK FRENCH FASHION LADY,** painted br. eyes, closed mouth, pierced ears w/gold earrings, leather body, arms & feet, 13¾" H. ............................ $300.00

*Row II, L to R*
**SWIVEL-HEAD LADY,** gray stationary eyes, closed mouth, leather body, Bisque arms, damage, 18½" H. ..... $600.00
**SHOULDER-HEAD GIRL,** lt. blue paperweight eyes rimmed in drk. blue, closed mouth, human-hair wig, leather body, Bisque arms, mkd. w/maroon paper label "Registered/MY SWEETHEART/Germany," damage, 20½" H. .... $150.00
**GERMAN SOCKET-HEAD CHARACTER,** painted br. eyes, closed mouth, jointed composition body, incised "K & H/520/6," 17½" H. ........... $2300.00

A-MA Oct. 1982 *Richard A. Bourne Co., Inc.*
DOLLHOUSE ACCESSORIES
*Row I, L to R*
**BUST FIGURE CIGARETTE HOLDERS,** pr., age cracks, 3½" H. ..... $20.00
**CHINA FIGURAL GROUP,** "A Present from Rhyl," 4" H. .............. $15.00
**CHINA FIGURAL GROUP,** "Looking Down Upon His Luck," 3½" H. ... $30.00
**CHINA COVERED BOX,** Little Red Riding Hood, replm., some wear to decor., 3¼" H. ........................ $10.00

*Row II, L to R*
**ROYAL COPENHAGEN GIRL FIGURE,** 3 Rivers cobalt blue mark, 5¼" H. ............................ $80.00
**DESK SET,** wear to decor., repr., 3¾" H. ............................ $50.00
**COVERED BOX IN FORM OF BASSINET,** reclining baby & rattle, slight roughness, 8" H. .............. $130.00
**SALT & PEPPER SHAKERS,** pr., Kate Greenaway-type figures, bottom stoppers are missing, tallest is 4" H. ....... $20.00

*Row III, L to R*
**COPENHAGEN CHINA FIGURE,** girl w/doll, 7¼" H. ................. $90.00
**CHINA PLATE,** Bavarian china w/comical transfer of sm. girl in wading pool, slight wear, 9" H. ................... $120.00
**COVERED CONTAINER,** glazed German bisque, 5½" H. ............. $60.00
**TRINKET BOX,** 5" H. ........ $30.00

A-MA Oct. 1982 *Richard A. Bourne Co., Inc.*
**BISQUE DOLLS,** Kewpie, lot of 2, painted eyes, blue wings, jointed at shoulders, incised mark at bottom of feet "O Neill," damage, 5" H., character doll has pointed googly eyes, button nose, Triangle-shaped mouth, painted blond hair, jointed at hips & shoulders, damage, 4¾" H. ............................ $40.00

A-MA Oct. 1982 *Richard A. Bourne Co., Inc.*
BISQUE DOLLS
*L to R*
**TWINS,** painted eyes, closed mouths, frowning eyebrows, blond hair wigs, jointed at shoulders, molded suits, each 4" H. ............................ $30.00
**CHILD,** painted blue eyes, turned-up nose, red line for mouth, molded lt. br. hair, seated position, left arm has molded baby bottle, right arm holds a kitten, 3¾" H. ............................ $60.00

A-MA Oct. 1982 *Richard A. Bourne Co., Inc.*
DOLL HEADS
*Row I, L to R*
**PARIAN SHOULDER-HEAD GIRL,** left shoulder broken & reglued, 5¼" H. ............................ $75.00
**CHINA SHOULDER-HEAD GIRL,** molded hair ................... $175.00
**SHOULDER-HEAD GIRL,** composition, mkd. "Patented/Holz Masse," face is badly worn, 4¾" H. ............. $60.00
*Row II, L to R*
**CHINA HEAD GIRLS,** lot of 3, 4, 5 & 5½" H. ............................ $60.00

A-MA Oct. 1982 *Richard A. Bourne Co., Inc.*
BISQUE DOLLS
*L to R*
**STATIONARY-NECK CHILD,** blue glass stationary eyes, closed mouth, feathered eyebrows, blond wig, 4 fingers missing, 8¼" H. ...................... $300.00
**STATIONARY-HEAD GIRL,** br. sleep eyes, open mouth, missing leg, sm. paint rub on cheek, 8½" H. ..... $100.00
**STATIONARY-NECK BOY,** painted blue eyes, closed mouth, mkd. "Germany/8," surface chips at stringing holes, flaw in cheek, 7" H. ................... $30.00

A-MA Oct. 1982    *Richard A. Bourne Co., Inc.*
*DOLLHOUSE MINIATURES*
*Row I, L to R*
**METAL VICTORIAN-STYLE LAMP TABLE,** leather inset top, cast in gold color to represent brass ......... $40.00
**BRASS-STYLE BED,** head & footboard, & bedspread .................... $50.00
**METAL VICTORIAN-STYLE LIBRARY TABLE,** marble-like top, bronze-like table, minor flaking .......... $60.00
*Row II, L to R*
**6-SOCKET CHANDELIER,** sockets slightly bent .................... $120.00
**METAL LAMP BASE,** drk patination, 2 feet broken off, top missing ...... $40.00
**METAL VICTORIAN TABLE LAMP,** base has drk. patination, brass-colored top fixture & shade ................ $150.00
**METAL VICTORIAN-STYLE 3-SOCKET CHANDELIER** ............. $20.00
*Row III, L to R*
**BRASS FRENCH PROVINCIAL-STYLE SHOWCASE,** beveled glass & 2 heavy glass shelves, top is loose ................................. $200.00
**METAL FIREPLACE & MANTLE,** chipped paint, dents & bends in metal ................................. $200.00
**WOODEN SHOWCASE,** painted gold, glass door & sides, contains several miniature figurines ............. $125.00

A-MA Oct. 1982    *Richard A. Bourne Co., Inc.*
*DOLLHOUSE ACCESSORIES*
*Row I, L to R*
**THREE CLOCKS,** 2 hanging pendulum clocks & 1 Empire shelf clock ... $160.00
*Row II*
**REGULATOR WALL CLOCK,** golden oak ......................... $50.00

A-MA Oct. 1982    *Richard A. Bourne Co., Inc.*
*L to R*
**EMPIRE DINING CHAIRS,** set of 9 (2 illus.), 1 armchair & 8 side chairs ................................. $50.00
**MARBLE-TOP TABLE,** top has sm. chips ........................ $30.00

A-MA Oct. 1982    *Richard A. Bourne Co., Inc.*
*DOLLHOUSE ACCESSORIES*
*Row I, L to R*
**VICTORIAN-STYLE HANGING LAMPS,** lot of 2, metal, blown glass shades ................................. $660.00
**MINIATURE ITEMS,** lot of 2, Victorian fluid lamp on stand, gr. glass shade & art deco table lamp .............. $125.00
*Row II, L to R*
**HANGING FLUID LAMP,** metal, incised decor. around base & brass reflector ................................. $80.00
**CHANDELIER,** metal, 3 light sockets & center candle, painted gold, some damage ................................. $12.00
**VICTORIAN DOUBLE-BRACKET LAMP,** metal, painted gold, some damage ................................. $40.00
**ART DECO CHANDELIER,** metal, some damage ................. $70.00
*Row III, L to R*
**CHANDELIER,** brass ........ $110.00
**CHANDELIER,** brass, some damage ................................. $60.00
**ART DECO CHANDELIER,** metal, some damage ................. $120.00

A-MA Oct. 1982    *Richard A. Bourne Co., Inc.*
*DOLLHOUSE FURNITURE*
*Row I, L to R*
**VICTORIAN-STYLE SIDE CHAIRS,** set of 6 (2 illus.), litho., upholstered, 1 chair has leg missing ................ $310.00
**SIDE CHAIRS,** set of 2, 1 is Victorian-style w/litho. back, other is litho. Empire-style w/gr. upholstery ........... $60.00
*Row II, L to R*
**BIEDERMEYER EMPIRE-STYLE SOFA,** stenciled decor., flowered upholstery ......................... $100.00
**VICTORIAN-STYLE ARM CHAIR,** litho. decor., arms are broken & cracked ................................. $70.00
**VICTORIAN-STYLE DRESSING TABLE,** litho. decor., back mirror ................................. $80.00
**MARBLE-TOP SERVER,** litho. decor., mirror is loose ................ $175.00
**CABINET,** litho. decor., some wear & chips ........................ $50.00

A-MA Oct. 1982    *Richard A. Bourne Co., Inc.*
*DOLLHOUSE ACCESSORIES*
*L to R*
**VICTROLA,** brass, on stand ... $110.00
**TIN LAVABO,** spigot handle is broken off, minor paint chips .......... $260.00
**GLASS GLOBE,** wire stand, globe has hole for liquid .................. $35.00
**DOUBLE-LIDDED BASKET,** brass handle, inscribed "J. Avery & Son/Reditch," minor dents ............. $20.00
**TIN VICTORIAN PARLOR STOVE,** wooden base & top, rust spots, chipped paint ........................ $45.00

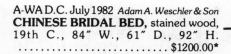

A-WA D.C. July 1982 *Adam A. Weschler & Son*
**CHINESE BRIDAL BED,** stained wood,
19th C., 84″ W., 61″ D., 92″ H.
.............................. $1200.00**\***

A-MA July 1982          *Robert W. Skinner Inc.*
**BENTWOOD HANGING CRADLE,**
Europe, ca. 1865, 56″ W., 68″ H.
.............................. $875.00**\***

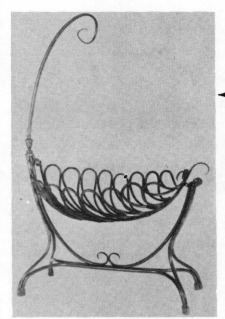

A-MA Nov. 1982    *Richard A. Bourne Co., Inc.*
**CHILD'S BED,** PA, 18th C., solid maple
posts, retains orig. drk. gr. paint over red,
78″ L., 35½″ W., 34″ H. ......... $900.00

A-MA Nov. 1982    *Richard A. Bourne Co., Inc.*
**LOW POSTER BED,** Am., early 19th C.,
pumpkin color w/br. graining, orig. finish,
retains all pegs for rope support, 50″ W.,
headboard 30½″ H. ........... $1000.00

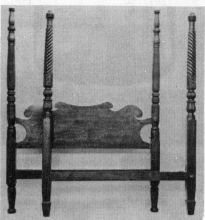

A-MA July 1982    *Richard A. Bourne Co., Inc.*
**TALL POSTER BED,** Am., ca. 1810-
1820, Am., maple, finished cond., 84″ H.
............................. $1000.00

A-MA Aug. 1983    *Robert C. Eldred Co., Inc.*
**EMPIRE FOUR POSTER BED,** Am.,
mahogany & mahogany veneer, 84″ H.
........................... $1100.00

A-MA July 1982    *Richard A. Bourne Co., Inc.*
**EMPIRE BED,** early 19th C., 41½″ H.
............................. $375.00

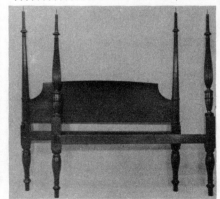

A-MA July 1982    *Richard A. Bourne Co., Inc.*
**SHERATON TESTER BED,** drk. finished curly maple footposts, ht. of posts:
62½″ H. ..................... $2200.00

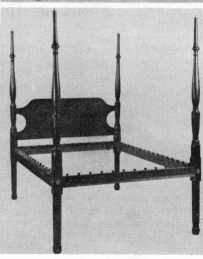

A-MA Nov. 1982    *Richard A. Bourne Co., Inc.*
**SHERATON HIGH POSTER BED,** PA,
ca. 1800, poplar, once painted, drk. natural
finish, 80½″ H., 78″ L., 54″ W. .. $2500.00

A-MA Aug. 1982       *Robert W. Skinner Inc.*
**FEDERAL BED,** N. Eng., ca. 1800, maple
& pine, shaped headboard w/pencil posts
& footboard w/matching posts, 78″ H.,
76½″ L. ................... $2300.00**\***

\*Price does not include 10% buyer fee.

*Left*

A-MA July 1982    *Robert W. Skinner Inc.*
**Q.A. WING CHAIR,** N. Eng., walnut, mid-18th C., 47″ H. ........ $10000.00*

*Right*

A-MA July 1982    *Richard A. Bourne Co., Inc.*
**CHIPPENDALE WING CHAIR,** Eng., ca. 1770-1780, in-the-rough cond. ............................. $700.00

A-MA July 1982    *Richard A. Bourne Co., Inc.*
*L to R*
**WINDSOR ARMCHAIR,** Am., ca. 1800, 7-spindle, orig. paint w/some wear ............................. $275.00
**WINDSOR SIDE CHAIR,** 18th C., RI, 7-spindle, seat altered & upholstered, repainted ..................... $300.00
**WINDSOR ROCKER,** Am., ca. 1800-1810, orig. paint .............. $300.00

A-MA July 1982    *Richard A. Bourne Co., Inc.*
*L to R*
**WINDSOR ARMCHAIR,** Am., 18th C., maple seat, oak legs & back, labeled "A.B. Oatman," ref. in natural wood .. $1500.00
**WINDSOR ARMCHAIR,** Am., 18th C., pine, oak, maple & fruitwood, ref. in natural wood ......................... $1100.00
**WINDSOR ARMCHAIR,** Am., ca. 1800, maple legs & oak back, ref. ..... $800.00

A-MA July 1982    *Richard A. Bourne Co., Inc.*
**WRITING ARM WINDSOR,** ca. 1760-1780, orig. candle slide, ref. in natural wood, traces of blue-gray paint, replaced drawer ..................... $12000.00

A-MA Nov. 1982    *Richard A. Bourne Co., Inc.*
*L to R*
**Q.A. CANDLESTAND,** southern NH, ca. 1800, old blk. paint ......... $750.00
**WINDSOR BOW-BACK ARMCHAIR,** N. Eng., 18th C., old blk. paint ... $800.00

A-MA July 1982    *Richard A. Bourne Co., Inc.*
*L to R*
**WINDSOR ARMCHAIR,** N. Eng., 18th C., pine seat w/oak back & legs, ref. ............................. $1500.00
**WINDSOR ARMCHAIR,** N. Eng., 18th C., pine seat w/maple legs & oak back, natural finish, darkened & worn on seat ............................. $1700.00
**WINDSOR ARMCHAIR,** Am., 18th C., maple seat & legs, oak spindles & arms, fruitwood bow, ref. in natural wood ......................... $1600.00

A-MA Nov. 1982    *Richard A. Bourne Co., Inc.*
**FAN-BACK WINDSOR SIDE CHAIRS,** set of 4, Am., ca. 1780, ash w/pine seats, old but not orig. natural finish, few old minor repr. ..... $2400.00

A-MA July 1982    *Richard A. Bourne Co., Inc.*
*L to R*
**WINDSOR ARMCHAIR,** N. Eng., 18th C., original cond., worn old gr. paint ............................. $3750.00
**WINDSOR SIDE CHAIR,** 18th C., RI, unrestor., painted drk. gr. over lt. gr. over traces of red, paint worn & flaking ............................. $3500.00
**CONTINUOUS ARM WINDSOR CHAIR,** ca. 1800, RI, orig. gr. paint, unrestor., watermarks on seat ... $950.00

A-MA Mar. 1983    *Robert W. Skinner Inc.*
**WINDSOR ARMCHAIR,** 18th C., N. Eng., bow back above 7 spindles, shaped seat, side & medial stretchers, 36″ H. ............................. $3000.00*

*Left*

A-MA July 1982    *Robert W. Skinner Inc.*
**WINDSOR LADY'S ARMCHAIR,** N. Eng., late 18th C., maple, ash & pine, 7-spindle, saddle seat ......... $2500.00*

*Right*

A-MA Nov. 1982    *Richard A. Bourne Co., Inc.*
**WINDSOR BOW-BACK ARM CHAIR,** PA, late 18th C., slightly cut down, old patch in seat, remains of old blk. paint on finish ..................... $700.00

*Price does not include 10% buyer fee.

A-MA Nov. 1982   *Richard A. Bourne Co., Inc.*
L to R
**WINDSOR COMB-BACK ROCKER,**
Am., early 19th C., orig. blk. paint
...................... $900.00
**COMB-BACK WINDSOR SIDE
CHAIR,** Am., early 19th C., 7-spindle, orig.
blk. paint, comb restored, 3 center spindles
repr. ........................ $150.00

A-MA Nov. 1982   *Richard A. Bourne Co., Inc.*
L to R
**FAN-BACK WINDSOR SIDE CHAIR,**
Samuel Vinson, Newport, RI, 18th C.,
"S.V." mark on bottom of seat, refin.
............................. $850.00
**FAN-BACK WINDSOR SIDE CHAIR,**
Hartford, CT, 18th C., "I. Clark" under
seat, probably Josiah Clark, refin.
............................. $1100.00

A-MA Mar. 1983   *Robert W. Skinner Inc.*
**WINDSOR SIDE CHAIRS,** set of 6 (3
illus.), N. Eng., ca. 1810, grain painted in red
& blk., 33" H. .............. $1050.00*

A-MA July 1982   *Richard A. Bourne Co., Inc.*
**WRITING ARM WINDSOR,** ca. 1800,
MA, pine & maple, areas of orig. gray paint,
orig. drawer, ref. ............. $3000.00

A-MA Nov. 1982   *Richard A. Bourne Co., Inc.*
L to R
**RI CONTINUOUS ARM WINDSOR
CHAIR,** ca. 18th C., natural wood
.......................... $2200.00
**RI CONTINUOUS ARM WINDSOR
CHAIR,** ca. 18th C., refinished
..................... $2300.00
**WINDSOR BOW-BACK SIDE CHAIR,**
N. Eng., 18th C., 9-spindle, bears chalked
letter "D" under seat, refinished
........................... $700.00

A-MA July 1982   *Richard A. Bourne Co., Inc.*
L to R
**COMB-BACK WINDSOR ARM-
CHAIR,** N. Eng., 18th C., ref. in natural
wood, minor restor. necessary
.......................... $1600.00
**BOW-BACK WINDSOR ARMCHAIR,**
N. Eng., 18th C., all of hardwood, ref. &
worn to nice patina, traces of old gr. paint
.......................... $1400.00
**WINDSOR BOW-BACK ARMCHAIR,**
N. Eng., ca. 1800, hardwood structure
w/pine seat, ref. w/traces of old blk. & blue
paint ........................ $1300.00

*Left*
A-MA Oct. 1982   *Robert W. Skinner Inc.*
**WINDSOR ARMCHAIR,** N. Eng., 18th
C., bowback, 37" H. ........ $1850.00*
*Right*
A-MA Oct. 1982   *Robert W. Skinner Inc.*
**WINDSOR ARMCHAIR,** N. Eng., 18th
C., painted blk., 36" H. ....... $1100.00*

A-MA Jan. 1983   *Robert W. Skinner Inc.*
**BIRDCAGE WINDSOR SIDE
CHAIRS,** set of 6 (3 illus.), N. Eng., ca.
1800, shaped plank seats, bamboo turned
legs, damage, 33" H. ......... $1600.00*

A-MA Mar. 1983   *Robert W. Skinner Inc.*
**WINDSOR CONTINUOUS BOW
BACK ARMCHAIRS,** set of 6 (3 illus.),
18th C., N. Eng., molded bow back above 7
spindles, shaped seats, side & medial
stretchers, 35" H. ........ $15,000.00*

A-MA Oct. 1982   *Robert W. Skinner Inc.*
**WINDSOR SIDE CHAIRS,** pr., N. Eng.,
18th C., 36" H. .............. $1700.00*

*Price does not include 10% buyer fee.

A-MA July 1982          *Robert W. Skinner Inc.*
**CHIPPENDALE STYLE CHAIRS**, set of six (two illus.), Am., ca. 1880, mahogany, one arm & five side chairs, upholstered sq. seats, 39½" H. . . . . . . . . . . . . . $1900.00*

*Left*
A-MA July 1982          *Robert W. Skinner Inc.*
**TURNED ASH ARMCHAIR**, ca. 1690, MA, restor., 42¼" H. . . . . . . . . $1100.00*

*Right*
A-MA July 1982          *Robert W. Skinner Inc.*
**CHILD'S LADDERBACK HIGH-CHAIR**, maple, Delaware Valley, 18th C., 38½" H. . . . . . . . . . . . . . . . . . $2500.00*

*Left*
A-MA Nov. 1982    *Richard A. Bourne Co., Inc.*
**CHILD'S CARVER CHAIR**, Am., 17th C., 28¼" H. . . . . . . . . . . . . . . . . $4000.00

*Right*
A-MA July 1982          *Robert W. Skinner Inc.*
**CHILD'S PAINTED HIGHCHAIR**, N. Eng., 18th C., painted, remnants of old paint, 35½" H. . . . . . . . . . . . . . $800.00*

*Left*
A-MA July 1982          *Robert W. Skinner Inc.*
**CARVER ARMCHAIR**, ca. 1680, MA, curly maple & ash, chair pieced at base, 43" H. . . . . . . . . . . . . . . . . . . . . $1800.00*

*Right*
A-MA Aug. 1982          *Robert W. Skinner Inc.*
**ARMCHAIR**, MA, ca. 1680, oak & ash, 43" H. . . . . . . . . . . . . . . . . . . . . $7000.00*

A-MA July 1982          *Robert W. Skinner Inc.*
**CHIPPENDALE SIDE CHAIRS**, set of 10 (2 illus.), Am., ca. 1930, upholstered slip seats, 38½" H. . . . . . . . . . . . . . $1300.00*

A-MA Oct. 1982          *Robert W. Skinner Inc.*
**CHIPPENDALE SIDE CHAIRS**, pr., N. Eng., ca. 1760, maple, Spanish feet . . . . . . . . . . . . . . . . . . . . . . . . . . $1100.00*

A-MA Nov. 1982    *Richard A. Bourne Co., Inc.*
**SIDE CHAIRS**, pr., mahogany, by William Fiske, Boston, MA, ca. 1788-1793, brand "WF" inside of back seat rail. . $37,500.00

*Left*
A-MA Nov. 1982    *Richard A. Bourne Co., Inc.*
**BANISTER-BACK ARM CHAIR**, N. Eng., early 18th C., old worn blk. paint over red . . . . . . . . . . . . . . . . . . . . . $3250.00

*Right*
A-MA July 1982    *Richard A. Bourne Co., Inc.*
**SHERATON WING CHAIR**, maple, pine & oak, needs reupholstering . . . . . . . . . . . . . . . . . . . . . . . . . . $2250.00

*Left*
A-MA Aug. 1982          *Robert W. Skinner Inc.*
**TURNED ASH ARMCHAIR**, S.E. MA, 17th C., repr., 43" H. . . . . . . . . $2000.00*

*Right*
A-MA Aug. 1982          *Robert W. Skinner Inc.*
**TURNED SLAT BACK ARMCHAIR**, N. Eng., last qtr. 17th C., old blk. paint over red, 41½" H. . . . . . . . . . . . . . $14,000.00*

*Price does not include 10% buyer fee.

*Left*
A-NY June 1982                          *Christie's*
**Q.A. SIDE CHAIR,** ca. 1745, walnut, 21"
W., 37" H. ................. $11000.00

*Right*
A-MA Aug. 1982         *Robert W. Skinner Inc.*
**WM. & MARY SIDE CHAIR,** North
Shore, MA, 1st qtr. 18th C., uphol-
stered back & seat on block, 43" H.
.......................... $2000.00*

A-MA Dec. 1982          *Robert W. Skinner Inc.*
**CHIPPENDALE-STYLE SIDE
CHAIRS,** set of 6 (2 illus.), Am., ca. 1900,
mahogany, 39" H. .......... $1600.00*

*Left*
A-OH April 1983          *Garth's Auctions, Inc.*
**CHIPPENDALE SIDE CHAIR,** mahog-
any, attrib. to Gilbert Ash, orig. old drk.
finish, frame is loose, some repr., pale gr.
damask slip seat ............. $4000.00

*Right*
A-OH April 1983          *Garth's Auctions, Inc.*
**Q.A. TO CHIPPENDALE SIDE
CHAIR,** walnut, slip seat has leather
covering under pale gr. damask, ref.
........................... $9000.00

*Left*
A-MA Aug. 1982         *Robert W. Skinner Inc.*
**WM. & MARY SIDE CHAIR,** Boston,
first qtr. 18th C., maple, upholstered, blk.
paint, 45½" H. .............. $1300.00*

*Right*
A-MA Aug. 1982         *Robert W. Skinner Inc.*
**WM. & MARY SIDE CHAIR,** N. Eng.,
ca. 1700, maple, 44" H. ....... $1200.00*

A-MA Aug. 1982          *Robert W. Skinner Inc.*
**WM. & MARY SIDE CHAIRS,** pr., 1st
qtr. 18th C., blk. paint, some repr., 46" H.
.......................... $2200.00*

*Left*
A-MA Aug. 1982         *Robert W. Skinner Inc.*
**WM. & MARY SIDE CHAIR,** N. Eng.,
first qtr. 18th C., banister back
.......................... $800.00*

*Right*
A-MA Aug. 1982         *Robert W. Skinner Inc.*
**SLAT BACK SIDE CHAIR,** possibly CT,
ca. 1700, restor., 43½" H. ...... $600.00*

A-OH April 1983         *Garth's Auctions, Inc.*
**HEPPLEWHITE SIDE CHAIRS,** set of 6
(3 illus.), shield back, mahogany, seats
upholstered in reproduction horsehair,
old worn finish, some breaks & repr.
.......................... $7800.00

A-OH April 1983         *Garth's Auctions, Inc.*
**HEPPLEWHITE SIDE CHAIRS,** pr.,
mahogany, seats upholstered in reproduction blk. horsehair w/decor. brass
studs, old finish, some breaks, repr.
.......................... $6000.00

A-WA D.C. Sept. 1982 *Adam A. Weschler & Son*
**VICTORIAN SIDE CHAIRS,** pr., ca.
1855, laminated rosewood, attrib. to John
Henry Belter, caster feet ...... $1000.00*

*Price does not include 10% buyer fee.

*Left*
A-MA Oct. 1982     *Robert W. Skinner Inc.*
**GUSTAV STICKLEY SIDE CHAIR,** ca. 1903, oak, brass detail, 47¾" H., 18½" W., 15½" D. .................... $2000.00*

*Right*
A-MA Oct. 1982     *Robert W. Skinner Inc.*
**GUSTAV STICKLEY SIDE CHAIR,** oak, designed by Harvey Ellis, seat missing, rough cond., 42½" H., 16¾" W., 21½" D. .................... $1250.00*

*Left*
A-MA Oct. 1982     *Robert W. Skinner Inc.*
**GUSTAV STICKLEY SPINDLE MORRIS CHAIR,** oak, unsgn., 37¼" H., 33" W., 28" D. .............. $5000.00*

*Right*
A-MA Oct. 1982     *Robert W. Skinner Inc.*
**GUSTAV STICKLEY RECLINING CHAIR,** unsgn., cushions need repr., replaced seat peg, 39½" H., 30" W., 36" D. .................... $1500.00*

A-MA Oct. 1982     *Robert W. Skinner Inc.*
**CHARLES STICKLEY LIVING ROOM SET,** 3 pcs., ca. 1910, minor damage to decal sgn., settee 36½" H., 49½" W., 22½" D. ................ $1050.00*

A-MA July 1982    *Richard A. Bourne Co., Inc.* →
*L to R*
**LADDER-BACK ARMCHAIR,** N. Eng., early 18th C., curly maple, restor. & ref. .................... $500.00
**LADDER-BACK ARMCHAIR,** early to mid 18th C., restor. & ref. ...... $350.00

*Left*
A-MA Dec. 1982     *Robert W. Skinner Inc.*
**GUSTAV STICKLEY SPINDLE RE-CLINING ARMCHAIR,** ca. 1910, NY, oak, replm., missing peg, new cushions, sgn., 27½" W., 24" D., 37½" H. .................... $1700.00*

*Right*
A-OH Oct. 1982     *Garth's Auctions, Inc.*
**LADDERBACK ARMCHAIR,** walnut, old drk. reddish-br. finish, replm. .................... $3250.00

*Left*
A-MA July 1982     *Robert W. Skinner Inc.*
**LADDERBACK ARMCHAIR,** N. Eng., ca. 1680, turned ash, 45" H. ... $1100.00*

*Right*
A-MA July 1982     *Robert W. Skinner Inc.*
**LADDERBACK ARMCHAIR,** N. Eng., ca. 1700, old blk. paint, minor repair to feet, 47" H. .................... $1600.00*

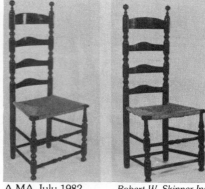

A-MA July 1982     *Robert W. Skinner Inc.*
*L to R*
**LADDERBACK SIDE CHAIR,** N. Eng., early 18th C., old blk. paint, 45" H. .................... $850.00*
**LADDERBACK SIDE CHAIR,** N. Eng., early 18th C., old blk. paint, 44½" H. .................... $900.00*

A-MA July 1982     *Robert W. Skinner Inc.*
*L to R*
**LADDERBACK SIDE CHAIR,** N. Eng., early 18th C., old blk. paint, 46" H. .................... $700.00*
**LADDERBACK SIDE CHAIR,** N. Eng., early 18th C., old blk. paint, 45" H. .................... $800.00*

A-OH April 1983     *Garth's Auctions, Inc.*
**Q.A. WING CHAIR,** mahogany base, banty feet, old finish, reupholstered in burnt orange .................. $9500.00

*Price does not include 10% buyer fee.

*Left*
A-MA Aug. 1982     *Robert W. Skinner Inc.*
**WM. & MARY BANISTER BACK SIDE CHAIR,** MA, 1st qtr. 18th C., carved & scrolled cresting, painted blk. & gilt, 43" H. .......................... $1100.00*

*Right*
A-MA Aug. 1982     *Robert W. Skinner Inc.*
**WM. & MARY BANISTER BACK CHAIR,** N. Eng., 1st qtr. 18th C., carved Prince of Wales crest, Victorian yellow paint & striping which is ended out, 45" H. .......................... $1100.00*

*Left*
A-MA Aug. 1982     *Robert W. Skinner Inc.*
**WM. & MARY BANISTER BACK SIDE CHAIR,** Eastern MA, 1st qtr. 18th C., 47" H. .......................... $1300.00*

*Right*
A-MA Aug. 1982     *Robert W. Skinner Inc.*
**WM. & MARY BANISTER BACK SIDE CHAIR,** N. Eng., 1st qtr. 18th C., sunflower & geometric shaped crest, repr., 43" H. .......................... $1100.00*

A-MA Aug. 1982     *Robert W. Skinner Inc.*
**CORNER CHAIR,** N. Eng., 18th C., maple & ash, 33½" H. ........ $2600.00*

*Left*
A-MA July 1982     *Robert W. Skinner Inc.*
**WM. & MARY BANISTER-BACK SIDE CHAIR,** N. Eng., ca. 1720, Dutch carved & pierced crest, rush seat, painted blk., 44" H. ................. $1200.00*

*Right*
A-MA July 1982     *Robert W. Skinner Inc.*
**W,M & MARY BANISTER-BACK ARMCHAIR,** N. Eng., ca. 1700, multi-cyma curve shaped crest, orig. blk. paint w/gold striping, sm. repair to hand hold, 44" H. ........................ $11500.00*

*Left*
A-MA July 1982     *Robert W. Skinner Inc.*
**WM. & MARY BANISTER BACK SIDE CHAIR,** N. Eng., ca. 1720, Dutch carved & pierced crest, painted blk., 44" H. .......................... $7200.00*

*Right*
A-MA July 1982     *Robert W. Skinner Inc.*
**WM. & MARY BANISTER BACK SIDE CHAIR,** N. Eng., ca. 1720, Dutch carved & pierced crest, rush seat, old blk. paint, 44" H. ..................... $3300.00*

---

*Left*
A-MA Aug. 1982     *Robert W. Skinner Inc.*
**SLAT BACK SIDE CHAIR,** possibly CT, ca. 1700, 42½" H. ............. $475.00*

*Right*
A-MA Aug. 1982     *Robert W. Skinner Inc.*
**SLAT BACK ARMCHAIR,** N. Eng., last qtr. 17th C., turned maple & ash, mushroom hand holds, old ref., 45" H. .......................... $6000.00*

*Left*
A-MA July 1982     *Robert W. Skinner Inc.*
**WM. & MARY BANISTER BACK SIDE CHAIR,** N. Eng., ca. 1730, old blk. paint, rush seat, 44½" H. .......... $2100.00*

*Right*
A-MA July 1982     *Robert W. Skinner Inc.*
**WM. & MARY SIDE CHAIR,** N. Eng., ca. 1700, banister back, rush seat, minor restor., 48" H. .............. $2200.00*

*Left*
A-MA July 1982     *Robert W. Skinner Inc.*
**WM. & MARY BANISTER-BACK ARMCHAIR,** maple & ash, ca. 1740, rush seat, 50" H. ................. $2100.00*

*Right*
A-MA July 1982     *Robert W. Skinner Inc.*
**WM. & MARY SIDE CHAIR,** ca. 1700, carved Prince of Wales crest & stretcher, upholstered leather back & seat, painted blk., 47½" H. .............. $6500.00*

*Left*
A-MA July 1982    *Robert W. Skinner Inc.*
**Q.A. ARMCHAIR,** N. Eng., ca. 1740, maple, Spanish feet, 40½" H. . . . $2000.00*

*Right*
A-MA July 1982    *Robert W. Skinner Inc.*
**Q.A. ARMCHAIR,** N. Eng., ca. 1750, rush seat, Spanish feet . . . . . . . . . . . $1700.00*

*Left*
A-MA July 1982    *Robert W. Skinner Inc.*
**Q.A. SIDE CHAIR,** N. Eng., ca. 1730, Spanish feet, rush seat, old blk. paint, 41" H. . . . . . . . . . . . . . . . . . . . $650.00*

*Right*
A-MA July 1982    *Robert W. Skinner Inc.*
**Q.A. SIDE CHAIR,** ca. 1730, MA, grain painted, 39½" H. . . . . . . . . . . . $4400.00*

*Left*
A-MA Aug. 1982    *Robert W. Skinner Inc.*
**TURNED SLAT BACK ARMCHAIR,** N. Eng., last qtr. 17th C., retains 19th C. grain paint, 42" H. . . . . . . . . . . $1600.00*

*Right*
A-MA Aug. 1982    *Robert W. Skinner Inc.*
**TURNED SLAT BACK ARMCHAIR,** N. Eng., last qtr. 17th C., mushroom hand holds, old varnish stain, loss of ht., 45½" H. . . . . . . . . . . . . . . . . . . . . . . . . . $1750.00*

*Left*
A-MA July 1982    *Robert W. Skinner Inc.*
**Q.A. SIDE CHAIR,** N. Eng., mid 18th C., Spanish feet, orig. blk. paint, 42" H. . . . . . . . . . . . . . . . . . . . . . . . . . $750.00*

*Right*
A-MA Nov. 1982    *Richard A. Bourne Co., Inc.*
**Q.A. SIDE CHAIR,** MA, ca. 1760, walnut, minor repr. only, good finish . . . . $5000.00

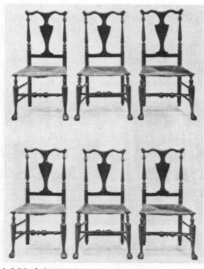

A-MA July 1982    *Richard A. Bourne Co., Inc.*
**Q.A. SIDE CHAIRS,** set of 6, orig. seats, early 19th C., drk. finish . . . . . $11,000.00

A-MA July 1982    *Richard A. Bourne Co., Inc.*
**Q.A. SIDE CHAIRS,** set of 3, Am., ca. 1700-1725, two w/drk. finish, one w/lt. finish, serviceable old replacement rush seats . . . . . . . . . . . . . . . . . . . . . . $5500.00

A-MA July 1982    *Richard A. Bourne Co., Inc.*
*L to R*
**Q.A. SIDE CHAIR,** Am., ca. 1700-1725, curly maple, ref. w/replaced rush seat . . . . . . . . . . . . . . . . . . . . . . . . . . $775.00
**Q.A. SIDE CHAIR,** curly maple, Am., ca. 1700-1725, feet built up, ref., rush seat . . . . . . . . . . . . . . . . . . . . . . . . . . $625.00

*Left*
A-MA Aug. 1982    *Robert W. Skinner Inc.*
**Q.A. SIDE CHAIR,** N. Eng., third qtr. 18th C., maple, painted blk. w/gilt striping, 40" H. . . . . . . . . . . . . . . . . . . . $1000.00*
*Right*
A-MA Mar. 1983    *Robert W. Skinner Inc.*
**Q.A. SIDE CHAIR,** ca. 1700, walnut, upholstered seat on cabriole legs, pad feet, 40" H. . . . . . . . . . . . . . . . . . . . . $2300.00*

A-MA Nov. 1982    *Richard A. Bourne Co., Inc.*
**Q.A. SIDE CHAIRS,** pr. (1 illus.), MA, ca. 1730, seats recovered in needlepoint, fine old finish . . . . . . . . . . . . . . . . . . . . $2500.00

*Price does not include 10% buyer fee.

A-MA July 1982 *Robert W. Skinner Inc.*
**DOWER CHEST,** painted basswood, PA, ca. 1780, reduced in ht., 51″ W., 25″ D., 21″ H. ...................... $1300.00*

A-MA July 1982 *Robert W. Skinner Inc.*
**MINIATURE BLANKET BOX,** pine, N. Eng., ca. 1700, lift top w/dovetailed const., orig. color, 17″ W., 9″ D., 8″ H. ........................... $1800.00*

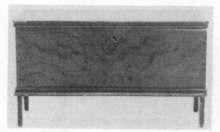

A-MA Aug. 1982 *Robert W. Skinner Inc.*
**MINIATURE BLANKET BOX,** N. Eng., ca. 1800, pine, 10¾″ H., 18″ W., 7¾″ D. ........................... $800.00*

A-MA Jan. 1983 *Robert W. Skinner Inc.*
**BLANKET CHEST,** N. Eng., early 19th C., grain-painted pine, mustard, gr. & umber fan designs, 37¼″ W., 17″ D., 37″ H. ........................... $11500.00*

A-MA Nov. 1982 *Richard A. Bourne Co., Inc.*
**BLANKET CHEST,** PA, late 18th C./ early 19th C., pine, blk. on red, orig. jaw lock & hinges, 52″ L., 25½″ H., 22½″ W. ........................... $3500.00

A-MA July 1982 *Richard A. Bourne Co., Inc.*
**DOWER CHEST,** mid 18th C., PA, orig. unicorn decor., restor., 50½″ L., 23″ D., 21″ H. ........................... $29,000.00

A-MA Aug. 1982 *Robert W. Skinner Inc.*
**CHEST,** N. Eng., last qtr. 17th C., oak & pine, old worn red color, repr. to top, 26½″ H., 40″ W., 19½″ D. ......... $2100.00*

A-OH Jan. 1983 *Garth's Auctions, Inc.*
**BLANKET CHEST,** PA, orig. blue paint, flowers in red, yellow, gr. & wh., German inscription "Johannes Schweinhardt, Jung, Anno 1802," minor damage, 48½″ W., 21½″ D., 23¾″ H. ................. $7600.00

A-MA Nov. 1982 *Richard A. Bourne Co., Inc.*
**LIFT TOP STORAGE CHEST,** Am., early 18th C., pine, old natural finish, orig. brass butterfly escut., lock missing, shrinkage cracks in wood, 49½″ L., 22¾″ H., 17½″ W. ........................... $1000.00

A-MA Aug. 1982 *Robert W. Skinner Inc.*
**PINE 6-BOARD CHEST,** N. Eng., last qtr. 17th C., front panel initialed D.B., old red color, missing drawer & side panel, 30″ H., 46″ W., 18½″ D. ......... $3500.00*

A-MA Mar. 1983 *Robert W. Skinner Inc.*
**BLANKET CHEST,** early 19th C., N. Eng., grain painted pine, decor. w/gr., red & mustard colors, paint loss & brasses replaced, 39″ W., 18″ D., 36½″ H. ........................... $2200.00*

A-MA Mar. 1983 *Robert W. Skinner Inc.*
**DOWER CHEST,** 18th C., PA, painted pine, lift top, 52″ W., 23″ D., 25″ H. ........................... $750.00*

*Price does not include 10% buyer fee.

A-MA July 1982    *Richard A. Bourne Co., Inc.*
**LOWBOY,** walnut, 18th C., PA, restor., 32½" W. ..................... $2500.00

A-MA July 1982    *Richard A. Bourne Co., Inc.*
**SHERATON SWELL-FRONT BUREAU,** mahogany, MA, replaced hardware, 45" W., 41" H. ...... $1200.00

A-MA Mar. 1983    *Robert W. Skinner Inc.*
**Q.A. LOWBOY,** ca. 1750, PA, walnut, restor., 33½" W., 20½" D., 30½" H. ......................... $10,500.00*

A-MA July 1982    *Richard A. Bourne Co., Inc.*
**SM. CHIPPENDALE BUREAU,** Hartford area, ca. 1760-1770, cherry, orig. brasses, 32" W. ............ $13,000.00

A-MA Aug. 1982    *Robert W. Skinner Inc.*
**WM. & MARY CHEST OF DRAWERS,** N. Eng., 1st qtr. 18th C., bun feet, minor restor., 35½" H., 37" W., 20¼" D. ........................... $3000.00*

A-MA Mar. 1983    *Robert W. Skinner Inc.*
**Q.A. TALL CHEST,** ca. 1760, PA, walnut, restor., 43½" W., 23¼" D., 58" H. ......................... $1600.00*

A-MA July 1982    *Richard A. Bourne Co., Inc.*
**CHIPPENDALE CHEST OF DRAWERS,** Am., ca. 1760-1770, tiger maple, finished cond., repl. hardware, 37¾" L. ............................. $4500.00

A-MA Aug. 1982    *Robert W. Skinner Inc.*
**WM. & MARY CHEST OF DRAWERS,** N. Eng., first qtr. 18th C., birch, 38" H., 37" W., 18¾" D. ............... $3700.00*

A-MA Mar. 1983    *Robert W. Skinner Inc.*
**CHIPPENDALE TALL CHEST,** ca. 1780, N. Eng., cherry, replm., 39¼" W., 20½" D., 57" H. ............ $2900.00*

*Price does not include 10% buyer fee.

A-MA July 1982       *Robert W. Skinner Inc.*
**Q.A. HIGHBOY,** maple, N. Eng., ca. 1760, 2-part, engraved batwing brasses, 36½″ W., 19″ D., 67″ H. ...... $5500.00*

A-MA July 1982       *Robert W. Skinner Inc.*
**WM. & MARY HIGHBOY,** ca. 1700, NY, poplar & maple, two split drawers above three graduated drawers, lower case w/single long drawer, red paint, 34″ W., 18½″ D., 57″ H. ............ $9250.00*

A-MA Nov. 1982   *Richard A. Bourne Co., Inc.*
**CHIPPENDALE BUREAU,** CT, late 18th C., cherry, missing 1 knob, 36″ W .......................... $3700.00

A-MA July 1982   *Richard A. Bourne Co., Inc.*
**CHIPPENDALE BUREAU,** Am., 18th C., made from highboy top, ref., two drawer pulls missing, small split in wood, 36″ W., 20½″ D., 35⅝″ H. ....... $350.00

A-MA July 1982   *Richard A. Bourne Co., Inc.*
**CHIPPENDALE HIGHBOY,** ca. 1780, CT, cherry, old finish, orig. bail brasses, 38″ W., 18″ D., 80″ H. .......... $31000.00

A-MA July 1982   *Richard A. Bourne Co., Inc.*
**CHIPPENDALE CHEST-ON-CHEST,** attrib. to Aaron Roberts, ca. 1780-1790, cherry, completely orig., 38″ W., 18¾″ D., 83″ H. ..................... $22500.00

A-MA Nov. 1982   *Richard A. Bourne Co., Inc.*
**Q.A. SLIPPER FOOT LOWBOY OR DRESSING TABLE,** attrib. to John Goddard, Newport, RI, ca. 1760, bears "J. Goddard" on underside of top, bottom part of shell has sustained a break & has brace behind it, back 2¾″ of pull-out slide is replm., orig. hardware, orig. finish, 32″ W., 31″ H., 18⅞″ D ............. $42500.00

*Price does not include 10% buyer fee.

A-MA Nov. 1982    *Richard A. Bourne Co., Inc.*
**Q.A. SLIPPER FOOT HIGHBOY,** N.
Eng., ca. 1760, curly cherry, hardware is
orig., 71⅛″ H., 38¾″ base W., 19¼″ D.
. . . . . . . . . . . . . . . . . . . . . . $26,000.00

A-MA Aug. 1983    *Richard A. Bourne Co., Inc.*
**CHIPPENDALE HIGHBOY,** cherry,
CT, 18th C., married pc., 39½″ W., 20″ D.,
86″ O.H. . . . . . . . . . . . . . . . . . . . $5000.00

A-MA Nov. 1982    *Richard A. Bourne Co., Inc.*
**Q.A. SLIPPER FOOT HIGHBOY
W/BONNET TOP,** Goddard Townsend
School, Newport, RI, ca. 1760, mahogany,
cleaned & waxed, orig. hardware, finial is
orig. except the bottom inch which is repr.
w/replm. turning, upper 6½″ probably orig.,
85″ H., 38″ base W., 19½″ D.
. . . . . . . . . . . . . . . . . . . . . . $92,500.00

A-MA July 1982    *Robert W. Skinner Inc.*
**WM. & MARY HIGHBOY,** Am., ca.
1710, maple & pine, two part, orig. brass,
cockbeaded skirt, 40″ W., 21″ D., 60″ H.
. . . . . . . . . . . . . . . . . . . . . . $7500.00*

A-OH Jan. 1983    *Garth's Auctions, Inc.*
**Q.A. HIGHBOY,** maple, poplar & pine,
repr., ref., 36″ W. at waist, base: 39″ W., 20″
D., 69″ H. . . . . . . . . . . . . . . . $6000.00

A-MA Aug. 1983    *Richard A. Bourne Co., Inc.*
**Q.A. HIGHBOY,** N. Eng., 18th C., curly
maple & birch, repl. legs, orig. hdw., 38″ W.,
19″ D., 17½″ H. . . . . . . . . . . . . $3500.00

*Price does not include 10% buyer fee.

A-MA Nov. 1982    *Richard A. Bourne Co., Inc.*
**SHERATON SIDEBOARD,** Am., early 19th C., mahogany, some loss of veneer around top edge, 64⅜" L. ....... $200.00

A-MA July 1982    *Richard A. Bourne Co., Inc.*
**CHIPPENDALE SECRETARY BOOK-CASE,** curly maple, made from 2 pcs. of furniture, base a bureau w/sliding walnut lid, finished cond., 36⅜" W., 19¼" D., 72¾" H. ........................... $600.00

A-MA June 1983    *Robert W. Skinner Inc.*
**PROVINCIAL COURT CUPBOARD,** France, late 18th C., walnut, restor., minor wood damage, 62" W., 24" D., 83½" H. .......................... $2000.00*

A-WA D.C. Sept. 1982 *Adam A. Weschler & Son*
**FEDERAL SIDEBOARD,** ca. 1815-20, cherry, one shelf in int., 61½" W., 20" D., 57½" H. .................... $1000.00*

A-MA July 1982    *Richard A. Bourne Co., Inc.*
**SHERATON CUPBOARD SECRETARY,** inlaid mahogany, ca. 1800, Am., 38½" W., 49¾" H. ............ $3500.00

A-MA Nov. 1982    *Richard A. Bourne Co., Inc.*
**HEPPLEWHITE-STYLE SECRETARY,** tiger maple, reconstructed piece made from old desk, minor veneer repr. necessary, 78" H., 38½" W., 17¼" D. ............................. $650.00

A-MA Oct. 1982    *Robert W. Skinner Inc.*
**CHIPPENDALE SERPENTINE SECRETARY,** Salem, MA, ca. 1800, mahogany & mahogany veneer, document drawer replm., 97¼" H., 42½" W., 23½" D. ........................ $10,000.00*

*Price does not include 10% buyer fee.

A-WA D.C. July 1982 *Adam A. Weschler & Son*
**DOUBLE CABINET ON STAND,**
Chinese, 19th C., 30″ W., 16″ D., 48″ H.
............................... $350.00*

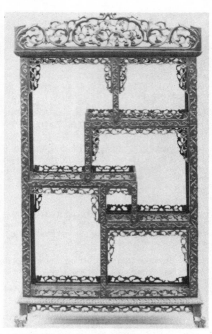

A-WA D.C. Sept. 1982 *Adam A. Weschler & Son*
**CHINESE DISPLAY CABINET,** 19th
C., carved teakwood, 35″ W., 15″ D., 61″ H.
............................ $650.00*

A-WA D.C. July 1982 *Adam A. Weschler & Son*
**VICTORIAN WARDROBE,** ca. 1870,
VA, labeled S. A. Green, mahogany, 60″
W., 22″ D., 103″ H. ........... $800.00*

A-WA D.C. Sept. 1982 *Adam A. Weschler & Son*
**GEORGE III DUMBWAITER,** ca. 1810,
mahogany, casters, 18″ W., 16″ D., 52″ H.
......................... $1300.00*

A-MA July 1982          *Robert W. Skinner Inc.*
**FEDERAL STYLE SECRETARY,** Am.,
ca. 1920, mahogany & mahogany veneer,
full inlaid drawers, brass finials, 37″ W.,
18¾″ D., 79″ H. ............. $1400.00*

A-WA D.C. Dec. 1982 *Adam A. Weschler & Son*
**VICTORIAN ETAGERE,** walnut, mirror
flanked by 8 shaped shelves, serpentine
rouge marble base, 52″ W., 84″ H.
............................. $900.00*

*Price does not include 10% buyer fee.

A-MA Aug. 1982 *Robert W. Skinner Inc.*
**WM. & MARY SLANT FRONT DESK,** N. Eng., ca. 1700, maple, supported by bun feet which are restor., 38" H., 18¾" D., 29¾" W. ...................... $7000.00*

A-MA Oct. 1982 *Robert W. Skinner Inc.*
**CHIPPENDALE SERPENTINE SLANT TOP DESK,** N. Eng., ca. 1780, mahogany, restoration, missing document drawer, 44" H., 51" W., 23" D. .......... $3800.00*

A-MA July 1982 *Richard A. Bourne Co., Inc.*
**MINI. WM. & MARY SLANT-LID DESK,** N. Eng., ca. 1700-1720, pine case w/poplar & chestnut subwoods, retains orig. ball feet, minor damage, 18½" W. ............................ $2500.00

A-MA July 1982 *Richard A. Bourne Co., Inc.*
**CHIPPENDALE SLANT-LID DESK,** cherry, replaced lid hinges, small pc. broken off lid, repl. hdw., 39⅞" L. ............................ $2600.00

A-MA Nov. 1982 *Richard A. Bourne Co., Inc.*
**SLANT-LID DESK,** Goddard Townsend School, Newport, RI, ca. 1760-1770, mahogany, base is replm., hardware is replm., minor piece of molding missing, 35⅞" W. .................... $5000.00

A-WA D.C. Dec. 1982 *Adam A. Weschler & Son*
**HOUSE OF REPRESENTATIVES SLANT-TOP DESK,** carved oak, hinged lid, "America" within scrolling work frieze, 30" W., 21" D., 36" H. ........ $3000.00*

A-OH Jan. 1983 *Garth's Auctions, Inc.*
**Q.A. DESK ON FRAME,** cherry, old finish, repr., replm., 33½" W., 19¾" D., 33¾" writing ht. .............. $5750.00

A-MA July 1982 *Richard A. Bourne Co., Inc.*
**SLANT-LID DESK,** cherry, late 18th C., new hdw. w/brass gallery added to top, replaced lip on bottom drawer, 36½" L. ............................ $1900.00

A-WA D.C. Dec. 1982 *Adam A. Weschler & Son*
**VICTORIAN SCHOOLMASTER'S DESK,** ca. 1865, walnut, hinged-lid writing surface, 41" W., 26" D., 38" H. ............................ $775.00*

*Price does not include 10% buyer fee.

A-OH April 1983    *Garth's Auctions, Inc.*
**CUPBOARD,** pine, 4 int. shelves, old
yellow & br. graining shows drk. br. paint
beneath, 51½″ W., 17¼″ D., 72″ H.
.............................. $250.00

A-OH July 1982    *Garth's Auctions, Inc.*
**CORNER CUPBOARD,** pine, two-piece,
scalloped stiles on doors, dentil molded
cornice, feet repl., other repr., old worn
yellow repaint, 44″ W., 89¼″ H.
............................. $900.00

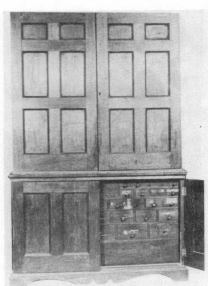

A-OH Mar. 1983    *Garth's Auctions, Inc.*
**CUPBOARD,** walnut, one pc., contains
43 dovetailed apothecary drawers, old
finish, 56″ W., 18¼″ D., 89″ H. .. $4200.00

A-OH April 1983    *Garth's Auctions, Inc.*
**CORNER CUPBOARD,** pine, one pc.,
extensive alter. lt. natural finish, 33″ W.,
83½″ H. ...................... $475.00

A-OH July 1982    *Garth's Auctions, Inc.*
**WALL CUPBOARD,** 2 pc., poplar, orig.
faded red graining, panels have blue steel
comb graining over wh., moldings have
worn blk. paint, 50¼″ W., 29″ D., 74½″ H.
............................. $1600.00

A-OH April 1983    *Garth's Auctions, Inc.*
**CORNER KAS,** walnut, 1 pc., int. has one
shelf & 7 turned hooks, poplar secondary
wood, replm., repr., damage, 43½″ W., 77″
H. .......................... $5750.00

A-OH Feb. 1983        *Garth's Auctions, Inc.*
**PIE SAFE,** poplar, worn weathered surfaces stained a drk. cherry color, some damage & rust, 39" W., 18½" D., 52¼" H.
.............................. $395.00

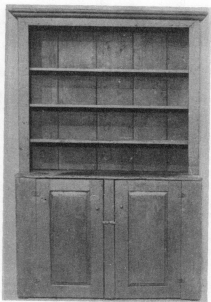

A-OH Feb. 1983        *Garth's Auctions, Inc.*
**WALL CUPBOARD,** one pc., pine, repr., replm., old red paint, 53" W., 18½" D., 86" H. ........................... $1150.00

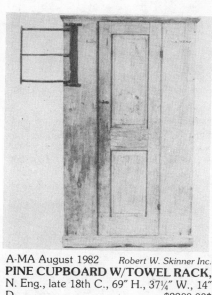

A-MA Aug. 1982        *Robert W. Skinner Inc.*
**HANGING CUPBOARD,** N. Eng., late 18th C., pine, old red paint, 31" H., 48" W., 12" D. ..................... $4200.00*

A-MA August 1982        *Robert W. Skinner Inc.*
**PINE CUPBOARD W/TOWEL RACK,** N. Eng., late 18th C., 69" H., 37¼" W., 14" D. ........................ $2200.00*

A-OH Mar. 1982        *Garth's Auctions, Inc.*
**CORNER CUPBOARD,** one pc., pine, wavy glass, blue repaint, 38" W., 90" H.
.............................. $1350.00

A-MA Aug. 1982        *Robert W. Skinner Inc.*
**BARREL-FRONT CORNER CUPBOARD,** N. Eng., mid-18th C., pine, old natural color, 73" H., 34" W., 19" D.
........................... $3300.00*

A-OH July 1982        *Garth's Auctions, Inc.*
**CORNER CUPBOARD,** cherry, ref., repr., sm. patch missing, W. PA orig., 52" W., 85½" H. ................ $2000.00

*Price does not include 10% buyer fee.

A-MA Nov. 1982    *Richard A. Bourne Co., Inc.*
**PRESERVE CUPBOARD,** Am., early 19th C., pine, pierced tin panels, red painted int., old natural finish, 62″ H., 42½″ W., 18″ D. ..................... $900.00

A-MA Aug. 1982       *Robert W. Skinner Inc.*
**PINE CUPBOARD,** N. Eng., last qtr. 18th C., painted old blue, base repr., 66½″ H., 34½″ W., 19″ D. ............. $6500.00*

A-MA Oct. 1982    *Robert W. Skinner Inc.*
**GUSTAV STICKLEY CHINA CLOSET,** ca. 1907, oak, 62½″ H., 36″ W., 15″ D. ..................... $1000.00*

A-MA Aug. 1982       *Robert W. Skinner Inc.*
**COUNTRY PINE CUPBOARD,** N. Eng., 18th C., old blue paint over red, 66″ H., 28½″ W., 13½″ D. ........ $800.00*

A-OH July 1982       *Garth's Auctions, Inc.*
**CORNER CUPBOARD,** 2-pc., walnut, Ogee feet, paneled doors & 12 pane door, dentil molded cornice, top is old, base is replm. & is handmade using old wood, 42″ W, 88½″ H. .................. $1250.00

A-MA Nov. 1982   *Richard A. Bourne Co., Inc.*
**CORNER CUPBOARD,** PA, 18th C., poplar, gr. painted int. ext. has been refinished, 90½″ H., 44″ W., 24″ D. ............................. $4100.00

*Price does not include 10% buyer fee.

A-MA Nov. 1982    *Richard A. Bourne Co., Inc.*
**PIE SAFE OR PRESERVE CUP-BOARD**, pine, screened panels, old natural wood finish, screening at sides has rusted through in areas, 44½″ H., 26⅝″ W., 17″ D. ...................... $550.00

A-MA July 1982    *Richard A. Bourne Co., Inc.*
**HUTCH CUPBOARD**, pine, 2-part, ref. in natural wood, normal wear, 19¼″ D., 44½″ L., 80¾″ H. ............. $375.00

A-WA D.C. Sept. 1982  *Adam A. Weschler & Son*
**FEDERAL CORNER CABINET**, ca. 1800-10, cherry, 50″ W., 21″ D., 84″ H. ......................... $1100.00*

A-MA Nov. 1982    *Richard A. Bourne Co., Inc.*
**CORNER CUPBOARD**, PA, early 19th C., cherry, gr. painted int., natural finish, 1 glass cracked, minor break in wood of 1 arch, 74½″ H., 46½″ W., 23″ D. ............................ $1700.00

A-OH April 1983      *Garth's Auctions, Inc.*
**CORNER CUPBOARD**, walnut, one pc., ref., repr., replm., 52½″ W., 84½″ H. ............................ $1350.00

A-WA D.C. Dec. 1982  *Adam A. Weschler & Son*
**VICTORIAN CHINA PRESS**, ca. 1870, walnut, two parts, flush base, 54″ W., 18″ D., 100″ H. ................. $1300.00*

*Price does not include 10% buyer fee.

*Left*
A-MA July 1982         *Robert W. Skinner Inc.*
**Q.A. MIRROR,** Am., ca. 1760, mahogany, minor veneer damage, 14″ W., 24¼″ H.
...................................... $1650.00*

*Right*
A-MA July 1982    *Richard A. Bourne Co., Inc.*
**Q.A. MIRROR,** Am., ca. 1760, orig. painted decor., orig. gold striping on drk. blue-gr. paint, worn, 13½″ H. ... $5100.00

*Left*
A-MA Aug. 1982         *Robert W. Skinner Inc.*
**Q.A. MIRROR,** possibly Am., early 18th C., high shaped crest, molded & painted red, pine frame, orig. glass, upper left corner of glass missing, 19¼″ H.
...................................... $2300.00*

*Right*
A-MA July 1982    *Richard A. Bourne Co., Inc.*
**FEDERAL ARCHITECTURAL MIRROR,** orig. label of E. Tothrop, Boston, ca. 1822, 24½″ H. .................. $700.00

*Left*
A-MA July 1982    *Richard A. Bourne Co., Inc.*
**CHIPPENDALE MIRROR,** Am., late 18th C., mahogany over pine w/inlay & gilded crest, replacement glass, minor restor. to ears, 31¾″ H. ....... $3100.00

*Right*
A-MA Aug. 1982         *Robert W. Skinner Inc.*
**CARVED GILT "CAPE COD" COURTING MIRROR,** early 18th C., rectangular frame, crest w/bird & flowers, shaped pendant below, in orig. case, written history on back, 20″ H., 8½″ W.
........................... $2000.00*

*Left*
A-MA July 1982    *Richard A. Bourne Co., Inc.*
**SMALL Q.A. MIRROR,** Am., early 18th C., traces of orig. blk. & gold Japanned finish, orig. glass, upper third of crest missing, 15½″ H. .............. $675.00

*Right*
A-MA Aug. 1982         *Robert W. Skinner Inc.*
**Q.A. MIRROR,** possibly Am., early 18th C., high shaped crest, small bolection-molded frame, painted blk., orig. glass, 2 scrolls missing, 17¾″ H. ...... $1600.00*

*Left*
A-MA July 1982         *Robert W. Skinner Inc.*
**WM. & MARY MIRROR,** Eng., ca. 1720, walnut, etched crown decor., backboard replaced, 36″ x 17″ ........... $900.00*

*Right*
A-MA July 1982         *Robert W. Skinner Inc.*
**WM. & MARY MIRROR,** ca. 1730, mahogany, two part beveled glass, 18″ W., 46″ H. ..................... $1350.00*

*Left*
A-MA July 1982    *Richard A. Bourne Co., Inc.*
**Q.A. MIRRORED SCONCE,** ca. 1740-1750, walnut over pine w/orig. beveled glass, minor loss of veneer, 22½″ H.
........................... $14500.00

*Right*
A-MA July 1982    *Richard A. Bourne Co., Inc.*
**Q.A. MIRROR,** ca. 1730-1750, walnut, 39¾″ H. ..................... $6750.00

←

*Left*
A-MA July 1982    *Richard A. Bourne Co., Inc.*
**SHERATON TABERNACLE MIRROR,** orig. reverse painted glass, frame repainted w/bronze-colored paint, 41½″ H.
........................... $125.00

*Right*
A-MA July 1982    *Richard A. Bourne Co., Inc.*
**CHIPPENDALE MIRROR,** ca. 1770, mahogany veneered on pine, orig. glass, old finish w/gilt paint over gold leaf, few minor repr., 45″ H. .......... $1700.00

A-MA July 1982 *Robert W. Skinner Inc.*
**ROCOCO REVIVAL SOFA,** Am., ca. 1865, rosewood, 59½″ L., 46″ H. ......................... $1100.00*

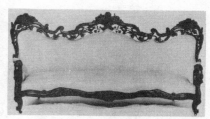

A-MA July 1982 *Robert W. Skinner Inc.*
**ROCOCO REVIVAL SOFA,** ca. 1855, NY, attrib. to J. H. Belter, pierced & carved laminated rosewood, Cornucopia patt., 68″ L. ......................... $10000.00*

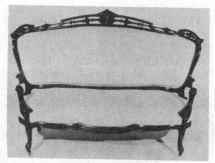

A-MA July 1982 *Robert W. Skinner Inc.*
**ROCOCO REVIVAL SOFA,** laminated rosewood, NY, ca. 1865, 66½″ L., 46½″ H. ......................... $900.00*

A-MA July 1982 *Richard A. Bourne Co., Inc.*
**VICTORIAN SOFA,** Am., mid-19th C., finger-carved walnut or rosewood legs, burgundy tufted velvet upholstery, 68″ L. ......................... $100.00

A-WA D.C. July 1982 *Adam A. Weschler & Son*
**LOUIS XV STYLE SALON SET,** 3 pcs. (2 illus.), carved & gilt wood, late 19th C., floral Aubusson upholstery ..... $800.00*

A-MA Jan. 1983 *Robert W. Skinner Inc.*
**CLASSICAL REVIVAL CARVED SOFA,** ca. 1820, mahogany, 82″ W., 27″ D., 36½″ H. ................. $5000.00*

A-MA Mar. 1983 *Robert W. Skinner Inc.*
**FEDERAL SOFA,** ca. 1810, N. Eng., mahogany, upholstered, satinwood inlay on turned round reeded tapering legs, 33″ L., 74″ H. ................. $3500.00*

A-MA Mar. 1983 *Robert W. Skinner Inc.*
**FEDERAL SOFA,** ca. 1810, Am., mahogany, upholstered, 8 reeded legs on brass casters, 77½″ W., 27″ D., 38½″ H. ......................... $800.00*

A-MA July 1983 *Robert W. Skinner Inc.*
**ROCOCO REVIVAL PARLOR FURNITURE,** 3 pcs. (1 illus.), walnut, Am., late 19th C. ................. $1600.00*

A-MA Oct. 1982 *Robert W. Skinner Inc.*
**GUSTAV STICKLEY SETTEE,** oak, spindle back, seat missing, branded, 31″ H., 49½″ L., 27¾″ D. ........... $8000.00*

A-MA Oct. 1982 *Robert W. Skinner Inc.*
**L. & J.G. STICKLEY SETTEE,** ca. 1910, oak, 34″ H., 76″ W., 31″ D. .... $850.00*

A-MA July 1982 *Richard A. Bourne Co., Inc.*
**HITCHCOCK SETTEE,** w/fold-out bed, early 19th C., blk. w/gold stencil decor., normal wear, 72″ L. ........... $1000.00

A-MA July 1982 *Richard A. Bourne Co., Inc.*
**MINI. SETTEE,** early 19th C., PA, orig. stencil decor., minor repair, 26″ L. ......................... $2300.00

A-MA Aug. 1983 *Richard A. Bourne Co., Inc.*
**SHERATON SOFA,** MA, ca. 1810-1815, mahogany, upholstered, some restor., 77″ O.L. ......................... $3900.00

*Price does not include 10% buyer fee.

A-NY June 1982 *Christie's*
**Q.A. DROP-LEAF TABLE,** ca. 1755, Goddard-Townsend School, RI, walnut & mahogany, distinctive cross bracing, knuckle joint, overlapping gate-leg, 3 knee brackets are missing, top extends to 55¾", 58" W., 27" H. .............. $37400.00

A-MA July 1982 *Richard A. Bourne Co., Inc.*
**SHERATON CARD TABLE,** inlaid mahogany ................... $2500.00

A-MA July 1982 *Richard A. Bourne Co., Inc.*
**HEPPLEWHITE CARD TABLE,** late 18th C., VT, cherry table w/mahogany veneered skirt, minor restor. necessary ........................... $1200.00

A-MA July 1982 *Richard A. Bourne Co., Inc.*
**HEPPLEWHITE BOW-FRONT SIDE-BOARD,** Am., 18th C., inlaid mahogany, restor., minor imperfections, 63" L., 22" D., 38⅝" H. ..................... $1200.00

*Left*
A-MA July 1982 *Robert W. Skinner Inc.*
**WINDSOR TAVERN TABLE,** Am., 18th C., restor., top: 20" x 34", 24" H. . . $550.00*
*Right*
A-MA July 1982 *Robert W. Skinner Inc.*
**Q.A. PORRINGER TOP TABLE,** N. Eng., ca. 1750, maple, top: 34" x 26", 26" H. ........................... $3250.00*

A-MA July 1982 *Richard A. Bourne Co., Inc.*
**HEPPLEWHITE DROP-LEAF TABLE,** inlaid cherry, ca. 1790-1800, orig. natural finish, replaced hinges, 42⅛" L., open: 40½" W., closed: 18" W., 27" H. ...... $700.00

A-MA Oct. 1982 *Robert W. Skinner Inc.*
**FEDERAL BANQUET TABLE,** N. Eng., ca. 1810, cherry, brass caps & casters, 29½" H., 81" L., 29½" W. ..... $1650.00*

*Left*
A-NY June 1982 *Christie's*
**Q.A. CARD TABLE,** ca. 1750, walnut, foldover top, small patch to skirt, 30½" W., 29½" H. ..................... $8250.00
*Right*
A-MA Oct. 1982 *Robert W. Skinner Inc.*
**GUSTAV STICKLEY TABLE,** oak, 29" H., 36" D. ................... $300.00*

A-MA Aug. 1982 *Robert W. Skinner Inc.*
**WM. & MARY TAVERN TABLE,** N. Eng., 1st quarter 18th C., pine & maple, 26" H., 30" W., 15½" D. ......... $1200.00*

A-MA Aug. 1982 *Robert W. Skinner Inc.*
**WM. & MARY TAVERN TABLE,** N. Eng., 1st quarter 18th C., restor., 26" H., 43½" W., 25½" D. .......... $1600.00*

A-MA July 1982 *Richard A. Bourne Co., Inc.*
**HEPPLEWHITE 3-PART BANQUET TABLE,** Am., late 18th C., string inlaid mahogany, restor., 42" W., 92" O.L., 28⅜" H. ........................... $2750.00

*Price does not include 10% buyer fee.

A-MA July 1982 *Robert W. Skinner Inc.*
**SMALL HUTCH TABLE,** N. Eng., early
18th C., pine, old red color, storage space,
30½" D., 26" H. ............ $3000.00*

A-MA Nov. 1982 *Richard A. Bourne Co., Inc.*
**HUTCH TABLE,** N. Eng., 18th C., pine &
maple, restor. & ref., 45" D., 26¾" H.
.......................... $1400.00

A-MA July 1982 *Richard A. Bourne Co., Inc.*
**HUTCH TABLE,** N. Eng., 18th C., pine &
oak, ref., top: 46" x 66½", 26½" H.
.......................... $4250.00

A-MA Aug. 1982 *Robert W. Skinner Inc.*
**WM. & MARY TAVERN TABLE,** N.
Eng., ca. 1700, pine & maple, red paint, 26"
H., 37¼" W., 24" D. ......... $7000.00*

A-MA Aug. 1982 *Robert W. Skinner Inc.*
**WM. & MARY GATE-LEG TABLE,** N.
Eng., 1st qtr. 18th C., maple, restor., 26"
H., 46" W., 32¾" D. ......... $2300.00*

A-MA July 1982 *Richard A. Bourne Co., Inc.*
**GATE-LEG TABLE,** early 18th C.,
walnut w/hard pine subwoods, period
brasses on drawers, hinges, 28" L., 19¼"
W., 29¼" H. ............... $13000.00

A-MA Aug. 1983 *Richard A. Bourne Co., Inc.*
**LRG. SHAKER WORK TABLE,** dove-
tailed drawers, orig. worn down finish, 37"
W., 69½" L., 29½" H. ........ $2000.00

A-MA July 1982 *Richard A. Bourne Co., Inc.*
**OVAL TAVERN TABLE,** N. Eng., early
18th C., single drawer, ref. w/stains on top,
2 legs built up, 33" L., 23" W., 25½" H.
.......................... $2100.00

A-MA Aug. 1982 *Robert W. Skinner Inc.*
**WM. & MARY DROP LEAF TABLE,** N.
Eng., 1st qtr. 18th C., drawer missing,
restor., 36½" H., 40¼" W., 42½" D.
.......................... $2400.00*

A-MA Nov. 1982 *Richard A. Bourne Co., Inc.*
**SPLAY LEG TAVERN TABLE,** Am.,
18th C., pine & maple, 35¼" L., 26½" H.,
21¾" W. .................... $1750.00

← A-MA Nov. 1982 *Richard A. Bourne Co., Inc.*
**OVAL TAVERN TABLE,** N. Eng., 18th
C., pine & maple, orig. red paint, 33¾" L.,
25¼" H., 22⅝" W. ........... $3400.00

*Price does not include 10% buyer fee.

A-MA Aug. 1982        *Robert W. Skinner Inc.*
**WM. & MARY TUCKAWAY TABLE,**
Eng., 1st qtr. 18th C., one stretcher
broken, 24″ H., 32″ W., 24″ D.
......................... $3000.00*

A-MA Jan. 1983        *Robert W. Skinner Inc.*
**WM. & MARY TAVERN TABLE,** N.
Eng., ca. 1720, pine & maple, reduced
in ht., 21½″ W., 30″ D., 23½″ H.
......................... $1300.00*

A-MA Aug. 1982        *Robert W. Skinner Inc.*
**WM. & MARY TAVERN TABLE,** N.
Eng., ca. 1700, cherry & pine, 26″ H., top:
24″ x 30″ .................. $3800.00*

A-MA Aug. 1982        *Robert W. Skinner Inc.*
**WM. & MARY TAVERN TABLE,** N.
Eng., 1st qtr. 18th C., maple, restored,
25½″ H., 25″ W., 34″ D. ...... $5000.00*

A-MA Jan. 1983        *Robert W. Skinner Inc.*
**WM. & MARY TAVERN TABLE,** N.
Eng., early 19th C., pine & maple, 23″ W.,
32″ D., 25″ H. .............. $4000.00*

A-MA Aug. 1982        *Robert W. Skinner Inc.*
**WM. & MARY TAVERN TABLE,** N.
Eng., first qtr. 18th C., scrub top, old red
paint, reduced in ht., 23″ H., 43½″ W., 22½″
D. ......................... $3600.00*

A-MA Aug. 1982        *Robert W. Skinner Inc.*
**TAVERN TABLE,** N. Eng., ca. 1700, pine
& maple, repl. top, 25″ H., 30″ W., 18″ D.
......................... $2400.00*

*Left*
A-MA Aug. 1982        *Robert W. Skinner Inc.*
**WM. & MARY TAVERN TABLE,** N.
Eng., 1st qtr. 18th C., pine & maple, 24″ H.,
29″ W., 26″ D. ............ $10,500.00*

*Right*
A-MA Jan. 1983        *Robert W. Skinner Inc.*
**WM. & MARY TAVERN TABLE,** N.
Eng., early 18th C., pine & maple, top split
& braced, 29″ W., 22″ D., 26½″ H.
......................... $3400.00*

A-MA Aug. 1982        *Robert W. Skinner Inc.*
**WM. & MARY TAVERN TABLE,** N.
Eng., first qtr. 18th C., pine & maple, old
blk. paint, top repr., 22½″ H., 23½″ W.,
17½″ D. .................... $1500.00*

A-MA Jan. 1983        *Robert W. Skinner Inc.*
**Q.A. TAVERN TABLE,** ca. 1750, maple
& pine, old red paint on base, 34″ W., 27″
D., 28½″ H. ................ $3250.00*

*Price does not include 10% buyer fee.

A-MA Oct. 1982    *Robert W. Skinner Inc.*
**LIMBERT TABLE**, oak, 47½″ L., 36″ W.,
29″ H. . . . . . . . . . . . . . . . . . . . . . $1150.00*

A-MA Oct. 1982    *Robert W. Skinner Inc.*
**LIMBERT TABLE**, ca. 1910, oak,
branded trademark, 29″ H., 45″ W., 30″ D.
. . . . . . . . . . . . . . . . . . . . . . . . . $550.00*

A-MA Aug. 1982    *Robert W. Skinner Inc.*
**Q.A. TAVERN TABLE**, N. Eng., ca.
1750, br. paint, 26″ H., top 33″ x 24″
. . . . . . . . . . . . . . . . . . . . . . . . . $6000.00*

A-MA Oct. 1982    *Robert W. Skinner Inc.*
**WM. & MARY TAVERN TABLE**, N.
Eng., 2nd quarter 18th C., maple & pine,
26½″ H., 40″ W., 27″ D. . . . . . . $2250.00*

A-MA Nov. 1982    *Richard A. Bourne Co., Inc.*
**Q.A. TRAY TOP TEA TABLE**, CT, ca.
1740-1750, maple, orig. old finish, top 29″ x
20¼″, 25½″ H. . . . . . . . . . . . . . $7000.00

A-MA Oct. 1982    *Robert W. Skinner Inc.*
**Q.A. TABLE**, N. Eng., ca. 1794, dated on
bottom "1794," 26″ H., 39¼″ W., 30½″ D.
. . . . . . . . . . . . . . . . . . . . . . . . . $4800.00*

A-MA Nov. 1982    *Richard A. Bourne Co., Inc.*
**STRETCHER BASE TAVERN TABLE**,
Buxton, ME, 18th C., maple, top paint
worn off, orig. drk. red paint remains on
base, 33″ L., 26½″ W., 26¼″ H.
. . . . . . . . . . . . . . . . . . . . . . . . . $7500.00

---

A-MA July 1982    *Robert W. Skinner Inc.*
**Q.A. TAVERN TABLE**, N. Eng., ca.
1750, maple, restor., 26½″ W., 23″ D.,
31″ H. . . . . . . . . . . . . . . . . . . . . . $1500.00*

A-MA July 1982    *Richard A. Bourne Co., Inc.*
**HEPPLEWHITE CARD TABLE**, late
18th C., MA, inlaid mahogany, orig.
. . . . . . . . . . . . . . . . . . . . . . . . . $1050.00

A-MA July 1982    *Richard A. Bourne Co., Inc.*
**HEPPLEWHITE CARD TABLE**, inlaid
mahogany, orig. & unrestor., finish water-
stained w/scratches . . . . . . . . . . $1600.00

*Left*

A-MA Aug. 1982　　*Robert W. Skinner Inc.*
CANDLESTAND, N. Eng., 19th C., 28¼"
H., 16¼" W., 15¼" D. ......... $175.00*

*Right*

A-MA July 1982　　*Richard A. Bourne Co., Inc.*
CANDLESTAND, curly maple, NH, late
18th or early 19th C., orig. finish, restor.
............................. $1800.00

A-MA July 1982　　*Richard A. Bourne Co., Inc.*
FEDERAL CANDLESTAND, Am.,
early 19th C., tiger maple ....... $625.00

*Left*

A-MA July 1982　　*Richard A. Bourne Co., Inc.*
CANDLESTAND, ca. 1800, CT, cherry,
2 repairs, age split in top, top needs ref.
............................. $1300.00

*Right*

A-MA July 1982　　*Richard A. Bourne Co., Inc.*
Q.A. CANDLESTAND, Am., ca. 1740-
1760, hardwood w/drk. finish, 2-way
drawer, age split in top, replaced drawer
pulls, base reglued ............. $950.00

A-MA Nov. 1982　　*Richard A. Bourne Co., Inc.*
*L to R*

Q.A. CANDLESTAND, Am., 18th C.,
maple, retains old finish w/some water
stains on top & minor repr. to split in top,
27" H., 14½" D. ............... $475.00
Q.A. CANDLESTAND, oval tilt-top
maple & curly maple, oval top is delicate &
thin, 26½" H., 22" L., 14½" W. .. $1800.00
Q.A. CANDLESTAND, birch, old
probably orig. finish, 27" H., 13" square
............................. $400.00

A-MA Nov. 1982　　*Richard A. Bourne Co., Inc.*
STANDING CANDLESTAND, N.
Eng., ca. 1700-1725, maple, screw adjust-
ment, small piece broken out of screw,
35½" H. ..................... $2900.00

*Right*

A-MA Aug. 1982　　*Robert W. Skinner Inc.*
CROSS BASE CANDLESTAND, N.
Eng., 1st qtr. 18th C., pine & maple, old red
paint, 24½" H., top 12¼" D. .... $5000.00*

*Left*

A-MA Aug. 1982　　*Robert W. Skinner Inc.*
CHIPPENDALE CANDLESTAND, N.
Eng., ca. 1770, maple & pine, Marlborough
legs, old br. finish, 26" H., top: 15½" x 14½"
............................. $1900.00*

*Right*

A-OH April 1983　　*Garth's Auctions, Inc.*
CHIPPENDALE TILT TOP TEA
TABLE, mahogany, orig. finish, 33" D.,
28¼" H. ..................... $13500.00

A-MA July 1982　　*Robert W. Skinner Inc.*
CHIPPENDALE CANDLESTAND, N.
Eng., ca. 1770, cherry, old red paint, 13¼"
W., 13¾" D., 24" H. ........... $575.00*

A-MA Aug. 1982　　*Robert W. Skinner Inc.*
FEDERAL CHERRY SHAPED TOP
CANDLESTAND, N. Eng., ca. 1810, 24"
H., 16½" W., 16¾" D. ......... $700.00*

A-MA Aug. 1982　　*Robert W. Skinner Inc.*
T-BASE CANDLESTAND, N. Eng., last
qtr. 18th C., pine & hardwood, traces
of red paint, 26" H., top: 14" x 15"
............................. $1800.00*

*Price does not include 10% buyer fee.

A-WA D.C. Dec. 1982 *Adam A. Weschler & Son*
**VICTORIAN BUREAU,** ca. 1865, walnut,
marble top, on casters, 48" W., 24" D., 89"
H. . . . . . . . . . . . . . . . . . . . . . . . . . . $575.00*

A-WA D.C. Dec. 1982 *Adam A. Weschler & Son*
**VICTORIAN SIDEBOARD,** ca. 1870,
walnut, marble top, 61" W., 23" D., 77½" H.
. . . . . . . . . . . . . . . . . . . . . . . . . . . $1200.00*

A-MA Dec. 1982 *Robert W. Skinner Inc.*
**RENAISSANCE REVIVAL BED-
ROOM SET,** Am., ca. 1860, walnut & burl
veneer, bed & mirrored bureau, dropped-
well bureau w/wh. marble, bed: 58" W., 76"
L., 92" H.; bureau: 60½" W., 18½" D., 82½"
H. . . . . . . . . . . . . . . . . . . . . . . . . $2500.00*

A-MA Dec. 1982 *Robert W. Skinner Inc.*
**RENAISSANCE REVIVAL BOOK-
CASE-BUREAU,** Am., ca. 1870, walnut &
burl veneer, glazed doors flanked by flat
pilasters, stepped base contains 6 burl-
paneled drawers w/pulls carved in the form
of leather straps, (2 handles incorporate
hearts), 54" W., 18" D., 98¼" H.
. . . . . . . . . . . . . . . . . . . . . . . . . . . $1500.00*

A-WA D.C. Dec. 1982 *Adam A. Weschler & Son*
**VICTORIAN DOUBLE BEDSTEAD,**
ca. 1870, walnut, 93" H. . . . . . . . $850.00*

A-MA July 1982 *Robert W. Skinner Inc.*
➔ **RENAISSANCE REVIVAL SIDE-
BOARD,** Am., ca. 1865, walnut, marble
top . . . . . . . . . . . . . . . . . . . . . . . $2400.00*

*Price does not include 10% buyer fee.

A-OH July 1983 *Early Auction Co.*
*Row I, L to R*
**VASE,** double handled, standard glaze, floral decor., sgn. Matt A. Daly, ca. 1888, 13″ H. ...................... $700.00
**VASE,** iris glaze w/wild rose decor., E. Diers, ca. 1904, 8½″ H. ........ $700.00
**VASE,** standard glaze w/raised decor., Rookwood, M. A. Daly, ca. 1886, 15″ H. ........................... $900.00

*Row II, L to R*
**PLAQUE,** rural scene, artist Fred Rothenbusch, 13½″ x 8¾″ ......... $1750.00
**EWER,** standard glaze, raised yellow decor., A. B. Spraque, ca. 1888, 6½″ H. ........................... $170.00
**LRG. BISQUE URN,** mkd. Rookwood, ca. 1882, 12″ D., 23″ H. ....... $5000.00
**HISTORICAL PITCHER,** Rookwood, Cinti, OH, ribbon mark, ca. 1881, 10½″ H. ........................... $2200.00

*Row III, L to R*
**VASE,** iris glaze w/wh. decor., Lenora Ashbury, ca. 1907, 9½″ H. ..... $1750.00
**NEWCOMB POTTERY BOWL,** blue w/raised pink trumpet flower, sgn. ........................... $675.00
**LRG. VASE,** Matt Daly, high glaze w/trumpet vines on gold ground, ca. 1888, 12″ H. ....................... $850.00
**VASE,** standard glaze w/blk.-eyed susans, S. Markland, ca. 1896, 5″ H. .... $350.00
**VASE,** woodland scenic vellum, E. Diers, ca. 1909, 10″ H. ............... $850.00

*Row IV, L to R*
**VASE,** mat glaze w/lilac decor., sgn. A. R. Valentien, ca. 1901, 15″ H. ...... $550.00
**SQUATTY VASE,** standard glaze, apple blossom decor., K. C. Matchette, ca. 1894, 2½″ H. .......................... $330.00
**VASE,** tiger eye w/fish & seaweed, ca. 1885, 6″ H. ................... $525.00
**VASE,** iris glaze w/grapes & vines, Charles S. Todd, ca. 1910, 6″ H. ........................... $650.00
**VASE,** vellus glaze w/woodland scene, sgn. Ed Diers, ca. 1917, 14″ H. ........................... $3100.00
**TEAPOT,** standard glaze w/raised jonquils, C. A. Baker, age line, ca. 1894, 7½″ H. ........................... $400.00
**VASE,** iris glaze on wh. clay w/lavender floral, S. Sax, ca. 1906, 8″ H. .... $750.00
**NEWCOMB POTTERY VASE,** blue, artist Julia Michel, 6¼″ H. ...... $600.00

*Row V, L to R*
**VASE,** aerial blue, shiny glaze, O. G. Reed, wheat decor., ca. 1896, 7″ H. .. $1075.00
**JUG,** exhibition pc., high glaze, ca. 1882, 10″ H. ...................... $850.00
**SAKI POT,** decor. w/oriental water scene, ca. 1882 ..................... $425.00
**NEWCOMB POTTERY PITCHER,** blue & tan, high glaze, sgn. Maria R. LeBlanc, 8½″ H. .............. $1300.00
**NEWCOMB POTTERY BOWL,** blue w/pink buds, 5″ D. ............ $475.00

A-MA June 1983 *Robert W. Skinner Inc.*
*L to R*
**COLOGNE BOTTLE,** gr. cut to clear glass, attrib. to C. Dorflinger & Sons, PA, ca. 1890, Montrose patt., ground rim, 7¾″ H. ........................... $400.00*
**CUT GLASS PLATES,** set of 8 (1 illus.), attrib. to C. Dorflinger & Sons, PA, ca. 1900, Am. patt., some chips, 7½″ D. ........................... $400.00*
**HAWKES COLOGNE BOTTLES,** pr. (1 illus.), NY, ca. 1890, Venetian patt., unsgn., minor chips, 6″ H. ..... $350.00*

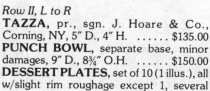

A-MA July 1982 *Richard A. Bourne Co., Inc.*
CUT GLASS
*Row I, L to R*
**CREAMER & OPEN SUGAR,** creamer w/handle check, slight handle roughage ........................... $50.00
**GOBLETS,** set of 6 (1 illus.) .... $300.00
**WINES,** set of 8 (1 illus.) ....... $200.00
**LEMONADE TUMBLERS,** set of 6 (1 illus.) ........................ $120.00

*Row II, L to R*
**TAZZA,** pr., sgn. J. Hoare & Co., Corning, NY, 5″ D., 4″ H. ...... $135.00
**PUNCH BOWL,** separate base, minor damages, 9″ D., 8¾″ O.H. ...... $150.00
**DESSERT PLATES,** set of 10 (1 illus.), all w/slight rim roughage except 1, several w/minor chips, 6¼″ D. ........ $100.00

*Row III, L to R*
**ICE CREAM TRAY,** Cane patt., minor grinding for sm. chips, 17¾″ L., 10¼″ W. ........................... $300.00
**DESSERT PLATES,** set of 10 (1 illus.), Daisy & Button patt., minor chips, 7″ D. ........................... $270.00

A-MA Dec. 1982 *Robert W. Skinner Inc.*
**TWO-PART CUT GLASS PUNCH BOWL,** Am., ca. 1900, sawtooth, scalloped rim w/slight flair on body cut w/sunbursts, hobstars & cane bands, raised corresponding base, 15¾″ W., 13½″ H. ........................... $1400.00*

A-MA July 1982 *Richard A. Bourne Co., Inc.*
CUT GLASS
*Row I, L to R*
**HAWKES SHALLOW BOWL,** sgn., 9⅛″ D. ........................... $275.00
**COMPOTE,** cut & etched flowers, 9⅛″ D., 8⅛″ H. ..................... $70.00
*Row II, L to R*
**COVERED BOWL,** deep bowl w/flat cover, shallow cut floral design, 8″ D., 5″ O.H. ........................... $100.00
**SM. COMPOTE,** cut & etched fruit, sm. rim nicks, 6¼″ D., 3¾″ H. ........ $50.00
**TALL COMPOTE,** tulips & daisies, 6⅞″ D., 6⅝″ H. ..................... $70.00

A-WA D.C. July 1982 *Adam A. Weschler & Son*
**CUT GLASS GOBLETS,** set of 8 (4 illus.), Am., early 20th C., stenciled Libbey, pineapple & diamond cut, 6″ H. ........................... $425.00*

*Price does not include 10% buyer fee.

A-OH July 1983      *Early Auction Co.*
*Row I, L to R*
**QUEZAL CLASSICAL FORM VASE,**
gr. ground w/silver feather design, 10½" H.
.................................................. $2300.00
**DURAND VASE,** blue feather on opal,
gold liner, 9" H. .................. $800.00
**TIFFANY DESK LAMP,** sgn. Tiffany
Studios N.Y., T & D Co. logo .. $1550.00
**WATER PITCHER,** pink slag, inverted
fan patt. ............................ $500.00
**TIFFANY COUNTERBALANCE
DESK LAMP,** gold dore, reticulated metal
shade w/leaded glass liner, sgn., 14" H.
.................................................. $1500.00

*Row II, L to R*
**ALBERTINE BISCUIT JAR,** pink
w/beaded decor., Mt. Washington paper
label mkd. Albertine, silver top... $650.00
**MT. WASHINGTON CAMEO VASE,**
rosaline over wh., 13" H. ...... $875.00
**WHEELING PEACHBLOW MOR-
GAN VASE,** shiny w/repro. holder
.................................................. $800.00
**TIFFANY FLOWER FORM VASE,** gold
to wh. opalescent base, gr. stem terminat-
ing into lrg. petal leaves at top of gold
opalescent bowl, sgn. L.C.T., 12" H.
.................................................. $5000.00
**FRENCH CLOCK,** Japy Freges & Co.,
Exposition 1855 .................. $1500.00
**N. ENG. PEACHBLOW D.Q. VASE,**
satin w/sq. top, 6" H. .......... $375.00

*Row III, L to R*
**STEUBEN AURENE VASE,** sgn., blue
w/silver paper label, 10¼" H. .. $800.00
**WEBB CITRON VASE,** 10" H.
.................................................. $2400.00
**DAUM NANCY CAMEO VASE,** sgn.,
orange lily decor. .............. $550.00
**MT. WASHINGTON VASE,** satin finish,
cream color ground, 12" ..... $550.00
**WEBB CITRON CAMEO VASE,** wh.
flowers & leaves, 5" H. ........ $450.00
**DURAND VASE,** sgn., gr. w/wh. feather
design, 12½" H. ................ $800.00
**HOLLY AMBER COVERED JELLY
COMPOTE,** 4" D. ............ $775.00

*Row IV, L to R*
**PINK SLAG JELLY COMPOTE**
.................................................. $375.00
**DURAND VASE,** irid. drk. pink w/gold
liner, 9½" H. .................. $1900.00
**GOLDEN AGATE DOLPHIN**
.................................................. $450.00
**STEUBEN COMPOTE,** calcite w/inside
gold stretch border, 7" H. ...... $600.00
**PINK SLAG TOOTHPICK** .... $400.00
**FRENCH CAMEO VASE,** sgn.
Lamartine, 9" H. ............... $800.00
**BOWL,** gr. w/gold pull up feather design,
mkd. L. C. Tiffany, 5" H. ...... $325.00
**NORTHWOOD VASE,** pink overlay on
pedestal w/applied decor., 19" H.
.................................................. $1400.00
**MINI. LAMP,** clear & rainbow, metal band
base & 4 ball feet ............. $300.00
**WEBB CAMEO VASE,** 3-color w/
hammered base & lid, 7½" H. ... $800.00

*Row V, L to R*
**PATE-SUR-PATE VASES,** pr., apricot,
mkd. Autumn & Summer, 6" H.
.................................................. $250.00
**DURAND VASE,** blue w/applied decor.
.................................................. $500.00
**DURAND VASE,** gr. irid. triple overlay,
sgn. "Durand 1812-6," gold liner, 7½" H.
.................................................. $1500.00
**HOLLY AMBER CREAM PITCHER**
.................................................. $600.00
**PINK SLAG CRUET** .... $1400.00
**STEUBEN FOOTED TRUMPET
VASE,** gold aurene & alabaster, 8" H.
.................................................. $450.00

A-WA D.C. Dec. 1982 *Adam A. Weschler & Son*
**WATERFORD CUT CRYSTAL
STEMMED TABLE SERVICE,** 16 water
goblets, 16 wine glasses & 16 champagnes
(1 of ea. illus.), gilt lip above floral cut
banding & sawtooth body ..... $1100.00*

A-WA D.C. July 1982 *Adam A. Weschler & Son*
**CUT GLASS TABLE SERVICE,** Scot-
tish, 53-pcs. (1 place setting illus.)
.................................................. $350.00*

A-WA D.C. July 1982 *Adam A. Weschler & Son*
**CUT GLASS TABLE SERVICE,**
French, 52-pcs. (1 place setting illus.),
retailed by Tiffany & Co., NY .. $550.00*

A-MA July 1982    *Richard A. Bourne Co., Inc.*
*STIEGEL GLASS*
*Row I, L to R*
**BLOWN MOLDED FLIP,** decor. w/birds
& flowers in various colors including the
stiegel gr., 3⅞" H. ............. $300.00
**CLEAR FLIP GLASS,** plain w/etched
band, 5⅜" H. .................. $90.00
**CLEAR BLOWN FLIP GLASS,** 3-mold,
5¾" H. ....................... $200.00
*Row II, L to R*
**CLEAR PANEL FLIP,** molded w/etched
band, 6¼" H. .................. $125.00
**CLEAR PANEL FLIP,** molded w/etched
band, 6⅜" H. .................. $150.00
**CLEAR BLOWN FLIP,** molded w/etched
band, glass w/greenish tint, 6¼" H.
.................................................. $100.00

A-MA July 1982    *Richard A. Bourne Co., Inc.*
*FLINT GLASS*
*L to R*
**COMPOTE,** clear w/Diamond Point patt.,
Boston & Sandwich Glass Co., small chips,
10½" D., 9" H. ................ $80.00
**PITCHER,** Thumbprint patt., w/heavy
applied handle, 9" H. .......... $160.00
**COVERED COMPOTE,** Thumbprint
patt., cover w/roughage, 8¼" D., 14½"
O.H. ......................... $140.00

A-MA July 1982    *Robert W. Skinner Inc.*
**HAWKES GLASS PUNCH BOWL
SET,** nine cups (two illus.), Corning, NY,
ca. 1920, gr. cut to clear, wheel cut floral
swags, flower & petal cut border, hobstar
cut base, cups w/floral swag rim, 14" D.
.................................................. $2700.00*

*Price does not include 10% buyer fee.

A-OH July 1983                    *Early Auction Co.*
*Row I, L to R*
**QUEZAL TABLE LAMP,** sgn., gold vines
& gr. leaves, 17″ H. .......... $1300.00
**QUEZAL BOWL,** peacock blue on
bronze finish base, mkd. Oscar B. Bach,
NY, 10″ H. ................. $450.00
**HUMIDOR,** mkd. Nakara "Cigar," 5½″ H.
.............................. $525.00
**CANDLESTICKS,** pr., gold, sgn.
Aurene, 7″ H. ............... $800.00
**GALLE VASE,** sgn., pink, yellow, olive gr.
& lt. blue, 16″ H. ........... $1150.00

*Row II, L to R*
**STEUBEN VASE,** rosaline cut to
alabaster, 10″ H. ............. $750.00
**VASE,** blue overlay w/applied amber
decor., 8″ H. ............... $225.00
**CROWN MILANO DRESSER BOX,**
shiny, mkd., orange & red floral decor.
.............................. $700.00
**SQUATTY V. DURAND VASE,** blue,
sgn. ......................... $375.00
**STEUBEN A.C.B. BOWL,** plum jade,
5¾″ D. ...................... $1600.00
**PINK SLAG WATER PITCHER,** inverted fan patt. .............. $500.00

*Row III, L to R*
**GALLE VASE,** sgn., decor. w/purple
clematis, leaves & vines, 8″ H. .. $625.00
**AURENE CENTER BOWL,** gold w/8
fold openings for floral arrangements, 8″ H.
.............................. $400.00
**TIFFANY FAVRILE STICK VASE,**
peacock blue w/gr. hearts & vines, 6″ H.
.............................. $1600.00
**CROWN MILANO ROSE BOWL,**
cream color w/enamel floral decor.
.............................. $375.00
**TRUMPET VASE,** bluish-gold, sgn. L. C.
Tiffany-Favrile, 13½″ H. ....... $850.00
**STEUBEN A.C.B.,** nedra design, blk. jade
over alabaster, 7″ H. ......... $1600.00
**WEBB CITRON CAMEO STICK
VASE,** deep cut wh. floral & leaf decor.,
9¼″ H. ...................... $475.00

*Row IV, L to R*
**DURAND ROSE BOWL,** sgn., on footed
base, orange w/drk. gr. swirls, 5″ H.
.............................. $850.00
**M.O.P. WATER PITCHER,** blue satin
herringbone .................. $240.00
**TIFFANY FLOWER BOWL,** gold irid.,
intaglio cut gr. leaves, sgn., 10″ D.
.............................. $750.00
**TIFFANY VASE,** gold irid., sgn., 4½″ H.
.............................. $425.00
**SMITH BROS. MAYONNAISE,** sgn.,
floral decor. w/silver top & handle
.............................. $170.00
**K.P.M. PORCELAIN,** mkd., framed,
10½″ x 7½″ ................. $550.00

*Row V, L to R*
**TIFFANY CANDLE LAMP BASE,** sgn.,
gold, 7″ H. .................. $150.00
**ROSE FINDLAY PITCHER,** check in
handle ....................... $200.00

**HOLLY AMBER PARFAIT** ... $375.00
**CROWN MILANO VASE,** 2-handled
w/cross stitch design .......... $500.00
**PINK SLAG PUNCH CUP** .... $175.00
**DURAND VASE,** sgn., butterscotch
w/gr. leaf & vine decor., 8″ H. ... $550.00

A-MA July 1982          *Robert W. Skinner Inc.*
**CUT GLASS PUNCH BOWL,** 2-part,
Am., ca. 1900, cross hatched bull's eyes
surrounded by hobstars & stepped motif,
14¼″ D., 15⅝″ H. ............ $1800.00*

A-WA D.C. Dec. 1982  *Adam A. Weschler & Son*
*L to R*
**FIGURE OF OWL,** German, molded &
frosted crystal, modeled by Gunther R.
Granget, 12″ H. ............. $125.00*
**FIGURE OF EAGLE,** lalique molded &
frosted crystal, 9¾″ H. ........ $250.00*

A-MA Dec. 1982          *Robert W. Skinner Inc.*
**LIBBEY EIGHT-SIDED BOWL,** ca.
1920, cut & engraved glass, Wisteria patt.,
7¾″ D., 3″ H. ................ $650.00*

A-MA June 1983          *Robert W. Skinner Inc.*
**MOSER VASE,** ca. 1920, amber glass,
gilded, 13½″ H. .............. $750.00*

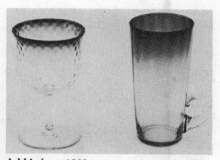

A-MA June 1983          *Robert W. Skinner Inc.*
*L to R*
**ALEXANDRITE WINE GLASS,** Eng.,
ca. 1900, Quilted patt., 4½″ H.
.............................. $500.00*
**AMBERINA PARFAIT GLASS,** N. Eng.
Glass Co., MA, late 19th C., loop handle,
Optic patt., 4¾″ H. ........... $150.00*

A-MA July 1982       *Richard A. Bourne Co., Inc.*
*L to R*
**STIEGEL BLOWN GLASS CREAM-
ER,** cobalt blue w/applied handle & opaque
wh. rim, 3⅞″ H. .............. $250.00
**SMALL AMETHYST PATT. GLASS
LAMP,** Loop patt., applied handle & single
drop whale oil burner, orig. pewter collar,
3″ H. ........................ $300.00

*Price does not include 10% buyer fee..

A-OH July 1983     *Early Auction Co.*
*Row I, L to R*
**DAUM NANCY VASE,** sgn., Pate-De-Verre, 11″ H. ............... $2350.00
**STEUBEN A.C.B. VASE,** yellow jade, drilled for lamp, 10″ H. ...... $2600.00
**CROWN MILANO EWER,** enamel beaded floral decor., 12½″ H. ... $950.00
**WHEELING PEACHBLOW PITCHER,** shiny, 10½″ H. ........... $1100.00

*Row II, L to R*
**COVERED ROYAL FLEMISH ROSE JAR,** decor. w/Roman coins, repr.
................................ $1750.00
**STEVENS & WILLIAMS VASE,** bluish-gr. swirl w/pink liner, 8¾″ H. ... $375.00
**NAILSEA FAILY LAMP,** blue w/ruffled base ...................... $350.00
**A.C.B. 3-LAYER BOWL,** plum jade, 8″ D., 7¼″ H. ................. $1750.00
**STEVENS & WILLIAMS PERFUME,** red & gr. w/swirled silver top .... $600.00

*Row III, L to R*
**WATERCREST BOX,** mkd., gr., mounted on footed base, 8″ D. .. $775.00
**FAN VASE,** bluish-gold decor., sgn. Steuben Aurene & numbered .. $1600.00
**STEUBEN LAMP,** pink decor. w/gold vines & pods, orig. wh. base, 24½″ H.
................................ $1750.00
**WEBB BURMESE FAIRY LAMP,** acid finish, base mkd. "S. Clarke-Trademark-Fairy," 5″ H. ............. $525.00
**RIBBED FLOWER FORM VASE,** sgn. L. C. Tiffany-Inc.-Favrille," bluish-gold, 12½″ H. ................... $600.00
**GALLE CAMEO VASE,** cut w/bleeding hearts, 8″ H. ................ $600.00

*Row IV, L to R*
**WEBB MINI. CAMEO LAMP,** red, 9½″ H. ......................... $1550.00
**CROWN MILANO VASE,** mkd., 11″ H.
................................ $1000.00
**CROWN MILANO COOKIE JAR,** pink satin w/raised starfish decor., silver embossed lid, paper label, 8″ D. .... $600.00
**D.Q.M.O.P. BRIDE'S BOWL,** mounted on metal base, bowl stamped Thos. Webb & Sons, 10″ D. ................ $275.00

*Row V, L to R*
**ENG. CAMEO VASE,** blue ground w/wh. decor., 5″ H. ............ $900.00
**HANDLED VASE,** peacock blue, sgn. Louis C. Tiffany Furnaces Corp.-Favrile, 9½″ H. ....................... $900.00
**CENTER BOWL,** gold w/gr. lily pads, sgn. L. C. Tiffany-Favrile, frog mkd. same w/some repair ................. $475.00
**WEBB CAMEO BOWL,** blue w/wh. floral decor., labeled Phillips & Pierce, London, rim chip, 3¾″ H. ...... $425.00
**WEBB CAMEO COLOGNE,** ivory w/dragon decor., embossed floral silver top w/hallmark ................... $800.00
**ROSE FINDLAY CELERY** .... $950.00

A-MA July 1982    *Richard A. Bourne Co., Inc.*
**MERCURY GLASS**
*Row I, L to R*
**FOOTED SALTS,** lot of 7, inc. application of silver finish to 3 of the pcs.
................................ $50.00
**CREAMER,** etched ferns & clear applied handle, 6½″ H. ........... $100.00
**CREAMER,** etched grape vines, clear applied handle, 6¾″ H. ........ $110.00
*Row II, L to R*
**VASES,** pr., frosted palm trees & flowers, gold lustre int., 10¼″ H. ....... $120.00
**TAZZA,** etched birds & leaves, 5¾″ D., 2¾″ H. ....................... $45.00
**COMPOTE,** etched ferns, attrib. to Boston & Sandwich Glass Co., 8″ D., 8½″ H. ........................... $130.00

A-WA D.C. July 1982   *Adam A. Weschler & Son*
L to R
**LOETZ GLASS VASE,** ca. 1900, gold irid., mkd., 11¾″ H. ........ $650.00*
**STEUBEN GLASS PINCH VASE,** ca. 1905-20, unsgn., gold irid., 6½″ H.
................................ $100.00*

A-MA July 1982     *Robert W. Skinner Inc.*
**GALLE GLASS MUG,** France, enameled & applisqued, applied handle, pink & amber shading to gr. w/acid etched decor., sgn., 5½″ H. ............... $500.00*

A-MA July 1982    *Richard A. Bourne Co., Inc.*
*Row I, L to R*
**MT. WASHINGTON MUFFINEER,** fired-on Burmese coloring on oqaque wh. glass, decorated w/daisies ....... $100.00
**HEAVY ART GLASS BASKET,** attrib. to Cape Cod Glass Co., mottled cranberry & gr. on opaque wh. ground, clear handle, 5¼″ D., 7″ O.H. ............... $90.00
**GREGORY JEWELRY BOX,** sapphire blue, orig. lining ............... $160.00
**RUBINA ATOMIZER BOTTLE,** incised design, 6¾″ H. ............... $130.00
*Row II, L to R*
**CASED ART GLASS VASES,** pr., peach-blow color, applied amber leaves & stems, 8¾″ H. ................. $125.00
**MT. WASHINGTON BURMESE LILY VASE,** ruffled rim, 14″ H. ...... $325.00

A-MA July 1982    *Richard A. Bourne Co., Inc.*
*Row I, L to R*
**CUP PLATE,** opalescent blue, four scallops chipped off, shallow upper rim chip, usual roughage ....... $70.00
**CUP PLATE,** cobalt blue, three large rim chips .......................... $60.00
**CUP PLATE,** blue, Eagle patt., Midwestern ...................... $200.00
**CUP PLATE,** violet blue, Heart patt., one small nick..................... $175.00
*Row II, L to R*
**CUP PLATE,** opalescent, Sunburst patt., one scallop chipped away, slight roughage
................................ $50.00
**CUP PLATE,** opalescent, Heart patt., minute rim roughage ........... $55.00
**CUP PLATE,** opaque wh., Heart patt., minute rim roughage ........... $80.00
**MARBLED OBLONG SALT,** fiery opalescent, sgn., N. Eng. Glass Co., small chip
................................ $325.00

*Price does not include 10% buyer fee.

A-WA D.C. Dec. 1982 *Adam A. Weschler & Son*
**BURMESE WARE**
*Row I*
**CROWN VASE,** trellising vine & leaf field, 4½" H. ..................... $400.00*
*Row II, L to R*
**VASE,** raised gilt & painted flowers & leaves, 7½" H. .............. $600.00*
**VASE,** raised enameled & painted floral boughs, 4½" H. ............. $300.00*
**INDIAN PORTRAIT VASE,** 3 tepees on other side, 4" H. ........... $300.00*
**INDIAN PORTRAIT CREAMER,** Indian chief surrounded by tepees on a footed base, 3¾" H. ................. $400.00*
**EGYPTIAN VASE,** desert scene w/2 antelopes within trees & pyramids, 4½" H. ................................... $550.00*
**ELEPHANT PITCHER,** 2 elephants, raised gilt trappings centering palm trees, 5½" H. .......................... $1900.00*

*Row III, L to R*
**ARCTIC VASE,** whalers in pursuit of sperm whale on one side, other side has whaler & anchor centering a polar bear, 4" H. ....................... $1100.00*
**VASE,** trellising vine & leaves centering 2 armorial crests, gilt enameled rim, 8½" H. ................................... $500.00*
**BUD VASES,** pr. (third & fifth items), floral spray & trellising vine, long neck, 7½" H. ................................... $500.00*
**FISH-IN-THE-NET VASE,** (fourth item), 5 fish in raised gilt enameled net & painted coral, 5" H. ................... $500.00*
**CHINOISERIE VASE,** bat & ribbon within clouds, long neck, gilt enameled rim, 8" H. ................... $400.00*
**VENETIAN VASE,** gondola on Grand Canal, raised gilt enameled cartouche, crown foliate top, 4½" H. ...... $700.00*

*Left*
A-MA Dec. 1982          *Robert W. Skinner Inc.*
**GALLE THREE-COLOR CUT CAMEO STICK VASE,** France, ca. 1890, lavender & pale gr. floral cut design on pale pink, sgn., 13½" H. .......... $950.00*

*Right*
A-MA Dec. 1982          *Robert W. Skinner Inc.*
**ART GLASS VASE,** Am., ca. 1920, blue irid., irid. gold int., baluster-shaped body, lt. blue pullup design of leaves on blue ground, 9½" H. ....................... $425.00*

A-WA D.C. Dec. 1982 *Adam A. Weschler & Son*
**BURMESE WARE**
*Row I, L to R*
**LACY RIM BASKET,** jeweled enamel, silver plated footed housing, mkd. "Aurora Silver Plated Manufacturing Co.," 8" D., 4½" H. ..................... $750.00*
**PLATE,** raised gilt, copper & gold crane in flight, above a floral landscape w/butterfly, 9" H. ....................... $750.00*
*Row II, L to R*
**TRIFID LION VASE,** raised on trifid celery stalk feet, 5" H. ....... $2200.00*
**LACY RIM BOWL,** thorny vines & raised enameled flowers, 9" D., 5" H. ................................... $650.00*
**VERSE PITCHER,** M. W. Glass Co., Shakespeare verse, mkd. "Burmese Mt. Washington Glass Co.," 6" H. ................................... $2500.00*

A-WA D.C. Dec. 1982 *Adam A. Weschler & Son*
**CROWN MILANO**
**VASE,** floral spray field, raised gilt enameled scroll, floral cartouche shoulder, printed monogram mark, mkd. "6555," 4" H. ......................... $250.00*
**TWO CUPS & SAUCERS,** M.W. Glass Co., each has raised gilt flowers & vine w/matching saucers, one is handleless, each monogramed, one mkd. "602," ................................... $850.00*
**EWER,** intertwined rope handle, floral medallion within a raised gilt enameled C-scroll cartouche, painted gilt floral ground, 10" H. ....................... $950.00*

A-MA Dec. 1982          *Robert W. Skinner Inc.*
**NIPPON PUNCH BOWL,** Japan, ca. 1900, gilt & scenic painted, 12 near-matching sherbet dishes, bowl: 13" D., 9" H.; dishes: 3¾" D., 2¾" H. ..... $425.00*

A-WA D.C. Dec. 1982 *Adam A. Weschler & Son*
*L to R*
**STEUBEN AMETHYST CUT CRYSTAL CANDLESTICKS,** pr., mkd. "Steuben," 20" H. ............. $2500.00*
**STEUBEN AMETHYST CUT CRYSTAL CENTER BOWL,** ca. 1921, boat-shaped, sq. base, 19½" L., 9½" H. ................................... $2900.00*

*Price does not include 10% buyer fee.

A-MA July 1982    *Richard A. Bourne Co., Inc.*
*Row I, L to R*
**POMONA CREAMER,** 2nd-grind, pansy
& butterfly decor., without color, 4″ H.
................................. $80.00
**POMONA SMALL FOOTED BOWL,**
1st-grind, plain body w/amber stain, 3¾″
D. .................................. $40.00
**ART GLASS AM. FOOTED VASE,**
opalescent, one small chip, 5½″ H.
................................. $30.00
**BOHEMIAN DRESSER BOX,** amber,
hinged lid & brass fittings, 3¾″ L., 2¾″ D.,
2⅞″ H. ..................... $150.00
*Row II, L to R*
**PAPERWEIGHT,** canes & bubbles, 2¾″
D. ................................ $100.00
**SANDWICH PAPERWEIGHT,** Broken
Cane patt., 2½″ D. ........... $100.00
**BACCARAT FACETED PAPER-
WEIGHT,** sulfide bust of young Q. Vic-
toria, very rough, check, needs polishing,
3½″ D. ......................... $50.00
**BACCARAT FACETED PAPER-
WEIGHT,** sgn., sulfide Capricorn Sign of
Zodiac, cobalt blue ground, 2¾″ D.
................................. $60.00
*Row III, L to R*
**WAVECREST ART GLASS JEWELRY
BOX,** sgn., wh. cartouch w/pale pink
flowers on pale blue ground, 5¼″ L.
................................. $200.00
**SMALL WAVECREST DRESSER
BOX,** sgn., hinged lid, orange flowers on
wh., 3⅛″ D. .................. $130.00
**MT. WASHINGTON COVERED JAR,**
holly on wh. & gr. ground, sgn., inside
plated silver cover, 5″ D. ....... $135.00

A-MA Dec. 1982    *Robert W. Skinner Inc.*
*L to R*
**TWO-COLOR CUT CAMEO VASE,**
Eng., ca. 1890, wh. band of triangle &
mixed flowers on cranberry ground, 3¼″ H.
................................. $1300.00*
**TWO-COLOR CUT CAMEO VASE,**
Eng., ca. 1890, wh. floral branches on pink
ground, 3½″ H. ............. $1300.00*

A-MA July 1982    *Richard A. Bourne Co., Inc.*
*Row I, L to R*
**WEBB PEACHBLOW VASE,** satin
finish ......................... $90.00
**MOTHER-OF-PEARL GLASS VASE,**
blue satin finish, Raindrop patt., ribbon
candy rim, 8½″ H. ............. $75.00
**ART NOUVEAU ART GLASS VASE,**
Austrian, mottled glaze, 8½″ H. .. $50.00

*Row II, L to R*
**TALL MOTHER-OF-PEARL GLASS
VASES,** pink satin finish, diamond-quilted,
ribbon candy rims, applied thorn handles,
13¾″ H. ..................... $150.00
**MT. WASHINGTON PICKLE JAR,**
plated silver holder, jar w/painted-on Burmese coloring on opaque glass w/enamel
decorated flowers, fork missing, holder
needs replating, 10½″ H. ....... $160.00

*Left*
A-OH July 1982    *Early Auction Co.*
**EPERGNE,** cranberry to wh., 3 holders
w/applied clear rigaree decor.
................................. $250.00*
*Right*
A-OH July 1982    *Early Auction Co.*
**DAUM NANCY CAMEO VASE,** sgn.,
winter scene, 9½″ H. ......... $900.00*

*Left*
A-MA July 1982    *Robert W. Skinner Inc.*
**TIFFANY FAVRILLE VASE,** ca. 1920,
NY, gold & irid. blue, sgn., 9¼″ H.
................................. $450.00*

*Right*
A-WA D.C. July 1982 *Adam A. Weschler & Son*
**GALLE CAMEO GLASS MONU-
MENTAL VASE,** ca. 1900, frosted yellow
& pale lavender body, golden br. overlay
cut, sgn., 29¾″ H. .......... $1400.00*

A-MA July 1982    *Richard A. Bourne Co., Inc.*
*Row I, L to R*
**CORNUCOPIA FLASK,** olive-amber,
½-pt. ......................... $90.00
**RAILROAD FLASK,** olive-amber,
pt. ............................ $175.00
*Row II, L to R*
**SNUFF BOTTLE,** deep clear olive-gr., 5″
H. ............................ $70.00
**EAGLE CORNUCOPIA FLASK,** olive-
amber ......................... $130.00
**QUART FLASK,** red-amber, slight wear
................................. $90.00

*Price does not include 10% buyer fee.

A-WA D.C. Dec. 1982 *Adam A. Weschler & Son*
L to R
**VASE,** Stevens & Williams, cranberry-to-opaque glass, 11″ H. .......... $350.00*
**VASE,** Thomas Webb & Sons, cased glass, gilt & silver trellising vine & leaves, opaque enameled beaded butterflies, ruby body on applied fruit-form feet, 13″ H.
............................ $700.00*

A-WA D.C. Dec. 1982 *Adam A. Weschler & Son*
L to R
**BURMESE FISH-IN-THE-NET VASE,**
12″ H. ...................... $1300.00*
**LONG-NECK VASE,** rainbow m.o.p. & enameled, 12″ H. ............. $600.00*
**BURMESE VERSE VASE,** verse by Sir Walter Scott, stenciled "Queen's Burmese Ware Patented Thomas Webb and Sons," 12″ H. ...................... $800.00*
**BURMESE VASE,** stenciled "Queen's Burmese Ware, Patented Thomas Webb and Sons," 10½″ H. ........... $800.00*
**CROWN MILANO JEWELED BISCUIT BOX,** raised coral ground, gold & silver ferns & sprays, repousse silvered metal top surmounted by butterfly & swivel bail handle, mkd. "Crown Milano Mt. W.G. Co.," 5½″ H. .................. $900.00*
**BURMESE & BRASS STUDENT LAMP,** Guba ducks in flight above a lily pond, electrified, 23″ H. ...... $1900.00*
**CROWN MILANO EWER,** one side has gilt cartouche enclosing boughs of flowers, other side has complementary boughs, printed monogram, mkd. "567," 9″ H.
............................ $1500.00*
**BURMESE JACK-IN-THE-PULPIT VASE,** lacy rim, enameled floral sprays, 12″ H. .................... $600.00*
**BURMESE JACK-IN-THE-PULPIT VASE,** lacy rim, enameled floral sprays, 12″ H. .................... $600.00*
**ROYAL FLEMISH VASE,** one side has birds perched on stem, other side has floral spray, printed monogram mark, mkd. "426," 12½″ H. ............... $600.00*

A-WA D.C. Dec. 1982 *Adam A. Weschler & Son*
L to R
**BURMESE VASE,** raised gilt & painted flowering branches w/butterflies, stenciled "Queen's Burmese Ware, Patented Thomas Webb and Sons," 10½″ H.
............................ $500.00*

**BURMESE VERSE VASE,** verse by James Montgomery, centered by a butterfly & floral bouquets, 12″ H. .. $1200.00*

**CROWN MILANO JEWELED BISCUIT BOX,** jeweled medallion, raised gold & silver ferns & sprays, repousse silvered metal top surmounted by butterfly & swivel bail handle, 5″ H. ............. $900.00*

A-MA June 1983        *Robert W. Skinner Inc.*
**SM. TEPLITZ VASE,** Austria, ca. 1900, 6⅞″ H. ...................... $90.00*

*Left*
A-WA D.C. Dec. 1982 *Adam A. Weschler & Son*
**GALLE CAMEO GLASS VASE,** ca. 1900, frosted yellow & gray ground overlaid in shaded cherry red, sgn. "Galle," 18¼″ H.
............................ $1250.00*

*Right*
A-WA D.C. Dec. 1982 *Adam A. Weschler & Son*
**GALLE CAMEO GLASS VASE,** ca. 1910, overlay red leafage, lavender trellising vine on frosted ground, sng. "Galle," 26″ H.
............................ $2000.00*

*Left*
A-WA D.C. Sept. 1982 *Adam A. Weschler & Son*
**DAUM NANCY MOLD BLOWN CAMEO GLASS VASE,** ca. 1910-20, lavender tree trunks, flowering branches viewing a clearing of frosted-to-gold-to-lavender sky & landscape, 11½″ H.
............................ $1300.00*
*Right*
A-MA Nov. 1982   *Richard A. Bourne Co., Inc.*
**PEKING GLASS WATER POT,** gr. glass lined w/heavy enameled material, Ju-i lappet metal border around neck, inlaid w/small jades, teakwood stand, carving of chrysanthemums, prunus blossoms & branches, 4¼″ H. ............. $300.00

*Price does not include 10% buyer fee.

*Left*
A-MA Dec. 1982    *Robert W. Skinner Inc.*
**KEW BLAS GLASS PITCHER,** ca. 1900, irid., gold & gr. feathering on spherical wh. body, scrolled molded handle, 4⅛" H.
........................... $650.00*

*Right*
A-MA Dec. 1982    *Robert W. Skinner Inc.*
**TIFFANY FAVRILE GLASS PUNCH BOWL,** ca. 1920, NY, gold irid., pale gr. & gold swirled pullup, minor imperfections, 15" D., 10" H. .............. $1900.00*

A-MA June 1983    *Robert W. Skinner Inc.*
*L to R*
**CROWN MILANO EWER,** Mt. Washington Glass Co., MA, late 19th C., gilt detail on cream, sgn. "CM," 10" H.
............................. $1350.00*
**BURMESE VASE,** Mt. Washington Glass Co., MA, late 19th C., 11¾" H.
............................. $1500.00*
**AMBERINA VASE,** N. Eng. Glass Co., MA, late 19th C., decorated enamel, 10" H.
............................. $250.00*

A-MA July 1983    *Robert W. Skinner Inc.*
**ROYAL FLEMISH EWER,** Mt. Washington Glass Co., MA, ca. 1890, unsgn., earthtone colors accented w/gilt highlights, 8½" H. ..................... $1800.00*

A-OH July 1983    *Early Auction Co.*
**NORTHWOOD VASE,** pink overlay on matching pedestal stand w/applied fruit, leaves & flowers, 19" H. ........ $975.00

A-OH July 1983    *Early Auction Co.*
**COVERED VASE,** cranberry Moser w/gold decor., portrait of Empress Elizabeth, 21" H. ................. $600.00

A-MA July 1982    *Richard A. Bourne Co., Inc.*
*Row I, L to R*
**SANDWICH ART GLASS BASKET,** blue w/clear applied handle, 7½" H.
............................. $90.00
**ART GLASS SET,** silver plated w/two rubina paneled blown glass bowls w/applied rigaree, 9½" O.H. ....... $160.00
**ART GLASS BOWL,** mottled pink & wh., clear applied & twisted thorn-style handle, 6" D., 5" H. ............. $90.00
*Row II, L to R*
**SANDWICH ART GLASS BASKET,** blue w/ribbon candy rin & clear twisted thorn handle, 7¾" L., 6" W., 6½" H.
............................. $150.00
**CASED ART GLASS BASKET,** blue w/clear twisted applied handle & hobnail rim, 7¼" x 6", 7" H. ............. $60.00
**SANDWICH ART GLASS BASKET,** pink w/clear applied thorn handle & ribbon candy rim, 7" x 6¼", 7" H. ...... $170.00
*Row III, L to R*
**DECORATED CASED GLASS BRIDE'S BASKET,** peachblow color, orig. silver plated stand, stand replated, 11½" D., 9½" H. ............... $170.00
**SANDWICH ART GLASS VASES,** pr., matched, 1-blue, 1-pink, clear applied handles, ribbon candy rims, minor chips, 8½" H. ...................... $135.00

A-OH July 1983    *Early Auction Co.*
*L to R*
**SQ. COOKIE JAR,** covered, mkd. w/rampant lion, Smith Bros. .... $700.00
**HUMIDOR,** mkd. Nakara "Cigar" ............................. $525.00
**ALBERTINE BISCUIT JAR,** pale pink w/beaded decor., Mt. Washington paper label, mkd. Albertine, silver top .. $650.00

*Price does not include 10% buyer fee.

**AGATA GLASS** was patented by Joseph Locke of the New England Glass Company of Cambridge, Massachusetts, in 1877. The application of a metallic stain left a mottled design characteristic of agata, hence the name.

**AMBER GLASS** is the name of any glassware having a yellowish-brown color. It became popular during the last quarter of the 19th century.

**AMBERINA GLASS** was patented by the New England Glass Company in 1833. It is generally recognized as a clear yellow glass shading to a deep red or fuschia at the top. When the colors are opposite, it is known as reverse amberina. It was machine-pressed into molds, free blown, cut and pattern molded. Almost every glass factory here and in Europe produced this ware, however, few pieces were ever marked.

**AMETHYST GLASS** - The term identifies any glassware made in the proper dark purple shade. It became popular after the Civil War.

**ART GLASS** is a general term given to various types of ornamental glass made to be decorative rather than functional. It dates primarily from the late Victorian period to the present day and, during the span of time, glassmakers have achieved fantastic effects of shape, color, pattern, texture and decoration.

**ADVENTURINE GLASS** - The Venetians are credited with the discovery of Aventurine during the 1860s. It was produced by various mixes of copper in yellow glass. When the finished pieces were broken, ground or crushed, they were used as decorative material by glassblowers. Therefore, a piece of Aventurine glass consists of many tiny glittering particles on the body of the object, suggestive of sprinkled gold crumbs or dust. Other colors in Aventurine are known to exist.

**BACCARAT GLASS** was first made in France in 1756 by La Compagnie des Cristalleries de Baccarat—until the firm went bankrupt. Production began for the second time during the 1820s and the firm is still in operation, producing fine glassware and paperweights. Baccarat is famous for its earlier paperweights made during the last half of the 19th century.

**BOHEMIAN GLASS** is named for its country of origin. It is ornate, overlay, or flashed glassware, popular during the Victorian era.

**BRISTOL GLASS** is a lightweight opaque glass, oftentimes having a light bluish tint, decorated with enamels. The ware is a product of Bristol, England—a glass center since the 1700s.

**BURMESE** - Frederick Shirley developed this shaded art glass at the now-famous old Mt. Washington Glass Company in New Bedford, Massachusetts, and patented his discovery under the name of "Burmese" on December 15, 1885. The ware was also made in England by Thomas Webb & Sons.

Burmese is a hand-blown glass with the exception of a few pieces that were pattern molded. The latter are either ribbed, hobnail or diamond quilted in design. This ware is found in two textures or finishes; the original glazed or shiny finish, and the dull, velvety, satin finish. It is a homogeneous glass (single-layered) that was never lined, cased or plated. Although its color varies slightly, it always shades from a delicate yellow at the base to a lovely salmon-pink at the top. The blending of colors is so gradual that it is difficult to determine where one color ends and the other beings.

**CAMBRIDGE** glasswares were produced by the Cambridge Glass Company in Ohio from 1901 until the firm closed in 1954.

**CAMEO GLASS** can be defined as any glass in which the surface has been cut away to leave a design in relief. Cutting is accomplished by the use of hand cutting tools, wheel cutting and hydrofluoric acid. This ware can be clear or colored glass of a single layer, or glass with multiple layers of clear or colored glass.

Although Cameo glass has been produced for centuries, the majority available today dates from the late 1800s. It has been produced in England, France and other parts of Europe, as well as the United States. The most famous of the French masters of Cameo wares was Emile Galle.

**CANDY CONTAINERS** were used for holding tiny candy pellets. These were produced in a variety of shapes—locomotives, cars, boats, guns, etc. for children.

**CARNIVAL GLASS** was an inexpensive, pressed, iridescent glassware made from about 1900 through the 1920s. It was made in quantities by Northwood Glass Company, Fenton Art Glass Company and others, to compete with the expensive art glass of the period. Originally called "Taffeta" glass, the ware became known as "Carnival" glass during the 1920s when carnivals gave examples as premiums or prizes.

**CORALENE** - The term Coralene denotes a type of decoration rather than a kind of glass—consisting of many tiny beads, either of colored or transparent glass—decorating the surface. The most popular design used resembled coral or seaweed—hence the name.

**CRACKLE GLASS** - This type of art glass was an invention of the Venetians that spread rapidly to other countries. It is made by plunging red-hot glass into cold water, then reheating and reblowing it, thus producing an unusual outer surface which appears to be covered with a multitude of tiny fractures, but is perfectly smooth to the touch.

**CRANBERRY GLASS** - The term "Cranberry Glass" refers to color only, not to a particular type of glass. It is undoubtedly the most familiar colored glass known to collectors. This ware was blown or molded, and oftentimes decorated with enamels.

**CROWN MILANO** glass was made by Frederick Shirley at the Mt. Washington Glass Company, New Bedford, Massachusetts, from 1886-1888. It is ivory in color with satin finish, and was embellished with floral sprays, scrolls and gold enamel.

**CROWN TUSCAN** glass has a pink-opaque body. It was originally produced in 1936 by A. J. Bennett, president of the Cambridge Glass Company of Cambridge, Ohio. The line was discontinued in 1954. Occasionally referred to as Royal Crown Tuscan, this ware was named for a scenic area in Italy, and it has been said that its color was taken from the flesh-colored sky at sunrise. When trans-illuminated, examples do have all of the blaze of a sunrise—a characteristic that is even applied to new examples of the ware reproduced by Mrs. Elizabeth Degenhart of Crystal Art Glass, and Harold D. Bennett, Guernsey Glass Company of Cambridge, Ohio.

**CUSTARD GLASS** was manufactured in the United States for a period of about thirty years (1885-1915). Although Harry Northwood was the first and largest manufacturer of Custard glass, it was also produced by the Heisey Glass Company, Diamond Glass Company, Fenton Art Glass Company and a number of others.

The name Custard glass is derived from its "custard yellow" color which may shade light yellow to ivory to light green glass that is opaque to opalescent. Most pieces have fiery opalescence when held to light. Both the color and glow of this ware come from the use of uranium salts in the glass. It is generally a heavy type pressed glass made in a variety of different patterns.

**CUT OVERLAY** - The term identifies pieces of glassware usually having a milk-white exterior that has been cased with cranberry, blue or amber glass. Other type examples are deep blue, amber or cranberry on crystal glass, and the majority of pieces has been decorated with dainty flowers. Although Bohemian glass manufacturers produced some very choice pieces during the 19th century, fine examples were also made in America, as well as in France and England.

**DAUMNANCY** is the mark found on pieces of French Cameo glass made by August and Antonin Daum, after 1875.

**DURAND ART GLASS** was made by Victor Durand from 1879 to 1935 at the Durand Art Glass Works in Vineland, New Jersey. The glass resembles Tiffany in quality. Drawn white feather designs and thinly drawn glass threading (quite brittle) applied around the main body of the ware,

are striking examples of Durand creations on an iridescent surface.

**FLASHED WARES** were popular during the late 19th century. They were made by partially coating the inner surface of an object with a thin plating of glass or another, more dominant color—usually red. These pieces can readily be identified by holding the object to the light and examining the rim, as it will show more than one layer of glass. Many pieces of "Rubina Crystal" (cranberry to clear), "Blue Amberina" (blue to amber), and "Rubina Verde" (cranberry to green), were manufactured in this way.

**FINDLAY or ONYX** art glass was manufactured about 1890 for only a short time by the Dalzell Gilmore Leighton Company of Findlay, Ohio.

**FRANCISWARE** is a hobnail glassware with frosted or clear glass hobs and stained amber rims and tops. It was produced during the late 1880s by Hobbs, Brockunier and Company.

**FRY GLASS** was made by the H. C. Fry Company, Rochester, Pennsylvania from 1901, when the firm was organized, until 1934 when operations ceased. The firm specialized in the manufacturing of cut glassware. The production of their famous "Foval" glass did not begin until the 1920s. The firm also produced a variety of glass specialties, oven wares and etched glass.

**GALLE** glass was made in Nancy, France by Emile Galle at the Galle Factory founded in 1874. The firm produced both enameled and cameo glass, pottery, furniture and other Art Nouveau items. After Galle's death in 1904, the factory continued operating until 1935.

**GREENTOWN** glass was made in Greentown, Indiana by the Indiana Tumbler and Goblet Company from 1894 until 1903. The firm produced a variety of pressed glass wares in addition to milk and chocolate glass.

**GUNDERSON** peachblow is a more recent type art glass produced in 1952 by the Gunderson-Pierpoint Glass Works of New Bedford, Massachusetts, successors to the Mt. Washington Glass Company. Gunderson pieces have a soft satin finish shading from white at the base to a deep rose at the top.

**HOBNAIL** - The term hobnail identifies any glassware having "bumps"—flattened, rounded or pointed—over the outer surface of the glass. A variety of patterns exist. Many of the fine early examples were produced by Hobbs, Brockunier and Company, Wheeling, West Virginia, and the New England Glass Company.

**HOLLY AMBER**, originally known as "Golden Agate," is a pressed glass pattern which features holly berries and leaves over its glossy surface. Its color shades from golden brown tones to opalescent streaks.

This ware was produced by the Indiana Tumbler and Goblet Company for only six months, from January 1, to June 13, 1903. Examples are rare and expensive.

**IMPERIAL GLASS** - The Imperial Glass Company of Bellaire, Ohio, was organized in 1901 by a group of prominent citizens of Wheeling, West Virginia. A variety of fine art glass, in addition to Carnival glass, was produced by the firm. The two trademarks which identified the ware were issued in June, 1914. One consisted of the firm's name, "Imperial," and the other included a cross formed by double-pointed arrows. The latter trademark was changed in September of the same year from the arrow cross to what was known as a "German" cross. The overlapping "IG" cipher was adopted by Imperial in 1949, and appears on practically all of their present production—including reproduced Carnival glass.

**LATTICINO** is the name given to articles of glass in which a network of tiny milk-white lines appear, crisscrossing between two walls of glass. It is a type of Filigree glassware developed during the 16th century by the Venetians.

**LEGRAS GLASS**, cameo, acid cut and enameled glasswares were made by August J. F. Legras at Saint-Denis, France from 1864-1914.

**LOETZ GLASS** was made in Austria just before the turn of the century. As Loetz worked in the Tiffany factory before returning to Austria, much of his glass is similar in appearance to Tiffany wares. Loetz glass is oftentimes marked "Loetz" or "Loetz-Austria."

**LUTZ GLASS** was made by Nicholas Lutz, a Frenchman, who worked at the Boston and Sandwich Glass Company from 1870 to 1888 when it closed. He also produced fine glass at the Mt. Washington Glass Company and later at the Union Glass Company. Lutz is noted for two different types of glass—striped and threaded wares. Other glass houses also produced similar glass and these wares were known as Lutz-type.

**MARY GREGORY** was an artist for the Boston and Sandwich Glass Company during the last quarter of the 19th century. She decorated glass ware with white enamel figures of young children engaged in playing, collecting butterflies, etc. in white on transparent glass, both clear and colored. Today, the term "Mary Gregory" glass applies to any glassware that remotely resembles her work.

**MERCURY GLASS** is a double-walled glass that dates from the 1850s to about 1910. It was made in England as well as the United States during this period. Its interior, usually in the form of vases, is lined with flashing mercury, giving the items an allover silvery appearance. The entrance hole in the base of each piece was sealed over. Many pieces were decorated.

**MILK GLASS** is an opaque pressed glassware, usually of milk-white color, although green, amethyst, black, and shades of blue were made. Milk glass was produced in quantity in the United States during the 1880s, in a variety of patterns.

**MILLEFIORI** - This decorative glassware is considered to be a specialty of the Venetians. It is sometimes called "glass of a thousand flowers," and has been made for centuries. Very thin colored glass rods are arranged in bundles, then fused together with heat. When the piece of glass is sliced across, it has a design like that of many small flowers. These tiny wafer-thin slices are then embedded in larger masses of glass, enlarged and shaped.

**MOSER GLASS** was made by Kolomon Moser at Carlsbad. The ware is considered to be another type of Art Nouveau glass as it was produced during its heyday—during the early 1900s. Principal colors included amethyst, cranberry, green and blue, with fancy enameled decoration.

**MOTHER-OF-PEARL**, often abbreviated in descriptions as M.O.P., is glass composed of two or more layers, with a pattern showing through to the outer surface. The pattern, caused by internal air traps, is created by expanding the inside layer of molten glass into molds with varying designs. When another layer of glass is applied, this brings out the design. The final layer of glass is then acid dipped, and the result is Mother of Pearl Satin Ware. Patterns are numerous. The most frequently found are the Diamond Quilted, Raindrop and Herringbone. This ware can be one solid color, a single color shading light to dark, two colors blended or a variety of colors which include the rainbow effect. In addition, many pieces are decorated with colorful enamels, coralene beading, and other applied glass decorations.

**NAILSEA GLASS** was first produced in England from 1788 to 1873. The characteristics that identify this ware are the "pulled" loopings and swirls of colored glass over the body of the object.

**NEW ENGLAND PEACHBLOW** was patented in 1886 by the New England Glass Company. It is a single-layered glass shading from opaque white at the base to deep rose red or from opaque white at the base to deep rose-red or raspberry at the top. Some pieces have a glossy surface, but most were given an acid bath to produce a soft, matte finish.

**NEW MARTINSVILLE PEACHBLOW GLASS** was produced from 1901-1907 at New Martinsville, Pennsylvania.

**OPALESCENT GLASS** - The term refers to glasswares which have a milky white effect in the glass, usually on a colored ground. There are three basic types of this ware. Presently, the most popular includes pressed glass patterns found in table settings. Here the opalescence appears at the top rim, the base, or a combination of both. On blown or mold-blown glass, the pattern itself consists of this milky effect—such as Spanish Lace. Another example is the opalescent points on some pieces of hobnail glass. These wares are lighter weight. The third group includes opalescent novelties, primarily of the pressed variety.

**PAMONA GLASS** was invented in 1884 by Joseph Locke at the New England Glass Company.

**PEKING GLASS** is a type of Chinese cameo glass produced from the 1700s, well into the 19th century.

**PHOENIX GLASS** - The firm was established in Beaver County, Pennsylvania during the late 1800s, and produced a variety of commercial glasswares. During the 1930s the factory made a desirable sculptured gift-type glassware which has become very collectible in recent years. Vases, lamps, bowls, ginger jars, candlesticks, etc. were made until the 1950s in various colors with a satin finish.

**PIGEON BLOOD** is a bright reddish-orange glassware dating from the early 1900s.

**PRESSED GLASS** was the inexpensive glassware produced in quantity to fill the increasing demand for tablewares when Americans moved away from the simple table utensils of pioneer times. During the 1820s, ingenious Yankees invented and perfected machinery for successfully pressing glass. About 1865, manufacturers began to color their products. Literally hundreds of different patterns were produced.

**ROSALINE GLASS** is a product of the Steuben Glass Works of Corning, New York. The firm was founded by Frederick Carter and T. C. Hawkes, Sr. Rosaline is a rose-colored jade glass or colored alabaster. The firm is now owned by the Corning Glass Company, which is presently producing fine glass of exceptional quality.

**ROYAL FLEMISH ART GLASS** was made by the Mt. Washington Glass Works during the 1880s. It has an acid finish which may consist of one or more colors, decorated with raised gold enameled lines separating into sections. Fanciful painted enamel designs also decorate this ware. Royal Flemish glass is marked "RF," with the letter "R" reversed and backed to the letter "F," within a four-sided orange-red diamond mark.

**SANDWICH GLASS** - One of the most interesting and enduring pages from America's past is Sandwich glass produced by the famous Boston and Sandwich Glass Company at Sandwich, Massachusetts. The firm began operations in 1825, and the glass flourished until 1888 when the factory closed. Despite the popularity of Sandwich Glass, little is known about its founder, Deming Jarvis.

The Sandwich Glass house turned out hundreds of designs in both plain and figured patterns, in colors and crystal, so that no one type could be considered entirely typical—but the best known is the "lacy" glass produced here. The variety and multitude of designs and patterns produced by the company over the years is a tribute to its greatness.

**SILVER DEPOSIT GLASS** was made during the late 19th and early 20 centuries. Silver was deposited on the glass surface by a chemical process so that a pattern appeared against a clear or colored ground. This ware is sometimes referred to as "Ssilver overlay."

**SLAG GLASS** was originally known as "Mosaic" and "Marble Glass" because of its streaked appearance. Production in the United States began about 1880. The largest producer of this ware was Challinor, Taylor and Company. The various slag mixtures are: purple, butterscotch, blue, orange, green and chocolate. A small quantity of Pink Slag was also produced in the Inverted Fan and Feather pattern. Examples are rare and expensive.

**SPANISH LACE** is a Victorian glass pattern that is easily identified by its distinct opalescent flower and leaf pattern. It belongs to the shaded opalescent glass family.

**STEUBEN** - The Steuben Glass Works was founded in 1904 by Frederick Carter, an Englishman, and T. G. Hawkes, Sr., at Corning, New York. In 1918, the firm was purchased by the Corning Glass Company. However, Steuben remained with the firm, designing a bounty of fine art glass of exceptional quality.

**STIEGEL-TYPE GLASS** - Henry William Stigel founded America's first flint glass factory during the 1760s at Manheim, Pennsylvania. Stiegel glass is flint or crystal glass; it is thin and clear, and has a belt-like ring when tapped. The ware is quite brittle and fragile. Designs were painted free-hand on the glass—birds, animals and architectural motifs, surrounded by leaves and flowers. The engraved glass resulted from craftsmen etching the glass surface with a copper wheel, then cutting the desired patterns.

It is extremely difficult to identify, with certainty, a piece of original Stiegel glass. Part of the problem resulted from the lack of an identifying mark on the products. Additionally, many of the craftsmen moved to other areas after the Stiegel plant closed—producing a similar glass product. Therefore, when one is uncertain about the origin of this type ware, it is referred to as "Stiegel-type" glass.

**TIFFANY GLASS** was made by Louis Comfort Tiffany, one of America's outstanding glass designers of the Art Nouveau period, from about 1870 to the 1930s. Tiffany's designs included a variety of lamps, bronze work, silver, pottery and stained glass windows. Practically all items made were marked "L. C. Tiffany" or "L.C.T." in addition to the word "Favrille"—the French word for color.

**TORTOISE SHELL GLASS** - As the name indicates, this type of glassware resembles the color of tortoise shell and has deep rich brown tones combined with amber and cream-colored shades. Tortoise Shell Glass was originally produced in 1880 by Francis Pohl, a German chemist. It was also made in the United States by the Sandwich Glass Works and other glass houses during the late 1800s.

**VAL ST. LAMBERT** Cristalleries, located in Belgium, was founded in 1825 and the firm is still in operation.

**VASA MURRHINA** glassware was produced in quantity at the Vasa Murrhina Art Glass Company of Sandwich, Massachusetts during the late 1900s. John C. DeVoy, Assignor to the firm, registered a patent on July 1, 1884, for the process of decorating glassware with particles of mica flakes (coated with copper, gold, nickel or silver) sandwiched between an inner layer of glass which is opaque, and an outer layer of clear or transparent colored glass. The ware was also produced by other American glass firms and in England.

**VASELINE GLASS** - The term "Vaseline" refers to color only, as it resembles the greenish-yellow color typical of the oily petroleum jelly known as Vaseline. This ware has been produced in a variety of patterns both here and in Europe—from the late 1800s. It has been made in both clear and opaque yellow, Vaseline combined with clear glass, and occasionally the two colors are combined in one piece.

**WAVECREST GLASS** is an opaque white glassware made from the late 1890s by French factories and the Pairpoint Manufacturing Company at New Bedford, Massachusetts. Items were decorated by the C. F. Monroe Company of Meriden, Connecticut, with painted pastel enamels. The name Wavecrest was used after 1898 with the initials of the Company "C.F.M. Co." Operations ceased during World War II.

**WEBB GLASS** was made by Thomas Webb & Sons of Stourbridge, England during the late Victorian period. The firm produced a variety of different types of art and cameo glass.

**WHEELING PEACHBLOW** - With its simple lines and delicate shadings, Wheeling Peachblow was produced soon after 1883 by J. H. Hobbs, Brockunier and Company at Wheeling, West Virginia. It is a two-layered glass lined or cased inside with an opaque, milk-white type of plated glassware. The outer layer shades from a bright yellow at the base to a mahogany red at the top. The majority of pieces produced are in the glossy finish.

A-MA Nov. 1982    *Richard A. Bourne Co., Inc.*
*Row I, L to R*
**POWDER FLASK,** brass, stamped "Sykes," orig. dulled copper color lacquer finish, spring retains most of orig. bright blue, 3¾" H. ................... $50.00
**POWDER FLASK,** brass, both sides embossed w/pheasant surrounded by scroll patt., top possibly old replm., spring is replm., body has several minor dents, 1 seam very slightly split, 4½" H. ... $40.00
**POWDER FLASK,** brass, embossed on both sides w/spread-winged eagle on hummock clutching flask & pistol, 4½" H. ...................... $60.00
**POWDER FLASK,** embossed on both sides w/spread-winged eagle on hummock clutching flask & pistol, flask has been taken apart to repr. damage at seams, top carelessly remounted w/some traces of soldered repr., spring is modern replm., body of flask w/traces of repr. to minor dents, 4½" H. ................... $40.00
**POWDER FLASK,** wh. metal, 2 small carrying rings, both sides embossed w/reclining dog surrounded by tendrils of foliage, fitted w/plain brass top & spout, 5¼" H. ........................ $25.00

*Row II, L to R*
**COMPARTMENT FLASK,** copper, brass top & bottom, both compartment covers restored, 4" H. ......... $40.00
**COMPARTMENT FLASK,** brass, body embossed on both sides w/leaf pattern, covered w/aged shellac or lacquer finish, 4¾" H. ...................... $40.00

**FLASK,** brass, both sides embossed w/fluted patt., top stamped "G * J.W/ Hawksley," internal dispensing spring broken or missing, body retains traces of orig. lacquer finish within fluted patt., 5" H. ............................... $40.00

**FLASK,** brass, both sides embossed w/shell patt., traces of orig. lacquer finish in protected areas, 4⅝" H. ......... $45.00
**FLASK,** brass, several minor dents on 1 side, orig. dispensing spring lightly pitted overall, 3⅛" H. ................. $50.00

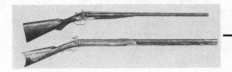

A-MA Nov. 1982    *Richard A. Bourne Co., Inc.*
*Row I, L to R*
**COLT-TYPE PISTOL FLASK,** 4⅞" overall, brass body embossed on both sides, several bad dents on 1 side, seam on 1 side partially split ............. $50.00
**COLT-TYPE POWDER FLASK,** 4" overall, brass body embossed on both sides, 2 small dents in bottom .... $70.00
**COLT-TYPE POWDER FLASK,** 3¾" overall, brass body embossed on both sides, dispensing spring is old replm., seam on 1 side w/slight traces of old resoldering repr. ....................... $50.00
**PISTOL FLASK,** 4¼" overall, brass bodied ........................ $45.00
**ENG. FLASK,** 5" overall, brass bodied, spout mkd. "DIXON & SONS," 1 side w/⅜" dent ..................... $45.00

*Row II, L to R*
**POWDER FLASK,** 5" overall, brass bodied, embossed on both sides w/beaded fluted patt., seam w/small dent & partial split opening in lower edge of 1 side ............................. $50.00
**COLT-TYPE POWDER FLASK,** 4½" overall, brass body embossed on both sides w/spread winged eagle on hummock, body has very deep ¼" dent on 1 side & several shallow dents on other side ...... $55.00
**COLT-TYPE PISTOL FLASK,** 4¾" overall, brass body embossed on both sides, top missing 1 small attaching screw, seam of 1 side slightly split for approximately 1", nozzle of spout has several small dents ......................... $55.00
**COLT-TYPE PISTOL FLASK,** 4⅝" overall, brass body embossed on both sides, dispensing spout a restor., body has several minor dents on both sides ................................ $55.00
**PISTOL FLASK,** 4½" overall, brass body embossed on both sides ........ $90.00

---

A-WA D.C. July 1982    *Adam A. Weschler & Son*
*Top to Bottom*
**TRAP GUN,** L.C. Smith, NY, ca. 1880, 12-gauge double barrel shotgun, walnut checkered stock & forearm, engraved lock & trigger guard, barrel 30" L. .. $350.00*
**CAP & BALL MUZZLE LOADING RIFLE,** Am., lock engraved & stamped A. McComas, last quarter 19th C., mahogany stock fitted w/brass patchbox & cheek rest, 51" L. ................... $350.00*

A-MA Nov. 1982    *Richard A. Bourne Co., Inc.*
*Row I, L to R*
**U.S. NAVY FOULED ANCHOR FLASK,** both sides embossed w/an anchor & rope over "U.S.N.," top stamped "N.P. Ames," dated 1843 above script "JL," seam on bottom very slightly split, body retains br. lacquer finish which is now aged encrested & slightly marred by tiny spots of wh. paint, nozzle has several dents, 9¾" H. ................. $325.00
**BATTY PEACE FLASK,** both sides embossed, top stamped "BATTY," "MS," dated 1853 w/"A.P.K." inspection mrk., spout is replm., 1 seam has evidence of splitting, body has minor dents, 9¾" H. ............................. $120.00
**PEACE FLASK,** body embossed on both sides, top stamped "N.P. Ames," "MS," dated 1838, 1 seam open, body has minor dents, 9½" H. ............... $110.00
**FLASK,** brass, embossed on both sides, top stamped "AM. FLASK & CAP CO," 2 lower carrying rings & studs repl., body has minor dents, 10" H. ............. $40.00
**FLASK,** brass, both sides embossed, traces of orig. lacquer finish, 1 side of body has large dent, 10" H. ........... $50.00
*Row II, L to R*
**POWDER FLASK,** both sides embossed, neck & top of flask made of German silver, stamped "G & J.W. HAWKSLEY/SHEFFIELD," dispensing spring is replm., 8¼" H. ............................... $120.00
**POWDER FLASK,** copper, embossed on 1 side, top is possibly old replm., back has minor dents, 8¾" H. ......... $60.00
**POWDER FLASK,** copper, both sides embossed, bottom fitted w/German silver stud & carrying ring, neck & top finely worked German silver, top stamped "DIXON & SONS/PATENT," neck has 4 small stampings, dispensing spring is probably replm., 8¼" H. ........ $110.00
**POWDER FLASK,** brass, both sides embossed, top stamped "AM. FLASK & CAP CO," missing 2 screws that attach neck to body, 8⅜" H. ........... $60.00
**FLASK,** brass, embossed on both sides, several minor dents, 8" H. ....... $35.00

A-MA Nov. 1982    *Richard A. Bourne Co., Inc.*
**WINCHESTER MODEL 63 22LR AUTOMATIC RIFLE,** Serial Number 102453, checkered at forend & wrist ............................. $210.00

*Price does not include 10% buyer fee.

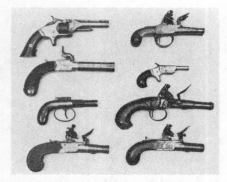

A-MA Nov. 1982    *Richard A. Bourne Co., Inc.*
*Left, Top to Bottom*
**SMITH & WESSON FIRST MODEL SECOND ISSUE 22 REVOLVER,** Serial Number 94777 .................. $80.00

**ENG. BOX LOCK PERCUSSION MUFF PISTOL,** 7″ overall, 2⅞″ octagonal, 50 caliber, smooth bore barrel stamped w/Birmingham proofs, half-cock sear defective, spring broken or missing ........................... $110.00

**AM. CENTER BAR HAMMER PERCUSSION DERRINGER,** 4¾″ overall, 2″ part-round, part-octagonal barrel, all steel construction w/varnished walnut grips ............................... $140.00

**FR. FLINTLOCK CENTER HAMMER MUFF PISTOL,** 6⅜″ overall, 2″ iron barrel, engraved left side "Bertheas/VCie," right side "a S. Etienne," some lt. pitting ............................... $160.00

*Right, Top to Bottom*
**DOUBLE-BARRELED FLINTLOCK PISTOL,** 5⅝″ overall, 1⅛″ screw-off iron cannon barrels, all steel, left side engraved "SEGALAS," right side engraved "LONDON" .................. $300.00

**DERRINGER,** unmkd., 22 caliber, Serial Number 1260, 4⅛″ overall, 2⅛″ part-octagonal barrel ................ $55.00

**ENG. Q.A. FLINTLOCK PISTOL,** 7⅝″ overall, 3¾″ iron barrel stamped w/London proofs, engraved "London" below frizzen spring, top of barrel sgn. "Stanton," hammer & frizzen spring poor replm., stock w/several repr. .......... $150.00

**ENG. BOX LOCK FLINTLOCK MUFF PISTOL,** 6″ overall, 1⅝″ round iron barrel, iron center hammer frame engraved "Wm/WILLIAMS," upper tang screw repl., barrel w/old reblue, checkering on butt shows wear & possibly old varnish refinish ............................... $130.00

A-MA Jan. 1983    *Robert W. Skinner Inc.*
**RIFLE,** N. Eng., ca. 1830, full stock, mkd. "J. Cooper," damage, 35½″ L. ...................... $375.00*

A-MA Nov. 1982    *Richard A. Bourne Co., Inc.*
*Top, L to R*
**FLASK,** 7″ overall, brass body embossed on both sides w/leaf pattern, partially obscured by lt. oxidation ........ $80.00
**FLASK,** 8″ overall, brass body embossed on both sides w/hanging dead game scene & fitted w/2 carrying rings, missing dispensing ring & retaining screw ..................................... $35.00
**FLASK,** 7½″ overall, brass body embossed on both sides w/shell pattern, shallow dent on 1 side ..................... $30.00
**FLASK,** 7½″ overall, brass body embossed on both sides w/leaf & beaded pattern, 4 carrying rings, dispensing spring old replm. ..................................... $50.00

*Bottom, L to R*
**FLASK,** 7½″ overall, brass body embossed on both sides w/shell pattern, body slightly marred w/lt. dents .............. $30.00
**FLASK,** 7¼″ overall, brass body embossed on both sides w/dead game & scrolls, evidence of disassembly & extensive resoldering at seams, body recolored ..................................... $35.00
**FLASK,** 7¼″ overall, brass body embossed on both sides w/dead game scene, disassembled for extensive repr. to seams & removal of dents ................ $30.00
**FLASK,** 6¼″ overall, brass body embossed on 1 side w/2 panels, dispensing spring old replm. ..................... $35.00

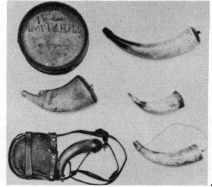

A-MA Nov. 1982    *Richard A. Bourne Co., Inc.*
*Row I, L to R*
**CONFEDERATE CANTEEN,** wooden, iron bound, 7¼″ D., 1 side carved "John L/Mitchell/May 14, 1862/NC/CSA," other side carved "JL/JL Mitchell," missing spout ........................ $450.00

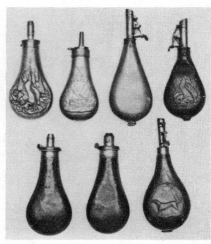

A-MA Nov. 1982    *Richard A. Bourne Co., Inc.*
*Top, L to R*
*LOT OF 2 FLASKS & 2 SHOT DISPENSERS*
**FLASK,** 7½″ overall, brass body embossed on both sides w/hanging dead game, seams carelessly resoldered, numerous dents, dispensing nozzle repl.
**REPRODUCTION "COLTS PATENT" NAVY FLASK,** 7″ overall, seams carelessly resoldered, numerous dents.
**LEATHER SPOT POUCH,** 9″ overall, brass dispenser mkd. "AM FLASK & CAP CO," leather body mkd. "3/lbs."
**LEATHER SHOT FLASK,** 8″ overall, body w/embossed hanging dead game scene on each side, brass dispenser mkd. "AM. FLASK & CAP CO" ....... $65.00
*Bottom, L to R*
*LOT OF 2 FLASKS & 1 SHOT DISPENSER*
**FLASK,** 7¾″ overall, body covered w/br. pigskin, brass top stamped "DIXON & SONS/PATENT," missing 1 screw at top.
**FLASK,** 7¾″ overall, br. pigskin covered body, brass top mkd. "IMPROVED/BEST/QUALITY" & "SYKES/PATENT," leather seams frayed & torn.
**LEATHER SHOT POUCH,** 9″ overall, embossed on both sides, brass dispenser top .......................... $40.00

---

**HORN,** 10¼″ overall, engraved w/Eng. coat of arms "Col Webb Trent" & "Ye Kings/Agent/1767," map scene from Western PA area .............. $110.00
*Row II, L to R*
**POWDER HORN,** 8″ overall, both sides engraved, 1 side inscribed "L. French/B. Hawk/C.T. 1867," some worm damage w/several holes ................ $275.00
**PRIMING HORN,** 5½″ overall, wood base engraved w/initials "WI" ........ $30.00
*Row III, L to R*
**HUNTING POUCH W/ATTACHED POWDER HORN,** late 19th C., pouch is 5″ x 5″, horn is 6″ overall w/orig. leather attaching straps ............... $120.00
**POWDER HORN,** 7½″ overall, old wooden base, engraved "Jonathan hall 1747" ........................ $140.00

*Price does not include 10% buyer fee.

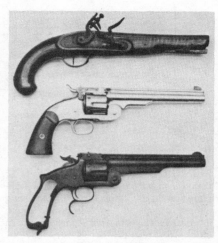

A-MA Nov. 1982 *Richard A. Bourne Co., Inc.*
*Top to Bottom*
**AM. FLINTLOCK HOLSTER PISTOL,**
8″ round brass barrel stamped "Crown & Crossed Scepter" proofs, top of barrel stamped "London," orig. engraved flat lockplate w/gooseneck hammer sgn. below the pan "Drepperd/Lancaster," full stock w/lt. applied tiger striping, fitted w/brass furniture, 2 ramrod pipes, lt. engraved trigger guard, 2 escut. for the lock screws, oval wrist escut. & butt for the lock screws, oval wrist escut. & butt plate, missing hammer screw, overall 13½″ L.
............................ $800.00
**FIRST MODEL SMITH & WESSON SCHOFIELD REVOLVER,** Serial Number 306, round dot stuck on butt, small flat spot on bottom rear of barrel mkd. w/small letters "lp," rear of cylinder stamped w/same letters, frame stamped w/letter "L"
............................ $900.00
**RUSSIAN MODEL SMITH & WESSON REVOLVER,** missing main spring, grips & part of ejector mechanism, covered w/deep age br. patina w/sections of orig. blue finish & some scaling rust
............................ $275.00

A-MA July 1982 *Richard A. Bourne Co., Inc.*
*Left, Top to Bottom*
**CASED PERCUSSION PISTOL,** Eng., mkd. "A.N. Wart/Son & Co. London," orig. leather-covered & lined case w/ accessories .................. $225.00
**TROUSSE SET,** brass-bound sheath containing knife, fork & skewer, ca. 1808, normal signs of wear .......... $95.00
*Right, Top to Bottom*
**FLINTLOCK TINDER LIGHTER,** mkd. "Wooiley," frizzen spring broken, lt. pitting
............................ $750.00
**FLINTLOCK TINDER LIGHTER,** unmkd., normal wear & patination
............................ $650.00
**BRASS POWDER TESTER,** mkd. "1590" .......................... $325.00
**BREECHBLOCK FOR HALL FLINTLOCK RIFLE,** mkd. "U.S./S. North/Midltn/Conn./1835," top jar & screw replm. .......................... $70.00

A-MA Nov. 1982 *Richard A. Bourne Co., Inc.*
*Left, Top to Bottom*
**COLT MODEL 1911 A 1 ARMY ISSUE 45 AUTOMATIC PISTOL,** Serial Number 864675, orig. parkerized finish, about-mint checkered br. plastic grips
............................ $375.00
**STURM RUGER BEARCAT SINGLE ACTION REVOLVER,** 22 caliber, Serial Number 1098, 4″ barrel, orig. blue crisp, brass trigger guard ............ $175.00
**SMITH & WESSON MODEL 34 KIT GUN,** 22 caliber, Serial Number 21081, 4″ barrel, 4-screw side plate, orig. blue finish w/slight wear at muzzle & minuscule wear at edges of cylinder ............ $175.00
*Right, Top to Bottom*
**WALTHER MODEL PPK/S 22LR AUTOMATIC PISTOL,** Serial Number 114713, in orig. cardboard carton w/lid missing, spare extension magazine, orig. instruction booklet, brass cleaning rod, 3 cleaning brushes, & blk. leather holster
............................ $275.00
**COLT MODEL 1908 .380 AUTOMATIC PISTOL,** Serial Number 93332, fitted w/orig. checkered walnut grips w/"Colt" medallions, orig. bright blue finish, Audley patent leather holster
............................ $290.00

A-MA Nov. 1982 *Richard A. Bourne Co., Inc.*
**ITHACA NO. 4 TRAP 12-GAUGE SHOTGUN,** Serial Number 278687, 34″ barrel w/orig. ventilated rib, Monte Carlo stock fitted w/blk. triple magnum pad, trigger guard tang w/age spotting to blue finish ........................ $800.00

→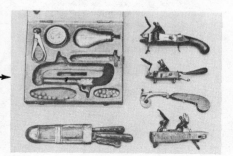

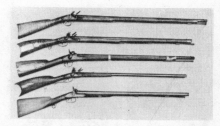

A-MA Nov. 1982 *Richard A. Bourne Co., Inc.*
*Top to Bottom*
**AM. FLINTLOCK FOWLER,** 37⅛″ round iron barrel, initials "S.M." on breech, fitted w/brass furniture, wrist inlaid w/German silver plate, barrel w/pitting in area of touch hole only, forend cap restored, 53″ overall ........... $350.00
**FAKE SUPERIMPOSED LOCK KENTUCKY STYLE RIFLE,** 33¾″ octagonal barrel, stamped on top flat "I. Scholb. 1782," 48¼″ overall ............ $225.00
**U.S. MODEL 1851 MISSISSIPPI RIFLE,** mfg. by Robbins, Kendall & Lawrence, Windsor, VT in 1847, barrel dated w/"US/JAQ/P" inspection mark, 55 caliber, smooth bore, sling swivel & studs removed, barrel w/welded repr. to dents, half-cock sear defective ........ $325.00
**FAKE DOUBLE-BARRELED HALF STOCK KENTUCKY STYLE FLINTLOCK RIFLE,** 30″ full octagonal barrels, mkd. on rib "W*G*M," locks poorly made, some splits in wood, 47″ overall .. $100.00
**DOUBLE-BARRELED PERCUSSION SHOTGUN,** 30″, 10 gauge barrels, a sliver of wood repr. w/small screw on bottom front of lockplate, forend w/stress crack, 46″ overall .................... $110.00

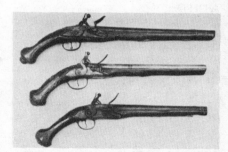

A-MA Nov. 1982 *Richard A. Bourne Co., Inc.*
**MEDITERRANEAN FLINTLOCK HOLSTER PISTOL,** barrel secured to stock near muzzle w/1″ flat brass sheet, missing several minor chips of wood, steel parts w/moderate age br. patina, 21¼″ L.
............................ $100.00
**MEDITERRANEAN FLINTLOCK HOLSTER PISTOL,** 12½″ half-round, half-octagonal barrel, missing a 2″ chip of wood at bottom front of lockplate, stock is missing minor chips of wood about the buttcap, 19″ L. ................. $125.00
**MEDITERRANEAN FLINTLOCK HOLSTER PISTOL,** 11½″ iron barrel, stock is missing minor old chips of wood, tip of left buttcap tang missing, steel parts w/lt. br. age patina, 18½″ L. ...... $90.00

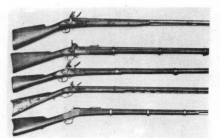

A-OH Oct. 1982        *Garth's Auctions, Inc.*
**KENTUCKY RIFLE,** ca. 1835, curly maple stock, sgn. "B. Samples," untouched cond., 43" barrel, 59" L. ....... $800.00
**KENTUCKY RIFLE,** ca. 1840, curly maple half-stock, by Ephraim Sonnedecker, Salem, OH, 29⅝" barrel, 45" L. ............................ $1800.00
**WRT. IRON LATCH,** N. Eng., dated 1824, pc. missing, 17" L. ....... $170.00
**IRON TRADE AXE PIPE,** pitted & some damage, 8½" L. ............... $125.00
**KENTUCKY RIFLE,** 20th C., curly maple stock, sgn. "Wm. Buchele," 43" barrel, 58½" L. ............... $1600.00
**BOWIE KNIFE,** Sheffield blade, stag horn handle, leather sheath, 11¾" L. ... $75.00
**KENTUCKY RIFLE,** ca. 1820, curly maple stock, sgn. "A. Koop," 40½" barrel, 56" L. ..................... $1900.00
**WRT. IRON LATCH,** N. Eng., 18th C., pc. missing, 21" L. ............. $115.00
**WRT. IRON TULIP LATCH,** 18th C., sgn. "F. Stone," 14¼" L. ........ $575.00
**WRT. IRON LATCH,** 18th C., tulip design, pc. missing, 13¼" L. ..... $350.00

A-OH Oct. 1982        *Garth's Auctions, Inc.*
**POWDER HORN,** engraved, 12½" L. ............................. $125.00
**KENTUCKY PERCUSSION PISTOL,** ca. 1835, curly maple stock, restor., 10" barrel, 14½" L. ................ $550.00
**KENTUCKY PISTOL,** converted, maple stock, brass trigger guard, 10¼" barrel, 17¼" L. ..................... $150.00
**POWDER HORN,** engraved, ca. 1750-70, by Samuel More of Poughkeepsie, NY, 10" L. ............................. $700.00
**POWDER HORN,** engraved, "Black Hawk," eagle w/"E. Pluribus Unum," dated "1833," Ohio horn by Tinsel, 8¾" L. ..................... $625.00
**POWDER FLASK,** embossed copper & brass, eagle, mkd. "H. P. Ames, 1846," 8¾" L. ............................. $175.00
**POWDER HORN,** brass cap, carved tip, 8" L. ........................ $40.00
**POWDER HORN,** turned wooden cap, 9⅝" L. ......................... $30.00
**HORN POWDER FLASK,** brass base, measuring spout, 7¼" L. ........ $85.00
**POWDER HORN,** engraved "Nov. 1823," 5¾" L. ........................ $40.00
**POWDER HORN,** engraved, "H. M. S. Zacs, 1812, Willcox, Java," 14" L. ............................. $375.00

A-MA Nov. 1982    *Richard A. Bourne Co., Inc.*
*Top*
**HUNTING BAG,** late 19th C., blk. leather 9½" H., 8" W., attached to carrying strap is 8½" horn engraved w/map scene, engraved w/numerous towns, pouch holds 19th C. hunting knife, 5¾" blade, 10" overall w/iron head 4¾" H., 12¾" overall ....... $360.00

*Bottom, L to R*
**POWDER HORN,** inscribed "JOHN/ CAMPBELL.S/HORN/MADE./DECMr 1830," 13" overall .............. $100.00

**ENG. POWDER HORN,** mid 19th C., carving near nozzle, main body engraved w/wide range of patt., fitted w/wrt. iron carrying ring at nozzle ......... $350.00

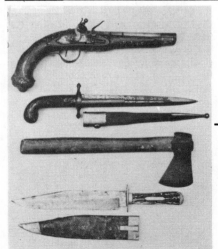

A-MA Nov. 1982    *Richard A. Bourne Co., Inc.*
*Top to Bottom*
**FLINTLOCK FOWLING PIECE,** 60½" round iron barrel, Brown Bess style lock-plate stamped "Galton," trigger guard tang almost completely broken away, some internal lock parts repl., partial split in stock, 76½" overall ............. $375.00
**CIVIL WAR ENG. PERCUSSION RIFLED MUSKET,** 39" round barrel, 577 caliber rifled, brass forend cap, trigger guard & butt plate, lockplate stamped "TOWER/1862," bore has some lt. pitting, 55½" overall ................... $500.00
**U.S. SPRINGFIELD MODEL 1795 FLINTLOCK MUSKET,** 41⅛" barrel, lockplate mkd. "1808," butt plate dated "1807," lockplate w/scattered pitting, ramrod is old wooden replm., 55¾" overall .................. $325.00
**KENTUCKY FLINTLOCK RIFLE,** 40½" full octagonal barrel, 44 caliber rifled, mkd. on top flat "C. HUGHES," barrel reconverted to flintlock, wood in top of stock repl. at wrist, forend missing 3 of 4 brass flat barrel keys, 56¾" overall .................. $700.00
**CIVILIAN REMINGTON ROLLING BLOCK MUSKET,** 43 caliber Spanish, 35" full round barrel, steel-tipped forend secured w/3 barrel bands, action tang stamped "E REMINGTON & SONS ILION N.Y." w/patent dates through March 16th, 1874, 50¼" overall .................. $275.00

A-MA Nov. 1982    *Richard A. Bourne Co., Inc.*
**NORTH AFRICAN FLINTLOCK PISTOL,** 7¼" round iron barrel, crudely engraved at breech, 13½" L. ..... $90.00
**DOUBLE-BARRELED PERCUSSION DIRK,** 9⅜" double edged blade, 3⅜" round Damascus steel, 36 caliber, 7" of blade on each side etched, raised carved walnut handles, leather scabbard w/steel mounts, stitching on seam of leather scabbard broken, 13⅞" L. ............... $2000.00
**IRON AXE HEAD,** stamped on right side w/early maker's mrk., heart w/raised letter "H" within, fitted w/worn 13½" handle, axe head has deep age patina, 4½" overall, 2¾" W. ............................. $60.00
**IXL BOWIE KNIFE,** stamped at ricasso "IXL," reverse side of blade stamped "G. WOSTENHOLD & SON/WASHINGTON WORKS/SHEFFIELD," rectangle plate scratched "MAReel," orig. red Morocco leather scabbard embossed w/tight diamond pattern & impressed "1*XL" in gold letters, German silver mounts, 13½" overall, 9⅛" blade .............. $550.00

A-OH July 1982      *Garth's Auctions, Inc.*
*Row I, L to R*
**TREEN BOX,** w/wire bail & wooden handle, old varnish finish, 3⅜″ H.
................................ $205.00
**MAPLE BOWL,** w/some burl, glued rim break, 3¼″ D., 1½″ H. ......... $65.00
**TREEN TURNED BOX,** w/lid, old age cracks in side of bowl, orig. red finish, 2½″ D., 2⅛″ H. .................... $235.00
**BURL BOWL,** w/foot & rim detail, 2″ D., 1⅛″ H. ....................... $185.00
**MINI. BURL BOWL,** very thin w/slightly protruding lip & foot, 3⅜″ D., 1⅛″ H.
................................ $475.00
**BUTTER PRINT,** round, w/turned handle, stylized tulip & leaves, 2¾″ D., 2⅞″ L. ............................... $50.00

*Row II, L to R*
**BURL FOOTED BOWL,** 3⅛″ H.
................................ $105.00
**MINI. TREEN BUTTER PADDLE,** w/backward looking bird on end of handle, 6″ L. .......................... $175.00
**BURL FOOTED BOWL,** scrubbed ext. & drk. int., 4¾″ D., 2″ H. ...... $175.00
**TREEN CUP,** hand carved from maple, old red varnish finish, age cracks, 3″ D., 2″ H. .............................. $55.00
**TREEN BOX,** w/threaded cap, age cracks, 3¼″ H. ................. $40.00

*Row III, L to R*
**WOODEN BUTTER PRINT,** round, tulip & leaf design, has had inserted handle, minor age cracks, 4″ D. ......... $55.00
**MINI. BOX,** curly maple, sgn. in several places, "S.P. Freeman, Fort Wayne, 1846," lid has minor corner damage & is slightly warped, 3″ x 3½″ x 5″ ............ $380.00
**WOODEN BUTTER PRINT,** round, deeply cut tulip & heart design, 3¾″ D.
................................ $150.00

A-MA Aug. 1982      *Robert W. Skinner Inc.*
**WOODEN PIGGIN,** Am., 18th C., locked laps, 6½″ H., 7½″ D. .... $250.00*
**TURNED WOODEN CHARGER,** 18th C., wide rim, 18½″ D. ........ $950.00*
**TURNED COVERED WOODEN BOWL,** Am., 18th C., 5″ H., 5½″ D.
................................ $1150.00*

A-OH July 1982      *Garth's Auctions, Inc.*
*Row I, L to R*
**WOODEN BUTTER PRINT,** round, small age cracks, 3½″ D., 5¾″ L.
................................ $125.00
**WOODEN BUTTER MOLD,** round cased, 4⅝″ D. .................. $50.00
**BURL BOWL,** w/protruding rim & foot, 7⅜″ D., 2¼″ H. ............... $350.00
**WOODEN BUTTER PRINT,** round cased, 3½″ D. .................. $100.00
**WOODEN BUTTER PRINT,** round, deeply cut double tulip & heart, age crack in center, 4¼″ D., 4¾″ L. ........ $55.00

*Row II, L to R*
**TREEN CHALICE,** old chip on base, 5¾″ H. ................................ $5.00
**WOVEN SPLINT BASKET,** w/bent reed handle, 5¼″ H. .......... $30.00
**WOVEN SPLINT BASKET,** a little wear, 8″ D., 3¾″ H. plus wooden handle
................................ $65.00
**WOVEN SPLINT BASKET,** w/bent reed handle, br. stain, 6½″ H. .... $25.00
**WOODEN BUTTER PRINT,** Star of David, age cracks & chips, 3¼″ D., 5½″ H.
................................ $8.00

*Row III, L to R*
**WOVEN SPLINT BASKET,** w/wooden mellon ribs, faded red stripe, 8½″ x 9″, 4″ H. ............................... $155.00
**WOODEN JEWELRY BOX,** openwork vintage base, some edge damage on lid & base, old drk. finish, 5½″ x 8½″, 6″ H.
................................ $85.00
**WOVEN SPLINT BUTTOCKS BASKET,** a little wear, 8″ x 8¾″, 5″ H. plus wooden handle ................. $85.00

A-OH July 1982      *Garth's Auctions, Inc.*
**WOODEN BUTTER PRINT,** primitive eagle, worn old red paint, 4″ D.
................................ $300.00
**WOODEN BUTTER PRINT,** small eagle, broken & glued, 3″ D. ..... $50.00
**WOODEN BUTTER PRINT,** turned handle attached w/wood screws is an old addition, rim chips, 5″ D. ....... $135.00
**WOODEN BUTTER PRINT,** small eagle, worn old red paint, age cracks, 3⅜″ D. ................................ $200.00
**WOODEN BUTTER PRINT,** eagle, 3¾″ D. ................................ $200.00
**CAST IRON DOOR KNOCKER,** in form of hand & ball, painted blk., 6¼″ L.
................................ $22.50
**WOODEN BUTTER PRINT,** pineapple & tulips, 1 pc. turned wooden handle has old filled-in repr., edge chipped, 3¾″ D.
................................ $65.00
**COPPER PEACOCK MOLD,** worn tin lining, 4¼″ H. ................. $85.00
**WOODEN BUTTER PRINT,** 1 pc., edge wear, 3¾″ D. ................. $140.00
**WOODEN BUTTER PRINT,** cross shape design w/squares of chip carving, 4¾″ D. ........................ $125.00
**WOODEN BUTTER PRINT,** 1 pc., w/carved wooden handle, 4¼″ D.
................................ $175.00
**MAPLE PADDLE,** w/burl bowl, 7½″ L.
................................ $210.00

A-MA Aug. 1983      *Richard A. Bourne Co., Inc.*
*Row I, L to R*
**TREENWARE SPOONS,** pr., fruitwood
................................ $80.00
**SM. BURLED BOWL,** 7″ D. .. $100.00
**SM. OVAL BURLED BOWL,** 11¾″ L.
................................ $225.00
*Row II, L to R*
**LIGNUM VITAE MORTAR & PESTLE,** 6½″ H. .............. $90.00
**LRG. TURNED WOODEN BOWL,** slight age split, 19½″ D. ......... $70.00

*Price does not include 10% buyer fee.

A-MA Aug. 1982          *Robert W. Skinner Inc.*
**MINIATURE CAST IRON TEA KETTLE,** Am., early 19th C., cover w/brass finial, gooseneck spout, 3 feet, 4½" H. ........................ $600.00*
**CAST IRON TILTING TEA KETTLE,** Am., 18th C., gooseneck spout, back sgn. "W:S.3" in an oval, 9½" H. ...... $700.00

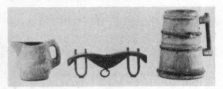

A-MA Aug. 1982          *Robert W. Skinner Inc.*
**WOODENWARE,** 2-pcs., Am., early 19th C., carved pitcher, 5" H., goose yoke, 10½" L. ........................... $125.00*
**WOODEN TANKARD,** Am., 18th C., hickory hoops, 9" H. .......... $325.00*

A-MA Aug. 1982          *Robert W. Skinner Inc.*
**FOOTED COVERED WOODEN SALT,** Am., 18th C., 5¼" H., 3¼" D. ........................... $250.00*
**SHALLOW WOODEN BOWL,** 18th C., 3" H., 8" D. ................... $150.00*
**OPEN BURL SALT,** Am., 18th C., 1½" H., 2" D. .................... $150.00*

A-MA Aug. 1982          *Robert W. Skinner Inc.*
**WOODEN BOX,** early 19th C., compass & chip carved hearts & circles, base mkd. "D.X.B.," no paint, 4¼" x 5½" .. $425.00*
**WOODEN BOX,** N. Eng., early 19th C., painted & grained imitation rosewood, old repr., 9¼" x 11¾" ............. $300.00*
**WOODEN PANTRY BOXES,** 3-pcs., N. Eng., early 19th C., 1 round blue-gray w/1 finger, 1 slightly oval drk. gray w/3 fingers & 1 round in old blue paint, 3¾" D., 7½" D., oval: 4½" x 5½" ................. $525.00*

A-MA Aug. 1982          *Robert W. Skinner Inc.*
**COVERED WOODEN BOWL,** Am., late 18th C., painted wh., 5¼" H., 3" D. ............................ $325.00*
**CARVED WOODEN BOX,** Am., rectangular w/sliding lid, mkd. "L.M. 1731," painted gr., 3¼" H., 6¾" L., 3½" D. ............................ $2100.00*
**BURL BOWL,** Am., 18th C., bottom stained, 2" H., 5¼" D. ......... $225.00*

A-MA July 1982          *Robert W. Skinner Inc.*
*L to R*
**WOODEN BUTTER MOLD,** Europe, 19th C., double shield eagle decor., 6¼" D. ............................ $210.00*
**WOODEN BUTTER MOLDS,** lot of 2, Am., 19th C., 1 w/eagle, other w/star & leaf decor., 4" D. ................ $160.00*
**WOODEN BUTTER MOLD,** Am., 19th C., double sided pinwheel & tulip decor., 4½" D. ...................... $150.00*

A-MA Aug. 1982          *Robert W. Skinner Inc.*
**TURNED WOODEN CUP,** Am., 19th C., painted red, 2¾" H., rim 4⅛" D. ............................ $150.00*
**WOODEN BUTTER WORKER,** N. Eng., early 19th C., hand carved, 5¼" L. ............................ $380.00*
**WOODEN TURNED DIPPER,** N. Eng., early 19th C., 8" L. ........... $130.00*
**WOODEN CUP-SHAPED DIPPER,** N. Eng., early 19th C., string repr. rim, 3¾" D. ............................ $160.00*

A-MA Aug. 1982          *Robert W. Skinner Inc.*
**TURNED WOODEN WINE CUP,** Am., early 19th C., br. & yellow sponge decor., 3½" H. ...................... $210.00*
**TURNED WOODEN COVERED SUGAR,** N. Eng., early 19th C., incised line decor., painted deep blue gr., 4⅛" H., rim 3¼" D. ................... $375.00*
**TURNED WOODEN COVERED SUGAR,** N. Eng., early 19th C., cover repr., sponge painted decor., 3½" H. ............................ $225.00*
**TURNED WOODEN COVERED SUGAR,** N. Eng., early 19th C., painted yellow-br., sponge style, 3¼" H. ............................ $370.00*

A-OH July 1982          *Garth's Auctions, Inc.*
**WOODEN BUTTER PRINT,** "Lolly-Pop," stylized tulip, 9" L. ....... $325.00
**WOODEN BUTTER PRINT,** round, pot of flowers w/"M," 3⅜" D. ........ $45.00
**STEEL FORKS,** set of 6, 2-tine w/carved bone handles, slight deterioration on ends & one metal cap is gone, 6½" L. .. $25.00
**WOODEN BUTTER PRINT,** round, double w/stylized tulip & leaves on one side & star flower on other, 3¾" D. .. $55.00
**MAPLE PADDLE,** w/curved handle & some curl, 8¼" L. .............. $60.00
**WOODEN BUTTER PRINT,** rectangular, stars, hearts & leaf pinwheel, 3½" x 5⅞" ......................... $145.00
**WOODEN BUTTER PRINT,** stylized tulip & other flowers, curved back & finger grips & initials "M.L.," 3⅞" D. ... $175.00
**WOODEN BUTTER PRINT,** almond shaped, double, sides are carved "M.C." & "P.R.C.," 3¾" x 6¾" ............. $325.00

A-MA July 1982          *Robert W. Skinner Inc.*
*L to R*
**BURL SCOOP,** N. Eng., 18th C., 5" D. ............................ $250.00*
**BURL BOWL,** Am., 18th C. .. $225.00*

A-MA Aug. 1983    *Richard A. Bourne Co., Inc.*
*BURLED WOOD ITEMS*
*Row I, L to R*
**DIPPER,** some wear to edges of bowl, 6½" L. ........................... $200.00
**BOWL,** carved handles on side, slight roughage to edge of bowl, 18¼" L. ............................ $900.00
**BOWL,** 10½" D. .............. $225.00
*Row II, L to R*
**BOWL,** carved foot & outer edge, 22¼" D. ............................ $1600.00
**LRG. BOWL,** carved molded outer edge, 19¼" D. ...................... $800.00

A-OH Jan. 1983    *Garth's Auctions, Inc.*
**WRT. IRON FORK,** tooling on handle, 16½″ L. ................... $25.00
**LADLE,** wrt. iron & brass, 15″ L. ............................ $50.00
**BUTTER WORKING PADDLE,** maple, some curl, 11¾″ L. ........... $55.00

**TIN COOKIE CUTTER,** Dutch woman, 5¼″ L. ...................... $25.00
**SKIMMER,** wrt. iron & brass, 17¾″ L. ......................... $55.00
**TIN COOKIE CUTTER,** greaser fig 148, some damage, 5¼″ L. ......... $25.00
**TIN COOKIE CUTTER,** horse, 5¾″ L. ............................ $50.00
**TIN COOKIE CUTTER,** pig w/long snout, 5″ L. .................. $75.00
**TIN COOKIE CUTTER,** hobby horse, damage, 5¼″ L. .............. $35.00
**BUTTER PADDLE,** curly maple, 9″ L. ........................... $95.00
**TIN COOKIE CUTTER,** dog, 4″ L. ............................... $30.00
**TIN COOKIE CUTTER,** pig, 4½″ L. .............................. $45.00
**TIN COOKIE CUTTER,** horse head, dog legs & fat bobbed tail, damage, 6⅝″ L. ......................... $45.00
**TIN COOKIE CUTTER,** elephant, 4½″ L. ......................... $105.00
**TIN COOKIE CUTTER,** lion, 3⅞″ L. ............................. $12.50

A-OH April 1983    *Garth's Auctions, Inc.*
*PEWTER ICE CREAM MOLDS*
**MEDALLION W/COUPLE,** 3¾″ D. ................................. $20.00
**CHICKEN,** "E & Co. N.Y.," 3½″ H. ............................. $15.00
**BATTLESHIP,** "E & Co. N.Y.," 7¼″ L. .......................... $22.50
**ROADSTER,** rumble seat, 4¾″ L. ............................... $20.00
**TURKEY,** 4¾″ H. .............................................. $20.00

A-OH Feb. 1983    *Garth's Auctions, Inc.*
*PEWTER ICE CREAM MOLDS*
**SCALLOPED BASKET,** 5″ ..... $40.00
**CLOVER,** "E & Co N.Y.," 5″ .... $50.00
**COW,** 4½″ ................... $100.00
**CABBAGE,** 3½″ ............... $35.00
**BOOK,** "Pat. applied for 1888. E & Co. N.Y.," 4½″ ................. $35.00
**DAHLIA,** 4″ ................. $40.00
**CAT,** 3½″ ................... $70.00
**GEORGE WASHINGTON IN HATCHET HEAD,** "E & Co N.Y.," wire hangers added, 3¾″ ..... $50.00
**MAN IN TOP HAT,** "E & Co. N.Y.," 5″ H. ...................... $45.00
**AIRPLANE,** "E & Co. N.Y.," 5″ ............................... $65.00
**DESK W/MAN & WOMAN,** 3¾″ D. ................................ $55.00
**CANNON,** 4¼″ L. ............. $30.00
**HORSESHOE,** "E & Co. N.Y.," 4¾″ L. .......................... $60.00
**OLD CONVERTIBLE,** "E & Co. N.Y.," 4¾″ L. .................... $55.00
**JACK-O-LANTERN W/TOP HAT,** "E & Co. N.Y. Pat. applied, 3½″ L. .................. $55.00
**HEART W/CUPID,** 3″ ......... $75.00
**THREE PANSIES,** "E & Co. N.Y.," 4½″ L. ...................... $45.00
**CHICKEN,** 3¾″ L. ............ $55.00
**STEAMER,** "E & Co. N.Y.," 7″ L. ............................. $40.00
**CABIN CRUISER,** 5½″ L. ...... $50.00

---

**AIRPLANE,** "E & Co. N.Y.," 4¾″ L. ........................... $17.50
**THREE FLOWERS,** "E & Co. N.Y.," 5″ L. ....................... $20.00
**EGGS,** embossed rabbits, "Made in Germany," 6½″ L. ............ $20.00
**STRAWBERRY,** 3″ H. ......... $22.50
**BUNCH OF GRAPES,** 5″ L. ... $15.00
**LAMB,** "E & Co. N.Y.," 3¼″ L. .. $20.00
**THREE-PART TULIP,** 3″ H. ... $20.00
**DOE,** 3½″ L. ................. $45.00
**SCROLLED BASKET,** "E & Co. N.Y.," 5″ L. ..................... $20.00
**WITCH ON BROOM,** 5½″ H. .. $77.50
**CABBAGE,** 3¾″ L. ............ $20.00
**HATCHET HEAD,** bust of Washington, "E & Co. N.Y.," 3⅜″ H. .......... $3.00
**CAMEL,** 5″ L. ............... $20.00
**JACK-O-LANTERN,** cigar & hat, "E & Co. N.Y. Patent Applied," 3⅝″ H. ................. $52.50
**BOY IN SAILBOAT,** 4¾″ H. ... $42.50

A-MA Aug. 1983    *Robert W. Eldred Co., Inc.*
**PEWTER MEASURES,** set of 7, 1½″ H. ........................... $280.00

A-MA Aug. 1983    *Richard A. Bourne Co., Inc.*
L to R
**LRG. COVERED WOODEN JAR,** sgn. "TP White Painesville, OH, June 16th 1871," turned from 1 pc. of fruitwood w/matching lid, base handle, 12¾″ D., 9½″ H. ............................... $1200.00
**SM. WINDSOR CRICKET,** Am., early 19th C., famboo turned legs, stripped & ref., traces of old chrome yellow paint ............................ $150.00

*Left*
A-MA July 1982    *Robert W. Skinner Inc.*
**WOODEN CANDLE BOX,** Am., 18th C., leather hinges, 12¼″ L. ..... $425.00*
*Right*
A-MA July 1982    *Robert W. Skinner Inc.*
**ROUND BURL BOWL,** Am., 18th C., rectangular handles, 11½″ D. ... $450.00*

A-MA July 1982    *Robert W. Skinner Inc.*
**HANGING SPOON RACK,** pine, N. Eng., 18th C., old natural color, 11¾″ W., 26¼″ H. .................... $950.00*

*Price does not include 10% buyer fee.

A-OH Feb. 1983     *Garth's Auctions, Inc.*
**STEEL FLATWARE,** set of 24 (2 illus.), 12 forks & 12 knives, bone handles w/pewter inlay, mkd. "New York Knife Co. Walden N.Y.," 9" L. ............... $70.00
**PEWTER TEA SPOONS,** 5, faint mark on one, 5¾" L. ................. $25.00
**BUTTER MOLD,** 4-part wooden, primitive house design, missing parts & age crack, 3½" x 4¼" x 5" .......... $155.00
**BUTTER PADDLE,** curly maple, varnished, 12½" L. ............... $135.00
**PEWTER SPOONS,** 3 w/seal handles, 6½" L. ................. $22.50
**PEWTER TABLESPOONS,** 3, similar to above, one mkd. "J. Sabadie," 8" L. ................................................. $30.00
**CASED BUTTER PRINT,** rectangular, chip-carved geometric design w/4 stars, scrubbed finish, 5" x 9" .......... $75.00
**PEWTER LADLES,** pr., "Shaw & Fisher, Sheffield," 6½" L. ............... $30.00
**WAFER IRON,** for a cook stove, star, people, umbrella, etc., broken hinge, 4½" D. ................................. $30.00
**STEEL FLATWARE,** 6 forks & 6 knives, (2 illus.), bone handles, 4½" L. .... $50.00
**PEWTER FORKS,** 4, 6¾" L. .... $35.00

A-MA Aug. 1983     *Robert C. Eldred Co., Inc.*
*Row I, L to R*
**TURNED WOOD MORTAR & PESTLE** .......................... $40.00
**TURNED MORTAR & PESTLE,** elm, 4" H. ................................. $45.00
**TURNED WOOD MORTAR & PESTLE,** elm, 9" H. ............ $70.00
*Row II, L to R*
**TURNED MORTAR & PESTLE,** in Lignum Vitae, 8" H. ........... $130.00
**TURNED WOOD MORTAR & PESTLE,** elm, 8" H. ....... $110.00
**TURNED WOOD MORTAR & PESTLE,** 8" H. ............... $120.00

A-OH Jan. 1983     *Garth's Auctions, Inc.*
**SEWER PIPE TURTLE,** break reglued, 7¾" L. ........................ $15.00
**SEWER PIPE,** miniature clay 4-part, impressed "The H.B. Camp Co Aultman, O," flakes, 4" L. ................. $10.00
**SEWER PIPE DESK SET,** hand tooled, 8¾" W., 3¾" H. ................ $220.00
**SEWER PIPE PAPERWEIGHT,** Minerva head, impressed "The Nelsonville Sewer Pipe Co, Nelsonville, Ohio," edge flakes, 4½" L. ................. $25.00
**SEWER PIPE PLAQUE,** 2 roses, 6" D. ................................................. $15.00
**SEWER PIPE PLAQUE,** cherubs, 5¼" D. ................................................. $15.00
**SEWER PIPE DISH,** impressed "Adams, Allison & Co, Manufacturers, Middleburg, Summit Co, O," 3" D. .......... $20.00
**THREE CLAY MARBLES,** Rockingham glaze .......................... $12.00
**SEWER PIPE ADVERTISING WHIMSEY,** horseshoe, "Sample of body and glaze, N.V. Walker, Clay Manfg' Co. Vitrified Sewer Pipe, Walkers, Ohio," flakes, 10" L., 6½" H. .......... $40.00
**CLAY PIPE,** reed stem ........ $10.00
**SHOE,** Ohio wh. clay, 5" L. ..... $12.50
**SEWER PIPE PAPERWEIGHT,** mkd. "The Crown Co, Canal Dover, Ohio," 3" x 4½" ......................... $22.50
**WHITE CLAY INDIAN,** amber glaze, incised "March 26, 1910, L.H.," minor flakes & imperfections, 7" H. ..... $45.00
**SEWER PIPE STRING HOLDER,** man's head, edge flakes & wear, 6¾" L., 5¾" H. ........................ $225.00
**SEWER PIPE DESK SET,** chips & flakes, 5" D., 2¼" H. .................. $17.50

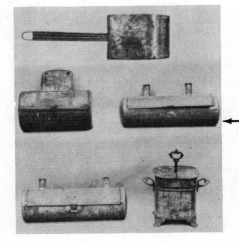

A-OH Jan. 1983     *Garth's Auctions, Inc.*
*Row I, L to R*
**WHITE CLAY FROG,** clear glaze w/amber spots, incised "W. O'Brien, 1907," 3⅜" L. ........................ $140.00
**MINIATURE JUG,** gray & br., Akron, OH, flakes, 1¾" H. ............. $15.00
**WHITE CLAY HORSESHOE W/ HORSE'S HEAD,** drk. br. glaze, 2⅛" L. ............. $15.00
**WHITE CLAY BOOT,** metallic tan glaze, flakes, 1⅜" H. ................. $10.00
**SEWER TILE FROG,** 3¾" L. .... $35.00
*Row II, L to R*
**TWO TINY JUGS,** wh. & br., Akron, 11/16" & 13/16" ................. $75.00
**MINIATURE SEWER TILE WASHBOARD,** Akron, ½" x 1" ....... $130.00
**TWO TINY JUGS,** joined, Akron, 13/16" H. ................................. $20.00
**BOOT CHARM,** 2-tone br., clear glaze, flakes, 1⅛" H. ................. $15.00
**CHAMBER POT,** attached lid, wh. clay, clear glaze, ⅞" H. ............. $45.00
**CHAMBER POT,** attached lid, cobalt blue glaze, mkd. "Thomas Pottery," ¾" H. ................................. $105.00
*Row III, L to R*
**MINIATURE SEWER TILE FROG,** 2" L. ................................. $100.00
**TWO-HANDLED FLATTENED JUG,** embossed, wh. clay, clear glaze, 1" H. ................................. $30.00
**MINIATURE BELL TILE TRAP,** mkd. "National Sewer Pipe Co. Akron, O.," 3⅞" L. ................................. $20.00
**PRIMITIVE POTTERY DOMINO,** attrib. to Foster Pottery, Mt. Eaten, OH, 1⅜" L. ................................. $30.00
**FLATTENED JUG,** br. glaze, 1⅝" H. ................................. $5.00

A-MA July 1982     *Richard A. Bourne Co., Inc.*
*Row I*
**TIN COVERED SCOOP,** 21½" L. ................................. $110.00
*Row II, L to R*
**TIN HANGING CANDLE BOX,** hanger is weak, 9¾" L. ................. $90.00
**TIN HANGING CANDLE BOX,** tag inside "Candle Box Which Came From Gov. Tichnor's House," 4¼" D., 14" L. ................................. $150.00
*Row III, L to R*
**TIN CANDLE BOX,** 4¼" D., 14" L. ................................. $160.00
**TIN EGG COOKER,** 19th C., 10" H. ................................. $75.00

A-OH Feb. 1983    *Garth's Auctions, Inc.*
**TREEN DIPPER,** handmade, 20th C., 12"
L. . . . . . . . . . . . . . . . . . . . . . . . . $60.00
**TRAMMEL,** brass, bird's head, late 19th
C., 16¾" L. . . . . . . . . . . . . . . . $125.00
**DIPPER,** brass & wrt. iron, cutout handle
design, 12¼" L. . . . . . . . . . . . . $75.00
**FORK,** wrt. iron, good detail, 13½" L.
. . . . . . . . . . . . . . . . . . . . . . . . . . $90.00
**SCOOP,** walnut w/some burl, 20th C.,
9¼" L. . . . . . . . . . . . . . . . . . . . $105.00
**SPATULA,** wrt. iron, blade is a little
uneven, 13¾" L. . . . . . . . . . . . . $35.00
**TASTER,** copper, slender wrt. iron
handle, worn tinning, 9¾" L. . . . . . $95.00
**PIPE TONGS,** wrt. steel, stamped "J.K.,"
16" L. . . . . . . . . . . . . . . . . . . . . $200.00
**DIPPER,** wrt. iron, nicely flared handle,
worn tinning, 16¼" L. . . . . . . . . . . $15.00
**TREEN DIPPER,** pouring spout, nicely
made, 12¼" L. . . . . . . . . . . . . . $175.00
**DOUGH SCRAPER,** wrt. iron, some
damage, 3⅜" W. . . . . . . . . . . . . $75.00
**SHAKER TREEN PINCUSHION,**
w/table clamp, worn orig. yellow varnish &
worn old red plush covering, age cracks,
repr., 5⅛" H. . . . . . . . . . . . . . . . $75.00
**TREEN PINCUSHION,** w/table clamp,
worn orig. striping, worn old br. plush
covering, 2½" L. . . . . . . . . . . . . . $60.00
**BUTTER WORKER,** primitive birch, 9½"
L. . . . . . . . . . . . . . . . . . . . . . . . . $45.00

A-OH Jan. 1983    *Garth's Auctions, Inc.*
**NAIL RAKE,** wrt. iron, 10½" L.
. . . . . . . . . . . . . . . . . . . . . . . . . . $35.00
**YELLOWWARE FOOD MOLD,** 6-petal
flower, 3" D. . . . . . . . . . . . . . . . . $35.00
**THREE QUILT PATTERNS,** tin, largest
is 4" . . . . . . . . . . . . . . . . . . . . . . $50.00
**YELLOWWARE FOOD MOLDS,** pine-
apple, 4¾" x 7" . . . . . . . . . . . . . $135.00
**COOKIE OR CANDY BOARD,** maple,
rooster, 3" x 3¾" . . . . . . . . . . . . $135.00
**TIN COOKIE CUTTER,** bird, 3¼" L.
. . . . . . . . . . . . . . . . . . . . . . . . . . $25.00
**BURL BUTTER SCOOP,** ash, 9¼" L.
. . . . . . . . . . . . . . . . . . . . . . . . . $105.00

A-OH July 1982    *Garth's Auctions, Inc.*
**LIGHTING DEVICE,** wood & wrt. iron,
spring candle clip, 28½" L. . . . . . . $75.00
**SPATULA,** brass & wrt. iron, 15" L.
. . . . . . . . . . . . . . . . . . . . . . . . . . $55.00
**CARVED WOODEN BUTTER PRINT,**
round, eagle design, glued break, weath-
ered surface, turned handle, 4" D.
. . . . . . . . . . . . . . . . . . . . . . . . . . $85.00
**STICKING TOMMY CANDLE HOLD-
ER,** wrt. iron, 12" L. . . . . . . . . . . $95.00
**CARVED WOODEN BUTTER PRINT,**
round, eagle design w/star, old drk. finish,
4½" D. . . . . . . . . . . . . . . . . . . . . $300.00
**FORK W/WIDE HANDLE,** wrt. iron,
stamped "F.B.S. Canton, O. Pat Jan 26,
'86," 15⅞" L. . . . . . . . . . . . . . . . $65.00
**PEWTER PORRINGER,** Am., cast "Old
Eng."-type handle, 4½" D. . . . . . $200.00
**FOOD CHOPPER,** crescent blade,
turned wooden handle, brass ferrules, 6"
W. . . . . . . . . . . . . . . . . . . . . . . . . $15.00
**PEWTER PORRINGER,** Am., cast floral
handle, 5½" D. . . . . . . . . . . . . . . $225.00
**WOODEN BUTTER PRINT,** round,
bird w/raised wings, turned handle, 3¾" D.
. . . . . . . . . . . . . . . . . . . . . . . . . $260.00
**WOODEN BUTTER PRINT,** round
eagle w/star, turned handle, worn surface,
3⅜" D. . . . . . . . . . . . . . . . . . . . . $225.00
**WOODEN BUTTER PRINT,** round,
baby eagle w/arrows in talons, turned
handle, 4½" D. . . . . . . . . . . . . . . $295.00
**WOODEN BUTTER PRINT,** round,
stylized tulip, turned inserted handle, 4⅛"
D. . . . . . . . . . . . . . . . . . . . . . . . . $195.00
**WOODEN BUTTER PRINT,** round tulip
& leaves, turned handle and letter "J," sm.
age cracks, 4⅜" D. . . . . . . . . . . . $45.00
**FORK W/LONG TWISTED HANDLE,**
wrt. iron, turned wooden hand hold, 27" L.
. . . . . . . . . . . . . . . . . . . . . . . . . . $10.00

**TIN COOKIE CUTTER,** tailed bird, 4¾"
. . . . . . . . . . . . . . . . . . . . . . . . . . $35.00
**CAST IRON TRIVET,** cat's head, adj. 5th
leg for tilting, 8¾" L. . . . . . . . . . $145.00
**WRT. IRON FORK,** 10" L. . . . . . $50.00
**TASTER,** wrt. iron & copper, 10¼" L.
. . . . . . . . . . . . . . . . . . . . . . . . . $110.00
**WRT. IRON FORK,** 9¾" L. . . . . . $65.00
→ **COOKIE BOARD,** 20th C., 3-section
carved, wooden, flag, fox & flower, 2" x 6½"
. . . . . . . . . . . . . . . . . . . . . . . . . . $25.00
**CUTOUT WOODEN BIRD,** tack eyes,
orig. br., wh., blk. & yellow paint, some
wear, cracks & chips, 9" L. . . . . . . $35.00
**IRONSTONE FOOD MOLD,** pine-
apple, 3¼" L. . . . . . . . . . . . . . . . $45.00

A-OH Mar. 1983    *Garth's Auctions, Inc.*
**STRAP HINGES,** pr. (1 illus.), wrt. iron,
18" L. . . . . . . . . . . . . . . . . . . . . . $10.00
**GREASE LAMP,** wrt. iron, pan w/wick
support, sawtooth trammel hanger, adj.
from 24" L. . . . . . . . . . . . . . . . . . $175.00
**TWO-TINE FORK,** wrt. iron, 14½" L.
. . . . . . . . . . . . . . . . . . . . . . . . . . $12.50
**CANDLE HOLDER,** wrt. iron, spring-
held trammel, repr., hole, 23" L.
. . . . . . . . . . . . . . . . . . . . . . . . . $375.00
**TWO-TINE FORK,** wrt. iron, 16¼" L.
. . . . . . . . . . . . . . . . . . . . . . . . . . $12.50
**SKIMMER,** wrt. iron, some wear on bowl,
22" L. . . . . . . . . . . . . . . . . . . . . . $12.50
**WIND CHIME,** tin, 3 dimensional steam
locomotive & 5 flat engines, some damage
& wear, top engine is 4" L. . . . . . $175.00
**CANDLE HOLDER,** wrt. iron, sawtooth
trammel hanger, adj. from 27" . . . $805.00

A-MA July 1982    *Richard A. Bourne Co., Inc.*
*Top to Bottom*
**BRASS LADLE,** ca. 1829, touch of
Richard Lee or Richard Lee, Jr., 10¾" O.L.
. . . . . . . . . . . . . . . . . . . . . . . . . $475.00
**BRASS LADLE,** touch of Richard Lee or
Richard Lee, Jr., 10¼" L. . . . . . . $175.00
**BRASS SKIMMER,** touch of Richard Lee
or Richard Lee, Jr., 14½" L. . . . . $250.00
**BRASS SKIMMER,** slightly bent, un-
known maker, 19⅜" L. . . . . . . . . . $125
**BRASS SPOON,** unknown maker, worn,
10½" L. . . . . . . . . . . . . . . . . . . . . $30.00

A-MA July 1982　　*Richard A. Bourne Co., Inc.*
*Row I, L to R*
**BURL BOWL W/COVER,** 11″ D.
. . . . . . . . . . . . . . . . . . . . . . . . . . . . $1200.00
**CHOPPING BOWL W/HANGER,** 1
pc., weathered, some age cracking, 16½″
x 18⅛″ . . . . . . . . . . . . . . . . . . . . . $1100.00
*Row II*
**BURL LONG-HANDLED DIPPER,** 1
pc. of wood, 9½″ D., 21″ O.L. . . . $500.00
*Row III, L to R*
**BALANCE SCALES,** ivory & iron
w/brass pan & brass counterweight, orig.
container w/sliding cane ring, untouched,
14¾″ O.L. . . . . . . . . . . . . . . . . . . . $300.00
**WOODEN RAZOR BOX,** 10½″ L.
. . . . . . . . . . . . . . . . . . . . . . . . . . . . $200.00

A-MA Aug. 1982　　*Robert W. Skinner Inc.*
*L to R*
**PAINTED COVERED BUCKET,** Am.,
early 19th C., flat fitted cover, straight
tapering sides w/stave construction over-
lapped wythes, bail handle, painted red,
8½″ H. . . . . . . . . . . . . . . . . . . . . $500.00*
**PINE CANTEEN,** Am., late 18th C.,
drum-shaped w/interlocking wythes,
pewter mouthpiece, 9¾″ D. . . . . $120.00*
**OAK BARREL CANTEEN,** Am., late
18th C., narrow staves w/overlapped
wythes (1 missing), initialed, 9¾″ H.
. . . . . . . . . . . . . . . . . . . . . . . . . . . . $90.00*

A-MA July 1982　　*Robert W. Skinner Inc.*
**HANDLED WOODEN BURL BOWL,**
N. Eng., 18th C., small hole on one side, 14″
x 15″ . . . . . . . . . . . . . . . . . . . . . . $825.00*

A-MA Aug. 1982　　*Robert W. Skinner Inc.*
*L to R*
**PAINTED COVERED BOWL,** Am.,
18th C., 7″ H., 7½″ D. . . . . . . . . $700.00*
**WOODEN PLATE,** Am., 18th C., 12″ D.
. . . . . . . . . . . . . . . . . . . . . . . . . . . . $225.00*
**WOODEN MIXING BOWL,** Am., 18th
C., outside w/wh. paint . . . . . . . $500.00*

A-MA Aug. 1982　　*Robert W. Skinner Inc.*
*L to R*
**MINI. TURNED WOODEN BOWL,** N.
Eng., late 18th C., incised line decor. &
footed base, rim 3⅝″ x 3⅛″, 1¾″ H.
. . . . . . . . . . . . . . . . . . . . . . . . . . . . $200.00*
**MINI. TURNED BURL BOWL,** N. Eng.,
late 18th C., rim 4¼″ D. . . . . . . . $260.00*
**BURL HANDLED CUP,** N. Eng., early
19th C., straight tapered sides, handle in
form of horse's head, 2¾″ H. . . . $325.00*

A-MA Aug. 1982　　*Robert W. Skinner Inc.*
*L to R*
**WOODEN SPICE BOXES,** 3-pcs., N.
Eng., early 19th C., two painted lt. gray-gr.,
the smallest unpainted, 3⅝″ L., 5½″ L. &
5⅞″ L. . . . . . . . . . . . . . . . . . . . . . $525.00*
**SHAKER THREE-FINGERED BOX,** N.
Eng., early 19th C., painted deep gr.,
copper tacks, 11″ L. . . . . . . . . . . $525.00*
**COVERED SPICE BOX,** N. Eng., early
19th C., gray & blk. smoke grained decor.,
narrow yellow band on cover rim & base,
4⅝″ L. . . . . . . . . . . . . . . . . . . . . . $180.00*

A-MA Aug. 1982　　*Robert W. Skinner Inc.*
*L to R*
**WOODEN SPICE BOXES,** 3-pcs., N.
Eng., early 19th C., two painted blue-gray,
one red, 3¼″ D., 4″ D. & 5⅜″ D.
. . . . . . . . . . . . . . . . . . . . . . . . . . . . $400.00*
**WOODEN PANTRY BOXES,** 2-pcs., N.
Eng., early 19th C., worn gray-gr. paint,
copper tacks, 5⅛″ L., 6¼″ L., 3¾″ W. & 4¾″
W. . . . . . . . . . . . . . . . . . . . . . . . . . $325.00*
**SHAKER WOODEN BOX,** N. Eng.,
early 19th C., three-fingered, painted drk.
gr., 8⅜″ x 11⅛″ . . . . . . . . . . . . . . $375.00*

A-MA Aug. 1982　　*Robert W. Skinner Inc.*
*L to R*
**COVERED TURNED WOODEN
BOWL,** Am., early 19th C., low domed
fitted cover w/knob finial, slightly spherical
body on pedestal base, old yellow-ochre
paint, 7¼″ H., 6¾″ D. . . . . . . . . . $600.00*
**DEEP PLATTER,** N. Eng., 18th C., curly
maple, wide flat rim, sharp shoulder, deep
center section, warped, rim chips, 14″ D.
. . . . . . . . . . . . . . . . . . . . . . . . . . . . $900.00*
**COVERED TURNED WOODEN CAN-
ISTER,** Am., 19th C., urn finial, flat cover,
barrel-shaped body, reeded wythes at top
& bottom, traces of old paint, old string
repr., 9″ H. . . . . . . . . . . . . . . . . . $400.00*

A-MA Aug. 1982　　*Robert W. Skinner Inc.*
*L to R*
**WOODEN CHOPPING BOWL,** N.
Eng., early 19th C., hollowed block of
chestnut w/slight footed base, old tin repr.
at one end, 3¾″ H., 8¾″ x 12″ . . . $140.00*
**WOODEN DEEP DISH,** N. Eng., possibly late 18th C., well turned chestnut
w/flat smooth rim, deep flat bottom, 2⅜″
H., 15″ D. . . . . . . . . . . . . . . . . . $1100.00*
**TURNED WOODEN CHOPPING
BOWL,** N. Eng., early 19th C., shallow
thin-walled bowl, narrow rim, yellow
painted underside, leather thong serves as
a repr. & also as a hanger, 12¾″ H.
. . . . . . . . . . . . . . . . . . . . . . . . . . . . $150.00*

A-MA Mar. 1983　　*Robert W. Skinner Inc.*
**LARGE SHALLOW BURL BOWL,**
18th C., oval w/raised ends & shaped
handle holds, flat rim, sm. nicks, crack, 16″
x 21½″ . . . . . . . . . . . . . . . . . . . . $1000.00*

*Price does not include 10% buyer fee.

A-MA Nov. 1982    *Richard A. Bourne Co., Inc.*
**PEWTER**
*Row I, L to R*
**ROY OR WINE-TASTER PORRING-ER**, 2⅛″, attrib. to Richard Lee or I.C. Lewis, ca. 1800-1820 .......... $150.00
**PORRINGER**, 3⅛″, unmkd., Am., ca. 1810, old Eng. style handle w/wedge & triangle bracket ............... $50.00
**PORRINGER**, 3-3/16″, attrib. to Richard Lee or Roswell Gleason, reverse "R" cast in back of handle, minor pitting ..... $75.00
**PORRINGER**, 3¼″, attrib. to Richard Lee or Roswell Gleason, reverse "R" cast in back of handle, minor pitting ..... $90.00
**BASIN PORRINGER**, 3¾″, by Samuel Danforth, Hartford, CT, 1795-1816, Eng. style handle .................. $550.00
*Row II, L to R*
**PORRINGER**, 3-3/16″, unmkd. but attrib. to Danforths, late 18th/early 19th C. ................................. $125.00
**PORRINGER**, 4⅛″, by samuel E. Hamlin, old Eng. handle ............... $650.00
**BASIN PORRINGER**, 4½″, s/"T.D. & S.B.," touch of Thomas D. & Sherman Boardman .................. $250.00
**BASIN PORRINGER**, 4½″, early 19th C., old Eng. handle w/initials "E.C." cast in back, possibly E. Crossman, Taunton, MA or Newport, RI ................ $350.00
*Row III, L to R*
**PORRINGER**, 4½″, unmkd., Eng. geometric handle of type made in early 18th C. ................................. $250.00
**PORRINGER**, 4″, N. Eng., ca. 1800, initials "W.N." cast in back of handle, possibly by William Northey, Lynn, MA, 1764-1804 ..................... $375.00
**PORRINGER**, 4″, N. Eng., ca. 1800, initials "W.N." cast in back of handle, possibly William Northey, Lynn, MA, 1764-1804, slight pitting on inside ..... $275.00

A-MA July 1982    *Robert W. Skinner Inc.*
**WRT. IRON TRIVET**, Am., 18th C. ........................... $800.00*

A-MA July 1982    *Richard A. Bourne Co., Inc.*
**PEWTER**
*Row I, L to R*
**BASIN**, by Thomas Danforth, ca. 1777-1818, little pitting, two old repairs, 9⅛″ D. ................................. $125.00
**BASIN**, by Thomas Badger, MA, ca. 1737-1815, scratches & minor denting, 8″ D. ................................. $325.00
**BASIN**, by S. Stafford & Co., NY, ca. 1794-1830, 7⅞″ D. ............. $400.00
*Row II, L to R*
**BASIN**, by David Melville, Newport, ca. 1755-1793, some wear, 8″ D. .... $225.00
**BASIN**, by Samuel Hamlin or Samuel Hamlin, Jr., touch similar to scroll touches, 7¾″ D. ................... $425.00
**BASIN**, by Samuel Danforth, CT, ca. 1795-1816, 8″ D. ............... $425.00

A-MA July 1982    *Richard A. Bourne Co., Inc.*
**PEWTER**
*Row I, L to R*
**SAUCER-BASED CANDLESTICK**, mkd., Am., orig. snuffer by Flagg & Homan, OH, some surface scratching, 4″ H. ................................. $400.00
**FLUID LAMP**, unmkd., Am., double divergent brass camphene burner, two holes in bottom, complete w/brass caps, 2½″ H. ...................... $30.00
**PORRINGER**, by Samuel Hamlin, Sr., surface scratches from abrasive cleaning, 4½″ H. ...................... $225.00
**PORRINGER**, unmkd., attrib. to Danforth, CT, scratched surface due to abrasive cleaning, 5″ H. ........ $175.00
*Row II, L to R*
**BASIN**, by Frederick Basset, some denting, split in side, 8″ D. .......... $200.00
**BASIN**, by Frederick Basset, repair to bottom, 8″ D. .................. $200.00
**TEAPOT**, unmkd., Am., needs cleaning, 8¼″ H. ........................ $70.00

*Left*
A-MA July 1982    *Richard A. Bourne Co., Inc.*
**PEWTER BASIN**, by Josiah Danforth, ca. 1825-1837, 6″ W. ............. $475.00
*Right*
A-MA July 1982    *Richard A. Bourne Co., Inc.*
*L to R*
**PEWTER DESSERT SPOON**, by George Coldwell, NY, ca. 1787-1811, engraved handle .................. $350.00
**PEWTER DESSERT SPOON**, by George Coldwell, NY, ca. 1787-1811, engraved handle ................. $400.00

A-WA D.C. July 1982  *Adam A. Weschler & Son*
**PEWTER BALUSTER-FORM MEASURES**, set of 8, Eng., 19th C., ½-gill to 1-qt. capacity, 2″ to 6″ H. ......... $225.00*

A-MA July 1982    *Richard A. Bourne Co., Inc.*
**PEWTER**
*L to R*
**PORRINGER**, by Josiah Danforth, ca. 1825-1837, CT, 4″ L. .......... $900.00
**PORRINGER**, by Samuel E. Hamlin, Jr., ca. 1801-1856, repr. to rim, some pitting, 5¼″ L. ...................... $325.00

A-OH July 1982          Garth's Auctions, Inc.
**WRT. IRON & COPPER UTENSIL,** copper blade has drilled holes & worn tinning, 23½″ L. ............... $55.00
**WRT. IRON LADLE,** w/wooden handle, 15½″ L. ..................... $20.00
**WRT. IRON FORK,** w/large curved hanging hook, 20½″ L. ......... $25.00
**WRT. STEEL SUGAR NIPPERS,** minor wear on blades, 9″ L. .......... $45.00
**WRT. IRON DIPPER,** w/straining bowl, 18½″ L. ..................... $25.00
**BRASS SKIMMER,** w/decor. piercing in handle & blade, 20½″ L. ........ $105.00
**WRT. IRON PASTRY CUTTER,** w/wooden handle, 7¼″ L. ........ $25.00
**WRT. IRON & BRASS SKIMMER,** edge splits in blade, 22″ L. ..... $45.00
**WRT. IRON SPATULA,** 17½″ L. ............................. $75.00
**WRT. IRON & BRASS SKIMMER,** w/wide bowl, polished, 24″ L. .... $75.00

A-MA Aug. 1982          Robert W. Skinner Inc.
**IRON DUTCH OVEN,** Am., late 18th C., 6¾″ H., 9¼″ D. ............. $375.00*
**WRT. IRON CAMP STOVE,** Am., 18th C., turned wooden handle, 5¼″ H., 12″ L., 6″ W. ..................... $375.00*

A-MA Aug. 1982          Robert W. Skinner Inc.
**WRT. IRON HANGING GRIDDLE W/RIM,** Am., 18th C., 16″ H., 13″ D. ............................. $175.00*
**WRT. IRON TOASTER,** Am., 18th C., ram's horn handle, 17½″ L., 13½″ W. ............................. $300.00*

A-OH Feb. 1983          Garth's Auctions, Inc.
*TRIVETS*
**TREE & QUADRUPED,** cast brass, sm. break in tree ................... $32.50
**SCROLLED DESIGN,** cast brass, central interlocked medallion, 7½″ L. ........................... $40.00
**SCROLLED,** cast brass, 7¼″ L. ........................... $15.00
**LEAFY FOLIAGE,** cast brass, Eng. registry mark, break in metal, 6¾″ L. ........................... $15.00
**CURVED LATTICE DESIGN,** cast brass, 8½″ L. ................. $10.00
**SHEET BRASS W/IRON FEET,** simple cutout design, 9″ L. ............. $55.00
**SCROLL WORK,** cast bronze, 9″ L. ........................... $15.00
**MASONIC,** cast brass ......... $75.00
**SHEET BRASS W/TURNED FEET,** cutout star & clover, 9¼″ L. ..... $70.00

A-MA July 1982     Richard A. Bourne Co., Inc.
*Row I, L to R*
**LADLE,** copper bowl w/wrt. steel handle, normal denting, 19″ O.L. ...... $120.00
**SKIMMER,** copper bowl w/wrt. steel handle, 18¼″ L. ............... $130.00
**LADLE,** copper plated steel, 19¾″ L. ................................. $35.00

*Row II, L to R*
**JAM KETTLE,** copper w/iron bail handle, 12¾″ D. ..................... $140.00
**POT,** copper w/ring hanger, mkd. "EM," 10″ D., 6½″ H. ................. $150.00
**TEA KETTLE,** Am., 19th C., 12″ O.H. ................................. $375.00

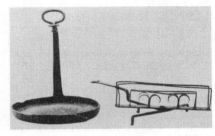

*Left*
A-MA Aug. 1982          Robert W. Skinner Inc.
*L to R*
**3-TINED WRT. IRON FORK,** Am., late 18th C., center tine reticulated, shaft finished by a whitesmith, 19″ L. ............................. $175.00*
**WRT. IRON SPOON,** Am., late 18th C., shaft w/chevron design, 21″ L. .. $50.00*
**BRASS SKIMMER,** Am., early 19th C., wrt. iron handle, 16½″ L. ...... $120.00*

*Right*
A-MA Aug. 1982          Robert W. Skinner Inc.
*L to R*
**BRASS SKIMMER,** Am., late 18th C., wrt. steel handle, 20½″ L. ...... $150.00*
**LONG HANDLED WRT. IRON SKIMMER,** Am., 18th C., 27½″ L. ............................. $130.00*
**WRT. IRON RATCHET PAN LAMP,** Am., 18th C., 27″ L., extended 36″ L. ............................. $500.00*

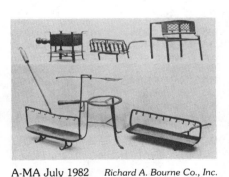

A-MA July 1982     Richard A. Bourne Co., Inc.
*Row I, L to R*
**CAMP STOVE,** type used by the Am. Army during Revolutionary War, 8½″ W., 14″ L., 7¾″ H. ................. $400.00
**WRT. IRON DOWN-HEARTH TOASTER,** 13″ W., 16″ L. ... $400.00
**IRON TRIVET,** does not stand evenly, pitted surface, 11″ W., 9″ D., 10¾″ H. ............................. $80.00

*Row II, L to R*
**DOWN-HEARTH SPIT,** for small game, rusted surface, 17¼″ L., handle: 22″ L. ............................. $375.00
**DOWN-HEARTH TRIVET & ADJ. SPIT,** trivet: 8″ D., 15″ L., 10″ H. ............................. $350.00
**DOWN-HEARTH SPIT,** for small game, normal rusting, 18″ L., 12″ handle ............................. $425.00

A-OH April 1983        *Garth's Auctions, Inc.*
**COOKIE BOARD**, pine, age cracks, metal fasteners, 19" x 29" . . . . . . . $17.50
**COOKIE CUTTER**, tin, Dutchman, 5" H. . . . . . . . . . . . . . . . . . . . . . . . . . . . $15.00

**COOKIE CUTTER**, tin, bird, handle missing, 4" L. . . . . . . . . . . . . . . . . . $15.00
**COOKIE CUTTER**, tin, scalloped circle, 4¼" D. . . . . . . . . . . . . . . . . . . . . . $7.00
**COOKIE CUTTER**, tin, horse, minor separation, 3⅝" L. . . . . . . . . . . . $12.00
**COOKIE CUTTER**, tin, simple Dutchman, 4½" H. . . . . . . . . . . . . . . . . $15.00

**COOKIE CUTTER**, tin, Dutchman in profile, mkd. "Germany," 3" H. . . . . $8.00
**COOKIE CUTTER**, tin, bird, 4" D. . . . . . . . . . . . . . . . . . . . . . . . . . . . . . $10.00

**COOKIE CUTTER**, tin, simple Dutchman in profile, 3⅝" H. . . . . . . . . $20.00
**COOKIE CUTTER**, tin, fish, slightly battered & resoldered, 4⅞" L. . . . . $4.00

**COOKIE CUTTER**, tin, rabbit, slightly battered, 4" L. . . . . . . . . . . . . . . $12.00
**COOKIE CUTTER**, tin, bear, 4¾" L. . . . . . . . . . . . . . . . . . . . . . . . . . . . . $7.00

**COOKIE CUTTER**, tin, stylized pine tree, 5" H. . . . . . . . . . . . . . . . . . . $27.50
**COOKIE CUTTER**, tin, hen, 4½" H. . . . . . . . . . . . . . . . . . . . . . . . . . . . . $6.00

**COOKIE CUTTER**, tin, simple bird, 3¼" L. . . . . . . . . . . . . . . . . . . . . . $13.00
**COOKIE CUTTER**, tin, simple Dutchman, 4⅜" H. . . . . . . . . . . . . . . . . $20.00

**COOKIE CUTTER**, tin, fish, 5" L. . . . . . . . . . . . . . . . . . . . . . . . . . . . . . $7.50
**COOKIE CUTTER**, tin, fish, 6" L. . . . . . . . . . . . . . . . . . . . . . . . . . . . . . $4.00

**COOKIE CUTTER**, tin, chick, 2⅝" L. . . . . . . . . . . . . . . . . . . . . . . . . . $12.00
**COOKIE CUTTER**, tin, Dutchman, 4½" H. . . . . . . . . . . . . . . . . . . . . . $20.00

A-OH April 1983        *Garth's Auctions, Inc.*
**SPATULA**, primitive, wrt. iron, European, 9¼" L. . . . . . . . . . . . . . . . . $22.50
**CAST IRON FROG**, worn old gr. paint, 5½" L. . . . . . . . . . . . . . . . . . . $25.00
**LEATHER CUTTING TOOL**, steel crescent blade mkd. "H.G. Gomph & Co. Albany, N.Y.," brass ferrule, rosewood handle, 6⅜" L. . . . . . . . . . . . . $15.00
**CAST IRON FROG**, worn layers of gr. & gold paint, 7" L. . . . . . . . . . . $50.00
**SPATULA**, primitive, wrt. iron, tooled handle, European, 10⅜" L. . . . $30.00
**WOODEN HANGING WALL POCKET**, old orange & gr. paint, 6" H. . . . . . . . . . . . . . . . . . . . . . . . . . . . . . . . $37.50
**LADYFINGER-SHAPED CHOCOLATE MOLD**, tin, embossed cats, 6¼" x 8" . . . . . . . . . . . . . . . . . . . . . . . . . . $20.00
**TOOL**, 3 rubber rollers, turned wooden handle, mkd. "Health Culture Co. New York, Pat'd Apr. 12, '82," 5½" L. . . . . . . . . . . . . . . . . . . . . . . . . . . . . . $10.00
**CAMEO MEDALLION**, woman in milk glass, tin surround, embossed edge, turned wooden back, 2" D., 4¼" L. . . . $5.00
**CUTOUT WOODEN ORNAMENTS**, (1 illus.), blk. boys, orig. polychrome paint, 20th C. folk art, 7" H. . . . . . . . . . . $10.00
**TRIVET**, cast iron, mkd. "Muster, Geschutz," worn nickel plating, 12" L. . . . . . . . . . . . . . . . . . . . . . . . . . . . . . $20.00
**TRIVET**, cast iron, old gold paint, 6½" H. . . . . . . . . . . . . . . . . . . . . . $30.00

A-OH Jan. 1983        *Garth's Auctions, Inc.*
*TIN COOKIE CUTTERS*
**PONY**, 4¾" L. . . . . . . . . . . . . . . . $77.50
**PITCHER**, 3¾" L. . . . . . . . . . . . . $80.00
**DEER**, 5" x 5½" . . . . . . . . . . . $245.00
**BIRD**, 5" L. . . . . . . . . . . . . . . . . $70.00
**HORSE**, resoldered, 4½" L. . . . . . $35.00
**SWAN**, handle removed, 4¾" L. . . . . . . . . . . . . . . . . . . . . . . . . . . . . . $17.50
**FLYING BIRD**, 3" L. . . . . . . . . . $15.00
**BEAR CUB**, 3¼" L. . . . . . . . . . . $25.00
**CAMEL**, handle removed, 4" L. . . . . . . . . . . . . . . . . . . . . . . . . . . . . . $40.00
**ROOSTER**, 4" L. . . . . . . . . . . . . $17.50
**FIREMAN**, 6¼" L. . . . . . . . . . . $450.00
**CROSS**, 4½" H. . . . . . . . . . . . . $15.00
**FISH**, handle removed, 4" L. . . . . . $8.00
**FISH**, 4" L. . . . . . . . . . . . . . . . . $35.00
**DUCK**, damage, 4½" L. . . . . . . . $20.00
**DOG**, 3" L. . . . . . . . . . . . . . . . . $32.50
**BOOT**, 3⅛" L. . . . . . . . . . . . . . $22.50
**DUCK**, 2¾" L. . . . . . . . . . . . . . $40.00
**EAGLE**, 4⅝" W. . . . . . . . . . . . . $32.50

A-OH April 1983        *Garth's Auctions, Inc.*
*TIN COOKIE CUTTERS*
**CHICKEN**, sq. back, 4½" sq. . . . . $30.00
**DUTCHMAN**, old resoldering, handle removed, 5⅛" H. . . . . . . . . . . . . . $15.00
**WALKING BEAR**, old resoldering, 6¼" sq. . . . . . . . . . . . . . . . . . . . . . . . . . . $90.00
**STANDING BEAR**, Teddy, brass handle, 3" x 4¾" . . . . . . . . . . . . . . . . . . . $50.00
**DOG**, 3⅝" x 4⅜" . . . . . . . . . . . . $40.00
**STYLIZED PINE TREE**, 4⅝" H. . . . . . . . . . . . . . . . . . . . . . . . . . . . . . $85.00
**STYLIZED CHICKEN**, 3¼" x 3⅝" . . . . . . . . . . . . . . . . . . . . . . . . . . . . . $10.00
**SMALL STYLIZED BIRD**, poorly soldered, 2¾" L. . . . . . . . . . . . . . . . $10.00
**PITCHER**, good handle, some separation, 5¼" H. . . . . . . . . . . . . . . . . . . . . . $95.00
**CAT**, handle removed, 5" H. . . . $115.00
**BIRD**, outstretched neck, 4" H. . . $30.00
**CAMEL**, 3¼" x 4" . . . . . . . . . . . $25.00
**STAR**, 3" D. . . . . . . . . . . . . . . . . $7.00
**RUNNING BEAR**, needs resoldering, 3⅞" L. . . . . . . . . . . . . . . . . . . . . . $22.50
**STYLIZED WOMAN**, enormous feet, 6" H. . . . . . . . . . . . . . . . . . . . . . . . . . $70.00
**SEATED DOG**, horse-like head, old resoldering, 3⅞" H. . . . . . . . . . . . . $45.00
**FISH**, 5" L. . . . . . . . . . . . . . . . . $25.00
**STYLIZED PRIMITIVE DEER**, 6" x 6¼" . . . . . . . . . . . . . . . . . . . . . . . . . . . $160.00
**STYLIZED BIRD IN FLIGHT**, 4" L. . . . . . . . . . . . . . . . . . . . . . . . . . . . . . $25.00
**STYLIZED CROW**, boots, 2½" x 6¼" . . . . . . . . . . . . . . . . . . . . . . . . . . . . . $50.00

*Left*
A-MA July 1982        *Richard A. Bourne Co., Inc.*
**BRASS FOOTED SKILLET**, by Cox of Tauton, VT, raised molded sgn. on handle, 6½" H. . . . . . . . . . . . . . . . . . . . . . $350.00

*Right*
A-MA Aug. 1982        *Robert W. Skinner Inc.*
**CAST IRON KETTLE**, Am., late 18th C., twisted wrt. iron bail handle, 6¼" H., 4¼" D. . . . . . . . . . . . . . . . . . . . . . . . . . $275.00*
**WRT. IRON HEARTH UTENSILS**, 2-pcs., Am., late 18th C., small spoon & spatula, both w/twisted rat-tail handles, 8" L. . . . . . . . . . . . . . . . . . . . . . . . . . $275.00*

*\*Price does not include 10% buyer fee.*

A-MA Aug. 1982 *Robert W. Skinner Inc.*
*L to R*

**COVERED WOODEN SPICE BOX,** N. Eng., early 19th C., cover has stenciled stylized floral spray surmounted by red rectangle w/initials "D.F.E.," stenciled, painted drk. gr., 3⅝" x 4¾" . . . . . $450.00*

**COVERED WOODEN BOXES,** 2-pcs., N. Eng., early 19th C., painted drk. gray-gr., single-finger construction, one w/rose-head tacks, 4⅝" x 6¼" & 6½" x 8⅞" . . . . . . . . . . . . . . . . . . . . . . . . . . . $575.00*

**SHAKER THREE-FINGER COVERED BOX,** N. Eng., early 19th C., painted deep gray-blue, copper tacks, 8¼" x 11½" . . . . . . . . . . . . . . . . . . . . . . . . . . . $375.00*

A-MA Aug. 1982 *Robert W. Skinner Inc.*
*L to R*

**MINI. WOODEN BUCKET,** Am., early 19th C., lapped loops, painted blue, 2¼" H., 1¾" D. . . . . . . . . . . . . . . . . . . . . . $230.00*

**CARVED BOOK BOX,** Am., early 19th C., spruce gum, hearts & geometric forms, cover missing, 4¼" H. . . . . . . . . . $260.00*

**CARVED WOODEN SPOON,** Am., 18th C., geometric designs below a hand & leaves, 6¼" L. . . . . . . . . . . . . . . . $180.00*

A-MA Aug. 1982 *Robert W. Skinner Inc.*
*L to R*

**WOODEN SUGAR BOWL,** N. Eng., early 19th C., slightly domed fitted cover, ovoid body on molded base, sponge paint decor., br., yellow & gr., small crack, 4½" H. . . . . . . . . . . . . . . . . . . . . . . . . . $275.00*

**TURNED WOODEN PLATE,** Am., 18th C., curved flange, raised ridge, 8" D. . . . . . . . . . . . . . . . . . . . . . . . . . . $160.00*

**WOODEN SCOOP,** N. Eng., 19th C., carved stylized floral design on handle, 8" L. . . . . . . . . . . . . . . . . . . . . . . . $140.00*

**MINI. HANGING WOODEN WALL BOX,** N. Eng., early 19th C., circular backboard extension w/hanging hole & high straight sides, unpainted, 6⅛" H., 3" x 3" . . . . . . . . . . . . . . . . . . . . . . . . . $275.00*

A-MA Aug. 1982 *Robert W. Skinner Inc.*
*L to R*

**BURL SCOOP,** Am., late 19th C., wide stubby handle, 5½" x 6½" . . . . . . $250.00*

**BURL BOWL,** Am., late 18th C., 3¾" H., 7½" x 10½" . . . . . . . . . . . . . . . . . . $325.00*

**BURL BOWL,** Am., late 18th C., 2¼" H., 4⅞" D. . . . . . . . . . . . . . . . . . . . . . $200.00*

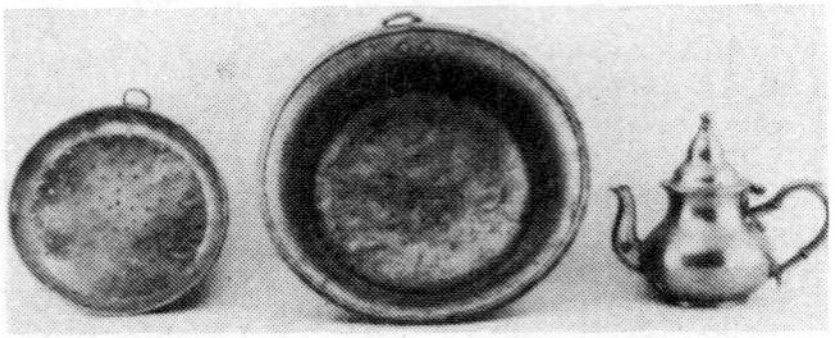

A-MA Aug. 1982 *Robert W. Skinner Inc.*
*L to R*

**BRASS COLANDER,** possibly Am., early 19th C., 1½" H., 8" D. . . . . . . . . $150.00*

**BRASS WASH BASIN,** possibly Am., early 19th C., break on rim, 4" H., 11½" rim D. . . . . . . . . . . . . . . . . . . . . . . . . . . $70.00*

**Q.A. TEA POT,** probably Eng., mid-18th C., damage to ring base, 7" H. . . . . . . . . . . . . . . . . . . . . . . . . . . . $260.00*

A-MA Aug. 1982 *Robert W. Skinner Inc.*
*L to R*

**TURNED WOODEN BOWL,** Am., 18th C., painted wh., 2½" H., 4½" D. . . . . . . . . . . . . . . . . . . . . . . . . . . $200.00*

**WOODEN PLATE,** Am., 18th C., 8½" D. . . . . . . . . . . . . . . . . . . . . . . . . . . $175.00*

**WOODEN BOWL,** Am., 18th C., worn gr. paint over wh., 1½" H., 4½" D. . . . . . . . . . . . . . . . . . . . . . . . . . . $220.00*

**OPEN PEDESTAL WOODEN SALT,** Am., 18th C., painted blue, 2¼" H., 2½" . . . . . . . . . . . . . . . . . . . . . . . . . . . $1075.00*

A-MA July 1982 *Richard A. Bourne Co., Inc.*

**DECORATED SPOON RACK,** late 19th C., pine, 15½" H. . . . . . . . . $125.00

A-OH July 1982 *Garth's Auctions, Inc.*

**CARVED WOODEN BUTTER PRINT,** tulip w/"M.M.," worn, cutout finger grips, 4¼" D. . . . . . . . . . . . . . . . . . . . . . . . $50.00

**CARVED WOODEN BUTTER PRINT,** tulip design, minor age cracks, handle missing, 4" D. . . . . . . . . . . . . . . . . $195.00

**CARVED WOODEN BUTTER PRINT,** pinwheel on one side, heart on other, minor age cracks, drk. finish, sm. protruding handle, 3½" D. . . . . . . . . . . . . . . . $200.00

**CARVED WOODEN BUTTER PRINT,** tulip design, handle, 3⅝" D. . . . . $100.00

**CARVED HARDWOOD COOKIE BOARD,** girl in fancy dress on one side, 2 parrots w/wreath initialed "JM" on other, 4½" W., 12" L. . . . . . . . . . . . . . . . $275.00

**CARVED WOODEN BUTTER PRINT,** cross-hatched tulip & other flowers, 3⅞" D. . . . . . . . . . . . . . . . . . . . . . . . . . . . $45.00

**ROLLER BUTTER PRINT,** carved wheel has leaf designs, age crack in wheel, worn red finish, 5½" L. . . . . . . . . $185.00

**CARVED BUTTER PRINT,** rectangular, two matching acorn & leaf designs, 2⅜" W., 4¾" L. . . . . . . . . . . . . . . . . . . . . . . $40.00

**CARVED BUTTER PRINT,** oblong, tulip & heart design, 3" W., 4½" L. . . . $345.00

**CARVED BUTTER PRINT,** round, eagle w/turned rim, handle, 4¾" D. . . . $195.00

**CARVED BUTTER PRINT,** round, chicken design, handle missing, 3⅞" D. . . . . . . . . . . . . . . . . . . . . . . . . . . . $252.50

**CARVED BUTTER PRINT,** oblong, tulip design, handle, 4½" W., 5" L. . . . . $115.00

**CARVED BUTTER PRINT,** round, tulip design, handle, worn & age cracks, 4¾" D. . . . . . . . . . . . . . . . . . . . . . . . . . . . $50.00

**CARVED BUTTER PRINT,** round, eagle w/leaf border, turned handle, sm. age crack, 3¾" D. . . . . . . . . . . . . . . . . $135.00

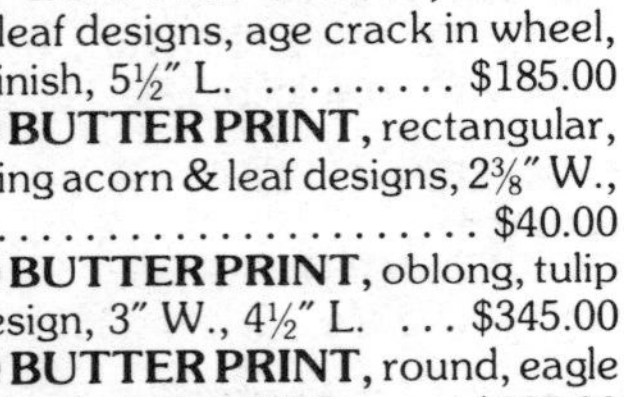

A-MA Nov. 1982 *Richard A. Bourne Co., Inc.*

**BRIDE'S BOX,** possibly PA or Scandinavian, early 19th C., laced w/rawhide, pine, 17¼" L., 10¾" W., 7¾" H. . . . . . . $750.00

*Price does not include 10% buyer fee.

A-OH Mar. 1983    *Garth's Auctions, Inc.*
**CAST IRON PORRINGER,** mkd. "Kenrick," 5½" D. ............. $55.00

**CAST IRON SKILLET,** 3 short feet, lid, 3½" D., 3" handle .............. $45.00

**CLAY PIPE CASE,** mahogany, stylized bird head on hinged opening, brass fittings, pipe mkd. "L. Fiolet," 9¼" L. .... $155.00

**NAUGHTY NELLIE BOOT JACK,** cast iron, traces of worn old paint, 8½" L. ...................................... $20.00

**CAST IRON PORRINGER,** 4¼" D. ...................................... $55.00

**CAST IRON PORRINGER,** mkd. "Kenrick. One Pint. No. 1," 5½" D. ...................................... $65.00

**CAST IRON TRIVET,** heart in hand & Odd Fellows insignia, 8¼" L. ..... $25.00

**CAST IRON TRIVET,** Minerva head, crack in neck, 9" L. ............. $15.00

**CAST IRON TRIVET,** eagle & heart in laurel wreath, 8¾" L. ........... $35.00

**CAST IRON TRIVET,** foliage scroll design, 9" L. ................... $20.00

**CAST IRON DOG,** worn old gr. & wh. paint, 3" L. .................... $70.00

**CAST IRON FROG,** worn old gr. paint, 5½" L. ....................... $75.00

**CAST PEWTER FROG,** worn stamped inscription "Frog in your throat? - the voice," one back foot is inc., 3" L. ................... $10.00

A-OH Sept. 1982    *Garth's Auctions, Inc.*
**WRT. IRON TRIVET,** 3½" D., 2⅛" H. ...................................... $75.00
**WRT. IRON TRIVET,** 2¼" D., 1" H. ...................................... $85.00
**COOKIE BOARD,** carved soapstone, eagle design, wooden frame, 12" W., 5" H. ...................................... $250.00
**DOUGH SCRAPER,** wrt. iron, sturdy handle, 4" W. ................. $45.00
**PEWTER ICE CREAM MOLD,** turkey design, 4½" H. ............... $35.00
**COOKIE CUTTER,** tin, cat design, 4¾" H. ...................................... $40.00
**CARVED COOKIE BOARD,** wooden, 8 scenes, animals, fruits, etc., age crack, 3" W., 7⅝" H. $95.00
**CARVED COOKIE BOARD,** wooden, cat on one side, dog on other, some damage, 6" W., 11¾" H. .... $450.00
**CARVED LEAF PRINTING BLOCK,** wooden, age cracks, 4¼" L. ...... $30.00
**FOOD MOLD,** tin, bunch of grapes, 7½" L. ...................................... $10.00
**COOKIE CUTTER,** tin, parrot-like bird, some damage, 6¼" L. ........... $50.00
**PEWTER ICE CREAM MOLD,** fruit design, 3" L. ................... $6.00
**CANDY MOLD,** tin, fish design, 4¾" L. ...................................... $12.50
**CHOCOLATE MOLD,** two-part, tin, rooster design, mkd. "Dresden," 4¼" H. ...................................... $35.00
**COOKIE CUTTER,** tin, pitcher, 3⅞" L. ...................................... $25.00

A-OH Jan. 1983    *Garth's Auctions, Inc.*
**PASTRY CUTTER,** brass, 6¼" L. ...................................... $45.00
**PASTRY CUTTER,** wrt. iron, 6⅞" L. ...................................... $65.00
**PASTRY CUTTER,** turned wooden handle, 6" L. ............. $45.00
**BRASS KITCHEN TOOL,** chicken's head, 5¾" L. ............. $22.50
**STEEL FLATWARE,** bone-handled, pewter inlay, 4 forks & 4 knives (2 illus.), mkd. "Brantford Cut. Co. U.S.A.," 9⅝" L. ...................................... $25.00
**BRASS KITCHEN TOOL,** hawk's head, 5¾" L. ...................................... $20.00
**PASTRY CUTTER,** wooden, 5½" L. ...................................... $5.00
**PASTRY CUTTER,** turned wooden handle, 7½" L. ................. $17.50
**PASTRY CUTTER,** turned wooden handle, 6⅞" L. ................. $25.00
**CAST IRON FOOD MOLD,** curved fish, 9" ...................................... $110.00
**CAST IRON COOKIE BOARD,** 12 sections, 5¼" x 5⅞" ............. $70.00
**CAST IRON CAN OPENER,** bull's head & tail, 6½" L. ................. $35.00
**CAST IRON CAN OPENER,** fish, 5" L. ...................................... $45.00
**CAST IRON CANDY MOLD,** makes 3 hands, 3" x 4¾" ............... $100.00
**TIN NUTMEG GRATER,** wooden handles, 5¼" L. ................. $35.00

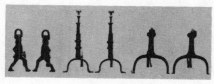

A-MA Aug. 1982    *Robert W. Skinner Inc.*
**HESSIAN SOLDIER IRON AND-IRONS,** pr., 18th C., 12" H. .... $250.00*

**WRT. IRON ANDIRONS,** pr., Am., brass knob finial, support w/spit holders, arched feet, 18" H. ......... $500.00*

**WRT. IRON GOOSENECK AND-IRONS,** pr., Am., 18th C., faceted knobs, arched feet, 12½" H. ......... $350.00*

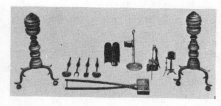

A-MA July 1982    *Richard A. Bourne Co., Inc.*
L to R
**MINI. BRASS ANDIRONS,** pr., ca. 1800, 8½" H. ...................................... $600.00
**MINI. FIREPLACE UTENSILS,** lot of 4, matched set, 3⅜" to 3¾" ..... $875.00
**MINI. LIGHTING DEVICES,** lot of 4, pcs. show considerable age ..... $775.00
**MINI. IRON WAFFLE IRON,** 8" L. ...................................... $150.00

A-MA July 1982    *Richard A. Bourne Co., Inc.*
**BRASS DOUBLE LEMON AND—IRONS,** pr., 23½" H. ......... $525.00
**SMALL BRASS DOUBLE LEMON ANDIRONS,** pr., few minor dents, 17½" H. ...................................... $325.00
**BRASS & WIRE FIREPLACE FENDER,** 43½" W., 18¾" H. ... $375.00

*Price does not include 10% buyer fee.

A-MA July 1982    *Richard A. Bourne Co., Inc.*
*PEWTER*
*Row I, L to R*
**TASTER PORRINGER,** mkd. "ICL & CO," ca. 1834-1852, 2¼" D. ..... $350.00
**TASTER PORRINGER,** minor signs of wear, 2½" D. ................. $150.00
**TASTER PORRINGER,** touch of Richard Lee, 2¼" D. ........... $400.00
**TASTER PORRINGER,** touch of Richard Lee, 2¼" D. ........... $450.00
**TASTER PORRINGER,** ca. 1770-1823, stag's-head touch, slight dents, 2¼" D. ..................................... $450.00
*Row II, L to R*
**TASTER PORRINGER,** 2½" D. .................................. $200.00
**TASTER PORRINGER,** Am., handle resoldered, 2⅛" D. ............. $50.00
**DOUBLE-HANDLED TASTER PORRINGER,** unmkd., 2⅛" D. ....... $75.00
**TASTER PORRINGER,** attrib. to Richard Lee, 2⅞" D. ........... $225.00
*Row III, L to R*
**PORRINGER,** old Eng. handle, minor denting, 3½" D. ............. $175.00
**PORRINGER,** attrib to Richard Lee w/reverse R molded into handle, 3¼" D. ......................... $175.00
**PORRINGER,** 3⅜" D. ......... $175.00

A-MA July 1982    *Richard A. Bourne Co., Inc.*
*PEWTER*
*Row I, L to R*
**PORRINGER,** N. Eng., attrib. to Roswell Gleason, ca. 1822-1871, mkd., sm. dent, 4½" D. ..................... $250.00
**BASIN,** deep pitting, 8" D. ..... $150.00
**PORRINGER,** N. Eng., 5¼" D. ..................................... $175.00
*Row II, L to R*
**TEAPOT,** by Boardman & Hart, NY, ca. 1805-1850, resoldering on bottom, 7¼" H. ..................... $125.00
**PORRINGER,** 3⅜" D. ......... $175.00
**PORRINGER,** 4" D. ......... $175.00
**TEAPOT,** by Dixon & Sons, Eng., early 19th C., 6" H. ............... $90.00

A-MA Nov. 1982    *Richard A. Bourne Co., Inc.*
*PEWTER*
*Row I, L to R*
**Q.A. STYLE TEAPOT,** by J. B. Woodbury, eastern MA or RI, late 1820's-1835, handle has been repainted, old repr. to lid, 7" H. ........................ $1100.00
**LIDDED SUGAR,** by Squire Hiram Yale, Yalesville, CT, 1824-1835, retains orig. ivory knob, 6" H. .............. $500.00
**TEAPOT,** by I. C. Lewis, Meriden, CT, 1834-1852, 6¾" H. ............. $225.00
*Row II, L to R*
**TEAPOT,** by J. Munson, Wallington, CT, 1846-1852, tiny hole in foot extension, handle repainted blk., 8" H. ..... $225.00
**LIGHTHOUSE COFFEE POT,** by Oliver Trask, Beverly, MA, 1825-1830, dome lid, hinge has been resoldered, smaller solder on inside bottom, handle repainted blk., 11" H. .......... $650.00
**TEAPOT,** by Freeman Porter, Westbrook, ME, 1835-1860, circular touch w/"No. 7," handle repainted blk., 6¾" H. ..................................... $275.00

A-MA Nov. 1982    *Richard A. Bourne Co., Inc.*
*PEWTER*
*Row I, L to R*
**PATENT WHALE OIL LAMP,** bulls-eye lenses, attrib. to Roswell Gleason, some pitting & mars, 8¼" H. ......... $425.00
**HAND LAMP,** by Morey Ober & Smith, Boston, MA, 1852-1855, orig. double divergent brass camphene burners w/pewter caps, 4½" H. ......... $275.00
**WHALE OIL LAMP,** by Smith & Co., Boston, MA, 1847-1849, orig. double-drop whale oil burner, 8" H. ......... $375.00
**TEAPOT,** by Eben Smith, Beverly, MA, 1813-1856, minor signs of wear, 7½" H. ..................................... $250.00
*Row II, L to R*
**BASIN,** 7⅞", faint touch mark of Thomas Danforth, III, some pitting ...... $125.00
**DEEP DISH,** 9¾", bearing double struck eagle touch of Thomas Danforth Boardman, heavily pitted, solder repr. on rim ..................................... $150.00
**PLATE,** 8½", by Frederick Bassett, New York City & Hartford, 1761-1800, pitted & cleaned ........................ $175.00

A-MA July 1982    *Richard A. Bourne Co., Inc.*
*PEWTER*
*Row I, L to R*
**LIDDED PITCHER,** by James Stimpson, ca. 1840's, MA, dented, 12" H. .. $150.00

**TEAPOT,** raised shield w/"MAD" engraved & dated 1760, 14½" O.H. ..................................... $400.00

**DEEP DISH,** by Jacob Whitmore, ca. 1758-1790, CT, double touch, sm. areas of pitting ........................ $400.00

*Row II, L to R*
**COFFEE URN,** by Roswell Gleason, ca. 1822-71, orig. finial needs refastening, 14¾" H. ..................................... $150.00

**COFFEE URN,** by Reed & Barton, 19th C., MA, complete w/burner, 18" H. ..................................... $125.00

**Q.A. STYLE URN,** w/spigot, Am., unmkd., on ebonized wooden feet, minor dents, 14½" H. ................. $250.00

*Left*
A-MA July 1982    *Robert W. Skinner Inc.*
**PEWTER PORRINGER,** Samuel Danforth, CT, ca. 1800-10, buffed, 4¼" D. ..................................... $300.00*

*Right*
A-MA July 1982    *Richard A. Bourne Co., Inc.*
**PEWTER PORRINGER,** by Frederick Bassett, NY, ca. 1761-1800, clear touch under handle, handle needs resoldered, 4¼" L. ..................... $900.00

A-MA July 1982    *Richard A. Bourne Co., Inc.*
*SILVER*
*Row I, L to R*
**CONTINENTAL REPOUSSE TEA-POT,** ebonized handle, Hallmarks "WM" & "12," 8-oz. troy, 7¼" O.H. .... $300.00
**GERMAN BASKET,** clear crystal liner, 7½-oz. troy, 6" D. ........ $120.00
**SHEFFIELD CANDLESTICKS,** pr., copper showing beneath on high points, needs repair, 8¼" H. .......... $60.00
*Row II, L to R*
**LIDDED SUGAR BOWL,** Am., unmkd., sleeping swan finial, handle slightly bent, 28-oz. troy, 8¾" O.H. ...... $350.00
**CONTINENTAL COMPOTES,** pr., un-ascribed Hallmarks, few minor dents, 4-oz. troy, 8" D., 6½" H. ............ $250.00

A-MA July 1982    *Richard A. Bourne Co., Inc.*
*SILVER*
*Row I, L to R*
**CONTINENTAL CANDLE SNUF-FER,** non-matching silver oblong tray, 5-oz. troy .............. $80.00
**MUFFINEER,** Eng., ca. 1902, 5-oz. troy
.......................... $70.00
**CUP,** Eng., unknown maker's mrk. "EV," 2½-oz. troy ................ $50.00
**OPEN SUGAR BOWL,** gold washed int., 7-oz. troy .................. $90.00
*Row II, L to R*
**REPOUSSE TAZZA,** pr., by S. Kirk & Son, 18-oz. troy, 6½" D., 3" H. .. $300.00
**COMPOTE,** Continental, 19th C., crudely made, 7½-oz. troy, 7" D., 5" H. .. $100.00

A-NY June 1982    *Christie's*
**SILVER DEMITASSE SERVICE,** ca. 1925, 9¾" H., tray diameter: 11"
.......................... $990.00

---

A-MA July 1982    *Richard A. Bourne Co., Inc.*
*Row I, L to R*
**SILVER MARROW SCOOP,** by Robert Evans, Boston, ca. 1812, 5" L. ... $130.00
**SILVER TEASPOON,** mkd. "EB," 4½" L.
.......................... $130.00
*Row II, L to R*
**SILVER TABLESPOON,** by John Edwards, Boston, ca. 1700, mkd. "MD," minor dents, slightly worn, 7¼" L.
.......................... $375.00
**SILVER TABLESPOON,** mkd. "ILC," slightly worn, 7¼" L. .......... $175.00
**SILVER RATTAIL TABLESPOON,** by Daniel Russell, Newport, ca. 1698-1771, mkd. "IH," very worn, 7¼" L. ... $110.00
**SILVER RATTAIL TABLESPOON,** by Ephraim Cobb, Boston, ca. 1708-1777, 8" L. .......................... $320.00
**SILVER RATTAIL TABLESPOON,** by Moody Russell, Barnstable, MA, ca. 1694-1761, mkd. "SDM," 8" L. ....... $375.00

A-MA July 1982    *Richard A. Bourne Co., Inc.*
*Row I, L to R*
**SHEFFIELD PLATED SILVER COVERED VEGETABLE DISH,** hot water compartment, armorial engraving, handle fits loosely, minor dents, copper showing through at high points, 15" O.L.
.......................... $130.00
**LRG. PLATED SILVER TRAY,** 23¼" L.
.......................... $30.00
*Row II, L to R*
**PLATED SILVER CANDELABRA,** pr., 4-branch, flame finials, 14" H. ... $175.00
**LRG. CANDELABRA,** flame finial, silver plated on copper, slight wear showing copper beneath, 21½" H. ........ $70.00

---

A-WA D.C. Sept. 1982    *Adam A. Weschler & Son*
*Left*
**VICTORIAN SILVER CRUET STAND,** ca. 1893, Bailey & Co., 4 cut crystal bottles, stand: 8½" H. .... $150.00*
*Right*
**GEORGE III SILVER CASTER STAND,** ca. 1816, Samuel Hennell, London, 4 cut crystal sterling mounted casters, 9" H. .............. $350.00*

A-NY June 1982    *Christie's*
**SILVER COVERED COMPOTES,** pr., ca. 1870, by William Forbes for Ball, Black & Co., engraved crest, mkd., 7" H. & 9" H.
.......................... $1760.00

A-MA July 1982    *Richard A. Bourne Co., Inc.*
*SILVER FLATWARE*
*Top to Bottom*
**TABLESPOON,** by Paul Revere, monogram on handle, bowl worn, slight denting ...................... $600.00
**TABLESPOONS,** pr. (1 illus.), by Joseph Loring, engraved monogram on handle
.......................... $100.00
**GEORGIAN STUFFING SPOON,** monogram on handle, by Thomas Deacty
.......................... $90.00
**SPOONS,** pr. (1 illus.), by William Roe, monogramed handles, worn slightly
.......................... $100.00
**TABLESPOONS,** pr. (1 illus.), initialed "LC" by Luther Bradley ....... $70.00
**GEORGIAN SILVER LADLE,** made in NY, ca. 1800 by H. Prince & Co., initialed "JHM," 6 oz. troy ............ $200.00

---

*Price does not include 10% buyer fee.

A-MA July 1982    *Richard A. Bourne Co., Inc.*
*Row I, L to R*
**BRASS FLUID LAMP,** late 18th/early
19th C., minus burner, 6⅛″ H. .. $75.00
**BRASS SAUCER-BASED CANDLE-
STICKS,** pr., w/pushups, minor break to
1, 6″ H. .. $200.00
**BRASS CANDLESTICKS,** pr., Eng., ca.
1820, pushups, minor bending around
bases, 7½″ H. .. $130.00

*Row II, L to R*
**BRASS CANDLESTICKS,** pr., Eng., ca.
1820, pushups, minor dents in 1, 7⅝″ H.
.. $140.00
**HOUR GLASS,** brass frame, 8″ H.
.. $275.00
**BRASS CANDLESTICKS,** pr., Eng., ca.
1820, pushups, 1 needs resoldering, other
w/sm. dents, 9″ H. .. $70.00

*Row III, L to R*
**BRASS CANDLESTICKS,** pr., Eng.,
17th C., 9½″ H. .. $1600.00
**BRASS CANDLESTICKS,** pr., Eng., ca.
1820, pushups, 10¾″ H. .. $175.00

A-OH July 1982    *Garth's Auctions, Inc.*
*Row I, L to R*
**TIN PETTICOAT PEG LAMP,** whale oil
burner, traces of orig. br. japanning, 4½″ H.
.. $75.00
**TIN TINDERBOX,** candle socket, flint &
steel missing from damper, seam separ-
ation, 4¼″ D. .. $65.00
**TIN SPOUT LAMP,** snuffer cap on
spout, attrib. to Shakers, 5¼″ H.
.. $40.00
**TIN CANDLESTICK,** sq. saucer base,
4½″ sq. .. $27.50
**TIN PETTICOAT PEG LAMP,** whale oil
burner, orig. br. japanning, some wear, 4¼″
H. .. $85.00

*Row II, L to R*
**CANDLESTICK,** wrt. iron spiral push-up
stem, turned wooden base, 8″ H.
.. $130.00
**TIN LAMP FILLER,** attrib. to Shakers, 6″
H. .. $55.00
**TIN PEG LAMP,** lemon-shaped font,
whale oil burner, 4″ H. .. $140.00
**TIN LAMP FILLER,** rust damage,
modern blk. paint, attrib. to Shakers, 5½″
H. .. $45.00
**CANDLESTICK,** wrt. iron spiral push-up
stem, turned wooden base, age cracks in
base, 8½″ H. .. $140.00

*Row III, L to R*
**TIN BETTY LAMP,** on standard w/
saucer base, dents & damage, blk. paint,
8¾″ H. .. $110.00
**PINE CANDLEHOLDER,** metal socket,
wire spring clip, 7″ H. .. $65.00
**FOUR-TUBE TIN CANDLE MOLD,**
edge has rust damage, blk. paint, 10¾″ H.
.. $50.00
**TIN OIL CAN,** corked filler hole, attrib. to
Shakers, 6⅝″ H. .. $55.00
**TIN BETTY LAMP STAND,** crimped
edge pan, saucer base w/high straight
sides, 8″ H. .. $215.00

A-OH Feb. 1983    *Garth's Auctions, Inc.*
*Row I, L to R*
**DOUBLE CRUSIE LAMP,** wrt. iron,
replm., damage, 5½″ H. .. $40.00
**TANKARD,** sheet brass, slightly battered
& damaged, 4⅞″ H. .. $17.50
**CHAMBER STICK,** tin, pushup, 4″ H.
.. $35.00
**HOT WATER BOTTLE,** copper, brass
ring handle & cap, 6¾″ x 10¼″ .. $55.00
**DOUBLE CRUSIE LAMP,** wrt. iron,
twisted hanger, 6½″ H. .. $45.00

*Row II, L to R*
**VICTORIAN CANDLESTICK,** brass
w/pushup, 7″ H. .. $65.00
**SCHOOL BELL,** brass, wooden handle
.. $70.00
**LAMP,** marble base, brass stem, clear
hexagonal font, oval punty, 10⅝″ H.
.. $35.00
**CLEAR FLINT LAMP,** brass collar,
whale oil burner, flaking & staining, 9¾″ H.
.. $110.00
**CANDLESTICK,** heavy early brass, 8″ H.
.. $175.00

*Row II, L to R*
**CANDLE MOLD,** 8 tubes, 10½″ H.
.. $55.00
**CANDLESTICK,** pewter, Cincinnati,
unmkd., 10″ H. .. $175.00
**COACH LAMP,** tin & brass, worn blk.
paint & nickel plating, beveled glass in 2
sides, rear has ruby lens, orig. oil burner,
11″ H. .. $50.00
**VICTORIAN CANDLESTICK,** brass,
pushup, 9¾″ H. .. $65.00
**CANDLE MOLD,** 6 tubes, tin w/handle
.. $45.00

A-MA July 1982    *Richard A. Bourne Co., Inc.*
*PEWTER*
*L to R*
**CANDLESTICKS,** pr. (1 illus.), by
Taunton Britannia Mfg. Co., MA, ca. 1830-
1835, minor pitting, 1 resoldered around
base, 8″ H. .. $200.00
**CANDLESTICKS,** pr. (1 illus.), Am.,
unmkd., 1 bent slightly, 9¾″ H. .. $200.00
**CANDLESTICKS,** pr. (1 illus.), Am.,
unmkd., 9¾″ H. .. $225.00

A-MA Aug. 1982    *Robert W. Skinner Inc.*
**Q.A. BRASS CANDLESTICKS,** early
18th C., near-matching, elongated candle
sockets above octagonal supports, square
base, 7″ H. .. $500.00*

A-OH Oct. 1982    *Garth's Auctions, Inc.*
*Row I, L to R*
**MINIATURE TAPER STICKS,** pr., brass, 3¾" H. ................. $45.00
**SPOUT LAMP,** brass, brass & iron hanger, 6¼" H. plus hanger ...... $25.00
**GIMBOL CANDLESTICKS,** brass, 5½" H. ............................. $55.00
**DOUBLE CRUSIE LAMP,** wrt. iron, 6" H. plus hanger ............... $65.00
**MINIATURE TAPER STICKS,** pr., brass, 4" H. .................. $85.00

*Row II, L to R*
**CANDLESTICKS,** pr., brass, open double spiral stems, 6⅛" H. ...... $35.00
**LAMP,** brass, pear-shaped font, tubular wick support, thumb screw mkd. "A. R. Depose," damage, 10" H. ....... $145.00
**LAMP,** clear pressed font, brass stem & collar, marble base, 8" H. ........ $50.00
**LAMP,** brass, pear-shaped font, tubular wick support, unmkd., damage, 9¼" H. ....... $50.00
**CANDLESTICKS,** neoclassic, pushups, 6" H. ......................... $55.00

*Row III, L to R*
**CHAMBERSTICK,** tin, pushup, damage, 4⅛" H. ......................... $45.00
**CANDLESTICK,** brass, scalloped base & pushup, 6¾" H. ............. $115.00
**LAMP,** clear bull's-eye font, brass stem & collar, marbleized slate base, 9" H. ......................... $65.00
**PEWTER LAMP,** saucer base, whale oil burner, unmkd., 5⅞" H. ......... $115.00
**IRON HOG SCRAPER CANDLE-STICK,** pushup (stamped signature), lip hanger is bent, 9⅜" H. .......... $65.00

A-MA Aug. 1982    *Robert W. Skinner Inc.*
*L to R*
**TIN WALL SCONCES,** pr., Am., early 19th C., oval crimped-edge reflector, single candle socket, 11½" H. ........ $500.00*
**TIN WALL SCONCE,** Am., early 19th C., cylindrical reflector w/incised lines, large cylindrical crimped-edge pan w/single candle socket, 11½" H. ...... $250.00*
**TIN WALL SCONCE,** Am., early 19th C., cylindrical incised-line reflector, single arm below w/glass peg, 10½" H. ......................... $400.00*

*Price does not include 10% buyer fee.

A-OH July 1982    *Garth's Auctions, Inc.*
*Row I, L to R*
**BETTY LAMP,** wrt. & cast iron, swivel hook on front cover, brass shield on hanger, 3½" H. plus hanger ...... $195.00
**REDWARE PAN LAMP,** single spout, int. glaze, rim chips, 3" D. ....... $15.00
**TINDER LIGHTER,** pistol grip, flint lock, replm. of front support foot & taper socket on side, small break in fore stock, 7" L. ......................... $220.00
**CLASSICAL-STYLE LAMP,** copper w/brass handle w/lion's head, mkd. "Gorham Co.," 4¾" L. ..................... $30.00
**WHITE CLAY LAMP,** early primitive, 6½" L. ......................... $30.00
*Row II, L to R*
**TIN DARKROOM LAMP,** cracked red lens, oil burner, dents, some rust, 7½" H. ......................... $4.00
**EARTHENWARE FAT LAMP,** Albany slip-type glaze, saucer base, ear handle, 2 spouts, one spout is chipped, repr. to saucer base, 6" H. ............. $550.00
**WRT. IRON LAMP,** rectangular pan w/2 candle sockets, one w/hook, one w/ferrule for wooden handle, 13¾" L. ..... $190.00
**WITCHES' LAMP,** cast iron, inside of lid mkd. "Carbon, No. 1 & 2, B.L.," 8" L. ......................... $385.00
**PENNSYLVANIA KETTLE LAMP,** wrt. iron, center wick support w/pick & chain, 7½" H. ................. $290.00
*Row III, L to R*
**CANDLE HOLDER,** 4 wire birdcage-like supports w/sliding push-up, lip handle, turned wooden base, 9½" H. .... $295.00
**TIN CAMPAIGN TORCH,** 3-spout burner, ferrule for wooden handle is missing, 5¾" H. ................ $25.00
**TIN PATENT LARD LAMP,** int. mkd. "I. Smith" but patent date is not clear, replm. on wing nut holding top, 5¾" H. .. $60.00
**TIN LAMP ON BASE,** inc., 6¼" H. ......................... $15.00
**TIN LAMP,** weighted conical base, clear blown font w/opening for drop burner, 10½" H. ...................... $295.00

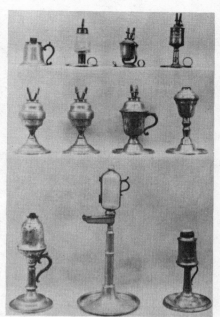

A-MA July 1982    *Richard A. Bourne Co., Inc.*
*Row I, L to R*
**BELL-SHAPED HAND LAMP,** Am., unmkd., orig. weighted patented burner, resoldered around bottom, minor dent, 3½" O.H. ..................... $100.00
**FLUID LAMP,** cut & etched sandwich glass font w/pewter base, touch of Smith & Co., orig. single brass camphene burner, burner slightly bent, 6½" O.H. ... $275.00
**HAND LAMP,** Am., unmkd., 5¼" O.H. ......................... $250.00
**FLUID LAMP,** Am., unmkd., needs re-soldering at stem, 7¼" O.H. ..... $100.00
*Row II, L to R*
**FLUID LAMPS,** pr., Am., unmkd., weighted bases, minor resoldering & slight dents, 7¾" O.H. ............... $375.00
**FLUID LAMP,** Am., unmkd., 8" O.H. ......................... $150.00
**FLUID LAMP,** Am., sgn. by Capen & Molineaux, burner missing, buffed, 7¾" H. ......................... $125.00
*Row III, L to R*
**FLUID LAMP,** Am., unmkd., 5-molded C-handle, weighted base, 10" H. ......................... $100.00
**TIME LAMP,** German, blown molded glass reservoir & pan-style burner, minor denting, 15¼" O.H. ............. $225.00
**FLUID LAMP,** sgn. by Fuller & Smith, ca. 1850, CT, lamp minus burner, needs cleaning, 8" H. ................ $225.00

A-MA July 1982    *Richard A. Bourne Co., Inc.*
*L to R*
**IRON HANGER,** for roasting game birds, normal pitting, 10" D., 10" H. ... $275.00
**IRON CHANDELIER,** 3-light, normal pitting, 10" O.H. .............. $300.00

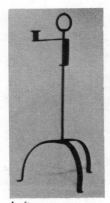

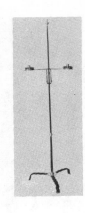

A-MA Aug. 1982     *Robert W. Skinner Inc.*
**WOOD & IRON CHANDELIER,** 18th C., turned wooden support w/gr. paint, 6 scrolling wrt. iron arms w/cylindrical candle sockets & drip cups, 16½″ H., 26″ D.
........................... $6100.00*

A-MA Nov. 1982    *Richard A. Bourne Co., Inc.*
**HANGING SCONCES,** pr., tin, shield-back reflectors, slight film of rust on surface as is normal, 12¼″ H. ......... $425.00
**CANDLE SCONCES,** pr., tin, decor. reflecting designs, 13″ H. ....... $475.00

A-MA July 1982     *Robert W. Skinner Inc.*
**IRON CHANDELIER,** early 19th C., 19″ D. ...................... $350.00*

*Left*
A-MA July 1982     *Robert W. Skinner Inc.*
**IRON STANDING CANDLEHOLDER,** Am., 18th C., adj. stem w/candle socket & arm, 29″ H. ................. $375.00*

*Right*
A-MA Nov. 1982    *Richard A. Bourne Co., Inc.*
**STANDING CANDLESTAND,** Am., 18th C., iron, brass sockets, drip pans, finials & decor., 58½″ H. ...... $3000.00

A-MA Aug. 1982     *Robert W. Skinner Inc.*
**TINWARE WALL SCONCE,** Am., early 19th C., 9¾″ H. .............. $275.00*
**TINWARE WALL SCONCE,** Am., early 19th C., encased w/glass, restor. candle drip pan socket, 9¾″ H. ...... $1000.00*
**TINWARE WALL SCONCES,** pr., Am., early 19th C., 6¾″ H. ......... $700.00*

A-MA July 1982    *Richard A. Bourne Co., Inc.*
*L to R*
**TIN HANGING CANDLE LAMP,** two candleholders, rusted, 26¾″ H.
........................... $425.00
**PIERCED TIN HANGING CHANDE-LIER,** Am., ca. 1820, three chanleholders, old blk. paint, small areas of surface rust, 24½″ H. ...................... $500.00

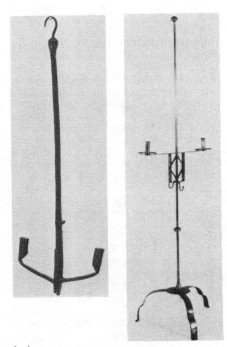

*Left*
A-MA Aug. 1982     *Robert W. Skinner Inc.*
**WRT. IRON HANGING CANDLE & SPLINT HOLDER,** Am., 18th C., double candle arm divided by a splint holder, adjustable, 25″ L., extended 42″ L.
........................... $1000.00*

*Right*
A-MA Aug. 1982     *Robert W. Skinner Inc.*
**WRT. IRON LIGHTING DEVICE,** Am., late 18th C., sliding horizontal arm w/snuf-fer hooks, cylindrical sockets, drip pans, arched tripod base, 5′3″ H. ... $6500.00*

A-MA Nov. 1982    *Richard A. Bourne Co., Inc.*
**CHRISTMAS CANDLE,** PA, 19th C., holds 13 pricket-type candles, 1 drip pan does not fit properly, 29½″ H. ... $500.00
**CANDELABRA,** PA, 19th C., tin, 24 candleholders, 23 of which are supported by serpentine-shaped metal arms, old gr. paint, 1 arm is replm. & is made of brass, 40″ H. ...................... $650.00

A-MA July 1982     *Robert W. Skinner Inc.*
**TIN WALL SCONCE,** Am., 19th C., single socket & fluted drip, 15″ H.
........................... $275.00*

*Price does not include 10% buyer fee.

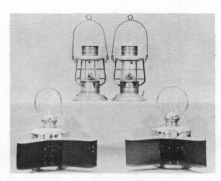

A-MA Mar. 1983 *Richard A. Bourne Co., Inc.*
**BRASS PERKO DECK LANTERNS,**
pr., 11″ H. .................... $100.00
**BRASS PORT & STARBOARD
LAMPS,** pr., made by The Boesch Lamp
Company of San Francisco, CA, includes
port & starboard lamps & retain their orig.
fluid lamps within, 11″ H. ....... $250.00

A-MA July 1982     *Richard A. Bourne Co., Inc.*
*Row I, L to R*
**FLUID LAMPS,** pr., by Boston & Sand-
wich Glass Co., clear pressed fonts,
yellowish-jade gr. opaque glass bases, gold
decor. on top & bottom, shows wear, 8½″
H. ............................ $350.00
**SANDWICH OVERLAY FLUID
LAMP,** marble base, triple-cut font, clear
to cranberry to opaque wh., brass electric
fixture in collar, 10″ H. ......... $350.00
*Row II, L to R*
**OPAQUE WHITE FLUID LAMP,** sgn.,
N. Eng. Glass Co., orig. fixture, heavy
roughage & small chip, 16½″ H.
............................ $500.00
**SANDWICH PRESENTATION FLUID
LAMP,** opalescent base, opaque wh. font,
gold decor., 14″ H. ............ $200.00

A-MA July 1982     *Richard A. Bourne Co., Inc.*
*Row I, L to R*
**SANDWICH BLOWN GLASS
WHALE OIL LAMP,** minus collar, 4½″ H.
............................ $70.00
**WHALE OIL LAMP,** minus collar, small
chips, 6⅝″ H. ................. $60.00
**WHALE OIL LAMPS,** pr., attrib. to N.
Eng. Glass Co., ca. 1820, similar but non-
matching pewter collars, double-drop
whale oil burner, small nicks, 8″ & 8¼″ H.
............................ $200.00
*Row II, L to R*
**BLOWN HAND LAMP,** fitted w/double
drop whale oil burner, no collar, 8½″ H.
............................ $200.00
**WHALE OIL LAMP,** no collar, slight
roughage, one chip around base, 9″ H.
............................ $90.00
**PEWTER CASTER SET,** Am., unmkd.,
four matched blown 3-mold caster bottles,
one w/small nick, minus its cover
............................ $150.00

A-MA July 1982     *Richard A. Bourne Co., Inc.*
**TIN CHANDELIER,** 19th C., 14 candleholders, ornamented w/rosettes & stars,
27″ O.H. ................... $2600.00

A-WA D.C. July 1982   *Adam A. Weschler & Son*
**HEISSEY PRESSED GLASS SPERM
OIL LAMPS,** pr., late 19th C., each
w/standard molded "H" monogram, 14¼″
H. ......................... $200.00*

A-MA July 1982     *Richard A. Bourne Co., Inc.*
*Row I, L to R*
**SMALL TIN LANTERN,** pierced design
on top, rusted, 8″ H. ........... $50.00
**TIN HAND LANTERN,** bull's-eye lens,
orig. whale oil lamp, slight loss of orig.
finish, 6¾″ H. ................. $70.00
**TIN CANDLE LANTERN,** provision for
four candles, frosted glass pane on back
side, glass cracked, 12″ L., 9½″ H.
............................ $175.00

*Row II, L to R*
**BRASS LANTERN,** mkd. "James
Monroe, Chief Engineer," globe reglued,
12″ H. ...................... $275.00
**DIETZ RAILROAD LANTERN,** bull's-
eye lens, slightly rusted, 12″ H. ... $40.00
**LANTERN,** N. Eng. Glass Co., ca. 1854,
orig. lamp, slightly rusted surface, 12″ H.
............................ $170.00

*Price does not include 10% buyer fee.

A-OH July 1982          *Garth's Auctions, Inc.*
**BRASS LANTERN**, probably New England Glass Co., remov. base w/font & burner missing, 16″ H. including ring handle
.............................. $1600.00

A-MA Nov. 1982     *Richard A. Bourne Co., Inc.*
*Row I, L to R*
**CHAMBER LAMPS**, pr., saucer based, pewter, by Meriden Britannia Mfg. Co., ca. 1850-1860, orig. double-drop whale oil burners, 4″ H. ................ $325.00
**SPARKING LAMPS**, pr., pewter, unmkd., by Allen Porter, Westbrook, ME, 1830-1840, single drop whale oil burners, 3½″ H. ........................ $350.00
*Row II, L to R*
**WHALE OIL LAMP**, pewter, by Smith & Co., Boston, MA, ca. 1840, orig. double drop whale oil burner, 5½″ H. .... $225.00
**WHALE OIL LAMP**, pewter, Am., ca. 1850, orig. brass divergent camphene, 5½″ H. ........................ $250.00
**WHALE OIL LAMP**, pewter, Am., unmkd., saucer base, high standard stem w/attached handle & orig. double drop whale oil burner .............. $400.00

A-MA Nov. 1982     *Richard A. Bourne Co., Inc.*
*Row I, L to R*
**IRON BETTY LAMP**, wrt. iron hanger, old gr. paint & decor. possibly orig.
.............................. $150.00
**SPIRAL CANDLESTICKS**, pr., wrt. iron, wood base, 7½″ H. & 6⅞″ H.
.............................. $250.00
**CANDLE SCONCE**, tin, small damage in top above hanging hole, 12¼″ H.
.............................. $175.00
*Row II, L to R*
**CANDLE LANTERN**, tin, orig. gr. & gold decor. ........................ $100.00
**LANTERN**, tin, 3 shaved horn panels, minor damage in 1 horn panel, 16″ H.
.............................. $325.00
**CANDLE LANTERN**, onion-shaped globe, repainted gold which is worn, 10″ H.
.............................. $250.00

A-MA July 1982     *Richard A. Bourne Co., Inc.*
*Row I, L to R*
**SM. PEWTER HAND LAMPS**, pr., thumb tabs at tops of handles, both w/double drop whale oil burners, 2½″ H.
.............................. $275.00
**IRON BETTY LAMP**, brass rooster & embossed brass plate, orig. hanger, 6″ O.H. ........................ $275.00
**IRON CRUSIE**, orig. fuel still, 7½″ L.
.............................. $90.00
**BRONZE HAND LAMP**, holes & minus cover, 4″ L. ................... $30.00
**SM. TIN MINER'S CAP LAMP**, orig. wick, 4″ H. .................... $75.00

A-MA Aug. 1982          *Robert W. Skinner Inc.*
*L to R*
**IRON KETTLE LAMP**, Am., early 19th C., cylindrical base, 8″ H. ...... $310.00*
**TIN WHALE·OIL LAMPS**, pr., Am., early 19th C., pear-shaped fonts, cylindrical supports & bases, 7¼″ H. ..... $220.00*
**TIN TINDER BOX W/CANDLE HOLDER**, Am., late 18th C., w/accessories, 2″ H., 4¼″ D. ......... $275.00*

A-MA Aug. 1982          *Robert W. Skinner Inc.*
*L to R*
**CAST IRON BAKER'S GREASE LAMP**, Am., late 18th C., saucer-base, 3½″ H., 9″ L. .................... $500.00*
**ONION CANDLE LANTERN**, Am., late 18th C., tin & clear glass, 11″ H.
.............................. $425.00*
**TIN BETTY LAMP ON STAND**, Am., late 18th C., 9½″ H. ........... $325.00*

A-MA Mar. 1983          *Robert W. Skinner Inc.*
**THREE-ARM CHANDELIER**, early 19th C., Am., tin, end of one arm partially crushed, approx. dia. 22″ ...... $800.00*

---

*Row II, L to R*
**TUMBLER LAMP**, Star patt. .. $275.00
**CIRCULAR TIN CANDLE LAMP**, box for flint & striker, 4½″ D., 3½″ H.
.............................. $130.00
**CANDLEHOLDER**, walnut, stained drk. w/oil, 4¾″ H. ................. $110.00
**TIN SPOUT LAMP**, painted, 7¾″ O.H.
.............................. $300.00
*Row III, L to R*
**IRON TRUNNION LAMP**, early 19th C., PA, sliding reservoir cover & hanger, complete & orig., 10″ H. ........ $400.00
**IRON TRUNNION-MOUNTED KETTLE LAMP**, early 19th C., PA, complete w/pickwick, 6¾″ H. ........... $400.00
**WRT. IRON RUSH LIGHT**, 9¾″ H.
.............................. $350.00
**IRON ADJ. CANDLEHOLDER**, 5 positions, pitting of iron, 9½″ H.
.............................. $200.00
**WRT. IRON RUSH LIGHT**, mounted on wooden block, 12″ H. ......... $150.00

A-MA July 1982    *Richard A. Bourne Co., Inc.*
*Row I, L to R*
**FLUID LAMPS,** pr., blown & pressed, by N. Eng. Glass Co., 1 minus its collar, 8" H. ....................................... $275.00
**WHALE OIL LAMP,** Flint glass, Bigler patt. w/brass collar, no burner, 9" H. ....................................... $100.00
**FLUID LAMP,** blown & pressed glass, sm. chips near corners of base, 10" H. ....................................... $75.00
**WHALE OIL LAMP,** Flint glass, Ellipse & Punty patt., minute base roughage, 10½" H. ....................................... $100.00
*Row II, L to R*
**WHALE OIL LAMPS,** pr., Flint glass, N. Eng. Glass Co., ca. 1840, minor base roughage, 11" H. ............... $275.00
**WHALE OIL LAMP,** Flint glass, Boston & Sandwich Glass Co., Star & Punty patt., slight roughage, orig. brass collar, 10" H. ....................................... $125.00
**FLUID LAMP,** Presentation glass, Boston & Sandwich Glass Co., gold decor., brass stem, 10½" H. ................. $150.00

*Left*
A-MA Dec. 1982    *Robert W. Skinner Inc.*
**TIFFANY THREE-LIGHT LILY LAMP,** ca. 1920, NY, adj. base, gold irid. ribbed shades, mkd. "L.C.T. Favrile," marred, 22¼" H. ........... $2000.00*
*Right*
A-WA D.C. Dec. 1982 *Adam A. Weschler & Son*
**GALLE CAMEO TABLE LAMP,** ca. 1900, glass & gilt bronze, shade has frosted glass overlay, br. amber foliage, trellising vine w/leafage, body is blue-to-frosted ground, trellising amber vines, deep cherry amber base, sgn. "Galle," diameter of shade 9¾", 21¾" H. .......... $2500.00*

A-MA July 1982    *Richard A. Bourne Co., Inc.*
*Row I, L to R*
**BRASS CANDLE LAMP,** heavy mirror-cut flint glass globe, normal roughness, base needs refastened, 11" H. ... $300.00
**SM. BRASS LAMP,** heavy pressed flint glass bull's-eye lens, orig. single drop whale oil lamp, 10¾" O.H. ........... $375.00
*Row II, L to R*
**HALL LAMP,** candle burner & cranberry cut overlay globe w/frosted cutting, 16" O.H. ....................................... $675.00
**RAILROAD-TYPE LANTERN,** by H. & J. Sangster, ca. 1852, orig. tin fluid lamp & heavy pressed glass globe in grape patt., 12" H. ....................................... $400.00

A-MA Mar. 1983    *Robert W. Skinner Inc.*
**WHALE OIL FIRE DEPARTMENT LANTERN,** ca. 1847, sheet iron lantern, pyramid top w/smoke ventilators, one side contains "Perseverance Engine No 5, 1847" in gilt on blk., includes fireman's badge, Hose "5," Beverly ............. $400.00*

*Left*
A-WA D.C. Dec. 1982 *Adam A. Weschler & Son*
**AMERICAN TABLE LAMP,** ca. 1910-20, leaded glass & patinated metal, attrib. to Duffner & Kimberly, diameter of shade 18", 30" H. ..................... $1100.00*

*Right*
A-WA D.C. Dec. 1982 *Adam A. Weschler & Son*
**JEFFERSON TABLE LAMP,** early 20th C., painted glass & patinated metal, mkd. "Jefferson" & "6247," diameter of shade 14", 22¼" H. ................. $600.00*

A-WA D.C. Sept. 1982 *Adam A. Weschler & Son*
**TIFFANY FAVRILLE SCARAB DESK LAMP,** ca. 1892-1900, glass & bronze, impressed monogram "Tiffany Glass and Decorating Company, number 28630" & "Tiffany Studios, New York," 9" H. ....................................... $2600.00*

A-MA Dec. 1982    *Robert W. Skinner Inc.*
**BURMESE CRICKET LIGHT,** late 19th C., three branches, simulated brass Corinthian column on stepped sq. base, 3 acid-finished fairy lamp shades, 13½" W., 19" H. ....................................... $650.00*

*Price does not include 10% buyer fee.

A-MA July 1982    *Richard A. Bourne Co., Inc.*
L to R
**ART NOUVEAU TABLE LAMP,** gr. onyx stem & sq. gr. glass leaded shade w/red flowers on each side, 23½" H. ..................................... $225.00
**ART NOUVEAU TABLE LAMP,** unsgn., cut-out Grape Vine patt., shade: 22" H. ........................... $375.00

A-MA July 1982    *Richard A. Bourne Co., Inc.*
L to R
**TIFFANY BRONZE DESK LAMP,** sgn., irid. blue & gr. Favrile shade, 13" O.H. ............................. $850.00
**BRONZE HANGING WALL LAMP,** turtleback leaded shade, unknown origin, small chips, 14⅛" W., 10¼" H. ... $350.00
**TIFFANY TABLE LAMP,** gold bronze mountings, sgn. "Louis C. Tiffany Furnaces Inc./Favrile/91," body of lamp w/irid. blue & gold paneled glass, orig. Tiffany finial, 21" H. ............................. $550.00

*Left*
A-WA D.C. July 1982 *Adam A. Weschler & Son*
**TIFFANY TURTLE-BACK DESK LAMP,** bronze & gr. irid., ca. 1905, impressed Tiffany Studios, NY, 15" H. ............................. $1700.00*

*Right*
A-WA D.C. July 1982 *Adam A. Weschler & Son*
**ART DECO BRONZE TABLE LAMP,** ca. 1925, shade: 21" D., 22" O.H. ............................. $700.00*

*Left*
A-MA July 1982    *Robert W. Skinner Inc.*
**BRASS OIL LAMP,** ca 1880, lithophane polychrome decor., one panel cracked, 17½" H. ..................... $500.00*

*Right*
A-WA D.C. July 1982 *Adam A. Weschler & Son*
**GALLE CAMEO GLASS LAMP,** ca. 1900, frosted yellow ground overlaid w/shaded cherry red, sgn., shade: 11½" D., 22½" H. ..................... $6800.00*

*Left*
A-MA July 1982    *Robert W. Skinner Inc.*
**PAIRPOINT TABLE LAMP,** MA, reverse painted w/amber & lavender decor., minor chip, shade: 16" D. ...... $650.00*

*Right*
A-MA July 1982    *Robert W. Skinner Inc.*
**PAIRPOINT BLOWN-OUT BOUDOIR LAMP,** ca. 1901, MA, pink & yellow decor. on ribbed wh. shade w/rose on top, 8¼" D., 15" H. ....... $1050.00*

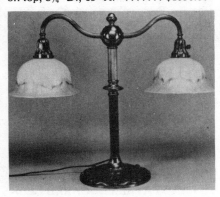

A-OH July 1982    *Early Auction Co.*
**DOUBLE STUDENT LAMP,** ornate metal base w/10" gold sgn. Quezal shades, wh. & gold feather design decor., 24" H. ............................. $1100.00*

*Left*
A-OH July 1982    *Early Auction Co.*
**CROWN MILANO G.W.T.W. HALF SHADE LAMP,** jeweled floral decor., base has age line, shade has slight chip on base ...................... $1050.00*

*Right*
A-OH July 1982    *Early Auction Co.*
**DAUM NANCY LAMP,** sgn., dome shade 9½" D., base & shade decor. w/gr. grapes on lighter gr. background .......................... $2500.00*

A-MA July 1982    *Richard A. Bourne Co., Inc.*
**FR. TOLE LAMP,** weighted base, electrified & redecor., 20" H. ......... $550.00

A-MA Oct. 1982    *Robert W. Skinner Inc.*
**TIFFANY SHADE,** NY, ca. 1920, 18th C., oriental bronze base, shade sgn. "Tiffany Studios, New York," lamp 22" H., shade 18" D. ................. $3500.00*

*Price does not include 10% buyer fee.

A-MA July 1982   Richard A. Bourne Co., Inc.
L to R
**ADJ. BRASS STUDENT LAMP,** single
decorative glass shade, electrified, shade
is modern replacement, 22½″ O.H.
.............................. $325.00
**BRASS DOUBLE STUDENT LAMP,**
pigeon's blood red shades, modern electrified shades, 22″ H. ............ $275.00

A-MA July 1982   *Richard A. Bourne Co., Inc.*
L to R
**LITHOPHANE SHADE,** 5-panel, 6½″
O.H. ........................ $400.00
**LITHOPHANE SHADE,** 5-panel, 6½″ H.
............................ $400.00
**LITHOPHANE SHADE,** umbrella-
shaped, 7½″ D. ............... $450.00

A-MA Aug. 1983   *Richard A. Bourne Co., Inc.*
L to R
**LRG. TABLE LAMP,** attrib. to Tiffany &
Co., bronze base & leaded shade, minor
cracks to leaded glass, shade 24″ D., lamp
29″ H. ...................... $3100.00
**ART NOUVEAU TABLE LAMP,**
bronze tree trunk base w/wisteria leaded
shade, minor damage to pcs. of leaded
glass, shade 24″ D., lamp 29″ H.
............................ $2400.00

*Left*
A-WA D.C. Dec. 1982 *Adam A. Weschler & Son*
**TIFFANY FAVRILE LINEN-FOLD
TABLE LAMP,** ca. 1910, glass & bronze,
mkd. "Tiffany Studios New York 1927
Patent Applied For," diameter of shade
19½″, 22″ H. ............... $1400.00*

*Right*
A-MA Dec. 1982   *Robert W. Skinner Inc.*
**PAIRPOINT REVERSE PAINTED
SCENIC TABLE LAMP,** ca. 1900,
Copley shade, base painted in blue & gr.,
sgn. "H. Fisher," minor chips, 19½″ D.,
25½″ H. ................... $2200.00*

A-MA Aug. 1983   *Richard A. Bourne Co., Inc.*
L to R
**TABLE LAMP,** metal bronze base
w/leaded shade, minor damage to pcs. of
leaded glass, shade 19½″ D., lamp 24½″ H.
............................ $350.00
**TABLE LAMP,** metal bronze base
w/leaded shade, minor damage to pcs. of
leaded glass, shade 20″ D., lamp 27″ H.
............................ $400.00

A-MA Aug. 1983   *Richard A. Bourne Co., Inc.*
**LAMP,** Pairpoint Glass Co., reverse
painted & frosted shade, sgn., turned wood
base w/brass decor., shade 15″ D., lamp
19½″ O.H. ................. $1800.00

A-OH July 1983          *Early Auction Co.*
**G.W.T.W. OVERLAY LAMP,** red
w/enamel poppy & painted leaf decor.,
Tam-O-Shanter shade .......... $95.00

A-OH July 1983          *Early Auction Co.*
**LAMP,** peacock blue aurene shade on
bronze tree trunk base, 13″ D. .. $875.00

*Price does not include 10% buyer fee.

A-OH July 1982          *Early Auction Co.*
**PAIRPOINT LAMP,** 14″ shade, puffy
roses, poppies & butterflies, base sgn.
"Pairpoint, #B3029" ......... $2000.00*

A-OH July 1982          *Early Auction Co.*
**TABLE LAMP,** leaded 18″ shade, decor.
w/apple blossoms, base made by Aladdin
Mfg. Co., Muncie, IN ........ $1250.00*

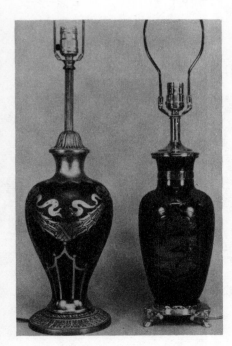

A-OH July 1983          *Early Auction Co.*
*L to R*
**STEUBEN AURENE LAMP,** bluish-
gold, cloth shade, 33″ H. ...... $1500.00
**STEUBEN TABLE LAMP,** plum jade,
A.C.B. oriental village scene .... $1900.00

A-MA June 1983    *Richard A. Bourne Co., Inc.*
**HANDEL LAMP,** w/frosted & decorated
umbrella shade, bronzed white metal base,
shade is reverse painted w/sunset landscape, sgn. on inner rim of shade, has slight
inner rim roughage and 2 slight inner rim
flakes, 22½″ H., shade 14″ D.
............................ $400.00

A-MA Aug. 1983    *Richard A. Bourne Co., Inc.*
**HANDEL TABLE LAMP,** sgn., re-
verse painted & frosted shade, 24¼″ H.
............................ $1000.00

---

A-MA Aug. 1983    *Richard A. Bourne Co., Inc.*
*L to R*
**ART NOUVEAU TABLE LAMP,**
bronze base & leaded glass shade, minor
cracks to glass, shade 17½″ D., lamp 23″ H.
............................ $350.00
**SM. PAIRPOINT TABLE LAMP,** sgn.
on base, sm. chips to shade, shade 9¼″ D.,
lamp 14¼″ H. ................ $1000.00

A-MA June 1983    *Richard A. Bourne Co., Inc.*
**HANDEL TABLE LAMP,** w/leaded and
gold bronze finished metal base, sgn. on
inner upper rim of shade, shade is smoky
amber color w/ruby diamonds around rim,
20″ H., shade 14½″ D. .......... $600.00

A-MA June 1983          *Robert W. Skinner Inc.*
**VICTORIAN OIL LAMP BASE,** ca.
1862, 2-color, 9½″ H. ......... $350.00*

A-MA Aug. 1983*Richard A. Bourne Co., Inc.*
**BUILDER'S HALF MODEL OF "THE IRON BARQUE MARGARET LONGTON,"** mounted on mahogany plank, bow sprit piece is missing, 39½" L., overall length of panel 51½" L. . . . . . . . . . . . . . . . $700.00

*L to R*
A-MA Aug. 1982 *Richard A. Bourne Co., Inc.*
**SHIP'S FIGUREHEAD,** female figure in Moorish style hat w/blue cape, repainted, large age split running vertically from neck through the billet head at the bottom
. . . . . . . . . . . . . . . . . . . . . . . . . . . $500.00

A-MA Aug. 1982 *Richard A. Bourne Co., Inc.*
**VICTORIAN CAST IRON UMBRELLA STAND,** depicting sailor holding ring which holds the umbrellas atop a trophy of crossed paddles, anchors, cargo & other marine objects, 27¾" H.
. . . . . . . . . . . . . . . . . . . . . . . . . . . $625.00

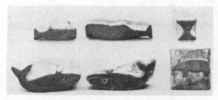

A-MA Aug. 1982 *Richard A. Bourne Co., Inc.*
*Row I, L to R*
**CARVED WOODEN WHALE STAMP,** figure of sperm whale w/square in center
. . . . . . . . . . . . . . . . . . . . . . . . . . . $400.00
**CARVED WOODEN WHALE STAMP,** figure of sperm whale . . . . . . . . . . . $375.00
**DOUBLE CARVED WOODEN WHALE STAMP,** whale's tail at each end
. . . . . . . . . . . . . . . . . . . . . . . . . . . $275.00

*Row II, L to R*
**CARVED WOODEN WHALE STAMPS,** pr., 2 different types of whales
. . . . . . . . . . . . . . . . . . . . . . . . . . . $600.00
**WHALE STAMP,** w/figure of hog
. . . . . . . . . . . . . . . . . . . . . . . . . . . $500.00

A-MA Aug. 1982 *Richard A. Bourne Co., Inc.*
**SCRIMSHAW GAME SET,** on top are initials "T.E.M.," & word "HOPE" on the other side, made of wood w/whalebone inlays, whalebone feet & whalebone card holders & handles, minor damage to decor. on one corner, 3 pawns are missing, dominoe set incom., 14½" L., 6⅞" W., 8" H.
. . . . . . . . . . . . . . . . . . . . . . . . . . . $1700.00

A-MA Aug. 1982 *Richard A. Bourne Co., Inc.*
*Top to Bottom*
**DOUBLE SAILOR'S VALENTINE,** made up entirely of seashells, 9⅛" across the flats . . . . . . . . . . . . . . . . . . . . . $600.00
**SAILOR'S VALENTINE,** made entirely of native seashells, case is missing its hinges & the 2 pcs. are separated, 14¼" across the flats . . . . . . . . . . . . . . . . . . . . . $900.00

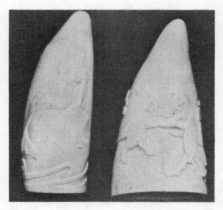

A-MA Aug. 1982 *Richard A. Bourne Co., Inc.*
*L to R*
**SCRIMSHAW WHALE'S TOOTH,** carved w/mermaid on one side & fish on other side, sm. chips in bottom only, 6" L.
. . . . . . . . . . . . . . . . . . . . . . . . . . . $550.00
**SCRIMSHAW WHALE'S TOOTH,** carved w/an African hunting scene, 5½" L.
. . . . . . . . . . . . . . . . . . . . . . . . . . . $500.00

A-MA Aug. 1982 *Richard A. Bourne Co., Inc.*
*L to R*
**SCRIMSHAW ITEMS,** lot of 6, mounted on velvet & framed w/early Victorian frame, items include small needly case, jagging wheel, broach carved w/bird, 2 sewing knives & a button, jagging wheel has been reglued for a break, frame has plaster applique which has been chipped, overall size of frame is 13" x 11"
. . . . . . . . . . . . . . . . . . . . . . . . . . . $400.00
**SCRIMSHAW ITEMS,** lot of 11, mounted on velvet & framed in oval Victorian frame, items include small whale's tooth, ring, pr. of napkin rings, 3 buttons, wheels from a jagging wheel, 2 bodkins & a sewing knife, frame is 13½" x 11½" . . . . . . . . . . . . . . . . . . . . . . . $200.00

A-MA Aug. 1982 *Richard A. Bourne Co., Inc.*
**WALRUS TUSK,** relief carving of a brig w/the word "ERA" on a banner above it, the date of 1899 below it, flowers & scrollwork run the length of the tusk, 20½" L. . . . . . . . . . . . . . . . . . . . . . . . . . $700.00

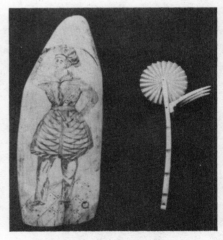

A-MA Aug. 1982 *Richard A. Bourne Co., Inc.*
*L to R*
**SCRIMSHAW WHALE'S TOOTH,** portrait of Fanny Campbell, 7½" L.
. . . . . . . . . . . . . . . . . . . . . . . . . . . $750.00
**SCRIMSHAW JAGGING WHEEL,** open carved handle of hearts & clubs fitted w/3-tined fork, 6½" L. . . . . . . . . . $600.00

A-MA Aug. 1982    *Richard A. Bourne Co., Inc.*
**SAILOR'S VALENTINE IN DOUBLE CASE,** 15¾" D. across flats ..... $550.00

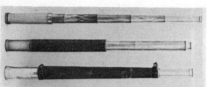

A-MA Aug. 1982    *Richard A. Bourne Co., Inc.*
*Top to Bottom*
**FIVE-DRAW TELESCOPE,** made by J. Ramsden/London, retains orig. wooden tube, 39½" L. ................. $500.00
**SINGLE-DRAW SPYGLASS,** by Dollond London, orig. leather covering, 20¾" L. ......................... $250.00
**SINGLE-DRAW SPYGLASS,** leather covered, made by John Bruce & Sons, South Castle Street, Liverpool, tube slightly bent, retains orig. lens cap, 30½" L. (closed) ...................... $250.00

A-MA Aug. 1982    *Richard A. Bourne Co., Inc.*
**BUILDER'S LAMINATED HALF MODEL OF AN UNIDENTIFIED SAILING SHIP,** small damage at tip of bow sprit, mounted on mahogany w/molding on edge which is chipped, model 27½" L., overall 35¾" L. ............. $750.00

A-MA Nov. 1982    *Richard A. Bourne Co., Inc.*
**DOUBLE SCRIMSHAW SWIFT,** whalebone & ivory, tied w/red & wh. ribbons, 21" H. ................. $950.00

A-MA Nov. 1982    *Richard A. Bourne Co., Inc.*
*L to R*
**CARVED WHALE FIGURE,** yellow & blk. glass eyes, bears maker's initials "JB," paint shows little wear, hole drilled for mounting, 32" L. .............. $300.00
**BARBER POLE,** Am., 19th C., red, wh. & blue striped, shows ravages of time & abuse, probably repainted number of times, 52" H. including mount, barber pole 45" H. ...................... $200.00
**VICTORIAN GAS CIGAR LIGHTER,** words at base "Do Not Touch," traces of orig. paint, 26" H. .............. $300.00
**WOODEN PHARMACIST'S SIGN,** ca. 19th C., orig. paint, 22½" H. .... $350.00

A-MA Nov. 1982    *Richard A. Bourne Co., Inc.*
*L to R*
**SCRIMSHAW BIRD CAGE,** walnut w/whalebone bars, finials & feeding stations, bars are loose on top due to shrinkage, 1 bar at top is broken, 18" L., 17" H., 13" W. ................... $1700.00
**MOUNTED SCRIMSHAW SWIFT,** 12 arms mounted on octagonal base, 1 real drawer, 7 false drawers, minor imperfections, 17½" H. ............. $2300.00

A-MA Aug. 1982    *Richard A. Bourne Co., Inc.*
**"WHALESHIP" SIGN,** in form of sperm whale, well preserved orig. paint, 36" L.
.......................... $125.00

*Left*
A-MA Nov. 1982    *Richard A. Bourne Co., Inc.*
**SCRIMSHAW SEWING BOX,** mahogany, inscribed "D. R. Benton 1853," sides & top have inlays of ivory, m.o.p. & ebony or baleen, 12" L., 9½" W., 4⅝" H. .. $450.00

*Right*
A-MA Nov. 1982    *Richard A. Bourne Co., Inc.*
**SCRIMSHAW SEWING BOX,** mahogany w/inlays of tortoiseshell, whale ivory, m.o.p. & various woods, 15⅝" L., 10½" W., 6½" H. ...................... $1100.00

A-MA Aug. 1982    *Richard A. Bourne Co., Inc.*
**CAMPHORWOOD SEA CAPTAIN'S DESK,** brass mounted w/unusual roll top activated by opening drawer to reveal small compartments, mounted on custom made base, 20½" W., 17" D., 11½" H., overall ht. (including base) 37½" H., writing ht. 33"
........................... $1500.00

A-MA Aug. 1982    *Richard A. Bourne Co., Inc.*
**SCRIMSHAW ON PANBONE,** depicting a view of Boston Harbor, few natural age cracks, placed in modern frame, 7½" x 12¼" ........... $3500.00

A-MA Aug. 1982    *Richard A. Bourne Co., Inc.*
*L to R*
**SCRIMSHAW WALRUS TUSKS,** pr., engraved w/a ship, children's portraits, a sailor, nesting birds, 7 engravings in all, normal age cracks in ivory, 16½" L. .................................... $500.00
**SCRIMSHAW WHALE'S TOOTH,** pinpoint work half figure portrait of a woman, 5½" L. ................. $275.00
**SCRIMSHAW WHALE'S TOOTH,** engraved w/full figure portraits of ladies on each side, 6" L. ............... $575.00

A-MA Aug. 1982    *Richard A. Bourne Co., Inc.*
*Top*
**SCRIMSHAW WHALE'S TOOTH,** engraving on both sides, tooth has a chip on one side of tip, 6½" L. ......... $2000.00
*Bottom, L to R*
**SCRIMSHAW WHALE'S TOOTH,** engraving of 4 scenes encompassing both sides of tooth, small chip in tip of tooth, 5½" L. .......................... $1000.00
**SCRIMSHAW WHALE'S TOOTH,** engraved on both sides, tooth was apparently once mounted on a base, 5⅜" L. .... $1000.00
**SCRIMSHAW WHALE'S TOOTH,** engraved on both sides, some use of red color, slight age crack on side w/ship, slightly chipped on bottom, 6¾" L. .............................. $2000.00

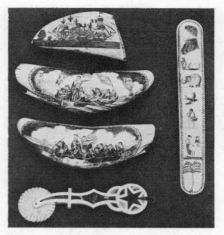

A-MA Aug. 1982    *Richard A. Bourne Co., Inc.*
*Top, L*
**SCRIMSHAW WHALE'S TOOTH,** depicting a naval battle at sea between French & Dutch ships, small chip at broad end of tooth of minor importance, 3½" W., 6¾" L. .......................... $2100.00

*Center, L*
**WHALE'S TEETH,** pr., ca. 1920, engraved w/famous Am. historical scenes, work done by Clarence W. deMontigny, New Bedford, MA, 9½" L. ..... $3750.00

*Bottom, L*
**SCRIMSHAW JAGGING WHEEL,** whale ivory w/tortoise shell inlays, broken on one side near wheel, 8⅜" L. .............................. $1600.00

*Right*
**SCRIMSHAW CORSET BUSK,** engraved on one side, old age splits, 13" L. .............................. $450.00

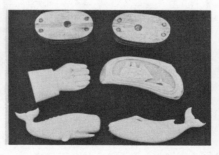

A-MA Aug. 1982    *Richard A. Bourne Co., Inc.*
*Top*
**DOUBLE SHIP'S BLOCKS,** pr., whalebone, 4¼" L. ................. $550.00
*Center, L to R*
**IVORY WHALEBONE SCULPTURE,** in form of clenched hand complete w/sleeve, 4½" H. .............. $250.00
**WHALE'S TOOTH,** late sculpture work of ship chasing a whale, 6¼" L. .. $450.00
*Bottom*
**CARVED WHALEBONE WHALES,** pr., a sperm whale & a humpback whale, sperm whale is 6¼" L., humpback whale is 7¼" L. ....................... $400.00

A-MA Aug. 1982    *Richard A. Bourne Co., Inc.*
*Row I, L to R*
**SCRIMSHAW WHALE'S TOOTH,** engraved on one side w/portrait of George Washington, mounted on a block, 6¾", overall ht. 7" ................ $1150.00
**SCRIMSHAW MANTLE ORNAMENT,** form of a pr. of whale's teeth, each engraved w/an Am. ship, each tip carved into eagle's head, mounted on mahogany stand w/whalebone legs, teeth 5½" L., stand 10¼" L., overall 7½" H. .. $1100.00

*Row II, L to R*
**WHALE'S TOOTH,** hand-carved, in form of bearded man w/stocking cap, 3½" ................................ $300.00
**SCRIMSHAW SCULPTURE WHALE'S TOOTH,** carved in form of an eagle's head, mounted on whalebone & whale ivory stand w/rings of wood between, attrib. to William Perry, eagle's head 4" L., 3½" H. ...................... $400.00
**SCRIMSHAW CANE HEAD,** form of hand clasping a ball, carved from whale ivory, mounted on piece of whalebone, 3¾" H. .............................. $200.00
**SCRIMSHAW WHALE'S TOOTH,** engraved on one side w/portrait of Charles W. Morgan & mounted on block of rough hewn mahogany, tooth sgn. "Hulina," 5" L., overall ht. 6⅜" ................ $200.00

A-MA Aug. 1982    *Richard A. Bourne Co., Inc.*
*L to R*
**SCRIMSHAW WHALE'S TOOTH,** mounted on whalebone base, engraved on one side, 6½" L., overall ht. 7½" .......................... $1600.00

**SCRIMSHAW WHALE'S TOOTH,** engraved on both sides, red & blk. ink, 7" L. .............................. $950.00

**SCRIMSHAW WHALE'S TOOTH,** engraved on one side, 5½" L. ...... $350.00

A-MA Aug. 1982    *Richard A. Bourne Co., Inc.*
*Top*
**WHALE'S TOOTH,** late engraving of an old Nantucket harbor scene, 8″ L.
............................... $850.00
*Center*
**WHALE'S TOOTH,** late engraving of excursion steamer Peter Stuyvesant, sgn. by artist R.M., 6¾″ L. ......... $450.00
*Bottom, L to R*
**WHALE'S TOOTH,** late engraved whaling scene, sgn. MJB, 4½″ L.
............................... $225.00
**WHALE'S TOOTH,** colored engravings of an Eskimo fishing through ice, sgn. CM, 5⅛″ L. ...................... $325.00
**SCRIMSHAW WHALE'S TOOTH,** late engraving of paddle, steam & sail vessel & rough seas, sgn. RM, 6¼″ L. .... $350.00

A-MA Aug. 1982    *Richard A. Bourne Co., Inc.*
**SCRIMSHAW WHALE'S TOOTH,** engraved w/naval scenes on both sides, one minor chip at broad end, 5⅞″ L.
............................... $1900.00
**SCRIMSHAW WHALE'S TOOTH,** engraved overall depicting a naval engagement on one side & a portrait of the warship Isis on the other, 6″ L.
............................... $2900.00

A-MA Aug. 1982    *Richard A. Bourne Co., Inc.*
*Top to Bottom*
**SCRIMSHAW POWDER HORN,** engraved w/rosettes overall, 22″ L.
............................... $325.00
**EARLY POWDER HORN,** engraved w/various animals, birds, designs & bearing the initials "ARK," complete w/orig. wooden plug, 11½″ L. ... $200.00

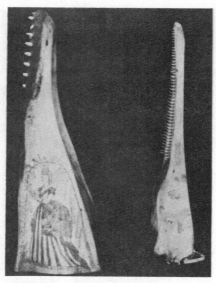

A-MA Aug. 1982    *Richard A. Bourne Co., Inc.*
*L to R*
**BLACKFISH JAW,** engraved on both sides the full figure portrait of a lady standing beneath a flowering bush, 2 of teeth are chipped, 16″ H. ....... $450.00
**PORPOISE JAW,** w/teeth, engraved on one side of jawbone w/a figure of a lion or leopard & some birds, 2 of teeth are missing, 15″ L. ................ $175.00

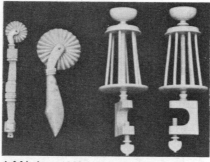

A-MA Aug. 1982    *Richard A. Bourne Co., Inc.*
*L to R*
**JAGGING WHEEL,** bone w/abalone shell squares & diamonds, 6½″ L.
............................... $400.00
**SCRIMSHAW JAGGING WHEEL,** whale ivory handle, wheel 2⅜″ D., 6″ L.
............................... $425.00
**ELEPHANT IVORY WINDERS,** pr., w/clamps, 8″ L. ............... $450.00

A-MA Aug. 1982    *Richard A. Bourne Co., Inc.*
*Top, L to R*
**SCRIMSHAW WHALE'S TOOTH BY FRANK,** depicting the Bark Wonderer on one side, the other side left rough, 7″ L.
............................... $500.00
**SCRIMSHAW WHALE'S TOOTH BY FRANK,** depicting the Bark Wonderer w/a whale in the foreground, sgn. center left, 6½″ L. ................... $400.00
*Center, L to R*
**WHALE'S TOOTH,** late engraving of an Am. clipper ship on one side, 5⅞″ L.
............................... $225.00
**SCRIMSHAW WHALE'S TOOTH,** late engraving of a Pacific whaling scene on one side, 5½″ L. ................... $175.00
**WHALE'S TOOTH,** late engraving of a whaling scene done after "The Capture," 4¾″ L. ...................... $140.00
*Bottom, L to R*
**SCRIMSHAW WHALE'S TOOTH BY FRANK,** depicting the ship "Resolution 1772," sgn. lower left, 6¼″ L. .... $375.00
**SCRIMSHAW WHALE'S TOOTH,** late engraving of eagle w/trophy of arms & flags, 4¼″ L. .................. $150.00
**WHALE'S TOOTH,** w/large active whaling scene, 4⅝″ L. ........... $325.00
**WHALE'S TOOTH,** late engraving around its entire circumference depicting whaling scene, a village, coastal shipping, etc., sgn. "Lyons" at top, 4¾″ L.
............................... $180.00
**WHALE'S TOOTH,** engraved on one side a naval engagement between an Am. & a British ship, on other an Am. sailor holding the Am. flag, slight crack, 4¼″ L.
............................... $250.00

A-MA Aug. 1982    *Richard A. Bourne Co., Inc.*
**SHIP'S WOODEN WHEEL,** brass hub & rivets, 52½″ D., not including spokes
............................... $825.00

A-MA Nov. 1982    *Richard A. Bourne Co., Inc.*
*L to R*
**SAILOR'S VALENTINE,** orig. case w/decor. of Am. sloop under sail on tin cover, 10″ D. ................. $550.00
**SCRIMSHAW CANDLESTICKS,** pr., whalebone, 8″ H. ............. $450.00

*Left*
A-MA July 1982    *Richard A. Bourne Co., Inc.*
**SCRIMSHAW SPERM WHALE'S TOOTH,** engraved w/patriotic & political decor., age cracks, 7¼″ L., at base: 3⅞″ W. ............................. $1300.00

*Right*
A-MA July 1982    *Richard A. Bourne Co., Inc.*
*L to R*
**SCRIMSHAW JAGGING WHEEL,** whale ivory, repr. w/small chips, 5¼″ O.L. ................................ $250.00
**SCRIMSHAW JAGGING WHEEL,** whale ivory, handle w/billethead-like scroll, 4¾″ L. ............ $300.00
**SCRIMSHAW CORSET BUSK,** engraved on one side, 13⅝″ L. ..... $550.00
**SCRIMSHAW SPERM WHALE'S TOOTH,** initialed "AP," small chips, 5″ L. ................................ $175.00

A-MA Aug. 1982    *Richard A. Bourne Co., Inc.*
**BUILDER'S PLATE,** for U.S. Revenue Steamer "Gallatin," red paint has been mostly scraped from the large letters, 15¾″ L., 12″ H. ................... $750.00

A-MA Aug. 1982    *Richard A. Bourne Co., Inc.*
**SCRIMSHAW WHALE'S TOOTH,** by Frederick Myrick, engraving is the ship Barclay of Nantucket, very slight age crack near bottom & one near the tip, 6″ L., 3⅛″ W. ........................ $14000.00

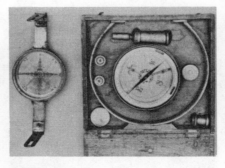

A-MA Aug. 1982    *Richard A. Bourne Co., Inc.*
**JOURNAL LOG BOOK,** kept on board the ship Mary, Edgartown, MA, orig. cover w/spine worn & pages loose .... $6000.00

A-MA July 1982    *Richard A. Bourne Co., Inc.*
*L to R*
**CASED SURVEYOR'S INSTRUMENT,** made by W. & L.E. Gurley Co., tripod missing, 13¼″ x 12¼″ .... $1100.00
**BRASS SURVEYOR'S COMPASS,** Eng., made by J. Gilbert, needle off its pivot, 12″ L., 5⅜″ D. .......... $325.00

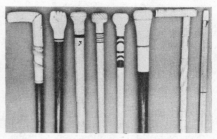

A-MA Aug. 1982    *Richard A. Bourne Co., Inc.*
*L to R*
**SCRIMSHAW CANE,** wooden shaft, carved bone & ivory handle w/serpent, 2 small chips in the snake's body, 35½″ L. ............................... $175.00
**SCRIMSHAW CANE,** island wood shaft & carved whale ivory handle in form of a hand, thumb chipped off at end, 33″ L. ............................... $190.00
**SCRIMSHAW CANE,** whalebone shaft & turned whale ivory head, heavy brass tip has been added later, 31⅛″ L. ... $250.00
**SCRIMSHAW CANE,** rope carved whalebone shaft & rope carved whale ivory knob set w/silver coin, 35½″ L. ............................... $360.00
**SCRIMSHAW CANE,** whalebone shaft, wood inlays, turned whale ivory knob, 33½″ L. ........................... $300.00
**SCRIMSHAW CANE,** island wood shaft & heavy whale ivory neck & knob at neck is cracked, 34″ L. ............... $120.00
**SCRIMSHAW CANE,** shaft made up of 18 pcs. of cylindrical carved bone w/matching bone handle, 32¼″ L. ....... $200.00
**SCRIMSHAW YARDSTICK,** wood w/ivory & wood inlays & initials "MFY" ............................... $120.00

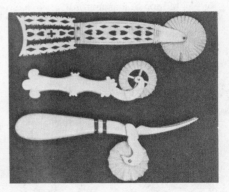

A-MA Aug. 1982    *Richard A. Bourne Co., Inc.*
*Top to Bottom*
**SCRIMSHAW JAGGING WHEEL,** w/ reticulated handle, 7½″ L. ...... $750.00
**SM. SCRIMSHAW JAGGING WHEEL,** broken & reglued at end of handle where it holds the wheel, 5½″ L. ............................... $170.00
**SCRIMSHAW JAGGING WHEEL,** whale ivory w/3-tined fork & wheel holder in form of turkey's head, 7½″ L. ............................... $450.00

A-MA Aug. 1982    *Richard A. Bourne Co., Inc.*
*L to R*
**SCRIMSHAW DITTY BOX,** w/wooden cover & bottom, panbone sides, embellished w/small cartouche of a whale & inlaid on the cover w/banners which read "R.V.C." & another which has the date "1852" & a whale in between them, 8" L. ............................. $800.00

**WHALEBONE LANTERN,** for a candle, 8¼" H. ..................... $1500.00

**SCRIMSHAW DITTY BOX,** w/mahogany top & pine bottom w/dovetail like fingers joining it, some damage to fingers, an old piece of paper on the bottom penned w/"The box & contents the property of Maud North," 9¼" L. .......... $525.00

A-MA Aug. 1982    *Richard A. Bourne Co., Inc.*
**SCRIMSHAW DITTY BOX,** baleen w/wooden bottom & padded top w/painted apple blossoms on it, cover has a damage where the 2 bands come together & has been reglued & repr. crudely, 8" L. ............................. $250.00

A-MA Aug. 1982    *Richard A. Bourne Co., Inc.*
*L to R*
**SCRIMSHAW WHALE'S TEETH,** pr., engravings in color on both sides, 5¼" L. ............................. $850.00

**SCRIMSHAW WHALE'S TOOTH,** engraved on each side w/representations of birds, tooth has been broken in half vertically & reglued, 4½" L. ..... $150.00

A-MA Aug. 1982    *Richard A. Bourne Co., Inc.*
*Row I, L to R*
**SCRIMSHAW LADY'S POCKET-BOOK,** in form of ditty box, engraved w/whaling scene on one side, sturdy wood & bone handle, 4 bone feet, lined w/suede, 7" L. ............................. $800.00
**NANTUCKET POCKETBOOK,** sgn. "Farnum/79," w/scrimshaw simulated bone or ivory top, minor unraveling at back needs restoration .............. $125.00
*Row II, L to R*
**SCRIMSHAW DITTY BOX,** mahogany top & bottom w/whalebone sides to box & cover, int. retains old plaid material in the cover, 7¾" L. ................. $700.00
**SCRIMSHAW DITTY BOX,** mahogany bottom & top, sides of both cover & box are panbone & made w/5 almost human-like fingers at side, bottom wood may be replm., 6" L. ................. $700.00

A-MA Aug. 1982    *Richard A. Bourne Co., Inc.*
**SCRIMSHAW TRAVEL DESK,** walnut w/whalebone feet, knobs & trim, 11½" W., 9½" D., 9¼" H. .............. $1000.00

A-MA Aug. 1982    *Richard A. Bourne Co., Inc.*
**WHALE'S TOOTH,** carved & engraved on wooden mounting, showing ship Charles W. Morgan & initials "CWM," 5⅜" L. ............................. $325.00

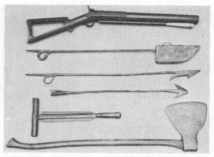

A-MA Aug. 1982    *Richard A. Bourne Co., Inc.*
*Top to Bottom*
**IRON BRAND BOMB HARPOON GUN,** ramrod is a replm. ...... $450.00
**DARTING HARPOON FOR AN EBEN PIERCE DARTING GUN,** complete w/sheath made of wood w/canvas covering, retains traces of orig. orange paint ............................. $150.00

**EBEN PIERCE DARTING HARPOON,** traces of orange paint ..... $100.00
**ARROWHEAD ARCTIC DOUBLE FLUE HARPOON,** worn, rusted & bent ............................. $100.00

**MINCING KNIFE,** w/handles at each end & blades on both sides ......... $175.00
**BROAD AXE** ................. $125.00

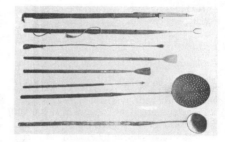

A-MA Aug. 1982    *Richard A. Bourne Co., Inc.*
*Top to Bottom*
**EBEN PIERCE DARTING HARPOON GUN,** mounted on orig. pole, 81½" L. ............................. $1300.00
**LONG-HANDLED BLUBBER FORK,** mounted on orig. pole, traces of orig. orange paint, 85" L. ............ $350.00

**LANCE,** bent & rusted, broken off at pole, 67½" L. ..................... $50.00
**HEAD SPADE,** mkd. D. Gray, mounted as a deck spade w/shorter handle, retains orig. handle, 74" L. ............. $80.00

**BONE SPADE WORK DOWN,** mounted for use as deck spade, retains orig. pole, 60½" L. .............. $70.00
**ARROWHEAD HARPOON,** 58½" L. ............................. $70.00

**SKIMMER,** retains orig. pole, 88" L. ............................. $500.00
**DIPPER,** mounted on orig. pole, 85½" L. ............................. $275.00

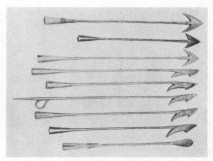

A-MA Aug. 1982 *Richard A. Bourne Co., Inc.*
*Top to Bottom*
**DOUBLE-FLUE ARCTIC HARPOON,**
normal rusting, 34″ L. ......... $300.00
**DOUBLE-FLUE ARCTIC HARPOON,**
retains orig. blk. protective paint, 27″ L.
............................. $150.00
**DOUBLE-FLUE ARCTIC HARPOON,**
initials of maker faintly visible, normal
rusted surface, 34¾″ L. ........ $275.00
**TEMPLE TOGGLE HARPOON,** normal rusted surface, ½″ of tip is broken off,
36″ L. ..................... $125.00
**TOGGLE HARPOON,** less rust than
usual, 33″ L. .................. $150.00
**DARTING TOGGLE HARPOON,** has
been straightened & still shows bend,
traces of orig. orange rustproofing paint,
39½″ L. ..................... $200.00
**TOGGLE HARPOON,** less than normal
rusting, 35½″ L. ............... $150.00
**TOGGLE HARPOON,** blk. preservative
paint well preserved, 32½″ L. .... $175.00
**SHORT KILLING IRON OR LANCE,**
normal rust & pitting, some blk. preservative paint still in evidence, 29″ L.
............................. $175.00

A-MA Aug. 1982 *Richard A. Bourne Co., Inc.*
*Top to Bottom*
**MINCING KNIFE,** bearing the name V.
Doane & initials V.D. on sheath, blade
mkd. "Brades Co Cast Steel," 37″ L.
............................. $350.00
**CUTTING SPADE,** bears the name
Snow & Paddington, 21½″ L. ... $125.00
**FLENSING KNIFE,** unmkd., wood
handle & canvas covered wooden sheath,
sheath deteriorating, canvas is rotted away
at both ends, 60½″ L. ......... $375.00
**LANCE OR KILLING IRON,** bearing
the name of the maker G & EH Giffold,
mkd. Charlestown below the name, orig.
pole & rope, 133″ L. .......... $325.00
**DECK SPADE,** orig. a bone spade, orig.
handle, 51⅝″ L. .............. $150.00
**TOGGLE HARPOON,** orig. pole & rope
work, bent from use & normal pitting from
rust, 100¾″ L. ................ $225.00

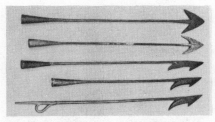

A-MA Aug. 1982 *Richard A. Bourne Co., Inc.*
**DOUBLE-FLUE ARCTIC HARPOON,**
normal surface pitting due to salt water,
34¾″ L. ..................... $250.00
**DOUBLE-FLUE ARCTIC HARPOON,**
more than ½ of shaft has been repl., normal
surface rust, 33½″ L. .......... $125.00
**TEMPLE TOGGLE IRON,** mkd. "BSB"
on one side & Roman numeral "III" on the
other & the maker's mark "D" & "S,"
retains part of orig. wrapping, point is
slightly blunted, 35″ L. ......... $400.00
**TOGGLE HARPOON,** mkd. "BR" on
one side of blade & the maker's mark
"JDD," 29¼″ L. ............... $175.00
**TOGGLE HARPOON FOR DARTING
GUN,** maker's mark "JDD" on one side of
blade, 35-3/5″ L. .............. $300.00

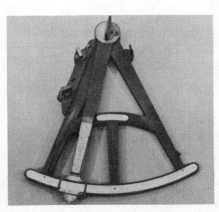

A-MA Aug. 1982 *Richard A. Bourne Co., Inc.*
**QUADRANT,** 18th C., inlaid ivory calibrations & name plate, bears the name
Benjamin E. Gorton, engraved brass piece
mounted on arm, number of parts missing
............................. $875.00

A-MA Aug. 1982 *Richard A. Bourne Co., Inc.*
**CASED QUADRANT,** 18th C., bearing
ivory label which reads "Made by John
Hardy-Ratcliff-London/*For Joseph-
Green-1774*," orig. oak case ... $2000.00

A-MA Aug. 1982 *Richard A. Bourne Co., Inc.*
**CASED QUADRANT,** ivory nameplate
of E & G W Blunt, complete w/oak case &
ivory engraved calibrations, minor damage
to ivory...................... $700.00

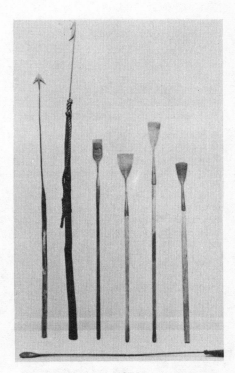

A-MA Aug. 1982 *Richard A. Bourne Co., Inc.*
*L to R*
**ARCTIC OR DOUBLE FLUE HARPOON,** orig. pole, typical rust surface,
bent from use, 85″ L. ......... $225.00
**TOGGLE HARPOON,** orig. pole
w/rope, traces of orig. orange preservative
paint, 104″ L. ................ $200.00
**DECK SIZE BONE SPADE,** orig. pole,
64¾″ L. ..................... $50.00
**HEAD SPADE,** cut down for deck use,
60½″ L. ..................... $90.00
**BLUBBER SPADE,** orig. pole, cut down
to deck size, 71″ L. ............ $80.00
**DECK SPADE,** orig. pole, blade is
chipped, shows much wear & use, 58″ L.
............................. $60.00

*Bottom*
**LANCE OR KILLING IRON,** mounted
on orig. pole, mkd. "Cast Steel," retains
some orig. orange preservative paint, 126″
L. .......................... $175.00

A-MA Aug. 1982    *Richard A. Bourne Co., Inc.*
**OIL ON CANVAS,** William H. Yorke, British 19th C., portrait of the steam sail ship George Fisher, unsgn., 23½" x 35½" ............................ $2300.00

A-MA Aug. 1982    *Richard A. Bourne Co., Inc.*
**WATERCOLOR ON PAPER,** Antoine Roux, Fr. 1765-1835, "Paul Pry, CAPtn J Foster 1828," sgn. lower right "Ant. Roux Mars Ile 1828," painting is foxed overall & slightly faded, framed, w/4-page letter written in Fr. w/seals & labels, mkd. on envelope "Property of H.I. Chapelle Cambridge Maryland," w/envelope attached, 13" x 17" ........... $1600.00

A-MA Aug. 1982    *Richard A. Bourne Co., Inc.*
**OIL ON CANVAS,** James Gale Tyler, Am. 1855-1931, U.S.S. Constitution at Sea, modern replm. frame, 24" x 33" ............................ $1100.00

A-MA Aug. 1982    *Richard A. Bourne Co., Inc.*
**LITHOGRAPH,** Gordon Grant, The Whale Hunt, orig. sgn., paper has toned slightly, 9" x 10" .............. $250.00

A-MA Aug. 1982    *Richard A. Bourne Co., Inc.*
**OIL ON CANVAS,** William Kimmins McMinn, 1854-1880, Liverpool, Eng., unsgn., relined, replm. frame, 20" x 30" ............................ $3500.00

A-MA Aug. 1982    *Richard A. Bourne Co., Inc.*
**SHADOW BOX MODEL OF A BARQUE SAILING BY A LIGHT-HOUSE,** 1 sail has come unglued & needs repr., 16½" H., 22½" L., 4" D. ... $275.00

A-MA Aug. 1982    *Richard A. Bourne Co., Inc.*
**PAINTED PANBONE,** oil painting on bone, border is painted in gr. scroll work w/gold flowers, 10¾" x 20", image size 8" x 17" .................... $4500.00

A-MA Aug. 1982    *Richard A. Bourne Co., Inc.*
**OIL ON CANVAS,** possibly South African school, "View of the 'Artisan' of Boston-Smith, COMdr off Queenstown 1871," unsgn., title on brass plate affixed to orig. walnut frame, frame has gold liner, 27" x 40" ...................... $3000.00

A-MA Aug. 1982    *Richard A. Bourne Co., Inc.*
**OIL ON PAPER,** William Y. Yorke, 19th C., sgn. lower right "W.H. Yorke" & dated 1867, backed on heavy pasteboard which has number of knife marks on reverse side, slight evidence of one slice having gone through painting, 11" x 17½" .... $2500.00

A-MA Aug. 1982    *Richard A. Bourne Co., Inc.*
**PAINTING,** D. McFarlane, "Portrait of the American ship Weymouth off the English coast," maple frame, 19" x 27¾" ............................ $4000.00

A-MA Aug. 1982    *Richard A. Bourne Co., Inc.*
**OIL ON CANVAS,** Antonio Jacobsen, Am. 1850-1921, portrait of the ship San Domingo, sgn. lower left "A. Jacobsen 1888/705 Palisades Av. West Hoboken, NJ," framed under glass, 24" x 42" ............................ $5750.00

A-MA Aug. 1982    *Richard A. Bourne Co., Inc.*
**OIL PAINTING,** Earl Collins, "Flying Cloud," orig. driftwood style frame, tilted & sgn. lower right, 24" x 36" ....... $850.00

A-MA July 1982    *Richard A. Bourne Co., Inc.*
**ENGRAVED MAP,** Italian, ca. 16th C., sm. tear, lightly foxed, 17″ x 21″
............................ $300.00

A-MA July 1982    *Richard A. Bourne Co., Inc.*
**LRG. FOLIO LITHO,** "The Trotting Gelding Frank w/J. O. Nay, His Running Mate," pub. by Currier & Ives in 1884, orig. blk. walnut frame ............. $450.00

A-MA Aug. 1982    *Richard A. Bourne Co., Inc.*
**OIL ON CANVAS,** Antonio Jacobsen, Am. 1850-1921, "Tugboat Komuk," sgn. lower right "A. Jacobsen 1888/705 Palisade Av West Hoboken, NJ," replm. frame, 21¾″ x 36″ ................... $5500.00

A-MA July 1982    *Richard A. Bourne Co., Inc.*
**CURRIER & IVES LITHO.,** "The Stray-Yard Winter," slightly faded & foxed, paper toned, later bird's-eye maple frame
............................ $350.00

A-MA July 1982    *Richard A. Bourne Co., Inc.*
**CURRIER & IVES LITHO.,** "On The Hudson," paper toned a soft tan color, faded slightly, period Victorian frame
............................ $140.00

A-MA Aug. 1982    *Richard A. Bourne Co., Inc.*
**OIL ON CANVAS,** Am., 19th C. school, "Brem. Ship Elizabeth. Capt----," part of title is missing due to flaking, orig. gilt frame, 22″ x 33″ ............. $4000.00

A-MA Aug. 1983    *Robert C. Eldred Co., Inc.*
**OIL ON MASONITE PAINTING,** framed, "No School Today," sgn. Moses, 24″ x 36″ ................... $65000.00

A-MA Aug. 1982    *Richard A. Bourne Co., Inc.*
**OIL ON CANVAS,** William Kimmins McMinn, "The James Longton," sgn. left "W. K. McMinn," dated 1863, relined, replm. gilt frame, 20″ x 30″ ..... $4000.00

A-MA Aug. 1982    *Richard A. Bourne Co., Inc.*
**WATERCOLOR,** sgn. "Ant Roux Marseille 1821," very slight foxing, orig. frame w/repr. to gesso, 17″ x 23″ ..... $4750.00

A-MA Aug. 1983    *Richard A. Bourne Co., Inc.*
**OIL ON CANVAS,** by Antonio Jacobsen, sgn., gilt frame, 23¾″ x 42″ ..... $7000.00

A-MA Aug. 1982    *Richard A. Bourne Co., Inc.*
**OIL ON HEAVY PASTEBOARD,** Fred Pansing, Am., "Battleship at Sea," sgn. lower right "Fred Pansing," 7″ x 10″
............................ $425.00

A-MA Aug. 1982    *Richard A. Bourne Co., Inc.*
**OIL ON CANVAS,** William Kimmins McMinn, "The Margaret Longton," unsgn., relined, 20″ x 30″ ............ $3500.00

A-MA Aug. 1982     *Richard A. Bourne Co., Inc.*
**OIL ON CANVAS,** mounted on beaver-board, Chinese, 19th C. school, "City of Peking," restor. for crazing, relined, framed in a period Victorian walnut frame, 18" x 23½" ...................... $1850.00

A-MA Aug. 1982     *Richard A. Bourne Co., Inc.*
**OIL ON CANVAS,** Am., 19th C. school, "SCHr. Star of West-Dennis Browning B. Crowell Master," retains orig. gold liner as a frame, unsgn., 20" x 30" ...... $2200.00

A-MA Aug. 1982     *Richard A. Bourne Co., Inc.*
**OIL ON CANVAS,** Am., 19th C. school, "An American Steam Frigate Heading Out To Sea," unsgn., modern replm. frame, 20" x 30" ...................... $3250.00

A-MA Nov. 1982     *Richard A. Bourne Co., Inc.*
**OIL ON CANVAS,** British School, 19th C., "Vancouver - A.M. Lunt Comdr," faint signature visible at lower right, relined, no frame, 20" x 30" ............. $4250.00

A-MA July 1982     *Richard A. Bourne Co., Inc.*
**OIL ON CANVAS,** mkd. "L. F. Porter/ 1922," 19" x 14" ............. $100.00

A-MA July 1982     *Richard A. Bourne Co., Inc.*
**OIL ON CANVAS,** by Walter White, "The Sea," sgn., old frame, 18" x 24" ............................. $300.00

A-MA July 1982     *Richard A. Bourne Co., Inc.*
**WATERCOLOR ON PAPER,** by Louis K. Harlow, sgn., paper toned, faded, orig. frame & matting, 7¾" x 19¾" .... $100.00

A-MA July 1982     *Richard A. Bourne Co., Inc.*
**OIL ON CANVAS,** Am., 19th C., "The Reception of Lafayette at Mount Vernon," unframed, relined, 19½" x 27½" .. $250.00

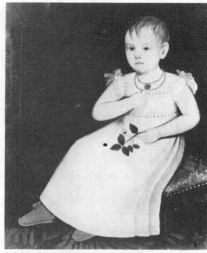

A-MA Oct. 1982     *Robert W. Skinner Inc.*
**OIL ON CANVAS,** Ammi Phillips, Am., 1788-1865, "Portrait of Mary Margaret Deuel," orig. repainted frame lacking corner moldings, 29¾" x 23¾" ......................... $90,000.00*

A-MA Aug. 1982     *Robert W. Skinner Inc.*
**OIL ON CANVAS,** possibly NY or PA, early 19th C., "Portrait of a woman wearing a blk. dress w/a wide lace collar," areas of restoration, unframed, 28" x 24" ............................. $400.00*

A-MA Aug. 1982     *Richard A. Bourne Co., Inc.*
**OIL ON CANVAS,** Am., 19th C. school, "Brave Old Kearsarge," relined, modern replm. frame, 20" x 30" ........ $3250.00

*Price does not include 10% buyer fee.

A-MA Aug. 1982    *Richard A. Bourne Co., Inc.*
**OIL ON HEAVY PASTEBOARD,** Fred Pansing, Am., late 19th C., "Warship Yorktown," unsgn., 7" x 9" ...... $325.00

A-MA July 1982    *Richard A. Bourne Co., Inc.*
**PORTRAITS,** pr., attrib. to Benjamin Greenleaf, oil reverse painted on glass, ca. 1810, minor flaking, orig. molded pine frames, 13½" x 9½" ........... $2200.00

A-MA Nov. 1982    *Richard A. Bourne Co., Inc.*
**FOLIO CURRIER & IVES LITHOGRAPH,** "The Nearest Way In Summer Time," from painting by T. Creswick, RA, minor foxing & knot holes in back, orig. Victorian gilt frame............. $375.00

A-MA July 1982    *Robert W. Skinner Inc.*
**FRAKTUR,** early 19th C., PA, inscription in circular motif flanked by tulips and birds, tear, 7½" x 12½" .............. $425.00*

A-MA July 1982    *Richard A. Bourne Co., Inc.*
**BUCKRAM EAGLE,** ca. 1850, gold & yellow bird perched on three squares which are red, wh. & blue, Victorian shadow box frame, 17" x 15" ............... $80.00

A-OH July 1982    *Garth's Auctions, Inc.*
**CUT SILHOUETTE,** lady seated in chair, back of modern frame is mkd. "Lise Isaac, 1850," 7¼" x 9¼" ............... $85.00
**HOLLOW CUT SILHOUETTE,** woman, hair, collar & bodice are rendered in blue & blk. watercolor, gilded brass matt is old, gilded frame is replm., 6" x 6⅞" ................... $250.00
**CUT SILHOUETTE,** full length of young gentleman w/cigar, wh. backing paper is wrinkled & trimmed, framed, 6⅝" x 9⅝" ............................... $25.00

**HOLLOW CUT SILHOUETTE,** gentleman in tin type case, blk. cloth backing, 3¼" x 3⅝" ......................... $15.00
**SILVER PILL BOX,** oval, embossed basket of flowers, mkd. "800," 1" x 1⅜" ............................ $155.00

A-MA July 1982    *Richard A. Bourne Co., Inc.*
*Row I, L to R*
**PORTRAIT SILHOUETTE,** young man, paper toned & frail, sm. pc. missing in lower left, orig. crude hand-carved frame, 2¾" x 2½" ........................ $70.00
**SILHOUETTES,** pr., Am., 19th C., children w/penciled highlighting, paper slightly toned, orig. simple carved frame, 3½" x 2½" ....................... $60.00
**SILHOUETTE,** gentleman, painted on ivory w/incised hair & wh. collar, orig. lacquered frame, 2½" x 2" ........ $90.00
*Row II, L to R*
**SILHOUETTE,** gentleman, gold painted glasses & hair details, paper toned warm br., orig. lacquered frame, 2⅞" x 2⅛" ................................ $70.00
**SILHOUETTE,** gentleman, gold hair & highlights, paper toned, orig. lacquered frame, 3⅝" x 2⅝" ................. $100.00
**PORTRAIT SILHOUETTE,** gentleman, gold highlights of hair, beard & coat details, paper toned, orig. lacquer frame, 3¼" x 2⅝" ................................ $90.00

A-MA July 1982    *Richard A. Bourne Co., Inc.*
**PORTRAIT,** attrib. to Benjamin Greenleaf, ME, ca. 1810-1817, orig. gilt frame, accompanied by matching frame, oil reverse painted on glass, 16¼" x 11½" ............................... $850.00

**PAPER DOLL,** printed in satin & lace dress & bonnet, shadowbox frame, 5" x 7¾" ........................ $55.00
**CUT SILHOUETTE,** boy, "James McKenzie July 29, 1846," shadowbox frame, 8" x 9¾" ............... $100.00

**GLASS SILHOUETTE,** youth, reverse painted, wh. is flaked, inlaid frame has damage, 4½" sq. ............... $40.00
**HOLLOW CUT SILHOUETTE,** young man, collar is done in pencil, 4⅝" x 5⅞" ............................ $30.00

*Price does not include 10% buyer fee.

A-MA Aug. 1983    *Richard A. Bourne Co., Inc.*
**COVERLET,** blue & wh., sgn. & dated
1833, sm. holes, 73" x 83" . . . . . . . $250.00

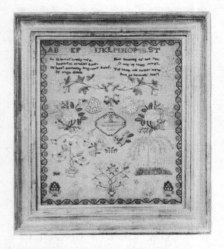

A-MA Aug. 1983    *Richard A. Bourne Co., Inc.*
**NEEDLEWORK SAMPLER,** unsgn.,
early 19th C., framed, overall discoloration,
16" x 19" . . . . . . . . . . . . . . . . . . . . . $500.00

A-MA Aug. 1983    *Richard A. Bourne Co., Inc.*
**NEEDLEWORK SAMPLER,** ca. 1819,
framed, modest fading, 16½" x 17"
. . . . . . . . . . . . . . . . . . . . . . . . . $1100.00

A-MA Aug. 1983    *Richard A. Bourne Co., Inc.*
**NEEDLEWORK SAMPLER,** ca. 1817,
framed, 17" sq. . . . . . . . . . . . . . . . $900.00

A-MA Aug. 1983    *Robert W. Eldred Co., Inc.*
**APPLIQUED FRIENDSHIP QUILT,**
Am., sgn. & dated 1850-52, matching
pillow, 6' x 6' . . . . . . . . . . . . . . . . $2800.00

A-MA Aug. 1983    *Richard A. Bourne Co., Inc.*
**NEEDLEWORK SAMPLER,** Eng., ca.
1840, framed, overall discoloration & deterioration of silk, 13½" x 20" . . . . $600.00

A-MA Aug. 1983    *Richard A. Bourne Co., Inc.*
**NEEDLEWORK SAMPLER,** ca. 1831,
framed, overall discoloration, damage to
background, 13½" x 16" . . . . . . . . $450.00

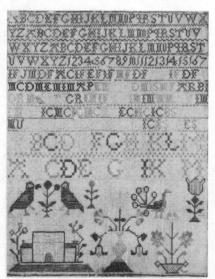

A-MA Aug. 1983    *Richard A. Bourne Co., Inc.*
**NEEDLEWORK SAMPLER,** Eng., ca.
1837, framed, 22" x 23" . . . . . . . . $800.00

A-MA Aug. 1983    *Richard A. Bourne Co., Inc.*
**NEEDLEWORK SAMPLER,** unsgn.,
Eng., early 19th C., framed, modest
damage, 13" x 17½" . . . . . . . . . . . $200.00

A-MA Oct. 1982          *Robert W. Skinner Inc.*
**APPLIQUE QUILT,** PA, ca. 1860, gray, red, blk., yellow, 84″ sq. ....... $800.00*

A-MA Nov. 1982     *Richard A. Bourne Co., Inc.*
**APPLIQUED & NEEDLEWORK QUILT,** 19th C., sgn. "MM," minor stains on back, 86″ x 87″ ........... $5600.00

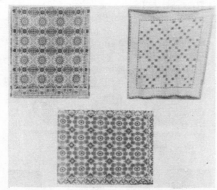

A-OH Jan. 1983          *Garth's Auctions, Inc.*
*Row I, L to R*
**TWO-PIECE JACQUARD COVER-LET,** single weave, red, blue, wh. & gr., dated "1857," minor wear, 74″ x 88″
.............................. $300.00
**PIECED QUILT W/TRAPUNTO,** faded red calico on wh., stains, worn, 74″ x 82″
.............................. $325.00
*Row II*
**TWO-PIECE JACQUARD COVER-LET,** single weave, red, wh. & 2 shades of blue, sgn. "Wove by D. Smith," wear, stains & patch, 70″ x 88″ ............ $150.00

A-MA Aug. 1982          *Robert W. Skinner Inc.*
**SILK MEMORIAL,** framed, embroidered & painted, a woman standing in a scenic setting beside an urn monument inscribed "Sacred to the memory of Mary Lindsay, aged 3 years, May 14, 1823," variety of colors, reverse label "William Shermer, 30 Arch St., Philadelphia," 20½″ x 23″
.......................... $1100.00*

A-MA Mar. 1983          *Robert W. Skinner Inc.*
**NEEDLEWORK SAMPLER,** 18th C., Philadelphia school, "Catherine Goodman, her work made in the 13th year of her age March 29th --," finely worked in a variety of stitches, silk yarns on natural linen gauze, 22¼″ x 17¼″ ................. $4500.00*

A-MA Nov. 1982     *Richard A. Bourne Co., Inc.*
**FRIENDSHIP QUILT,** Baltimore, ca. 1840's, appliqued & quilted, areas of wear w/few minor repr., orig. wh. toned to slightly tan color, 97¾″ x 95¾″ .. $5500.00

A-MA Jan. 1983          *Robert W. Skinner Inc.*
**NEEDLEWORK SAMPLER,** 18th C., signature vase sgn. "Elizabeth Sheffield, October 11, 1784" ........... $8500.00*

A-OH Feb. 1983          *Garth's Auctions, Inc.*
**QUILT,** pieced & appliqued, 12 star designs, blue gr., goldenrod, br. & multi-colored prints, machine stitched applique, hand quilted, 86″ x 109″ ........ $275.00

A-MA Aug. 1982          *Robert W. Skinner Inc.*
**APPLIQUED & EMBROIDERED HEARTH RUG,** N. Eng., early 19th C., filling a red basket is a spray of madder red & buff colored flowerheads, interspersed between drab gr. & tan leaves, all of hand woven wool fabrics appliqued in place w/buttonhole stitch on blk. wool, some mends in background fabric, 5′ x 2′4″
.......................... $5750.00*

A-OH April 1983    *Garth's Auctions, Inc.*
**PIECED AMISH QUILT,** blue & gr. on a
blk. ground, embroidered initials in each
sq., 81″ x 87″ . . . . . . . . . . . . . . . . . $210.00

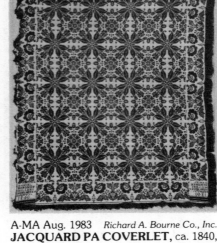

A-MA Aug. 1983    *Richard A. Bourne Co., Inc.*
**JACQUARD PA COVERLET,** ca. 1840,
sgn., 103″ x 88″ . . . . . . . . . . . . . . . $900.00

A-WA D.C. Sept. 1982 *Adam A. Weschler & Son*
**APPLIQUE QUILT,** ca. 1860, turquoise,
red & yellow, on trapunto ground, 96″ sq.
. . . . . . . . . . . . . . . . . . . . . . . . . . . $425.00*

A-OH Feb. 1983    *Garth's Auctions, Inc.*
**PIECED QUILT,** star design in wh.
homespun & calico, red, blue, yellow, pink
& medium br., 99″ x 103″ . . . . . . . $465.00

A-MA Aug. 1983    *Richard A. Bourne Co., Inc.*
**JACQUARD COVERLET,** some wear,
wh. areas turned to beige, 82″ x 86″
. . . . . . . . . . . . . . . . . . . . . . . . . . . $500.00

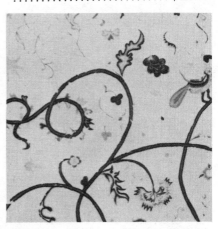

A-MA Aug. 1982    *Robert W. Skinner Inc.*
**CREWEL EMBROIDERY TEXTILE
FRAGMENTS,** 2-pcs., one 18th C.,
scrolling vine & floral Arabesques, portions
missing yarns, 22″ x 29″, the other w/small
vine & floral designs, badly damaged
. . . . . . . . . . . . . . . . . . . . . . . . . . $1600.00*

A-OH Feb. 1983    *Garth's Auctions, Inc.*
**APPLIQUE HOMESPUN QUILT,** gr.,
pink (faded red) & goldenrod, colors other
than red are in reasonably good cond., 69″
x 85″ . . . . . . . . . . . . . . . . . . . . . . . $150.00

A-MA June 1983    *Robert W. Skinner Inc.*
**APPLIQUE ALBUM QUILT,** Am., late
19th-early 20th C., printed cotton red,
yellow, gr. & lavender w/wh. backed
cotton, 6′8″ x 6′8″ . . . . . . . . . . . . $900.00*

A-MA July 1982    *Richard A. Bourne Co., Inc.*
**COVERLET,** double weave, drk. blue &
wh., 7′6″ x 6′ . . . . . . . . . . . . . . . . . $600.00

*Price does not include 10% buyer fee.

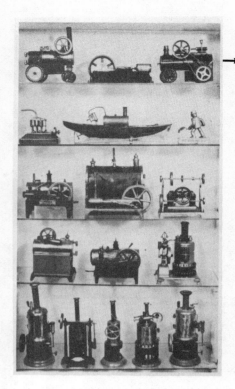

**A-OH Sept. 1982**   *Garth's Auctions, Inc.*
*CAST IRON TOYS*
*Row I, L to R*
**FIRE PUMPER,** Kenton, 3 horses & driver, 13″ L. .................. $125.00

**SURREY,** Kenton, fringed cloth top, 2 horses, driver & passenger, 11½″ L. ................................ $50.00

*Row II, L to R*
**OVERLAND CIRCUS,** Kenton, 2 horses, driver, 6 musicians, some damage, 15½″ L. ...................... $200.00

**HANSON CAB,** Kenton, horse, driver & passenger, orig. box, unused, 15¾″ L. ................................ $210.00

*Row III, L to R*
**FARM WAGON,** Kenton, 14½″ L. ................................ $100.00

**OVERLAND CIRCUS WAGON,** Kenton, 2 horses, outriders, driver, polar bear, orig. box, unused, 14″ L. .. $275.00

**A-OH Sept. 1982**   *Garth's Auctions, Inc.*
*Row I, L to R*
**TRACTOR,** marked Weeden, inc., 6½″ L. ........................... $65.00
**HORIZONTAL MILL ENGINE,** Eng., mkd. "Stuart," 8½″ L. ......... $215.00
**STEAM-DRIVEN ENGINE,** cast iron wheels, tin frame, steel boiler, horizontal engine, flywheel, chain drive, mkd. "B. W. Germany," stack & burner missing, 7″ L. ................................ $300.00

*Row II, L to R*
**MARINE ENGINE,** brass & steel, 2 cylinders, wooden base, 5″ H. .... $85.00
**TIN STEAMBOAT,** Weeden model #1, brass boiler, angled engine w/propeller, repr., missing parts, 14½″ L. .... $225.00
**ADVERTISING PAPERWEIGHT,** "The Iron Fireman," 4½″ H. ......... $25.00

*Row III, L to R*
**STEAM ENGINE,** Weeden, electric fired, horizontal brass boiler, cast iron base, flywheel, belt governor, inc., 7″ L. ................................ $25.00
**STEAM ENGINE,** ca. 1887, Weeden model 60, nickel plated frame, brass boiler, sheet metal cover, flywheel & governor, damage, 8¼″ L. .............. $125.00
**ELECTRIC DYNAMO,** Weeden, shaft, pulleys, old drk. red paint, nickel plated base & trim, 6″ L. .............. $65.00

*Row IV, L to R*
**STEAM ENGINE,** Weeden model 702, electric fired, horizontal brass boiler, top-mounted horizontal cylinder w/flywheel, stack missing, 7″ H. ............ $20.00
**STEAM ENGINE,** German, cast iron base, horizontal brass boiler, side-mounted engine, flywheel & governor, 7″ L. ................................ $110.00
**STEAM ENGINE,** ca. 1887, mkd. "Weeden Mfg Co.," model 17, vertical brass boiler, tin base, cast wh. metal feet & fittings, governor & flywheel, 8½″ H. ................................ $150.00

*Row V, L to R*
**UPRIGHT STEAM ENGINE,** ca. 1887, mkd. "Weeden," brass boiler, side-mounted engine, flywheel, kerosene burner, replm., repaint, 11⅝″ H. ................................ $45.00
**UPRIGHT STEAM ENGINE,** unmkd., Weeden Dart, brass boiler, side-mounted vertical engine, top-mounted flywheel, worn old paint, needs a burner, 9⅝″ H. ................................ $45.00
**UPRIGHT STEAM ENGINE,** ca. 1887, sheet metal boiler, mkd. "Weeden," hole in boiler & damage, 9¼″ H. ........ $25.00
**UPRIGHT STEAM ENGINE,** ca. 1887, Weeden model #2, brass boiler, top-mounted horizontal engine, repr., missing parts, 8¾″ H. .................. $35.00
**UPRIGHT STEAM ENGINE,** Weeden model #26, brass boiler mkd. "Big Giant," side-mounted vertical engine, kerosene burner, 10⅜″ H. ................ $45.00

**A-MA Dec. 1982**   *Robert W. Skinner Inc.*
*L to R*
**MARX POPEYE ECCENTRIC AIRPLANE,** ca. 1940, NY, excellent working cond., orig. carton, 7½″ L. ..... $410.00*
**MARX MERRY MAKERS,** ca. 1929, NY, 4-mouse jazz & dance combo, excellent working cond., orig. carton..... $500.00*
**MARX CHARLIE McCARTHY IN HIS BENZINE BUGGY,** ca. 1938, NY, excellent working cond., orig. carton, 7¾″ L. ................................ $300.00*

**A-MA Dec. 1982**   *Robert W. Skinner Inc.*
**CLOCK WORK CAT,** late 19th C., painted tin, two rats in cage, 7⅞″ L., 6½″ H. ................................ $675.00*

**A-MA Dec. 1982**   *Robert W. Skinner Inc.*
**LIONEL DONALD DUCK & PLUTO HAND CAR,** ca. 1936, NY, clock work, quacking mechanism, red base, gr. roof, track & carton, mechanism needs work ................................ $650.00*

**A-MA Dec. 1982**   *Robert W. Skinner Inc.*
**LIONEL SANTA & MICKEY MOUSE HAND CAR,** ca. 1935, NY, red base, clock work mechanism, track, instruction & carton, flaking............ $1150.00*

A-OH Sept. 1982        *Garth's Auctions, Inc.*
*Row I, L to R*
**STEAM ENGINE,** "Weeden" model 14, horizontal brass boiler, old repaint is green w/gold striping, red flywheel & blk. trim, minor wear, 7″ L. . . . . . . . . . . . . $55.00
**HORIZONTAL MILL,** Eng., mkd. "S" for Stuart, orig. paint, 6½″ L. . . . . . . . $100.00
**STEAM TRACTOR,** "Weeden," flywheel, some parts missing, 9¼″ L. . . . . . . . . . . . . . . . . . . . . . . . . . . $105.00

*Row II, L to R*
**HORIZONTAL ELECTRIC STEAM ENGINE,** chrome plated, red base, some parts missing, 8″ L. . . . . . . . . . . . . . $35.00
**STEAM ENGINE ACCESSORY,** bucket pump & operator, mkd. "Germany," repr. & repaint, 5¼″ H. $105.00
**WALKING STEAM ENGINE,** homemade wooden base, inc. & damage, 10¼″ L. . . . . . . . . . . . . . . . . . . . . . . . . . $55.00

*Row III, L to R*
**BRASS STEAM ENGINE,** "Weeden's Upright Engine No 1, Pat May 19, 1885," 9½″ H. . . . . . . . . . . . . . . . . . . . $185.00
**HIGH-PRESSURE BOILER,** Eng., attrib. to Stuart, "Bassett-Lowke" pressure gauge, sheet metal base, brass fittings, 11¾″ L. . . . . . . . . . . . . . . . . . . . $155.00
**HOT AIR UNIFLO ENGINE,** one cylinder, 2 flywheels, "Pat Nov 20, 1930," old worn red repaint, 6″ L. . . . . . . . $75.00
**HOT AIR CYLINDER UPRIGHT ENGINE,** "Weeden," 2 flywheels, tin, worn blk. paint, japanning, repr., 8¾″ H. . . . . . . . . . . . . . . . . . . . . . . . . . $150.00

*Row IV, L to R*
**TRAIN,** 3 pcs., steam powered, Weeden engine, brass boiler, 2 cylinders, embossed labels "Dart 1887. W. Mfg. Co.," coal car has "I & A.R.R.," brass & tin, old repaint, cars are all tin, engine: 7¾″ L., overall length: 22½″. . . . . . . . . . . . . . . . $300.00
**VERTICAL ENGINE,** German, cast iron sheet metal boiler & nickel plated fittings, base mkd. "J.F. 524," some parts missing, 8½″ H. . . . . . . . . . . . . . . . . . . . . $65.00

A-OH Sept. 1982        *Garth's Auctions, Inc.*
*Row I, L to R*
**TIN WINDUP,** man sharpening scissors on grinding wheel, steam engine accessory, orig. litho., 5½″ H. . . . . . . . . . . $85.00
**WATER WITCH STEAM-POWERED BOAT,** tin, model 3, brass boiler, wear & damage, 14½″ L. . . . . . . . . . . . . . $180.00
**COMPRESSED AIR ENGINE,** twin inverted cylinders & flywheel, 5⅜″ H. . . . . . . . . . . . . . . . . . . . . . . . . . . $45.00

*Row II, L to R*
**ELECTRIC CYNAMO,** Weeden, shaft & pulleys, old repaint, 6″ L. . . . . . . . $110.00
**STEAM ENGINE,** ca. 1887, Weeden, inverted vertical single action, brass boiler, cylinder, flywheel, replm., 7¾″ x 8¾″ . . . . . . . . . . . . . . . . . . . . . . . . . $85.00
**MARINE ENGINE,** brass & polished steel, 2 cylinders, wooden base is 3½″ x 6″ . . . . . . . . . . . . . . . . . . . . . . . . $155.00

*Row III, L to R*
**HORIZONTAL STEAM ENGINE,** brass boiler, bottom mkd. "Empire," 6¼″ x 8″, 8⅝″ H. . . . . . . . . . . . . . . . . $65.00
**VERTICAL HOT AIR ENGINE,** Weeden, 2 flywheels, parts missing, 8⅞″ H. . . . . . . . . . . . . . . . . . . . . . . . . $150.00
**STEAM TRACTOR,** ca. 1887, flywheel & slide valve, replm., parts missing, 9″ L. . . . . . . . . . . . . . . . . . . . . . . . . . $125.00

*Row IV, L to R*
**VERTICAL STEAM ENGINE,** walking beam & brass boiler, sliding plate valve, embossed label "W. Mfg Co," 8½″ H. . . . . . . . . . . . . . . . . . . . . . . . . $175.00
**HORIZONTAL STEAM ENGINE,** ca. 1920, Weeden, cast iron base, brass boiler, old red & blk. paint, parts missing, 6¾″ L. . . . . . . . . . . . . . . . . . . . . . . . . . $55.00
**VERTICAL STEAM ENGINE,** Weeden, brass boiler, damage, parts missing, 6¾″ H. . . . . . . . . . . . . . . . . . . . . . $35.00

A-OH Sept. 1982        *Garth's Auctions, Inc.*
*Row I*
**STEAM-POWERED TRAIN,** 3 pcs., Weeden Dart engine mkd. "W. Mfg Co & 1887," 7¾″ L., 21¾″ L. overall. . . . . . . . . . . . . . . . . . . . . . . . . $425.00

*Row II, L to R*
**HOT AIR ENGINE,** burner, cast iron base, metal plate "--Corporation, Dayton Ohio, 9″ L. . . . . . . . . . . . . . . . $125.00
**ENGINE,** Stuart, cast steel & brass, vertical cylinder, wooden base, part missing, 7″ H. . . . . . . . . . . . . . . . $65.00
**ENGINE,** German, horizontal brass boiler, cast iron base, flywheel, old worn blk. paint w/orange striping, 7″ L. . . . . . . . . . . . . . . . . . . . . . . . . . $50.00

*Row III, L to R*
**STEAM ENGINE,** Weeden, tin frame & boiler w/"W" & "Favorite," vertical cylinder, horizontal pump, 6″ H. . . $105.00
**TURBINE ENGINE,** electric fired boiler, side-mounted turbine, "Quality Brand, Great Northern Mfg Co. Chicago," 9¼″ L. . . . . . . . . . . . . . . . . . . . . . . . . $135.00
**UPRIGHT ENGINE,** ca. 1887, Weeden model #1, tin base & boiler, top-mounted engine, unpainted, no burner, 8″ H. . . . . . . . . . . . . . . . . . . . . . . . . $115.00

*Row IV, L to R*
**UPRIGHT ENGINE,** Weeden, brass boiler, side-mounted vertical cylinder, mkd. "Weeden Mfg Co.," repr., 8¾″ H. . . . . . . . . . . . . . . . . . . . . . . . . $55.00
**UPRIGHT ENGINE,** Weeden model #340, ca. 1900, damage, 6″ H. . . . . $20.00
**ELECTRIC FIRED ENGINE,** Weeden model #58, nickel plated boiler & stack, horizontal engine, flywheel & governor, 8¾″ H. . . . . . . . . . . . . . . . . . . . . . $85.00

A-OH Sept. 1982 *Garth's Auctions, Inc.*
**CAST IRON TOY CAP PISTOL,** tip of hammer is broken, 7¾" L. ........ $7.00
**PAPIER MACHE BIRDS,** pr. (1 illus.), one has old red paint, one has old gr. paint, repr., 6¼" L. .................... $20.00
**CAST IRON TOY CAP PISTOL,** "Super, Pat Sept 11, 23," old yellow varnish, 8½" L. ............... $15.00
**CAP PISTOL,** nickel plated, in shape of padlock, Hubley, 4½" L. ...... $35.00
**CAST IRON TOY CAP PISTOL,** "Scout, Patd June 17, 1890," 7" L.
.......................... $12.50
**TIN SPARKING TOY,** bust of man w/turban, gold earrings, "Made in Germany," 4½" H. .............. $12.50
**CAST IRON STILL BANK,** bust, lion, unicorn, "Our Kitchener Bank," Eng., 6¾" H. .......................... $105.00
**TIN WINDUP,** summersaulting mice on wheels, by Schucco, mkd. "Made in Germany," orig. cloth on mice, 7" L.
.......................... $65.00
**CAST IRON STILL BANK,** horse head in horseshoe, "Tally-Ho Bank," 4½" H.
.......................... $105.00
**CAST IRON STILL BANK,** baby in cradle, nickel plated top, bronzed ends & tin underside are painted blk., 3⅞" L.
.......................... $925.00

A-OH April 1983 *Garth's Auctions, Inc.*
*Row I, L to R*
**TIN FRICTION TOY,** man in speedboat, "Made in Germany," worn orig. paint, working cond., 11¾" L. ......... $95.00
**TIN WINDUP TOY,** duck & 3 ducklings on wheels, "Made in Japan," worn orig. paint, 12" L. .................... $10.00
**TIN TOY,** hen that clucks & lays eggs, "Baldwin Mfg. Co.," no eggs, rusted orig. paint, 5½" L. .................... $10.00
*Row II, L to R*
**TOY TRAIN ACCESSORY,** Mickey Mouse Hand Car," composition bodies, windup motor, orig. paint, some damage, no key, 9" L. ................. $200.00

A-OH Sept. 1982 *Garth's Auctions, Inc.*
**TWO TIN PENNY TOY BEETLES,** Germany, one mkd. "A souvenir from the Universal Theatres Concession Co, Chicago Ill.," other unmkd. 2¾" L. ... $17.50
**TIN WINDUP TOY,** snake on wheels, spring slips, some wear, 11" L. ... $65.00
**TIN PENNY TOY,** matador & bull, mkd. "Germany" & "Cko," 6" H. ...... $55.00
**CAST IRON STILL BANK,** orig. bronze finish & brass padlock, "Postal Savings Mail Box. U.S.," wooden back, orig. paper label, "Nicol's Latest Creation," 6¾" H.
.......................... $55.00
**FELIX THE CAT WALKING STICK TOY,** tin, minor wear, stick is missing, 7½" H. .......................... $75.00
**CAST IRON STILL BANK,** shelf clock, replm., 5⅝" H. ............... $105.00
**CAST IRON STILL BANK,** A. C. Williams clock bank, 6⅛" H. .... $285.00
**CIRCULAR REGISTERING BANK,** tin, "The Copper Mine, Girard Model Wks. Inc.," 5½" D. ............... $35.00
**CAST IRON GLOOMY GUS,** worn paint, 4¾" H. ............... $65.00
**TIN SPARKING TOY,** clown coming out of chimney, "Made in Germany," some wear, 5" H. .................... $22.50
**CAST IRON STILL BANK,** Eng., hanging Santa, "Save and Smile," 7½" H.
.......................... $400.00
**TIN STRING TOY,** man tips hat, "Made in Germany CKO," 3⅝" H. ...... $20.00
**CAST IRON STILL BANK,** A. C. Williams, "U.S. Mail Bank," 5¼" H.
.......................... $75.00

→ **FRICTION TOY,** wood & cast iron, steam locomotive, worn old blk. & gold paint, 13" L. .................... $75.00
**WINDUP TOY,** celluloid, walking Mickey Mouse, mkd. "W. D. Japan," some wear & damage, working cond., 7½" H. .. $75.00
**SHEET METAL BANK,** "Uncle Sam's Register Bank," orig. red enamel w/gold & blk. labels, good cond., 6¼" H. ... $30.00
*Row III, L to R*
**TIN WINDUP TOY,** woman sweeping, "Made in Germany," working cond. 7½" H. .......................... $310.00
**SHEET METAL FRICTION TOY,** fire truck, worn red & gold paint, damage, 13" L. .......................... $65.00
**WINDUP TIN TOY,** "Charleston Trio," "Louis Marx & Co.," worn orig. paint, working cond., 8¼" H. ........ $325.00

A-MA Dec. 1982 *Robert W. Skinner Inc.*
**DIONNE QUINTUPLETS,** ca. 1930's, wooden crib, Madame Alexander, jointed composition bodies, 3 have name bibs, replm., crib: 19¾" L. ......... $425.00*

A-MA Dec. 1982 *Robert W. Skinner Inc.*
**WIRE CARRIAGE,** Am., ca. 1880, tin horses, bisque shoulder-head doll, roughness, wear & rust, 14¼" & 7½" L.
.......................... $400.00*

A-MA Mar. 1983 *Robert W. Skinner Inc.*
**LONE RANGER FARM,** 20th C., carved & painted, barn 27" W., 39" D., 33" H.
.......................... $1000.00*

A-OH Sept. 1982 *Garth's Auctions, Inc.*
**JUMBO ELEPHANT,** ca. 1920, by Steiff, orig. plush covering, red felt blanket, glass eyes, working noise maker, "Steiff" button in one ear, 30" H., 35" L. ....... $625.00
**JUMBO DUTCH GIRL POLLY DOLLY,** Schoenhut, head turns, minor wear, 15" H. .................... $255.00

*Price does not include 10% buyer fee.

A-OH Sept. 1982          *Garth's Auctions, Inc.*
*CAST IRON*
*Row I, L to R*
**COACH,** miniature Fageol, worn paint & chips, 3⅝" L. ................. $10.00
**HORSE-DRAWN CLOWN CART,** repr., wear & rust, 7½" L. .... $170.00
**TWO COUPES,** worn silver, damage, worn gr., 3½" L. ............... $25.00

*Row II, L to R*
**TWO TOY CARS,** Fageol coaches, one is blue w/steel wheels, one is blk. repaint, rusted wheels, 5" L. & 4⅞" L. .. $30.00
**TOY CAR,** rubber tires, old gr. paint, cracked tires, 6½" L. ........... $55.00
**TAXI,** mkd. "Arcade," old orange & blk. paint, 5" L. ................. $195.00

*Row III, L to R*
**TOY CARS,** mini convertible w/rubber wheels, worn old gr., 2-door w/old blk. & red repaint, 4" L. & 4⅛" L. ...... $40.00
**GASOLINE TRUCK,** old worn red, steel wheels, 2 nozzles, 5" L. ........ $85.00
**FARM TRUCK,** worn old blue paint, steel wheels, 4¾" L. ............... $47.50
**MODEL T,** no paint, 4" L. ...... $35.00

*Row IV, L to R*
**TOY CAR,** Ford sedan, mkd. "Arcade Mfg Co.," old red paint, steel wheels, some wear, 5" L. .................. $95.00
**STILL BANK,** auto w/passengers, 5¾" L. ............................. $275.00
**STILL BANK,** armored W.W. I car, 7" L. ............................. $435.00

A-MA Oct. 1982     *Richard A. Bourne Co., Inc.*
*Row I, L to R*
**PULL TOY,** papier-mache & wood boy figure, 8½" L. ................. $850.00
**UNCLE TOM'S CABIN,** dissected, litho. cabin w/puzzle pcs. inside, some pcs. may be missing ..................... $50.00
*Row II, L to R*
**ROOSTER ON SQUEEZE BOX,** papier-mache, works, 6¾" H. ......... $125.00
**ROOSTER,** papier-mache, bellows of squeeze box broken ......... $300.00
**BIRD,** corn husks, papier-mache & felt, on squeeze box, some fading, 7½" H. ............................. $70.00

A-MA Oct. 1982     *Richard A. Bourne Co., Inc.*
*Top to Bottom*
**EARLY TIN CARRIAGE,** upper chauffeur's seat, 2 lower seats, drawn by 2 metal horses on metal stands w/cast wheels, some crazing & flaking, 15" L. ............................. $2400.00
**TIN CARRIAGE,** convertible passenger section, chauffeur's section, drawn by 2 br. metal horses on metal stands w/cast wheels, some damage ........ $2100.00
**TIN CARRIAGE,** fold-down convertible top, side lanterns, drawn by 2 br. horses, some wear, 20" L. ........... $2900.00

A-MA Oct. 1982     *Richard A. Bourne Co., Inc.*
*L to R*
**MERRY-GO-ROUND,** 19th C., tin, cloth fringed top, flaking & wear, 13½" H. ............................. $900.00
**WALTZING COUPLE,** tin, windup mechanism, some flaking, 8" H. ............................. $375.00

A-OH April 1983          *Garth's Auctions, Inc.*
*Row I, L to R*
**TIN PULL TOY,** horse on embossed base, cast iron wheels, worn orig. wh. paint w/red & blk., split in base, 6½" L. ............................. $200.00
**TIN PULL TOY,** 4-part train, worn orig. paint, engine in blk. & yellow w/gr. & red, tender in gr. & yellow, cars in orange, red w/blue Japanned roofs, 21" L. ... $650.00

*Row II, L to R*
**TIN LEVER ACTION TOY,** boy on dog, orig. paint, working cond., rusting, 6¾" H. ............................. $225.00
**TIN PULL TOY,** goat on scalloped base, worn orig. gold Japanning, red trim & gr. base, 5½" L. .................. $275.00
**TIN PULL TOY,** house w/gingerbread detail, worn old repaint, replm., wear & damage, back door missing, 6½" H. ............................. $125.00
**TIN PULL TOY,** sheep w/bell, worn gold Japanning, gr. base, 6½" L. ..... $225.00
**TIN PULL TOY,** rabbit, worn old wh. & gr. paint, damage, 6½" L. ....... $250.00

*Row III, L to R*
**TIN PULL TOY,** lion, orig. paint, 8½" L. ............................. $375.00
**TIN PULL TOY,** horse & wagon, worn orig. paint, old resoldering, 12½" L. ............................. $340.00
**TIN PULL TOY,** camel, worn orig. paint, 9¼" L. ..................... $400.00

A-MA Aug. 1982     *Robert W. Skinner Inc.*
*L to R*
**STUFFED ELEPHANT PULL TOY,** Am., late 19th C., br. cloth body, wooden tusks & platform, cast metal wheels, some wear & damage, 9" H. ........ $280.00*
**STUFFED TOY PIG,** Am., 19th C., camel-colored wool, some wear, 10" L. ............................. $300.00*
**STUFFED COW PULL TOY,** Am., late 19th C., plush br. & wh. body, leather hooves, wooden wheels, worn & some damage, 11" H. ............. $290.00*

*Price does not include 10% buyer fee.

A-MA Oct. 1982    *Richard A. Bourne Co., Inc.*
CAST IRON TOYS
*Row I, L to R*
**AUTOMOBILES,** lot of 3, good orig. paint showing some flaking & rusting, 4" to 6" L. . . . . . . . . . . . . . . . . . . . . . . $150.00

*Row II, L to R*
**TRACTORS,** lot of 2, by Arcade, 1 has orig. Arcade tires, minor flaking & rusting, 3" & 5¼" L. . . . . . . . . . . . . . . . . . . $25.00
**VEHICLES,** lot of 2, motorcycle, sm. automobile, slight wear & rusting, 4" & 3¾" L. . . . . . . . . . . . . . . . . . . . . . . . . . $50.00

*Row III, L to R*
**AIRCRAFT,** lot of 3, 2 dirigibles & Lucky Boy single-engine plane, 4½" to 6" L. . . . . . . . . . . . . . . . . . . . . . . . . . $180.00

A-MA Aug. 1982    *Robert W. Skinner Inc.*
*L to R*
**STUFFED TOY BULL,** Am., late 19th C., wooden horns & legs, metal nose ring, some wear, 5½" H. . . . . . . . . . . $180.00*
**ARTICULATED STUFFED TOY MONKEY,** probably Germany, early 20th C., red felt cap & jacket, blk. pants, tail moves to swivel head, jointed shoulders & hips, slight moth & wear damage, 13½" H. . . . . . . . . . . . . . . . . . . . . . . . . . $170.00*
**STUFFED TOY DOGS,** set of 2 (1 illus.), Am., late 19th & 20th C., one cloth poodle w/fuzzy ears, tail & feet, some wear, damage, 6" H & 7" H. . . . . . . . . $90.00*

A-MA Dec. 1982    *Robert W. Skinner Inc.*
**SCHOENHUT TOYS,** ca. 1925, "Speedy Felix" auto pull toy, Borgfeldt label, 12" L.; jointed Felix figure mkd. "Felix," copyright labels, needs new elastic, 5½" H.; cartoon litho. tin pail, rust . . . . . . . . . . . . $375.00*

A-MA Oct. 1982    *Richard A. Bourne Co., Inc.*
CAST IRON TOYS
*Row I, L to R*
**SLEIGH,** drawn by wh. horse, gr. decor. w/gold highlighting on sleigh, cast figure of woman in sleigh, paint flaking & rusting, 15" L. . . . . . . . . . . . . . . . . . . . . . . . . $200.00

**BELL PULL TOY,** clown seated in a wagon drawn by a pig, heart molded cast wheels, 6½" L. . . . . . . . . . . . . . . . $70.00

**BELL PULL TOY,** alligator perched on a log, blk. boy seated on top, slight wear, 6" L. . . . . . . . . . . . . . . . . . . . . . . . . $750.00

*Row II, L to R*
**SURREY,** drawn by wh. horse, 19th C., tin, damage, 9" L. . . . . . . . . . . . . $160.00

**TIN HORSE,** early 19th C., mounted on tin base, cast iron wheels, molded tin man in riding outfit seated on horse, some flaking, 6¼" L. . . . . . . . . . . . . . . . $500.00

**CIRCUS WAGON,** 19th C., tin, drawn by 2 horses, damage, 11½" L. . . . . . $1000.00

*Row III, L to R*
**FARM WAGON,** blk. man driving & standing inside wagon, drawn by a blk. donkey, minor flaking & rusting, 10½" L. . . . . . . . . . . . . . . . . . . . . . . . . $170.00

**FARM WAGON,** blk. man driving, drawn by blk. donkey, flaking & rusting, 10¼" L. . . . . . . . . . . . . . . . . . . . . . . . . $170.00

A-MA Dec. 1982    *Robert W. Skinner Inc.*
**SCHOENHUT CIRCUS,** ca. 1925, painted eyes, elephant, buffalo, zebra, camel, leopard, tiger, lion, 2 horses, donkey, rhinoceros, hippopotamus, giraffe, monkey, cow, ringmaster, Chinaman, 2 clowns, Negro dude, girl bare-back rider, farmer, circus wagon, 3 chairs, 3 ladders, 7 assorted stands, barrel, 2 balls & reduced size elephant, clown, barrel & stand, some damage & loss . . . . . . . . . . $2150.00*

A-MA Oct. 1982    *Richard A. Bourne Co., Inc.*
CAST IRON TOYS
*Top to Bottom*
**HOOK & LADDER,** drawn by 1 wh. & 2 blk. horses, some replm., flaking & wear, 19½" L. . . . . . . . . . . . . . . . . . . . $125.00
**HOOK & LADDER,** drawn by 1 br. & 1 blk. horse, paint flaking & rusting, 94½" L. . . . . . . . . . . . . . . . . . . . . . . . . $450.00

A-MA Oct. 1982    *Richard A. Bourne Co., Inc.*
TOYS
*L to R*
**GIRL ON TRICYCLE,** clock-work-type mechanism, china-head girl, horse head of tin, some damage, 8½" H. . . . . . $1700.00
**STUFFED BEAR MUSIC BOX,** crank handle, paper-covered box, some wear damage, 10½" H. . . . . . . . . . . . . . $375.00
**DOLL ON TRICYCLE,** papier-mache head, tin hands & legs, stenciled tin over mechanism, some damage, 8" H. . . . . . . . . . . . . . . . . . . . . . . . . $1500.00

A-MA Dec. 1982    *Robert W. Skinner Inc.*
**SCHOENHUT CIRCUS W/TENT,** ca. 1925, tent has wooden ring base, replm., loss & damage, ring master w/whip is 8½" H. . . . . . . . . . . . . . . . . . . . . . . . $800.00*

A-MA Oct. 1982    *Richard A. Bourne Co., Inc.*
**DOLL'S PIANO,** "Crandall's Florence of Montrose," 10¼" H., 20" L. . . . . . $150.00
**SCHOENHUT GRAND PIANO,** keys work, some paint flaking, 8½" H., 13" D. . . . . . . . . . . . . . . . . . . . . . . . . . $50.00

*Price does not include 10% buyer fee.

A-OH Sept. 1982     *Garth's Auctions, Inc.*
*Row I, L to R*
**CAST IRON STILL BANK,** bulldog, 5¼"
H. .............................. $80.00
**CAST IRON STILL BANK,** lion, 5½" L.
.............................. $40.00
**CAST IRON STILL BANK,** "Liberty
Bell" w/bust of Washington, 3⅞" H.
.............................. $25.00
**CAST IRON STILL BANK,** elephant,
3¾" H. ......................... $60.00
**CAST IRON STILL BANK,** scottie by
Hubley, 5⅛" H. ................ $85.00

*Row II, L to R*
**CAST IRON STILL BANK,** elephant
w/howdah, old repaint, 6¾" L. ... $45.00
**CAST IRON STILL BANK,** Crosley
radio, mkd. "Kenton Toys," 4⅜" H.
.............................. $105.00
**STEEL BANK,** "Lincoln Bank," log on
sawbuck, hatchet & saw, paint wear,
handle missing, 8¼" L. .......... $25.00
**CAST IRON STILL BANK,** "Junior"
cash register, mkd. "Manufactured by The
J & E Stevens Co, Cromwell, Conn.," 4¼"
H. .............................. $30.00
**CAST IRON STILL BANK,** lion, 5⅛" H.
.............................. $55.00

*Row III, L to R*
**ORGAN MUSIC BOX,** hand crank,
cathedral case, "J. Chein," some wear, 9¼"
H. .............................. $22.50
**HOOK & LADDER TRUCK,** tin driver,
3 wood & metal ladders, old worn red paint,
19½" L. ....................... $150.00

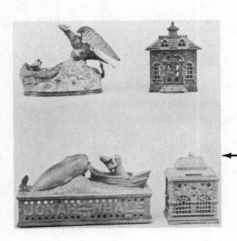

A-OH Sept. 1982     *Garth's Auctions, Inc.*
*BANKS*
*Row I, L to R*
**CAST IRON,** mechanical dog, worn orig.
bronze gilding, 7" L. ........... $220.00
**CAST IRON,** still, seated cat by Arcade,
4⅛" H. ......................... $100.00
**CAST ALUMINUM,** still, inside label
"There's money in Aberdeen Angus," worn
blk. paint, 7½" L. .............. $85.00
**CAST IRON,** still, rabbit by A. C.
Williams, 5" H. ................ $75.00
**NICKEL PLATED,** still, pig, 7¼" L.
.............................. $40.00

*Row II, L to R*
**WHITE METAL CLOCK,** "A Schadow
& Son N.Y. Pat 1913," clock mechanism &
2 coin slots, worn gold paint, 5⅞" H.
.............................. $32.50
**CAST IRON,** still, Billiken, 6⅜" H.
.............................. $65.00
**CAST IRON,** still, Buster Brown & Tige,
"Fidelity Trust Vault, Counting House,
Cashier," 6½" H. .............. $335.00
**CAST IRON,** mechanical, crowing
rooster, old worn paint, 6⅛" H. .. $220.00
**CAST IRON,** mechanical, "Automatic
Coin Savings Bank," orig. bronze finish,
replm., 7¼" H. ................ $615.00

*Row III, L to R*
**CAST IRON,** still, Gen. Sherman on
rearing horse, Arcade, 6" H. .... $385.00
**CAST IRON,** still, bear w/pot by Hubley,
6¾" H. ......................... $70.00
**CAST IRON,** mechanical, 2 frogs, worn
orig. paint, replm., 9" L. ....... $575.00
**CAST IRON,** still, "Thrifty, the Wise Pig,"
6¾" H. ......................... $45.00
**CAST IRON,** still, prancing horse
on rectangular base, Arcade, 7¾" H.
.............................. $75.00

A-MA Oct. 1982   *Richard A. Bourne Co., Inc.*
*BANKS*
*Row I, L to R*
**MECHANICAL BANK,** eagle w/eaglets
.............................. $400.00
**STILL BANK,** State Bank Building
.............................. $30.00
*Row II, L to R*
**JONAH & THE WHALE,** mechanical,
6-pc. const., paint flaking & rusting
.............................. $100.00
**STILL BANK,** Bank Building .... $40.00

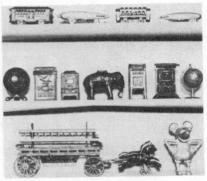

A-OH Sept. 1982     *Garth's Auctions, Inc.*
*Row I, L to R*
**CAST IRON STILL BANK,** street car,
"Main Street," 6¾" L. .......... $170.00
**CAST IRON STILL BANK,** "Graf
Zeppelin," 8" L. ............... $200.00
**CAST IRON STILL BANK,** trolley car,
Kenton, ca. 1911, 5¼" L. ....... $185.00
**CAST IRON STILL BANK,** "Graf
Zeppelin," 6¾" L. .............. $100.00

*Row II, L to R*
**CAST IRON STILL BANK,** Globe safe
on ball & claw foot tripod, Kenton, ca.
1920, "The Globe," 5¼" H. ...... $85.00
**CAST IRON STILL BANK,** "U.S. Mail"
w/eagle, 5¼" H. ............... $45.00
**STILL BANK,** cast iron & steel, stove,
4½" H. ......................... $70.00
**CAST IRON BANK,** elephant, 6¼" L.
.............................. $65.00
**CAST IRON BANK,** mailbox w/"U.S. Air
Mail" & eagle, 5½" H. .......... $40.00
**STILL BANK,** cast iron & steel, "Save
your money and buy a gas stove," 5½" H.
.............................. $50.00
**CAST IRON STILL BANK,** globe on arc
stand, 5⅜" H. ................. $70.00

*Row III, L to R*
**HOOK & LADDER,** cast iron, 3 horses,
one (of 2) drivers, 2 wooden ladders
(unpainted), old repaint, replm., 22¼" L.
.............................. $90.00
**STILL BANK,** cast aluminum, Mickey
Mouse, unpainted, 8¼" H. ...... $115.00

A-OH Sept. 1982     *Garth's Auctions, Inc.*
**CAST IRON STILL BANK,** Dot stove,
4" H. ......................... $65.00
**CAST IRON STILL BANK,** "GE" re-
frigerator, 4¼" H. ............. $45.00
**ALUMINUM MECHANICAL BANK,**
"Bill E. Grin," recast, 4⅜" H. .... $25.00
**CAST IRON STILL BANK,** ice cream
freezer, "Richmond Cedar Works, Rich-
mond Va.," 4⅜" H. ............ $85.00
**CAST IRON STILL BANK,** "GE" refrig-
erator, 3¾" H. ................ $40.00

**A-OH April 1983**    *Garth's Auctions, Inc.*
*BANKS*
*Row I, L to R*
**HOUSE,** cast iron, worn old gold paint, 3″
H. ........................... $30.00
**BANK BUILDING,** cast iron, traces of
old silver paint, 3¼″ H. ......... $17.50
**CAT & BALL,** cast iron, worn old blk.
paint, 5½″ L. ................. $140.00
**BANK BUILDING,** cast iron, cupola,
worn old gr. & orange paint, 3¼″ H.
................................ $35.00
**TWO-FACED BLACK BOY,** cast iron,
worn old blk. & gold paint, 3⅛″ H.
................................ $45.00

*Row II, L to R*
**BANK,** cast nickel steel, sheet metal sides
& back, 3″ H. ................. $15.00
**PIG,** cast iron, worn old flesh-colored
paint, 4½″ L. ................. $70.00
**HORSESHOE & HEAD,** cast iron, wire
mesh center, old gold paint, 3¼″ H.
................................ $45.00
**SMALL JUMBO ELEPHANT,** cast iron,
old gold paint, 3″ L. ............ $35.00
**BANK BUILDING,** cast iron, traces of
old paint, 3¾″ H. ............. $15.00

*Row III, L to R*
**ROOSTER,** cast iron, traces of old paint,
4¾″ H. ........................ $55.00
**BUILDING,** cast iron, worn old gold paint,
3″ H. ......................... $15.00
**CAMEL & BABY ON ROCKERS,** cast
iron, Oriental, old gray paint, gr. rockers &
gold trim, minor wear, 5″ L. ..... $545.00
**BUILDING,** cast iron, worn old gold paint,
3½″ H. ....................... $20.00
**RABBIT,** cast iron, no paint, minor rust,
4⅝″ H. ....................... $22.50

**BUILDING,** cast iron, the "Deposit,"
worn old gold paint, 4″ H. ....... $40.00
*Row III, L to R*
**HOUSE,** cast iron, old silver & red paint,
some wear, 4⅛″ H. ........... $35.00
**CRYSTAL BANK,** cast iron & glass,
worn old gold paint on iron frame, 3¾″ H.
................................ $20.00
**HORSE,** horseshoe, Buster Brown &
Tige," "Good Luck," old gold & blk. paint,
label "An Arcade Toy," 4¼″ H. .. $180.00
**CRYSTAL BANK,** cast iron, wire mesh,
old gold & blk. paint, 4″ H. ...... $22.50
**HOUSE,** cast iron, old aluminum paint,
some wear, 4⅛″ H. ........... $25.00

**A-OH April 1983**    *Garth's Auctions, Inc.*
*BANKS*
*Row I, L to R*
**CAST IRON,** house, old silver & gold
paint, red chimney, 4⅛″ H. ...... $20.00
**CAST NICKEL STEEL,** safe, some rust,
4″k H. ........................ $15.00
**CAST IRON,** two-faced black boy, old
blk. & gold paint has been varnished, 4″ H.
................................ $65.00
**CAST IRON,** "White City Puzzle Safe,"
partial paper label "Nicol & Co. Chicago,"
locking mechanism is inc., 4″ H. .. $35.00
**CAST IRON,** bank building, old aluminum
repaint, 4¾″ H. ............... $10.00
*Row II, L to R*
**CAST IRON,** "Liberty Bell Sesquicenten-
nial, 1926," orig. bronze finished highlights,
3¾″ H. ....................... $25.00
**CAST IRON,** clown, worn old gold paint,
6″ H. ......................... $11.00
**CAST IRON,** ox, traces of old blk. paint,
5¼″ L. ....................... $47.50
**CAST IRON,** Boy Scout, worn old gold
paint, 5⅞″ H. ................. $65.00
**CAST IRON,** "Liberty Bell," worn old
bronze/dull gold finish, 3¾″ H. ... $32.50
*Row III, L to R*
**CAST IRON,** "Security Safe Deposit,"
"Pat. Feby 15, '81, March 1, '87" .. $10.00
**CAST IRON,** seated Boston bull, traces of
old gold & red paint, 4½″ H. ..... $87.50
**CAST IRON,** seated rabbit, worn old gold
paint, 5¼″ H. ................. $72.50
**CAST IRON,** rearing horse on oval base,
old blk. paint, 5⅛″ H. .......... $15.00
**CAST IRON,** bank building, worn old
paint, rust, 3⅛″ H. ............ $10.00

**TWO-FACED BLACK BOY,** cast iron,
old blk. paint, 3⅛″ H. .......... $25.00
**CROWN,** cast brass, souvenir bank mkd.
"Coronation, 1952," "Made in England,"
4¼″ H. ....................... $35.00
**TWO-FACED BLACK BOY,** cast iron,
worn old blk. & gold paint, 3⅛″ H.
................................ $55.00
**SAFE,** cast iron, "Pat. June 2, 1896," worn
old gold paint, has key, 3¼″ H. ... $25.00
*Row II, L to R*
**BILLIKEN GOOD LUCK,** cast iron,
worn old gold paint, 4¼″ H. ... $22.50.00
**ELEPHANT,** cast iron, worn old blue
paint, 4¼″ L. ................. $30.00
**BUFFALO,** cast iron, worn old gold paint,
4¼″ L. ....................... $15.00

**A-OH Sept. 1982**    *Garth's Auctions, Inc.*
*STILL BANKS*
*Row I, L to R*
**CAST IRON,** "Porky" pig, 5¾″ H.
.............................. $165.00
**CAST WHITE METAL,** "Beaky,"
"W.B.C.," for Warner Brothers, no trap,
4½″ H. ....................... $45.00
**CAST WHITE METAL,** "Daffy,"
"W.B.C.," no trap, 4¼″ H. ...... $75.00
**CAST WHITE METAL,** pirate, repaint,
6″ H. ......................... $25.00

*Row II, L to R*
**CAST WHITE METAL,** Amish boy
w/pig, 4⅝″ H. ................. $65.00
**CAST IRON,** circus elephant, Hubley,
3⅞″ H. ....................... $45.00
**CAST WHITE METAL,** Dutch girl, 5⅝″
H. ........................... $30.00
**CAST WHITE METAL,** "Elmer,"
"W.B.C.," for Warner Brothers, 5½″ H.
................................ $65.00
**CAST WHITE METAL,** elephant, 5¼″
H. ........................... $10.00
**CAST IRON,** Mammy, Hubley, 5¼″ H.
................................ $75.00

*Row III, L to R*
**CAST WHITE METAL,** "Porky,"
"W.B.C.," 4⅜″ H. .............. $55.00
**CAST WHITE METAL,** "Bugs Bunny,"
"W.B.C.," 5¾″ H. .............. $75.00
**CAST WHITE METAL,** "Beaky,"
"W.B.C.," 4¼″ H. .............. $75.00
**CAST WHITE METAL,** "Sniffles,"
"W.B.C.," break in base, no trap, 5¼″ H.
................................ $30.00
**CAST WHITE METAL,** Elmer at stump,
"W.B.C.," no trap, 5½″ H. ....... $45.00

**A-OH April 1983**    *Garth's Auctions, Inc.*
*BANKS*
*Row I, L to R*
**BANK BUILDING,** cast iron, replm., old
silver & gold repaint, 3⅝″ H. ...... $6.00

A-OH April 1983        *Garth's Auctions, Inc.*
**BANKS**
*Row I, L to R*
**BUILDING,** cast iron, old br. & gold repaint, 5⅜″ H. ................. $17.50
**ST. BERNARD,** cast iron, "I Hear a Call," "Copyright July 20th, 1900," worn old blk. paint, replm., 8″ L. ........... $20.00
**NATIONAL SAFE,** nickel steel, 4¾″ H.
.............................................. $20.00
**PUP ON A PILLOW,** cast iron, "Fido," worn old polychrome paint, 5½″ H.
.............................................. $165.00
**BANK BUILDING,** cast iron, worn old paint, repr., 5″ H. ....... $12.50
*Row II, L to R*
**CHARLIE McCARTHY, INC.,** cast aluminum, worn old paint, bottom is missing, 7½″ H. ................. $45.00
**FLAT IRON BUILDING,** cast iron, worn old aluminum paint, 5½″ H. ...... $67.50
**FIRE PUMPER WAGON,** cast iron, driver & 2 horses, worn old paint, repr., 17″ L. ........................... $175.00
**SHARE CROPPER,** cast iron, worn old paint, 5⅜″ H. ................... $70.00
**PERSHING,** cast iron, "Patented July 10, 1918," worn bronze finish, minor rust, 7¾″ H. ........................... $85.00
*Row III, L to R*
**ROCKET SHIP,** cast aluminum, "Astro Mfg, E. Detroit," worn red trim, 11″ H.
.............................................. $4.00
**BANK,** sheet metal, "Home Budget Bank, Tudor Metal Prod. Corp.," worn old red & blk. paint, 6¼″ x 6″, 7½″ H. ....... $5.00
**OSCAR,** cast iron, seams are welded, old blk. paint, 7¾″ H. ............. $47.50
**BANK,** sheet steel, painted blk. 4¼″ x 5¼″, 4½″ H. ........................... $2.00
**JOLLY NIGGER,** cast aluminum, "Starkie's patent," worn old paint, tongue & eyes missing, 6¾″ H. ............. $17.50

A-OH Sept. 1982        *Garth's Auctions, Inc.*
**CAST IRON BANKS**
*Row I, L to R*
**LITTLE RED RIDING HOOD & WOLF,** mkd. "Copyright by J. M. Harper 1907," blk. paint, 5″ H. ........ $1425.00
**PROFESSOR PUG FROG,** 3¼″ H.
.............................................. $220.00
**SANTA AT CHINMEY,** mechanical, 6″ H. ......................... $1000.00
**SCOTTIE,** 3⅛″ H. ............. $210.00
**CAT W/BOWTIE,** 4⅜″ H. ..... $155.00

*Row II, L to R*
**CAMEL W/PACK,** 5″ L. ...... $200.00
**THE DAISY,** safe, Japanned & gold, 2-3/16″ H. ...................... $45.00
**PRANCING HORSE W/BELLY BAND,** 4½″ H. ................. $95.00
**THE DAISY,** safe, red & gold, 2-3/16″ H.
.............................................. $45.00
**SEAL,** 4¼″ L. ................. $200.00

*Row III, L to R*
**TWO KIDS,** goat variety, restor., 4½″ H.
.............................................. $500.00
**CAPITALIST,** 5″ H. .......... $625.00
**MECHANICAL BANK,** "Dog Tray, 1880 Bank," wear, 4¼″ H. ....... $1425.00
**POLICEMAN,** mkd. "Copyright by J.M. Harper, 1907," 5⅜″ H. ...... $1225.00
**ORIENTAL CAMEL,** 4″ H. .... $600.00

A-OH Sept. 1982        *Garth's Auctions, Inc.*
**CAST IRON**
*Row I, L to R*
**STILL BANK,** "Bank" building, 5½″ H.
.............................................. $50.00
**STILL BANK,** Blackpool Tower, 7½″ H.
.............................................. $85.00
**STILL BANK,** General Butler, "Patd Nov 12, 1878," Stevens, 6½″ H. ...... $550.00
**STILL BANK,** mascot, Hubley, boy on baseball, "American and National League Ball," 5¾″ H. .................. $1425.00
**STILL BANK,** parlor stove, 7″ H.
.............................................. $110.00
**STILL BANK,** "Home Savings Bank," 5⅞″ H. ......................... $85.00

*Row II, L to R*
**MECHANICAL BANK,** ca. 1885, "Speaking Dog Bank," Stevens, 7¾″ L.
.............................................. $550.00
**STILL BANK,** "Independence Hall Tower," 9½″ H. .............. $175.00
**MECHANICAL BANK,** pig baby in high chair, mkd. "atd Aug 24, 1897," nickel plated, 5¾″ H. ................. $475.00
**STILL BANK,** castle w/3 turrets & 2 coin slots, Eng., 7″ H. .......... $375.00
**MECHANICAL BANK,** ca. 1885, "Trick Pony," 7¾″ H. ................. $625.00

*Row III, L to R*
**STILL BANK,** "100th Anniversary, Battle of Gettysburg, Commemorative Bank," 7½″ L., 4¾″ H. ................ $40.00
**TOY FIRE PUMPER,** ca. 1880, 3 horses & pumper w/eagle finial & driver, 21½″ L.
.............................................. $475.00

A-OH April 1983        *Garth's Auctions, Inc.*
*Row I, L to R*
**CAST IRON BANK,** elephant w/Howdah, worn old gold paint, minor break, 4⅛″ L. ........................... $12.50
**GLASS BANK** tin cap, shape of a baseball, wh. w/red transfer Indian head & Pegasus, 3⅛″ H. ................ $10.00
**SHEET METAL BANK,** register bank shaped like a cooking pot, worn orig. bronze finish, 3⅜″ D., 2⅜″ H. ..... $5.00
**TOY CANDY CONTAINER,** shaped like a lantern, clear glass globe, red tin top & base, 3¾″ H. ................. $3.00
**CAST IRON BANK,** lion, no paint, 3⅝″ H. .......................... $22.50
*Row II, L to R*
**CAST IRON BANK,** "Tank Bank U.S.A. 1918," worn old gold paint, minor rust, 4⅜″ L. ........................... $85.00
**CAST WHITE METAL BANK,** Indian head, orig. bronze finish, 4⅛″ H.
.............................................. $10.00
**CAST WHITE METAL BANK,** treasure chest w/pirate head, worn finish, 4¼″ L.
.............................................. $5.00
**CAST WHITE METAL BANK,** house labeled "American Union Bank, New York," worn finish, 3⅞″ L. ....... $17.50
**CAST IRON BANK,** pig, worn old gold paint, 3″ H. ................. $15.00
*Row III, L to R*
**CAST IRON TOY,** plane, propeller missing, worn old blue paint, 5¾″ L.
.............................................. $20.00
**CELLULOID NODDING BANK,** "NICKY," worn paint, br. plus hair, silver foil paper hat, 4¾″ H. ............. $2.00
**CAST IRON BANK** donkey, worn old red paint, 4½″ H. ............. $15.00
**CAST IRON BANK,** "Crystal Bank," wire mesh sides, worn old gold paint, 4″ H.
.............................................. $5.00

A-OH Sept. 1982 *Garth's Auctions, Inc.*
*STILL BANKS*
*Row I, L to R*
**CAST IRON,** "Bank" building, 3" H. ............................... $40.00

**CAST ALUMINUM,** girl & dog cart, mkd. "Sixpenny piece bank," unpainted, 3¼" H. ........................... $45.00
**CAST IRON,** "Campbell Kids," 3⅜" H. ............................... $175.00

**CAST IRON,** lamb, old silver repaint, 3⅛" H. ........................... $120.00
**CAST IRON,** "Home Savings Bank," 3⅝" H. ............................... $45.00

*Row II, L to R*
**CAST IRON,** rabbit, by A. C. Williams, 3¾" H. .......................... $85.00

**CAST IRON,** dog on tub, A. C. Williams, 4⅛" H. .......................... $75.00
**CAST IRON,** squirrel w/nut, 4⅛" H. ............................... $400.00

**CAST IRON,** elephant on bench on tub, A. C. Williams, 3⅞" H. ......... $195.00
**CAST IRON,** seated pug, 3½" H. ............................... $85.00

*Row III, L to R*
**CAST IRON,** cat on tub, A. C. Williams, 4⅛" H. .......................... $175.00

**CAST IRON,** horse on tub, A. C. Williams, 5⅜" H. ............. $110.00
**CAST IRON,** bear, "Teddy" on side, 3⅞" L. ............................... $80.00

**CAST IRON,** "Middy Bank," 5⅜" H. ............................... $100.00
**CAST IRON,** lion on tub, A. C. Williams, 4¼" H. .......................... $135.00

A-OH Sept. 1982 *Garth's Auctions, Inc.*
*CAST IRON*
*Row I, L to R*
**STILL BANK,** nickel plated, "U.S. Mail," 4" H. ............................ $45.00
**STILL BANK,** rabbit, 4⅝" H. .... $95.00
**STILL BANK,** automobile, 6¾" L. ............................... $300.00
**STILL BANK,** Eng., bulldog, 3⅞" H. ............................... $75.00
**STILL BANK,** "City Bank," Japanned, 4" H. ............................... $62.50

*Row II, L to R*
**STILL BANK,** "World's Fair Adm. Bldg. 1893," replm., 5¾" H. ......... $350.00
**STILL BANK,** Woolworth Building, 8" H. ............................... $65.00
**STILL BANK,** deer, 9" H. ..... $105.00
**STILL BANK,** Statue of Liberty, 9½" H. ............................... $175.00
**MECHANICAL BANK,** "Recording Dime Bank," mkd. "The National Recording Bank Patented Apl 7, '91," orig. bronze finish, 6⅝" H. ................. $175.00

*Row III, L to R*
**TOY,** hook & ladder, 3 horses, driver & bucket, some damage, 22½" L. ............................... $150.00
**STILL BANK,** elephant, Hubley, solid cast feet, 4¾" H. ............... $80.00

A-OH Sept. 1982 *Garth's Auctions, Inc.*
*STILL BANKS*
*Row I, L to R*
**CAST IRON,** dog, 3¾" H. ...... $40.00
**CAST IRON,** "Radio Bank," "Kenton Toys, Kenton Ohio," 4¾" H. ..... $45.00
**CAST IRON,** horse, "My Pet," 4¼" H. ............................... $105.00

*Row II, L to R*
**CAST IRON,** Mammy w/spoon, A.C. Williams, 5¾" H. ................. $75.00
**CAST IRON,** boat w/child, "Mermaid," 4⅛" H. ............................... $275.00
**CAST IRON,** elephant on wheels w/bell, converted to bank, by N. N. Hill Brass Co., trunk unpainted, blk. body, red wheels, 5½" L. ............................... $175.00
**CAST IRON,** boat w/child, "Dolphin," 4½" H. ............................... $325.00
**CAST IRON,** share cropper, A. C. Williams, 5½" H. ............... $90.00

*Row III, L to R*
**CAST IRON,** Dutch girl, 6½" H. ............................... $330.00
**CAST IRON,** Rumplestiltskin "Do You Know Me?" 6" H. ............. $225.00
**CAST IRON,** horse on tub, A. C. Williams, 5⅜" H. ............. $175.00
**CAST IRON,** water wheel, 4½" H. ............................... $750.00
**CAST IRON,** "Billiken Shoes Bring Luck," 4⅛" H. ............. $65.00
**CAST IRON,** lion on tub, A. C. Williams, 5½" H. ............. $100.00
**CAST IRON,** golly wog, 6⅛" H. ............................... $200.00

A-OH April 1983 *Garth's Auctions, Inc.*
*BANKS*
*Row I, L to R*
**BANK,** cast iron, upside label "Security Safe, Deposit," repr., repaint, 5" H. ............................... $10.00
**LION,** cast iron, old wh. repaint, 5" H. ............................... $10.00
**CAROUSEL,** cast iron, traces of red & blk. on base, top has worn red paint, 4¾" H. ............................... $10.00
**ELEPHANT W/HOWDAH,** cast iron, traces of paint, 4⅝" H. .......... $15.00
**SAFE,** cast iron, old repaint, no key, 4" H. ............................... $10.00

*Row II, L to R*
**POLLY WOG,** worn old paint, 6¼" H. ............................... $185.00
**BANK BUILDING,** cast iron, old silver & gold paint, 5½" H. ............. $50.00
**REARING HORSE,** worn old blk. paint, 7⅜" H. ............................... $37.50
**SKYSCRAPER,** cast iron, worn old gold & silver paint, 6½" H. ........... $70.00
**GEORGE WASHINGTON,** contemporary, orig. polychrome paint, 6½" H. ............................... $10.00

*Row III, L to R*
**SANTA ASLEEP IN CHAIR,** cast wh. metal, worn orig. polychrome paint, "Wyandotte Savings Bank," 6" H. ............................... $30.00
**SUN BONNET BABY,** cast iron, worn orig. paint, 7½" H. ............. $135.00
**ARTILLERY BANK,** mechanical, cast iron, worn orig. bronze finish, trigger lever broken, 6" H. ............ $395.00
**POLICEMAN,** cast iron, old gold paint, 5½" H. ............................... $5.00
**JOLLY NIGGER,** cast iron mechanical, worn old blk. & red paint, 6½" H. ............................... $100.00

A-OH Sept. 1982 *Garth's Auctions, Inc.*

*CAST IRON STILL BANKS*

*Row I, L to R*

**HORSE,** 2⅞" H. .............. $155.00
**ELEPHANT W/HOWDAH,** 2½" H. .............................. $45.00
**THREE MONKIES,** 3¼" H. ..... $255.00
**PIG,** 4" L. .................... $55.00
**ELEPHANT,** political slogan w/busts "Prosperity McKinley, Teddy," 2½" H. ............................ $475.00

*Row II, L to R*

**RHINO,** arcade, 5" L. ......... $425.00
**BRONZE PLATED,** "Smiling Jim, Peaceful Bill," replm., 4" H. .......... $545.00
**MARY & LITTLE LAMB,** 4½" H. ............................ $550.00
**EAGLE,** 4" H. ................. $425.00
**BILLY POSSUM,** 4⅞" H. ..... $1525.00

*Row III, L to R*

**ELEPHANT ON TUB,** A. C. Williams, 5⅜" H. ..................... $90.00
**MUTT & JEFF,** 5¼" H. ....... $120.00
**LOG CABIN,** 2⅝" H. ......... $175.00
**ANDY GUMP ON STUMP,** arcade, 4½" H. ......................... $775.00
**ELEPHANT ON TUB,** A. C. Williams, 5½" H. ....................... $105.00

A-MA Oct. 1982 *Richard A. Bourne Co., Inc.*

*MECHANICAL BANKS*

*Row I, L to R*

**ELEPHANT W/HOWDAH,** trunk's release mechanism is missing, paint flaking & rusting ........................ $10.00
**TAMMANY,** spring mechanism is not working ....................... $75.00
**THE OUTHOUSE,** bottom penny catch is missing, paint flaking & rusting ............................ $110.00
**THE HALL'S EXCELSIOR BANK,** paint flaking & rusting ........... $40.00

*Row II, L to R*

**CREEDMORE,** paint rusting, bottom penny catch is missing .......... $225.00
**WILLIAM TELL,** most of paint worn off, bottom penny catch is missing .... $50.00

A-OH April 1983 *Garth's Auctions, Inc.*

*Row I, L to R*

**CAST IRON BANK,** bank building, worn old gr. & gold paint, 4⅝" H. ...... $15.00
**CAST IRON BANK,** skyscraper, worn old gold & silver paint, 4½" H. .... $15.00
**CAST NICKEL STEEL BANK,** "State Safe," sheet metal sides, 4⅛" H. .. $15.00
**CAST IRON BANK,** prancing horse, old blk. paint, repr., 4¼" H. ......... $20.00
**CAST IRON BANK,** safe, worn old red & gold paint on front, sides & top are unpainted, some rust, 4" H. ...... $10.00
**CAST IRON BANK,** skyscraper, worn old gold & silver paint, one corner of tower is glued, 4½" H. ................ $10.00
**CAST IRON BANK,** bank building, old silver & gold repaint, 4¼" H. ...... $5.00

*Row II, L to R*

**CAST IRON BANK,** elephant w/Howdah, worn old red paint, 4⅞" H. ............................ $10.00
**CAST IRON TOY,** sled w/pr. of horses & driver, old repaint, 16" L. ....... $100.00
**CAST WHITE METAL BANK,** pirate & treasure chest, worn orig. polychrome paint, minor cracks, 6" H. ....... $35.00

*Row III, L to R*

**CAST IRON BANK,** Boston bulldog, worn old paint, 5⅜" H. .......... $75.00
**CAST IRON BANK,** horse, no paint, 4⅛" H. ........................... $10.00
**SHEET METAL BANK,** "Uncle Sam's Register Bank," worn orig. blk. paint, 6⅛" H. ............................ $3.00
**CAST IRON BANK,** doe, traces of old blk. paint, 5" H. ............... $17.50
**CAST IRON BANK,** stag, worn old gold paint, 5¾" H. ................. $40.00

A-OH Sept. 1982 *Garth's Auctions, Inc.*

*L to R*

**OWL,** replm., "Be Wise, Save Money," 5" H. ........................... $75.00
**RADIO,** 4½" H. ................ $65.00
**CAT W/BALL,** 5⅝" L. ........ $145.00
**RADIO,** mkd. "Kenton Toys," 4½" H. ............................ $35.00
**STATUE OF LIBERTY,** 6" H. ............................ $50.00

A-OH April 1983 *Garth's Auctions, Inc.*

*Row I, L to R*

**CAST IRON FIRE TRUCK,** worn orig. red paint, "Made in U.S.A.," ladders are missing, rubber wheels cracked, 3½" L. ............................. $5.00
**CAST IRON BANK,** side-wheel steam boat, "ARCADE," no paint, pitted from rust, 7½" L. .................. $27.50
**CAST IRON TOY,** farm truck, no paint, 4¾" L. ....................... $15.00

*Row II, L to R*

**CAST WHITE METAL BANK,** stump w/elf, worn old paint, repr., inc. ornament, 2⅝" H. ........................ $95.00
**CAST IRON BANK,** bank building, old gold repaint, 3¾" H. ............ $7.00
**CAST WHITE METAL BANK,** Casey Jones, worn bronze finish, 5⅜" L. ............................ $20.00
**CAST IRON BANK,** bank building, no paint, 3⅛" H. ................. $20.00
**CAST IRON BANK,** building, gr. & gold repaint, 2⅞" H. ................ $9.00

*Row III, L to R*

**CAST IRON BANK,** bank building, no paint, 3" H. .................... $12.50
**CAST IRON BANK,** U.S. Mail, worn old aluminum paint w/red, 3½" H. ..... $9.00
**BRASS BANK,** windmill, engraved surface & cast vanes, originally silver plated, bottom retains silver, 3⅜" H. ..... $50.00
**CAST IRON BANK,** Home Savings Bank, worn old gr. & red paint, 3½" H. ............................ $20.00
**CAST IRON BANK,** turkey, worn old br. finish w/red, 3½" H. ............ $92.50
**SHEET METAL BANK,** safe, worn old blk. paint, 4" H. ................ $10.00

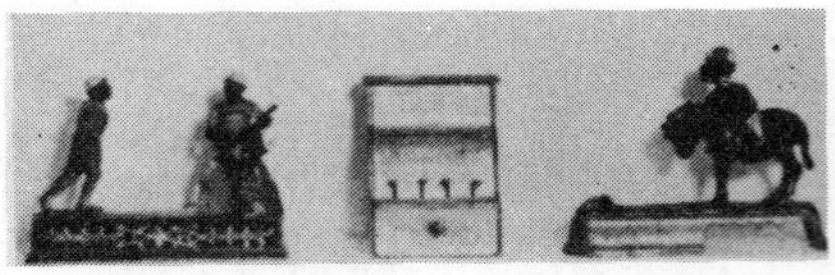

A-OH Sept. 1982 *Garth's Auctions, Inc.*

*L to R*

**MECHANICAL BANK,** "Dark Town Battery," repr., 9⅞" L. ......... $975.00
**MECHANICAL BANK,** "National," old gold & silver paint w/wear, 6¾" H. ............................ $450.00
**MECHANICAL BANK,** "Always Did 'spise a Mule," wear, 10¼" L. .... $425.00

A-OH July 1982     *Garth's Auctions, Inc.*
*Row I, L to R*
**CAST IRON PENNY BANK,** ball player w/bat, worn old repaint, 5¾" H. .. $85.00
**CAST LEAD FIGURE,** man in driving clothes, mkd. "England," worn orig. paint, 2" H. ............................ $10.00
**CAST IRON TOY ROCKER,** worn old red paint, 2¾" H. ............... $12.50
**CAST WH. METAL TOY,** man on motorcycle, "Barclay, Made USA," worn old paint, 3½" L. ............... $25.00
**CAST IRON MECHANICAL BANK,** cabin w/blk. man, worn orig. paint, 3¾" H. ...................................... $275.00
**CAST IRON AMISH GIRL ON SWING,** orig. paint w/some rust, late, 4⅞" H. ................................ $40.00
**CAST IRON AMISH MAN BOOK END,** orig. paint w/some rust, late, 4¾" H. ........................................ $25.00

*Row II, L to R*
**CAST IRON MAN IN ROADSTER,** orig. paint, late, 7¼" L. .......... $75.00
**WOODEN NOAH'S ARK,** w/orig. painted decor., 11 carved & painted animals (animals have some damage), 7¾" L. ..................................... $275.00

*Row III*
**TOY TRAIN,** cast iron engine w/old blk., red & gold paint, 7¾" L.; tin coal car 4" L.; 3 tin passenger cars, 1 each in red, blue & wh., 8½" L. ................... $215.00

---

A-MA Nov. 1982    *Richard A. Bourne Co., Inc.*
*Row I, L to R*
**MECHANICAL BANK "JONAH & THE WHALE,"** iron, orig. paint w/some wear, door at bottom missing .... $800.00
**MECHANICAL BANK "TRICK DOG,"** iron, orig. paint w/some flaking, door in bottom missing ................. $275.00
**"DARK TOWN BATTERY" BANK,** iron, door on bottom missing .... $850.00

*Row II, L to R*
**MECHANICAL BANK "DANCING BEAR,"** iron, orig. paint w/some re-touching...................... $850.00
**MECHANICAL BANK "EAGLE & EAGLETS,"** cast iron, orig. paint, door at bottom missing ............... $275.00
**MECHANICAL BANK "PUNCH & JUDY,"** iron, orig. paint, slight possibility of retouching of gold on front .... $475.00

A-MA Nov. 1982    *Richard A. Bourne Co., Inc.*
BANKS
*Row I, L to R*
**FROG,** mechanical, iron, orig. paint, door in bottom missing .............. $425.00
**BULLDOG SAVINGS BANK,** pat. August 13, 1878, key wind, small dor in bottom missing, orig. finish ...... $750.00
**MOSQUE,** iron, hand crank .... $450.00

*Row II, L to R*
**UNCLE SAM,** mechanical, iron, orig. paint w/retouching, door at back missing ........................................ $400.00
**PADDY & PIG,** mechanical, iron, orig. paint, door in bottom missing .... $500.00
**LEAPFROG,** mechanical, iron, orig. paint, replm. of 1 bolt in back, door missing ........................................ $675.00
**MAGIC,** mechanical, iron, orig. paint ........................................ $400.00

A-OH Sept. 1982    *Garth's Auctions, Inc.*
*CAST IRON BANKS*
*Row I, L to R*
**BANK BUILDING,** 3⅜" H. ..... $55.00
**PIG,** mkd. "Deckers Iowana," 4½" L. ........................................ $75.00
**LIBERTY BELL,** 2¾" H. ........ $65.00
**ELEPHANT W/HOWDAH,** A. C. Williams, 3" H. ................. $45.00
**CLOCK W/TIN SIDES,** "A Money Saver," Arcade, 3½" H. ......... $60.00
*Row II, L to R*
**CANNON,** 6½" L. ........... $1225.00
**FACE** Eng., w/"Save and Smile Money Box" on hat, 4⅛" H. .......... $250.00
**CABIN,** mechanical, wear, 3⅝" H. ........................................ $325.00
**TURKEY,** 3½" H. ............... $75.00
**DONKEY,** 4½" H. .............. $70.00

A-MA Nov. 1982    *Richard A. Bourne Co., Inc.*
*Row I, L to R*
**MECHANICAL BANK "HALL'S LILLIPUT,"** iron, w/tray, orig. paint, door in bottom missing .............. $275.00
**MECHANICAL "ORGAN" BANK,** iron, orig. paint ................. $250.00
**"SANTA CLAUS" BANK,** iron, orig. paint worn away on high spots ... $675.00
**MECHANICAL BANK "CHIEF BIG MOON,"** iron, orig. paint ....... $600.00
*Row II, L to R*
**MECHANICAL BANK "WILLIAM TELL,"** cast iron .............. $350.00
**MECHANICAL BANK "I ALWAYS DID 'SPISE A MULE,"** orig. paint, replm. door, left-hand rein needs resoldered ........................................ $275.00

A-OH Jan. 1983    *Garth's Auctions, Inc.*
*BANKS*
*Row I, L to R*
**PIG,** wh. clay, chips, 3⅝" L. ..... $35.00
**APPLE,** redware, orig. drk. red paint, sm. flakes, 2½" H. ................. $75.00
**SPHERE & DOG,** Ohio wh. clay, bubbles & crack, 4⅞" H. .............. $125.00
**PEACH,** wh. clay, flakes, 2⅝" H. ................................ $45.00
**PIG,** sponge decor., br. & blue on wh., chips, roughness, 3⅝" L. ........ $85.00
*Row II, L to R*
**PIG,** sponge decor., drk. blue & br. on cream, chips, 5¾" L. ............ $85.00
**FROG,** wh. clay, amber & gr. glaze, flaking, 4" H. ................. $65.00
**ACORN,** yellowware, Rockingham glaze, chips, 3" H. ................... $40.00
**PIG,** sponge decor., blue & br. on cream, chips, 6" L. .................... $95.00
*Row III, L to R*
**CAT HEAD,** wh. clay, chips, flakes, 4" H. ........................................ $85.00
**ACORN,** wh. clay, Rockingham glaze, 3½" H. ................................ $35.00
**MONKEY HEAD,** gr. glaze, flakes, 3¾" H. ................................ $55.00
**STONEWARE JUG,** wh. porcelain glaze, flake, 4⅜" H. ................... $30.00
**DOG HEAD,** wh. clay, amber glaze, br. & tan sponging, minor flakes, 3¾" H. ........................................ $75.00

A-OH Nov. 1983    *Garth's Auctions, Inc.*
*Row I, L to R*
**BLOWN GLASS CLOWN,** worn red, gr., amber, 3¾″ H. .............. $8.00
**BLOWN GLASS BUNCH OF GRAPES,** red, blue, amber & silver, sm. chips, 3¾″ H. ............... $35.00
**BLOWN GLASS OWL ON BALL,** red, pink & wh. w/blk. eyes, 3¾″ H. ... $20.00
**BLOWN GLASS BOY,** blue, amber & red, 5″ H. .............. $75.00
**BLOWN GLASS DOG,** on ball, worn red & blk. on silver, 3¾″ H. ........ $55.00
**BLOWN GLASS SANTA,** metal spring clip, worn red & wh., 3½″ H. ..... $25.00
**BLOWN GLASS SHOE,** amber, red, blue & silver, 3½″ H. ........... $55.00
**BLOWN GLASS COO-COO CLOCK,** red, blue, gr. & silver, paper face, 3½″ H. ................................... $50.00
*Row II, L to R*
**BLOWN GLASS COTTAGE,** amber, red, blue, gr. & silver w/snow, 3″ H. ................................... $8.00
**BLOWN GLASS HORN,** pastel floral design, 4½″ H. ............. $7.50
**CAST IRON TREE HOLDER,** old metallic gr. repaint w/gold & silver, mkd. "Germany," 12″ D., 5″ H. ........ $30.00
**BLOWN GLASS CHILD'S HEAD,** glass eyes, worn red scarf, 3″ H. ................................... $85.00
**BLOWN GLASS OWL,** worn yellow, magenta & blk., 3½″ H. ......... $22.50
**BLOWN GLASS HORN,** worn floral decor., 5″ H. .............. $7.50
*Row III, L to R*
**BLOWN GLASS ORNAMENT,** in tinsel basket, 3¾″ H. ................... $3.50
**BLOWN GLASS FRUIT,** gr., rose & wh., 3¾″ H. .............. $5.00
**TIN CANDLE LANTERN ORNA-MENT,** worn red & wh. coated glass sides, 3¼″ H. .......................... $30.00
**BLOWN GLASS HORN,** magenta, 4″ L. ................................... $8.00

A-OH Nov. 1983    *Garth's Auctions, Inc.*
*CHRISTMAS ORNAMENTS*
*Row I, L to R*
**BLOWN GLASS TREE FINIAL,** silver w/red horns & Santa, minor wear, 13½″ H. ................................... $25.00

A-OH Nov. 1983    *Garth's Auctions, Inc.*
*CHRISTMAS ORNAMENTS*
*Row I, L to R*
**BLOWN GLASS PEACHES,** set of 2 (1 on second row), greenish opaque w/red highlights & pink, 2½″ H. ........ $25.00
**BLOWN GLASS COTTAGE,** silver w/red & gr., 2½″ H. ............. $7.50
**BLOWN GLASS DUCK,** silver w/red & blue, 3″ H. .............. $55.00
**PRINTED PAPER SANTA,** pink angel hair, some wear, 12″ H. .... $15.00
**BLOWN GLASS SNOWMAN,** sanded w/red, blue & gold, 3″ H. ........ $55.00
**BLOWN GLASS COTTAGE,** silver w/red & gr., 3″ H. ............. $10.00
**BLOWN GLASS ORNAMENT,** pale gold, 2½″ H. ................... $10.00

*Row II, L to R*
**BLOWN GLASS BALLOON,** printed paper Santa w/applied tinsel, 4¾″ H. ................................... $90.00
**BLOWN GLASS BABY ON BALL,** gold & red, 3¼″ H. ................... $65.00
**GLASS BULB,** Santa, red, blue, yellow & blk. paint w/wear, 4″ H. ......... $15.00
**CLOTH DOLL,** caroler w/felt body & comp. face, 4″ H. .............. $40.00
**BLOWN GLASS ORNAMENT,** basket of fruit, polychromed, 2¾″ H. .... $25.00

*Row III, L to R*
**BLOWN GLASS ORNAMENT,** fruit w/metal clip candleholder, sanded yellow & orange, 4¼″ H. .............. $30.00
**BLOWN GLASS BIRD,** angel hair tail, silver w/blue & red, spring clip, 4½″ L. ................................... $40.00
**BLOWN GLASS FISH,** silver w/blue & red, 3¼″ L. ................... $50.00
**BLOWN GLASS BIRD,** spring clip & angel hair tail, wh., gr. & red, 5½″ L. ................................... $10.00
**BLOWN GLASS PIPE,** silver w/red, blue & gold, end taped, 4½″ L. .... $25.00
**BLOWN GLASS UMBRELLA,** gold w/tinsel, 5″ L. ................... $35.00

**BLOWN GLASS PIPE,** silver w/red & gr., 4″ L. ...................... $12.50
**GLASS BULB,** snow topped cottage, 2¾″ H. ................................... $6.00
**GLASS BULB,** parrot, pink & gr. w/some wear, 3¼″ H. ............. $8.00
**GLASS BULB,** Santa, red, gr., yellow & blk., 4¼″ H. ................... $12.50
**GLASS BULB,** clown, magenta, gr. & blue w/wear, 3¾″ H. ............. $8.00
**GLASS BULB,** bull dog, red & blk. w/wear, 2¾″ H. ............... $25.00
**GLASS BULB,** pouter pigeon, magenta w/blue, wear, 3″ H. ......... $15.00
**BLOWN GLASS FRUIT,** yellow w/leaves, 2¾″ H. ................. $3.00
**BLOWN GLASS TREE FINIAL,** silver w/gr., applied tinsel & sm. silver balls, 10½″ H. ................................... $10.00

*Row II, L to R*
**BLOWN GLASS PEACOCK,** spread angel hair tail & spring clip, gr. & silver w/gold, 4″ H. ................... $35.00
**BLOWN GLASS PINE CONES,** set of 12 (2 illus.), silver w/tinsel, 3″ H. ................................... $50.00
**GLASS BULB,** blimp w/Am. flag, red & gr. plus flag, 2½″ L. ........... $40.00
**BLOWN GLASS BIRD,** spring clip, wh. w/salmon & blk., tail missing, 3½″ L. ................................... $10.00
**BLOWN GLASS REVOLVER,** silver w/pink grip, 5¼″ L. ............. $140.00

*Row III, L to R*
**BLOWN GLASS ROSE,** silver w/worn pink, 5¼″ L. ................... $8.00
**BLOWN GLASS GRAPES,** silver, 4″ H. ................................... $40.00
**TIGER,** comp. w/calf skin covering, glass eyes, blk. stripes, wear, 5″ L. ..... $20.00
**BLOWN GLASS ORNAMENT,** red, blue & yellow on silver, 3½″ H. .... $5.00

A-OH Nov. 1983    *Garth's Auctions, Inc.*
**ENGRAVING,** blk. & wh., "Washington & His Generals," some foxing, 32¾″ x 44¼″ ................................... $100.00
**MAMMIES BENCH,** old red & blk. graining w/yellow striping & stenciled decor., rockers removed & castors added, orig. finish, 72″ L. ............. $300.00

A-MA June 1983    *Robert W. Skinner Inc.*
*L to R*
**VICTORIAN LADY'S DESK &
CHAIR,** Eng., ca. 1870, bamboo, 23½" W.,
18" D., 40" H. ............... $300.00*
**VICTORIAN CORNER WHAT-NOT,**
Eng., ca. 1870, bamboo w/lacquered
decor., 12" D., 62" H. ........ $150.00*

A-MA Aug. 1983    *Richard A. Bourne Co., Inc.*
**BRIDE'S BOX,** 18th C., 11¾" W., 19¼" L.,
7" H. ....................... $1150.00

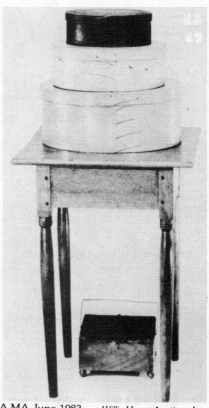

A-MA June 1983    *Willis Henry Auctions Inc.*
*SHAKER ITEMS*
**OVAL BOX,** 4 fingers, orig. green paint,
3⅜" H., 9" L. .............. $650.00*
**OVAL BOX,** 4 fingers, yellow paint, 4½"
H., 12" L. .................. $900.00*
**OVAL BOX,** 5 fingers, tangerine paint
over powder blue, stamped "J. Power,"
6¼" H., 14¾" L. ............. $900.00*
**STAND,** birch, turned leg, New Lebanon,
NY, ca. 1830, 26¾" H., 18" W., 16¾" D.
........................... $1000.00*
**FOOTWARMER,** pine, footed, dove-
tailed, velvet top, grain painted, tin interior
w/oil burner, wire bail handle, 5" H., 8¼"
W., 7¼" L. .................. $125.00*

A-MA Aug. 1983    *Richard A. Bourne Co., Inc.*
**FLAX WHEEL,** Am., 18th C., retains
most of orig. grain paint ....... $425.00

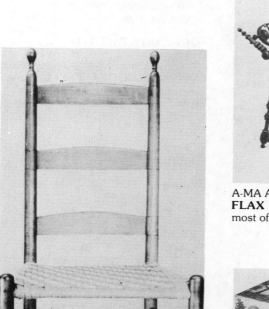

A-MA June 1983    *Willis Henry Auctions Inc.*
**SHAKER SIDE CHAIR,** 3 slats, taped
seat, orig. finish, 37½" O.H., 14" seat Ht.
........................... $950.00*

A-MA Aug. 1983    *Richard A. Bourne Co., Inc.*
**DECORATED PINE BOX,** Am., early
19th C., orig. fabric lining w/sm. red polka
dots, normal signs of wear, 8" W., 14" L., 8"
H. ......................... $7000.00

A-MA June 1983    *Willis Henry Auctions Inc.*
*L to R*
*SHAKER ITEMS*
**ROCKER,** #6, 4 slats, shawl bar, mush-
room arm, taped seat, old blk. finish
........................... $900.00*
**ROCKER,** #5, 3 slats, shawl bar, trans-
itional mushroom arm, orig. blue taped
seat, natural finish ........... $900.00*

*Price does not include 10% buyer fee.

A-OH Nov. 1983          *Garth's Auctions, Inc.*
*Row I, L to R*
**CAST IRON CANDY MOLD,** makes 3
Santas, 2½″ x 6¾″ . . . . . . . . . . . . . $65.00
**WOODEN CLAMPS,** set of 2, mkd.
"Bulldog Blanket Clamp," attrib. to
Shakers, 6½″ L. . . . . . . . . . . . . . . $20.00
**SM. WOODEN BELLOWS,** embossed
brass top plate & brass nozzle, releathered,
15″ L. . . . . . . . . . . . . . . . . . . . . $105.00
**SHAKER GLOVE STRETCHER,** 11½″
L. . . . . . . . . . . . . . . . . . . . . . . . $55.00
**WOODEN MATCH HOLDER,** carved
eagle, 7¼″ H. . . . . . . . . . . . . . . . $55.00

*Row II, L to R*
**TIN STAR ORNAMENT,** punched
edges & cut-out curled design, 10″ D.
. . . . . . . . . . . . . . . . . . . . . . . . . $30.00
**SHAKER HORSEHAIR BRUSH,** turned
wooden handle, 9½″ L. . . . . . . . . . $30.00
**SHAKER CLOTHES PIN,** 6¼″ L.
. . . . . . . . . . . . . . . . . . . . . . . . . $55.00
**CAST IRON SHAKER TRIVETS,** set of
2 (1 illus.), similar but not a pair, 3⅜″ x 4⅜″
. . . . . . . . . . . . . . . . . . . . . . . . . $40.00

*Row III, L to R*
**FOLDING TIN CHOCOLATE MOLD,**
Santa, 6¾″ H. . . . . . . . . . . . . . . . $55.00
**ROUND WOODEN BUTTER PRINT,**
sheaf design, 1 pc. w/turned handle, age
cracks, 4″ D. . . . . . . . . . . . . . . . . $50.00
**SHAKER WOODEN SCOOP,** 9½″ L.
. . . . . . . . . . . . . . . . . . . . . . . . . $70.00
**PEWTER ICE CREAM MOLD,** Santa,
"E & Co.," 4⅝″ H. . . . . . . . . . . . . $45.00

A-OH Nov. 1983          *Garth's Auctions, Inc.*
**SINGLE WEAVE JACQUARD
COVERLET,** 2 pc., red, blue, gr. & wh.,
sgn., 76″ x 80″ . . . . . . . . . . . . . . $350.00
**WOODEN HAY FORK,** 63″ L.
. . . . . . . . . . . . . . . . . . . . . . . . $110.00
**SHAKER SWIFT,** old yellow varnish,
restor., 22″ H. . . . . . . . . . . . . . . $135.00
**SHAKER LADDER-BACK ROCKER,**
orig. drk. finish w/orig. burgandy plush
seat, seat worn . . . . . . . . . . . . . . $225.00
**TILTED SHAKER WORK BOX,**
mahogany w/birdseye veneer, printed
paper covered int., old finish w/some wear,
7¾″ x 11″, 3¾″ H. . . . . . . . . . . . $55.00
**CANDLESTAND,** cherry, 1 board top
w/applied gallery, ref. w/old repairs, orig.
top reattached, 16″ x 16½″, 26¾″ H.
. . . . . . . . . . . . . . . . . . . . . . . . $275.00

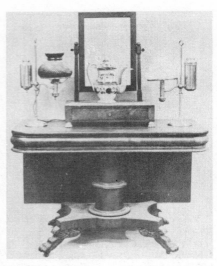

A-OH Nov. 1983          *Garth's Auctions, Inc.*
**EMPIRE SHAVING MIRROR,**
mahogany veneer, repl. frame, 20¾″ W.,
11″ D., 27″ H. . . . . . . . . . . . . . . . $75.00
**BRASS STUDENT LAMP,** gr. enameled
ribbed shade, electrified, mkd., polished,
repr. to base, chips in shade, 21″ H.
. . . . . . . . . . . . . . . . . . . . . . . . $200.00
**BRASS STUDENT LAMP,** opaque wh.
shade w/enameled floral decor., burner
missing, sm. flakes on rim of shade, 20½″ H.
. . . . . . . . . . . . . . . . . . . . . . . . $150.00
**SOFT PASTE TALL POT,** leads decor.,
stains & hairline, sm. chips, 10⅝″ H.
. . . . . . . . . . . . . . . . . . . . . . . . $300.00
**EMPIRE BANQUET TABLE,** 2-part,
mahogany, old alligatored varnish, open:
44″ x 88½″, 30¼″ H. . . . . . . . . . . $500.00

A-OH Nov. 1983          *Garth's Auctions, Inc.*
**DOUBLE STUDENT LAMP,** brass
w/gr. shades cased in wh., mkd., electrified,
sm. edge flakes, 29″ H. . . . . . . . . $700.00
**COVERED COMPOTE,** clear flint,
sawtooth, lid w/edge flakes, 8¼″ D., 12″ H.
→ . . . . . . . . . . . . . . . . . . . . . . . $50.00
**COVERED COMPOTE,** clear flint,
sawtooth, sm. check & minor flakes, 9″ D.,
14″ H. . . . . . . . . . . . . . . . . . . . $115.00
**HEPPLEWHITE CHEST,** cherry, ref.,
repl. oval brasses, 40¾″ W., 19¾″ D., 41¾″
H. . . . . . . . . . . . . . . . . . . . . . . . $800.00

A-OH Nov. 1983          *Garth's Auctions, Inc.*
**MULE CHEST,** poplar, 6-board const.,
orig. engraved brass hdw., ref., 40¾″ W.,
18″ D., 30¾″ H. . . . . . . . . . . . . . $425.00
**TIN REVERE CANDLE LANTERN,**
punched design, some rust, old flaking blk.
paint, 12½″ H. . . . . . . . . . . . . . . . $45.00
**STONEWARE JUG,** brushed cobalt blue
decor., hairline, 15½″ H. . . . . . . . $125.00
**TIN REVERE LANTERN,** 2 blown
bullseye lens, made to be electrified, 12½″
H. . . . . . . . . . . . . . . . . . . . . . . . . $30.00

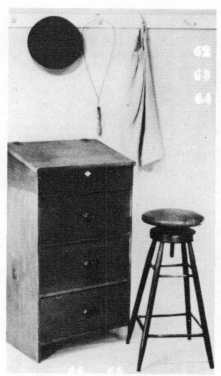

A-MA June 1983   *Willis Henry Auctions Inc.*
*SHAKER ITEMS*
**DESK**, pine, stand-up, slant lid over 3 drawers, interior shelf, stained red finish, 46" H., 25" W., 18" D. . . . . . . . . $850.00*
**SIEVE**, horse hair woven in checkerboard patt., wooden straight lapped side, by Shaker Hands, 5" H., 13½" D. . . . $55.00*
**RUG BEATER**, partial label, "Levi Shaw -Mt. Lebanon". . . . . . . . . . . . . . . . $95.00*
**APRON**, cotton homespun, brown & white check, initialed "N.S. . . . . . $25.00*
**STOOL**, birch, turned & joined base, leather cushioned adjustable seat, 33" O.H. . . . . . . . . . . . . . . . . . . . . . . . . . . $1500.00*

A-MA June 1983   *Willis Henry Auctions Inc.*
*L to R*
*SHAKER ITEMS*
**CHILD'S ARMCHAIR**, rare #0, 3 slats, old blk. paint, orig. wh. & tan taped seat, 23" H., seat Ht. 7½" . . . . . . . . . $1100.00*
**ROCKER**, #4, taped seat & back, orig. light finish . . . . . . . . . . . . . . . . $600.00*
**CHILD'S ROCKER**, rare #0, shawl bar, 3 slat, orig. finish, transfer on rocker, orig. red & blk. taped seat, 23" H., seat Ht. 9" . . . . . . . . . . . . . . . . . . . . . . . . . . . $800.00*

**5**

A-MA June 1983   *Willis Henry Auctions Inc.*
**SHAKER WOODBOX**, pine, hooded, old ivory, colored paint, peg on side, 43¾" H., 27½" W., 18½" D. . . . . . . . . $700.00*

A-MA June 1983   *Willis Henry Auctions Inc.*
**SHAKER FLAX WHEEL**, sgn. "S.R.A.L." Samuel Ring, Alfred, ME, orig. cinnamon color paint . . . . . . . . . $375.00*

A-MA June 1983   *Willis Henry Auctions Inc.*
*SHAKER ITEMS*
**CHEST OF DRAWERS**, butternut & poplar, 5 drawers, orig. wooden threaded knobs, arched bracket base, Enfield, CT, 49" H., 45¾" W., 17½" D. . . . . . $2200.00*
**BASKET**, splint gathering basket, hoop handle, round top, square bottom, 9" H., 14" D. . . . . . . . . . . . . . . . . . . . . . . $100.00*
**BRUSHES**, 3 whisk brooms . . . $70.00*
**TABLE TOP DESK**, poplar, slant lid, dovetailed constr., orig. red finish, 6¼" H., 16" W., 13" D. . . . . . . . . . . . . . . $170.00*

A-OH Nov. 1983   *Garth's Auctions, Inc.*
**CURRIER & IVES LITHO.**, shadow box frame w/some flaking, 26½" x 30½" . . . . . . . . . . . . . . . . . . . . . . . . . . . $550.00
**TREEN BOX**, poplar w/age cracks, old ref., 8½" H. . . . . . . . . . . . . . . . . . $135.00
**FACTORY DECOY**, canvasback hen, glass eyes, old paint, 16¼" L. . . . . $35.00
**FACTORY DECOY**, mate to above, glass eyes cracked, split in head, 16¼" L. . . . . . . . . . . . . . . . . . . . . . . . . . . . $30.00

A-MA Aug. 1983   *Richard A. Bourne Co., Inc.*
→ **BLANKET CHEST**, early 19th C., painted & decorated pine, dovetailed construction, 16" D., 39" L., 16" H. . . . . . . . . . . . . . . . . . . . . . . . . . . . $850.00

*Price does not include 10% buyer fee.

A-MA June 1983    *Willis Henry Auctions Inc.*
**SHAKER STOVE,** New Lebanon, NY, door professionally repl. & sgn. by Wm. Sensency, 23½″ H., 13¼″ W., 30″ L.
............................ $500.00*

A-MA June 1983    *Willis Henry Auctions Inc.*
*SHAKER ITEMS*
**CHEST,** poplar, 4 drawers w/bonnet drawer top, tall tapered foot, yellow wash finish, Enfield, CT, 44″ H., 45″ W., 18″ D.
............................ $1000.00*
**BASKET,** ash splint, double wrapped rim, used for drying herbs, 2 carved side handles, 5½″ H., 25¾″ D. ...... $275.00*
**DOCUMENT BOX,** figured butternut, ivory escutcheon, "R. H. Van Deusen, P.O. Shaker Station, Conn. (Hartford County," 4½″ H., 12½″ W., 7¼″ D. ...... $450.00*
**BONNET & BONNET BOX,** bonnet - poplar w/blue silk lining, pleated collar & matching ribbon; bonnet box - mahogany w/pine bottom, dovetailed lid & case, 10¼″ H., 11½″ W., 12½″ D. ......... $700.00*
**FOOT STOOL,** maple & cherry, label transfer, Mt. Lebanon, NY ..... $250.00*

A-MA June 1983    *Willis Henry Auctions Inc.*
*SHAKER ITEMS*
**TABLE,** maple, pine & poplar, turned leg, 27½″ H., 30″ W., 16″ D. ...... $250.00*
**GLOVE BOX,** Bird's eye maple, dovetailed construction, brass push latch, 3¾″ H., 10½″ W., 4⅜″ D. ......... $170.00*
**SHOVELS,** stove ash shovel, hand wrought, iron; miniature shovel, cast iron, brass acorn finial ............. $95.00*
**FUNNEL,** used for witch hazel, Canterbury, NH, old red paint ........ $50.00*

A-MA June 1983    *Willis Henry Auctions Inc.*
*SHAKER ITEMS*
**TWO-DRAWER WORK TABLE,** pine & butternut, tapered & slightly splayed legs, dovetailed drawers, cherry threaded knobs, 2 board pine top, breadboard ends, Enfield, NH, ca. 1820, 30″ H., 52″ W., 32″ D.
............................ $1000.00*

**APOTHECARY CHEST,** 12 drawers, pine, dovetailed drawers, old red & black paint, Alfred, ME, 16″ H., 40¼″ W., 11½″ D.
............................ $700.00*

**BASKET,** splint, carved handles, double wrapped, sgn. "Sisters Basket," 38″ O.L., 18½″ H., 26″ W. ............. $450.00*

A-MA June 1983    *Willis Henry Auctions Inc.*
**SHAKER COBBLER'S BENCH,** butternut & pine, contains shoe lasts, iron shoe anvil, 18 awls & punches, heel dye, cobbler's hammer, asst. tools in drawers, chalk board ................. $3300.00*

A-MA June 1983    *Willis Henry Auctions Inc.*
**STOVE,** w/orig. elbow pipe, 10½″ H., 11″ W., 30″ O.L. .................. $600.00*

*Price does not include 10% buyer fee.

A-OH July 1982        *Garth's Auctions, Inc.*

**HOGSCRAPER CANDLESTICK,** w/pushup, 6⅜" H. ............. $55.00
**TOLE DEED BOX,** dome top, traces of orig. drk. br. ground, floral decor. in red, yellow & gr. is still visible, orig. brass bale, 8½" L. ........................ $65.00
**HOGSCRAPER CANDLESTICK,** w/pushup, rim w/small handle is loose, old blk. paint, 5" H. ................ $65.00
**TIN FOOD MOLD,** fish, mkd. "Germany," 12" L. .................. $20.00
**DESK,** pine, w/old red repaint, 29" W., 19¾" D., 35" H. ............... $130.00
**LADDERBACK SIDE CHAIR,** old blue repaint shows red beneath, new splint seat has wear .................... $40.00
**CHILD'S LADDERBACK ARM CHAIR,** has old repr. & worn drk. red paint, 24" H. ................... $35.00
**TIN SIGNAL LANTERN,** w/brass trim & orig. oil burner, 12" H. ....... $20.00

A-OH July 1982        *Garth's Auctions, Inc.*

**WATERCOLOR,** winter scene w/2 hunters, sgn. "John Hammer '51," birdseye frame, 8½" x 11" ............... $85.00
**OIL ON CANVAS,** 3-masted clipper ship flying an Am. flag, faded inscription on back of canvas, "Of The Seas, Built At Boston," orig. stretcher, modern gilded frame, 23¼" x 33¾" ..................... $2800.00

**Q.A. SIDE CHAIR,** old worn blk., front leg has repr., Spanish feet have lost some detail, repr. to crest ........... $300.00
**BRASS Q.A. CANDLESTICK,** scalloped base, polished, 8" H. ..... $375.00

**BRASS FOOTED SALVER,** w/turned wooden handle & brass ferrule, 7" D., 5½" handle ...................... $175.00
**BRASS Q.A. CANDLESTICK,** scalloped base, socket flange is battered, 7¾" H. .......................... $325.00

**Q.A. TAVERN TABLE,** maple, oval curly top, old ref., orig. 2 board top has been reattached some time ago, 26¾" x 35", 26¾" H. .......................... $3250.00
**SPUN BRASS PAIL,** w/iron bale handle, mkd. "Waterburg," battered w/soldered repr. in base, polished, 8¼" D., 6" H. .............................. $75.00

**HANGING SALT BOX,** pine, red, 10½" W., 7" D., 17" H. .............. $85.00

A-OH July 1982        *Garth's Auctions, Inc.*

**WALL CUPBOARD,** 2-pc., pine, ref. & brasses repl., repr. to feet & base molding, 46¾" W., 13¼" D., 83¼" H. .... $1900.00
**ROCKINGHAM PIE PLATE,** 12¼" D., 1¾" H. .... $115.00
**STONEWARE CHURN,** 5-gal., cobalt blue laurel wreath & "5," has wooden dasher & stoneware lid w/Albany slip, rim hairline, 17" H. plus dasher ...... $200.00
**ROCKINGHAM PIE PLATE,** some glaze wear & hairline, 11¼" D., 1½" H. .............................. $20.00

A-MA Nov. 1982   *Richard A. Bourne Co., Inc.*

**ARTIST'S SKETCH,** done for Parker Gun Co., gray & blk. watercolor, framed in silver-colored wood 18" x 25" w/gray matte, sketch is 13" x 19½", titled "THE PARKER GUN/A DREAM," sgn. "Sketch/Burns/Millington,/New Jersey/Box 102" .......................... $400.00

A-WA D.C. Sept. 1982 *Adam A. Weschler & Son*

**THIRD LIBERTY LOAN POSTER,** ca. 1918, WWI, published by Edwards & Deutsch, Litho. Co., Chicago, 54" W., 34" H. .......................... $75.00*

A-MA Nov. 1982   *Richard A. Bourne Co., Inc.*

**REMINGTON ADVERTISING BROADSIDE,** 18" x 25½", print mkd. "COPYRIGHT 1923, BY REMINGTON ARMS COMPANY, INC.," old gilt wood frame 20" x 27½" ............. $140.00

*Price does not include 10% buyer fee.

A-OH July 1982        *Garth's Auctions, Inc.*
*Row I, L to R*
**YELLOWWARE CREAMER,** tiny edge flakes, 4⅛" H. . . . . . . . . . . . . . . . . $12.50
**ROCKINGHAM SOAP DISH,** 4¼" D. . . . . . . . . . . . . . . . . . . . . . . . . . $40.00
**SPONGE CUSPIDOR,** blue & wh., 7¼" D., 5" H. . . . . . . . . . . . . . . . . . . $70.00
**SPONGE BOWL,** blue & wh., small glaze flakes & rim has filled in chips, 6¼" D. . . . . . . . . . . . . . . . . . . . . . . $60.00
**ROCKINGHAM FIGURAL CREAMER,** man in tri-corner hat, 6" H. . . . . . . . . . . . . . . . . . . . . . . . . $120.00
*Row II, L to R*
**ROCKINGHAM BOWL,** has wear & int. glaze flakes, 8" D., 4" H. . . . . . . . $30.00
**YELLOWWARE TEA POT,** br. & gr. sponge spatter decor., chips on base & tip of spout, lid flange has small chips, 6½" H. . . . . . . . . . . . . . . . . . . . . . . $25.00
**ROCKINGHAM BOWL,** minor wear, 8½" D., 3⅝" H. . . . . . . . . . . . . . . . . $40.00
*Row III, L to R*
**SPONGE SPATTER PITCHER,** shape of keg, gr. & br. sponging, 7½" H. . . . . . . . . . . . . . . . . . . . . . . . . . $40.00
**YELLOWWARE PRESERVING JAR,** w/orig. lid, hairline in lid, 6¼" H. . . . . . . . . . . . . . . . . . . . . . . . . . $45.00
**MAJOLICA HOUND HANDLED PITCHER,** w/hanging game, 8½" H. . . . . . . . . . . . . . . . . . . . . . . . . . $95.00
**SPONGE SPATTER PITCHER,** yellowware w/gr. & br. sponging, chips on rim & base, 7½" H. . . . . . . . . . . . . . . . . $35.00

A-MA July 1982        *Robert W. Skinner Inc.*
**GESCHUTZ BRONZE HEN & ROOSTER,** Austria, polychrome decor., ca. 1880's, 4½" & 4¾" H. . . . . . . $500.00*

A-OH July 1982        *Garth's Auctions, Inc.*
*Row I, L to R*
**TREEN BOX,** 5¼" D., 4½" H. . . . $25.00
**CERAMIC MATCH HOLDER,** silver insert, 3¾" H. . . . . . . . . . . . . . . . . $50.00
**FOLK ART CARVED DOG,** small old spling in one back leg, drk. finish, 5" H. . . . . . . . . . . . . . . . . . . . . . . . . . $40.00
**REDWARE MUG,** w/flared sides, gr. glaze w/orange spots, 3¼" H. . . . . $55.00
**REDWARE SUGAR BOWL,** w/applied handles & drk. br. pebbly glaze, 4¾" H. . . . . . . . . . . . . . . . . . . . . . . . . . $25.00
*Row II, L to R*
**FOLK ART BIRD ON PERCH,** orig. paint, glass eyes, 20th C., 9½" H. . . . . . . . . . . . . . . . . . . . . . . . . . $20.00
**MINI. OWL ON PERCH,**        7¼"H. . . . . . . . . . . . . . . . . . . . . . . . . . $20.00
**COOKIE BOARD,** pine, 6" x 12" . . . . . . . . . . . . . . . . . . . . . . . . . $200.00
**SHAKER BOX,** orig. drk. blue paint, 7½" D., 2¾" H. . . . . . . . . . . . . . . . . $185.00
**FOLK ART LION,** yellow w/red & blk. paint, initialed "W.J.G. 6¼" H. . . . $50.00
**BOX,** curly maple, wrt. iron strap hinges & push button lock, 3¾" x 4½" x 7½" . . . . . . . . . . . . . . . . . . . . . . . . . $350.00
*Row III, L to R*
**WOODEN DOG,** old wh. repaint w/br. & blk., has minor wear, 7¾" H. . . . . . $85.00
**HAND MIRROR,** pine, worn red finish, 3½" x 8½" . . . . . . . . . . . . . . . . . . . . $3.00
**MINI-FOOT STOOL,** w/boot jack legs & chip carved seat, old paint, 4¼" x 5" x 8" . . . . . . . . . . . . . . . . . . . . . . . . . $105.00
**SPICE BOX,** w/sliding lid, dovetailed curly maple, 4 part int., 3¼" x 4½" x 8" . . . . . . . . . . . . . . . . . . . . . . . . . $325.00

A-WA D.C. Sept. 1982 *Adam A. Weschler & Son*
**FOURTH LIBERTY LOAN POSTER,** ca. 1918, WWI, by J. Scott Williams, 53" W., 33" H. . . . . . . . . . . . . $175.00*

A-OH July 1982        *Garth's Auctions, Inc.*
*Row I, L to R*
**WOVEN SPLINT BUTTOCKS BASKET,** minor wear, 5" L. . . . . $105.00
**REDWARE DOG,** PA, clear glaze covers all but bottom of legs, very minor flakes, 3¾" H. . . . . . . . . . . . . . . . . . . . . $270.00
**WOVEN SPLINT BUTTOCKS BASKET,** minor wear, 6¾" D., 4" H. plus handle . . . . . . . . . . . . . . . . . . . . . $180.00
**CAST IRON PENNY BANK,** "Billiken," traces of old paint on base, 4¼" H. . . . . . . . . . . . . . . . . . . . . . . . . . $30.00
**REDWARE HANGING POCKET,** hairline at hole in crest is glazed over, 4¾" H. . . . . . . . . . . . . . . . . . . . . . . . . . $15.00
*Row II, L to R*
**STONEWARE DOG,** wh. glaze, glazed over break in base, 7¾" H. . . . . . . . $65.00
**PORCELAIN DOGS,** pr., wh., mkd. "Germany," 3⅛" H. . . . . . . . . . . . . . $10.00
**WOVEN SPLINT BASKET,** worn old gr. paint, very minor wear, 8½" D., 6" H. plus wooden handle . . . . . . . . . . . . . . . $65.00
**WHITE BISQUE DOG,** orig. painted decor., minor wear & small edge chips, 6" H. . . . . . . . . . . . . . . . . . . . . . . . . . $15.00
*Row III, L to R*
**CHALK DOG,** orig. paint & some old repaint, 8" H. . . . . . . . . . . . . . . . . $25.00
**NANTUCKET PURSE,** carved ivory-like whale & fitting, 7" x 8½" . . . . . . . $120.00
**SEWER TILE DOG,** old repr. break concealed by old paint, 7½" H. . . . $30.00

*Left*
A-MA Oct. 1982        *Robert W. Skinner Inc.*
**ROOSTER WEATHERVANE,** Am., late 19th C., cast iron body w/sheet iron tail, minor surface rust, 24" H., 23½" L. . . . . . . . . . . . . . . . . . . . . . . . $1100.00*
*Right*
A-MA Oct. 1982        *Robert W. Skinner Inc.*
**WEATHERVANE,** Boston, MA, mid 19th C., cast zinc head, molded sheet metal body, sgn. on 1 side "Harris & Co., Boston," orig. color, old repr., open seams, 27½" L. . . . . . . . . . . . . . . . . . . . . . $700.00*

*Price does not include 10% buyer fee. .

A-OH July 1982     *Garth's Auctions, Inc.*
**EMPIRE WALL CUPBOARD,** 2-pc., walnut & curly maple, sq. tapered legs are repl., raised diamond panel doors & 2 matching nailed drawers w/Rockingham knobs in base, repr. & ref. w/orig. slip pin hinges on base & repl. butt hinges on top doors, Indiana origin, 51″ W., 16½″ D., 90″ H. ............................ $900.00
**OGEE SHELF CLOCK,** mahogany veneer, painted tin face & orig. paper label, "Improved Brass Clocks, Made & Sold By Manross Prichard & Co, Bristol, Conn.," old mirror glass in bottom of door, old worn finish & Minor veneer damage, 15¾″ x 26½″ ............................ $125.00

A-OH July 1982     *Garth's Auctions, Inc.*
**ROPE BED,** poplar, old very drk. finish, 52½″ W. x 78¾″ L. ............. $290.00
**SHELF CLOCK,** mahogany veneer, orig. paper label "Patent Brass Eight Day Clocks, Manufactured by Birge, Gilbert & Co, Bristol, CT," face repainted, back of face inscribed "March 9th 1864, cleaned by Jas Smith, Piketon, O.," repl. feet, 36″ H. ............................ $310.00

A-OH July 1982     *Garth's Auctions, Inc.*
**LITHO,** hand colored, "Currier & Ives," "The Farmer's Friends," margins slightly trimmed, birdseye Ogee frame w/gilded liner, 13½″ x 17″ ............. $215.00
**LITHO,** hand colored, "Currier & Ives," "Mating In The Woods," margins slightly trimmed, birdseye Ogee frame, 12½″ x 16½″ ........................ $250.00
**BRASS DOUBLE STUDENT LAMP,** gr. shades cased in wh., polished & electrified, 21″ H. ............. $600.00
**WINDSOR ARM CHAIR,** pr., brace back, worn gr. repaint shows several shades of red beneath, repr. splits in seats, legs are made in 2 parts & pieced w/2 having glued breaks at splice, 18″ seat ht. ............................ $1900.00
**HEPPLEWHITE STAND,** birch, old repr. break in base where legs join, ref., 16½″ x 21¼″, 29½″ H. .......... $550.00

A-OH July 1982     *Garth's Auctions, Inc.*
**ROPE BED,** orig. rails & orig. red paint, 53″ x 77½″, 55″ H. ............. $425.00
**DOVETAILED POPLAR BOX,** orig. red & blk. graining has wear, iron lock & hasp old replm., 7¼″ x 9¼″ x 14½″ ..... $70.00
**PLATFORM,** w/cut out feet, 11¾″ H. ............................ $65.00

A-OH July 1982     *Garth's Auctions, Inc.*
*Row I, L to R*
**LEEDS SOFT PASTE CREAMER,** gaudy blue & wh. decor., glaze wear on spout, 3¾″ H. .................. $75.00
**LEEDS SOFT PASTE LOVING CUP,** double handles have leaf attachments, 3 color decor. w/flowers & "Robert Hill 1791," professional repr. on rim & one handle, 7⅞″ H. ................ $400.00
**MOCHA BOWL,** wh. w/drk. br., ochre & gr. gray decor., broken int. bubble & rim hairlines, 7¼″ D., 3¾″ H. ....... $325.00
**LEEDS SOFT PASTE CREAMER,** br. & yellow decor., small chips on foot & glaze wear on rim, 3⅜″ H. ........... $95.00
*Row II, L to R*
**SOFT PASTE PLATE,** yellow strawberry border design in br., gr., blue & orange, knife scratches & some glaze flakes, small chip on table ring, 8⅜″ D. ....... $200.00
**CREAM WARE MUG,** 5 color decor., 6″ H. ........................ $350.00
**STAFFORDSHIRE PLATE,** floral design in red, blk., gr. & ochre, 7½″ D. .. $65.00
**LEEDS SOFT PASTE SOUP BOWL,** gaudy blue & wh. floral decor., has wear & knife scratches, 8¼″ D. ......... $75.00
*Row III, L to R*
**LEEDS DAHLIA SOFT PASTE TEA POT,** 5 color floral decor. w/acorn finial, small hairline in rim, spout chips & crows foot in base, small flake on rim of lid, 6″ H. ............................ $75.00
**LIVERPOOL JUG,** blk. transfer w/polychrome enameling, ship w/"Success To Trade," eagles shield & "E. Pluribus Unum" & Jefferson quote "Anno Domini 1802," reverse has oval w/"The Memory Of Washington & The Proscribed Patriots Of America," has professional repr., 8″ H. ............................ $1650.00
**LEEDS SOFT PASTE TEA POT,** gaudy blue & wh. floral decor., hairlines & professional repr. to spout & lid, 7¼″ H. ............................ $250.00

A-MA Aug. 1982     *Richard A. Bourne Co., Inc.*
**BOMB HARPOON GUN,** unmkd., solid brass.................. $1200.00

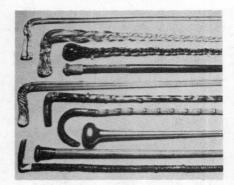

A-OH July 1982    Garth's Auctions, Inc.
**CANE,** clear glass w/red center stripe, tip is snapped, 49½" L. . . . . . . . . . . . . . $45.00
**CANE,** aqua glass, twisted, tip is snapped, 38½" L. . . . . . . . . . . . . . . . . . . . . $35.00

**CANE,** clear glass, twisted w/hollow center filled w/drk. red liquid, 51½" L. . . . . . . . . . . . . . . . . . . . . . . . . . $125.00
**SWORD CANE,** w/stag horn handle & silvered colored mountings, battered brass tip, 35" L. . . . . . . . . . . . . . . . . . . . . $125.00

**CANE,** aqua glass, twisted & straight ribs, tip is snapped, 59" L. . . . . . . . . . . . $40.00
**ROOT CANE,** w/silver colored studs & engraved plate "Compliments Of Niles Tool Works," 35½" L. . . . . . . . . . . $45.00

**CARVED WOODEN CANE,** eagle head handle & flying bird at base of handle, 35" L. . . . . . . . . . . . . . . . . . . . . . . . . . $65.00
**WALKING STICK,** clear glass w/gold int., 54½" L. . . . . . . . . . . . . . . . . . . $70.00

**WOODEN WALKING STICK,** silvered colored head has embossed panels of Oriental figures, bamboo & calligraphy, 33¾" L. . . . . . . . . . . . . . . . . . . . . . $36.00
**GNARLED WOODEN WALKING STICK,** stag horn handle & chased silver colored ferrule, 30¾" L. . . . . . . . . $30.00

A-OH July 1982    Garth's Auctions, Inc.
**LITHO,** hand colored, "Birds Eye View of Mt. Vernon," pub. in 1859 by G. & F. Bill, fold line & tears, margins are trimmed, framed, 20" x 23¾" . . . . . . . . . . . . . $75.00

**TURNED TREEN BOX,** orig. red sponged decor. on yellow ground, paint has wear & inside lid flange chipped, 6½" H. . . . . . . . . . . . . . . . . . . . . . . . . . $325.00

**TURNED TREEN BOX,** old red paint, 7¾" H. . . . . . . . . . . . . . . . . . . . . . $200.00

**TURNED TREEN BOX,** orig. red sponged decor. on yellow ground, some wear, 5" H. . . . . . . . . . . . . . . . . . $300.00

**HUTCH TABLE,** pine, old ref., some added glue blocks to base, top has some corrugated fasteners added, 36" x 46", 29" H. . . . . . . . . . . . . . . . . . . . . . . . . . $525.00

**WOVEN SPLINT BUTTOCKS BASKET,** minor wear, 14" x 14½", 9" H. plus wooden handle . . . . . . . . . . . $85.00

**BLANKET CHEST,** w/till, dovetailed pine, hinges repl. & lock missing, old red paint, 13½" x 23¼", 13" H. . . . . . . $175.00

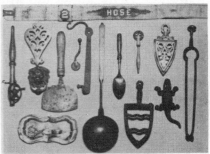

A-OH July 1982    Garth's Auctions, Inc.
**LEATHER FIRE BELT,** worn red & wh., "Hose 2," 36" L. . . . . . . . . . . . . . . . $25.00
**WIG MAKER'S TOOL,** wood & brass, 12½" L. . . . . . . . . . . . . . . . . . . . . . $15.00

**BRASS TRIVET,** 7¼" L. . . . . . . . $25.00
**FOOD CHOPPER,** w/turned handle & decor. cut out blade, 5½" W., 13" L. . . . . . . . . . . . . . . . . . . . . . . . . . $50.00

**WRT. IRON BAR LATCH,** 11¾" L. . . . . . . . . . . . . . . . . . . . . . . . . . . $30.00
**WRT. IRON DIPPER,** 19½" L. . . $25.00
**BRONZE SPOON,** w/wooden handle, 10" L. . . . . . . . . . . . . . . . . . . . . . . $7.50
**PASTRY CUTTER,** cast wh. metal wheel & wooden handle, 7" L. . . . . . . . . $12.50

**CAST BRASS TRIVET,** 8¼" L. . . . . . . . . . . . . . . . . . . . . . . . . . . . . $20.00
**WRT. IRON TONGS,** w/brass knob finial, 18¼" L. . . . . . . . . . . . . . . . . $15.00

**WRT. IRON PASTRY CUTTER,** 5¼" L. . . . . . . . . . . . . . . . . . . . . . . . . . $70.00
**CAST BRASS DOOR KNOCKER,** lion's head, 4½" H. . . . . . . . . . . . . . $17.50

**WRT. IRON TRIVET,** wh. shoe feet, 10" L. . . . . . . . . . . . . . . . . . . . . . . . $25.00
**CAST IRON ALLIGATOR,** old br. repaint, 7¾" L. . . . . . . . . . . . . . . . . $7.50
**BRASS SCISSOR WICK TRIMMERS & TRAY,** 9" L. . . . . . . . . . . . . . . . $45.00

A-WA D.C. July 1982  Adam A. Weschler & Son
**WOODEN HOBBY HORSE,** Am., late 19th C., carved & painted, 50" L., 45" H. . . . . . . . . . . . . . . . . . . . . . . . . . $350.00*

A-MA Nov. 1982   Richard A. Bourne Co., Inc.
**CHILD'S ROCKING HORSE,** Am., ca. 1840, orig. br. paint w/red striped base, 30" H. . . . . . . . . . . . . . . . . . . . . . . . $450.00

A-MA Oct. 1982    Robert W. Skinner Inc.
**ZEBRA CAROUSEL FIGURE,** Am., 19th C., repainted, 57½" H., 58" L. . . . . . . . . . . . . . . . . . . . . . . . . . $1150.00*

*Price does not include 10% buyer fee.

A-OH April 1983          *Garth's Auctions, Inc.*
*Row I, L to R*
**TREEN BOX,** turned detail, 4¼" H.
.................................. $175.00
**WHALE OIL LAMPS,** (2), brass, 6¼" H.
.................................. $160.00
**WHALE OIL LAMPS,** pewter, orig. single spout burner, 5⅜" H. ... $150.00
**TREEN BOX,** good turned detail, minor age crack in lid, 4¼" H. ........ $175.00
*Row II, L to R*
**LIGHTING DEVICE,** wrt. iron, adj. pan, adjusts from 6¾" to 10¼" H. .... $150.00
**PIP SQUEAK W/SEATED CAT,** composition, worn gray & salmon flocking, blk. striped, gr. painted eyes, damage & cracks, 6" H. ......................... $175.00
**DOOR STOP,** cast iron, cat w/arched back, old blk. repaint, gr. eyes, red mouth, 10¾" H. ......................... $65.00
**FOLK ART CARVED WOODEN HEAD,** turned base, orig. paint, 4½" H.
.................................. $65.00
**CAT,** cast iron, yellow glass eyes, old blk. repaint, 10" H. ............. $110.00
*Row III, L to R*
**TIN LANTERN,** glass front & back, burner missing, replm., indistinct label "Patent Apr. 1866, New York," 9" H.
.................................. $65.00
**CHAMBER STICK,** sheet iron, pushup, sgn. "SHAW," 5" H. ............ $85.00
**WHALE OIL LAMP,** pewter, twin magnifying lens, weighted base, 10¼" H.
.................................. $500.00
**CLEAR BLOWN PEG LAMP,** brass collar, 5¾" H. ................. $115.00
**CHAMBER STICK,** brass, long handle, threaded socket has been soldered, 3⅞" D.
.................................. $105.00
**TIN STRAINER,** holes punched in base, removable top w/small funnel attached, 9" H. ............................ $30.00

A-MA Nov. 1982   *Richard A. Bourne Co., Inc.*
**IRON FIREBACK,** 18th C., reputed to be 1 of 3 cast by Paul Revere, Masonic symbols ................... $20000.00

A-OH Oct. 1982          *Garth's Auctions, Inc.*
**OPEN CUPBOARD,** pine, one drawer, repr., replm., painted red, 54" W., 24" D., 71¾" H. ...................... $155.00
**BENTWOOD SPICE BOXES,** round, tin corners, stenciled labels, stamped "Patent Package Co., Newark New Jersey, Pat Aug 31, 1858," some damage, 9⅜" D.
.................................. $250.00
**REDWARE JAR,** mottled amber glaze, probably Galena, flaking, 7¾" H.
.................................. $30.00
**WOVEN SPLINT MARKET BASKET,** some wear, 13½" W., 16½" L., 9" H. plus handle ......................... $45.00
**STONEWARE JAR,** 4-gal., cobalt blue, stenciled decor., freehand "4," rim flakes, 14½" H. ........................ $75.00

---

A-OH Mar. 1983          *Garth's Auctions, Inc.*
**HANDCOLORED ENGRAVING,** "Yale College," "Pubd. for the Souvenir by P. Price Jr 1828," paper has wrinkles, matted & framed, 15½" x 18½" ... $40.00
**CUTOUT FIBER BOARD,** silhouette of a dog on wooden base, old wh. & blk. paint, 11¼" H. ....................... $17.50

**CANNISTER W/HINGED LID,** tin, drk. br. Japanning & stenciled "Sugar," 6" D., 5" H. ............................... $12.50
**PULL TOY HORSE,** wood & papier mache, on sm. cast metal wheels, orig. dapple gray paint, missing parts, replm., chipped & cracked, 10¾" L., 11¾" H.
.................................. $65.00
**BANNISTER BACK SIDE CHAIR,** blk. repaint, replm. ................. $425.00
**COUNTRY SCHOOL MASTER'S DESK,** walnut, primitive const., fitted int. w/3 nailed drawers, 30¾" W., 22" D., 45¼" H. ....................... $350.00
**STAVE-CONSTRUCTED CONTAINER,** oval w/slightly flaring sides, iron bands, old varnished finish w/traces of old red, 15½" x 20½", 16¾" H. ...... $325.00

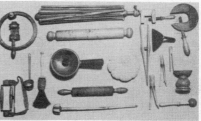

A-OH Jan. 1983          *Garth's Auctions, Inc.*
**SHAKER EMBROIDERY HOOP,** turned table clamp, age cracks, 7⅜" D.
.................................. $65.00
**SHAKER SWIFT,** table clamp, orig. yellow varnish, repr., replm., 24" L.
.................................. $95.00
**SHAKER EMBROIDERY HOOP,** table clamp (clamp is pictured), repr., 5½" D.
.................................. $30.00
**SHAKER ROLLING PIN,** ref. maple, scarring, 15" L. ................ $40.00
**SHAKER TIN DIPPER,** 6⅝" L.
.................................. $47.50
**SHAKER HORSEHAIR BRUSH,** turned handle, 10" L. ................. $24.00
**SHAKER MARKING INK CUP,** tin w/wooden ball, 5" D., 4" handle ... $35.00
**SHAKER PINCUSHION,** faded pink velvet, 5½" D. ................. $7.50
**SHAKER GLOVE STRETCHER,** 11" L.
.................................. $65.00
**SHAKER DOUGH SCRAPER,** wrt. iron, 4½" W. ..................... $35.00
**SHAKER BOOK STRAP,** repr., 6¼" W.
.................................. $40.00
**SHAKER NOODLE CUTTER,** 12¼" L.
.................................. $50.00
**THREE SHAKER CLOTHES PINS,** whittled wood, 2 have tin bands, 4¾" to 6" L. ............................. $115.00
**SHAKER TREEN SANDER & HAMMER,** sander has worn orig. yellow varnish, hammer does not, 3½" H.
.................................. $100.00
**SHAKER WHISK,** primitive, wooden, 14½" L. ....................... $40.00

A-WA D.C. Sept. 1982  *Adam A. Weschler & Son*
*Left*
**ZUNI JAR**, blackish-br. & red-orange painted over a wh. slip, base painted orange-red, 13″ D., 10½″ H. .... $350.00*
*Right*
**SAN IL DEFONSO BLACKWARE JAR**, polished slip, painted in an opaque band of bird's wings, inscribed "Lupita San il Defonso," 9½″ H. .......... $150.00*

A-MA Nov. 1982  *Richard A. Bourne Co., Inc.*
**GREAT LAKES BEADED CLOTH BANDOLIER BAG**, ca. 1890-1900, floral design, br. velvet backing & loomwork fringe w/wool tassels, several tears along belt, many beads missing, 41″ L.
...................... $475.00

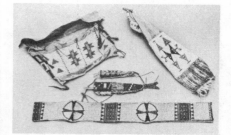

A-MA July 1982  *Richard A. Bourne Co., Inc.*
**BEADED TEEPEE OR TENT BAG**, Stone CA Sioux, red, blue, gr. & yellow on wh. ground, ornamented w/horsehair tassels, leather stiffened w/age, 12″ H.
........................ $500.00
**BEADED PIPE BAG**, red, gr., blue & yellow w/wh. ground, leather stiffened w/age, few beads missing, 25″ L.
........................ $425.00
**BEADWORK ITEMS**, lot of 2, blue, gr., red & wh., stiffened w/age, some beads missing ................ $450.00
**BEADWORK HORSE HANGING**, red, blue, gr., yellow on wh., 6′2″ L. .. $950.00

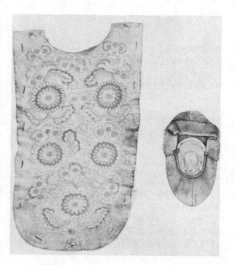

A-MA Nov. 1982  *Richard A. Bourne Co., Inc.*
**CREE SILK EMBROIDERED HIDE BIB**, 2 pcs., 19th C., floral design & buttonholes around perimeter, single cree silk embroidered ladies' moccasin, soiled, bib 18¾″ L. ................... $125.00

A-MA Nov. 1982  *Richard A. Bourne Co., Inc.*
**WOODEN CEREMONIAL PADDLES**, pr., Haida or Tsimshian, ca. 1880-1890, carved on both sides, one paddle has slight crack, 47¾″ L. ............... $1200.00
**MAN'S VEST**, Sioux, ca. 1890, fully beaded on hide .............. $2200.00
**SIOUX HIDE MOCCASINS**, pr., ca. 1800, calf length, few beads missing ............................ $700.00

A-MA Nov. 1982  *Richard A. Bourne Co., Inc.*
*Row I, L to R*
**PLAINS BEADED KNIFE & SHEATH**, ca. 1900, hide fringe of tinklers & wrapped quill work, knife is steel w/copper guard & wooden handle, few beads & tinklers missing, quill work faded, 10″ L.
........................... $525.00
**LOWER PLAINS BEADED HIDE MOCCASINS**, pr., ca. 1900, red & blue, some beads damaged or missing, soiled, 10¼″ L. ...................... $75.00
**PLAINS BEADED HIDE & CLOTH MEN'S MOCCASINS**, pr., ca. 1900, floral design on wh. ground, much wear & damage to beadwork, 11″ L. ..... $70.00
*Row II, L to R*
**EASTERN PLAINS BEADED HIDE TRIANGULAR PENNANT**, late 19th/ early 20th C., some soiling & general wear, 21½″ L. ................. $90.00
**PLAINS BEADED MEN'S HIDE MOC-CASINS**, pr., late 19th C., stripes of orange & red on wh. ground bordered by triangular motif, soiled, some beads missing, wear to hide, 11″ L. .... $175.00

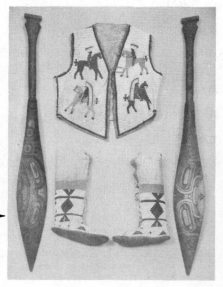

*Price does not include 10% buyer fee.

A-OH Mar. 1982    *Garth's Auctions, Inc.*
**HANDCOLORED ENGRAVING,** by W. H. Bartlett, "Lockport, Erie Canal, London, 1838," .............. $35.00
**HANDCOLORED ENGRAVING,** by C. H. Billings, "Custom-House, Boston 1850," 12" x 16" .............. $25.00

**PLATES,** set of 12 (2 illus.), medium blue transfer, "Copeland Spode's Italian, England," one has chip, 9" D. .... $90.75
**SOUP PLATES,** set of 5 (1 illus.), match above plates, 3 have hairlines, one has rim chip, 7⅝" D. ................... $25.00

**CREAM PITCHERS,** two (1 illus.), match above plates, also 2 saucers that can be used with creamers, flaking & hairlines, 3⅜" & 4" H. ................. $20.00
**EMPIRE CHEST,** cherry, some damage & repr., ref., 43½" W., 23¼" D., 48" H. ........................... $200.00

**STAFFORDSHIRE BOWL,** medium blue transfer, mkd. "Enoch Woods Castles, (Conway) Wood & Sons, England," 11" D., 3¼" H. ........ $25.00

A-OH Mar. 1982    *Garth's Auctions, Inc.*
**CARVED WOODEN BIRD,** orig. paint, mkd. "J.E.D.," & "Rock Dove made by John Olson, Elgin III. Artist, early 1900's," damage, 11" L. ............... $145.00
**DOLL-SIZED LADDERBACK ARM-CHAIR,** primitive, 12" H. ....... $65.00
**TABLE TOP WRITING BOX,** primitive walnut, lock missing, worn finish, edge wear & cracks, 25" W., 15" D., 9¼" H. ....................... $45.00
**DOLL-SIZED LADDERBACK SIDE CHAIR,** primitive, paper splint seat, 11¼" H. ............................. $20.00
**ROUND FISHSCALE MAT,** made from red, blk., blue, wh., gray & lavender wool felt, 34" ........................ $45.00
**HEPPLEWHITE DROPLEAF TABLE,** birch legs, mortised pine apron & pine top, worn finish, traces of old red, 17½" x 43", 9¼" leaves, 27½" H. ............ $400.00
**WOVEN SPLINT BASKET,** misshapen, some wear, 18½" D., 11" H. plus wooden handle ....................... $65.00

A-MA July 1982    *Robert W. Skinner Inc.*
**WOODEN PAINTED DECOY,** N. Eng., 20th C., dappled head w/orange bill, simulated gr. & wh. feathers .... $120.00*

A-OH Feb. 1983    *Garth's Auctions, Inc.*
**SPINNING WHEEL,** bobbin reel is missing, 44½" wheel, 59" H. ..... $150.00
**CARVED WOODEN COOKIE BOARD,** figures on both sides include animals, birds, cat, Santa Claus, various people, etc., early 20th C., 4⅝" x 26½" ........................... $225.00
← **SCOURING BOARD,** pine, old drk. patina, 7¾" x 18" ................. $67.50
**SHAKER WEAVER'S STOOL,** replm., old worn refinishing, 30" H. ..... $200.00
**APOTHECARY CUPBOARD,** primitive, 9 drawers, wire nail const., red repaint, damage, 21" W., 11½" D., 16¼" H. ............................. $85.00

A-OH Mar. 1982    *Garth's Auctions, Inc.*
**CAST IRON URNS,** pr., 8¼" D., 6¼" H. ........................... $35.00
**EARLY WRITING BOX,** oak, int. has primitive pigeon holes, replm., repr., some edge damage, finish has traces of old red, 22½" W., 16¾" D., 10" H. ...... $350.00
**CHEST OF DRAWERS,** pine, repr., red repaint, 37¼" W., top 20" x 41¼", 41" H. ........................... $1025.00

A-OH Feb. 1983    *Garth's Auctions, Inc.*
**WATERCOLOR THEOREM,** French, free-hand & stenciled work of flowers in basket, "Mary-Anne Oigault ou Couvent de la Presentation de Marie St. Cesaire 1859," good colors, some wear, old frame, 21¾" x 26" .................... $275.00
**ROPE BED,** turned maple post w/a little curl, poplar headboard, replm., ref., some age cracks, 52¾" x 81½", 58" H. ........................... $225.00
**TIN CANDLE MOLD,** 12 tubes, side handles, 11" H. ............... $65.00
**BLANKET CHEST,** pine, wrt. iron strap hinge, side handles & escut., lock missing, orig. rose-mulled decor. on red ground, "Ole Zuren" & "Ano 1823" on front, replm., Alpine, 27" W., 13½" D., 16½" H. ............................. $425.00

A-OH July 1982    *Garth's Auctions, Inc.*
**LITHO,** hand colored, "Currier & Ives," "The Great Fire at Boston," stains & small edge tear in right margin, framed, 12½" x 16½" ...................... $190.00

**DOUBLE STUDENT LAMP,** brass w/embossed vining foliage w/orig. gr. patina finish, gr. ribbed shades cased in wh. are new, electrified, 24" H. ...... $800.00

**BOWBACK WINDSOR ARM CHAIR,** ref., 16¾" seat ht. ............. $900.00

**HEPPLEWHITE STAND,** curly maple & butternut w/poplar secondary wood, ref. & repl. brass pulls, 17½" x 22" ..... $500.00

**WATCH HUTCH,** carved oak, in form of tall case clock, facade is one piece of wood w/carved relief, old drk. finish, 15¼" H. ................................. $115.00

*Left*
A-MA July 1982    *Robert W. Skinner Inc.*
**PIPE BOX,** N. Eng., 18th C., cherry, 7¼" W., 5" D., 20½" H. .......... $1350.00*

*Right*
A-MA July 1982    *Robert W. Skinner Inc.*
**WOODEN PIPE BOX,** Am., 18th C., single drawer, gr. paint, 21½" H. ........................... $1100.00*

A-MA July 1982    *Richard A. Bourne Co., Inc.*
**HEPPLEWHITE KNIFE BOXES,** pr., inlaid mahogany, complete w/orig. liners, minor loss of veneer, 15½" H. .. $1450.00

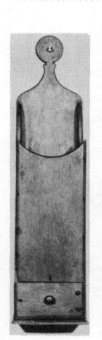

*Right*
A-MA Aug. 1982    *Robert W. Skinner Inc.*
**CHERRY PIPE BOX,** Am., late 18th C., circular hanger, shaped backboard, sides, front, bottom w/drawer, 21½" H., 5½" W. ........................... $1600.00*

*Left*
A-MA Aug. 1982    *Robert W. Skinner Inc.*
**MAHOGANY PIPE BOX,** Am., late 18th C., drawer restored, 24½" H., 6¼" W. ........................... $1700.00*

A-MA July 1982    *Richard A. Bourne Co., Inc.*
**MINI. PORTRAIT OF VIRGIN MARY,** painted on porcelain, mounted on carved walnut frame w/bracket, 18" O.H. ................................. $60.00

A-MA July 1982    *Garth's Auctions, Inc.*
**CUPBOARD,** one pc., pine & poplar, ref., back feet restor. w/one broken out, molding replm., 41¾" W., 15¾" D., 61½" H. ................................. $260.00

**LOOM LIGHT,** wrt. iron, adj., rush light holder & candle socket counterbalance, adj. from 27" L. .............. $500.00

**SHAKER PIE LIFTER,** 18" L. ... $25.00

**LIGHTING DEVICE,** adj., wrt. iron rush light holder, candle socket counterbalance, wooden base replm., 38½" H. ... $200.00

**WOVEN SPLINT BASKET,** stylized floral design, faded purple & gr., varnished, 8¾" H. plus wooden handle ...... $65.00

*Price does not include 10% buyer fee.

A-MA Mar. 1983   *Robert W. Skinner Inc.*
**NANTUCKET BASKETS,** nest of 4, late 19th C., MA, bottoms mkd. on inside "R. Folger, Maker, Nantucket, Mass.," largest basket has minor breaks, diameters 5½", 8½", 10½" & 14" . . . . . . . . . . . . $2300.00*

A-MA Aug. 1982   *Robert W. Skinner Inc.*
*L to R*
**WALL SPLINT BASKET,** N. Eng., early 19th C., polychrome painted, 10" H., 10" L., 9" W. . . . . . . . . . . . . . . . . . . . . $500.00*
**WALL SPLINT BASKET,** N. Eng., early 19th C., 11" H., 12" L., 5" W. . . $460.00*
**WALL SPLINT BASKET,** N. Eng., early 19th C., 7" H., 10½" L., 4" W. . . $260.00*

A-MA Aug. 1982   *Robert W. Skinner Inc.*
*L to R*
**COVERED SPLINT BASKET,** N. Eng., early 19th C., red painted bands, 6½" H., 10" L., 6½" D. . . . . . . . . . . . . . . $130.00*
**SPLINT BASKET,** N. Eng., early 19th C., 7" H., 12" L., 8½" D. . . . . . . . . . $500.00*
**SPLINT BASKET,** N. Eng., early 19th C., cone fixed handle, 7½" H., 7½" L., 6½" D. . . . . . . . . . . . . . . . . . . . . . . . $380.00*

A-MA Aug. 1982   *Robert W. Skinner Inc.*
*L to R*
**OPEN WEAVE SPLINT TWO-TIER WALL BASKET,** N. Eng., early 19th C., painted gr., 7½" H., 8½" L., 3" D. . . . . . . . . . . . . . . . . . . . . . . . . . $190.00*
**WALL SPLINT BASKET,** N. Eng., early 19th C., blk. painted dots, diamonds, 9½" H., 9½" L., 4" D. . . . . . . . . . . $850.00*
**WALL BASKET,** N. Eng., 19th C., polychrome painted, 6" H., 5½" L., 3" D. . . . . . . . . . . . . . . . . . . . . . . . . $550.00*

A-OH July 1982   *Garth's Auctions, Inc.*
**LITHO,** hand colored, "Currier & Ives," "Prairie Fires of the West," tear in right side, framed, 17¼" x 21½" . . . . . . . $150.00
**HANGING WRT. IRON UTENSIL RACK,** w/scroll work & 5 hooks, 16" W. . . . . . . . . . . . . . . . . . . . . . . . . $105.00
**WRT. IRON FORK,** w/walnut handle, 16½" L. . . . . . . . . . . . . . . . . . . . $45.00
**WRT. IRON SPOON,** 13½" L. . . . . . . . . . . . . . . . . . . . . . . . . . . $25.00
**WRT. IRON FORK,** w/eye hanger, tooled initials "W.E.M.," 23½" L. . . . . . $35.00
**WRT. IRON LADLE,** 14¾" L. . . . $22.50
**WRT. IRON FORK,** 16½" L. . . . . $25.00
**WINDSOR WRITING ARM CHAIR,** drawer under arm & under seat have both been rebuilt, old repr. & brace where scrolled arm joins post, ref., 17¾" seat ht. . . . . . . . . . . . . . . . . . . . . . . . . . $800.00
**APOTHECARY CHEST,** dovetailed pine, w/10 cockbeaded dovetailed drawers w/orig. tooled brass pulls, old mellow ref., 20" W., 8½" D., 20" H. . . . . . . . . $775.00
**CAST IRON TEA KETTLE,** 9½" H. . . . . . . . . . . . . . . . . . . . . . . . . . $30.00

A-MA Nov. 1982   *Richard A. Bourne Co., Inc.*
**WINCHESTER ADVERTISEMENT,** 34½" x 25", orig. blk. stained oak frame 41½" x 32", gilt liner, top of frame painted in gold, 1¾" letters "WINCHESTER" . . . . . . . . . . . . . . . . . . . . . . . . $425.00

A-OH July 1982   *Garth's Auctions, Inc.*
**WRT. IRON STRAP HINGE,** 29½" L. . . . . . . . . . . . . . . . . . . . . . . . . . $6.00
**WRT. IRON STRAP HINGE,** 24" L. . . . . . . . . . . . . . . . . . . . . . . . . . $6.00
**WRT. IRON STRAP HINGES,** 2 similar but not pr., 21" L. . . . . . . . . . . . . $6.00
**TURNED CHILD SIZE ROLLING PIN,** 9" L. . . . . . . . . . . . . . . . . . . $40.00
**STRAP HINGE,** "Y" shaped w/pin, 10" L. . . . . . . . . . . . . . . . . . . . . . $17.50
**WRT. IRON KETTLE BALE,** w/attaching ears, 10½" W. . . . . . . . . . . . . $20.00
**CAST IRON LION HEAD,** 8½" D. . . . . . . . . . . . . . . . . . . . . . . . . . $75.00
**"H" HINGES,** 2 pr., w/decor. ends, old gray paint, 7¾" L. . . . . . . . . . . . . $5.00
**WRT. IRON STRAP HINGE,** 16" L. . . . . . . . . . . . . . . . . . . . . . . . . . $6.00
**WRT. IRON BARN DOOR HINGES,** pr., jamb plate on one has old damage, 15¾" L. . . . . . . . . . . . . . . . . . . . $20.00
**WRT. IRON TRIVET,** heart shaped, 11" L. . . . . . . . . . . . . . . . . . . . . . $85.00
**CARVED WOODEN BUTTER PRINT,** heart shaped, edge wear, 4" x 5" . . $65.00
**CAST IRON FROG,** old gr., 7" L. . . . . . . . . . . . . . . . . . . . . . . . . . $102.00
**WRT. IRON TRIVET,** triangular, 10" L. . . . . . . . . . . . . . . . . . . . . . . . $75.00
**TURNED WOODEN NEEDLE CASE,** 9½" L. . . . . . . . . . . . . . . . . . . . $45.00

A-OH April 1983   *Garth's Auctions, Inc.*
**NEEDLEWORK BUREAU BOX,** Eng., ca. 1665, Charles II, pine, needlework on silk panels, various scenes on all sides, front fitted w/drawers & top compartment has lift-out trays for ink wells, etc., faded colors, some wear, replm., 8" x 8½" x 11½" . . . . . . . . . . . . . . . . . . . . . . . $3250.00

*Price does not include 10% buyer fee.

A-MA July 1982    *Richard A. Bourne Co., Inc.*
TOLEWARE
*Row I, L to R*
**TRAYS,** pr., 6¼″ D. ........... $475.00
**TRAY,** coffin lid shaped, decor. w/red tulips, 9⅛″ L. ................ $250.00
*Row II, L to R*
**TRAY,** coffin lid shaped, decor. w/red fruit & gr. leaves, small break, 8¾″ L.
.................................. $125.00
**TEA CANISTER,** sgn. "Sawyer," decor. w/tiger lilies, 7½″ H. ........... $100.00
**SPICE BOX,** double folding lids w/3-compartments, darkened w/age & dust, 7¼″ W., 9¼″ L. 5″ H. ........... $130.00
*Row III, L to R*
**OVAL BASKET,** red, yellow & gr. w/tulips, 12¼″ L. .............. $425.00
**OVAL BASKET,** red, yellow & gr. fruit & leaves, minor paint loss, 12″ L. .. $175.00

A-MA July 1982    *Richard A. Bourne Co., Inc.*
**STONEWARE JUG,** br. decor., age cracks & discoloration ......... $425.00
**STONEWARE CROCKS,** lot of 2, one mkd. "Bennington, VT," other mkd. "E. Bennington," cracks & chips, discolored
.................................. $125.00
**SAWBUCK TABLE,** N. Eng., late 18th-early 19th C., birch base w/pine single plank top, ref., minor scratches, 90¼″ L., 25⅛″ W., 29¼″ H. ............. $900.00

A-WA D.C. July 1982   *Adam A. Weschler & Son*
**HUNTING CASE RAILWAY TIME KEEPER,** Eng., 18 karat yellow gold, Joseph Johnson, ca. 1825, 19-jewel detached lever movement, chain driven
........................... $650.00*

A-MA Oct. 1982    *Garth's Auctions, Inc.*
**PEWTER LADLE,** sm. indistinct mark, 13¼″ L. ...................... $27.50
**SCISSOR WICK TRIMMERS,** silver plated steel, damage, 6½″ L. ..... $10.00
**HORN SNUFF BOX,** silver-colored fittings, lid engraved "F.E. Lindquist," 3⅝″ L.
.................................. $33.00
**ICE PICK,** wrt. iron, ram's horn, 12¼″ L.
.................................. $50.00
**SHAKER HORSEHAIR BRUSH,** turned handle, mkd. "Adams 53," 11¾″ L.
.................................. $30.00
**TURNED WOODEN BUTTER PRINT,** handle, stylized flower w/leaves, age cracks, 4″ D. ................. $37.50
**TURNED WOODEN BUTTER PRINT,** handle, foliage design, age crack, 3⅞″ D.
.................................. $25.00
**HANGING BOX,** pine, carving of stylized flowers, orig. alligatored varnish w/br. molding, wire nail const., wear, 10⅞″ H.
.................................. $65.00
**COOKIE CUTTER,** tin, full-length woman, 3¾″ W., 5½″ H. ......... $25.00
**COOKIE CUTTER,** tin, fish, 2¾″ W., 6¾″ H. .................................. $25.00

A-MA July 1982    *Richard A. Bourne Co., Inc.*
**COROMANDEL SCREEN,** Chinese, ca. 19th C., incised polychromed floral scenes, blk. ground, normal loss of lacquet, 72¼″ H.
.................................. $700.00

A-MA Oct. 1982    *Garth's Auctions, Inc.*
**WOVEN SPLINT BASKET,** br. potato print design, 12″ sq., 4½″ H. ..... $15.00
**ROCKINGHAM PITCHER,** embossed hunter, dogs & deer, crack in base, 9½″ H.
.................................. $30.00
**MINIATURE DOVETAILED BLANKET CHEST,** pine, turned feet & till, butternut lid, ref., replm., 20¾″ W., 8½″ D., 9″ H. ......................... $80.00
**ROCKINGHAM PITCHER,** embossed dogs & hunter, 9¾″ H. .......... $25.00
**REDWARE PITCHER,** strap handle & ribbed neck, wear & flaking, 7¾″ H.
.................................. $45.00
**DOVETAILED BLANKET CHEST,** pine, turned feet, old ref., damage, 49½″ W., 22″ D., 23″ H. ............. $160.00
**SEMI-CYLINDRICAL CANDLE LANTERN,** sliding glass front & hinged door in back, 11¾″ H. ........... $90.00
**CANDLE MOLD,** 36 tubes, tin, double handles, 12″ H. ........... $200.00
**CYLINDRICAL CANDLE LANTERN,** tin, punched conical top, tooled signature over door "T. Wm. 1890," 13¾″ H.
.................................. $65.00

A-MA July 1982    *Richard A. Bourne Co., Inc.*
*L to R*
**TEA CHEST,** rosewood, complete w/ Waterford cut glass bowl, 12¾″ L.
.................................. $300.00
**CASED SET OF LIQUOR BOTTLES,** set of six qt. bottles, Eng., 18th C., orig. to chest, chest w/mahogany veneer & domed top, two brass feet missing, 11¼″ L.
.................................. $425.00
**CASED SHEFFIELD STEEL FLATWARE,** by J. Russel & Co., "Gr. River Works," 3-pc. carving set, 12 dinner knives, 12 luncheon knives, all w/solid ivory handles, rosewood case ....... $150.00

*Price does not include 10% buyer fee.

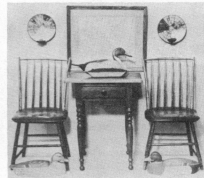

A-OH April 1983          *Garth's Auctions, Inc.*

**TIN SCONCES,** pr., round mirrored reflectors, candle sockets w/crimped pans, old blk. paint, has been electrified at one time, soldered repr., replm., 9½" D.
............................ $190.00

**HANDCOLORED ENGRAVING,** "Map of the Middle States of America by J. Russell. Published in London. Dec. 13, 1794," damage & repr., minor stains, burlap mat, wormy chestnut frame, 22" x 26". ..................... $152.50

**WINDSOR SIDE CHAIRS,** pr., bamboo turnings, old worn br. repaint, yellow striping shows traces of gr. beneath, seat 16¾" H. ..................... $450.00

**PINTAIL DRAKE,** by Bill Enright (1913-1979), cork body, wooden head & tail, tack eyes, old worn repaint, old split, 19" L.
............................ $35.00

**STAND,** cherry & poplar, repr., ref., 20" x 22½", 28¼" H. ................. $145.00

**MALLARD HEN,** by Cecil Rollins, contemporary working decoy w/stamped feathers, glass eyes & orig. paint, 18" L.
............................ $50.00

**MALLARD DRAKE,** by Cecil Rollins, 17½" L. ....................... $50.00

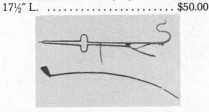

A-MA Aug. 1982          *Robert W. Skinner Inc.*

**WRT. IRON PIPE TONGS,** Am., 18th C., 17½" L. .................. $850.00*

**WRT. IRON CHURCH WARDEN'S PIPE,** Am., 18th C., 17" L. .... $550.00*

A-OH April 1983          *Garth's Auctions, Inc.*

**Q.A. CANDLESTICK,** brass, 6¾" H.
............................. $250.00

**Q.A. CANDLESTICK,** brass, 7" H.
............................. $300.00

**SALT GLAZE DISH,** Eng., embossed design, reticulated rim, flaking, slightly crooked, 11⅜" D., 2" H. ........ $375.00

**SALT GLAZE OVAL BOWL,** Eng., underplate, crack, minor flaking, 8½" x 10", 3¼" H. ..................... $475.00

**CHIPPENDALE LOWBOY,** cherry, orig. brasses, old mellow color, repr., case 31⅝" W., top 18½" x 35½", 28⅝" H.
............................. $10000.00

**HISTORICAL STAFFORDSHIRE PLATTER,** drk. blue transfer, arms of "North Carolina," impressed "T. Mayer," repr., 11½" x 14¾" ........... $2000.00

*Left*
A-WA D.C. Sept. 1982 *Adam A. Weschler & Son*
**GEORGE III CELLARETTE ON STAND,** ca. 1790, mahogany, fitted bottle int., 12 bottle compartments, 18" sq., 30" H.
........................... $800.00*

*Right*
A-MA Nov. 1982     *Richard A. Bourne Co., Inc.*
**CHILD'S LADDER-BACK ARM-CHAIR,** N. Eng., 18th C., orig. blk. paint, seat needs repr. ............. $1500.00

A-MA July 1982     *Richard A. Bourne Co., Inc.*
L to R
**TAVERN TABLE,** Am., mid 18th C., maple w/oval pine top, ref. in natural wood, few surface scratches, 27½" L., 21" W., 24¾" H. ..................... $1200.00

**Q.A. SIDE CHAIR,** Am., ca. 1700-1725, maple, feet built up, replaced rush seat, chair finished in natural wood.... $500.00

A-MA Aug. 1982          *Robert W. Skinner Inc.*
L to R

**MINI. WOODEN TOWEL RACK,** N. Eng., early 19th C., w/linen napkin, old worn red paint, hand-woven tan & blue plaid linen napkin, initialed "R.B.," rack 11½" H., napkin 21" Sq. ...... $1200.00*

**MINI. WOODEN BOX,** N. Eng., early 19th C., made from block of wood w/sliding cover, red & blk. painted geometric carving, 1¼" H., 3⅛" x 1½" ........ $200.00*

**MINI. WOODEN FIRKIN & BARREL,** N. Eng., early 19th C., fitted cover, tapered sides, copper tacks, painted blue-gray, mini. barrel cut from one piece of wood, painted blue & blk., firk 2¾" H., barrel 2½" H. ........................... $325.00*

**MINI. PINE FOOTSTOOL,** N. Eng., early 19th C., flat top, notched ends, deep scalloped skirt, bootjack ends, painted, 3⅜" H., top: 6⅛" x 3¼" ............ $275.00*

A-OH Feb. 1983          *Garth's Auctions, Inc.*
**STONEWARE JUG,** stenciled cobalt label "John Weaver, Stoneware, Cincinnati, O.," 11" H. ................ $75.00

**SHAKER DRYING RACK,** mortised construction, one spindle is broken out, 20" x 30" ....................... $350.00

**STONEWARE JAR,** "One" & nice flourish in cobalt, flake, 9½" H. .... $85.00

**MULE CHEST,** pine, 6-board, replm., old red repaint, lock missing, orig. staple hinges, 38" W., 18" D., 38¾" H.
............................. $750.00

A-OH April 1983    *Garth's Auctions, Inc.*
**OIL ON CANVAS PAINTING,** prim- itive, country landscape, sgn. "Elsie Earl," good orig. cond., cleaned, orig. stretcher, old gilded frame, 28½" x 33½".... $650.00
**CAMPAIGN TORCH,** tin, sq., star- shaped air holes, circular glass lights, pierced vent top, sliding door, on wooden pole, 60" H. ................. $200.00

**BURL BOWL,** ash, cracks & hole, 9½" D., 3¾" H. ........................ $90.00
**BURL MORTAR & PESTLE,** ash burl, poplar pestle, wear, cracks, 5½" D., 5¼" H. ................................ $85.00
**BURL BOWL,** ash, cracks, repr., 11½" D., 2⅞" H. ......................... $75.00
**Q.A. TAVERN TABLE,** birch base, pine breadboard top, old worn refinishing, 23¼" x 36¾", 25¾" H. ............ $2500.00
**BENTWOOD BOXES,** stack of 4, orig. br. graining, some wear, 5¾" D., 7¾" D., 8¾" D., 9¾" D. ................. $900.00
**STONEWARE OVOID JUG,** impressed "H & G. Nash, Utica," faded leaf in cobalt blue, some wear, hairline in neck, 11¼" H. ........................... $125.00
**STONEWARE JUG,** 2-gal., impressed "Fresh Tomatoes," tomato & foliage in cobalt blue brush work, hairlines in neck, chips, 13¼" H. ................. $425.00

A-MA Aug. 1982    *Robert W. Skinner Inc.*
**MELON BASKET,** N. Eng., early 19th C., gr. paint, 4" H., 8" L., 6" W. .... $475.00*
**DOUBLE MELON SPLINT BASKET,** N. Eng., early 19th C., orange paint, 5½" H., 20½" L., 8½" W. .............. $775.00*
**MELON SPLINT BASKET,** N. Eng., early 19th C., hinged lidded, drk. gr. paint, 4" H., 6" L., 6" W. ........... $600.00*

A-OH Feb. 1983    *Garth's Auctions, Inc.*
**STUDENT LAMP,** brass, opaque wh. shade, font mkd. "C.F.A. Hinrighs, Patd Dec 1, 1874," never electrified, burner missing, 21½" H. .............. $217.50
**CRUCIFIX CANDLESTICK,** milk glass, 7⅛" H. ....................... $15.00
**CRUCIFIX CANDLESTICK,** milk glass, some damage, 9½" H. ........... $10.00
**CRUCIFIX CANDLESTICK,** milk glass, minor roughness, 12⅝" H. ....... $20.00
**STUDENT LAMP,** brass, opaque wh. shade, mkd. "Kaiser," and "German Student Lamp Co.," chimney ring mkd. "New York, B.B. Schneider," lamp is electrified, font altered, damage on ring, 20½" H. ..................... $175.00
**VICTORIAN CHEST OF DRAWERS,** walnut, ref., 42¾" W., 19" D., 40" H. plus crest .......................... $245.00
**STICK SPATTER IRONSTONE PLATTER,** blk. transfer rabbits around rim, Gaudy floral center in red, blue, gr., & yellow, minor wear, 14¾" L. ..... $225.00

A-OH Oct. 1982    *Garth's Auctions, Inc.*
**PENNSYLVANIA GERMAN FRAK- TUR,** birth certificate in watercolor, attrib. to York County, stains & minor creases, 15¼" x 18½" ................... $595.00
**LUDLOW BOTTLE,** blown olive amber, some wear & flaking, 9¾" H. ..... $75.00
**MINIATURE HEPPLEWHITE CHEST OF DRAWERS,** cherry, ref., replm., 16" W., 8½" D., 14¾" H. ......... $750.00
**BOWBACK WINDSOR SIDE CHAIR,** old splits, ref., 18" seat ht. ....... $75.00
**COUNTRY SHERATON STAND,** curly maple, replm., ref., warping, 22½" W., 17¼" D., 28½" H. .............. $575.00
**LUDLOW BOTTLE,** blown olive gr., 13⅜" H. ...................... $175.00

A-OH Sept. 1982    *Garth's Auctions, Inc.*
**WEATHER VANE,** sheet iron silhouette horse & sulky, base of directionals, 50" W., 58½" H. ..................... $2500.00

**WOVEN SPLINT BASKET,** wooden lid, orig. cast iron handles, mkd. "Moore Whitmore Co. So. Milwaukee, Wis, Pat Sept 2, 1890," 22½" W., 32" L., 22½" H. ............................. $125.00

**GALENA POTTERY CROCK,** red- ware, clear greenish glaze, applied handles, tooled lines, impressed "5," some damage, 13¾" H. ........................ $80.00

**STONEWARE CROCK,** cobalt "3" w/flourish, hairline crack, 10¾" H. ............................. $30.00

A-MA July 1982    *Richard A. Bourne Co., Inc.*
*Row I, L to R*
**HOGSCRAPER STEEL CANDLE-STICK**, mkd., by Shaw, orig. hanger, 5¼″ H. ............................ $90.00
**HOGSCRAPER STEEL CANDLE-STICK**, mkd. "A Shaw/Birm.," rusted, hanger broken off, 7″ H. ........ $50.00
**STEEL HOGSCRAPER CANDLE-STICK**, complete w/hanger, 6″ H. ................................ $80.00
**"MAKE-DO" LAMP**, broken pewter whale oil lamp mounted on solid pine block, 5½″ H. .................... $40.00
*Row II, L to R*
**TIN HANGING CANDLE SCONCE**, punch work design, 13½″ H. .... $175.00
**TIN CANDLE MOLD**, 12-tube, somewhat bent, slightly rusted, minus handle ................................ $60.00
**WRT. IRON BROILER**, 18th C., fat drain included, 14″ W., 12½″ D., 9″ handle ............................ $170.00

*Left*
A-MA July 1982    *Robert W. Skinner Inc.*
**PAINTED BOOK STAND**, Am., ca. 1800, polychrome floral decor., 8½″ H. ............................ $470.00*
*Right*
A-MA July 1982    *Richard A. Bourne Co., Inc.*
**IVORY DIPTYCH DIAL**, German, 17th C., mkd. "Welsch VR" on one side & "Nirenperger/VHR" on other, 4¾″ x 2-15/16″ x ¾″ ................ $5100.00

A-MA July 1982    *Richard A. Bourne Co., Inc.*
**WOODEN SCULPTURE**, Am., 19th C., eagle on book, repainted, 16½″ H. ............................ $5500.00

A-OH July 1982    *Garth's Auctions, Inc.*
**BRASS TRANSIT LEVEL**, w/wooden tripod base & dovetailed case, "Gurley Engineering Instruments, Troy, N.Y.," worn blk. finish, instrument is 19½″ L. ............................ $325.00

A-MA July 1982    *Richard A. Bourne Co., Inc.*
*L to R*
**VICTORIAN PARLOR STOVE**, made by S. H. Ranson & Co., Albany, NY, 29″ O.H. ............................ $150.00
**TINY VICTORIAN FIREPLACE STOVE**, by Taylor & Flagier of Peekskill, NY, cracks, 26″ O.H. ......... $100.00

A-MA July 1982    *Richard A. Bourne Co., Inc.*
**OVAL COVERED BOX**, early 19th C., orig. decor., somewhat faded, 17½″ L. ............................ $450.00

A-OH July 1982    *Garth's Auctions, Inc.*
**TIN EAGLE**, embossed, old drk. gr. patina, edges are battered, 29″ W. ............................ $375.00
**PEWTER PLATE**, Eng., w/several touch marks, rim has stamped initials, surface is corroded, 9″ D. ................ $75.00
**PEWTER CHARGER**, Eng., "Made in London" touch & "___ & Compton," 12″ D. ............................ $175.00
**PEWTER PLATE**, Eng., small indistinct touch marks, 8¾″ D. ........... $75.00
**PEWTER CANDLESTICK**, Am., base mkd. "T. Wildes, N. York," soldered repr. at stem & remov. bobeche, 9¾″ H. ................................ $115.00
**PEWTER COMMUNION CHALICES**, pr., Am., unmkd., 8⅛″ L. ....... $700.00
**PEWTER FLAGON**, Am., unmkd., 10½″ H. ............................ $225.00
**PEWTER CANDLESTICK**, Am., unmkd., remov. bobeche, dents in stem, 9¾″ H. ............................ $125.00
**BLANKET CHEST**, tulip wood 6 board, orig. red graining applied over unfinished wood w/old varnish, 40¾″ W., 21″ D., 29¼″ H., back is dated "1828" ....... $2100.00
**WRT. IRON KNIFE BLADE ANDIRONS**, pr., w/penny feet, brass plate in base & brass urn finials, 24½″ H. ............................ $700.00

A-MA July 1982    *Richard A. Bourne Co., Inc.*
**HETCHEL**, walnut w/brass borders, incised decor., ca. 1795, minus box cover ............................ $150.00

A-MA July 1982    *Richard A. Bourne Co., Inc.*
*Top to Bottom*
**PLAQUE,** bronze & gold inlaid, Japanese, 19th C., 12″ D. .............. $700.00
**DAGGER,** Japanese, 19th C., tip of blade slightly rusted, handle loose, 15″ O.L. ................................ $75.00
**DAGGER,** Japanese, 19th C., blade nicked, basketry weave partly broken away, scabbard minus its tip, needs restor., 19½″ O.L. .................... $125.00

A-MA Aug. 1982    *Robert W. Skinner Inc.*
**BRASS WARMING PAN,** Am., 18th C., wrt. iron handle, pan has etched star, 44″ L. ............................ $600.00*

A-MA July 1982    *Richard A. Bourne Co., Inc.*
*Row I, L to R*
**HANGING CANDLE BOX,** oak, sliding cover, Am., 18th C., old finish, 17⅛″ L. ................................ $200.00
**HOUR GLASS,** orig. sand, oak & maple frame, sand leaks, 4⅜″ D., 8½″ H. ................................ $125.00
**SEWING BOX,** hand-decorated, sm. tray missing from int., 12″ L. ........ $225.00
*Row II, L to R*
**TOLE DOCUMENT BOX,** orig. floral & fruit decor., finish worn on domed top, 9½″ L. ................................ $125.00
**MORTAR & PESTLE,** solid maple, remains of orig. gr. paint, slight age cracking, mortar 6⅞″ H. ......... $80.00
**CARVED WOODEN CHEST,** Am., 17th C., Diamond patt. w/traces of old gold decor., dovetail const., minor damage, 8½″ L. ................................ $350.00

A-MA July 1982    *Robert W. Skinner Inc.*
**BRONZE FIGURE,** bird, France, late 19th C., sgn. "F. Pautrot," 5″ H. ............................ $350.00*

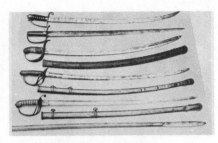

A-MA July 1982    *Richard A. Bourne Co., Inc.*
*Top to Bottom*
**CONFEDERATE SWORD,** turned wooden handle & iron hilt, 40″ O.L. ............................ $250.00
**BRASS-MOUNTED SWORD,** spiral carved wooden grip, minor pitting, grips missing wire wrapping, 40″ O.L. ............................ $80.00
**MANUFACTORY SWORD,** unmkd., wooden grips missing leather covering & most of wire wrapping, 40″ O.L. ............................ $250.00
**BRASS-MOUNTED SABER,** Civil War period, lt. pitting, most of wire wrapping missing from grip, traces of orig. finish, 40¼″ O.L. .................... $100.00
**SWORD,** mkd. "S. Isaac/Campbell & Co./71 Jermyn/London," patches of pitting, some orig. finish, 41½″ O.L. ............................ $225.00
**PIKE,** Civil War period, cone-shaped brass mounting on end, 71½″ O.L. .... $150.00

A-MA Aug. 1982    *Richard A. Bourne Co., Inc.*
**FR. BRASS TELESCOPE ON STAND,** by Charles Chevalier/Paris, mounted on tripod w/folding feet attached to spotting scope, length at focal length 40+″ ............................ $1800.00

A-MA July 1982    *Richard A. Bourne Co., Inc.*
**SWISS MUSICAL BIRD IN BOX,** gold bronze w/enamel, working order, 3½″ x 2½″ ...................... $1650.00

A-MA July 1982    *Richard A. Bourne Co., Inc.*
*L to R*
**IRON WAFFLE MAKER,** for Easter waffles, normal surface rust, 28″ O.L. ............................ $75.00
**WAFFLE IRON,** mkd. "B. Phreaner," stylized leaf design, surface rust, 28″ L. ............................ $125.00

A-OH July 1982    *Garth's Auctions, Inc.*
**WALL CUPBOARD,** poplar w/orig. red paint, molded cornice is repr. & inc., unusual inset hinges have broken out in top doors, 49″ W., 17½″ D., 78½″ H. ............................ $1300.00
**CARVED WOODEN DECOY,** Mason's Bluebill drake, glass eyes & old working repaint w/shot scars, 13½″ L. .... $40.00
**PEWTER PLATE,** 10½″ D. ..... $65.00
**CARVED WOODEN DECOY,** factory Redhead drake, Saginaw Bay, MI, glass eyes & old working repaint, 12½″ L. ............................ $30.00

*Price does not include 10% buyer fee.

A-OH July 1982   *Garth's Auctions, Inc.*
**DOUBLE WEAVE JACQUARD
COVERLET,** 2 pc., has some wear &
fringe removed, end edges are rebound,
80" x 84" ..................... $200.00
**PUNCHED TIN CANDLE SCONCES,**
similar but not pair, varnished, 10½" H.
................................ $70.00
**LITHO,** colored, advertising print of
Indian shooting buffalo, "Prairie," sponged
frame has edge chip, 11" x 13" .... $65.00
**BRASS EAGLE,** embossed, w/arrows &
foliage in tallons, tin back has holes for
flags, slightly battered, 26¼" L. .. $105.00
**SHERATON BENCH,** old worn blk.
paint w/yellow striping & yellow & gold
decor. on back .............. $1700.00
**CARVED WOODEN DECOY,** alert
head, old worn paint & repl. glass eyes,
homemade copper tag, "A. & H. Lindsay,
Green St, Harrisburg Pa," 18" L.
................................ $110.00
**CARVED WOODEN DECOY,** redhead
drake w/turned head, tack eyes & old
working repaint, 13" L. ......... $75.00

A-OH July 1982   *Garth's Auctions, Inc.*
**TIN CANDLE SCONCE,** 9¾" H.
................................ $75.00
**TIN CANDLE SCONCE,** 9¾" H.
................................ $75.00
**WOVEN SPLINT BASKET,** w/lid, some
wear, Woodlands Indian orig., 10" D., 8" H.
................................ $25.00
**LADDERBACK SIDE CHAIR,** old drk.
red finish, new woven splint seat
................................ $45.00
**TABLE,** curly maple, 25½" x 26", 30" H.
................................ $845.00
**CARVED WOODEN DECOY,** canvas-
back drake, attrib. to Hank Fralie, 15" L.
................................ $20.00
**WOVEN SPLINT BASKET,** Cherokee,
13" H. ...................... $40.00

*Left*
A-MA Nov. 1982   *Richard A. Bourne Co., Inc.*
**HANGING CANDLE BOX,** Am., ca.
late 18th C./early 19th C., retains old red
paint overall, front panel has crack, 15" L.,
11½" H., 7" D. ................ $400.00
*Right*
**PRISONER-OF-WAR STRAW-WORK
BOX,** elaborate scene of village w/ship on
cover, minor loss of straw, 10⅞" L., 7½" W.,
3¼" H. ...................... $350.00

A-OH July 1982   *Garth's Auctions, Inc.*
**LITHO,** hand colored, "Currier & Ives,"
"Fruits Autumn Varieties," tears in margins
& cleaned, w/printing on bottom margin
inc., 17" x 21" ................ $25.00
**BRASS CANDLESTICK,** octagonal
base w/screw in stem w/octagonal
baluster, 6⅛" H. .............. $175.00
**TURNED TREEN FOOTED BOX,**
worn old yellow varnish finish, 6¾" H.
................................ $110.00
**BRASS CANDLESTICK,** 6¼" L.
................................ $135.00
**SHERATON CHEST OF DRAWERS,**
cherry, brasses are old replm., poplar
secondary wood, ref., 42¾" W., 21" D.,
41¼" H. ...................... $800.00

A-OH July 1982   *Garth's Auctions, Inc.*
**TOLE CANNISTERS,** set of 4, orig. blk.
paint w/gilded striping & labels outlined in
red & wh., "Must. Seed," "Saltpetre," "W.
Pepper," & "Cayenne," paint has wear, 9"
H. ........................... $140.00
**BLANKET CHEST,** w/till, pine & poplar,
boot jack legs w/applied front brackets &
base molding, orig. drk. gr. paint, 41½" W.,
16½" D., 24¾" H. ............. $325.00
**STONEWARE PRESERVING JAR,**
blurred stenciled cobalt blue floral decor.,
old base chips, 9¼" H. ......... $40.00

**STONEWARE JAR,** mkd. "Binghamton,
N.Y.," polka dot bird on branch in cobalt
blue slip, rim hairlines & chips on handles,
8" H. ......................... $200.00
**STONEWARE PRESERVING JAR,**
w/cobalt blue floral decor., 9¼" H.
................................ $65.00

A-OH July 1982   *Garth's Auctions, Inc.*
**OIL ON CANVAS,** folk art painting of
cherry pickers, 20th C., framed, 25" x 34¾"
................................ $650.00
**HIRED MAN'S ROPE BED,** old gr. paint
w/red beneath, single size w/cushion upholstered in blue & wh. coverlet material,
32" x 75¾" ................... $425.00
**WOODEN WHIRRLY-GIG,** Indian in
boat w/animated oars driven by sheet
metal vanes, old weathered polychrome
paint w/light bulb in bow, 20" L.
................................ $235.00

**WOODEN HORSE PULL TOY,** orig.
wh. paint w/horse hair tail, base is gr. &
wheels are red, 23" L. ......... $525.00
**TOY TANKER WAGON,** iron, wood &
tin, orig. red & gr. paint w/striping in
yellow, blk. & silver, 15" L. plus tongue
................................ $185.00

A-OH April 1983          *Garth's Auctions, Inc.*
*Row I, L to R*
**BURL BOWL,** scrubbed finish, wear on int., 8½" D., 2⅝" H. ............ $300.00
**DECORATED BOX,** orig. red & blk. graining, stenciled foliage, fruit & flowers in gr., red, blk. & gilt, 4" x 4¼" x 8¾" ............... $195.00
**BURL BOWL,** good turned detail, scrubbed finish, 6⅞" D., 2¾" H. ............... $155.00
*Row II, L to R*
**BURL MORTAR & CURLY MAPLE PESTLE,** wear, top irregular, 6¼" H. ............... $155.00
**BURL PORRINGER,** bird's-eye figure in bowl, handle has some curl, scrubbed finish, age cracks, 5¼" D., 2¼" H. ............... $300.00
**WOODEN FOLK ART CARVING,** jumping horse, orig. wh. paint w/blk. detail, red strap & blk. leather tail & ears, house-shaped base has old red, 9¾" O.H. ............... $150.00
**TURNED BURL BOX,** filled-in age crack, 7½" H. ............... $85.00
**TURNED BURL BOX,** 7½" H. ............... $350.00
*Row III, L to R*
**FOLK ART HORSE,** carved from one pc. of wood, old worn wh. paint w/blk., gr. & red, chip, 10⅛" H. ............... $275.00
**CARVED WOODEN HORSE PULL TOY,** pine, repr., inc., 9¼" L. ... $250.00
**BURL GAME BALL,** some wear, 3¼" D. ............... $95.00
**FOOTED BURL SALT,** good turned detail, 4" D., 2⅞" H. ............... $200.00
**WOODEN QUAIL,** primitive, laminated body, worn paint, wire legs, rosewood base, 7¾" H. ............... $250.00

A-MA Aug. 1982          *Robert W. Skinner Inc.*
**WOVEN SPLINT BASKET CHAIR,** N. Eng., 19th C., br. paint, pad, 25" H., 6" L., 18" D. ............... $575.00*

A-OH April 1983          *Garth's Auctions, Inc.*
**LIGHTING DEVICE,** wrt. iron, adj. shallow pan w/8 spouts held by a spring clip, can be hung, 17" H. ...... $200.00
**CANDLESTAND,** tin, adj. crimped pan w/4 sockets, circular spring clip under pan, 22½" H. ............... $750.00

**HANGING CANDLE HOLDER,** 2 sockets, semicircular brace, iron rod has finial, sm. holes in pan, 26½" H. ............... $350.00
**LIGHTING DEVICE,** wrt. iron, 2-part adj. pan w/spout on each end, circular spring clip, can be hung, 18" H. ............... $250.00

**BLANKET CHEST,** decor., PA, poplar, wrt. iron strap hinges, orig. paint w/br. sponging on an ochre wash, old glued splits, 53" W., 23¼" D., 24" H. ............... $4500.00

A-OH Jan. 1983          *Garth's Auctions, Inc.*
**CORNER CUPBOARD,** one-piece, cherry & poplar, ref., repaint, 54⅝" W., 82" H. ............... $2400.00
**STONEWARE BATTER PITCHER,** impressed "H. Purdy, 4," minor chips, 16" H. ............... $575.00

A-OH Mar. 1983          *Garth's Auctions, Inc.*
**STONEWARE JAR,** drilled & fitted as lamp, brushed cobalt blue, shade old band box w/orig. wallpaper covering, 24½" O.H. ............... $195.00
**HANDCOLORED LITHOGRAPH,** by Currier & Ives, "Trotting Gelding Harry Wilkes," faded colors, cork mat, modern cherry frame, 16¾" x 20¼" ...... $75.00
**BOW BACK WINDSOR ARMCHAIR,** old break, modern repaint is antiqued blue, 18" seat ht. ............... $575.00
**HEPPLEWHITE STAND,** worn old red paint, 23" x 24", 27½" H. ...... $1150.00
**WOVEN SPLINT BASKET,** minor wear, 16" D., 8" H. plus wooden handle ............... $55.00
**STONEWARE JAR,** mkd. "Cowden & Son, Harrisburg," old rim chip, 7¼" H. ............... $20.00

A-OH Sept. 1982          *Garth's Auctions, Inc.*
**PRIMITIVE BIRD,** wooden, outstretched wings & spread tail, old blk. & wh. paint, 35" W., 12½" H. ............... $50.00
**BIRD CAGE,** wooden, old drk. finish, top folds & roof is removable, cutout wooden lattice, hinged doors, removable balcony & gate on front, some damage to lattice, 54" W., 31" D., 62" H. ............... $425.00
**TOLE BIRD CAGE,** old wh. paint, floral decor., damage, 15" H. ............... $40.00

A-OH Mar. 1983    *Garth's Auctions, Inc.*
**HOOKED RAG RUG,** 24" x 48"
..................................... $525.00
**REDWARE TURK'S HEAD MOLD,** gr.
glaze w/orange spots, chips, 10¼" D., 3½"
H. .................................... $95.00
**BLANKET CHEST W/TILL,** pine, orig.
reddish-br. graining on yellow ground,
worn paint, lid is inc., 48½" W., 18" D., 25"
H. .................................... $285.00
**SPIDER POT,** cast iron, 6¼" D., 6" handle
.................................... $15.00
**SPIDER POT,** cast iron, 5¼" D., 5½"
handle ................................ $25.00
**SPIDER POT,** cast iron, worn old red, 5¼"
D., 4½" handle .................. $25.00
**SPIDER POT,** cast iron, crack at handle,
5" D., 4¾" handle .............. $10.00

A-OH Oct. 1982    *Garth's Auctions, Inc.*
**PIECED YOUTH QUILT,** star in tum-
bling block design, multicolor satin, worn,
62" sq. ................................ $175.00
**CHEESE PRESS,** primitive, mortised
frame, adj. lever, old worn red, drain board,
4 round Bentwood molds, minor damage,
52" H. ................................ $95.00
**SPLINT HALF-BUSHEL BASKET,**
wooden bottom, tin band, 15" D., 8½" H.
plus handle ...................... $45.00
**HANGING SCOURING BOX,** poplar,
cut-out crest, branded "J. Lawrence," drk,
br. paint, damage, 10" W., 4" D., 15" H.
.................................... $65.00
**FRYING PAN,** iron, 20" D., 23½" handle
.................................... $20.00
**BLACKSMITH HORSESHOEING
BOX,** primitive pine, iron legs, damage,
14¾" x 20" ...................... $55.00
**HANGING BOX,** primitive, pine, simple
crest, wear & damage, 13½" W. .. $40.00

A-OH Jan. 1983    *Garth's Auctions, Inc.*
**SHAKER ALL WOOD RAKE,** old worn
blue paint, 67" L. ............. $145.00
**BED WARMER,** copper, turned wooden
handle 12¼" D., 44" L. ......... $300.00
**SHAKER SPINNING WHEEL,** stamped
"J.A.," (John Anderson), 45" D., 61" H.
.................................... $175.00
**STONEWARE CHURN,** impressed
"Pat'd June 23, 1896," & Manufactured by
Fredk H. Weeks, Akron, Ohio," flake, 17½"
H. plus wooden dasher ......... $65.00
**SHAKER SUGAR BUCKET,** stave &
copper nail const., orig. worn lt. gray paint
.................................... $100.00
**CARVED MAPLE SUGAR CANDY
MOLD,** walnut, 28 depressions, cracks &
wear, 9¾" x 17¾" ............. $165.00

A-MA Aug. 1982    *Robert W. Skinner Inc.*
**MELON BASKET,** N. Eng., early 19th C.,
painted red, 13" H., 24" L., 18" D.
.................................... $900.00*
**MELON SPLINT BASKET,** N. Eng.,
early 19th C., fixed handle, 12" H., 15" D.
.................................... $425.00*
**MELON SPLINT BASKET,** N. Eng.,
early 19th C., fixed handle, 9½" H., 13½" L.,
12" D. ............................. $290.00*

A-MA Aug. 1982    *Robert W. Skinner Inc.*
**CYLINDRICAL COVERED SPLINT
BASKET,** N. Eng., early 19th C., poly-
chrome painted, 7" H., 13" D. .. $375.00*
**CYLINDRICAL HANDLED COV-
ERED SPLINT BASKET,** N. Eng., early
19th C., polychrome painted, 10½" H., 16"
D. .................................. $375.00*
**CYLINDRICAL PEAKED COVERED
SPLINT BASKET,** N. Eng., early 19th C.,
polychrome painted, 10½" H., 19" D.
.................................... $500.00*

A-OH April 1983    *Garth's Auctions, Inc.*
**ANALYTICAL BALANCE SCALES,**
blk. enameled metal case, blk. glass
platform, scales are brass, iron & other
metals, mkd. "Wm Ainsworth & Sons Inc.
Denver, Col.," complete w/weights, wear,
18" W., 9" D., 19" H. ........... $75.00
**MICROSCOPE,** German, orig. blk.
enamel, brass trim, mkd. "Ernst Leitz,
Wetzlar," binocular & single scopes,
complete in case w/accessories, 12½" H.
.................................... $180.00

**HANGING LATTICE-WORK SHELF,**
2 basket-like containers, worn old gr. paint,
minor edge damage, 28" W., 43" H.
.................................... $185.00
**AMISH QUILT,** solid navy blue on one
side, gr. on the other w/yellow calico
binding, elaborate quilting in wh. thread has
stylized tulips, stars, leaves, quilting &
binding is all hand-stitched, seams in blue &
gr. are machine-stitched, 72" x 82"
.................................... $160.00
**STOCKING STRETCHERS,** pr.,
wooden, 17" L. ................. $50.00
**LADDERBACK ARMCHAIR ROCK-
ER,** ref., woven splint seat ...... $250.00
**WOVEN SPLINT BUTTOCKS
BASKET,** minor wear, 10½" x 11½", 6" H.
plus wide wooden handle ...... $120.00
**COUNTRY STAND,** walnut, repr., worn
old finish, 14½" x 23¾", 26¼" H. .. $90.00

A-OH Mar. 1982        *Garth's Auctions, Inc.*
*Top, L to R*
**METAL BELL,** cast bell, mkd. "Saignele-gier Chiantel Fondeur 1878," damage, replm., 5¼" H. ................. $25.00
**FOLK ART CARVED BEAR,** metal bead eyes, worn gold paint, 6" H. ...... $15.00
**DECORATIVE DECOY,** miniature, contemporary carving of mallard drake, orig. paint, sm. chip on bill, 3⅜" L. ................................ $7.50
**FOLK ART CARVING OF SPREAD-WING EAGLE,** old drk. br. finish, 8¼" W., 7¾" H. ........................ $170.00
**DECORATIVE DECOY,** miniature, contemporary carving, orig. paint, gr. wing teal, 4¼" L. ................. $12.50
**DECORATIVE DECOY,** miniature, contemporary carving of pintail, orig. paint, 3⅝" L. ................. $12.50
**STRING HOLDER,** cast iron, reticulated sphere on triangular base, old blk. repaint, 6½" H. ..................... $25.00
**STRING HOLDER,** cast iron, beehive, worn old blk. paint, 4½" H. ...... $20.00
*Bottom, L to R*
**STRING HOLDER,** cast iron, adj. holder for cone & arm mkd. "J. Anstice & Co, Inc. Rochester N.Y.," 10¾" H. ........ $6.00
**HANGING STRING HOLDER,** cast iron, old blk. paint, worn floral decor., 4¼" H. ........................... $40.00
**STRING HOLDER,** cast iron, wire bail fastener, old blk. repaint, 4¾" H. ................................ $25.00
**DOOR STOP,** cast iron, basket of flowers, orig. polychrome paint, 8" H. ................................ $60.00
**STRING HOLDER,** cast iron, dome-shaped w/intersecting arches, 5" H. ................................ $35.00
**STRING HOLDER,** cast iron, made to be wall-mounted, "Patd Oct 21, 1893," 5" H. ................................ $15.00
**STRING HOLDER,** cast iron, heavy reticulated dome for cone of string, 8½" H. ................................ $30.00

A-MA Aug. 1982        *Robert W. Skinner Inc.*
*L to R*
**SPLINT BASKET,** N. Eng., early 19th C., painted blk. bands, 7" H., 17½" L., 15" W. ................................ $375.00*
**SPLINT BASKET,** N. Eng., early 19th C., lt. br. paint w/blk. dots, 8½" H., 25½" L., 17" W. ........................... $625.00*

A-OH Feb. 1983        *Garth's Auctions, Inc.*
**STRAP HINGES,** 4 (1 illus.), wrt. iron, worn old wh. paint, 24" L. ...... $70.00
**WALL CUPBOARD,** one pc., pine, dry sink well, top has int. drawers, old red repaint, 33" W., 25½" D., 74" H. ................................ $335.00
**IRON BROAD AXE,** replm., 12" blade ................................ $30.00
**IRON BROAD AXE,** replm., stamped signature on 9" blade ........... $32.50
**STONEWARE CROCK,** 3 gal., impressed "Burger & Lang, Rochester N.Y.," "3," feather design in cobalt slip, glued crack, 10½" H. ................. $95.00

A-OH Mar. 1982        *Garth's Auctions, Inc.*
**JINNY LIND SHAVING MIRROR,** cast iron, old repaint in red, wh. & blue, worn silvering on glass, old break in one branch, 20¾" H. ..................... $95.00
**JIGSAW WORK FRAME,** walnut, wavy glass, alligatored varnish finish, late 19th C., can be hung, 16" x 20" ...... $115.00
**BLANKET CHEST,** pine, poplar & chestnut, has till & orig. yellow paint w/smoked decor., hinges reset, 45¼" W., 18" D., 23½" H. ................. $280.00
**BUCKET,** spun brass, iron bail handle, slightly battered, 11¼" D., 7¾" H. ................................ $35.00
**BOWL,** spun brass, iron rim handles, dents, 10" D., 5" H. ............ $40.00

A-OH Feb. 1983        *Garth's Auctions, Inc.*
*Row I, L to R*
**TURNED TREEN CHALICES,** pr. (1st & last items), sm. age cracks, 2⅝" H. ................................ $20.00
**SHEEP,** pr., wood & composition, flocked coats, 4" L. ................. $40.00
**STEER,** wood & composition, flocked br. coat, glass eyes, some wear, 6¼" L. ................................ $25.00
**TIN CANDY MOLD,** hen on nest, pc. missing, 3¼" L. ................. $12.50
*Row II, L to R*
**SNUFF BOX,** tin lining, hinged lid, 3½" L. ................................ $12.50
**TREEN FOOTED SALT,** 3⅛" D., 3" H. ................................ $20.00
**CANDLESTICKS,** pr., brass, mid 19th C., 3¾" H. ..................... $90.00
**TREEN SANDER,** figured wood, branded in 3 places "S. Davis," 3⅛" D., 3¼" H. ................................ $80.00
**BOX,** mahogany, in form of a snub nose wood plane, old reddish-br. varnish, 3⅞" L. ................................ $75.00
*Row III, L to R*
**TREEN BOX,** simple geometric inlay in lid, 2⅝" H. ..................... $12.50
**TREEN CHALICE,** old alligatored red varnish, minor age cracks, 3¾" H. ................................ $5.00
**CHOCOLATE MOLD,** tin, horse, hinged at top, 5¼" L. ............ $87.00
**TREEN SANDER,** boxwood, 2½" H. ................................ $40.00
**TURNED WOODEN TRAMMELL,** glass insert, orig. blk. paint w/gilt decor. & applied caduceus, 2⅝" D., 1¾" H. ................................ $70.00

*Price does not include 10% buyer fee.

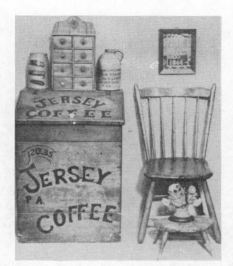

A-OH Feb. 1983        *Garth's Auctions, Inc.*
**HANGING SPICE BOX,** 8 shelves, wire nail construction, age splits, edge damage, worn finish, 9¾″ W., 5″ D., 16½″ H.
..................................... $115.00
**STONEWARE PRESERVING JAR,** 3 slashes of cobalt blue, 8″ H. ...... $70.00
**STONEWARE JUG,** stenciled cobalt label "L. Sternberger, Wines & liquors, 3rd Ave Bet 10 & 11st Huntington, W. Va.," traces of blk. paint, 9″ H. ....... $125.00
**SIGNATURE BLOCK FROM A COVERLET,** red, blue & wh., "Philip Bysel Shanesville, Ohio 1844," framed, 8½″ x 10½″ ........................ $45.00
**COFFEE BIN,** blk. painted label "Jersey Coffee 120 lbs.," 22½″ W., 17¼″ D., 32″ H.
..................................... $325.00
**BAMBOO WINDSOR SIDE CHAIR,** ref., age cracks, 15¾″ seat ht. .... $55.00
**CAST IRON DOOR STOP,** basket of flowers, old polychrome repaint, 9½″ H.
..................................... $35.00
**FOOT STOOL,** wear & cracks, 6½″ x 12″, 7″ H. ..................... $55.00

A-OH Mar. 1982        *Garth's Auctions, Inc.*
**CHALKWARE SEATED DOG,** orig. red & blk. paint, repr., 9″ H. ..... $55.00
**SMALL BOX,** poplar, base & lid molding, orig. graining is imitation of bird's-eye maple, 6″ x 7″ x 10″ ........... $195.00
**CHALKWARE SEATED DOG,** good detail, worn orig. blk., yellow & red paint, 8″ H. ................................ $95.00
**CHIPPENDALE HIGH CHEST,** maple, some curl in top & sides, replm., repr., warm old br. finish, 44″ W., 19¼″ D., 52½″ H. ......................... $1650.00

A-OH April 1983        *Garth's Auctions, Inc.*
**CANDLESTICKS,** pr., brass Victorian, pushups inc., repr., split in lip of one, 7⅝″ H.
..................................... $35.00
**CHARGER,** Eng., pewter, touchmarks "Townsend" & "Giffin," worn & corroded, damage, 15″ D. .............. $45.00
**TEA KETTLE,** copper, dovetailed seams, gooseneck spout, mkd. "I.B.K.," battered, replm., repr., 7¾″ H. ........... $45.00
**SHERATON CHEST,** cherry, ref., replm., 45″ W., 24¼″ D., 45⅝″ H.
..................................... $325.00
**STONEWARE JAR,** brushed cobalt blue floral decor., worn, lime deposits, 10″ H.
..................................... $80.00
**RINGBILL HEN,** glass eyes, orig. paint, 12¾″ L. ...................... $45.00
**MALLARD DRAKE,** Victor factory, glass eyes, orig. paint, 15¼″ L. ........ $25.00

A-OH Feb. 1983        *Garth's Auctions, Inc.*
**WEATHER VANE,** copper, embossed eagle & sphere, brass arrow, iron paint & cast iron directionals, repr., 33″ wingspan, 41″ H. ..................... $250.00
**COUNTRY WORK TABLE,** poplar worn old gray paint, 25¼″ x 78″, 28″ H.
..................................... $495.00
**FIRE TOOLS,** iron & brass, shovel & tongs, 33″ L. .................. $150.00
**BENCH,** pine, weathered surface w/age cracks, 11¾″ x 48″, 16″ H. ...... $115.00
**TEA KETTLE,** copper, wrt. iron handles, repr., replm., 7½″ H. plus handle
..................................... $65.00

A-OH Feb. 1983        *Garth's Auctions, Inc.*
**BUTTER PRINT,** rectangular, hinged frame, glued & ref., 5½″ x 6″ ..... $55.00
**WOODEN COOKIE BOARD,** turned handle, 2 nut-shaped depressions, 9″ L.
..................................... $85.00
**FOOD CHOPPER,** crescent blade, wooden handle, 8″ W. .......... $45.00
**BUTTER PADDLE,** wooden, 4 primitively-carved compass stars, age crack in blade, 3½″ x 9¼″ ............... $240.00
**BUTTER PRINT,** rectangular, primitively-carved sheaf, 4¼″ x 7″ .... $110.00
**BUTTER PRINT,** spade-shaped, simple chip-carved designs, worn, 4¼″ L.
..................................... $45.00
**MATCHBOX W/EAGLE,** cast iron, worn old gilt & blk. paint, 4¾″ W.
..................................... $55.00
**BUTTER PRINT,** chip carving on 3 surfaces, whittled handle, 4⅜″ L.
..................................... $65.00
**COOKIE BOARD,** carved poplar, 6 designs include deer, cherries, cornucopia, flower, pineapple & building, ref., 3¼″ x 6¼″
..................................... $55.00
**BUTTER SCOOP,** maple, well made, good color, 7″ L. .............. $125.00
**CARVED WOODEN WHIMSEY,** pastry cutter wheel at one end, 4-prong pick at other, ball in cage shaft, repr., 11″ L.
..................................... $85.00
**PASTRY CUTTER,** wooden, turned handle, sm. chip, 6″ L. .......... $35.00
**ICE CREAM MOLD,** pewter, bust of George Washington, "S & Co.," 3½″ x 3⅞″
..................................... $50.00
**COOKIE BOARD,** carved cherry, 9 designs include fish, flowers, swan, buildings, compote w/fruit & corncopia, ref., 4¾″ x 6¼″ ................. $190.00

A-OH Feb. 1983          *Garth's Auctions, Inc.*
**YELLOWWARE BOWL,** br. sponging, 9¼″ D., 4¼″ H. ................ $40.00
**PEWTER CHARGER,** inc. crowned rose mark, wear, 13¾″ D. .......... $125.00
**SPONGE SPATTER PITCHER,** blue & wh., embossed medallion of child & dog, 9″ H. ............................ $160.00
**SPONGE SPATTER BOWL,** blue, br. & wh., 6¼″ D., 4¼″ H. ............. $45.00
**SLANT FRONT DESK,** walnut, fitted pine int. w/9 dovetailed drawers, replm., repr., 43″ W., 21″ D., 30″ H. .... $500.00
**FOOT SCRAPER,** cast iron, dachshund, 20½″ L. ...................... $65.00

A-OH Mar. 1982          *Garth's Auctions, Inc.*
**HATCHEL,** on cutout poplar board, worn old patina, 8½″ x 23¾″ .......... $15.00
**HANDCOLORED LITHOGRAPH,** by "Haskell & Allen," "Fruit Piece," faded colors & stains, matted & framed, 16″ x 20″ ............................ $17.50

**TAPE LOOM,** maple, traces of old red, 11¼″ x 22″ ................. $295.00
**DOME-TOP BOX,** dovetailed pine, orig. br. graining w/"Maria Burtner 1835" in yellow, wear & break, 9¾″ x 10″ x 16½″ ............................ $95.00

**HEPPLEWHITE WORK TABLE,** orig. red paint, inc., splits, 31½″ x 42½″, 30″ H. ............................ $575.00
**WOVEN SPLINT BASKET,** bentwood rim handles, damage & wear, 22″ D., 11″ H. ............................ $45.00

A-OH Mar. 1982          *Garth's Auctions, Inc.*
**WATERCOLOR THEOREM,** mahogany frame, 13½″ x 16¼″ ........ $145.00
**EMPIRE MIRROR,** 2-part, orig. blk. paint & gilding, embossed brass rosettes, 15½″ x 32″ ......................... $65.00

**GAUDY WELSH COMPOTE,** floral decor. w/purple luster, decor. int., glaze wear, 10¼″ D., 5¾″ H. ........ $200.00
**ARROWBACK WINDSOR ROCKER,** worn orig. reddish-tan paint w/yellow striping & floral decor. on arrows & crest, rockers worn flat ............ $100.00

**STAND,** maple & poplar, worn orig. red paint, 20¾″ x 22¾″, 29″ H. ...... $190.00
**DECORATED BELLOWS,** orig. red paint w/yellow striping, freehand & stenciled shell & foliage decor. in gold, yellow & blk., brass nozzle, worn old releathering, split, 17½″ L. ................. $100.00

A-OH Mar. 1982          *Garth's Auctions, Inc.*
**HOOKED RAG RUG,** dog w/rose border in shades of red, gr., br. & blue on lt. gray ground, 18″ x 39½″ ........ $325.00
**BANNISTER BACK SIDE CHAIR,** repr., br. repaint, replm. ........ $350.00
**ROCKINGHAM BOWL,** wear, flaking, hairline, 9″ D., 4″ H. ............. $25.00
**ROCKINGHAM BOWL,** hairline in rim & crow's foot in foot, 13″ D., 6¼″ H. ............................... $40.00
**ROCKINGHAM BOWL,** flaking, 8½″ D., 3¾″ H. ...................... $25.00
**BLANKET CHEST,** pine, old yellow paint w/smoke graining shows earlier red beneath, has till, 43½″ W., 16½″ D., 20¼″ H. ............................ $325.00
**SPATTERWARE JARDINIERE,** blue & wh., gr. rim flecked in gold, 11″ D., 8¼″ H. ............................ $75.00

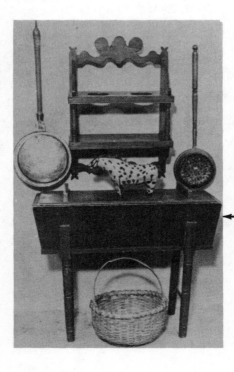

A-OH Mar. 1982          *Garth's Auctions, Inc.*
**BED WARMER,** brass, short turned wooden handle, engraved lid, splits in rim, end of handle is inc., 12″ D., 23″ L. ............................ $105.00
**HANGING SHELVES,** pine, ref., repr., 21″ W., 8¼″ D., 32″ H. ........ $175.00

**CHESTNUT ROASTER,** brass, turned wooden handle, 9″ D., 22″ handle ............................ $125.00
**WOODEN HORSE,** primitive, cut from one pc. of pine, gray wash, blk. dots, fur tail & mane, steel upholstery tack eyes, cord halter, 20th C. folk art, 14″ L. .... $95.00

**DOUGH BOX,** poplar, matching lid, orig. int. dividing board, old red paint, 15″ x 36″, 28½″ H. ...................... $300.00
**WOVEN SPLINT BASKET,** some rim wear, 15½″ D., 8″ H. plus wooden handle ............................ $55.00

A-OH Jan. 1983 *Garth's Auctions, Inc.*
**NAVAHO RUG,** drk. br., gold & beige on natural ground, wear, 38" x 60" ... $45.00
**VICTORIAN ARCHITECTURAL BRACKET,** used as hanging shelf, old red & wh. repaint, 24" H. .......... $45.00
**FANBACK WINDSOR ARMCHAIR,** ref., 16¼" seat ht. ............. $650.00
**INDIAN POTTERY VASE,** red clay, designs in red & blk., wear, chips, 8¾" H. ................................ $70.00
**COVERED RYE STRAW BASKET,** wear, handles missing, 19½" D., 10" H. ................................. $55.00
**NORTHWEST COAST INDIAN BASKET,** br., orange, yellow & tan, minor wear, 5" D., 4⅜" H. ......... $150.00
**HUTCH TABLE,** maple base, pine seat, pine top, damage, ref., 44" D., 29" H. ................................. $950.00
**SPUN BRASS BUCKET,** 13½" D., 9" H. ................................. $50.00
**SPUN BRASS BUCKET,** stamped label "Hayden's Patent 1851, Manufactured by Waterbury Brass Co.," 11½" D., 7¾" H. ................................. $45.00
**SPUN BRASS BUCKET,** slightly battered, 10" D., 6½" H. ........... $45.00

A-OH Jan. 1983 *Garth's Auctions, Inc.*
**PUNCHED TIN CHANDELIER,** late 19th C., riveted const., 32" ..... $250.00
**PRIMITIVE WATERCOLOR,** red, blue, gr., & yellow, minor stains, framed, 9" x 11" ................................ $400.00

A-OH April 1983 *Garth's Auctions, Inc.*
**HOOKED RAG RUG,** stylized floral design, rich drk. colors, lt. ground, blk. hooked velvet border, 18½" x 36" ................................. $35.00
**ROPE BED,** poplar, ref., minor age cracks, 50½" x 78½", 41½" H. .... $90.00
**SNOW GOOSE,** contemporary stickup field decoy, laminated body, glass eyes, orig. paint, slightly weathered, some separation, 27" L., 22¾" H. ......... $50.00
**CANVASBACK BOBTAIL,** Detroit River area, brass tack eyes, old working repaint, 17" L. ................ $35.00
**MALLARD DRAKE,** working decoy, orig. paint, glass eyes, relief carving, mkd. "D.W.S.," 17½" L. .............. $30.00

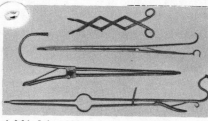

A-MA July 1982 *Richard A. Bourne Co., Inc.*
*Top to Bottom*
**HAND WRT. IRON PIPE TONGS,** 18th C., rusted surface, spring worn, 24½" L. ................................. $300.00
**WRT. IRON TONGS,** 19" L. .. $225.00
**IRON PIPE TONGS,** 19" L. ... $175.00
**EXTENSION PIPE TONGS,** rusted surface, 11¼" L. ................ $75.00

___

**SHAKER LADDERBACK ROCKER,** orig. drk. br. finish, stenciled "Mt Lebannon, N.Y.," replm. .......... $375.00
**SHAKER TIN DIPPER,** some rust, 7½" D., 4½" H. .................... $25.00
**TIN BUCKET,** lid & wire handle, 7½" D., 6" H. ........................ $15.00
**SHAKER SORTING TABLE,** old red repaint, 20¾" x 26", 30⅜" H. ... $1000.00
**ROUND WOVEN SPLINT BASKET,** some wear, 16" D., 10" H. plus Bentwood handle ...................... $85.00
**CARVED WOODEN DECOY,** mallard hen, glass eyes, old paint, 17¾" L. ................................. $105.00

A-OH Jan. 1983 *Garth's Auctions, Inc.*
**HANDCOLORED LITHOGRAPH,** Currier & Ives, "The Old Homestead," old stains & foxing, 17" x 21" ...... $205.00
**BOWBACK WINDSOR ARMCHAIR,** worn old blk. & red grained repaint, repr., seat ht. 16" .................. $1050.00
**TURTLEBACK BELLOWS,** orig. red paint, brass nozzle, some wear, 18¼" L. ................................. $85.00
**OHIO YELLOWWARE DOG,** Rockingham glaze, chips, 10¼" H. ...... $195.00
**HEPPLEWHITE STAND,** cherry, ref., warping, 18½" x 19", 25¾" H. .. $200.00
**SPONGEWARE BOWL & PITCHER SET,** blue & olive gr. on wh., blue bands, handle separation, 11⅝" D., 8½" H. ................................. $324.00

A-OH Jan. 1983 *Garth's Auctions, Inc.*
**REDWARE DOGS ON BASES,** pr., flaking, 8" H. ................. $390.00
**SEATED DOG,** sewer pipe, hand tooling, greenish amber glaze, 11½" H. .. $225.00
**Q.A. HIGH CHEST,** curly maple & pine, replm., 35¾" W., 19⅝" x 39¼" at cornice, 50½" H. .................... $3600.00
**STONEWARE JAR,** impressed "O.L. & A.K. Ballard, Burlington Vt.," minor flaking, 10¾" H. ................... $215.00

A-OH Mar. 1983        *Garth's Auctions, Inc.*
**SINGLE-WEAVE JACQUARD COV-ERLET,** red, yellow, blue, gr. & wh., sgn., some stains, wear & holes, 86" x 90"
.................................... $150.00
**SETTLE BENCH,** pine, paneled base w/lift lid, old but not orig. br. & yellow graining, 54" W., 17½" D., 53½" H.
.................................... $925.00
**STONEWARE PITCHER,** br. Albany slip, rim flakes, 12" H. .......... $25.00
**DOVETAILED BRASS KETTLE,** heavy wrt. iron bail handle, battered, split, repr., 15" D., 11" H. ................. $100.00
**CAST BRONZE RABBIT,** 2 pcs., 11¼" H. ...................................... $50.00

A-OH Sept. 1982        *Garth's Auctions, Inc.*
**HAND-COLORED LITHOGRAPH,** "J. & E. Gould," "Nestor Productus," trimmed & framed, 15¾" W., 21½" H. ..... $45.00
**TAVERN SIGN,** sheet metal of zinc in wooden frame, wrt. iron frame on 3 sides, "Phipps House," sgn. "H. Smith," bird is blk., wh., & br. on wh. sky, base is gold & drk. red, some damage, 39" W., 40½" H.
.................................... $650.00

**HAND-COLORED LITHOGRAPH,** "J. Gould & H. C. Richter," "Nestor Esslingii," trimmed & framed, 15½" W., 21½" H.
.................................... $35.00
**WOODEN HOBBY HORSE,** orig. br. & yellow graining, gr. rockers, leather harness & saddle, branded label "B. P. Crandall, Griland St N.Y.," some damage & replm., 54" L. ............... $725.00

**DAY BED,** maple, spool turnings, fitted as a couch, some wear, 25" W., 60½" L., 23¾" H. .......................... $375.00
**TOY ANIMALS,** stuffed, leatherized cloth bodies, bear, giraffe, kangaroo, camel & polar bear, up to 16" H. ...... $100.00

A-OH Jan. 1983        *Garth's Auctions, Inc.*
*Row I, L to R*
**SHOE W/CAT,** Ohio wh. clay, drk. br. glaze, embossed, 5" L. .......... $30.00
**YELLOWWARE MINIATURE CHAMBER POT,** wh. stripes, 3⅜" D., 2" H.
.................................... $20.00
**BOOT TOOTH PICK,** Ohio wh. clay, drk. br. Albany slip glaze, chips, 3" H.
.................................... $10.00
**MINIATURE BEAN POT,** Rockingham, chips, 2½" H. ................. $17.50
**SHOE,** Ohio wh. clay, orig. paint, embossed, 5" L. ................... $15.00
*Row II, L to R*
**POTTERY BIRD,** br. glaze, embossed, replm., 3⅝" H. ................. $12.50
**MINIATURE YELLOWWARE CHAMBER POT,** br. & wh. stripes, flaking, 2⅝" D., 1⅞" H. ...................... $25.00
**ROCKINGHAM PIG BANK,** embossed "J.A.," 5⅝" L. ................... $30.00
**MINIATURE YELLOWWARE CHAMBER POT,** blue mottled glaze, flaking, 2⅝" D., 1¾" H. ...................... $45.00
**REDWARE LAMB,** wh. & tan glaze, incised "C.E.Ohl 1936," 3½" H. .... $30.00
*Row III, L to R*
**HIGH BUTTON SHOE,** Ohio wh. clay, Albany slip glaze, chips, 6" H. .... $15.00
**INKWELL,** Ohio wh. clay, lion, drk. br. glaze, incised "T.G.W.H. Nov 24, 1868," chips, 5" L. .................... $95.00
**ROCKINGHAM SHOE BOTTLE,** flaking, 4" H. ...................... $25.00
**WHITE CLAY BANK,** child w/sword & rifle, olive gr. glaze, 6¼" H. ...... $25.00

A-OH April 1983        *Garth's Auctions, Inc.*
**SILVER SALVER,** rococo rim w/shell detail & hoof feet, London hallmarks for Henry Morris 1747-8, 6⅞" D. .... $350.00
**SILVER SALVER,** similar to above, London hallmarks for Wm. Peaston 1747-8, 7⅛" D. ..................... $650.00
**SILVER SALVER,** rococo rim w/shell detail & hoof feet, engraved rooster & rampant lion, London hallmarks for John Crouch & Thomas Hannam 1773-4, 9⅜" D.
.................................... $800.00
**SILVER SALVER,** similar to above, engraved diamond-shaped shield, London hallmarks for 1747-8, 11½" D. .. $1550.00
**CHIPPENDALE BLOCK FRONT CHEST OF DRAWERS,** mahogany, repr., orig. brasses & old finish, 32⅝" W., top 21¼" x 36", 29¾" H. ....... $9500.00

A-OH Jan. 1983        *Garth's Auctions, Inc.*
**OIL ON CANVAS,** curly maple veneer frame, gilded liner, repr., 32½" x 37½"
.................................... $750.00
**ROCKINGHAM MIXING BOWL,** minor wear & flaking, 10¼" D., 4¾" H.
.................................... $45.00
**WOVEN SPLINT BASKET,** Bentwood rim handles, some wear, 13¾" x 18"
.................................... $105.00
**ROCKINGHAM MIXING BOWL,** minor wear & flaking, 10¼" D., 4¾" H.
.................................... $45.00
**SHAKER PEMBROKE TABLE,** Hepplewhite, Union Village, OH, replm., 21¼" x 41", 10" leaves, 27" H. ......... $375.00
**WOVEN SPLINT BUSHEL BASKET,** round, Bentwood rim handles, wear, 19" D., 11½" H. .................... $65.00

A-OH Oct. 1982    *Garth's Auctions, Inc.*
**SAWTOOTH TRAMMEL**, wrt. iron, adj., 40½" L. .................... $40.00
**FOLDING SHOREBIRD**, tin, old worn paint, 11½" L., 19½" H. ........ $55.00
**PRIMITIVE CANDLESTAND**, wrt. iron, socket & spring holder, damage, 21" H. ...................... $225.00
**FOLDING SHOREBIRD**, tin, old worn paint, 9½" L., 17" H. ........... $55.00
**WRT. IRON PEAL**, 43" L. ...... $25.00
**REDWARE APPLE BUTTER JAR**, clear glaze, drk. orange color, minor damage, 7⅞" D., 6¼" H. ....... $20.00
**REDWARE APPLE BUTTER JAR**, clear glaze, br. specks, wear & flaking, 7¼" H. ........................ $20.00
**APOTHECARY CASE**, 15 drawers in 3 tiers, pine w/walnut drawer fronts, alter., wh. porcelain knobs, 48" W., 13¼" D., 25" H. ........................ $325.00
**LOW TABLE**, turned legs, top is gridded, old worn blk. paint, damage, 16½" W., 72" L., 18" H. .................... $175.00
**WOVEN SPLINT MARKET BASKET**, bleached finish, some wear, 10" W., 17½" L., 8" H. plus handle ........... $20.00

A-OH Jan. 1983    *Garth's Auctions, Inc.*
**SHAKER APPLE PICKER**, cherry & wrt. iron, old drk. patina, 10½" x 14½" ........................ $65.00
**WOVEN SPLINT BUSHEL BASKET**, Bentwood rim handles, good cond., 18" D., 12" H. plus handles ........... $245.00
**SHAKER TIN DUST PAN**, slightly battered, 8" x 15" ................. $40.00 ←
**SHAKER DRY SINK**, pine, yellow wash over red stain residue, replm., 51" W., 21¼" D., 37" H. .................... $1350.00
**OVOID STONEWARE JAR**, 2-gal., impressed "J. Bennage & J.A. Sutherland Springfield, Portage Co. Ohio," minor flaking, 13¼" H. .................... $65.00
**SHAKER SUGAR BUCKET**, wood w/staves, copper nail const., old drk. gr. paint, 14¼" D., 14" H. ......... $215.00
**OVOID STONEWARE JAR**, 2-gal., impressed "J. Bennage & J.A. Sutherland Springfield, Portage Co. Ohio," minor flaking, 13" H. ................ $135.00

A-OH April 1983    *Garth's Auctions, Inc.*
**WOODEN TRADE SIGN**, orig. blk. paint w/wh. letters "HATS, John P. Dyer," some wear, 11½" x 14¾" ....... $260.00
**WOODEN & SHEET METAL TRADE SIGN**, orig. yellow paint w/red handle & blk. letters "Saw Filling" on both sides, some wear, 45" L. ........... $275.00
**WINDSOR SETTLE BENCH**, replm., stripped of finish, worn gr. stain on base, 75" L. ...................... $1350.00
**CONESTOGA WAGON TOOL BOX LID**, wrt. iron hinges, hasp w/bird head-like detail on hasp, age cracks, traces of old blue, 10½" x 19" ............... $375.00

A-OH Jan. 1983    *Garth's Auctions, Inc.*
**TRIBAL MASK**, carved wood, monkey face, glass eyes, orig. blk., wh. & red paint, 6½" H. ..................... $65.00
**TRIBAL MASK**, carved wood, tiger face, orig. yellow, blk. & wh. paint, 8" H. ................................. $35.00 ←
**OHIO YELLOWWARE TEAPOT**, Rebecca at the well, blue mottled glaze, flaking & wear, 9¼" H. ......... $125.00
**MULE CHEST**, pine & maple, old reddish br. finish, replm., 38¾" W., 18¼" D., 43" H. ............................ $1000.00
**WOVEN SPLINT BASKET**, unusual rim detail, 11" x 14½", 7½" H. ....... $115.00

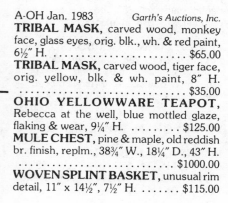

A-OH Jan. 1983    *Garth's Auctions, Inc.*
**APOTHECARY CUPBOARD**, one-piece walnut, reconst., 38" W., 12¾" D., 79¼" H. ...................... $600.00
**STONEWARE OVOID CHURN**, cobalt blue brush work, flakes & pitting, 15½" H. plus wooden dasher ........... $625.00
**STONEWARE CROCK**, turned wooden lid, chip, 8⅜" D., 7½" H. ........ $155.00
**STONEWARE OVOID CHURN**, cobalt, turned wooden lid, chips, 15½" H. .................... $375.00

A-OH July 1982 *Garth's Auctions, Inc.*
**DOUBLE STUDENT LAMP,** brass w/double rods, repl. gr. glass shades cased w/wh., polished, 29″ H. ....... $675.00
**PEWTER SALT & PEPPER SHAKERS,** pr., mkd. "Quaker Shaker Set Reg. 2064," 5⅜″ H. ...................... $35.00
**PEWTER SALT & PEPPER SHAKERS,** similar but not matched set, 4¾″ H. ............................. $60.00
**Q.A. WORK TABLE,** cherry, extensive alterations, ref., 32½″ x 48¼″, 28¼″ H. ................................... $725.00
**FIREPLACE TONGS & SHOVEL,** brass & iron, polished, 31″ L. ... $165.00
**STONEWARE CROCK,** w/brushed cobalt blue decor., both lid & base are stamped "John Bell Waynesboro," base cracked, lid has chips, 8¼″ D., 5″ H. ................................... $550.00
**CHILD'S SLEIGH,** wooden w/iron tipped runners, orig. blue gr. paint w/drk. br. & red & yellow stripping & decor., 32″ L. ................................. $390.00

A-OH July 1982 *Garth's Auctions, Inc.*
**KENTUCKY RIFLE,** curly maple, percussion lock w/engraved brass patch box, octagonal barrel, sgn. "B. Sells," old repr. & minor splits in stock, 34½″ barrel, 50½″ overall ...................... $675.00
**COPPER DOVETAILED SAUCE PAN,** w/wrt. copper handle, 7¾″ D., 9¼″ handle ...................... $100.00
**BURL BOWL,** 12¼″ D., 3¾″ H. ................................... $475.00
**HANGING BOX,** pine, cut out finials & woven splint sides & back, 10¼″ W., 4½″ D., 8½″ H. .................... $200.00
**WOODEN CUTTING BOARD,** w/chip carved edge, old worn br. finish, 13″ D. ................................... $100.00
**DOVETAILED COPPER SAUCE PAN,** w/wrt. copper handle, 8½″ D., 9¼″ handle ...................... $105.00
**BURL BOWL,** w/carved protruding rim, 7½″ D., 2¼″ H. ................. $425.00
**DOVETAILED COPPER SAUCE PAN,** w/wrt. copper handle, 10¼″ D., 10¾″ handle ...................... $115.00
**WOODEN BOWL,** w/hand painted int. landscape sgn. "R. Schulz," back mkd. "View Of The Hudson River," 15″ D., 4″ H. ................................... $85.00
**DOVETAILED COPPER SAUCE PAN,** w/wrt. copper handle, 9″ D., 10¾″ handle ...................... $80.00
**HANGING SHELF,** pine, old drk. alligatored finish & sq. nail construction, 46″ W., 11″ D., 16″ H. ............. $300.00

---

A-OH July 1982 *Garth's Auctions, Inc.*
**BRIDE'S BOX,** pine, oval, orig. blue gr. paint w/red & yellow flowers & foliage decor., name & "1852," box has edge wear & paint is worn in places, 12″ x 18½″ ................................... $400.00
**PENNSYLVANIA CUPBOARD,** 2-pc., poplar w/orig. red paint w/faded blk. graining, pine secondary wood, brass pulls are repl. & one brass "H" hinge moved ½″ from orig. position, 59″ W., 21″ D., 90¼″ H. ................................... $15000.00
**ROCKINGHAM BOWL,** rim & base chips, 13¼″ D., 3¾″ H. .......... $50.00
**ROCKINGHAM BOWL,** base is badly chipped, 11¾″ D., 5½″ H. ........ $35.00
**ROCKINGHAM BOWL,** ribbed ext., 11⅜″ D., 3¾″ H. ................. $65.00

A-OH July 1982 *Garth's Auctions, Inc.*
**APPLIQUE QUILT,** scalloped edge w/swags & rosettes in gr., red & Lemon yellow, feather quilted circle alternate w/9 laurel wreaths in red, gr. & goldenrod w/small dots of pink calico, 81″ x 83″ ...................... $675.00
**WINDSOR SIDE CHAIRS,** set of 3, orig. blk. paint w/worn foliage design on crest, 16½″ seat ht., chairs are very similar but not exact match ................... $330.00

A-OH July 1982 *Garth's Auctions, Inc.*
**OIL ON CANVAS,** 2 masted sailboat w/Am. flag, "Brenton's ReefNoll," rebacked w/minor repr., old gilded frame, 20″ x 26¼″ ...................... $675.00
**BRASS STUDENT LAMP,** sgn. "C. H. Covell, 450 Broadway, N.Y.," double wick burner has an electric socket added, polished, amber ribbed shade cased in wh., 21″ H. ...................... $450.00
**BOWBACK WINDSOR ARM CHAIR,** old worn alligatored br. paint shows blk. beneath, feet are worn down a bit, 16″ seat ht. ......................... $1725.00
**STAND,** 1-drawer, poplar w/turned butternut legs, country decor., worn orig. blk. paint, dovetailed drawer, 21″ sq., 30¼″ H. ................................... $325.00
**GENEVA STONEWARE JAR,** red clay w/salt glaze has tan color, brushed cobalt blue wavy lines & foliage w/"3," hairlines in base, 13¾″ H. ........ $190.00

A-OH July 1982    *Garth's Auctions, Inc.*
**HANDCOLORED LITHO,** "Washington Crossing The Delaware, Evening Previous To The Battle Of Trenton, Dec 25, 1776," birdseye frame, 14¼" x 17¾"
.............................. $90.00

**HANGING CANDLE BOX,** dovtailed hardwood, sliding lid, back board w/fishtail crest is ash or chestnut, old repr. age crack in lid, 18¼" H. ............ $250.00

**BURL BOWL,** w/protruding foot & lip, some wear in base & some old filled repr., 21" D., 8½" H. .............. $1500.00

**CERAMIC BIRD OF PREY,** glass eyes, mkd. "Germany, Fritz Hochendorfer," chips, 18" H. ................ $90.00

**BLANKET CHEST,** pine dovetailed, drawer overlap has repr. & brasses are old replm. & 2 are missing bales, 50¼" W., 22" D., 32" H. ................ $700.00

A-OH July 1982    *Garth's Auctions, Inc.*
**WOODEN SWIFT,** minor damage & ends of staves need retied, threads are worn on table clamp thumb screw, 18½" L.
.............................. $35.00

**WOVEN SPLINT HALF BUTTOCKS BASKET,** w/wooden handle, old drk. color, has wear, 10" W. ........ $85.00

**WOVEN SPLINT HALF BUTTOCKS BASKET,** w/wooden handle, some wear, 9" W. ........................ $130.00

**LADDER-BACK SIDE CHAIR,** old olive gr. repaint shows blk. beneath .... $25.00

**DECOR. BOX,** w/sliding lid, orig. blue paint & red decor. detail & initials "L.B.D.," 11¾" L. ........................ $185.00

**HEPPLEWHITE TAVERN TABLE,** walnut, old worn scrubbed finish, orig. bale, brace added to underside of top, 20" x 31¾", 29" H. .................. $475.00

**STONEWARE JAR,** 2 gal., mottled br., 12½" H. ........................ $25.00

**WINDSOR FOOT STOOL,** oval top, bamboo turnings, several layers of old gr. paint, 10½" x 13", 10½" H. ....... $45.00

**CARVED CONTEM. DECOY,** Bluebill drake, branded "DWH," 14¼" L.
.............................. $25.00

A-OH July 1982    *Garth's Auctions, Inc.*
**SHAKER WALL CUPBOARD,** 1 pc., poplar w/orig. old red paint, wide single board ends have cut out arches resulting in high feet, 35" W., 18½" D., 74" H.
.............................. $1000.00

**CHERRY KRAUT CUTTER,** w/applied molded edge & rounded hanging crest, 7⅝" x 19" ........................ $25.00

**OVOID STONEWARE JUG,** mkd. "T.D. Chollak, Cortland," brushed cobalt blue 3 & foliage design, 15½" H.
.............................. $105.00

**STONEWARE JUG,** Canadian, small chips on base, 11¾" H. ..... $35.00
**CHURN,** w/iron bands, 31" H.
.............................. $150.00

A-OH July 1982    *Garth's Auctions, Inc.*
**WOODEN PEAL,** poplar, old splits in blade, 70" L. .............. $27.50
**WOVEN SPLINT BASKET,** Woodlands Indian orig., has wear, 13" x 16½"
.............................. $17.50
**WORK TABLE,** walnut, wide overlap on drawer front has some edge damage, minor splits in top & in one back leg, 40" x 71¾", 30" H. .............. $550.00
**DOUGH BOX,** pine, ref., 17" x 24", 14½" H. .............. $100.00
**CARVED WOODEN DECOY,** canvasback drake from Saginaw Bay, MI, 16" L. .............. $20.00
**CARVED WOODEN DECOY,** canvasback hen from Saginaw Bay, MI, 16¼" L. .............. $20.00

A-OH July 1982    *Garth's Auctions, Inc.*
**BRASS DIPPER,** w/wrt. iron handle, brass has drk. patina, 20" L. ..... $65.00
**WRT. IRON SKIMMER,** 18½" L.
.............................. $30.00
**WAG ON WALL CLOCK,** brass works w/wooden plates & painted wooden face w/weights & pendulum, 12¼" x 17½"
.............................. $300.00
**TOLE DEED BOX,** orig. br. Japanning w/floral decor. in red, yellow & gr., paint has wear & a few small pierced holes in bottom, 9¼" L. .............. $125.00
**LADDERBACK ARMCHAIR,** cherry, hickory & maple, ref. & new woven splint seat, top slat is inc. .............. $75.00
**TAVERN TABLE,** pine, old drk. red paint is partially removed, Irish, 19" D., 30½" H.
.............................. $255.00

A-OH Oct. 1982          *Garth's Auctions, Inc.*
**HANGING SHELVES,** Eng., mahogany, scrolled ends, 2 dovetailed drawers, replm., repr., old finish, 18″ W., 6¼″ D., 28″ H. . . . . . . . . . . . . . . . . . . . . . . . . . . . . . . $200.00
**SEWER TILE,** 20th C., hand-molded cat on oval base, chip, 4¼″ L. . . . . . . $155.00
**HAND-CARVED PIPE,** primitive Indian chief design, glass eyes, blk. & gold paint w/natural pine, 6″ H., 17½″ L. . . . . . $5.00
**LIGNUM VITAE TURNED BOX,** age cracks & chips, 4″ H. . . . . . . . . . . . $20.00
**TURNED WOODEN CHALICE,** 4½″ H. . . . . . . . . . . . . . . . . . . . . . . . . . . . . . $2.00
**TREEN SANDER,** minor flaking, 3¼″ H. . . . . . . . . . . . . . . . . . . . . . . . . . . $17.50
**TREEN PIPE TAMP,** brass head, 3¼″ H. . . . . . . . . . . . . . . . . . . . . . . . . . . . $15.00
**TREEN SANDER,** worn orig. yellow varnish, 3⅜″ H. . . . . . . . . . . . . . . $55.00
**TREEN CHALICE,** chips, 5″ H. . . . . . . . . . . . . . . . . . . . . . . . . . . . . . . . $10.00
**EBONY MATCHBOX,** ("going to bed lamp"), turned ivory taper socket, smaller hole socket for matches, 4¼″ H. . . . . $10.00
matches, 4¼″ H. . . . . . . . . . . . . . . . $10.00

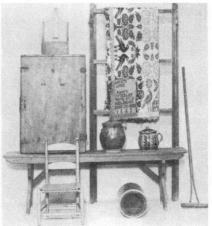

A-OH Jan. 1983          *Garth's Auctions, Inc.*
**SCOURING BOX,** poplar, wire nail const., old red paint, 9¼″ W., 4¼″ D., 17¾″ H. . . . . . . . . . . . . . . . . . . . . . . . . . . . $165.00
**MORTISED DRYING RACK,** pine, 3 sections, old br. patina, attrib. to Shakers, 30″ x 72″ . . . . . . . . . . . . . . . . . . . . . $105.00
**TWO-PIECE JACQUARD COVERLET,** blue, red & wh., "Louicy Long, Fancy Coverlet Wove by J. Heilbronn Ross Co, Ohio 1842," very worn, 72″ x 82″ . . . . . . . . . . . . . . . . . . . . . . . . . . . . . . $200.00
**SHAKER CUPBOARD,** pine, int. shelves, ref., split, 21″ W., 9½″ D., 33½″ H. . . . . . . . . . . . . . . . . . . . . . . . . . . . $375.00
**SHAKER HERB RAKE,** Union Village, 49½″ L. . . . . . . . . . . . . . . . . . . . . . $110.00
**REDWARE OVOID JAR,** chips, 11½″ H. . . . . . . . . . . . . . . . . . . . . . . . . . . $250.00
**REDWARE JAR,** chips & cracks, rim spout, 8¼″ H. . . . . . . . . . . . . . . . $150.00
**SHAKER CHILD-SIZE LADDER-BACK CHAIR,** ref., replm., Mt. Lebanon, 25½″ H. . . . . . . . . . . . . . . . . . $220.00
**BENCH,** pine, worn & weathered old gr. paint, 10¼″ x 60½″, 19¾″ H. . . . . . $225.00
**STONEWARE CHICKEN FOUNTAIN,** olive br. glaze, embossed "Manf'd by --- & Co Akron, O.," 9″ D., 9¾″ L. . . . . $35.00

---

A-OH Jan. 1983          *Garth's Auctions, Inc.*
**TIN HEART MOLD,** 9 sections, 9⅞″ x 11″ . . . . . . . . . . . . . . . . . . . . . . . . . . . $135.00
**HANGING CUPBOARD,** Shaker, chestnut, fitted for tools, modern red stain, 39¼″ W., 11″ D., 51″ H. . . . . . . . . $150.00
**SHAKER WOODEN SAW FRAME,** missing parts, 37″ L. . . . . . . . . . . . . $45.00
**SHAKER LADDERBACK CHAIR,** ref., replm. . . . . . . . . . . . . . . . . . . . . . . . $135.00
**OHIO POTTERY ROOF TILE,** chips, 6″ x 15″ . . . . . . . . . . . . . . . . . . . . . . . $25.00
**SUGAR BUCKET,** stave const., attrib. to Shakers, old red paint, 14″ D., 14″ L. . . . . . . . . . . . . . . . . . . . . . . . . . . . . . $45.00
**SHAKER BUCKET,** wooden w/sheet metal, 9″ D., 7″ H. . . . . . . . . . . . $75.00
**SHAKER BENTWOOD MEASURE,** turned handle, damage, 7″ D., 7″ handle . . . . . . . . . . . . . . . . . . . . . . . . . . . . . $45.00

A-OH Jan. 1983          *Garth's Auctions, Inc.*
**CHILD-LIKE WATERCOLOR,** German inscription, 11¾″ x 14½″ . . . . $185.00
**SHAKER ARMCHAIR ROCKER,** ref., new seat . . . . . . . . . . . . . . . . . . . . . $375.00
**WOVEN SPLINT BASKET,** old breaks, 12″ x 16″, 5″ H. . . . . . . . . . . . . . . . $65.00
**SHAKER WASHSTAND,** pine & poplar, ref., 20¼″ W., 17¾″ D., 29″ H. plus gallery . . . . . . . . . . . . . . . . . . . . . . . . . . $275.00
**SHAKER SEWING BOX,** inlaid wood lid, 3¾″ x 7⅞″ x 11″ . . . . . . . . . . . . . . . $55.00

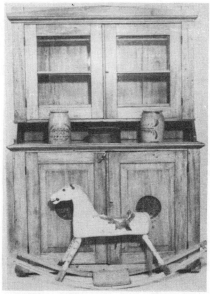

A-OH Feb. 1983          *Garth's Auctions, Inc.*
**WALL CUPBOARD,** 2 pcs., poplar & hardwood, 3 dovetailed drawers in top, alter. & additions, ref., 54″ W., 23″ D., 78″ H. . . . . . . . . . . . . . . . . . . . . . . . . . . $400.00
**STONEWARE PRESERVING JAR,** cobalt stenciled label "Williams & Reppert Greensboro, Pa.," 10″ H. . . . . . . . . $85.00
**STONEWARE PRESERVING JAR,** brushed cobalt foliage design & stripes, 9½″ H. . . . . . . . . . . . . . . . . . . . . . . . $85.00
**TURNED BOX,** poplar, age cracks in lid & base, old drk. ref., 10″ D., 4¾″ H. . . . . . . . . . . . . . . . . . . . . . . . . . . . . $45.00
**WOODEN HOBBY HORSE,** worn orig. dapple gray paint, harness & saddle partly missing, 54″ L. . . . . . . . . . . . . . . . $445.00

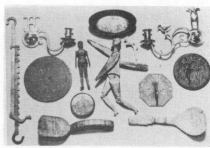

A-OH April 1983     *Garth's Auctions, Inc.*
**SAWTOOTH TRAMMEL,** brass, bird's head detail, adj. from 18″ L. ..... $150.00
**WALL SCONCE,** brass, polished & lacquered, extends 8¼″, 5½″ H.
.......................... $100.00
**TOLE TRAY,** orig. br. Japanning, floral decor., red, gr., yellow & wh., worn, 4″ x 7″, 1¾″ H. ....................... $145.00

**WALL SCONCE,** brass, bird on arm, polished & lacquered, extends 9½″, 6¼″ H.
.......................... $185.00
**WOODEN TOY,** jointed, some wear, 7¼″ H. ............................... $125.00
**WOODEN DANCING MAN,** jointed, primitive detail, worn patina, 12″ H.
.......................... $150.00

**CLAY PIPE,** wh. & blk. glazed cat on bowl, cast initials "D.G. and 1334," 3½″ L.
.......................... $20.00
**CARVED SUN DIAL,** primitive, slate, "John Neafsy 1845," chips, broken & glued, 7″ D. .................. $50.00
**COOKIE BOARD,** cast iron, eagle w/shield, 5½″ D. .............. $200.00

**SNUFF BOX,** papier mache, old blk. paint, decoupage blk. & yellow engraving of man in Dutch attire on lid, 3⅜″ D.
.......................... $45.00
**SMALL SUN DIAL,** cast bronze, engraved Roman numerals, octagonal, 5¼″
.......................... $85.00
**SCOOP,** curly maple, 10½″ L. ... $85.00
**BUTTER PADDLE,** curly maple, worn, cracks, 10¾″ L. ................ $65.00

A-OH July 1982     *Garth's Auctions, Inc.*
**SHAKER BENTWOOD MEASURE,** turned handle, old ref. w/traces of gr. on handle, Hancock, 7¼″ D., 7¼″ handle
.......................... $150.00
**SHAKER SIEVE,** oval, finger const., lid on each end, orig. woven horsehair, sm. holes, mellow finish, 9¼″ H., 12″ W.
.......................... $575.00
**SEWING BOX,** walnut, maple & cherry, w/drawer, old varnish finish, 5¼″ H., 7″ W.
.......................... $60.00
**PIE SAFE,** poplar, 12 tin panels w/ punched pinwheels, one drawer, old red repaint, 41¼″ W., 16½″ D., 55½″ H.
.......................... $450.00
**SHAKER REEL,** cherry hub & maple spokes, holder missing, 20″ D. ... $45.00
**DOUGH BOX,** poplar, worn orig. blue paint w/some red trim on lid, damage to one handle, 12″ W., 23½″ L. .... $115.00

A-OH April 1983     *Garth's Auctions, Inc.*
**GRAIN SHOVEL,** all wooden, minor age cracks, 46″ L. ................... $70.00
**AMISH CHILD'S DRESS, CAP & BONNET,** dress & bonnet are wool, cape is navy flannel, 29″ L. .......... $45.00
**CHESTNUT ROASTER OR BED WARMER,** wrt. iron & brass, some damage, 10″ D., 24″ handle ...... $60.00
**YARN WINDER,** maple & oak, geared counting mechanism w/click, ref., 29½″ D., 34″ H. ........................ $80.00
**BLUEBILL,** worn old paint, combed back, tack eyes, some damage, mkd. "J.W.," 13″ L. ....................... $25.00
**COMMODE,** cherry, ref., 13½″ x 15″, 15¼″ H. ....................... $7.50
**BLACK DUCK,** primitive, relief carving, brass tack eyes, old worn paint, age cracks, 13½″ L. ....................... $25.00

A-OH Oct. 1982     *Garth's Auctions, Inc.*
**BANISTER-BACK SIDE CHAIR,** ref., split ......................... $850.00
**STILL LIFE DRAWING,** pastel on paper, pine frame, 18¾″ x 20¼″ ... $75.00
**TOLE COFFEE POT,** orig. drk. br. japanning, foliage in red, wh., yellow & drk. br., minor wear, 8½″ H. ....... $1300.00
**TOLE COFFEE POT,** orig. drk. br. japanning, foliage in red, wh., yellow & drk. gr., minor wear, 8⅝″ H. .......... $1300.00
**TAVERN TABLE,** oval top, splayed maple base, top & apron in pine, ref., repr., 21½″ x 30″, 25″ H. ............ $2050.00

A-OH Feb. 1983     *Garth's Auctions, Inc.*
**HANDCOLORED ENGRAVING,** "Washington from Arlington Heights," published by Appleton in 1872, old walnut frame, 12½″ x 16½″ ............. $17.50
**HANDCOLORED ENGRAVING,** "City of Louisville," published by Appleton in 1872, old beveled frame, 12½″ x 16½″
.......................... $15.00

**BUTTERNUT BOX,** lift lid, ash drawer, porcelain knobs, sq. nail construction, ref., 14″ W., 8½″ D., 12″ H. .......... $85.00
**HUTCH TABLE,** poplar, replm., top is scarred & cracked, repr., drk. red repaint, 32½″ x 64½″, 27¾″ H. .......... $375.00

**MODEL AIRPLANE,** wood & tin, W.W. I biplane, sgn. "R. G. Mullin," orig. olive drab paint, red, wh. & blue emblems, "Look out Red Baron!" 24″ L. ............. $55.00
**BIPLANE MODE,** wood & wire, unsgn., old varnished finish, 21½″ L. ..... $70.00

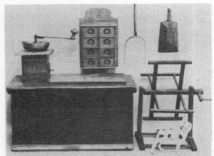

A-OH July 1982     *Garth's Auctions, Inc.*
**HANGING SPICE CUPBOARD,** 8 drawers, ash, flush turned knobs, wire nail const., ref., 11" W., 17½" H., 5" D. ............................ $120.00
**SHAKER PIE LIFTER,** wooden handle, 18" L. ........................ $30.00
**BEECH SCOOP,** Am., one piece of wood, 13" L. ................... $35.00
**COFFEE GRINDER,** brass hopper w/wrt. iron crank, dovetailed drawer, worn old finish, damaged edge, 12¼" D., 28½" W., 12" H. ................... $200.00
**BLANKET CHEST,** pine, dovetailed, orig. wrt. iron end handles, strap hinges replm., old red paint has some wear, 17" D., 33" L., 18" H. ................. $95.00
**HARDWOOD REEL,** mortised & pinned const. w/shoe feet, portion of handle repl., 19" D. wheel, 17" H. frame ....... $35.00
**DOOR STOP,** cast iron, Boston bull, old blk. & wh. repaint, 10" H. ....... $35.00

A-OH April 1983     *Garth's Auctions, Inc.*
**TOLE TRAY,** marbelized int., wh. band w/red & gr. fruit & foliage, 6⅞" x 11¾", 3" H. ............................ $55.00
**TOLE DOME-TOP DEED BOX,** orig. drk. br. Japanning, polychrome floral decor. in red, gr., yellow, wh. & blk., worn, brass hasp replm., orig. brass bail handle, 9½" L. ....................... $175.00
**TOLE DOME-TOP DEED BOX,** orig. drk. br. Japanning, floral & foliage decor. in yellow, red, gr. & blk., worn, ring handle missing, hasp replm., 9" L. ...... $135.00
**BLANKET CHEST,** pine, orig. br. vinegar painting on yellow ground, 4 pigeon holes in int., one backboard missing, 44" W., 19" D., 42" H. ............ $8000.00

A-OH Mar. 1983     *Garth's Auctions, Inc.*
**WALL CUPBOARD,** poplar, 2 pcs., int. shelf has cutouts for spoons, ref., int. painted wh., repr., replm., 48" W., 17½" D., 80¾" H. ....................... $990.00
**WASH BASIN,** Eng., pewter, mkd. "Townsend" & "London," 13⅛" D., 3½" H. ............................ $175.00
**BALUSTER MEASURE,** Eng., pewter, mkd. "½ Pint," slightly battered, 3⅝" H. ............................ $40.00
**SMALL CAST IRON GATE,** 30" W., 20" H. ............................ $55.00

A-OH Mar. 1983     *Garth's Auctions, Inc.*
**HOOKED RAG RUG,** colorful semicircle w/cat & kitten, flowers & "Welcome," 27" x 40" ........................ $510.00
**BENTWOOD STORAGE BOXES,** 3, nailed seams, splits & cracks, 6", 6¼" & 6½" D. ............................ $37.50
**BLANKET CHEST,** pine, replm., orig. reddish-br. sponge graining over a yellow ground, blk. feet, 48¾" W., 21¾" D., 27¾" H. ............................ $850.00

A-OH Mar. 1983     *Garth's Auctions, Inc.*
**FANBACK WINDSOR SIDE CHAIR,** modern gray-gr. repaint, sm. breaks, 18⅛" H. ............................ $450.00
**WATERCOLOR THEOREM,** fruit & vintage in basket, old blk. painted frame, 17¾" x 21¾" ................... $1325.00
**CANDLESTICK,** early brass, pushup, slightly battered, damaged, 6½" H. ............................ $65.00
**CANDLESTICK,** brass, 19th C., screw-off base, 9" H. ................. $75.00
**Q.A. TAVERN TABLE,** maple, old split on top, worn red paint on base, varnished finish on top, 23¼" x 28¾", 23½" H. ............................ $1500.00
**RYE STRAW BASKET,** some wear, 12" D., 8" H. ..................... $35.00

A-OH Feb. 1983     *Garth's Auctions, Inc.*
**HANDCOLORED LITHOGRAPH,** by "Kellogg & Thayer," "Hyde Park, Hudson River," tear, framed, 16½" x 21¼" ............................ $45.00
**HANDCOLORED LITHOGRAPH,** by "Currier & Ives," "Sunnyside, on the Hudson, presented by Dr. S. Vanmeter & Co. of Charleston, Illinois Infirmary," framed, 16¼" x 20¼" ........... $85.00
**STUDENT LAMP,** brass, sgn. "Miller's Ideal No 2 Burner, Made in U.S.A.," electrified, old gr. ribbed shade cased in wh., sm. flakes, 19¾" H. ........ $325.00
**HALF SPINDLE-BACK SIDE CHAIRS,** pr., bamboo turnings & plank seats, finish removed, split in crest on one ............................ $90.00
**VICTORIAN STAND,** walnut, ref., 19½" D., 30½" H. ..................... $65.00

A-OH Jan. 1983        *Garth's Auctions, Inc.*

**HANGING SHELVES,** cherry, N. Eng., 18th C., restor., old finish, 29¼″ W., 8″ D., 42¼″ H. ...................... $755.00

**FOLK ART CARVING,** fish on a panel, 6¾″ x 17″ ...................... $285.00

**WOVEN SPLINT BASKET,** lid, some wear, 4½″ x 4½″, 4″ H. plus handle ................................ $60.00

**TIN CHAMBERSTICK,** wrt. iron push up, no handle, 3¾″ H. ........... $50.00

**IRON HOG SCRAPER CANDLE-STICK,** push up & lip hanger, 6¼″ H. ................................ $95.00

**TIN BUCKET,** wire handles, 5″ D., 4″ H. ................................ $12.50

**TIN HOG SCRAPER CANDLESTICK,** push up mkd. "Ryton & Walton," 7″ H. ................................ $85.00

**IRON HOG SCRAPER CANDLE-STICK,** worn tin plating, brass ring, parts missing, 8⅛″ H. ............... $125.00

**ROUND WOVEN SPLINT BASKET,** minor wear, 10″ D., 4½″ H. plus handle ................................ $135.00

**TIN BETTY LAMP,** double burners, open font, 6½″ H. ............... $75.00

---

A-OH July 1982        *Garth's Auctions, Inc.*

**Q.A. SCROLL MIRROR,** Eng., mahogany on pine w/gilded liner, repr., old finish, 14¼″ W., 24″ H. ............... $375.00

**PEWTER PLATE,** Eng., touchmarks "Burford & Green," & "London," back engraved "M.D.," surface wear & scratches, 8¾″ D. ................... $95.00

**PEWTER PLATE,** Eng., touchmarks for "---Townsend & Thomas Griffin," 7⅝″ D. ................................ $40.00

**SLANT-TOP DESK,** walnut, fitted int. w/10 dovetailed drawers, extensive alter., 39¾″ W., 21¼″ D., 43″ H., 32¼″ writing ht. ................................ $1050.00

**PEWTER CHARGER,** Am., unmkd., worn surface, repr., 15″ D. ..... $125.00

A-OH Oct. 1982        *Garth's Auctions, Inc.*

**HOOKED RAG RUG,** 2 racing horses in gray, blk., gr., br., yellow & lavender, made by Sarah Esh, Lancaster Co., PA, ca. 1930-35, some wear, 1′10″ x 3′4″ ..... $325.00

**LADDERBACK ARMCHAIR ROCKER,** 4-slat back, ref. ........... $30.00

**BUTTER WORKING TABLE,** soft & hardwoods, mortised base, ref., 20″ W., 29″ D., 29″ H. ................... $85.00

**CHILD'S DRUM,** brass-colored tin, litho. on paper scene of Am. soldiers, 11″ D. ................................ $155.00

**HANGING BOX,** pine, 3 nailed drawers, slanted top compartment, replm., 5¼″ x 5½″, 12½″ H. ................... $45.00

A-OH April 1983        *Garth's Auctions, Inc.*

**Q.A. STYLE CHILD-SIZE HIGHBOY,** walnut, 8 dovetailed drawers, engraved brasses, 28½″ W., 17¾″ D., 56″ H. ............................ $3050.00

**DOVETAILED BOX,** pine & poplar, domed lid, orig. br. flame graining, brass bail handle, minor wear, 12″ L. .. $425.00

A-OH July 1982        *Garth's Auctions, Inc.*

**PINE & POPLAR WARDROBE,** int. has shelves & open area for garments, yellow & br. graining, minor damage, 64¼″ W., 23″ D., 84″ H. ................... $300.00

**SHAKER CHEESE DRAINER,** 25½″ D., 8¼″ H. ...................... $45.00

A-OH Jan. 1983        *Garth's Auctions, Inc.*
**Q.A. HIGHBOY,** maple & pine, ref. in br. color, replm., 35¾" W., 19¼" x 39¼" at cornice, 75¼" H. . . . . . . . . . . . . $9500.00
**KNIFE BLADE ANDIRONS,** pr., wrt. iron, penny feet, brass ball finials, 15¾" H. . . . . . . . . . . . . . . . . . . . . . . . . . . $185.00
**BAND BOX,** wallpaper-covered cardboard, minor wear, 14¾" x 18¼", 11½" H. . . . . . . . . . . . . . . . . . . . . . . . . . . $325.00

A-OH Jan. 1983        *Garth's Auctions, Inc.*
**SHAKER YARN REEL,** old br. patina, 25½" D., 46" H. . . . . . . . . . . . . . . $130.00
**SHAKER CARPET BEATER,** reglued break, 41½" L. . . . . . . . . . . . . . . . $75.00
**TOWEL RACK,** walnut, reglued, worn old finish, 25" W., 27½" H. . . . . . $275.00
**CAST IRON MORTAR & PESTLE,** 6¾" H. . . . . . . . . . . . . . . . . . . . . . . . . . $55.00
**FOOT STOOL,** pine, primitive, several layers of paint, 6⅞" x 13", 6¾" H. . . . . . . . . . . . . . . . . . . . . . . . . . . $75.00

A-OH Mar. 1983        *Garth's Auctions, Inc.*
**STONEWARE PRESERVING JAR,** mkd. "Rich," sm. flake on lip, 10½" H. . . . . . . . . . . . . . . . . . . . . . . . . . . $35.00
**OVOID STONEWARE JUG,** hairline in base of handle, 8¼" H. . . . . . . . . $30.00

**WOVEN SPLINT BASKET,** all wooden swivel handle, worn finish, slightly misshapen, 17½" D., 10½" H. . . . $135.00
**STONEWARE PRESERVING JAR,** cobalt stenciled label "A.P. Donaghho, Parkersburg, W. Va.," 8¼" H. . . . . $45.00

**OVOID STONEWARE JUG,** splash of blue at handle, wear & surface chips, 10¾" H. . . . . . . . . . . . . . . . . . . . . . . . $70.00
**APOTHECARY CHEST,** pine, some damage, repr., additions & replm., ref., 49" W., 13" D., 59" H. . . . . . . . . . . . . $850.00

**STONEWARE CHURN,** 6-gal., "6" & flourish in cobalt quillwork, turned wooden lid, no dasher, 17½" H. . . . . . . . . $65.00
**STONEWARE JUG,** "3" & primitive flower in cobalt, sm. flakes, 14" H. . . . . . . . . . . . . . . . . . . . . . . . . . . $85.00
**OVOID STONEWARE JAR,** 18¼" H. . . . . . . . . . . . . . . . . . . . . . . . . . . $55.00

A-OH Oct. 1982        *Garth's Auctions, Inc.*
**LITHOGRAPH,** blk. & wh., "L. Kurz, Chicago," "Mr. Lincoln. Residence and Horse," minor stains, shadowbox frame, gilded liner, 22½" x 27¾" . . . . . . . $160.00

**ROPE BED,** curly maple, turned post, bold urn finials, turned blanket bar, poplar headboard, old worn shellac, orig. side rails, 53" x 77½", 59" H. . . . . . . . $650.00

**CHILD'S SLEIGH,** wooden top, iron runners, wooden tongue, worn orig. red & gr. paint, worn paper label, 20" W., 43" L. . . . . . . . . . . . . . . . . . . . . . . . . . . $95.00

A-OH Oct. 1982        *Garth's Auctions, Inc.*
**HOOKED RAG RUG,** oval, 2 scotties, red ball, some wear, 24" W., 40" L. . . . . . . . . . . . . . . . . . . . . . . . . . . $85.00

**BALLOON-BACK SIDE CHAIRS,** set of 6 (1 illus.), stenciled flower & fruit on splat & crest, orig. br. paint, yellow & wh. striping, repr. on 4, some wear & fading . . . . . . . . . . . . . . . . . . . . . . . . . . $650.00

**DOME-TOP TOLE DEED BOX,** worn orig. blk. paint, red & yellow floral decor., some damage, 10" L. . . . . . . . . . . $15.00

**BED-SIDE STAND,** cherry, turned maple legs, dovetailed drawer, repr., ref., 17" D., 19¼" W., 27¼" H. . . . . . . . $105.00

**PUNCHED TIN FOOT WARMER,** wooden frame, turned posts, old red finish, repr., pan for coals, 8¼" D., 10¾" W., 8" H. . . . . . . . . . . . . . . . . . . . . . . . . . . $65.00

A-OH Jan. 1983          *Garth's Auctions, Inc.*
**JACQUARD COVERLET,** double weave, mkd. "Pyna Rose, Wove in Logan Co, Ohio by I. M. 1849," minor stains & wear, 37" x 85" ............... $85.00
**SAMPLER,** "A. D. 1835, John S. Mershon was born June 21, 1788, Abigale Mershon was born Dec 8, 1795, Ellen Scudder Mershon W. B. July 28, 1825, Ralph S. Mershon was bo. Feb 13, 1830," name of maker "Ellen S. Mershon, P. A. W.," pink, blue, 2 shades of gr., br., rust & wh., unframed, 17" x 17½" .......... $750.00

**SHAKER LADDERBACK CHAIR,** replm. ...................... $95.00
**STONEWARE BUTTER CROCK,** chips, 10" D., 5½" H. .......... $200.00
**CORNER WOOD BOX,** poplar, hinged lid, attrib. to Shakers, worn old gray repaint, 22" W., 21" D., 24¾" H. ........................... $180.00
**SEWER TILE PITCHER,** ca. 1911-15, impressed "½ G," 8¼" H. ........ $35.00

A-WA D.C. Sept. 1982 *Adam A. Weschler & Son*
*Left*
**GEORGE III CANTERBURY,** ca. 1800, mahogany, 4 compartments, caster feet, 19" W., 14" D., 20" H. ......... $800.00*

*Right*
**GEORGE III CANTERBURY,** ca. 1800, mahogany, 4 banister slats, caster feet, stretcher shelf, 16½" W., 13½" D., 19" H. ........................... $600.00*

A-OH Oct. 1982          *Garth's Auctions, Inc.*
**HAT BOX,** wallpaper-covered cardboard, mkd. "The Glad Tidings," & "Pittsburgh, September 24, 1836," wear, 13¾" x 15½", 9¼" H. ...................... $215.00

**TWO-PIECE WALL CUPBOARD,** old marriage, dovetailed cherry base, walnut top, top rebuilt, old red repaint, 57½" W., 18¾" D., 81¾" H. ............ $1200.00

**WOODEN HOBBY HORSE,** laminated const., worn orig. blk. paint, mane is missing, rocking frame missing, 30" L. ........................... $200.00

_____

A-OH Oct. 1982          *Garth's Auctions, Inc.*
**PENNSYLVANIA GERMAN VORS-CHRIFT,** pen, ink, & watercolor, sgn. "Elias Friedt 1814," framed, 15" x 19" ........................... $1500.00

**PAUL REVERE-TYPE LANTERN,** punched tin, Masonic design, hasp missing, slightly battered & damaged, 15" H. plus handle ...................... $450.00

**PEWTER CANDLESTICK,** push up, unmkd., 8" H. ............... $175.00

**PEWTER BASIN,** Am., scratches, repr., unmkd., 5¾" D., 1¾" H. ........ $95.00

**ARROWBACK ARMCHAIR,** worn orig. decor. ...................... $275.00

**COUNTRY SHERATON STAND,** birch, ref., replm., 16¾" x 20¾", 28" H. ........................... $390.00

**STONEWARE CHURN,** 2-gal., cobalt flower, flaking, 17" H. ......... $145.00

**PEWTER BASIN,** Am., minor repr., 8" D., 2" H. ..................... $95.00

A-OH Jan. 1983          *Garth's Auctions, Inc.*
*Row I, L to R*
**SHOOTING GALLERY BIRD ON BASE,** cast iron, old worn wh. paint, 4¼" H. ............... $47.50

**CAST LEAD DOORSTOP,** old red & gr. repaint, 5½" H. ............ $30.00

**CARVED WOODEN SEAGULL,** on piling, chip, 2¾" H. ........... $35.00

**CAST IRON NUTCRACKER,** wooden handle, mkd. "Easy Cracker, Sapulpa, Okla.," old worn blue paint, 4½" H. ........................... $32.50

**CAST IRON PRANCING HORSE,** on base, wh., blk. & red paint, 5¼" H. ........................... $110.00

*Row II, L to R*
**WOVEN SPLINT BASKET,** mkd. in pencil "Mar. 1890," 3½" D., 2½" H. plus handle ...................... $125.00

**BISQUE KITTEN,** orig. paint, 4" H. ........................... $25.00

**TREEN BOX,** old worn varnish, 1¾" H. ........................... $75.00

**OVAL SHAKER BOX,** finger constr., old worn flame graining, 3¼" x 4¼" .. $295.00

**POT W/LID,** Ohio wh. clay, tan glaze, 3¼" H. ........................... $7.50

**FOLDING BURL CASE,** 4-part, completely wood (maple burl & birdseye), 3¼" x 3½" ........................... $200.00

A-OH Feb. 1983          *Garth's Auctions, Inc.*
*Row I, L to R*
**TREEN FOOTED JAR W/LID,** made by Pease, 5¼″ H. . . . . . . . . . . . . . . . . $115.00

**INKWELL,** turned wooden, glass insert & cork stopper, some wear on orig. staining, gold stenciling, red wool bottom label "Manufactured by S. Silliman & Co. Chester, Conn.," 4½″ D., 2¾″ H. . . . . . . . . . . . . . . . . . . . . . . . . . . . $85.00

**PINE BOX,** worn old br. paint, int. lined w/oil cloth & pastor's work sheet dated 1885, Hasp Inc., 3¼″ x 5″ x 8¼″ . . . $65.00

**INKWELL,** turned wooden, same as above but w/old refinishing, 4⅜″ D., 2½″ H. . . . . . . . . . . . . . . . . . . . . . . . . . . . $50.00

**TURNED TREEN JARS,** (1 illus.), one w/worn yellow varnish, one w/laminated walnut & maple, each 3⅜″ H. . . . . $45.00

*Row II, L to R*
**TOLE,** 2 pcs., both have worn br. Japanning, syruper 6½″ H., sugar bowl 3¾″ H. . . . . . . . . . . . . . . . . . . . . . . . . . . . $35.00

**BUTTER PADDLE,** maple, stylized bird head handle, good color, 6¼″ L. . . . . . . . . . . . . . . . . . . . . . . . . . . . $342.50

**CHEST OF DRAWERS,** miniature, primitively const., worn orig. wallpaper covering replm., wooden cigar box bottom is mkd. in pencil "Yoder's Board," 5¼″ x 7¼″ x 10½″ . . . . . . . . . . . . . . . . . . . . . $35.00

**RUSH LIGHT HOLDER,** primitive wrt. iron, candle socket counterbalance, old wooden base has age cracks & insect damage, 9¾″ H. . . . . . . . . . . . . . . . $155.00

**HEXAGONAL TOBACCO JAR,** quarter sawed soft wood w/applied moldings, whittled handle on lid, old br. alligatored varnish, 7″ H. . . . . . . . . . . . . . . . . . $50.00

A-OH July 1982          *Garth's Auctions, Inc.*
**WOODEN CANDLESTAND,** late 19th C., sq. base, turned finial, adj. wooden arm, 64¼″ H. . . . . . . . . . . . . . . . . . . . . . $150.00
**WOVEN SPLINT BASKET,** round, lid, faded blue & orange, Woodland Indian origin, minor wear, 18″ D., 11½″ H. . . . . . . . . . . . . . . . . . . . . . . . . . . . $95.00
**YELLOWWARE PITCHER,** fluted sides, gr. & br. sponging, 5½″ H. . . . . . . . . . . . . . . . . . . . . . . . . . . . $50.00
**YELLOWWARE PITCHER,** embossed label "W. A. Garry, Ledyard, Iowa," 4½″ H. . . . . . . . . . . . . . . . . . . . . . . . . . . . $55.00
**PINE DESK,** dovetailed case & 3 dovetailed drawers, int. has 16 dovetailed drawers, ref., repr., fold-down lid, 37″ W., 21″ D. . . . . . . . . . . . . . . . . . . . . . . $400.00
**DOLL-SIZE WALL CUPBOARD,** top doors removed, old red repaint, 12½″ W., 23″ H. . . . . . . . . . . . . . . . . . . . . . . $105.00

A-OH July 1982          *Garth's Auctions, Inc.*
**LAUNDRY BASKET,** woven splint, rim handle holds, wear, rim is inc., 21″ W., 26½″ L., 9″ H. . . . . . . . . . . . . . . . . . . . . . $15.00
**OPEN PEWTER CUPBOARD,** pine & poplar, single board door, worn orig. blue paint, feet worn & one foot repl., 38¾″ W., 18¾″ D., 75″ H. . . . . . . . . . . . . . $2450.00
**TIN LANTERN,** clear blown spherical globe, remains of orig. blue Japanning, burner missing, some soldered repr., 15″ H. plus ring handle . . . . . . . . . . . . . . $100.00
**FLAT-BOTTOMED BUTTOCKS BASKET,** woven splint, a little wear, 11″ W., 18″ L., 7½″ H. . . . . . . . . . . . . $165.00

A-OH Sept. 1982          *Garth's Auctions, Inc.*
*STEAM WHISTLES*
*L to R*
**BRASS,** one tone, 7¾″ H. . . . . . . . $55.00
**BRASS,** one tone, 10¾″ H. . . . . . . $50.00
**BRASS,** one tone, mkd. "Buckeye Brass Works, Dayton, O.," 13¾″ H. . . . . $65.00
**BRASS,** one tone, 15½″ H. . . . . . . $55.00
**BRASS,** one tone, 17″ H. . . . . . . . $65.00

A-OH Feb. 1983          *Garth's Auctions, Inc.*
**PEWTER PLATES,** pr., faint crowned "X" touch, pitted & worn surface, 9″ D. . . . . . . . . . . . . . . . . . . . . . . . . . . . $100.00
**PEWTER CHARGER,** repr., damage, 15″ D. . . . . . . . . . . . . . . . . . . . . . . . . . . . $145.00
**SAWBUCK TABLE,** pine, replm., old drk. finish, 29″ x 57″, 28″ H. . . . . . $250.00
**HOBBY HORSE,** cast wh. metal, wooden frame, old repaint in wh. w/red & blk., 26″ L. . . . . . . . . . . . . . . . . . . . . . . . . . . . $145.00

*Row III, L to R*
**BLACKBALL BOX,** mahogany, 2 drawers, wire nail const., 4¾″ x 6″ x 8¾″ . . . . . . . . . . . . . . . . . . . . . . . . . . . $50.00

**SEWING BOX,** mahogany, sm. pullout easel mirror, thread compartment & pincushion top, 6¼″ x 8¾″, 9″ H. . . . $185.00

**TURNED TREEN JAR,** maple, glued age crack, 8″ D., 8″ H. . . . . . . . . . . . . $155.00

A-OH Feb. 1983          *Garth's Auctions, Inc.*
**PIECED QUILT,** 20 connecting star designs, colorful triangles, some wear, 66" x 82" .......................... $150.00
**CUPBOARD,** 1 pc., ref., int. painted pale blue, 38" W., 13" D., 70" H. ..... $500.00
**APPLE PEELER,** cast iron, "Bonanza," 16" H. ......................... $45.00

A-OH July 1982          *Garth's Auctions, Inc.*
**WRT. IRON LIGHTING DEVICE,** adj. extension arm, broken spring clip, base replm., 21½" H. ............... $120.00
**WRT. IRON RUSH LIGHT,** tripod base, 13" H. ........................ $275.00
**HOG SCRAPER CANDLESTICK,** brass ring & push up, sgn. "Shaw, Birm," 7¼" H. ......................... $270.00
**WRT. IRON LIGHTING DEVICE,** spouts & tripod base, hanging hook, 20" H. ............................. $200.00
**JELLY CUPBOARD,** maple, 2 dove-tailed drawers, old worn red paint, 45" W., 19¼" D., 45½" H. .............. $375.00
**OVOID REDWARE JAR,** strap handles, impressed "Solomon Way," sm. chips & worn glaze, 14" H. ........... $35.00
**STAVE BUCKET,** metal bands, orig. yellow paint w/br. blocked graining & vines, mkd. "Woodcock & Sawyer," 9½" H., 12" D. ..................... $95.00

A-OH Jan. 1983          *Garth's Auctions, Inc.*
**TWO-PIECE JACQUARD COVERLET,** blue & wh., "1844," wear & damage, 76" x 93" ..................... $200.00
**SHAKER TIN DUST PAN,** orig. br. Japanning, wear, 12¼" W. ........ $6.00

**SHAKER LADDERBACK ROCKER,** old gray repaint, wear, splits ...... $85.00
**OVAL BRIDE'S BOX,** pine, wear & damage, 10¼" x 17", 7" H. ...... $325.00

**SHAKER STAND,** walnut, old finish, 19" x 19¾", 26" H. ................ $250.00
**RABBIT GARDEN ORNAMENT,** cast iron, old gray repaint, 12" H. .... $115.00

A-OH July 1982          *Garth's Auctions, Inc.*
**SHAKER FOLDING BED,** maple & birch, slat missing, old drk. gr. repaint, repr., 53" W., 77" L., 35½" H. .. $1450.00
**TWO PIECE JACQUARD COVERLET,** double weave, blue & wh., "1852," some wear, 78" W., 92" L. ...... $200.00
**CASE OF DRAWERS,** cherry, dove-tailed drawers, hinged back compartment, wh. porcelain pulls, 10¾" W., 34" L., 8¾" H. ............................. $270.00

A-OH July 1982          *Garth's Auctions, Inc.*
**WOVEN SPLINT BASKET,** double handles, lid is missing, 14" D., 12" H. .................................. $5.00
**WOVEN SPLINT MELLON-RIB BASKET,** damage, repr., 15" W., 15½" L., 8" H. plus wooden handle ....... $40.00
**WALL CUPBOARD,** 2 pcs., pine, old red repaint, 53" W., 19¾" D., 76½" H. ◄ ............................ $265.00
**LITHOGRAPH,** handcolored, "Currier & Ives," "Fruits of the Golden Land," good color, modern frame, 20" W., 16" H. .................................. $5.00
**HOBBY HORSE,** laminated wooden const., worn orig. wh. paint w/red base, orig. leather bridle, worn saddle, harness replm., horsehair tail, mane is missing, 39" L. ............................. $260.00

A-OH July 1982 _Garth's Auctions, Inc._
**LADDERBACK ARM CHAIR,** old splint seat, add-on rockers removed from legs, old br. finish . . . . . . . . . . . . . . . . . . $55.00
**PIE SAFE,** poplar, worn old gr. repaint & minor molding replm. on one side, hardware repl., 48″ W., 17″ D., 54¾″ H. . . . . . . . . . . . . . . . . . . . . . . . . . . . . . . . $352.50
**BALSA & WOOD DECOY,** Canada goose feeder by Herters, old repaint, 20½″ L. . . . . . . . . . . . . . . . . . . . . . . . . . . . . $40.00
**STONEWARE JAR,** mkd. "Soloman Bell, Strasburg VA," old rim repr., 8½″ H. . . . . . . . . . . . . . . . . . . . . . . . . . . . . . . . $95.00
**WOVEN SPLINT BASKET,** w/carrying handles, faded colors, East Woodland Indian orig., 11½″ x 18″, 11½″ H. . . . . . . . . . . . . . . . . . . . . . . . . . . . . . . . $25.00
**OVOID STONEWARE JAR,** 1½ gal., mkd. "H. Smith & Co.," chips on handles & old rim repr., 10⅝″ H. . . . . . . . . . . $80.00

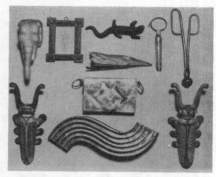

A-OH July 1982 _Garth's Auctions, Inc._
**FOLK ART CARVED WOODEN ELEPHANT HEAD,** old lt. blue & wh. paint w/rhinestone eyes, 7¾″ L. . . . . . . . $15.00
**TRAMP ART PICTURE FRAME,** w/old photograph of soldier, 4⅜″ x 5½″ . . . . . . . . . . . . . . . . . . . . . . . . . . . . . . . . . . . $25.00
**CAST IRON LIZARD,** old gr. repaint, 7″ L. . . . . . . . . . . . . . . . . . . . . . . . . . . . . $5.00
**IRON TOOL,** combination tack puller & watermelon plugger, 6¾″ L. . . . . $15.00
**STEEL TONGS,** 9¾″ L. . . . . . . . . $3.00
**WOODEN MEMO OR LETTER CLIP,** bird's head, old gold paint . . . . . . . $55.00
**PERSIAN BOX,** brass & silver, engraved & highly polished, 1¾″ x 4″ x 6″ . . . $80.00
**CAST IRON CRICKET BOOT JACK,** colorful old repaint, 10½″ L. . . . . . $20.00
**TIN NOODLE CUTTER,** 12½″ L. . . . . . . . . . . . . . . . . . . . . . . . . . . . . . . . $67.50
**CAST IRON CRICKET BOOT JACK,** colorful old repaint, 10½″ L. . . . . . . $27.50

A-OH July 1982 _Garth's Auctions, Inc._
_Row I, L to R_
**CHALK BANK,** dog w/snake in mouth, worn orig. red, tan & blk. paint, 4½″ H. . . . . . . . . . . . . . . . . . . . . . . . . . . . . . $135.00
**PIG BANK,** wh. clay, gr. & br. running glaze, 7″ L. . . . . . . . . . . . . . . . . . . . $90.00
**CHALK BANK,** horse w/orig. red & yellow paint w/br. harness, 4½″ H. . . . . . . . . . . . . . . . . . . . . . . . . . . . . . . $65.00

_Row II, L to R_
**CHILD'S ROCKINGHAM TEA SET,** 24-pcs. (7 shown), wh. clay w/embossed ribbing & br. amber glaze, teapot (spout & rim chips) 3⅞″ H., creamer 2¼″ H., open sugar, covered sugar, 8 plates (small chips) 3½″ D., 2 saucers (chipped) 3¼″ D., 10 cups (minor flakes) . . . . . . . . . . . . . . . . $165.00

_Row III, L to R_
**ROCKINGHAM CUP,** 2¾″ H. . . . . . . . . . . . . . . . . . . . . . . . . . . . . . . . $85.00
**MINI. ROCKINGHAM JAR,** small chips on lid & rim, 3″ H. . . . . . . . . . . . $25.00
**BENNINGTON BANK,** flint enamel, in form of Uncle Sam, minor flake on bottom is from kiln adhesion & does not show when upright, 4¼″ H. . . . . . . . . . $130.00
**MINI. OVOID JUG,** wh. clay w/drk. br. glaze, 2¾″ H. . . . . . . . . . . . . . . . . $25.00
**ROCKINGHAM MUG,** rim chip & hairline crack, 3¼″ H. . . . . . . . . . . $15.00

A-OH July 1982 _Garth's Auctions, Inc._
**WRT. IRON CHANDELIER,** made from an early utensil rack by the addition of candle sockets, 25¼″ D. . . . . . . . . $135.00
**TIN LANTERN,** w/clear blown globe, removable base has font but burner is missing, base & font have some small holes from rust damage, probably N.E. Glass Co. but unmkd., 11″ H. . . . . . . . . . $205.00
**PEWTER INKWELL,** 7″ D. . . . . . $70.00
**STONEWARE MILK BOWL,** w/rim spout & side handles, hairline in side, 12¾″ D., 5″ H. . . . . . . . . . . . . . . . . . . . . . $305.00
**PEWTER BASIN,** Am., unmkd., worn surface, 8″ D. . . . . . . . . . . . . . . . . . $115.00
**IRON HOGSCRAPER CANDLESTICK,** brass ring is battered, 8¾″ H. . . . . . . . . . . . . . . . . . . . . . . . . . . . . . $155.00
**Q.A. WORK TABLE,** maple, ref., 27¼″ x 42″, 26½″ H. . . . . . . . . . . . . . . . . . $1800.00
**OVOID STONEWARE JUG,** red clay w/gr. tan salt glaze, traces of red paint, old cork is firmly rooted in chipped neck, 15½″ H. . . . . . . . . . . . . . . . . . . . . . . . . . . . . $25.00
**REDWARE APPLE BUTTER JAR,** br. amber glaze has wear & flakes, 7″ H. . . . . . . . . . . . . . . . . . . . . . . . . . . . . . . $35.00
**BOWBACK WINDSOR ARMCHAIR,** base of one arm support has old repr., old blk. paint shows pale gray gr. beneath, 16¼″ H. . . . . . . . . . . . . . . . . . . . . $1550.00

A-MA July 1982 _Richard A. Bourne Co., Inc._
_L to R_
**VICTORIAN LAP DESK,** rosewood w/m.o.p. & abalone shell inlays, orig. velvet, sm. spring-loaded drawer in working cond., 14″ W. . . . . . . . . $160.00
**VICTORIAN LAP DESK,** elaborate inlays of m.o.p. & metal, 15″ L. . . . . . . . . . . . . . . . . . . . . . . . . . . . . . . $150.00

A-OH July 1982 _Garth's Auctions, Inc._
**BRASS CANDLESTICK,** pr., stem threads to base, 17¾″ H. . . . . . . . $150.00
**LITHO,** hand colored, "Currier & Ives," "The Young Brood," framed, 16½″ x 20½″ . . . . . . . . . . . . . . . . . . . . . . . . . . . . $85.00
**EMPIRE CARD TABLE,** curly maple, pedestal base w/folding swing top, ref., opens to 32¼″ x 34½″, 28″ H. . . . $525.00

A-OH July 1982          Garth's Auctions, Inc.
**BURL BOWL,** int. wear & old drk. finish, 15″ D., 6″ H. ....................... $750.00
**Q.A. HIGHBOY,** ref. w/warm br. color, brasses are repl., top & base are a closely matched marriage, top 36″ W., cornice 40½″ W., 21″ D., 71¾″ H. ...... $6100.00
**AQUA BLOWN JAR,** gr., lid is bluish, finial was left rough & w/open blister & has been ground smooth, small flake on lip, 14½″ H. ........................ $120.00

A-MA July 1982     Richard A. Bourne Co., Inc.
**CONTINUOUS ARM WINDSOR CHAIR,** 8-spindle, Am., ca. 1800, saddle seat & bamboo turnings, restorations, much of old paint visible ........ $325.00
**LRG. HAT BOX,** wallpaper covering, slight break in top, minor loss of paper, 17½″ L., 11″ H. ............... $210.00
**PASTEBOARD HAT BOX,** wallpaper covering, slight water staining, 12¼″ L., 9″ H. ............................. $35.00
**BLANKET CHEST,** pine, Am., late 18th C., orig. red paint, 2 minor chips, 23″ W. ............................. $600.00

A-OH July 1982          Garth's Auctions, Inc.
**STONEWARE PITCHER,** blue & wh., embossed bust of Indian, rim & spout chips, 8″ H. .................... $85.00
**WOODEN BOWL,** poplar, ext. has worn drk. red paint, int. has worn scrubbed finish, 22½″ x 23½″, 8″ H. ....... $300.00
**STONEWARE PITCHER,** yellow & gr., embossed bust of Indian, rim & spout chips, 8¼″ H. .................. $85.00
**WOODEN DECOY,** Herter's display special old squaw drake, in unused cond., mkd. "Herters Inc, 1893," 13″ L.
............................. $20.00
**HEPPLEWHITE WORK TABLE,** base has worn old red, top scrubbed, 32¼″ x 48″, 29¼″ H. ...................... $300.00
**DECOY,** balsa & pine, Herter's redhead hen, glass eyes & worn old working repaint, 16″ L. ........................ $15.00
**WOODEN SUGAR BUCKET,** br. color, copper nail const., 12″ D., 12″ H.
............................. $60.00
**DECOY,** balsa & pine, Herter's canvasback drake, glass eyes & worn old working repaint, 16½″ L. ................. $30.00

A-MA July 1982     Richard A. Bourne Co., Inc.
**ENGRAVED IRON STRONG BOX,** European, 15th or 16th C., key & working lock, 6″ L., 4″ W., 4″ H. ........ $500.00

A-OH July 1982          Garth's Auctions, Inc.
*GOING TO BED LAMPS*
*Row I, L to R*
**EBONY CASTLE TOWER,** threaded lid & turned ivory socket for match & larger one for taper, 4″ H. ............. $30.00
**TREEN,** w/ivory socket, blk. transfer of "The Abby, Windermere," 2″ H.
............................. $25.00
**TREEN,** w/ivory socket & plaid decoupage, "McPherson," 2½″ H.
............................. $20.00
**CAST IRON FIGURE,** youth w/bow & wine jug, basket on his arm is added & bow is broken, socket on base, 4⅞″ H.
............................. $20.00
**EBONY CASTLE TOWER,** threaded lid, socket missing, 2⅞″ H. ....... $37.50
**TREEN,** w/ivory socket, blk. transfer "Balmoral," 2⅛″ H. ............. $45.00
**DARK FIGURED WOOD,** threaded lid & ivory acorn socket, 3¾″ H. .... $30.00
*Row II, L to R*
**TOLE,** w/worn red Japanning, taper jack, 3¼″ H. ..................... $62.50
**EBONY CASTLE TOWER,** threaded lid, ivory socket damaged, age cracks, 2⅝″ H. .......................... $22.50
**TREEN,** w/ivory socket & pull out compartment, blk. transfer "The Nave, Fountain's Abbey, Yorkshire," 2¼″ L.
............................. $65.00
**TWO SHADES OF WOOD,** w/inlaid taper socket & ivory match socket, some wear, 3¾″ H. .................. $35.00
**TREEN,** w/ivory socket, blk. transfer "Royal Arch, Dundee Harbour," 1⅞″ H.
............................. $40.00
**EBONY,** w/ivory socket, threaded lid, 2⅝″ H. .......................... $40.00
**BRASS,** w/embossed floral design, 2¾″ H.
............................. $27.50
**CERAMIC CANNON,** in brass base, blue w/gilt trim & wh. reserve w/polychrome shield, helmet & arrows, rim repr., 3″ H. ....................... $100.00

A-MA Oct. 1982          Robert W. Skinner Inc.
**ROWBOAT W/3 FIGURES,** Am., mid 19th C., carved & painted, boat inscribed "Jim Crow," mounted on stand, boat 13½″ L. ....................... $2600.00*

A-OH July 1982     *Garth's Auctions, Inc.*
**PINE SWORDFISH,** w/heart cut out, worn surface has been varnish, 33″ L.
. . . . . . . . . . . . . . . . . . . . . . . . . . . . . $200.00
**CARVED WOODEN SHOREBIRD,** old paint & nail beak, 20th C., 11½″ H. on stand
. . . . . . . . . . . . . . . . . . . . . . . . . . . . . $110.00
**CARVED WOODEN LOON,** old blk. repaint w/wh. spots & tack eyes, 12½″ H. on stand . . . . . . . . . . . . . . . . . . . . . . $35.00
**BLANKET CHEST,** dovetailed poplar, orig. smoked graining on pale salmon ground, varnished, 31½″ W., 17½″ D., 24¼″ H. . . . . . . . . . . . . . . . . . . . . . . $575.00
**WOODEN DECOY,** old worn working repaint w/old damage & repr. to head, 12¾″ L. . . . . . . . . . . . . . . . . . . . . $40.00

A-OH July 1982     *Garth's Auctions, Inc.*
**BENNINGTON BOWL W/ROCK-INGHAM GLAZE,** impressed mark in almond shaped configuration is indistinct, large chip on underside of rim & small base flake, 12″ D., 4¼″ H. . . . . . . . . . . $75.00
**BENNINGTON HOUND HANDLED PITCHER W/ROCKINGHAM GLAZE,** embossed vintage & hunt scenes, small flake on lip & one on dog's ear, 11¼″ H.
. . . . . . . . . . . . . . . . . . . . . . . . . . . . . $150.00

**BOWL W/ROCKINGHAM GLAZE,** cracks in base, 10⅞″ D., 4½″ H. . . $50.00
**WALL CUPBOARD,** 2 pc., pine & poplar, ref., brasses are old replm., int. shelves w/plate rails & spoon rack, 58″ W., 20¼″ D., 88″ H. . . . . . . . . . . . . . $1800.00
**SEWER TILE SEATED DOG BANK,** old chips on base, loose mounted as a lamp w/burlap shade 9½″ H., 24″ O.H.
. . . . . . . . . . . . . . . . . . . . . . . . . . . . . $155.00

A-OH July 1982     *Garth's Auctions, Inc.*
**CARVED WOODEN DECOY,** primitive Bufflehead drake from MI, tack eyes, working repaint & old damage to bill, 13″ L.
. . . . . . . . . . . . . . . . . . . . . . . . . . . . . $20.00
**WOVEN SPLINT BASKET,** yellow w/red stripe, base mkd. "Made By Mary Mandoka, Potawattomi Indian," minor rim damage, 12″ x 20″, 6¼″ H. plus wooden handle . . . . . . . . . . . . . . . . . . . . . . $30.00
**CARVED WOODEN DECOY,** primitive duck w/glass eyes & orig. paint, carved "Arness," 12¼″ L. . . . . . . . . . . . . . . $25.00
**MULE CHEST,** pine, old alligatored mustard colored paint over old red, 37¼″ W., 19″ D., 43″ H. . . . . . . . . . . . . . $400.00
**CARVED WOODEN DECOY,** hollow pintail w/glass eyes & orig. paint, mkd. "Arness," 17½″ L. . . . . . . . . . . . . . . $45.00

A-MA July 1982     *Richard A. Bourne Co., Inc.*
L to R
**GEORGIAN POLE SCREEN,** Eng., 18th C., mahogany, oval needlework panel, normal signs of wear & age, 53¼″ H.
. . . . . . . . . . . . . . . . . . . . . . . . . . . . . $425.00
**MINI. SHERATON DRESSER,** Am., ca. 1800-1810, mahogany, 18¾″ L., 15⅝″ O.H.
. . . . . . . . . . . . . . . . . . . . . . . . . . . . . $350.00
**BUREAU,** Am., late 18th C., curly birch, ref., 1 brass knob missing, 37⅝″ W.
. . . . . . . . . . . . . . . . . . . . . . . . . . . . . $400.00

A-OH July 1982     *Garth's Auctions, Inc.*
**HOOKED RAG RUG,** gray cat w/red dish, 24″ x 36″ . . . . . . . . . . . . . . . . . $295.00
**SPINDLE BACK SIDE CHAIR,** ref. w/drk. br. color, new woven splint seat
. . . . . . . . . . . . . . . . . . . . . . . . . . . . . $30.00
**BRASS CANDLESTICK,** 5¼″ H.
. . . . . . . . . . . . . . . . . . . . . . . . . . . . . $195.00

**PEWTER TEA POT,** pear shaped, mkd. w/bee & "S.I.A.M.," finial inc. & hinge damage, 6¾″ H. . . . . . . . . . . . . . . $105.00
**CANDLESTAND,** birch & cherry, one foot broken & repr. & turned ring on column damaged, old drk. finish, 16″ D., 24¾″ H. . . . . . . . . . . . . . . . . . . . . $250.00
**CARVED WOODEN DECOY,** hollow gr. wing teal, turned head, glass eyes & orig. paints, unsgn., 12″ L. . . . . . . . $40.00

A-MA Nov. 1982    *Richard A. Bourne Co., Inc.*
**BRIDE'S BOX,** Am., early 19th C., orig.
gr. paint, fastened w/rawhide, 22" L., 14½"
W., 9¾" H. .................. $800.00

A-MA Nov. 1982    *Richard A. Bourne Co., Inc.*
**CIRCULAR BOX,** orig. painted decor.,
initials "HOS" & date 1808, orig. color was
red & has darkened w/age, decor. done in
blk., gray, yellow & red, fastened w/
rawhide ..................... $300.00

A-MA July 1982    *Richard A. Bourne Co., Inc.*
*Row I, L to R*
**CHINESE CARVED GLASS BOTTLE,**
carol-colored, complete w/spoon, base
chipped, 2⅝" H. ................. $50.00
**CARVED BONE FIGURE,** monkey, 3¼"
H. ............................. $80.00
**CHINESE IVORY SCULPTURE,** teak
stand, age crack, 4⅜" W., 4¼" O.H.
.............................. $100.00
**CARVED IVORY FIGURE,** old man,
Japanese, 19th C., sgn. on base, 4¾" H.
.............................. $90.00
*Row II, L to R*
**CHINESE CARVED CANDLE-
STICKS,** pr., turned wooden bases, 1
damaged & reglued, 16" H. ..... $150.00
**INDIAN IVORY SCULPTURE,** ele-
phant, 7" O.H. ................. $125.00

A-OH July 1982    *Garth's Auctions, Inc.*
**HANGING CORNER CUPBOARD,**
pine, orig. brass hinges & brass knob, ref.,
22" W., 29¼" H. ............... $360.00
**TIN LAMP,** conical weighted base &
cylindrical stem that is adjustable, 3
burning fluid burners, 1 snuffer cap
missing, adjusts from 13¼" H. ... $150.00
**WOODEN DECOY,** coot branded
"L.J.R." for Lawrence Reno, Detroit, old
weathered paint & glass eyes, 11" L.
.............................. $100.00
**FR. PUMP LAMP,** pewter, battered, 12¾"
H. ............................. $45.00
**HEPPLEWHITE WORK TABLE,** ref. &
drawer overlaps have repr., back of top
shows sgn. of having once had a drop leaf,
27" x 40¼", 29¾" H. ........... $175.00
**OVOID STONEWARE JUG,** 2 gal.,
mkd. "S. Hart Fulton" in cobalt blue &
good brushed "2" w/foliage design, 13½" H.
.............................. $125.00

A-OH July 1982    *Garth's Auctions, Inc.*
**HANGING DOUBLE LAMP,** brass,
Greek key design on font, polished &
electrified, gr. shades cased in wh., 36" W.,
21" H. ........................ $325.00
← **SHEET IRON WEATHERVANE,** Indian
w/bow & arrow, 20th C. folk art, red
mottled paint, 34" H. .......... $175.00
**PINE WEATHERVANE,** Indian w/bow
& arrow, age crack & old yellow varnish,
has some age, 17" H. ........... $100.00
**FOLK ART SHEEP,** w/curlique coat,
sgn. "T. Koss '79. Lebanon Ohio," base 5" x
18" .......................... $55.00

A-OH Mar. 1982    *Garth's Auctions, Inc.*
**WOODEN GATE,** mortised & pegged,
one side has orig. iron spring latch, worn
old wh. paint is grayish-yellow color, 43"
W., 39½" H. ................... $200.00
**TIN CANDLE SCONCE,** crimped pan,
sunburst ribbed reflector, 9¾" W., 9" H.
.............................. $215.00
**MELLON-RIBBED WOVEN SPLINT
BASKET,** good cond., 6¼" x 7", 3¾" H.
plus wooden handle ........... $135.00

**RUSTIC STAND,** tripod base is made
from saplings & has twig supports, top
edge is decor. w/split saplings, natural
vanished bark & br. paint w/gold detail,
13¼" x 13¾" .................. $45.00
**WOODEN CRADLE,** birch w/pine hood,
worn old red finish, one end is dovetailed,
one nailed, repr., 21¾" x 39", 26½" H.
.............................. $285.00

A-OH Feb. 1983    *Garth's Auctions, Inc.*
**PEGBOARD,** pine, 7 hooks, 83" L.
.............................. $150.00
**BUCKSAW W/BLADE,** old drk. patina,
replm., 33" L. .................. $45.00
**DRY SINK,** pine, old mellow refinishing,
72" W., 21½" D., 27" H. ........ $500.00
**RYE STRAW BASKETS,** 2, damage,
repr., wear, 12" D., 3½" and 6" H.
.............................. $40.00

**WOVEN SPLINT GATHERING
BASKET,** wear, 14" x 23½", 7" H. plus
wooden handle ................ $115.00
**SUGAR BUCKET,** all wooden, 3 wooden
bands w/interlocking fingers, worn red
paint, 12½" D., 15" H. ......... $105.00

**WOVEN SPLINT BUTTOCKS
BASKET,** worn old br. varnish, 14" x 17",
10" H. plus wooden handle ...... $155.00
**SUGAR BUCKET,** wooden, metal band
at base, splits, old refinishing, 12" D., 12" H.
.............................. $45.00

A-MA Oct. 1982     *Garth's Auctions, Inc.*
**CARVED WOODEN DECOY,** feeding gr. wing teal, glass eyes, old repaint, 17″ L.
.......................................... $55.00
**CARVED WOODEN DECOY,** mate to above, 14¼″ L. ................. $55.00
**CORK & CARVED WOODEN DECOY,** mallard drake, turned head, glass eyes, old repaint, 15¼″ L. ... $90.00
**PIE SAFE,** 12 tin panels w/punched star & circle design, sq. posts form legs, 1 dovetailed drawer in base, old yellow & br. comb graining, panel molding & cornice are br., some damage, 40″ W., 17¼″ D., 56¼″ H.
.......................................... $260.00
**WOVEN SPLINT BASKET,** double swivel handles, wear, 10″ W., 15½″ L., 10½″ H. .................................. $25.00
**STONEWARE PRESERVING JAR,** cobalt stenciled label "A.P. Donaghho, Parkersburg, W. Va.," 9½″ H. .... $25.00
**STONEWARE JAR,** "2" & lines in brushed cobalt, 12¼″ H. ......... $35.00

A-MA July 1982     *Richard A. Bourne Co., Inc.*
**BRASS SUN DIAL,** dated 1722, 8″ sq.
.......................................... $300.00

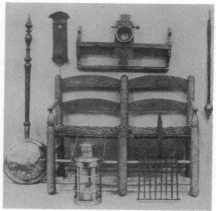

A-MA Oct. 1982     *Garth's Auctions, Inc.*
**COPPER BED WARMER,** turned walnut handle, engraved bird in flight, polished, some damage, 43″ L. ......... $210.00
**TIN CANDLE SCONCE,** crimped crest, some damage, 13¼″ L. ........ $145.00
**HANGING SPOON RACK,** pine, towel bar, mortar & pestle holder, replm., ref., 23½″ L. ...................... $90.00
**MORTAR & PESTLE,** metal & brass, 3¼″ H. ......................... $40.00
**CAMPAIGN TORCH,** brass font, thumb screw mkd. "The P & A Mfg Co.," turned wooden handle, worn blk. paint, 26½″ L.
.......................................... $25.00
**LADDERBACK WAGON SEAT,** turned posts, 2-slat back, woven splint seat, worn, ref., 35¼″ L. ........ $375.00
**BRASS SHIP'S LANTERN,** 5 glass panels, hinged top, removable kerosene burner, 14″ H. ................. $65.00
**WRT. IRON BOILER,** painted blk., 20½″ L. ........................... $35.00

A-OH July 1982     *Garth's Auctions, Inc.*
**SHERATON TALL POST BED,** curly maple, one head post is warped, w/springs & mattress, fish net canope & dust ruffle w/hand tied fringe, handmade repro., 54¼″ x 77¾″, 85″ H. ............... $1000.00
**OVERSHOT COVERLET,** 1-pc., blue & wh., some wear & stains, 92″ x 110″
.......................................... $130.00

A-OH July 1982     *Garth's Auctions, Inc.*
**SCROLL MIRROR,** mahogany w/pine, cut out crest, ogee frame & unusual "Comma" cut out on base of frame, orig. mirror glass, old repr. to top crest, 9½ x 15⅜″ ...................... $500.00
**REDWARE PLATE,** 3 line yellow slip decor. & coggled edge, slip has old blk. surface flakes, 9¼″ D. .......... $225.00
**REDWARE OVOID JAR,** w/applied handles mounted as lamp, br. glaze covers 2/3 of surface, yellow slip decor. w/3 lines at shoulder & "Sugar 1827," large rim chips & drilled, 12¼″ H., 28″ H. w/linen shade
.......................................... $250.00
**PIE PLATES,** pr., amber glaze & coggled edge, 8⅞″ D. ................... $75.00
**WINDSOR SIDE CHAIR,** brace back, ref., 17″ seat ht. .............. $1200.00
**Q.A. TAVERN TABLE,** oval 2 board top is old replm., ref. w/br. color, 23½″ x 35″, 26¾″ H. ...................... $900.00
**WOODEN MILKING STOOL,** 3 legs, legs puttied into place, old drk. finish, 7¼″ x 18″ ..................... $275.00
**CARVED WOODEN DECOY,** canvas-back hen w/orig. paint & glass eyes, old glued neck break, 14¾″ L. ...... $175.00
**WH. CLAY FLOWER POT,** w/attached saucer base & flared lip, unglazed, 7¼″ H.
.......................................... $6.00

A-MA July 1982     *Richard A. Bourne Co., Inc.*
*Row I, L to R*
**PATENT MODEL OF HAY MOWER,** orig. paint, 15″ L. .............. $1200.00
**PATENT MODEL OF RAKING DEVICE,** wood w/iron wheels, branded "H.M. Woodford," 7¼″ W., 7″ L. ...... $250.00
*Row II*
**IRON MODEL OF PLOW,** slightly rusted, 22¾″ L. ................. $450.00

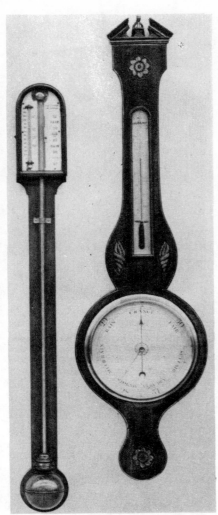

A-WA D.C. Sept. 1982 *Adam A. Weschler & Son*
*Left*
**GEORGE III STICK BAROMETER,** ca. 1800, mahogany, Robert Aitkin, Calashiels, 36" H. ..................... $675.00*
*Right*
**GEORGE III WHEEL BAROMETER,** ca. 1800, satinwood inlaid mahogany, Borini, Birmingham, 40" H. .... $675.00*

A-WA D.C. Dec. 1982 *Adam A. Weschler & Son*
**TOWER BELL,** Am., ca. 1899, wh. brass, supported by cast iron swivel arbor standard................... $1100.00*

A-MA Aug. 1982       *Robert W. Skinner Inc.*
*L to R*
**COVERED SPICE BOXES,** 3-pcs., N. Eng., early 19th C., different shades of gray-blk. paint on 2 & yellow-ochre over red on third, one & three finger construction, 3⅝" D., 3⅞" D., & 4¼" D. ......... $475.00*
**SHAKER COVERED WOODEN BOX,** N. Eng., early 19th C., four-fingered, painted drk. gr., 9⅞" x 13½ ..... $500.00*
**SHAKER COVERED BOXES,** set of 3, N. Eng., early 19th C., 2 largest w/three finger construction, 1 w/two finger, 5⅞" L., 8⅞" L., & 11½" L. ............ $1800.00*

*Left*
A-MA Aug. 1982       *Robert W. Skinner Inc.*
**NEEDLEWORK CASKET,** Eng., 17th C., silk panels of simple vase & floral motifs worked in polychrome silk, purled metallic yarns w/sequin embellishments, bordered by metallic braid, contains removable tray w/ink drawn landscape scene, a writing cabinet lined in salmon silk w/silver vials & 4 silk lined drawers .......... $1300.00*

*Right*
A-MA Aug. 1982       *Robert W. Skinner Inc.*
**NEEDLEWORK POCKETBOOK,** 18th C., overall geometric trellis design, yellow, pink, red, gr. & lavender, initialed "MC," wool yarns worked in tent stitch on linen canvas, bright peach colored glaze wool lining, 9" x 9" open ........... $375.00*

A-MA Nov. 1982   *Richard A. Bourne Co., Inc.*
*L to R*
**CHINESE STEATITE MOUNTAIN CARVING,** early to mid-19th C., temple garden showing individual thatched huts for priests of varying ranks, carved rocky stand, 5⅞" H., 11" L. ........... $175.00
**MOSS GREEN SPIRIT SCREEN,** ca. 17th or 18th C., both sides of jade plaque carved w/10 columns of calligraphy rubbed w/gold, mounted on 19th C., carved rosewood stand inlaid w/wh. jade, 14" H. ............................ $800.00
**MINIATURE LAC BURGAUTE PLAQUE,** 18th C., nacreous shell of Chinese garden around a lake, carved hardwood stand, cracking in center, only 3 small pcs. of shell missing ........ $90.00

*Left*
A-MA Aug. 1982   *Richard A. Bourne Co., Inc.*
**CARVED EAGLE,** mounted on a stand, full carved feathers, talons, beak, etc., finished in natural drk. wood, 33¾" H., wingspread approx. 28" W. .... $1700.00
*Right*
A-MA Aug. 1982       *Robert W. Skinner Inc.*
**CHERRY PIPE BOX,** Am., late 18th C., ivory inlaid heart, shaped backboard, shaped sides & front w/cut out star, 2 drawers below w/ivory pulls, 16" H., 6¼" W. ........................ $1600.00*

A-MA Aug. 1982       *Robert W. Skinner Inc.*
**WRT. IRON LATCH,** N. Eng., 18th C., w/spear ends, 18½" L. ........ $310.00*

A-OH Oct. 1982          *Garth's Auctions, Inc.*
**HOOKED RAG RUG,** clipper ship, Am. flag, drk. blue background, two red Chinese symbols, 2'5" x 3'7" ............. $70.00
**MINIATURE BLANKET CHEST,** pine, bracket feet, orig. drk. red flame graining, replm., some wear, 13" W., 7½" D., 7" H. .............................. $200.00
**HITCHCOCK-TYPE SIDE CHAIRS,** (set of 6), (1 illus.), orig. red & blk. graining w/yellow stiping & bronze powder stenciling of foliage & flowers in gold w/red, new cane seats on 3, damaged seats on 3, some wear, varnished ............... $150.00
**CHUCK WAGON FLOUR DISPENSING BOX,** poplar, old worn red varnish, cast iron hardware & side handles, 27¾" W., 15½" D., 29¾" H. .......... $75.00
**BEAN BAG TARGET,** wooden, decor., red flame graining on easel back, front is yellow w/blk. & red striping & foliage, 13" W., 26½" H. ..................... $55.00
**CAST IRON LAMB BAKING PAN,** bolt fasteners & small wrench, 12½" L. ......................................... $35.00

A-OH Oct. 1982          *Garth's Auctions, Inc.*
**CHIPPENDALE SCROLL MIRROR,** mahogany on pine, gilded phoenix, repr., replm., old ref. & regilding, 21¾" W., 38" H. .............................. $325.00
**SILHOUETTE,** inscription "Miss Fielde, with the H. N. A. Jervis, 18th April, 1827," remounted & recut, 10⅜" W., 12¼" H. .............................. $65.00
**SILHOUETTE,** inscription "Mrs Taylor 14 March 1827," remounted & recut, 11¼" W., 14¼" H. .............. $75.00
**TILT-TOP CANDLESTAND,** walnut, Mansfield, OH origin, repr., 19½" D., 26½" H. .............................. $260.00
**CHILD'S CORNER CHAIR,** early 20th C., Sheraton styling, old rush seat, old worn gilding over yellow paint, 19" H. .............................. $155.00

___

A-OH Jan. 1983          *Garth's Auctions, Inc.*
**HANGING VICTORIAN SHELF,** oak, orig. worn finish & decal, mkd. "Variety Bracket Works, South Bend Ind, Pat Sept 24-72," 13¾" x 26¼" ........... $145.00
**DRAWING OF THREE HUNTING DOGS,** charcoal on cream paper, framed, 18¼" x 22¼" ..................... $5.00
**BAMBOO WINDSOR SIDE CHAIR,** modern blk. paint, gold striping, 17" seat ht. .............................. $175.00
**MINIATURE HANDLELESS CUP & SAUCER,** blue spatterware, flakes .............................. $55.00
**BLUE SPATTERWARE TEAPOT,** stains & flakes, 6" H. ........... $95.00
**BLUE SPATTERWARE SUGAR BOWL,** minor flakes, 5¼" H. .... $60.00
**DECORATED STAND,** Rupp of York, PA, poplar & pine, orig. red flame graining, 19½" sq., 29½" H. ......... $550.00
**OVOID STONEWARE JAR,** impressed "A. DeHaven, Middlebury, Ohio, 2," tulip in cobalt blue, no lid, 12¼" H. ... $450.00

A-OH Oct. 1982          *Garth's Auctions, Inc.*
**HOOKED RAG RUG,** braided edge, multicolored, crowing rooster, purple border, wear, 2'5" x 3'7" ....... $100.00
**WINDSOR SIDE CHAIR,** bamboo, "H" stretcher, bird cage back, ref., 17¼" seat ht. .............................. $150.00
**TURNED WOODEN MORTAR & PESTLE,** old lt. gr. paint, 7¼" H. .............................. $100.00
**SHOE SHINE BOX,** pine, cut out feet, int. foot rest, one drawer, old worn paint of layers of br., gr. & tan, 16½" W., 14¼" D., 17½" H. .............................. $175.00
**OVAL WOVEN SPLINT BASKET,** drk. br. & natural, wear, 11" x 12", 5¾" H. .............................. $30.00

A-OH July 1982          *Garth's Auctions, Inc.*
**COBBLER'S BENCH,** pine, corner post holds cast iron shoe vise mkd. "T.D. Bailey No 4, Lowell, Mass, Pat'd Dec 21, 1858," orig. vise had foot pedal, this one does not, worn orig. blue paint, drawers have worn yellow graining on wh. ground, 37½" W., 22" D., 44" H. ................. $525.00

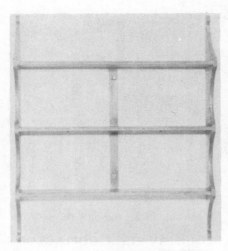

A-MA July 1982    Robert W. Skinner Inc.
**WAGON SEAT**, N. Eng., 18th C., 34" W., 15" D., 27½" H. . . . . . . . . . . . . . $1650.00*

A-MA July 1982    Richard A. Bourne Co., Inc.
**LOUIS XVI STYLE DRESSING TABLE**, marquetry inlaid tulipwood, minor repr., drawers stuck, 29¼" L. . . . . . . . . . . . . . . . . . . . . . . . . . . . $450.00

A-MA Aug. 1982    Robert W. Skinner Inc.
**WALL SHELF**, N. Eng., 18th C., grain painted, 3 tiers w/shaped sides, 38" H., 32" W. . . . . . . . . . . . . . . . . . . . . . $900.00*

A-MA July 1982    Richard A. Bourne Co., Inc.
**CENTENNIAL SHAVING STAND**, inlaid mahogany, ref., 26¼" L., 11" D., 26" H. . . . . . . . . . . . . . . . . . . . . . $135.00

A-MA Aug. 1982    Robert W. Skinner Inc.
**WM. & MARY CHAIR TABLE**, N. Eng., ca. 1st qtr. 18th C., sq. top w/rounded corners on base w/block & turned legs ending in turned feet joined by box stretchers, 22¼" H., 36½" W., 14½" D. . . . . . . . . . . . . . . . . . . . . . . . . . . . $3000.00*

A-MA July 1982    Richard A. Bourne Co., Inc.
L to R
**WINDSOR SIDE CHAIR**, N. Eng., 18th C., in-the-rough cond., old blk. paint badly flaking . . . . . . . . . . . . . . . . . . . . . . $275.00
**Q.A. SIDE CHAIR**, 18th C., drk. wood finish . . . . . . . . . . . . . . . . . . . . . . $1700.00

L to R
A-MA July 1982    Robert W. Skinner Inc.
**RENAISSANCE REVIVAL SEWING STAND**, walnut, Am. ca. 1870, int. mirror & compartments, gilt incised sides, lid needs regluing, 33½" H. . . . . . . $1700.00*

A-MA July 1982    Robert W. Skinner Inc.
**HANGING CUPBOARD**, painted pine, 18th C., 23" W., 9½" D., 27" H. . . . . $2400.00*

A-MA Aug. 1982    Robert W. Skinner Inc.
**MAHOGANY WALL CABINET**, N. Eng., 18th C., 21" H., 29¼" W., 8¾" D. . . . . . . . . . . . . . . . . . . . . . . . . . . . $1700.00*

A-MA July 1982    Richard A. Bourne Co., Inc.
**LEATHER-BOUND DOCUMENT BOX**, orig. lock, brass studs on front, 12" L., 7" D., 7" H. . . . . . . . . . . . . . . . $50.00
**TAVERN TABLE**, new single board pine top w/breadboard ends, maple base, worn, 26" L., 19¾" W., 26¼" H. . . . . . . $325.00
**Q.A. SIDE CHAIR**, N. Eng., early 18th C., fruitwood w/splat back & rush seat, natural finish, serviceable replacement seat . . . . . . . . . . . . . . . . . . . . . . . . . . . $100.00

*Price does not include 10% buyer fee.

A-WA D.C. July 1982 *Adam A. Weschler & Son*
**VICTORIAN ROCKING CRADLE,** on separate stand, walnut, ca. 1860, attrib. to Green & Bro., VA, 40″ L., 22″ W., 29″ H.
............................. $250.00*

A-WA D.C. Sept. 1982 *Adam A. Weschler & Son*
*Left*
**AUSTRIAN BENTWOOD CANED SETTEE,** late 19th C., 56″ L., 39″ H.
............................. $225.00*
*Right*
**AUSTRIAN BENTWOOD CANED ROCKER,** late 19th C., stenciled "Hofamn Bielitz-Austria" ............... $200.00*

A-WA D.C. July 1982 *Adam A. Weschler & Son*
**VICTORIAN FOLDING YOUTH'S HIGH CHAIR,** ca. 1875, attrib. to Green & Bro., VA, walnut, split reed seat, steel wheels ...................... $200.00*

A-MA Nov. 1982   *Richard A. Bourne Co., Inc.*
**CHIPPENDALE LOOKING GLASS,** Am., ca. 1770, mahogany veneered frame on pine, all orig., lower right scroll has been broken & reglued w/some loss of veneer, 31″ H. ...................... $475.00
**SPLAY LEG WORK TABLE,** Am., 18th C., maple, old natural finish .... $1100.00
**Q.A. DROP-LEAF TABLE,** Eng., 18th C., mahogany, orig. finish needs washing, tip of 1 foot broken & missing, 29″ sq., 27½″ H. ...................... $2500.00
**Q.A. TILT-TOP TEA TABLE,** maple, 27½″ x 28⅝″ top, 27½″ H. ...... $1600.00

A-MA Nov. 1982   *Richard A. Bourne Co., Inc.*
**BANISTER-BACK SIDE CHAIR,** N. Eng., early 18th C., seat has been repl., front stretcher shows wear ...... $350.00
**Q.A. TAVERN TABLE,** N. Eng., 18th C., maple, refinished ............. $2700.00

A-MA July 1982   *Richard A. Bourne Co., Inc.*
*L to R*
**VICTORIAN LADY'S ARMCHAIR,** Am., mid 19th C., walnut frame, burgundy velvet upholstery ......... $250.00
**VICTORIAN BIRDCAGE W/ STUFFED BIRD,** orig. red paint, minor repairs, 22¾″ H. ............... $500.00
**TOLE TEA CANNISTER,** redecorated, 23″ H. ...................... $100.00
**VICTORIAN GENTLEMAN'S CHAIR,** walnut frame, rose velvet upholstery, Am., mid 19th C. ................... $275.00

A-MA July 1982   *Richard A. Bourne Co., Inc.*
*L to R*
**LOUIS XV-STYLE COLLECTOR'S CABINET,** case w/bronze or ormolu mounts, middle shelf missing, 21″ sq., 49″ O.H. ...................... $500.00
**LOUIS XV-STYLE COLLECTOR'S CABINET,** bronze or ormolu mounts, mirrored glass shelf, quatrefoil shaped, marquetry inlaid, 21¾″ D., 37″ H.
............................. $550.00

A-MA July 1982   *Richard A. Bourne Co., Inc.*
*L to R*
**LOUIS XV-STYLED ARMCHAIR,** upholstered in muslin, minus cushion, framed stripped to natural wood ........ $125.00
**LOUIS XV-STYLE ARMCHAIR,** painted frame, gilt in frame flaking, upholstered in muslin ............. $175.00

A-MA July 1982   *Richard A. Bourne Co., Inc.*
*L to R*
**Q.A. ARMCHAIR ROCKER,** Am., ca. 1740-1760, new seat, rockers are addition, natural finish w/traces of red paint showing
............................. $200.00
**WINDSOR ROCKER,** Am., ca. 1800, old drk. finish, rockers worn flat on bottoms
............................. $350.00

*Price does not include 10% buyer fee.

A-OH Mar. 1982    *Garth's Auctions, Inc.*
**COW WEATHER VANE,** copper, sheet metal ears & cast horns, traces of old gilding, damage, modern stand, 25″ L., 17″ H. ............................ $550.00
**MULE CHEST,** poplar, replm., ref., 39¼″ W., 19″ D., 43″ H. ............. $550.00

A-MA Aug. 1982    *Robert W. Skinner Inc.*
*L to R*
**HANGING WATCH HUTCH,** N. Eng., early 19th C., pine, shaped backboard w/circular hanger, door w/circular glazed opening, wire hinges & hasp, red stain, 8½″ H. ........................... $625.00*
**HANGING HOUR GLASS,** Am., 18th C., two free blown glass bulbs, bound at joint w/oiled cloth, 6″ H. ....... $975.00*
**WOODEN BOX,** N. Eng., early 19th C., sliding cover, painted lt. gray w/drk. random brush strokes, 2¾″ H., 5″ x 1⅛″ ............................ $575.00*

A-MA Aug. 1982    *Richard A. Bourne Co., Inc.*
**CHILD'S SLED,** orig. red paint w/painted narwhale & name on lower end of front & "Norwhale" on other end, orig. paint ............................ $800.00

*L to R*
A-MA Mar. 1983    *Robert W. Skinner Inc.*
**TIMBY'S STICK BAROMETER,** ca. 1857, MA, long straight blk. walnut case, barometer in top section, thermometer in middle, date slot at base, "A.D. More, Boston," 41″ H. ............. $400.00*
A-MA Mar. 1983    *Robert W. Skinner Inc.*
**PIPE BOX,** mid 18th C., N. Eng., tiger maple, dovetailed drawer w/brass button pull, 7¼″ W., 16″ H. .......... $2000.00*

*L to R*
A-WA D.C. Sept. 1982 *Adam A. Weschler & Son*
**SPINNING WHEEL,** Am., ca. 1828, turned fruitwood & oak, inscribed "1818/HK/N883,"36″ H. ........... $200.00*
A-MA Mar. 1983    *Robert W. Skinner Inc.*
**PAINTED COFFEEPOT,** early 19th C., Am., tin, blk. base paint, stylized flower in bright colors on each side, 11″k H. ............................ $500.00*

*L to R*
A-WA D.C. Sept. 1982 *Adam A. Weschler & Son*
**ART NOUVEAU CENTER BOWL,** ca. 1900, patinated bronze, mounted as lamp, mottled gr. domed art glass shade is fitted w/oil font, 20½″ H. .......... $700.00*

A-MA Dec. 1982    *Robert W. Skinner Inc.*
**TIFFANY TURTLE-BACK PLANTER,** ca. 1910, NY, irid., patinated bronze round body, leaded glass surface, copper insert, sgn., 9¼″ D. ................. $1700.00*

*L to R*
A-WA D.C. Sept. 1982 *Adam A. Weschler & Son*
**GEORGE III KNIFE BOX,** ca. 1790, satinwood inlaid mahogany, divided stepped int., 14″ H. .......... $300.00*

A-MA Aug. 1982    *Robert W. Skinner Inc.*
**PINE HANGING WALL BOX,** N. Eng., 18th C., hanging handle above shaped backboard & sides, old red paint, 21⅜″ H., 7¾″ W. .................... $1500.00*
**OAK TAPE LOOM,** N. Eng., 18th C., shaped handle, initialed "S.C., M.C. & S.A.," old repr., 25½″ H. ...... $375.00*

A-OH Mar. 1983    *Garth's Auctions, Inc.*
**HANDCOLORED LITHOGRAPH,** by Currier & Ives, racing print "'Two-Twenty' on the Road," some damage, crude touch-up, matted & framed, 16¼″ x 20½″ ............................ $55.00
**EMPIRE ARCHITECTURAL MIRROR,** old gold repaint, 20″ x 33¼″ ............................ $30.00
**STUDENT LAMP,** brass, opaque wh. shade, embossed nameplate "Berlin," old electrification, repr., 20″ H. ..... $210.00
**BOSTON ROCKER,** orig. paint w/drk. graining & flame grained seat, red & yellow striping, freehand floral decor. on crest & splat, glued breaks, repr., touch-up paint ............................ $135.00
**COUNTRY EMPIRE STAND,** orig. mahogany graining, worn & scratched paint, 18¼″ x 20½″, 10¾″ leaves, 29¼″ H. ............................ $166.00

*Price does not include 10% buyer fee.

A-MA June 1983    *Robert W. Skinner Inc.*
**MANDARIN FAN,** China, ca. 1865, carved & pierced ivory sticks, gold on red lacquer box, not orig. box, 10¾" L.
............................... $325.00*

A-MA June 1983    *Robert W. Skinner Inc.*
**EMPIRE FAN,** France, ca. 1810, lovers w/ivory faces, sequin border & sides, horn sticks, very slight damage, 8¼" L.
........................... $1350.00*

A-MA June 1983    *Robert W. Skinner Inc.*
**FRAMED BALLOON FAN,** France, ca. 1784, painted silk, slight damage & splitting, 11" L. ....................... $950.00*

A-MA June 1983    *Robert W. Skinner Inc.*
**BRISE SILVER FILIGREE FAN,** 19th C., Europe, 2 sm. repairs, 8" L.
............................... $475.00*

A-MA June 1983    *Robert W. Skinner Inc.*
**BRISE FAN,** ivory w/engraved macaques, Japan, late 19th C., incised sgn. on guard, very slight warping, 10" L. .... $1700.00*

A-MA June 1983    *Robert W. Skinner Inc.*
**BRISE SILVER FILIGREE FAN,** China, mid 19th C., blue & gr. cloisonne enamel on filigree ground, brass guards & edges, needs new ribbon, 8" L. ....... $450.00*

A-MA June 1983    *Robert W. Skinner Inc.*
**L'ORCLE PRINTED FAN,** France, 19th C., silk, 11" L. ................ $175.00

A-MA June 1983    *Robert W. Skinner Inc.*
**TROMPE L'OEIL PAINTED FAN,** ca. 1770, ivory sticks, some damage & staining, 11" L. ........................ $750.00*

A-MA June 1983    *Robert W. Skinner Inc.*
*L to R*
**PLIQUE-A-JOUR STERLING SILVER SPOONS,** 2 (1 illus.), Am., late 19th C., both gold washed, stylized floral design enameled, 4-1/16" L. .......... $100.00*
**PLIQUE-A-JOUR & GILDED METAL SPOON,** Europe, 19th C., some enamel damage, 7¾" L. ............... $70.00*
**RUSSIAN SILVER & ENAMEL SPOON,** mkd. A. P., ca. 1890, gold washed, 6¼" L. .............. $140.00*
**SILVER & PLIQUE-A-JOUR SPOON,** Europe, late 19th C., gold washed, 5⅝" L.
............................ $60.00*

A-OH Nov. 1983    *Garth's Auctions, Inc.*
**HOOKED RAG MAT,** framed, 23" x 31"
........................... $225.00
**OH YELLOWWARE LION,** mottled blue glaze, old chip, 9½" L. ..... $400.00
**SHERATON CHEST OF DRAWERS,** pine & basswood, orig. yellow & br. glazing, orig. wooden pulls, escut. removed, 41½" W., 19½" D., 41" H.
........................... $1875.00
**WOVEN SPLINT BASKET,** 13" x 16", 7½" O.H. ..................... $155.00

*Price does not include 10% buyer fee.

A-MA Nov. 1982 *Richard A. Bourne Co., Inc.*
*SNUFF BOTTLES*
*Row I, L to R*
**MOTTLED AGATE,** late 19th C., collared carnelian stopper, 2⅝" H. . . . $75.00
**AGATE,** mid-19th C., carving in relief, minor chip at lip, 3⅛" H. . . . . . . . $250.00
**SMOKY QUARTZ,** late 18th C., 3" H. . . . . . . . . . . . . . . . . . . . . . . . . . . . . $250.00

*Row II, L to R*
**TIGER-EYE,** early 20th C., carved, minor chip at foot, 2⅜" H. . . . . . . . . . . . $125.00
**RHODONITE,** early 20th C., indented foot, 2⅝" H. . . . . . . . . . . . . . . . . . $150.00
**AGATE,** late 18th C., high relief carved, bird stopper, no cork or spoon, 2⅞" H. . . . . . . . . . . . . . . . . . . . . . . . . . . $125.00

*Row III, L to R*
**FOSSILFEROUS LIMESTONE,** late 19th C. or early 20th C., carved, 2½" H. . . . . . . . . . . . . . . . . . . . . . . . . . . . $50.00
**BLACK & WHITE JADE,** 18th C., mkd., stone on both sides, 2⅞" H. . . . . . $275.00
**AGATE,** late 19th C., carved on one side only, 2½" H. . . . . . . . . . . . . . . . . . $50.00

A-MA Nov. 1982 *Richard A. Bourne Co., Inc.*
*SNUFF BOTTLES*
*Row I, L to R*
**HONEY AGATE,** 19th C., carving of a Foo lion & a bat, 3" H. . . . . . . . . $425.00
**MACARONI AGATE,** 20th C., carved, chips on foot, 2⅜" H. . . . . . . . . . . $40.00
**BLUE CHALCEDONY,** late 19th C. or early 20th C., carved, minor roughness on edges, 2¾" H. . . . . . . . . . . . . . . . . $250.00

*Row II, L to R*
**TURQUOISE,** 20th C., 2⅞" H. . . . . . . . . . . . . . . . . . . . . . . . . . . $120.00
**ROOT AMBER,** late 19th C. or early 20th C., minor chip at neck, 2½" H. . . . $50.00
**MOSS AGATE,** 20th C., stone, 2¼" H. . . . . . . . . . . . . . . . . . . . . . . . . . . $70.00

*Row III, L to R*
**TIGER-EYE,** 20th C., stone, carved . . . . . . . . . . . . . . . . . . . . . . . . . . . $225.00
**TIGER-EYE SNUFF SAUCER,** 20th C., stone matches previous bottle, 1¾" L. . . . . . . . . . . . . . . . . . . . . . . . . . . $90.00
**BUTTERSCOTCH AGATE,** late 18th C., collared jade stopper, chips at neckline, 2⅝" H. . . . . . . . . . . . . . . . . . . . . . $25.00

A-MA Nov. 1982 *Richard A. Bourne Co., Inc.*
*SNUFF BOTTLES*
*Row I, L to R*
**GOURD,** early 19th C., 40-calligraphic character inscription, ivory stopper, 2" H. plus 1" stopper . . . . . . . . . . . . . . . . $550.00
**INLAID COPPER,** 20th C., w/silver & applied silver mask handles, 2⅛" H. . . . . . . . . . . . . . . . . . . . . . . . . . . . $50.00
A-MA Nov. 1982 *Richard A. Bourne Co., Inc.*
**AGATE,** 20th C., relief carving in yellow skin, coral stopper, 2 chips on lip, 2¾" H. . . . . . . . . . . . . . . . . . . . . . . . . . . . . $40.00

*Row II, L to R*
**JASPER,** late 19th C. or early 20th C., minor roughness at foot, 2¼" H. . . . . . . . . . . . . . . . . . . . . . . . . . . . $60.00
**YELLOW JADE,** late 18th C., basket weave design, 2½" H. . . . . . . . . . $800.00
**AMBER,** 20th C., carved chicken, chipping around lip & foot, 2½" H. . . . $80.00

*Row III, L to R*
**MOTHER-OF-PEARL INLAY,** 20th C., 2½" H. . . . . . . . . . . . . . . . . . . . . . . $120.00
**TUANSTONE,** probably late 18th C., shield design, roughness on lip, 3" H. . . . . . . . . . . . . . . . . . . . . . . . . . . . $50.00
**PUDDINGSTONE JASPER,** 20th C., natural flaw on foot, 2½" H. . . . . . $50.00

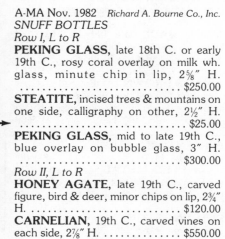

A-MA Nov. 1982 *Richard A. Bourne Co., Inc.*
*SNUFF BOTTLES*
*Row I, L to R*
**PEKING GLASS,** late 18th C. or early 19th C., rosy coral overlay on milk wh. glass, minute chip in lip, 2⅝" H. . . . . . . . . . . . . . . . . . . . . . . . . . . $250.00
**STEATITE,** incised trees & mountains on one side, calligraphy on other, 2½" H. . . . . . . . . . . . . . . . . . . . . . . . . . . $25.00
**PEKING GLASS,** mid to late 19th C., blue overlay on bubble glass, 3" H. . . . . . . . . . . . . . . . . . . . . . . . . . . . $300.00
*Row II, L to R*
**HONEY AGATE,** late 19th C., carved figure, bird & deer, minor chips on lip, 2¾" H. . . . . . . . . . . . . . . . . . . . . . . . . $120.00
**CARNELIAN,** 19th C., carved vines on each side, 2⅞" H. . . . . . . . . . . . . $550.00
**CHALCEDONY,** carved figure, bamboo & rock work, minor roughness on lip & neck, 3" H. . . . . . . . . . . . . . . . . . . $125.00
*Row III, L to R*
**YELLOW JADE W/BR. SKIN,** late 18th C., carved, jade stopper, no spoon, 2¾" H. . . . . . . . . . . . . . . . . . . . . . . . . . . $650.00
**GRAY MOTTLED JADE,** late 18th C. or early 19th C., coral stopper, 2⅞" H. . . . . . . . . . . . . . . . . . . . . . . . . . . $125.00
**SOOCHOW CARVED AGATE,** late 18th C. or early 19th C., monkeys & rock work, sgn. w/3 calligraphic characters, 2⅝" H. . . . . . . . . . . . . . . . . . . . . . . . . $600.00

A-MA Nov. 1982    *Richard A. Bourne Co., Inc.*
*SNUFF BOTTLES*
*Row I, L to R*
**HORN,** 20th C., silver inlay on both sides, drk. ivory stopper, 2⅞″ H. ....... $35.00
**PEKING GLASS,** early 20th C., overlay of jade gr., small chip on stopper, 2⅝″ H. ......................................... $25.00
**PORCELAIN,** late 19th C., lrg. crackle glaze in drk. gray w/small yellow crackle glaze, roughness in foot, 2½″ H. ......................................... $25.00
**IRON RED UNDERGLAZE PORCE-LAIN,** late 19th C., PoKu, 2⅝″ H. ......................................... $40.00
*Row II, L to R*
**METAL MOUNTED MONGOLIAN-TYPE,** 19th C., inset w/turquoise cabochons, 3¾″ H. .................... $100.00
**METAL MOUNTED MONGOLIAN-TYPE,** 19th C., inset w/turquoise cabochons, carved w/birds & flowers from ivory-tinted bone, 3⅞″ H. .............. $80.00
**METAL MOUNTED MONGOLIAN-TYPE,** 19th C., inset w/turquoise cabochons, neck bent, 4½″ H. .......... $90.00
**MONGOLIAN-TYPE SILVER,** 19th C., mounted w/turquoise & coral, filigree missing at base, 3″ H. .......... $25.00
*Row III, L to R*
**SERPENTINE,** late 18th C., cash design on both sides, calligraphy in relief on both sides, chipped, 3″ H. ............ $25.00
**CHALCEDONY,** late 19th C., raised panels on 4 sides, ground area corner, chipped, 2½″ H. ................ $25.00
**HISTORIC SOUVENIR OF 1972,** meeting between President Nixon & Chairman Mao Tse-Tung in 1972, ivory-colored porcelain w/underglaze blue & overglaze red, 2½″ H. .......... $75.00
**PUDDINGSTONE,** blk. & wh., 20th C., 2½″ H. ...................... $25.00
*Row IV, L to R*
**TURQUOISE MATRIX,** 20th C., colorful w/boy & dog, roughness, 2″ H. ... $75.00

A-MA Nov. 1982    *Richard A. Bourne Co., Inc.*
*SNUFF BOTTLES*
*Row I, L to R*
**HAIR CRYSTAL,** 18th C., finely dispersed hairs in flattened round form, metal collared coral stopper, 2-5/16″ H. ......................................... $150.00
**BLUE CHALCEDONY,** late 19th C., carved in relief of Chinese beauties, flowers, crane & deer, carved stopper, spoon missing ................. $400.00
**ROCK CRYSTAL,** 19th C., rounded ovate bottle w/4 columns of calligraphy on each side, mask handles, crystal stopper, 2½″ H. ......................................... $250.00
*Row II, L to R*
**ROSE QUARTZ,** late 18th C., carving of 2 birds & blossoms, matching carved stopper, 3″ H. ..................... $325.00
**CARVED PORCELAIN,** Chia Ch'ing (1796-1820), carving of scaly dragon on one side, phoenix on other, 2 small chips, 3⅛″ H. ......................................... $450.00
**PUDDINGSTONE,** mid to late 19th C., blk. collared carnelian stopper, 2½″ H. ......................................... $75.00
*Row III, L to R*
**WHITE JADE W/YELLOW SKIN,** mid-19th C., carving of millet & crabs, 3″ H. ......................................... $225.00
**WHITE JADE,** late 19th C., tinges of apple gr., flattened bottle, collared jade stopper, jade well worn, 2¼″ H. ......................................... $125.00
**GRAY & BROWN JADE,** late 19th C. or early 20th C., 2 circular panels on each side in br. area, chip on foot ring, minor rough area on lip edge, 2¾″ H. ........ $125.00

**SERPENTINE,** late 19th C., carved in stripes, 2½″ H. ................. $25.00
**ENAMELED METAL,** early 20th C., → w/blue, aubergine & turquoise depicting birds & blossoms, screw-in stopper, 3″ H. ......................................... $45.00
**PUDDINGSTONE,** early 20th C., in blues & grays, 2¼″ H. .......... $10.00

A-MA Nov. 1982    *Richard A. Bourne Co., Inc.*
*SNUFF BOTTLES*
*Row I, L to R*
**PORCELAIN,** sgn. w/4-character seal of Tao Kuang (1821-1850), minor chip, 2½″ H. ......................................... $75.00
**CHRYSOPRASE,** 20th C., uncarved, indented foot, 2¾″ H. .......... $200.00
**PORCELAIN,** 19th C., carved deer in wh. enamel, 3″ H. .................. $50.00

*Row II, L to R*
**SEAL-TYPE PEKING GLASS,** early 19th C., 3-color overlay, bug, flowers & rock work on one side, 2⅞″ H. .. $200.00
**YI-HSING,** late 18th C., deep blue, inset panel decor. w/enameled design of bird & flowers, silver mounted jade stopper, 2¾″ H. ......................................... $650.00
**ROSE QUARTZ,** early 20th C., carved overall, no spoon, minor chipping at lip & base, 3″ H. .................. $150.00

*Row III, L to R*
**MOTTLED JADE,** early 19th C., lt. br. w/touch of blk., collared coral stopper, 2⅜″ H. ......................................... $50.00
**PEKING GLASS,** 19th C., rare Peking glass imitation of agate, 3″ H. ... $200.00
**PORCELAIN,** late 19th C., blue & wh. underglaze, 2½″ H. ........... $120.00

A-MA July 1982    *Richard A. Bourne Co., Inc.*
*L to R*
**CINNABAR SNUFF BOTTLE,** orig. spoon, Chinese, 2¼″ H. ........ $60.00
**CINNABAR SNUFF BOTTLE,** orig. spoon, Chinese, 2⅞″ H. ......... $70.00

A-WA D.C. Dec. 1982 *Adam A. Weschler & Son*
**BRONZE SETTER,** on a carved wooden
base, 13″ L., 9″ H. . . . . . . . . . . . $375.00*

A-WA D.C. Dec. 1982 *Adam A. Weschler & Son*
**COMBAT de TAUREAUX ROMAINS,**
French, late 19th C., bronze, br. gr. patina,
26″ L., 20″ H. . . . . . . . . . . . . . $3800.00*

*Left*
A-OH July 1982     *Garth's Auctions, Inc.*
**BLACK BOY HITCHING POST,** cast
iron, polychrome repaint has some rust,
attrib. to Robert Wood & Co. Philadelphia,
43″ H. . . . . . . . . . . . . . . . . . . . . $500.00
*Right*
A-WA D.C. July 1982 *Adam A. Weschler & Son*
**FRENCH BRONZE "LA CHARITE,"**
late 19th C., br.-gold patina, 25″ H.
. . . . . . . . . . . . . . . . . . . . . . . . $1600.00*

A-WA D.C. Dec. 1982 *Adam A. Weschler & Son*
**APOLLO & DIANA,** pr., bronze busts,
on round socle, sq. base, gr. br. patina, 17″
H. . . . . . . . . . . . . . . . . . . . . . . . $450.00*

*Left*
A-WA D.C. Dec. 1982 *Adam A. Weschler & Son*
**BRONZE FIGURE "EVENING,"**
French, mkd. "Cillmary," molded rouge
marble base, br. patina, 28½″ H.
. . . . . . . . . . . . . . . . . . . . . . . . $850.00*

*Right*
A-WA D.C. Dec. 1982 *Adam A. Weschler & Son*
**NYMPH RIDING LION,** French, ca.
1900-25, bronze, on a mottled gr. marble
base, mkd. "P. Philippe," impressed
founder's mark of Goldscheider, numbered
RG12-1623, 8¾″ L., 9½″ H. . . . . $550.00*

A-WA D.C. Dec. 1982 *Adam A. Weschler & Son*
**ART NOUVEAU MAIDEN,** bronze, gr.
br. patina, 27″ H. . . . . . . . . . . . . $900.00*

A-OH July 1983     *Early Auction Co.*
**BRONZE FIGURES,** "Accolade," by P. J.
Mene . . . . . . . . . . . . . . . . . . . . $1500.00

A-WA D.C. July 1982 *Adam A. Weschler & Son*
**CONTINENTAL STEEL SUIT OF
ARMOR & SHIELD,** 19th C., engraved
floral motif, 72″ H. . . . . . . . . . . . $850.00*

*Price does not include 10% buyer fee.

# INDEX